PENGUIN CANADA

KNIGHTS OF THE BLACK AND WHITE

JACK WHYTE was born in Scotland and emigrated to Canada in 1967. He is an actor, orator, singer, poet, and the author of the critically acclaimed Dream of Eagles series of novels about King Arthur and his court. Whyte lives in Kelowna, British Columbia.

Also by Jack Whyte

A DREAM OF EAGLES

The Skystone

The Singing Sword

The Eagles' Brood

The Saxon Shore

The Sorcerer, Volume I:
The Fort at River's Bend

The Sorcerer, Volume II:
Metamorphosis

— • —

Uther

— • —

THE GOLDEN EAGLE

Clothar the Frank

The Eagle

BOOK ONE OF THE
TEMPLAR TRILOGY

KNIGHTS
OF THE BLACK
AND WHITE

JACK WHYTE

PENGUIN
CANADA

PENGUIN CANADA

Published by the Penguin Group

Penguin Group (Canada), 90 Eglinton Avenue East, Suite 700, Toronto, Ontario, Canada M4P 2Y3 (a division of Pearson Canada Inc.)

Penguin Group (USA) Inc., 375 Hudson Street, New York, New York 10014, U.S.A.
Penguin Books Ltd, 80 Strand, London WC2R 0RL, England
Penguin Ireland, 25 St Stephen's Green, Dublin 2, Ireland (a division of Penguin Books Ltd)
Penguin Group (Australia), 250 Camberwell Road, Camberwell, Victoria 3124, Australia
(a division of Pearson Australia Group Pty Ltd)
Penguin Books India Pvt Ltd, 11 Community Centre, Panchsheel Park, New Delhi – 110 017,
India
Penguin Group (NZ), 67 Apollo Drive, Rosedale, North Shore 0632, Auckland, New Zealand
(a division of Pearson New Zealand Ltd)
Penguin Books (South Africa) (Pty) Ltd, 24 Sturdee Avenue, Rosebank, Johannesburg 2196,
South Africa

Penguin Books Ltd, Registered Offices: 80 Strand, London WC2R 0RL, England

First published in a Viking Canada hardcover by Penguin Group (Canada),
a division of Pearson Canada Inc., 2006. Published simultaneously in the
United States by G. P. Putnam's Sons, Penguin Group (USA) Inc.
Published in this edition, 2007.

1 2 3 4 5 6 7 8 9 10 (OPM)

LIBRARY AND ARCHIVES CANADA CATALOGUING IN PUBLICATION

Whyte, Jack, 1940–
Knights of the Black and White / Jack Whyte.

(Templar trilogy ; bk. 1)
ISBN 978-0-14-301736-3

I. Title. II. Series: Whyte, Jack, 1940– Templar trilogy ; bk. 1.

PS8595.H947K55 2007   jC813'.54   C2007-902889-6

ISBN-13: 978-0-14-301736-3
ISBN-10: 0-14-301736-5

Visit the Penguin Group (Canada) website at **www.penguin.ca**

Special and corporate bulk purchase rates available; please see
www.penguin.ca/corporatesales or call 1-800-810-3104, ext. 477 or 474

... fresh fields and pastures new ...

*To my wife, Beverley, as always,
and to the other two women in my life,
Jeanne and Holly*

It has served us well, this myth of Christ.

—Pope Leo X

No other problem of our time is rooted so deeply in the past.

—Report of the Royal Palestine Commission of Inquiry, 1937

It is difficult to distinguish fact from legend … I have found no consensus on what is fact; it depends on the viewpoint. Interestingly enough, legend—which is by definition distorted—gives a far more acceptable view of events. Everyone agrees on legend, but nobody agrees on facts.

—Michael Coney,
The Celestial Steam Locomotive

AUTHOR'S NOTE

No other organization in history has captured the attention and curiosity of modern readers as completely and intriguingly as the medieval order of monks known as the Knights Templar. The beginnings of that popular fascination sprang from the 1982 publication of *Holy Blood, Holy Grail* by Michael Baigent, Richard Leigh, and Henry Lincoln. I know that my own interest in the Order of the Temple was kindled by reading that book, because although I had always been fascinated by the mystery and mysticism surrounding the Templars, it was only after reading *Holy Blood, Holy Grail* that I thought, *There has to be a truly great story hidden in there somewhere, if a guy could just strip away all the layers of obfuscation and find a way to really look at who these people were and what made them tick.* I had always believed that the Knights Templar were real, very human people, despite the fact that, back when I was a boy, the only pictures we had of them were stylized stone figures carved on medieval tombs, and the only reports we ever read of them told us they were a villainous and evil breed, condemned and excommunicated by the Church as heretics and apostates.

The grasping Norman knights in *Ivanhoe* were all

Templars, as were the lowering, black-visaged villains in several other tales I read in boyhood, and one seldom heard, or read, anything good about the Knights Templar. They were always evil, threatening stereotypes. And yet a quiet, logic-bound area of my awareness recognized other, seldom listed and infrequently mentioned aspects of Templar history: they existed as an order for less than two hundred years, and for most of that time they were the legitimate standing army of the Catholic Church; they invented and perfected the first sophisticated, credit-and-gold-bullion–based international banking system, and they financed all the kings and kingdoms of Christendom. They also amassed the largest and most impressive portfolio of real estate holdings known to history, and to protect their enormous trading fleet they developed the largest navy in the world. Their black and white naval ensign, a white skull and crossbones on a black field, struck the fear of God into pirates everywhere.

Most impressive of all, however, to a storyteller, was the awareness that their meteoric career effectively came to an end in a single day, on Friday the thirteenth of October 1307, a date, to paraphrase Franklin Roosevelt, that will live forever, if not in infamy, then at least in mystery. And so were born in my mind the elements of my tale of the Templars: The Beginnings, designed and brought about, history tells us, by nine penniless men—two of whose names we do not even know today—who spent years digging in the bowels of Jerusalem and unearthed a treasure that made them the most powerful and influential force on earth for two centuries; The Middle, when a corps of monks, all of them wearing the equal-armed cross of the Order of the Temple, formed a standing army in the Holy Land and fought to the death, hopelessly outnumbered by the swarming legions of Saladin's Saracens, in a vain attempt to preserve an impossible dream; and The End, when the order was overthrown in a single day by the sinister lieutenant of a grasping, ambitious king, and only a few escaped to foster and nurture a legend and a tradition of hope and regeneration.

In writing these novels for modern readers, I have had to deal with the French names of my major characters. All the original Templar knights were French and nobly born, which meant that their names all had a "de" in the middle, as in Geoffroi de Bouillon, André de Montbard, Hugues (Hugh) de Payens, etc. Family names, or surnames, as we know them today, were not in common use that long ago, and most of the identifiable names that existed came from the family's birthplace or region. If a man called Guillaume (William) was born in a certain town or city, such as Chartres in France, he would be known as William of Chartres ... Guillaume de Chartres. That makes for tough reading in modern English, and so I have made allowances, dropping the "correct" French names in many, although not all, instances, in favor of simplifying things for modern readers. I have given all my characters "modern" sounding names, simply by anglicizing their first names wherever possible and dropping the "de" between their first and second names.

Thus Geoffroi de St. Omer becomes simply Godfrey St. Omer, Archambaud de St. Agnan becomes Archibald St. Agnan, and Payen de Montdidier becomes Payn Montdidier, but Hugues de Payens, the founder of the Knights Templar, becomes Hugh, yet remains Hugh de Payens, because that is his historical identity.

I also made a note to myself, back when I first started writing these stories, to be sure to explain a few of the things that were normal eight or nine hundred years ago but would seem utterly alien and incomprehensible to modern readers. For example, no one—neither the clergymen who planned the Crusades nor the warriors who fought in them—ever heard the words *Crusades* or *Crusaders*. Those words came along hundreds of years later, when historians began talking about the exploits of the Christian armies in the Middle East. And the Crusaders' word for the Holy Land was *Outremer*—the land beyond the sea. In addition to that, medieval Europe was not called Europe. It was called Christendom, because all the countries in it were Christian. The name *Europe* would not come along for a few more centuries.

Even more difficult for modern people to grasp is the idea that there was no middle class in medieval Europe, and only one, all-powerful Church. There was no capacity for religious protest and no Protestants. Martin Luther would not be born for hundreds of years. There were only two kinds of people in Christendom: the haves and the have-nots (some things never change), otherwise known as aristocrats and commoners, and both were male, because women had no rights and no identity in the world of medieval Christianity. The commoners, depending on which country they lived in, were known as peasants, serfs, slaves, and mesnes, and they were uneducated and largely valueless. The aristocrats, on the other hand, were the men who owned and ruled the lands, and they were divided into two halves—knights and clerics. There were no other options. If you were firstborn, you inherited. If you were not first born, you either became a knight or a cleric. From clerics, we get the modern word *clergyman*, because all clerics were priests and monks, but we also get the modern word *clerk,* because all clerics were expected to be both literate and numerate. Knights had no need to be literate. Their job was fighting, and they could hire clerics to keep their records straight. Knights represented the worldly order, whereas clerics represented God and the Church, and there was no love lost between the two orders. On the most basic level, knights existed solely to fight, and clerics existed to stop them from killing. That entailed the most fundamental kind of conflict and led to anarchy and chaos.

The Knights Templar, for a multiplicity of reasons, became the first religious order ever entitled to kill in the name of God. They were the first and the greatest of their kind, and this is their story.

Jack Whyte
Kelowna, British Columbia, Canada
May 2006

BEGINNINGS

ONE

"**S**ir Hugh!"

As the guards on either side of the doors ahead came to attention and saluted him, not even the rattling clatter of their armor penetrated the awareness of the frowning, mop-headed young man who walked towards them. He was deep in thought, head down and moving slowly, a heavy, sheathed broadsword slung across the back of his neck like a yoke, and his arms extended so that his hands hung loosely over both ends of the long weapon, at hilt and point. It was the guards' movements that finally caught his attention as they stepped quickly forward and swung the wide, heavy doors open to admit him. He looked up, blinked, nodded cordially at the guard commander, and dropped one arm from the end of the sword, catching the hilt in his other hand at the same moment, so that the long blade swung upright before he allowed it to slope backward to rest on his shoulder again.

"Practicing, m'lord?" The guard commander's question was rhetorical, but Hugh de Payens stopped walking and glanced down at the sword he held, then flipped it forward, gripping the thick steel hilt with both hands and extending the sheathed blade straight-armed until its weight made the muscles in his enormous arms, neck, and shoulders stand out like ropes. Then he released it with his left hand and twirled it effortlessly with his right until the blade returned to rest on his right shoulder again.

"Practicing, Sergeant? Aye, but not with the sword, not this time. I've been practicing with my memory … thinking." He nodded to the other two guards and walked through the open doors, out of the bright afternoon light of the courtyard and into the castle's central tower, where he paused, momentarily blinded by the sudden darkness. Then, his face growing solemn again, he moved ahead into the immense space of the room, keeping his eyes lowered to the floor ahead of him as his stride lengthened, the sword still angled casually backward, over his shoulder.

Most young men his age would have strutted with such a magnificent sword, using its lethal beauty to enhance themselves, but Hugh de Payens did no such thing. He carried the weapon simply because he had set out with it earlier and thus had to continue carrying it until he could set it down somewhere without danger of its being lost, stolen, or forgotten, and now he headed towards his own quarters, where he could finally lay it down. He was so far removed from awareness of anything else that he walked past a group of brightly dressed, giggling young women huddled in one corner of the vast room without noticing them, despite their admiring glances and the greetings some of them called out to him.

He also failed to notice the tall, broad-shouldered man who came striding towards him as their paths converged almost in the exact center of the room, and it was left to the other to notice that Hugh was making no attempt to slow down or yield as they came together. The man stopped walking and drew himself up to his full height, his eyebrows rising in astonishment, then slowly raised one hand high, fingers spread, and stepped out of Hugh's way. Only as Hugh drew abreast of the taller man, who now reached out to grasp his shoulder, did he become aware of him, and he reared back as though under attack, whipping the sword down from his shoulder and seizing the sheath to pull it off, before looking to see who was accosting him. He grounded the point of his still-sheathed weapon immediately, his face flushing.

"My lord St. Clair! Forgive me, sir. I was ... woolgathering."

The big man's raised hand, even before Hugh's reaction, had been a signal to the single, armed bodyguard behind him to remain where he was, and now as he looked at the young man in front of him, a hint of something that might have been either a smile or a scowl tugged at one corner of his mouth. "I could see that," he replied, in a great, rumbling bass voice. "But even in the midst of grave concerns, young Hugh, a man should always try to keep one eye at least on his surroundings. What were you dreaming of, so many miles away?"

"Nothing, my lord ... I beg your pardon. I was practicing words in my head, for the Gathering tomorrow night. There is much to learn."

"Ah, the Responses. Aye, there is, as you say. Particularly for a young man in your position. But you have the best teachers you could have, and I know they are not unhappy with your efforts." His eyes dropped to the heavy, long-bladed weapon. "But why the sword, godson? Do you remember better with a weapon in your hand?"

Hugh looked down in mild bewilderment at the weapon he was still holding point down on the ground. "No, sir, no, not at all. I went out to walk to the butts, to practice, but I never reached them. I merely kept walking ... thinking about the work and practicing that instead."

"Aye, well, that sounds like time well used, considering how close you are to the testing. Where are you going now, then?"

"Back to my quarters, my lord, to rid myself of this." He indicated the sword.

"Here, give it to me and come and walk with me instead." St. Clair reached out and took Hugh's sword, then tossed it casually to the armored guard standing several paces behind him, bidding him remain and look after the weapon. As the mail-clad man saluted and stepped back, St. Clair turned back to Hugh. "I was on my way to visit the scene of your trial when you came along, and so I think your arrival might have been a signal that we should visit it together. Seeing the place thus, as sponsor and supplicant, might give us both food for thought, albeit different foods and vastly differing thoughts."

Listening to the deep voice, Hugh de Payens thought he might have detected a note of humor in those words, but such was his awe of the other man that he could not quite bring himself to believe him ordinary enough to use humor, and so he merely nodded, his eyes downcast again, although this time in humility. He stepped forward to walk beside and slightly behind St. Clair, too abashed and unsure of himself to make any attempt to speak. Hugh was eighteen years old, big for his years and normally irrepressible, but he was awestruck by the fame and the worldly status of the man with whom he was now walking, a man who was also, beyond doubt, the largest, most physically impressive man Hugh had ever seen.

Without looking back at his godson, St. Clair now reached out a hand until his extended palm found the nape of the younger man's neck, then urged him gently forward until they were walking side by side.

"Your father has high hopes for you, he tells me." The hand fell away from his neck. "Did you know that?"

Hugh shook his head, swallowing the awkward lump in his throat. "No, my lord," he said, his voice emerging as little more than a whisper.

"No, I thought not. Well, take it from me, he does. He is very proud of you. Prouder, I think, than I am of any of my own sons, although I like them all well enough. But like most fathers, yours will probably tell everyone else in the world about his pride and never think to mention it to you. It is a peculiarity common to fathers, I've been told. He will simply assume you know it, since you are his son and therefore so much like him—" He stopped, turned to look at Hugh keenly. "You *have* been down here before, have you not?"

They had paused at the top of the wide marble staircase that spiraled downward from the floor above and continued to the one beneath, and Hugh nodded. "Aye, my lord. Twice."

"Twice, of course. I knew that, had I but thought about it. Your First Summons and your First Advancement. Come you, then, let's make it a third time." The big man started down the stairs, and Hugh followed half a step behind him, still unable to believe that he was actually walking with, and talking with, Sir Stephen St. Clair, and that the great knight had recognized and remembered him. It mattered not that they were godfather and godson, for St. Clair, one of the most famous knights in all of Christendom, had many godsons, and young Hugh de Payens, although nominally a knight, had done nothing since being knighted, less than two years earlier, to distinguish himself from the ruck of his peers or to make himself memorable in any way. Nor did it matter, Hugh believed, that Sir Stephen had come here to Payens specifically to officiate as Hugh's sponsor at the forthcoming Raising—whatever that might be—for he knew the great knight would have come here anyway, on whatever excuse he could muster. He and Hugh's father, Hugo, the Baron de Payens, had been the closest of friends since boyhood, enjoying one of those rare relationships that make true friendship utterly independent of physical, geographical, or temporal separation. In consequence of that, the two missed no opportunity, ever, to spend time together.

The last time they had met was two years earlier, when Sir Stephen appeared in Payens unexpectedly, accompanied by his patron, who had once been known as William the Bastard but had since become both Duke of Normandy and William I, King of England. The two great men had been on their way home from Normandy, with unencumbered time at their disposal for once, and the King had expressed a wish to see Sir Stephen's family home in Anjou. Their route passed close by Payens, and so Sir Stephen had brought the King of England to call upon his friend the Baron of Payens, knowing that the two had met before, in 1066, when William invaded England.

William had died since then, in a riding accident, and his crown in England had been taken by one of his sons, another William, known as William Rufus because of his red hair and fiery temper. According to reports from England, Rufus was a tyrannical monster, detested by everyone, but somehow the lord of St. Clair, close as he had been to Rufus's father, had also found credibility and acceptance in the eyes of the son, something that few of the old king's favorites had been able to achieve.

Now, descending the stairs at St. Clair's shoulder, Hugh was unsurprised that the new English king should show respect for the great knight, because Sir Stephen St. Clair's reputation was stainless and his stature reflected his *dignitas*. Even walking one step below Hugh, the older man yet loomed over him, his height greater than Hugh's by almost a full hand's span. At the age of forty-two, he was barely out of his prime, physically towering above most other men but head and shoulders taller in moral stature, too. And he was here in Payens, in the flesh, to honor the son of his best friend and to make the occasion of his Raising a memorable one. This, Hugh had been informed, was a signal honor. It was an honor, however, that he accepted with certain reservations, for he had no idea, even at this late date, less than a day from the Gathering, what a Raising was or what it entailed. Yet he knew, because he had been told so very seriously and very convincingly, that despite its meaning nothing to him now, the Raising would be extremely important to his future.

When he had first heard his father use the term—the Raising—the sound of it, emerging from the Baron's mouth, had been portentous, the emphasis he used setting it apart. That had been nine months ago, and Hugh had immediately asked what it meant, but the Baron's answer had been no answer at all. He had blustered a little, attempting to dismiss it with a wave of his hand, and would say no more than that Hugh would find out all about it when the time came. In the meantime, however, he must begin to prepare for it, since it would be the most important event in Hugh's life. Hearing the Baron say that had silenced his son, who had until then believed that nothing could be more important than his achievement of knighthood, less than a year earlier. He learned otherwise in a very short time, however, for so important was this newly announced ceremonial, this Raising, that both his father the Baron and his mother's father, Lord Baldwin of Montdidier, had become his personal tutors, instructing him patiently and painstakingly on the matter of the Raising every day, and before he had even been permitted to begin working with them, he had had to swear never to reveal what he would learn, or even to mention the Raising itself to anyone.

Since then, for months on end, Hugh had worked harder than he had at anything else in his whole life. His task was to master, by rote and to perfection, the verbal responses required for the ceremony surrounding the Raising, and the doing of it was far more grievous and exhausting than the harshest weapons training. He had been struggling with the work for months now, achieving something close to fluency in his responses, but he had absolutely no idea of their meaning, at any level of understanding. And now he was within a day of the great occasion, when all the details and the mysteries—the Gathering itself, the importance of the ceremonies, the meaning of the rites and the significance of Sir Stephen's voyage from England to be present here as Hugh's sponsor—would be made clear to him.

"I feel feather-light," the big man said unexpectedly, speaking back over his shoulder as he swept nimbly down the wide, shallow stairway and bringing Hugh's attention sharply back to where he was. "No armor, and no weapons ..." He stretched his arms out to his sides at shoulder height, and the light material of the decorative cloak he was wearing billowed out behind him almost as though he were floating down the steps, so that Hugh thought, for the second time within minutes, of humor in association with the great man. "And no need of either of them," St. Clair continued, "although I can scarce believe that." He stopped suddenly, dropping his arms back to his sides, and when he spoke again all trace of levity had vanished from his voice. "I think I could never grow accustomed to not wearing armor, and I will certainly never be comfortable going weaponless, not even here in your father's house, where I know it is safe ... That is the difference between your life here today, lad, and ours in England."

England! There, in a single word, St. Clair had encapsulated all the mystery and legend surrounding himself and his phenomenal prowess. It had been twenty-two years since he had first set foot in England, along with Hugh's father, Hugo, landing on the south coast of the island as young, untried knights in the invading army of William, Duke of Normandy, in September 1066. Both young men had been Hugh's age at that time, and they had conducted themselves with distinction during the great battle that had been fought at Hastings two weeks later, in mid-October.

Sir Stephen St. Clair had achieved more than any of his fellows on that occasion—an accomplishment he was to repeat time and again through the decades that followed—for his had been the sword that struck down and killed the English king, Harold Godwinson, that day. He had not known the name or rank of the man he had killed—in the heat of combat he had merely recognized a cluster of enemy officers and attacked them—but his single-handed attack had been witnessed by Duke William himself, and later, when the identity of the dead man had been established beyond doubt, the Duke had known whom to thank, for this single death had cleared the way for William the Bastard to become King of England.

Soldiers' legend had it that Sir Stephen was reluctant to take credit for the victory, and that had it not been for the insistence of the Duke himself as witness, St. Clair would have accepted no reward. The battle that day had been fought between two very different armies. Duke William's was made up mainly of heavy Norman cavalry, generally attributed to be the finest in Christendom, backed up by massed bowmen, whereas the English army was a disciplined infantry force, acknowledged far and wide as the finest in the world. Among the English, however, only the leaders and senior commanders were mounted, which made them easy to recognize, and St. Clair, finding himself close enough to a group of them to attack, had done so. The enemy officers had bunched together defensively at his approach, but after the initial impact of his one-man charge, their much smaller mounts had been scattered by the superior weight of his enormous war horse. Their act of bunching together to forestall St. Clair's attack, however, had attracted the attention of a squadron of Norman archers, who had been trained to watch for sudden grouping of potential targets, and one arrow among the resultant shower of missiles had struck an English knight in the face, leaving him reeling in his saddle, weaponless and shocked, just as St. Clair crashed into their midst. St. Clair had seen the helpless man and struck at him in passing, sending him toppling to his death, but it was unclear later, and generally agreed to be unimportant, whether the fallen man—the English king, Harold—had died by the arrow or by the sword blow. What was important was that his death had cut the heart out of his army and resulted in the first conquest of Britain in hundreds of years.

Since then, through more than two decades of Norman settlement and occupation of a violently hostile England, Sir Stephen St. Clair had been one of King William's strongest and most loyal supporters and had been consistently and royally rewarded for his services, so that he now owned several vast estates throughout the conquered country. Thanks to the harsh lessons in treachery and duplicity he had learned during his days as William the Bastard, the King would never permit any of his powerful nobles, even the most trusted of them, to grow strong enough to be able to threaten him, and so their lands and holdings were always kept far apart from each other and surrounded by the holdings of their own greatest rivals. That, to St. Clair, made eminent sense. He was more than happy with his lot, and, thanks to that attitude, he had prospered even beyond his own belief.

The two men reached the bottom of the spiral stairs and walked forward several paces to where narrower steps sank straight downward through an opening in the floor, and the sound of their footsteps changed as they passed beyond the polished marble flooring and between the two guards who stood motionless at the top of the smooth sandstone steps. Neither man paid any attention to the table-filled banquet hall surrounding them, their attention tightly focused on the way ahead.

As they reached the bottom of the first stone flight and swung left to continue downward, St. Clair, still slightly ahead of the younger man, spoke again, his words floating back over his shoulder. "Believe me, young Hugh, you have no idea how fortunate you are to be living here, among civilized people you can usually trust not to try to kill you." He glanced back, and this time his teeth flashed in a definite grin before he began to move down the next flight of stairs. "Some of them always will, of course—try to kill you, I mean—but that is only to be expected, men being what they are no matter where one lives. Among the Franks, however, a man may sleep soundly in his own bed most of the time. In England, on the other hand, a Frank of any station is in constant danger, because to the English, all Franks are Normans. That is not true, of course, but it might as well be, since all the Frankish warriors now in England are in Norman employ. You would be surprised, I believe, to know how seldom I go anywhere without being fully armored. I could count on the fingers of one hand the number of times I've gone outside without it since last I was here." They reached the bottom of the last flight of steps and St. Clair raised one eyebrow questioningly. "Right, here we are. Are you ready for this?"

Hugh merely nodded, not trusting his voice, since his throat had swollen up with sudden apprehension halfway down the last flight. The stairs had changed direction three times as they descended, switching back on themselves so that the two men were now deep in the bowels of the castle, five floors below the point from which they had started. The steps of the last flight they had come down were wooden—as broad and sturdy as the stone they had replaced, and still shallow and easy to descend—and they ended in a very narrow, high-ceilinged vestibule that was nothing other than a rectangular pit, lit by half a dozen torches in sconces set at shoulder height into niches along the side walls. The stairs almost completely filled the length and breadth of the space, and the bare, high stone walls on either side were so close that Hugh knew, because he had tried it on a previous occasion, that he could barely have inserted his flattened fingers between the stair risers and the walls. A short walkway, barely three paces in length, stretched from the foot of the stairs to a pair of massive, iron-studded doors that blocked the way ahead as completely as the stairs filled the space at the rear.

Hugh knew enough of what went on down in this most private part of his father's castle to know that preparations were underway for the following night's Gathering. Had it been otherwise, the high, narrow chamber in which they now stood would have been inaccessible, because the wooden flight of stairs would not have been there. It would have been pulled up like the drawbridge it was, to rest flush against the high wall opposite, covering the doors, while a corresponding slab of equal size, cunningly contrived to look like solid, foot-worn flagstones, would have been lowered into place to cover the hole in the floor.

St. Clair stepped forward and used the pommel of his short dagger—the only weapon he carried—to hammer on the oaken doors, and while he awaited a response, he looked at Hugh again. "You have lived here all your life. Did you know this floor existed, before they brought you down the first time, for your initiation?"

"No, sir."

"That must have been a surprise, eh? To discover that there was a place in your own house you hadn't known was there?"

"Aye, and such a large place. I do remember the shock of it, my lord."

"You had no idea of its existence at all? No suspicions? Had you never been down here on the storage floors before? I find that hard to credit."

"Oh no, my lord. I'd been down here many times, on the floor above this one. We used to play there when I was small and the weather was too wet or stormy for us to be outside, and we enjoyed it because it was always dark and dusty and dangerous looking. But the floor up there was always the *floor* ... the ground. None of us knew there was anything beneath it. How could we?"

"And you know that now because you went looking for an entrance soon after your first visit here, eh?"

Hugh nodded, smiling sheepishly. "Yes, my lord. I did. I came down alone, the next day, and brought torches with me, sufficient to give me ample time to really look around. I could not believe that there was nothing to see. I thought I must have missed something before, some sign that would have shown me where to look. But even when I went back *knowing* there was an entrance, and knowing where to look for it, I could see nothing."

"Of course you couldn't. Because there is nothing there to be seen. You either know the secret of access or you do not. This place was built hundreds of years ago by people who knew how to hide the evidence of their work from profane eyes when they so wished. Aha! Someone is coming. Step away." He grasped Hugh's wrist and pulled him backward with him as he stepped away from the doors. There came a muffled sound from the other side of the heavy doors that suggested a solid bar being dragged aside, and then a tiny, windowlike aperture, smaller than a man's face, opened in the door on the left and someone looked out at them. Hugh had known that would happen, but even knowing and looking for it, he failed to see the outline of the spyhole before it swung open. Sir Stephen stepped forward, cupped his hands around the edges of the tiny window, and leaned forward to whisper. Moments later, the great door swung open on one side, and St. Clair stepped through, motioning to Hugh to go with him.

Hugh remembered this entrance well, for it had unsettled him when he had first used it. The thick, high doors opened outward rather than inward, and the space beyond them unexpectedly contained only a short passageway, less than two paces long, that was built purely for defense and shrank alarmingly on all sides, forcing everyone who passed through—and they could pass only one at a time—to crouch into an awkward, stooping shuffle by the time they reached the end of the passage to exit through yet another door. Beyond that lay another vestibule, this one octagonal, with doors, much smaller than but otherwise identical to the outer pair, set into every facet of the octagon, and even as Hugh emerged from the low entranceway he saw the nearest door to his left close behind the departing figure of the gatekeeper.

"Eight doors," St. Clair said. "All identical. You have been through two of them ere now. Do you remember which they were?"

Hugh nodded and pointed at two doors, one on his left and the other on his right.

"Good man. Now, which of the two do you remember better?"

"That one, the more recent." Hugh pointed again at the one on his left.

"Then that is the one we will use today." St. Clair stepped forward and pushed the door open easily, much to Hugh's surprise, since he had expected a guard on duty there, too. The knight stepped inside and the younger man followed him along the narrow, curving, dimly lit passageway that he remembered from his previous visit, until they reached a curtained doorway. Sir Stephen pulled the curtain aside and passed through into the space beyond, and Hugh followed him, knowing that what he was about to see, if he saw anything at all, would probably bear no resemblance to what he had seen on either of his two earlier visits to this place.

Sure enough, the place was shrouded in darkness, the only light being a dim glow from a single hanging lamp that seemed to be a great distance away from where he stood, although he suspected that was probably an illusion. Hugh stopped on the threshold, blinking his eyes and willing them to adjust quickly to the available light, and as they did so, he began to discern vague shapes and patterns in the surrounding darkness, the easiest of which to see was the pattern of the black and white squares of the tessellated floor. Most of what he could see, however, remained an indistinct collection of draped and shrouded shapes, one of which, close by where he stood, might have been a heavy, ornate chair.

"Stay you here now and don't move around, lest you blunder into things and knock something over. There is much in this room of great value, and your future brethren would not be pleased were anything to be broken through your clumsiness. I have some things to see to, and will return as soon as I am done. But I am not going anywhere. I will be here all the time and you will hear me moving about. You may not be able to see me, or what I am doing, but then you should not even be here, so nothing is lost ... unless, as I say, you knock something over, in which case we will both find ourselves in dire circumstances."

A short time later, the knight returned and led Hugh by the hand across a broad floor until they came to a row of seats, where he told Hugh to sit down, and then proceeded to catechize him on the questions and answers Hugh had been rehearsing with his father and grandfather for months. Hugh felt strange, sitting there in the darkness and responding by rote to the arcane questions being thrown at him. Many of them—questions and answers both—he did not understand at all, reciting his answers verbatim as he had been taught them and trusting blindly that their meaning would be revealed to him in due course, as his mentors had promised they would. Now, however, sitting in the darkness and going through his exercises with the massive knight who was to be his sponsor, he felt stranger than he ever had before, excited and apprehensive at the same time, and acutely aware of who and what he was at that moment, because he knew that, as the result of some mysterious process, he would never·again be the same man after the events of the following night.

He became aware then that St. Clair had said nothing since he answered the last question, apparently having no more to ask, and the knight confirmed that by clearing his throat softly and quietly saying, "I'm impressed, lad. I don't think I have ever heard a student answer better. I've heard many as good, but none better. I can see why your father is pleased with you. If you perform like that tomorrow night, you will have no difficulty with any part of the ceremonies. Now, ask me a question, anything you like."

"About the Gathering, you mean?"

"About anything you like, I said."

"Well, my lord, there is one thing. What ... what does a Raising mean? What is it?"

"Ha! I should have known you'd ask me the only question I can't answer. I can't tell you, boy. Not that. But come midnight tomorrow, you'll know anyway, and you'll know, too, why I could not tell you tonight. Now ask me something else."

"Well, sir, now that the other brethren know me as a student, some of them have been warning me that the Raising is dangerous, that there are great risks built into it. But I suspect that's only their way of cozening me, and I don't want to waste my question by asking about that ..."

"Then ask me something you do want to ask about."

Hugh nibbled at his upper lip, and then blurted, "Why me, my lord? Why not my brother?"

"Ah, so you know about that. I was wondering if you did." The dimly outlined shape across from Hugh stirred in its seat. "Who told you about it?"

"My father, and my grandfather, too. They warned me not to speak of it to William, because he knows nothing of the reality of the Gatherings and does not belong to the brotherhood. I asked them what brotherhood they were talking about, since William is my brother, but they would tell me nothing more. They said I would understand everything after my own

Raising, and that until then they could say no more. But they warned me that if I were to speak a word of this to William I would forfeit my own chance of belonging. I am not sure I want to belong to any brotherhood—and I care not what it does or what it means to others—if it requires me to deny my own brother."

St. Clair exhaled loudly. "There's no denial involved, Hugh, but I understand what you mean. I was in your shoes myself once, facing the exact same circumstances and for exactly the same reasons. My elder brother was passed over, just as William was."

"But for what reason?" There was anguish in the young man's voice. "There's nothing wrong with my brother. William is not a bad man, he is simply … young."

"Aye, *young*. That he is. And weak, too, whether you care to admit that or not." The voice coming from the darkness was heavy now, speaking slowly and clearly. "He is your elder by two years, Hugh, and you are already years senior to him in rank and prowess. How long can a boy continue to be a boy before becoming a man? Your William, like my own brother Richard before him, is still attempting, successfully it seems, to avoid achieving manhood. And manhood is what this is mainly about, Hugh."

"Aye, perhaps it is, but William will one day be Baron de Payens."

"And you will not. Do you resent that?"

Hugh blinked, surprised that he should be asked. "No, of course not. I have never thought to be Baron.

It simply seems to me that if he is judged fit to be the Baron of Payens, he should be deemed good enough to join this brotherhood of yours."

"Not at all." St. Clair's voice was flat. "There is no *judgment* involved in his being your father's heir. That is sheer chance. As firstborn, he is *blessed* among your father's sons, but he is not necessarily *best* among them. Should William prove to be a weak baron, or a foolish or even a tyrannical one, any damage that he does may be undone by his successor. On the other hand, should he prove to be a weak member of our brotherhood, the damage he could do might well destroy it.

"The event for which you are training now—your Raising—will grant you entry into the ranks of an amazing comradeship, Hugh, a fraternity dedicated to great ideals and the protection of dire secrets. Its roots are ancient and its history is shrouded in the earliest beginnings of antiquity, and you know nothing about it. Can you guess why you know nothing?"

Hugh shook his head, realizing as he did so that St. Clair probably could not see him. "No."

"Because it *is* secret, lad, and it has been that way since its beginnings. Secrecy is essential to its continued existence, and so we who guard its secrets must be constantly vigilant, particularly among ourselves. I tell you this now only because, having listened to you at your work, I know you will pass tomorrow's test with no difficulty, and that means you will be admitted to our fraternity tomorrow anyway. No one—*no* one, Hugh—who is loose-lipped can ever be admitted to our brotherhood. The danger of his drinking or whoring and then talking indiscreetly is too great. Your brother William drinks too much, and when he drinks even a little, he talks too much. He is a splendid fellow, a good companion with whom to share a flask of wine or a meal and a fit of laughter over amusing and trivial things, but he is weak willed, intemperate, quarrelsome at times, and always too talkative and indiscreet, and thus he was deemed unworthy of belonging."

"He was *deemed*? By whom? Who would be arrogant enough to deem the son of Baron Hugo de Payens unworthy?"

St. Clair sighed. "Your own tutors, lad. His father, the Baron de Payens himself, and his grandfather, the lord Baldwin of Montdidier. One person per family, Hugh, that's all that is permitted. One son from each generation of each of the families involved may be initiated into the mysteries, and the selection has nothing to do with the laws of primogeniture. The first boy born into a family will inherit, if he lives. That is the law. But the boy chosen from among his siblings to be of our brotherhood is chosen by merit, not by any accident of birth, timing or precedence, and therefore all the sons of all the families are watched closely by *all* the elders. There is no room for error or for carelessness."

He held up an open palm to forestall Hugh before he could interrupt. "I know what you are going to say—how can they judge such things? Well, eighteen is the youngest age at which a new member may join, and by then he has been closely watched and judged for suitability for years. Thus, if a family has seven sons, born even two years apart, and none of them shows distinctive and definitive qualifications for membership, the elders may simply defer making a choice among the seven until sufficient time has passed to form a judgment on the youngest one. The oldest boy will be fourteen when the seventh is born. By the time the youngest is eighteen, the eldest will still be only thirty-two years old, should the final choice revert upon him. But even then, if the elders are unable to decide, they may simply invite no one from that generation to join. Ours is a secret fraternity, so no one who is not of the brotherhood would know what had been done, and therefore no one would be slighted or offended. It would not be the first time that had ever happened. There are sufficient families to generate an intake for every generation, and a passed-over generation may easily provide worthy members the next time around."

"But—" Hugh bit off his response before it could emerge.

"But what? What were you going to say?"

"What would happen if the elders judged two or more members of the same generation of a family to be worthy of admission?"

Hugh could hear the smile in St. Clair's voice as the knight responded, "Then the family involved would have produced a fine crop of sons. It happens often, Hugh, far more so than you might think, but nevertheless, only one from each family is admitted in a generation. Therefore, as you can see, the matter of the final choice is one of delicacy and fine judgment, involving great debate and deliberation."

"Who are these elders, then?"

St. Clair stretched and stood up, the smile still evident in his voice, even though Hugh could not see his face. "They change from year to year, depending on who dies and who survives, and that, my young friend, must be your tenth and last question, since I permitted you only one."

"One more then, my lord, a brief one, if it please you. How long is it since you were Raised, and has it truly made a difference to your life?"

Hugh sensed the knight's shape grow still in the darkness, and when the deep voice spoke again it was quieter than it had been before. "I was eighteen, the age you are now, and that was a long time ago ... twenty-three years and more. As for whether it made a difference to my life, I must say that it has. Not because it generated any major change that I could identify with certainty, but because of all I have learned since, simply through belonging. I can tell you honestly that I believe myself to be a better man because of what the brotherhood has taught me, but more than that I cannot say until you yourself have been admitted to the fraternity." A sound from somewhere in the surrounding darkness made the knight look around him. "Come now, our brethren here are growing impatient to be gone, for they have been working down here all day, preparing for tomorrow's ceremonies. Besides, it must be close to dinnertime."

Together the two men retraced their steps until they passed through the last pair of doors and found themselves in the pit again, at the bottom of the wooden stairs. The torches in the sconces along the wall were beginning to gutter audibly and would soon burn themselves out, but everyone down here on this hidden level would have departed before then, and the stairs would have been removed and the stairwell disguised by the false flooring above. Neither man said another word until they reached the upper floor where they had met, and as Hugh collected his sword from Sir Stephen's waiting guard, the knight inclined his head graciously to his godson, bidding him farewell.

Before they could part, however, they were interrupted by the sound of young female voices calling their names, and Lady Louise de Payens, Hugh's younger sister, came gliding towards them with her best and dearest friend, Lady Margaret St. Clair, Sir Stephen's fifteen-year-old daughter, who had arrived with him from England the previous day. Extending a hand to each of the girls, Sir Stephen greeted them with an enthusiasm that might have surprised more than a few of the men who looked up to him as a paragon of stern military virtue. Before the girls could tug him away with them in the direction of the guest quarters, he pulled them to a standstill, gripping their wrists tightly, one in each hand, and using the pressure of his fingers to bid them silently wait until he had finished his dealings with Louise's brother.

"I will see you at the appointed time tomorrow, godson. On the other matter, the one you did not want to waste a question on before, look at it through the eyes of the tutors with whom you have been working, and ask yourself if they would endanger you in any way. The lads are teasing you, as you suspected. It's all a part of learning to belong, and of earning your place. You'll survive." He swung away to face the girls. "And now, young ladies, I am yours to command." The girls called goodbye to Hugh, then led Sir Stephen away, each of them holding one of his hands now, and neither of the two men had noticed the glance that passed between the girls as they listened to what the knight had said to Hugh.

TWO

B y the following afternoon, with less than an hour remaining between him and the test he must undergo, Hugh de Payens was beginning to doubt that he knew anything at all, more than half convinced that he must be suffering some kind of dementia, since his mind seemed to him to be no longer the one he had grown up with. Faced with what seemed like an interminable wait before he was hauled in to face his inquisitors, he had attempted to distract himself by reviewing the answers to the questions he would be asked, but to his horror he was unable to recall a single word of what he had fought so hard, and for so long, to learn. Not only was he unable to remember any of the responses, he was unable even to recall the basic catechism of questions that his father and grandfather had been hurling at him for months. Frustrated and suddenly close to panic, he imagined he could feel his entire skull, immense and empty, vaulted and grotesquely domed between his ears, too large and hollow, like an empty, echoing cavern. He wanted to weep, and a small voice inside him was telling him insistently to run away, but he did neither. He simply sat where he was, staring straight ahead and trying to empty his mind of everything that occupied it, as he waited to be summoned to the Gathering.

He became aware that he was no longer alone and raised his eyes to see Payn Montdidier, one of his closest friends and a cousin on his mother's side, smiling down at him, his amber eyes gentle and filled with humor. "Ready?" he asked, and Hugh stood up, blinking in mild disbelief.

"Crusty! I didn't expect to see you here! You can have no idea how glad it makes me, my friend—a familiar face. I have been dying here, by inches, of anticipation, mixed with terror."

Montdidier laughed. "I've come to know that mixture well since yesterday, so perhaps we may help each other."

Hugh frowned. "I don't follow. What d'you mean, since yesterday?"

"Anticipation and terror. It hit me for the first time yesterday, when I saw your sister's new friend. Who is she?"

Hugh's eyes went wide with surprise. "You mean Margaret? Louise's friend from England?"

"From England?"

"Aye, the tall, dark-haired girl."

"Wearing a bright yellow gown?"

"She was wearing yellow when I saw her yesterday, with her father and Louise. Is that the lady you mean?" He saw Montdidier's wide-eyed nod, and grinned. "She's the Lady Margaret St. Clair, daughter of my godfather, Sir Stephen. What nonsense are you spouting about anticipation and terror?"

Montdidier's face had fallen at the mention of St. Clair's name, and now he shook his head. "Anticipation of meeting her, and terror that she might ignore me ... And if she's the daughter of Sir William St. Clair, she *will* ignore me, most undoubtedly."

For the first time in days, Hugh had completely forgotten about the ordeal that lay ahead of him, captivated by the look on his friend's face and the emotions that were there to be read by anyone who cared to look. He was about to laugh, then realized that his friend might take his wonderment as ridicule and be hurt. "Crusty, are you smitten? And after seeing the lady only once? I have known Margaret for years. She is no beauty, but—"

"She has beauty enow for me, Hugh. Those eyebrows, that forehead, and that long neck. I have to meet her."

Now Hugh laughed aloud. "Well, that's easily arranged. You shall meet her tomorrow, and I will not permit her to ignore you ... not that she would be tempted for a moment to do such a thing. And I won't even tell Louise that you asked me to present you to her." Then his face grew somber again. "But in the meantime, there's tonight. Will I live through that?"

Montdidier grinned his old grin again. "By God, if my meeting Lady Margaret St. Clair depends upon that, then I'll fight to the death for you myself. But we are expected, and I have kept you standing here talking into tardiness. Shall we go?"

Hugh nodded, swallowed hard, and followed his friend. Payn Montdidier was known as Crusty to all his friends for two very fine reasons: Crusty was a word applied to bread, and the local word for bread, pai-yin, sounded very much like Payn, which, in its turn, was almost exactly similar in sound to Hugh's last name, de Payens. That similarity of sound had often led to much confusion before some wag started calling the young man Crusty several years earlier. The name had been amusing, and had stuck, and the confusion had been annulled.

The public functions at the Gathering were always held in the flagstone-floored hall directly beneath the main reception floor, at the foot of the castle's great spiral staircase, and as Crusty led him into the assembly, Hugh was surprised to see the size of the crowd. There must have been two hundred men in the vast room, perhaps more, not counting the army of servants and scullions who were moving around everywhere, and none of them paid the newcomers the slightest attention as Hugh followed Payn the length of the hall, to a table set for twelve that had been laid lengthwise in front of and abutting the very center of the head table. The table was already filled, but for a pair of vacant, high-backed chairs that sat empty, and as he approached, Hugh paid close attention to who would be sitting with them. There were two St. Clair brothers among them, Robert and Vincent, and that made him feel better immediately, although he could not have explained why. Robert, the elder of the two, was twenty-three, five full years older than Hugh, and yet he was his favorite among all the St. Clair brothers, the senior of four sons, the youngest of whom, Stephen, was fifteen, the same age as Hugh's sister, Louise. Vincent, sitting beside his elder brother and directly across from Hugh, was two years junior to Robert, and the remaining brother, William, named after the late king of England, was barely seventeen, still too young to attend the Gathering.

Hugh had been wondering for some time now whether Robert St. Clair might be one of the brotherhood, and as Sir Stephen's firstborn son, it had seemed likely to Hugh, in his ignorance, that he would be, but Robert's own father had said the night before that being firstborn did not entail membership in the fraternity, and so now Hugh bit his tongue, stifling his curiosity. Another of Hugh's friends was at the table, a nineteen-year-old cousin of some description. Hugh had never been able to come to an understanding of the varying degrees of kinship and consanguinity among the Friendly Families, as their clans were known, but Godfrey St. Omer and Hugh had been born less than a year apart and had been bosom companions since early childhood, when Hugh, incapable of pronouncing Godfrey's name, had called him Goff and the name had stuck. Now they did not even need to speak. Godfrey, lounging in his chair and listening to something his nearest neighbor was saying, merely smiled at Hugh's approach and closed one eye lazily in a long, welcoming wink.

The dinner passed quickly, and Hugh remembered little of it, even though it was the first Gathering dinner in which he had ever participated and, in its own way, the most important assembly he had ever attended. He met and spoke with all the other people at his table, most of whom were familiar to him by sight, and all of whose names he knew, although there were four of them, visitors from other regions, whom he had never actually seen before.

The meal seemed to end before it had time to get started, and as soon as the tables were cleared off, the entertainment began, with musicians, bards, jugglers, mummers, and dancers assembled from the great duchies of Anjou, Aquitaine, and Burgundy, and even a family of tumblers from the court of the King of France. The entertainers, however, were present only to provide an amusing and diverting background to the other activities that were now beginning throughout the hall, most of which involved copious drinking, the placing of wagers, and the setting of odds governing the real entertainment of the evening, which would be provided by the diners themselves.

Fully one quarter of the men in the hall, all of them young, had eaten sparely and drunk not at all during dinner, for they were to be the focal point of this night's activities. Their names had been chosen by lot, to the chagrin of their less fortunate peers who had not been picked, and when they were called upon later to step forward, they would fight against each other, singly and in groups, as though their lives depended upon the outcome, which, in one minor respect, at least, they did. They were the real entertainers here, but their performance and the abilities they demonstrated would be watched closely and critically judged by their peers and companions, for the competition among knights was always fierce and belligerent, and no aspect of anything they ever did could fail to reflect upon their reputations for competence and dependability.

Technically speaking, the combat in which they would engage was for sport alone, with wooden weapons and dulled practice swords so that there should be no risk of injury or death. The reality was, however, that many a knight had died in such events, trying too hard to snatch a victory from a stronger and more able opponent. Hugh was fully aware of the importance of the combative stage of the banquet, and he was unhappy that he himself would not be able to participate, or even to watch the fights, but he said nothing to anyone because he had no way of knowing who belonged to the brotherhood and who did not. And he knew, too, that it was during this stage of the activities that the real business of the Gathering was carried out in the secret chambers far below, while the attention of all the uninitiated was tightly focused on the contests being waged here. Most of the older knights had already begun to leave the hall after the meal, before the fighting began, although they would all have been welcome to remain and enjoy the activi-ties, but this part of the night's festivities had been carefully designed, and was now generally accepted, as the purview of the younger attendees at the Gathering, and tradition dictated that they be left to enjoy it without the inhibiting presence of their elders.

There was nothing casual or accidental about the regularly scheduled Gatherings and the activities that took place there, nor was there anything coincidental about the physical similarity of all the men in attendance. They were all knights, and that single distinction set them apart from other men in a number of ways that were plainly visible. They were all well born, for one thing, although no law or requirement stipulated that a knight must be of noble birth. It simply happened that the vast majority of knights were born into aristocratic, land-owning families. Of course, had they been born in different circumstances, they would have had their lives and all their working days laid out for them from the moment of birth, and they would have spent their days on earth as common working men, bound by the laws of feudalism to serve the owner of the land on which they lived, and struggling every day to provide for the families with which they would have been encumbered early in life.

Among the wealthy, land-owning families, under the law of primogeniture the holdings of the family, its land and wealth, passed from the father to the oldest surviving legitimate son. Other sons—younger and therefore lesser—were expected to make their own fortunes and were faced with selecting one of two professions: knighthood or priesthood. Most became knights and fought for their livelihood, espousing the causes of their feudal overlords; others, physically weaker, or disabled in some way, or even intellectually inclined and gifted, joined the Church, where, as clerics, they could live out their lives, often usefully, without being a burden on their families.

The vast majority of well-born young men, however, hundreds of thousands of them throughout all the countries of Christendom, were knights, and as such, they were trained to fight from their earliest boyhood. They were encouraged to fight, and expected to know everything that could be known about weaponry, horses, and armor, as well as to be proficient in every kind of fighting and warfare. The awareness that physical prowess is the only valid measure of a man's worth was hammered into them at every stage of growth from infancy. Paradoxically, however, under the stern and unyielding eye of the all-powerful Church and its ubiquitous clerics, they were simultaneously forbidden to fight, or even to brawl in public, and could be rigorously, even savagely, punished if they flouted the law. There was a very real need, therefore, for formal occasions like the Gatherings, at which young knights could fight among themselves legally, venting their pent-up frustration and energy while measuring themselves, publicly, against the best among their peers.

Hugh looked about him again, his eyes seeking the men who would fight that night. They were easy to find, for they were all sober, their demeanor serious, each of them withdrawn into himself, contemplating the strategies he would employ in the contest ahead, and as Hugh saw how they all resembled each other, his lips quirked in a tiny grin, for he knew that he himself, seen from behind, would have been indistinguishable from all of them, and yet instantly recognizable as a knight.

A knight was defined and could be instantly identified, in any country of Christendom, by his musculature; Englishman, German, Frank, Gaul, or Norman, it made no difference. All knights used similar weapons, wore virtually identical armor and trappings, and fought the same way, so that the only advantage any individual could gain over his peers was through constant and unflagging training and practice, involving the endless repetition of drills and exercise, hour after hour, day after day, month after month without respite, trying to go further, to endure more, and to last longer than any other man possibly could under the same circumstances. To do otherwise, to fail to train, was to die eventually on some field, your stamina and strength ground down and undermined until you fell, bested and beaten by someone who had simply worked harder and trained for longer and with more dedication and discipline than you had. And so no knight worthy of his title would ever contemplate allowing a day to pass without at least six hours of grinding, disciplined training of some kind.

A steel-hilted broadsword with a four-foot-long, three-inch-wide blade could weigh fourteen pounds. An unhorsed knight, afoot and encumbered by a sixty-pound coat of chain mail and all the padding and reinforcement that went with it, might have to stand and swing that sword one-handed, fighting for his life without rest and for minutes at a time. Thus the physical phenomenon known as the knight's build: neck and shoulder muscles, heavy and corded like ships' ropes, sloped down to enormously wide shoulders and gigantically muscled arms that projected sideways, pushed forward and into prominence by the massive bulges of chest, back, and torso; waists and hips were usually narrow and tight, above gargantuan thighs and tightly muscled calves that appeared to be constructed of slabs of meat. There were more than a hundred and a half such men gathered here in the banquet room, the only real difference between them being that some were longer of leg, and therefore taller, than others. Most of them could neither read nor write, preferring to leave such foolery to clerics, but without exception, they could all be relied upon to fight unflaggingly, at any time and without provocation, until their great strength had been exhausted and they collapsed senseless.

Looking about him now, Hugh saw that the crowd was good-natured and relaxed, the wines and ale were excellent and plentiful, and everyone in attendance was anticipating a marvelous night of entertainment. His father and grandfather had already left the hall, among the first to vanish, and they were now being followed by others, and although Hugh had been warned by his grandfather that this would occur and would not be remarked upon by anyone, it seemed to him at first that the exodus of elders and prominent knights was too obvious to go unnoticed. Fortunately, however, he also saw that their departures were masked, to a great extent, by a general pattern of movement as men began to change seats and to circulate among the tables, visiting friends and exchanging wagers on the outcome of the fights that would soon begin. After that, he was even able to relax slightly and breathe more calmly, until it dawned upon him that the time of his own inquisition was rapidly approaching.

It was his cousin, Godfrey St. Omer, who stood up eventually and clicked his fingers to capture Hugh's attention, and moments after that the two of them were headed down into the bowels of the castle, the din of the banquet hall fading rapidly behind them. Godfrey, normally irrepressible, was a silent, vigilant escort on this occasion, and he led Hugh quickly through the preliminary approaches to the secret assembly area and through the first set of doors, to stand in the circle of identical doors in the octagonal vestibule. He rapped on one with the hilt of his dagger, and when it swung open he stepped forward smartly and whispered something to the guard there, and then they both waved to Hugh to come forward. He did, and they asked him jointly for the password he had learned on his previous visit. He repeated it, resisting the urge to smile at their boyish earnestness, and they solemnly passed him forward alone from that point, to find his own way along a narrow, darkened, twisting passageway. At the end, Hugh found himself in a small room lighted by a single lantern and containing only a kneeling bench used for prayer that was draped with a drab-looking cloth that turned out to be a mendicant's robe. Hugh, remembering what he had learned from his two previous visits, dropped his own rich clothing to the floor and pulled on the beggar's threadbare tunic. Then, dressed more poorly than he had ever been in his life, he sat down in the bare wooden chair to await whatever might come next.

THREE

Hugh was more aware of impressions than of anything else during the time that followed his being summoned into the Chamber. He had no idea who the messenger who came to fetch him was, for the man was robed in black from head to toe, every vestige of individuality that might have identified him concealed from view. The passageway through which he led Hugh towards the Chamber was equally black and featureless, with not a single glimmer of light to relieve the darkness, so that Hugh, clutching the man's elbow and following him closely and with extreme caution, wondered how the fellow could possibly find his way without bumping into anything. He would discover later that there had been nothing to bump into, that there had been no passageway at all and that the serpentine, disorienting twists and turns they had taken had simply followed lines laid out on the wide floor of a single, black-painted anteroom. His guide had simply kept one hand on a black silken cord that led him unerringly towards his destination, the larger Chamber beyond.

Hugh knew they had reached the end of the passageway when they stepped through an unseen doorway into another place, for the silence there, though equally profound, had a different feel to it, a quality of spacious airiness. His guide stopped walking abruptly, and Hugh, following closely behind, walked right into him, striking him with his shoulder and almost unbalancing both of them. As he pulled himself to attention, holding his breath in his eagerness to hear anything that might be there for the noticing, a tiny gleam of light sprang into view far above them and grew steadily brighter and larger until it cast the faintest nimbus of light into the darkness that filled the Chamber. Hugh did not move his head to look about him, for he had done so on both of his earlier visits to this place and had been rewarded with pain for his temerity as his guide on each occasion had pierced his side with a goad of some kind, drawing blood both times. Now he merely strained to see and hear anything he could.

There were people here, he knew. He could sense them sitting or standing nearby, and that, too, he was familiar with from his previous visits, but this time it *felt* as though there were far more people out there than there had been on the first two occasions. Deprived of all sensory evidence, he had no true way of gauging how many people surrounded him. His mind was merely registering impressions, he knew, and those impressions must be influenced by his own knowledge of the numbers of people assembled for the Gathering.

He gritted his teeth, flexed his fingers, and forced himself to breathe deeply, seeking calm within himself and determined to allow the current of whatever events were scheduled here to carry him where he needed to go. It was, he thought at one point, the most difficult task he had ever assumed, for every aspect of his education and training demanded the exact opposite of what he was doing, and yet his father and grandfather had both been insistent that he needed to be passive now, and must simply let himself go along with whatever developed, ignoring the disciplines of his training and the fact that he had been taught to question everything he was told, and to fight against every effort made by anyone to manipulate him or to force him to do anything against his own good judgment. *Float,* he told himself now, *float!*

Someone approached him and stood close enough for Hugh to smell the heavy but not unpleasant sweetness of his breath, and began to chant in a language that Hugh had never heard before. It was a long incantation, and whatever it signified, as it progressed it seemed to Hugh that the air in the Chamber grew steadily brighter, so that he was soon able to see the shape of the man in front of him, and the dim outlines of others, many others, on the edges of the blackness around him. He saw, too, that his black-clad guide had vanished soundlessly from his side, no doubt at the moment when the cantor had stepped forward and claimed Hugh's attention.

At the conclusion of the opening chant, matters began to move more quickly, and Hugh was able to recognize, with more and more frequency, elements of what he had been learning for months. Throughout, he was conducted and led about by a succession of robed and hooded figures, to be positioned in various spots and then catechized by people whose differing, highly stylized modes of dress—defined in the darkness by shape and by bulk rather than detail—led him to believe they must be officers of the brotherhood. And still, continuously but infinitely slowly, the light in the Chamber continued to grow brighter. The single light source remained unaltered, a sole speck of brightness high above the assembly, but Hugh soon came to believe that it was being lowered, in infinitesimal increments, as the rites progressed, for he could increasingly see the outlines and shapes of individual people in the rows of seats surrounding the open floor of the Chamber, and although it was still far too dark to discern any of their features, he could clearly see the shadowy outlines of the alternating black and white squares in the floor.

Then, at the conclusion of a response that was one of the longest he had had to learn, he was forced to his knees by two men who held his wrists and pressed down on his shoulders. Kneeling thus, uncomfortably aware that he could not have resisted had he wished to, he was required to swear the most horrifying and baleful oath he could ever have imagined, calling down torture, dismemberment, death, and disgrace on himself and his loved ones should he ever recant and betray the secrets he was about to learn. He swore the oath, as required, and was allowed to rise to his feet again, surrounded by a number of men who laid hands on him and steered him gently towards what he could only believe to be a far corner of the Chamber. There he was turned again, and positioned with his chin raised towards the single source of light above, noticing that it was now framed between two high pillars that appeared to form a doorway or portal, and a new voice, stronger and more sonorous than any other he had heard, spoke in a language unknown to him.

He was aware of bodies pressing closer to him, and then there was a sudden scurry of movement in the surrounding darkness and several things happened at once, the worst and most unexpected of them bringing his heart leaping into his throat in terror. Some unknown man standing ahead of him suddenly broke away from the group and bent quickly, as though to snatch something up from the ground, then came rushing directly towards Hugh, raising a heavy club over his head and swinging it at Hugh's. As that happened the light went out, and Hugh felt himself being grasped from behind, hard and tightly, by many hands that held him rigid as they jerked him back and away from the murderous blow, pulling him down and lowering him helplessly, hard, towards the floor as the blow landed obliquely on his temple, hitting with a muffled thump rather than a bone-splintering crash. Stunned and disoriented, unable to move against the iron clutch of so many unseen hands, his heart pounding with breath-stopping fear, Hugh felt himself being lowered farther than he would have thought possible without meeting the floor, and then being pulled and tugged, turned one way and then another with no possibility of resisting, and for a disbelieving moment, he felt as though they were wrapping him in something.

So quickly that the speed of it unnerved him more than ever, all the gripping hands left him, all sounds and movement stopped, and the silence became absolute again. Terrified beyond anything he had ever known, Hugh lay motionless, holding his breath, his eyes clenched tightly shut as he tried to gauge what had happened to him. He knew he ought to be dead, for he had seen the size of the club his assailant had swung at him, and he had felt the impact of the blow, but no pain. And now there was nothing: no pain, no feeling at all, no sound, no light, nothing except the pounding of his own heart, reverberating in his chest and thudding in his ears. Could a dead man yet hear such things, or were they merely memories of life? Where was he now, if not in some anteroom of Heaven or Hell, awaiting the arrival of a judge?

Slowly, fearfully, he opened his eyes to see nothing but utter, stygian blackness, as deep and dark as the lack of light had been behind his tightly clenched eyelids. The dark, the silence, the profound stillness surrounding him, and the lack of pain or feelings combined to convince him that he really was dead, and as he allowed his mind to begin exploring that possibility, there came a tiny, metallic sound, and light exploded into the darkness as someone opened the closed door of a burning lamp.

Hugh went rigid with fear again, his heart leaping in his chest as he saw the person holding the lamp

insert a taper through its open door, and then other
tapers were extended towards the flame of the first, so
that the room filled rapidly with light. Hugh moved to
roll over and sit up, but found that he could not move,
and then a hand was pressed gently over his mouth
from above, bidding him to lie still. Moments later, he
found himself staring directly up at a ring of faces that
were looking down at him from high above. He was
flat on his back. Then the robed and hooded man
standing at his feet gave a signal, and the others knelt
quickly and reached down towards him, and once
again Hugh felt their hands grasp him and lift him,
exerting rigid control over him, so that his heels
remained on the ground while the rest of him was
swung upright, as stiff as a wooden board on a hinged
end, until he was standing erect. The hands left him
then, withdrawn in pairs, he thought, until he was
standing free, staring at the hooded man now facing
him, and knowing, from the man's immense height
and size, exactly who he was.

Sir Stephen St. Clair reached up and pulled off his
black hood, his face crinkled in a wide smile. "What are
you wearing?" he asked Hugh. Surprised by the
mundane question, Hugh looked down, then blinked
in confusion, never having seen this garment before. "I
don't know, my lord," he answered, shrugging his
shoulders and discovering that he was tightly bound in
a strange white robe, unable to move his arms.

"It is the cerement." St. Clair's face was grave again.
"You know what that is?"

Hugh glanced down again. "Aye, my lord. It is the shroud worn to the grave by a dead man."

"It is. And do you know why you are wearing it?"

"No, my lord."

"Turn around, then, and see where you have been."

Hands seized Hugh's arms and turned him slowly, bracing him as he reared back. Directly at his feet lay an open shallow grave containing a bleached human skull with a pair of thigh bones crossed beneath it. Hugh stood there stunned, gazing down into the pit. It was real, and he had lain in it. No wonder, he thought, that it seemed he had been lowered a long way.

"You died and were laid down," St. Clair said, "and then the light returned and you were raised up again to life. You are reborn, newborn, a different person, one of our ancient brotherhood. Your previous life now lies behind you, forsaken, finished, and abandoned, and you have been reborn into Enlightenment to serve the search for truth and restitution of that which was in our beginnings. Welcome therefore, Brother Hugh, to our fraternity, the Order of Rebirth in Sion. Now that you have been Raised to be one of us, you will have the opportunity to learn all that there is to know about our ancient and sacred trust, and the first step in that progression is to enrobe you in the vestments of the initiate."

"So mote it be!" Every man present spoke the words, their voices blending into a muffled thunder, and Hugh experienced, for the first time, the ancient blessing and ritual approval of the Brotherhood of the Order of Rebirth.

St. Clair motioned with his hand, and four white-clad men came forward to surround Hugh. They stripped him quickly of the shroud in which he had been wrapped, and of the coarse, jute tunic he had worn beneath it, and then they dressed him in a girdle made from the fleece of a lamb, over which they draped rich vestments of snowy white, and when they stepped away from him again, he saw that everyone else present had set aside the black cloaks they had worn earlier and were dressed in the same kind of brilliantly white garment that he wore. Some among them yet wore black, but only as adornments to their white garb, and Hugh quickly guessed that the black ornamentation signified rank of some kind, for all of them were different. The entire Chamber was now revealed in all its magnificence, and every element of it, ceiling, walls, furnishings, and floor, was either black or white or a combination of both.

Now St. Clair stepped forward with extended arms and embraced his white-clad godson, then stepped aside as Hugh's father and grandfather came next to welcome their family's latest member to the brotherhood. They were followed in turn by every other person there, and as Hugh accepted the acknowledgments of all of them, being enfolded in each one's arms in a welcoming gesture of brotherhood and recognizing some of them with great astonishment, he was thinking of what had happened, and of how many of the mysteries that had confounded him until tonight had suddenly become clear, and even as that thought occurred to him, he understood more and more as pieces continued to click into place within his mind.

Much later, when the last of the evening's rites had been concluded and the crowd had begun to disperse, Hugh found himself sitting in a brightly lit anteroom to the main chamber, sharing a jug of wine with his father, his two grandfathers, and his godfather, and at one point, when the conversation had reached a natural pause, Sir Stephen St. Clair set down his cup and crossed his arms over his broad chest, pushing himself back so that his chair rocked on its rear legs. Hugh waited, but St. Clair held his peace.

"Forgive me, my lord, but I think you wish to ask me something?"

St. Clair shook his head. "No, I want to tell you something, so listen carefully. We are brothers now, you and I, by virtue of tonight's proceedings, so we will have no more 'my lord' from you, especially here in the Chamber. If ever you feel a paralyzing need to be formal, you may call me Sir Stephen, but in the normal way of things, Stephen will suffice, as between natural brothers. You did well tonight, but we all knew you would. And last night, you may recall, I gave you leave to ask me any question that you wished. Now that you have been Raised, might you have another question in you?"

"Aye, I have, about the Order of Rebirth in Sion. The rebirth of what, or whom? Or does the name simply refer to the Raising ceremony? And where, or what, is Sion?"

"Aha!" St. Clair raised his feet, allowing his chair to drop onto all four legs again, and held out his hand to the Baron. Baron Hugo laughed ruefully, reached into the scrip at his belt, and threw his friend a purse of coins. The knight snatched it from the air with the speed of a pouncing cat and turned back to Hugh, grinning widely and holding the heavy purse in his extended palm. "I made this wager with your father yesterday, that you would ask me exactly what you did, with only one question available to you." He tossed the purse into the air and caught it again, then dropped it into his own scrip. "As for the answers to your question, you are now in a position to learn them for yourself, for they must be learned, earned, and won, just as your Raising was.

"Sion is the Hebrew name for the Holy Land, a place of safety, or sanctuary. That is common knowledge to anyone who thinks to ask. I cannot tell you more than that, however, nor can any other of our brethren, until you have earned the right to hear it. Even our most learned members have earned their right to know each secret. And you will earn those rights, one by one, as each of us here has learned them. That is how we function, and how we progress through the levels of our Order's knowledge: we study, and we learn the rituals—perfectly, word by word—from our brethren, the most revered of whom have spent their lives acquiring that knowledge, experience, and wisdom. We are carefully tested on our learning, and when we are ready, each of us at his own pace and according to his own wishes, we progress to the next level of awareness. Some progress further than others do, dependent upon intellect, abilities, and interests. There is no yardstick of judgment applied to the achievement of learning from this point onward; there is only the assessment of understanding and knowledge." A half-formed quirk at the corner of St. Clair's mouth hinted at the beginnings of a smile. "I can promise you, however, that you will enjoy earning those rights. The answers you find will excite you ... and the knowledge you will gain will astound you. I think, too, that once begun, you will learn quickly. And now we should rejoin the others upstairs."

"Wait, please, before we do. What happens next, here in Payens?"

"What happens next?" St. Clair glanced over at his friend Baron Hugo. "Well, as to you, I know not, but while we are here, your father and I will be seeing to other things, like marriages, for example. I have an unwed daughter and four sons, one of whom, at least, should marry soon, into a Friendly House. And your father has two daughters and two sons of marriageable age, one of whom is you. But I can see from your face that you had no thought of that in your mind. Speak up, lad, what are you thinking about?"

"The new Pope."

"The new Pope! Now yon's a dull topic. What about him? And why would a young knight from Anjou be thinking about a new *Pope*?"

Hugh shrugged his broad shoulders, but no trace of a smile touched his face. "Because he *is* new, and all men—all knights at least—should be thinking about him. I am told he has pledged himself to put an end to what he calls 'the problem of warring and contentious knights.'"

St. Clair was frowning now, looking from Hugh to Baron Hugo. "What's this? The *Pope* said that? I have heard nothing of this. What *problem* is he talking about?"

Baron Hugo answered him. "The same one that plagued us in our youth, Stephen, save that it's worse than ever. The problem of outlets for youthful energy. You would not be as aware of it in England today as we are here, because you have lived in a constant state of rebellion and insurrection, with continuous military activity over there for the past two decades, keeping your damned Saxons in their place. But the problem is real everywhere else throughout Christendom. And of course, although no one will ever admit it, its main cause, just as much now as it was in our day, is the Church itself, the damnable, officious zealotry of the priests. In England, surrounded by hostile Saxons, you have more than enough to keep your knights occupied and safely out of mischief, but over here knights are forbidden by law—which means of course forbidden by the Church, which *makes* the law—to fight among themselves in time of peace, or to brawl, or to break the civil amity in any way. And when they do—as they always do, being young and full of life and swarming everywhere one looks—the damn priests frown and punish them, fining them heavily, and sometimes even imprisoning them under pain of excommunication."

The Baron drew a deep breath, forcing himself to calm down. "Anyway, it is unhealthy and it has been going on for far too long and growing ever worse. But these last two decades, under Gregory as Pope, have been appalling. We are at the point of total anarchy and the entire situation is now untenable. The rule of law as we know it is being challenged and thwarted everywhere by the priests. That is how almost every knight at this Gathering would describe what is happening, and they would be echoed by their fellows everywhere in Christendom. But what is *truly* happening, the reality underlying the entire situation, is much more worrisome."

St. Clair had been listening closely, his eyebrows rising higher as the Baron went on, and now he flicked a hand in irritation. "I see where you are going, Hugo, but you are wrong. Gregory was an ambitious Pope, granted, but only for the spiritual dominion of the Church. His enthusiasm was for reform within the Church. And God knows it was needed."

"It is still needed, and Gregory is dead."

St. Clair paid no attention to the interruption. "But Gregory had no interest in governing the world. He was an autocrat—all popes are—but he was no would-be dictator. In his view of things, Rome should rule the world spiritually, through religion, but only after it had cleansed its own house of the stink and filth of corruption. And even then political government would always be the function of kings and ministers. He was not a comfortable man to be around, the Seventh Gregory—

and particularly so for errant priests and bishops—but his dreams were all of God's glory, not his own."

The Baron shrugged. "That may be true, but few of the characters surrounding him possessed his gifts or his vision, and only his strength held them under control. And now he has been dead for three years, and the man who took his place was a spineless nonentity who let the zealots run wild, doing what they wished. The upshot of three years of that is what we have in force today. The churchmen strut everywhere like peacocks, challenging the status quo everywhere and trying to wrest all power from the temporal lords in every land of Christendom."

He paused as though deliberating whether to continue, and then added, for St. Clair's benefit, "That, by the way, is what they have begun calling folk like you and me, were you aware of that? We are now designated 'temporal lords,' lords for the time being. Some clever little cleric in Rome doubtless came up with that piece of sophistry, undermining our ancient authority. They on the other hand, being anointed clerics and therefore God's personal representatives, are to be viewed as permanent and immutable." His voice became heavy with disgust. "It is a thing that has been building up for years now. I have discussed it with my lord the Count of Champagne, and with Count Fulk of Anjou, and several of the others, and there seems to be nothing we can do about it, other than resist in silence and refuse to suffer their damned arrogance."

The Baron glanced again from man to man, bringing all of them into what he was saying. "There is nothing of God in this, and I know you all know that. The breed of priests with whom we have to deal here care nothing for the things of God, save when it pleases them to wield His name as a weapon on their own behalf. They are all of this world, and hungry for the power and pleasures it contains. They buy their offices and live in fornication and they must stink in the nostrils of God.

"Gregory tried to stop all that, to reverse the trends, and he did well, for a while. But he was but one man, his reign too brief, and now they are back in power. This new Pope, Urban, is an unknown quantity. He may or may not align himself with the zealots. If he does, however, and if they win—if we permit them to win—then the whole world will be governed by priests and clerics, and men like us might as well lie down and die."

"But they won't win. They can't." St. Clair's voice was heavy with anger. "They are but priests, when all is said. That is iniquitous."

"Not so, Stephen. They believe otherwise. It is inevitable, in their eyes. It is the will of God, they say, and who is to contradict them, since only priests may speak with God to discover His wishes? But it is iniquitous. I will not disagree with you on that. And it is iniquity bred of greed and hypocrisy and the stench of corruption. But even if it comes to pass, it will require a long time to accomplish such an end.

"Urban was elected only recently, in March this year. He is very young and apparently full of ideals, according to the reports I have heard. He has sworn to put an end to all the nonsense—the publicly seen nonsense at the very least—and to resolve the matter of the knights and their uncontrolled violence. How he might do that without abolishing either the knighthood or the priesthood is a mystery to me, and to everyone else who even starts to think about it, but he has undertaken to do it."

Hugh had been listening avidly, thrilled to be a participant in a discussion of such depth, and now, emboldened by the fact that everyone plainly recognized his right to be there, he spoke up, surprising himself with the firmness of his own tone. "Well, he is the Pope. He could always start a war somewhere, in his own holy name. That would be nothing new, and it would give the knights something new to think about. They would all flock to a new war, and kill themselves off in admirable numbers. Of course, that would do nothing about the problem of the priests." Hugh was being facetious, but the Baron took him seriously.

"And where would he start this new war, boy? That's not a foolish idea, but it's impossible. There's no place to do it. This problem has infected all of Christendom. Everywhere. There's nowhere you can go to get away from it. There are only two kinds of men in our world—fighters and clerics, knights and priests. You do see that, do you not?"

Hugh nodded. "Aye, Father, I see it. Our world is, as you say, half-filled with knights, and in the eyes of those who fill the other half—the priests—they are become a plague." He looked to Sir Stephen St. Clair, who had been listening quietly, but had just reared upright in his chair, and now sat rigid, his eyes gazing off into some far distant place. After a few moments, he sat back again, beginning to scratch at his chin reflectively with one finger.

"You know, lad, you have just led me to a startling thought," he said. "You and your father, both. Christendom, the world, is full of knights, you said, and in the eyes of the Church they are become a plague. But not all the world is Christendom, and Christendom is sadly less than all the world ... and the Bible itself teems with plagues ..." His voice trailed away and he fell silent for a while. "I must think more on this, consult with people, and then, perhaps, I may talk to this new Pope. Perhaps. But not today. I have no wish to mix with clerics, and no need to go to Rome or Avignon, so let us talk now of other things. Have you heard about this new siege engine the Normans have developed, this trebuchet? I think that's what they are calling it. No, none of you? That surprises me. I have yet to see one of them myself, but by all accounts it is a fearsome device, capable of throwing a stone the size of a heavy man farther than anything else ever has."

FOUR

In the years that followed his Raising, from the age of eighteen until he was twenty-five, Hugh de Payens learned a great deal about life, while making rapid progress through the Levels of Learning of the Order of Rebirth, but he appeared to take little overt interest in any of the great changes that were occurring in the world around him. He was the kind of young man that people think of as being driven, impelled by a force that sets him apart and spurs him constantly to succeed in everything he attempts. Thus, when it came to his knightly responsibilities he fought like a lion, mastering sword, axe, dagger, mace, and spear, and even the crossbow, and was unbeatable either in the lists or in the butts, where his accuracy with the steel crossbow bolts quickly became a matter for awe. At the same time, he maintained a constant and focused attention to his studies within the Order of Rebirth, spending far more time with his tutors and elders than he did with people of his own age.

Commitment on such a scale carries a certain penalty, in that it leaves little time for things that are considered unimportant. Had anyone thought to ask for Hugh's opinion, they might have been perplexed to discover that, at such an early age, he considered relaxation or leisurely behavior of any kind unimportant and frivolous. He had no interest in carousing with his fellow knights, and he made no secret of the fact that he found the drinking of ale, for the mere sake of drinking until one grew drunk, to be a useless, feckless pursuit. That earned him little liking among his peers. But Hugh had friends enough, he believed; Godfrey St. Omer and Payn Montdidier had been his friends since boyhood, and even then he would have trusted them with his life. In later life he was to do exactly that, time and time again.

Godfrey's family, the St. Omer clan, held great estates in Picardy, and Godfrey had spent almost half his boyhood there, usually the winter months each year, obediently but under protest, since he was by far a younger son, fifth in line to inherit. He much preferred the other half of his life, where he spent the long summers in his mother's domain, which was close to Payens and the residence of her favorite cousin, Hugh's mother, and the friendship between their mothers had made it almost inevitable that the two boys should be friends, too.

Godfrey, much like Hugh in many things, was the perfect foil to him in others. The two were of an age, a mere ten months separating their births, with Godfrey the elder, and there was not a single item of physical similarity between them to indicate that they might be related to each other. Godfrey, with bright golden hair, had always appeared, at least from a distance, to be the more comely of the two youths, but on closer view, his blue eyes were set perceptibly closer together than were Hugh's brown ones, and although both lads had open, friendly countenances, the few girls of their acquaintance seemed to prefer Hugh's dark, saturnine appearance to Godfrey's sunny, golden one. The sole exception to that rule, as might be expected, was Hugh's younger sister, Louise, who had never had eyes for anyone other than Godfrey St. Omer since she grew old enough to recognize him from a distance. Godfrey, for his part, saw nothing out of place in that and was happy to return her high regard in equal measure.

Perhaps because of their close association with each other since childhood—Godfrey felt closer to Hugh than he ever had to any of his own brothers—they were equally skilled with weapons, although when he had to, Hugh could usually outfight Godfrey with swords. With the crossbow, however, a controversial weapon at the best of times since its distant and impersonal lethality seemed inconsistent with the spirit of chivalry, Godfrey always performed dismally and therefore tended to dismiss it contemptuously as being a weapon for old men and cripples. He was also as literate and well read as Hugh, thereby sharing an attribute that was viewed with deep suspicion by their fellow knights, most of whom were as ignorant as fence posts and regarded literacy as a clerical vice on a par with self-abuse and homosexuality. But where Hugh tended to be serious and single-minded to the point of sometimes appearing rigid and aloof, Godfrey was mercurial, with a sparkling wit, an irreverent, endearing, and never-failing sense of humor, and an inexhaustible willingness to see another person's point of view. He could cut through a conversational impasse or an awkward moment with a single barbed comment that usually brought laughter and averted unpleasantness.

The third and eldest member of their triumvirate, as they liked to call themselves, was Payn Montdidier, another Friendly Families scion and related somehow to both of them, although none of them ever bothered to inquire into the complexities of the cousinship; they were friends and that was all that mattered to any of them. Payn, like Hugh, was native to the County of Champagne. His father, like Hugh's own, was a senior and highly respected officer and tenant of Count Hugh, and Baron Hugo's wife was a Montdidier. Payn was a couple of months older than Goff and a year older than Hugh, and he had everything the others lacked in personal appearance and appeal. He was tall and slim, long legged, broad shouldered and narrow waisted even as a boy, and he had grown to manhood without losing any of his boyhood charm or his winning, affable ways. The tallest of the friends, a full head taller than Godfrey St. Omer, Payn had shoulder-length light brown hair, streaked with blond, and startling, amber-colored eyes that had frequently wrung sighs from the young women in their community.

Fortunately for everyone, Payn was genuinely unaware of his attractiveness, and his easy, informal friendliness and ready smile made it a simple thing for him to weave his way effortlessly through and around all the amatory threats that surrounded him constantly, without once giving serious offense to any of his disappointed lovers. Equally fortunately, for Payn himself, his fighting and riding skills set him sufficiently far above his more sullen and jealous rivals to ensure that he was never bothered by petty squabbles. He was a sound, solid friend, infinitely dependable, and Hugh and Godfrey felt deprived whenever he was not with them. In the year that followed Hugh's Raising, the three young men enjoyed what would be the most carefree time of their entire lives, and although much of their day, every day, was dedicated to duty and responsibilities, they nevertheless contrived to find ample time to enjoy themselves.

There was one more member of their group—one might have called him the fourth in the triumvirate, if such a thing were not logically impossible. As Sir Hugh de Payens, Hugh had an associate called Arlo, who was nominally and by birth a servant, but the two had been together for so long that Hugh simply accepted Arlo as a constant presence in his life, sharing most of his thoughts and activities first as a childhood friend and companion, then later as a classmate in learning to read and write, and later still, as both boys grew towards manhood, as his assistant, squire, bodyguard, and companion-at-arms.

The two of them were even closer to each other in age than Hugh was to Godfrey and Payn, and Arlo's father, Manon de Payens, had served Baron Hugo all his life. His eldest son, Arlo, had been born within three months and two hundred paces of young Hugh, and from the day of his birth it had been understood that Arlo, who also called himself de Payens because of his birth within the barony, would serve the future Sir

Hugh as his father had served Baron Hugo. Since then the two had been inseparable as boys and as men, sharing from the very outset of their lives that unique relationship, based upon total trust and mutual loyalty, that sometimes springs up between master and retainer. They had grown to know each other so well that frequently they had no need even to speak to each other, so close were they to thinking as one.

The Order of Rebirth was the sole topic proscribed among the four, never mentioned by any of the others in Arlo's hearing, and that had been an unforeseen development, starting at the moment of Hugh's first encounter with the Order. It was the only aspect of his new status that he did not enjoy wholeheartedly, since it meant that, after eighteen years of sharing every aspect of his life openly and fully with Arlo, he now found himself constrained to keep secrets from him. That he could understand and even justify the need for such secrecy did nothing at all to lessen his regret, but he had no other option than to accept that Arlo was not, and could never be, a member of the Order.

His dilemma resolved itself in a way that he could never have anticipated. He had been convinced that Arlo suspected nothing of what was going on, but there came a day when, for one reason after another, Hugh had had to shut Arlo out not merely once but three times in a single afternoon, and he grew angry at himself for not being able to do so less obviously, for it was clear that Arlo knew something untoward was going on. That night, however, in the period after dinner and before lights out, Arlo himself brought the matter up, in his own blunt, straightforward manner. It was a cool evening and they were outside, sitting alone by a well-established fire close to the stables, sharpening blades, Arlo with Hugh's sword and Hugh himself with a long, pointed dagger.

"Had a busy afternoon, today, didn't you?" Arlo spoke without raising his head from what he was doing. "You were scuttling around like a mouse in a miller's storehouse, frowning and biting your tongue all day."

Hugh stiffened as he wondered what was coming next.

"Days like that come and go, for all of us." Arlo straightened his back and laid the hilt of the sword against his knee before turning to look at Hugh.

"You're grumpy and you're upset. I can see that ... Everyone can see it. But you've been getting worse, that way at least, ever since you attended that big Gathering a few months ago." He held out the sword and squinted at the blade, looking for rust spots. "D'you know why *I* didn't attend that Gathering?" He glanced back just in time to see Hugh blink in astonishment at hearing such a question even asked. "'Course you do. I wasn't invited, that's why. And was glad to have it that way ... or I would have been glad, if I'd thought about it. It just isn't my place to attend such things. I wouldn't feel right, sitting there gawping among all you knights in all your fine clothes. Just the same way as you wouldn't feel right sitting around the kitchens with the scullions and the rest of us, eating the food we sometimes eat."

Hugh was frowning at him. "I am not sure I under-stand what you're saying, Arlo."

"Why not? It's plain enough." Arlo expelled a breath. "You and I are friends, Hugh, but before anything else, we're also master and servant—you the Baron's son, and me the Baron's servant's son. I never lose sight of that, but sometimes you do, and you shouldn't. Not ever. So now you're a man and you have new things to think about, things to which I can't be privy. I can sometimes see you fretting over it, like today. Well, you shouldn't, because I don't fret over it and I don't want to *know* whatever it is that keeps you so agitated. It's not my place to know about such things, and that pleases me." He looked Hugh straight in the eye. "I'm quite happy doing the things I have to do. I have enough of them to keep me occupied, I know how to do them all, and I can do them in my sleep if I have to. D'you hear what I'm saying to you?"

"Aye." Hugh had begun to smile. "You are telling me to mind my own affairs and keep them to myself, and to leave you to yours. I hear you."

"Good, because you're going to cut a finger off there if you don't start looking to what you're about."

WHEN THE TIME FINALLY CAME for Godfrey to marry Hugh's sister, Louise—Godfrey was almost twenty-one years old by that time, and tardy in taking up his spousal duties—the event had been so long awaited, its inevitability accepted, that it barely occasioned comment from Hugh and Payn; Louise had always been more of a friend than a sister to Hugh, and her relationship to Payn had been remarkably similar, in that they, too, were like brother and sister, so both men knew well that Godfrey's marriage to her would make little difference to the closeness they shared with him.

What no one expected, however, was that Payn, around the same time, would wed the Lady Margaret St. Clair. The two had met when Margaret accompanied her father on his visit to Champagne from England to attend Hugh's Raising, and although Payn had been far more enamored of Margaret than she of him, it became evident, much later, that he had none the less impressed her very favorably. So much so, as Hugh and his friends later discovered, that the Lady Margaret had done every-thing in her power, from the moment she returned home to England, to persuade her father to return with her to the civilized world of Champagne once again.

Sir Stephen, whose wife had died many years earlier, was utterly defenseless against both the wiles and the wishes of his only daughter, and had been so since the day of her birth, but he was unable to indulge her in this instance because of his duties and responsibilities to the King of England, William Rufus, son of William I, the Conqueror. But circumstances soon conspired with those same duties and responsibilities to oblige St. Clair, willing or no, to send Margaret back to Champagne without him. She arrived in the Barony of Payens in the early autumn of 1091, accompanied by a respectable retinue and bearing a heavy letter from her father to his old friend Baron Hugo, who was gracious enough to conceal any sense of misgiving he might have felt at the lady's unexpected reappearance, and to welcome her into his home and family. Then, once his wife and his ecstatic daughter had ushered her ladyship off to show her where she would be living and to distribute the people in her entourage among their own servants, the Baron sat down to read the letter from his friend. It was written on six sheets of heavy sheepskin vellum, carefully cured and scraped and softened with great care, then drafted with great precision, so that Hugo knew it had been dictated to one of Sir Stephen's scribes.

York
This Fifth Day of June, Anno Domini 1091
To Hugo, Baron of Payens in the County of
Champagne:

Greetings, my friend.

This missive, when it reaches you, will be accompanied by my greatest and most precious earthly possession, my daughter Margaret, and the mere fact of her presence there with you while I remain here in England will assure you that I am not making this approach to you lightly. Were I not deeply afraid for her safety now, I would never voluntarily part from her, nor would I impose upon you the task with which you are now faced: that of caring for another man's child. Margaret is no longer a child, however, and that is another contributing factor to this decision of mine.

Since the death of my wife, as you are aware, Margaret has been the light of my life, and she

has been saintly in her tolerance and acceptance
of the discomforts and indignities to which my
life, and my way of living it, have subjected her.
A castle such as mine is no fit place for a young
woman, as you are well aware. It is functional,
Spartan, and unlovely, its walls made of earth,
fronted by sharpened tree trunks, and its buildings
primitive, drafty, and mud-filled, containing no
amenities for a young, well-born woman. It is a
fortress, making no claim to being a home, and I
have finally come to see that, in merely keeping my
daughter here, I am condemning her, if not to
death, then at least to misery and squalor. We—
William's Normans—have now been here in
England for two decades and a half, and in this
region of York for sixteen years, and the local
Saxons are no less rebellious and savage now than
they were when first we came. I should have sent
my daughter far away from here years ago, but in
my own weakness and self-centered folly, I have
been afraid to part with her, for she provides my
only reminder of beauty in this rain-drenched,
sodden, chilly land.

Now, however, we are at war again, facing yet
another invasion from the north, and since I
cannot guarantee her safety, I have no other choice
but to send her to you, knowing that she could be in
no safer hands.

Malcolm Canmohr, the King of Scotland, has
come back to vanquish us—his third attempt in

*twenty years—and King William has decided yet
again that I should be the one to throw the fellow
out. I did it before, nine years ago, and we thought
to have done with it then, but now the Conqueror
is dead, and Canmohr—the name means Great
Chief, I am told—seems to believe the new king
will be easier to oust than his father was. Foolish
man. His wife, revered by her people as some kind
of saint, shares my daughter's name, but she is first
cousin to Egbert, the Saxon heir to the former
English throne, and thus she is unsaintly enough to
provoke her husband into squandering huge
numbers of men in trying to win back his
kingdom, not merely once, but thrice. And so I
must march in three days' time.*

*My army is assembling as I write, and will
consist of every available man I can conscript, and
one effect of that will be that I must leave my own
castle defenses to the care of a tiny skeleton crew
who will keep the gates closed until I return. Faced
with the inevitability of that, and with the real
possibility that I might not return at all from this
campaign, I have made arrangements to ship my
precious Margaret into your care. She and a small
party will leave tomorrow. The man in charge of
her party, appointed personally by myself, is called
Giscard, and he and his two sons, Michel and
Rombaud, are entrusted with sufficient gold, in
three sound chests, to dower the girl suitably for any
match you might arrange for her in future times.*

*I have no knowledge of when, or whether, you
might hear from me again, my friend, but neither
have I any doubt that my beloved daughter, in
your hands and under your supervision, could be
better served under any circumstances. Watch over
her for me, and I hope to see you both again soon.*

St. Clair

For the next three years, no word came out of
England concerning St. Clair. No one even knew if the
Scots invasion had been successful in the north. The
Normans in the south of the country were still in
power. That was common knowledge, but nothing was
known for sure about anything else, because William
Rufus willed it so and no one dared provoke his anger.
Unknowing then whether his old friend was dead or
alive, Baron Hugo had assumed full parental responsibility for the young woman by the end of her first full
year of residence with him, and treated her exactly as
he treated his own daughters, even going so far as to
arrange her marriage to young Payn Montdidier in the
autumn of 1092, as an eminently suitable match, advantageous to all parties, and one that he knew her father
himself would approve. The bridal couple were
nowhere near as visibly in love as Louise de Payens and
St. Omer had been, but they enjoyed and admired each
other, and everyone agreed that that was the required
basis for a lasting and successful marriage.

FIVE

For a time after that, life was idyllic for the three young men of the triumvirate. The two who were married lived in utter contentment, their wives the closest of friends, and Hugh, the unwed third, was more than satisfied to be able to work as hard as he wished on his studies of the Order of Rebirth without the distractions his now-preoccupied friends would normally have caused him.

The idyll came to an end on a day in May 1093, when Godfrey and Payn came to Hugh's quarters together, looking decidedly ill at ease. Hugh saw at first glance that something was seriously wrong, and he immediately set aside the book he had been studying and stood up.

"What has happened? What's wrong?"

Godfrey and Payn looked at each other—guiltily, was Hugh's first thought—and neither one appeared to have any wish to answer him.

Godfrey sank onto a bench against the wall by the window. "They know," he said.

"Who knows, and what?"

Payn cleared his throat. "The girls, Margaret and Louise. They know about the Order."

"They *what?*"

"They know about it," Godfrey muttered. "They've been talking about it, discussing and comparing their ideas, and they came right out and asked us about it, about what we do at the Gatherings."

"In God's name …" Hugh was barely able to speak, so profound was his shock. "What have you two done? How could you forget your oaths like that? Were they not awful enough, the dreadful penalties you undertook to suffer for betraying them?"

"We have done *nothing*, Hugh. We forgot nothing and we have said nothing. Neither one of us has as much as breathed a single word to anyone outside our Lodge. Believe me, we have asked each other every-thing there is to ask since we learned of this, and neither one of us has as much as whispered a word of anything to do with the Order."

"Yet your wives know of it." He waited, seeing only misery in their faces. "When *did* you discover this? How long ago did they ask you about it?"

"Today," Godfrey said, meeting Hugh's eye directly. "This afternoon, no more than an hour ago. We came to you immediately."

"And what exactly did they ask you?"

Payn looked bewildered. "I … I don't know … I can't remember. I felt such horror when I realized what they were saying that I was struck dumb. All I can remember thinking is, *They know. How could they know?*"

"I felt the same way." Godfrey was shaking his head, gazing into nowhere and frowning. "I didn't think about anything else once I had recognized what Louise was saying ... and I don't really remember now exactly what she *did* say."

"Then let's approach this from another side. What did you tell them in the first place?"

"Tell them? Have you not heard a word we said? We didn't tell them *anything,* Hugh. I certainly didn't, and I believe Payn when he says he didn't. But that's not important—even although it is. What we need to know is what we should do now."

His head still reeling, Hugh looked from one to the other of them, his lips pursed. "Well, at least that's easy to answer. We go to my father and ask him what's to be done. He will know, and he'll know what to do about the two of you, too. But we had better go now ... Did it occur to either one of you to warn your wives to say no more of this, to anyone?"

"Of course it did," Godfrey snapped. "We were appalled, but we were not rendered completely witless. They won't talk of it to anyone else, because we commanded them to say no more and they know how angry we are."

"Very well then, now let's make my father angry, too. Fortunately he is here. I saw him less than an hour ago, just about the time your wives were questioning you. Come on, then, let's go and find him."

Baron Hugo was in the smithy when they found him, supervising the shoeing of his favorite saddle horse. The beast was in its prime, but it had fallen on a treacherous slope the previous month, injuring its front right fetlock, and had been under the farriers' care ever since. It had been judged able only that morning to return to its full roster of duties, and when Hugh and his friends arrived they saw immediately that the Baron's attention was all for the horse and its new set of shoes, and he could barely conceal his impatience at their interruption, so that when he stumped off to a corner where they could speak with him in private, they followed him with unconcealed apprehension.

He listened to the first part of what his son had to say and then held up a hand, demanding silence. He looked at each of the three young knights in turn, then beckoned them to follow as he led them across the cobbled courtyard to his own chambers, where he dismissed the majordomo and his cleaning staff, then closed the doors securely behind them before waving to the three younger men to be seated. When they were all sitting, looking distinctly uncomfortable, the Baron cleared his throat and hooked a stool with his foot, dragging it closer to where he could sit on it, looking down at them.

"So," he said, after a silence that seemed endless to the three, "if I am correct in my understanding of what you have told me, your wives asked you about what you do at the Gatherings, but you do not recollect exactly what it was that they asked you?" The Baron's demeanor was remarkably calm, Hugh thought, for a man who had just discovered betrayal among his own family, and he admired his father's control even as he tried to gauge the fury that must be simmering and bubbling beneath that calm exterior. From the corner of his eye he saw his two friends nodding their heads.

"And you are both convinced that they are aware of, or that they at least suspect, the existence of our Order. You also believe absolutely that neither one of you said anything to either of them, at any time, that might have been intemperate, or ill considered, careless, or indiscreet?" Again both men shook their heads. "Well then," Hugo continued, "if neither one of you said anything you should not have said—and I believe you when you say you did not—how, then, could your wives have come by whatever information they have? Can you tell me?" He swung to look at his son. "Can you?"

"No, Father."

The Baron grunted. "Then I will tell you," he growled. "Because I know where their information probably sprang from. Your mother probably told them."

Hugh was aware that his jaw had dropped and he was sitting gaping, and he closed his mouth as his father said, "Think about it now, all of you, and think with your minds this time, not with your guts. Think about it logically and reasonably, and then accept what your intelligence tells you it means. The truth is there, right under your noses, and you are going to have to accept it and learn to live with it. I had to come to terms with it when I was your age. All of us have to, at one time or another, and for some men it is very difficult." He looked from face to face, but none of his listeners stirred. They sat stunned, and he spoke into the silence, aware that they would hear him now as never before.

"Our way of life teaches us to believe that women are less than we are in most things. They exist to bear our sons and to make our lives more comfortable and more pleasant. Is that not true? Of course it is, if you are a man. Women, however, tend to see things differently, through eyes and from strange viewpoints that men can never know. They believe they are more clever and more humane than men are, and from their point of view, they may have reason on their side to a great extent. They are certainly clever, in their own obscure ways, and they have little patience with our ways. They think of us, without exaggeration, as children who never grow up and never mature, despite the grayness in our beards and the wrinkles on our faces.

"Here is the truth, gentlemen, and whether you like it or not, you cannot change it: very few of our confraternity are wed to stupid women, and fewer yet are married to women who do not spring from the Friendly Families. And the Friendly Families, according to the Lore of our ancient Order of Rebirth, have been holding regular Gatherings for more than fifty generations. Fifty *generations*, my young friends, not merely fifty *years*. Can any of you truly believe that, in all that time, our women, our wives and mothers, sisters and cousins, have been unaware that their men are involved in something to which they are not privy? They know all about the secrecy surrounding what we do, and about the dedication and effort brought into being around the time of the Gatherings. They see, even if they do not acknowledge, the changes being wrought in their sons' lives and activities as they approach the age of eighteen. Any man who believes that a son's activities can be completely hidden from his mother is a fool. The most important knowledge they possess, however, is that whatever is involved, it is a thing for men, ancient beyond antiquity, in which women have no place and no involvement. They know that, and they accept it. Some accept it more easily and readily than others, and there are always the occasional few who, in their youth, seek to discover more than they are permitted to know. Those, fortunately, are very few, and eventually they are all discouraged by our total silence. Then they resign themselves to the realities of life.

"But never be tempted to believe they know nothing. That would be the worst kind of folly. They *know*. And we know they know, even if we never mention it among ourselves. But their knowledge is as close held as is our own. They never speak of it among themselves, to any great extent. They know, somehow, that it concerns an ancient trust of some description, and they are content, and even proud, that their men, their families, are strong enough and true enough to have earned that trust and to be worthy of it. And thus, in their silent knowledge, our strength grows the greater. Your young wives will learn that truth now, just as you are learning it, and you will see, no more will be said of any of it."

The Baron looked around at his three young listeners, and then smiled. "I would ask if you have any questions, but I know that it is still too soon for questions. What you all require now is time to think about what you have been told. Go then, and think."

"I HAVE A QUESTION." Godfrey sat up straight as he made his announcement. It was the same day, and the sinking sun was throwing elongated shadows across the grass in the meadow where the three of them had been lounging under a tree, their backs propped against a sloping, mossy bank for the previous hour and more, thinking deeply and saying little.

Hugh tilted his head and looked up at Godfrey from beneath an arched eyebrow. "For my father? I have no idea where he might be by now."

"No, not for your father, for you, because you're the one who has been studying all the lore." Godfrey was frowning, no trace of his usual levity present in his gaze.

"Ask away, then. I'm still a tyro but I'll answer if I can."

"What do you really think about all we've learned?"

Hugh remained motionless for several moments, his eyes closed, and then he pushed himself up and around so he could see Godfrey clearly. "What kind of a question is that? Are you asking me for my opinion of all we have learned since we were born? If that's what you mean, then let's fetch our practice swords and go to it right here. Better a healthy sweat than wasting an afternoon wondering about nonsense."

"No, that's not what I meant at all ... I'm not sure what I meant, Hugh, but it's important. What ..." Godfrey's face twisted in a frustrated grimace. "I know what I want to ask you, but I don't know how to put it into words properly. Let me think about it for a moment."

"Think for as long as you wish. I'll wait." Hugh lay back and closed his eyes again. Payn had not stirred.

Some time later, Godfrey tried again, "I wonder about what you believe."

Hugh did not even open his eyes. "How could that interest you in any way? Why should it? What I believe is in my own mind."

"Oh, come on, Hugh, don't be tiresome. I'm asking for your advice because I don't know what *I* believe."

That opened Hugh's eyes. "How can you not know that? That may be the silliest thing I have ever heard you say, Goff."

"It's not silly at all. You know me, Hugh. I am obedient to my elders and superiors in all things. And I believe whatever I'm told to believe—always have, since our first days in Brother Anselm's classroom, when we were all tads. After all, there was no option, was there? The Church tells us we have to believe what we are told. The priests tell us we're not clever enough to understand anything about God and His teachings without their help. They are God's interpreters, and only they are qualified to explain His mysteries, His words, and His wishes to us. It was always that way, and I always believed them. Until very recently …"

He sat staring into the distance for a while before he continued. "Now I don't know what to believe … and I don't know *why* I don't know. When I joined the brotherhood and was Raised and learned about the Order's origins, and about our ancestors being Jews and our Friendly Families springing from the priesthood of the Essenes, I had no difficulty with what I was learning, new and different as it was. Somehow, I managed to keep the two information sources separate. One was ancient history and the other was life today. I am amazed now, I admit, by how long I was able to keep doing that. But in the past few months I have lost my way. Everything is confusing now—the Church's teachings and the Order's, and how they fit and how they don't—and it has all been swarming in my mind so that now I don't know *what* I should believe. I have two sources of information, each appearing to be equally credible, each claiming supremacy, and each asserting itself as the One, True Way. And yet neither one of them makes complete sense."

He fell silent for a moment, and then added, in a strangely flat, emotionless voice, "Help me, Hugh."

Hugh opened his eyes and shifted his head slightly, looking up at his friend, but before he could say anything, Payn, whose eyes were still closed against the sun's brightness, added, "Yes, help him, Hugh, for the love of God, because then you'll help me, too. If Godfrey is as confused as he claims, I can but think him fortunate, since I myself am not confused by it at all ... I am utterly blind and deathly ignorant on exactly the same matters."

Hugh looked in amazement at Payn, who opened his eyes and spread his hands in a silent shrug.

"What should surprise you about that?" Payn said. "You know me well, my friend, better than any other. I am a knight, and that is all I wish to be. I am a warrior by birth, a fighter—a brawling, ignorant lout—and happy to be one. I have no time, and no wish, to fill my life with the kind of mystic, smoke-shrouded things that excite you ... all this mummery about the secrets and mysteries within the Order. To us it's all babble and bluster and we don't understand a word of it."

"Crusty's right, Hugh." Godfrey was nodding solemnly. "We don't know what to believe, but we both believe that *you* know what's right, and if you tell us what that is, we'll believe you."

Hugh had abandoned any pretense of laziness soon after Godfrey launched into this astonishing plea, and now he sat straight-backed and pale-faced, gazing at his two friends from wide, unblinking eyes. He made to speak, but although his mouth opened and his lips moved, nothing emerged. He pushed himself to his feet. Godfrey glanced worriedly at Payn and then spoke up again.

"Hugh, we're not asking you to sin, or to betray anything. This is very straightforward. Among the three of us, you are the one who knows most about this kind of matter. All we're asking you to do is tell us what you think, what you believe, based upon what you've learned since you joined the Order. That's all."

"That's all?" Hugh's voice sounded different to his own ears, husky and throaty. "That's *all*? You're asking me to be your priest, your spiritual guide, to direct you towards salvation. I can't do that, Goff. I don't know where salvation lies, even for myself."

"That's not true, Hugh." Payn's voice was urgent. "All we are asking you to do is talk to us, about what you *think* might be true. We believe the people we know within the Order, and we believe what they tell us. But we cannot understand any of it, once we move outside the ritual rooms. The Order is a secret world, Hugh. Out here, in the *real* world, among people who are not of the Order, we don't know who to trust ... who to believe."

Hugh de Payens stood there in the meadow, his back to the sinking sun, and looked at his two friends through new eyes, seeing the doubt, confusion, and misery in their faces.

"I have to walk," he said. "I can't think, standing here. Walk with me, and we'll see what comes into my mind."

Some time later, on the edge of a fast-flowing brook, he stopped and stood, his friends beside him, gazing down into the still waters by the bankside, searching for trout. "You asked me what I believe, but what I heard you asking me to do was to tell you the truth. That's why I was angry at first ... because I don't know what the truth is. Everything I believe might be completely wrong."

He turned away from the water then, and looked at each of his friends in turn. "So," he continued, "I am going to tell you what I believe. But I absolutely do not want either one of you to think, under any circumstances, that I'm convinced that what I tell you is the *truth*. Do you understand that? I am *not* telling you the truth, because as God is my witness, I do not know what the truth is, or even where it resides."

He waited until each of his friends had nodded in agreement, and then he walked away from them without looking back, allowing his next words to trail back over his shoulder.

"I believe in Jesus," he began. "I believe he lived and was crucified. But I do not believe he was the physical son of God, not now. I believe he was crucified for his political activities against the Romans and their allies—Herod and his clan. I believe he was a fighter in the cause of a free and unified Jewish nation, free of foreign occupation, and free to worship their own God in their own way. I also believe, because our Order has convinced me by *showing* me evidence—and not simply *telling* me about it and *ordering* me to believe—that Jesus was a member of the priestly sect known as the Essenes, whom some called Nazoreans, and that they formed a community that they called the Jerusalem Community, a brotherhood of what we would call monks today—a community of dedicated souls living in isolation and in voluntary poverty, practicing chastity and self-denial and striving to make themselves worthy in the eyes of their God, who was a stern and vengeful God with whom they held a covenant, an understanding that they would live their lives in strict commitment to His expectations ... Do you want to ask me any questions about any of that?"

He walked on in silence, waiting, and when nothing came from behind him, he began again. "I believe that Jesus was crucified and died. And after his death, his brother James, whom men called James the Just, continued to head their commune until his death. James was murdered on the steps of the Temple, and his death—far more so than the death of his brother Jesus—caused insurrection and rebellion, leading directly to the last Jewish war against Rome, when Titus destroyed the Jewish nation and those few who survived the destruction were scattered to the ends of the earth."

He stopped suddenly and turned on his heel to look back at them. "That is what I believe, and none of it should surprise you, for you have heard it all before, from your sponsors and tutors in the Order. We have evidence, within our Order, for all of it, but it might not all be true. Or it might be totally false, its interpretation lost over the centuries since our families first came here, after their flight from Jerusalem. In my own heart and mind, however, I believe it. But now comes the hard part. And it's the part, I know, that causes all the grief you feel over this."

He started walking again, more slowly this time, and his companions walked on either side of him, their heads bent.

"All our families, all of them who do not belong to the Brotherhood of the Order, are Christians, and that is what makes this all so difficult, because I also believe that the Christian Church, as it exists today, is built upon a myth created by the man called Paul. Paul was a gentile, we all know that, but nobody really knows today what a gentile was. Do you know, Goff?" Godfrey wrinkled his nose and shook his head, and Hugh smiled. "Well, a gentile was anyone who was not a Jew, and to the Jews, that was all that mattered. I believe that Paul was a friend of Rome, which is a spy, in the pay of the Empire, and I believe that he was an opportunist of the first magnitude. He never knew Jesus—although he knew the brother, James, and James knew *Paul*, and disliked and distrusted him.

"I believe, absolutely, that Paul somehow heard mention of the Raising ceremony practiced by the Essenes of the Community. He could never have witnessed it, for the Essenes' rites were practiced in secret and Paul was twice an outsider—a gentile and uninitiated—but I believe most certainly he heard of it, and he misunderstood everything he heard, except the most important part—the outline of the premise involved. He took the idea of resurrection that had been practiced in secret for centuries by learned men, and from it, and around his gross misunderstanding of it, he built an edifice that now rules the world in which we all live. He even invented a name for it after a time. He called it Christianity, based upon the Greek name he eventually dreamed up for the man Jesus—the *Christus*.

"Then, once he perceived the success of his message and could see where he might go with it, he stripped it, his fundamental idea, of everything Jewish that might be offensive to the Romans, and he constructed his new religion with great skill to appeal to Roman tastes, traditions, and superstitions, incorporating most of the favorite myths of Rome, and of Greece, and of Egypt, and all their gods.

"He took the story of the virgin birth, for one thing, from several sources. Mithras, the Roman soldiers' god, for example, was born in a stable, delivered of a virgin. And Horus, the god-son of Isis and Osiris, was born of a virgin, too, and destined to die to expiate the sins of mankind. Paul named Jesus the Son of God in that tradition, and cited his resurrection as the sign of his divinity. Paul the saint made Jesus the Christ an immortal. But the most blatantly untrue thing he did was to deny James's existence as Jesus' brother by denying his existence and transferring the power of the founding bishop to Peter the Rock."

"Tell us about this Mithras," Godfrey said. "I've never heard of him."

Hugh smiled. "Not surprising. He was a very powerful god in his day, the Lord of Light, worshipped by most of the soldiery of the Empire as the Soldier's God, but he was soon absorbed completely into Christianity and disappeared. Even the Cross that Christians revere today was his—the white, four-armed cross of Mithras, and it was an ancient symbol even before Mithras. It certainly was not the Cross that Jesus died on."

"What are you saying?" Payn sounded scandalized. "Are you telling us you don't believe Jesus was crucified?"

"No, Crusty, I am not. Jesus was crucified. There is no doubt in my mind of that. But he was crucified on the only kind of cross the Romans used, which was a simple T shape, with no upright above the crossbar."

Once again he looked from Godfrey's face to Payn's. "Now *that*—all that I've said about Mithras—is *true*. That evidence exists, and although it has been hidden from casual sight by the Church, they cannot destroy it, much as they might like to. It is historical fact backed by incontrovertible and indestructible evidence."

He looked squarely at each of his friends in turn, then twisted his lips into a grimace before continuing, his tone and demeanor more serious than at any time since this had begun.

"But that's all ancient history and Mithras does not concern us here, so to answer your questions as fully as I may, I will say this: I have become convinced, simply from reading what exists in our Order's Lore, that there is not one of the godly or miraculous events attributed to Jesus that was not in existence, and being marveled at, centuries before he was born, from the curing of lepers to raising the dead.

"The Jesus who lived in Galilee and died on the Hill of Skulls was a man—a patriot and a rebel. But he was not Jesus the Christ, because, as I said, the 'Christ' part of that name—the Greek *Christos,* or Savior—did not exist until Paul invented the name long after the man Jesus was dead … That, too, I believe.

"Most of all, however—and I think this is what you were asking me—I believe that the world has been led astray by men—ordinary, venal, and self-centered men—claiming to represent God and growing rich in wealth and worldly power in doing so. The evidence of that is everywhere, and a man does not have to be a saint to see it. The Church that Paul founded contains nothing today—a millennium later—that has not been created and propounded and promulgated by men, all of them claiming to have access to the ear of God, and most of them having no slightest resemblance to anything that might in any way be thought of as godly, pious, or holy, let alone *Christian*. They preach and pray about godly and Christian virtues, but few bishops or priests today even bother to conceal their venal worldliness. I believe—and I *know*, as do you two—that most people are aware of that, even although they dare not—*dare not*—speak of it to anyone. Despair walks the world today, my friends, and it wears clerical robes. But I believe, too—and more than anything else I believe this—that our ancient Order, the Order of Rebirth in Sion, contains the seeds of salvation that will one day cleanse the world and bring God back truly into the lives of men."

He saw the doubt and bafflement in his listeners' eyes, and he smiled. "Well, lads, you asked me, and I have told you, and now I can see you are obviously more confused than you were before, wondering about what you have learned that contains the seeds of salvation. Well, believe me when I tell you that you have learned it. You simply have not yet recognized what you have learned. But listen to me now, both of you, and I'll take you as far towards the light as I can go, because I myself can see it only hazily.

"Think of this. The Church tells us Jesus spoke of himself as being 'the Way,' and that he told others 'The Kingdom of Heaven is within you.' He asked them to follow him and that he would show them the Way, and he believed that, utterly and without doubt. But we in our Order believe he did not say it as the Son of God. He said it as an Essene, because it was part of his daily life, and the other Essenes of his community spoke the same way, because they believed that man carries God within himself, and that the Way to find God is to search within yourself.

"Now, if you think long and hard upon what that means, you might realize it means that you can talk to God in your own mind, and in your own prayers. And if you can do that, what need have you of priests? Think about that for a moment, and about what it means to our churchly fathers. If a man can talk to God in his own mind, and pray in the security of his own bosom, what need has he of priests, or of a Church—any church?"

He stopped then and remained silent, watching St. Omer and Montdidier as their faces showed what they were thinking, and he smiled more widely as he saw the conviction dawning in their eyes.

"You see it now? You see where our Order's power will someday lie? One day, our Lore—the knowledge that we have in our possession—will dictate and demonstrate the truth, incontrovertibly, that men have usurped God's covenant with mankind and placed the world in jeopardy while they pursue their own earthly power. It will come to pass, I promise you. There is no doubt in my mind."

"When?" Payn's voice was taut with urgency, but Hugh could only shrug.

"That I cannot tell you. We can do nothing to promulgate the solution yet, for we have no proof of what we know, and absolute proof will be demanded— demanded loudly and angrily by every corrupt priest and bishop in the world—as soon as we cast off our secrecy and speak out. But we have our Lore, and that Lore instructs us to return to Jerusalem one day, to find and recover the treasury of written records hidden there in ancient times by our forefathers, the founding fathers of what are now the Friendly Families. Those records— the written history of the Jerusalem Assembly served by the man Jesus and his brother James—will show the true beginnings of what would become the Christian Church, although Jesus and his companions called it simply the Way—the spiritual life, lived every moment of every day in the eyes of God and strengthened by the knowledge of the covenant between Him and the men who worship Him ... I believe that, too."

"Is there a map?"

Hugh turned to St. Omer. "A map?" He laughed. "I have no idea, Goff. There might be ... I don't know much more than you do, and I've mentioned nothing of the mysteries in what I have said. Everything I have told you, everything I've talked about, is common knowledge. I've simply been more patient in finding things out and piecing things together than you two have."

"Then when will we go? D'you believe we will?"

Hugh shrugged. "I believe someone will, someday. We three might be long dead by then, but I believe someone will go and find the treasure, and once that's done, the world will know salvation—from the clutches of the churchmen, if nothing else."

"And if we had the chance? Suppose we were to have the chance—the ability to sail off and search for this treasure—would you go?"

"Is that why you asked about a map?"

"Of course it is. Would you go?"

"I would. Before the words were out of the mouth of the person asking me. Do you think me mad enough *not* to go?"

Payn Montdidier crossed the two paces that separated him from Hugh and wrapped an arm about his friend's shoulder, holding out his free hand to Godfrey St. Omer, who moved quickly to join them.

"If you go, we'll be there with you. You see? That wasn't difficult at all, what you told us, was it? And yet it was exactly right. I feel as if all the priests in Anjou had been sitting on my chest and you just kicked them all off. Now I can breathe again. What about you, Godfrey?"

Godfrey St. Omer's smile spoke for him.

SIX

In the middle of September in the year 1095, Count Fulk of Anjou, the third of that name and one of the highest-ranked members of the Order of Rebirth, sponsored a great tourney, near the town of Blois, in honor of the coming of age of his second son, another Fulk, who would, in the course of time, become Count Fulk IV. The circumstances of this public celebration were highly scandalous, for the boy's mother, Bertrade de Montford, the Countess of Anjou, had deserted Count Fulk some time earlier and was living openly in an adulterous relationship with Philip I, the King of France, and this gaudy event was the Count's means of demonstrating how little he and his son cared about the faithless woman's desertion.

Hugh, Godfrey, and Payn, the latter two accompanied by their wives as a mark of special privilege, attended the celebrations among the entourage of their liege, Count Hugh of Champagne, who had considered it politically necessary to attend the festivities, and they enjoyed the activities hugely, as did Louise and Margaret. Now in their mid-twenties, the three friends acquitted themselves well during the tournament events, but were largely content to leave the most strenuous and tiring contests to the younger knights nowadays, while they themselves concentrated on those activities where skill and physical dexterity were more prized than brawn, bulk, and brute stamina. Godfrey, in particular, distinguished himself in the lists, using a long lance, from the back of a galloping horse, to collect a winning number of ring trophies. These rings were suspended from a pivoting arm counterbalanced by a swinging bag of sand that could whip around swiftly and unseat any passing rider who had failed to pick the ring perfectly from the ribbon suspending it, and Godfrey, to the unconcealed delight of his adoring wife, was the only contestant that afternoon who succeeded in picking the maximum possible number of rings without once being unseated, or even brushed, by a swinging weight.

Hugh and Payn waited for Godfrey to collect his prize money and turn his horse over to his groom, and then all three of them began to make their way towards one of the refreshment tents in search of the ladies, laughing and gazing around them in wonder at the riot of colors, music, noise, and movement that surrounded them. All of them had attended similar events before—there were usually two, sometimes even three, tourneys each year, within riding distance of the Barony of Payens—but none of them had ever seen anything quite as lavish as this display being mounted by the House of Anjou. They understood that this was not merely a tourney; it was a political statement of no great subtlety, a grand spectacle and a celebration of the county's success in a variety of ventures—including a public thumbing of the Count's

nose at the adulterous King of France made possible by
the annexation of Blois itself into the County of Anjou—
over the previous four years. Hundreds, and perhaps even
thousands, of people were in attendance from as far away
as Burgundy in the far northeast and Marseille in the
distant south, and the celebrations had continued for ten
days. Count Hugh's arrival had been a week earlier, and
they would be leaving again in another week's time to
make their way homeward.

They had stopped to stare in awe at a caged pair of
lions when Hugh's man Arlo found them and
summoned them to wait at once upon Baron Hugo in
his tent, and they obeyed him without comment,
curious but not alarmed, since Arlo had informed them
at the outset that the ladies were already there.

Louise and Margaret and several other women were
seated outside, but Baron Hugo was in his tent, dictat-
ing a letter to Charon, the elderly Greek scholar who
had been his amanuensis since before any of the three
younger knights were born, and when they entered
Hugo waved a hand, indicating that they should wait
and be silent until he was done, and then continued
pacing, rubbing his forehead with one hand and dictat-
ing his thoughts. As soon as he had finished, Charon
rose to his feet and left the tent. The Baron crossed to
a corner table and poured himself a cup of wine, making
no move to offer any to the others, then sipped at it,
frowning, before he spoke.

"We must leave here tomorrow. I trust you are all
sated with the pleasures Fulk has provided?"

The three friends looked at each other in surprise, but Hugh was the only one who responded. "Tomorrow, Father? Why? I thought we would be—"

"Because I have said so. Is that not reason enough?"

"It is, and forgive me. I meant no disrespect and had no thought of complaining. I was merely curious."

"I know, and I was merely being miserable. I have no more wish to leave early than you do, but we have little choice. The Count has ordered me to return to Payens, there to start making preparations for November."

"November? Am I permitted to ask the significance of November?"

"Aye, I suppose so. The Count has just received word, from Avignon, that the Pope, Urban, is here in our lands. He has been touring in the south and west since early last month, and he has just left Avignon, on his way north to Lyon, and thence into Burgundy. But while he was in Le Puy, en route to Avignon, he issued a decree that he will convene another great ecclesiastical council, like the one he held in March in Piacenza, in Italy. This one will be held in the Massif Central, in Clermont, and it will start in mid-November. Every churchman and every nobleman in all the lands and duchies has been summoned to attend, and apparently great things are to take place in the course of the assembly. What those great things may be, no one knows, but Count Hugh has charged me with organizing whatever will have to be done within his County of Champagne, and I, in turn, am deputizing you three to assist me. And I warn you, it will not be an easy task. There is much to be done, and alarmingly little time in which to see to it. Fortunately most of the harvest is already in, but the county is far from being ready to do anything quickly. And for that reason, we leave tomorrow, solely because it is already too late to leave today. Now, go and do what you have left to do, because I intend to be on the road by daybreak."

The six weeks that followed were indeed, as the Baron had promised, filled to capacity with every kind of exigency that could be imagined and many that could not, but by the time they came to leave for Clermont, everything that needed to be done had been accomplished, and the Count's party, more splendidly equipped and accoutered than any other that could be remembered by even the oldest resident of Champagne, set out with all due pomp and panoply to ride to join the Pope's convocation. Count Hugh's great friend Raymond, the Count of Toulouse, had added his own glittering entourage to the gathering, and the outgoing cavalcade was highly impressive. Once again, the triumvirate of Payens was in attendance, and finally relieved of the stresses under which they had been laboring for the previous six weeks, all three were in fine fettle and ready, they thought, to intercept and neutralize any theological missile the assembled priests might launch at them.

Speculation over the reason for the gathering had been rampant since the news of it broke, for at the previous council, in Italy, Urban had publicly declared an alliance between the western Church, represented by his own See of Rome, and the eastern Church, represented by the Byzantine emperor, Alexius Comnenus. Now people wondered what other momentous events were to occur in Clermont, and when the council began, they were not kept long in the dark. For the first nine days, the three hundred clerics in attendance debated a number of issues and made momentous decisions. Simony—the greatest bane of the Church at that time—was outlawed and declared anathema, involving as it did the buying and selling of priestly office or the exchange of spiritual favors and influence for monetary gain. Clerical marriage was also declared anathema, and to top everything off, King Philip I of France was excommunicated for his adulterous marriage to Count Fulk's wife.

On the very last day of the council, when the crowds hoping to see and hear the Pope had become too immense for the cathedral and its grounds, the gathering was moved to a field called the Champet, outside the church of Notre Dame du Port on the eastern edge of the city. It was the only open space large enough to accommodate all of those in attendance, and it was there, when everyone had reassembled, that Pope Urban unveiled his true purpose for convening the assembly. With the unerring instinct of a born performer, he did it spectacularly, creating chaos and fomenting a religious revolution with a single impassioned oration, unexpected and unprecedented, that inflamed everyone who heard it.

The Pope spoke with great eloquence, making it clear from the outset that he was speaking not only to the people assembled there but to all the Christian kingdoms of the West, and despite his initial skepticism, Hugh soon found himself caught up by the pontiff's passion as he talked about the terrible difficulties facing their Christian brethren in the East, struggling under the brutal repression of the Seljuk Turks. At one point, almost reeling from a vivid description of an atrocity he could visualize, he reached out and grasped Montdidier by the arm.

"They defile and desecrate our altars," Urban was saying, his voice ringing through the stunned silence of his listeners, reaching the culmination of a litany of horrors. "They circumcise Christians and pour the blood of the circumcised into the fonts. They will take a Christian—any Christian—and cut open his belly, then tie his intestines to a stake and force him to run, goaded with spears, until he pulls out his own entrails and falls dead." The Pope gazed out over the horrified crowd, watching the effect of his announcement. "I have heard many such reports, delivered to me from too many sources, and believe me when I say these are not isolated incidents. Throughout the East, from Jerusalem to Byzantium, these things are happening daily."

Again he paused, his eyes moving constantly, and then he said, "Let me remind you of the words of our beloved Savior, Jesus Christ. 'Whoever should abandon in my name his house or his brothers, his father or his mother, his wife or his children or his lands, will receive them again a hundredfold and will come to eternal life.'" The silence was absolute, because people were unable to believe what they had just heard from the lips of the Pope himself. But Urban was not yet done. He gazed around him and raised both arms wide. "Heed the words of God, my children, and you knights and men of prowess, hear the cries of your brethren in the eastern lands, dying beneath the heel of the ungodly. Think not about your petty quarrels here at home, among your friends, but turn your eyes towards true Glory ... the Holy City of Jerusalem itself cries out for deliverance! Take the road to the Holy Sepulcher as soldiers of God, and tear God's land from these abominable people!"

The silence lasted for perhaps another five heartbeats, just long enough for Godfrey St. Omer to turn, open mouthed, and look into Hugh's eyes. And then erupted a great, tumultuous shout of "God wills it! God wills it!"

Afterwards, no one could say how it began or who had started it, but the words, and the sentiment, exploded like a wind-driven fire in long, dry grass, almost as though the crowd had rehearsed it in advance and had been waiting for that moment to proclaim it. The Count and his entourage were as stunned as everyone else by the unexpectedness of what was happening, but Hugh was even more astounded by the reaction of Count Hugh himself.

It was plain that the Pope had planned his address carefully and with an eye to recruiting knights for the new war he had called for, because there were priests at the front of the crowd, close to the Pope's dais, who were well supplied with stocks of plain white cloth crosses, evidently prepared against the surge of expected volunteers. Hugh noticed them immediately, and his cynicism about anything the Church inspired ticked in recognition. It was equally clear, however, that no one, including the Pope himself, had anticipated the furious response that his speech and its emotional appeal provoked. Everyone, it appeared, every individual member of the multitude there—knights and common-ers, young and old and women and children—wanted to volunteer and rush off to attack and dismember the infidel Turks.

"Well," Godfrey said loudly, "that was worthy of a raised eyebrow, don't you think? Il Papa is an accom-plished orator."

"What did you expect, Goff?" Payn had to shout to make himself heard. "Think you he got to be Pope by being deaf and mute?"

"No, I don't, but he had me thinking, for a moment there, that I should rush away and fight the Turks like a good Christian knight anxious to please his bishop and earn a blessing or two. What did you think, Hugh?"

Before Hugh could respond, the Count's right-hand man, Pepin, interrupted. "His Grace requires your presence, gentlemen."

They followed Pepin through the cordon of guards surrounding the Count's party and found the Count himself among a group of his senior advisers, frowning and plucking at his lower lip. Although all of his advis-ers were looking at him, none of them were speaking, even among themselves. Pepin went directly to him and whispered in his ear, and the Count crooked a finger at the newcomers, then walked towards the high peak of the tent where his personal standard hung limp in the windless air. No one else moved to accompany them, and the Count opened the tent flap himself, holding it there while the three younger knights filed past him into the interior.

"Well," he said, as soon as he had followed them inside, "what did you think of that?" He waited half a heartbeat, then added, "Any one of you may speak, for I know you're all capable. Did the Pope stir your manly juices?"

"He was … persuasive, my lord," Godfrey murmured.

"And? Were *you* persuaded, St. Omer? Were any of you?"

"Not entirely, my lord." This was Payn.

The Count raised one eyebrow slightly. "Why not?"

Payn shrugged, not yet ready to respond, and Hugh spoke up.

"I believe it's a matter of learning, my lord. Our studies have shown us that anything related to, or instigated by, the Church exists for the benefit of the Church and its clerics only. That is why my friends and I hesitated in the first place."

"A matter of learning, you say. Have you learned nothing, then, about our Order?"

"My lord? I fear—"

"Aye, you fear you don't understand. I fear the same, that you do not understand. Now here is what I require you to do. I want you and your friends here to make your way directly to the bishops surrounding the Pope's dais and there volunteer for the Pope's new war. Each of you will take one of the white cloth crosses they are passing out and sew it onto your surcoat, immediately, this night, so that tomorrow you will be plainly seen and recognized as one of the Pope's Holy Warriors."

Hugh was astounded, and he could see his friends were, too, but the Count held up his hand to silence all of them. "Think! Think of the full name of our Order. Think now of what the Pope is suggesting. Think next of how long our Order has been planning a return to its place of origin. And think about where the Pope's war will lead. Now, do you not think a trip to Jerusalem might prove to be worthwhile for a member of our brotherhood?"

And thus it was that Hugh de Payens and his two friends were among the very first knights in Christendom to take the cloth cross from the hands of Pope Urban himself.

Hugh sewed the cross onto his surcoat that very day, aware of, but steadfastly refusing to consider, the ironies involved in their ancient and secretive Order's instant commitment to the new Christian cause. It was sufficient for him, and his friends, to know that Count Hugh had excellent reasons underlying the swift decision he had taken, and Hugh believed that he would be informed of those reasons when, and not before, the time was right. And so, being the man he was, he threw himself into his new duties and permitted himself to be swept up into the frenzy of the moment, so that, like almost everyone else in Clermont on that occasion, he began his personal odyssey to the Holy Land in a state of fevered commitment verging on ecstasy, screaming the instantly coined catchphrase "Deus le veult!" with everyone else.

"Deus le veult!" *God wills it!* It was a phrase Hugh de Payens would grow first to distrust, then to detest.

SEVEN

The hysteria unleashed on that final day of the Council of Clermont took everyone by surprise, including Pope Urban himself. He had been working hard for months, meticulously preparing what he would say to the assembly, and he had spent weeks struggling to find the very best way of couching his emotion-laden appeal so that it would be as close to irresistible as he could possibly make it to the hard-headed people for whom he intended it. Urban had hoped to spark enthusiasm for a real war, in a glorious cause, among the bored and fractious young Frankish knights and their aristocratic leaders, knowing that if he could win the commitment and involvement of the Franks, then all the other knights and lords of Christendom would run to join them. That had been Urban's sole objective, and in launching his initiative at the council in Clermont, he could have had no idea of what would happen.

The mood of the people, comprising equal parts of hopelessness, disillusionment, and despair, allied with the appalling conditions of poverty and moral deprivation under which they lived and their need for something tangible and visible in which they could believe, combined on that Tuesday afternoon, the twenty-eighth of November, 1095, to create the perfect tinder for the spark of Urban's impassioned appeal. The result was instant chaos, an incredible and utterly spontaneous explosion of raw emotion and popular enthusiasm that embraced every person present, irrespective of sex or social station, and then spilled outward to infect everyone who heard about it but had not been there to witness it. What happened was inconceivable and unprecedented, and within hours of the start of it, cool clerical heads were summoned to begin assessing how the groundswell should be handled and controlled, for it was plain, even from the outset, that something extraordinary had been set in motion. Special committees were established by the Pope and his clerics to accommodate the incredible outpouring of popular emotion and enthusiasm for the Pope's Holy War, and many things began to fall inexorably into place. The Pope's original call to arms was modified to ensure that the campaign to free the Holy Lands would be carefully coordinated to begin nine full months later, in August 1096, once the harvest was safely gathered in and stored.

While all of that feverish activity was going on among the legions of the Pope's clerical functionaries, the Governing Council of the Order of Rebirth had carefully analyzed the opportunity presented to them so unexpectedly by Pope Urban, and had begun to lay extensive plans to cover every contingency imaginable in ensuring that they would, in fact, achieve a return to the Holy Land. The Pope's campaign might fail; the armies, marching overland for the most part, might never reach the sacred places; or if they did, they might fail to oust the Muslim infidels, who had occupied the Holy City for more than four hundred years. But the Order's first priority was to ensure that if the Pope's armies were successful, and if Jerusalem were freed, the Order of Rebirth would have men and resources *in situ,* ready to do what must be done.

Count Hugh knew from the outset that he himself could not ride out to the Pope's war that year, simply because of the pressure of his own duties in Champagne, where he had not only recently married but also launched an ambitious program of improvements to his county, and so he instructed Sir Hugh de Payens and his fellow brethren in the Order, along with all the other, ordinary men from his County of Champagne who wished to ride to the Pope's Holy War, to prepare for their time away from home, commanding them to attend to their various responsibilities, to set their houses in order and arrange their marital and domestic affairs with care before leaving.

Then, at the appointed time, in October 1096, he dispatched a battle-ready expeditionary force to join the army commanded by Raymond, the veteran Count of Toulouse and Count Hugh's own sponsor and superior in the Order of Rebirth. Hugh de Payens and his two friends, the latter having acquired reluctant but dutiful permission from their wives, were proud to ride with Count Raymond, and Arlo rode with them, claiming that right as Hugh's lifelong personal attendant and bodyguard. All three of the triumvirate were happy that he had done so, for as Arlo himself remarked, had he not elected to go with them, the three of them alone would have been easy prey for the vultures within the army. Besides which, none of them had the slightest knowledge of how to cook and they would doubtless have starved to death in the midst of plenty.

From Toulouse, they marched southeastward to the Dalmatian coast and the port of Dyrrachium, where they took ship across the Adriatic Sea and then marched through Thessalonica towards Constantinople. They arrived in April 1097, as one of the four great armies from Christendom that arrived in the Byzantine capital that year, to be welcomed warmly by the Emperor Alexius, whose territories and possessions had been ravaged by the Turks in recent years and who was now ecstatic over his fortunate friendship with Pope Urban.

After remaining in Constantinople for only a short space of time, they were ushered across the Hellespont by Alexius's people into Turkey, where the four armies assembled into one great force, and Hugh and his two friends found themselves highly impressed to be part of a remarkably well-ordered army of forty-three hundred knights and thirty thousand infantry that struck out on foot shortly thereafter to cross Turkey and strike at the Muslim principalities of Syria, Lebanon, and Israel itself.

Everything went according to plan. They captured Nicea and Edessa, then won a great battle at Dorylaeum, and after that they marched across the brutalizing Anatolian desert to besiege the enormous city of Antioch.

That episode provided an object lesson in humility for all of them, and the three friends took note of how their expectations had been proved to be ludicrous. They had all heard of Antioch, a fabulous city in the mystical East, and they approached it expecting to find a biblical land flowing with milk and honey. Instead they found an overcrowded entrapment, a cesspool of filth and starvation that had been in the grip of brutal famine for years, and where inhuman conditions were made unbearable by chronic foul weather. From his first glimpse of the city, Hugh had known that the Frankish army could not hope to encircle it. It covered three square miles and was protected by high, thick walls, fortified by four hundred and fifty towers. Behind the city proper, but still within its walls, rose Mount Silpius, crowned with a citadel a thousand feet above the plains where Hugh and his fellows sat. Almost six thousand men and knights died of hunger during the eight months they spent outside Antioch's walls.

"Six thousand men ... Six *thousand* ..." The awe in Montdidier's voice reflected the stunned expressions on the faces of the others who sat beside him, staring into the fire they had built against the chill of the desert night. The fuel was smashed furniture, looted from an abandoned house in the city, and now they sat in front of it as if unwilling to look at one another, their minds occupied with the tidings they had just heard. Montdidier spoke again, looking this time at St. Omer, who had brought the word to them.

"Are you sure, Goff? Six thousand, *starved* to death? Impossible! How many were we, leaving Constantinople?"

It was Hugh who answered, glancing at St. Omer for confirmation, "More than thirty-five thousand, as I recall. So we have lost one man in six, providing that Goff's number is sound. Where did you hear it, Goff?"

"From Pepin, not half an hour ago. He said the commanders of the four armies ordered a census to be conducted shortly after the city fell. We all knew something of the kind was going on, because I remember we were together when the priests came by several days ago, asking all those questions about who among us had died, and how. Well, now we know why they were asking. The results were reported to Raymond of Toulouse today. Pepin had just heard the tidings before I met him, and he told them to me: six thousand men dead, some of the pestilence, but most of starvation. Now we have less than thirteen hundred knights remaining, and most of those have no horses."

"Not all of those starved, Goff, nor did the infantry. Those numbers tally total deaths, but we had heavy losses among our forces long before we came to Antioch. We lost too many men on the way here, before we learned to respect our enemies properly. We should have learned that lesson much sooner than we did."

"Aye, but still, Hugh, *six thousand* is a mass of dead men."

Hugh was suddenly impatient with Godfrey's awe. "Aye, it is," he snapped. "But there is nothing we can do to change that and we have little to gain from fretting over it. At least none of us is numbered among the dead. So we must simply shrug our shoulders, adjust to the loss of those six thousand and continue without them."

Neither of his friends responded, and Hugh hunched forward, staring into the flames, thinking that he had made more adjustments in the previous few months than he had in all the twenty-six years of his life before then. The siege of Antioch had forced him to confront his own mortality and to think about things that had never occurred to him before. Before reaching Antioch, what little philosophy he had pursued had all had to do with the Order of Rebirth, its requirements and its tenets. In front of this city's towering walls, however, he had been forced to realign his priorities and to re-examine his life, seeing it for the first time as what it really was—the life of an ordinary, mortal, and all too vulnerable man, prey, like all other men, to fears and doubts, to illness and to death from starvation and the dangers of drinking filthy waters. The famine that he and his fellows had found when they reached Antioch was something entirely new to all of them.

They had all heard of famine, he mused now, and had thought they knew what it was; they had all paid it lip service at one time or another, speaking of it in hushed tones and associating it with extraordinarily hard times. None of them, however, from the highest lord to the most base-born camp follower in the army, was equipped to imagine, or to deal with, the reality of a long-established famine that had resulted in the total absence of food of any kind over vast areas of land. The Franks, born and bred in green, lush lands, could not begin to imagine an absence of grass, and the first lesson they had to learn about that was that their beasts, deprived of fodder, died quickly. Thus they ended up eating their own livestock, aware that once the animals were all gone, they would have nothing else to eat—and the animals were dying in large numbers, which meant that most of their dead flesh was going to waste in the desert heat.

In addition to the famine afflicting the land, they had found the weather there on the plains of Antioch to be foul beyond belief, alternating freezing temperatures with high winds that stirred up suffocating sand storms, and long periods of high humidity that brought insects out by the millions and increased the intolerable discomforts facing the so-called besiegers, who were all by now aware of the ludicrous futility of what they were attempting.

Sickness had broken out quickly among the starving Frankish army, and once it did, it spread with terrifying speed. No one knew what to call the pestilence, and the few physicians among the Franks were powerless against it. When the scourge was at its height, Hugh, Godfrey, and Payn had all come down with it at the same time, leaving Arlo, who for some reason remained unscathed, to look after all of them. Godfrey had recovered quickly, back on his feet within a matter of days. Hugh had taken four days longer and recovered more slowly, but soon he, too, was strengthening noticeably. Montdidier, however, hovered close to death for more than fifteen days, and three times Arlo thought he had died, so still and motionless was he, his breathing imperceptible. But on each occasion Payn rallied and snatched another ragged breath, and on the eleventh night his fever broke. He had lost almost one quarter of his body weight by then, but once he began to grow stronger, his recovery was as rapid as the others' had been.

They had all survived, Hugh knew, because Arlo had somehow managed to acquire a sack of whole grain— half full and obviously stolen—and he guarded it jealously, grinding it in small portions, by hand, between two stones. He offered no explanation of where it had come from and no one asked him for one, all of them too grateful for the bounty contained in that simple jute bag and the bland but wholesome porridge it provided.

After eight months and a single day of siege, Antioch had collapsed in the course of one night, on the third of June, and it had fallen not through conquest but through corruption and treachery, when one of the tower guards, in exchange for a fortune in bribes, opened the water gate to Frankish infiltrators. By dawn more than five hundred Franks were inside the city, and the sound of their massed trumpets within the walls caused panic. The Muslim governor of the city fled through the rear gates with most of his army. Hugh was thinking of precisely that when Godfrey brought the matter up.

"I had a long talk with Pepin," he said. "He had just come off duty and was waiting for one of his friends to join him. I was surprised by what he had to say about our capturing the city."

Hugh smirked. "*Pepin* had *thoughts*?"

St. Omer shrugged in mock apology. "Well, you know what I mean ... the Count had thoughts. Pepin chanced to overhear them."

"So what did he say that surprised you?"

St. Omer wrinkled his nose. "He said that if the emir in charge of the city had rallied his men and stood his ground, we would not have stood a chance of taking the city, even although we were already inside."

"Hmm. He is probably correct. We barely had five hundred men inside, and they were tightly confined in one closed area. There were thousands of defenders in there who could have eaten us alive had they reacted differently. Did Pepin say anything about when we might be moving on, away from this hellhole?"

"I asked him that, but all he would say was that it won't be tomorrow or the day after. I think he was really saying that we might be here for a long time, regrouping and gathering our strength."

Hugh merely nodded at that, unsurprised, and returned to his musing. The six thousand deaths were now lodged in his mind, and he began to wonder about the numbers of men who had already died on both sides without a single Frankish warrior having yet set eyes upon Jerusalem. And as that thought came to him, he remembered his godfather St. Clair's suggestion, on the evening of his Raising, that the best thing that the new Pope, Urban II, might do to solve the problem of the

knights of Christendom and their ungovernable behavior would be to foment a war. Hugh found himself
recalling how Sir Stephen had talked that night about
speaking to the Pope concerning the idea because, as
St. Clair had observed, Christendom was not all the
world and not all the world was Christendom. Now that
it had come unbidden to his attention, Hugh found
the inference unavoidable, and he was surprised that the
connection had not occurred to him before, because
Sir Stephen St. Clair said nothing lightly. He was
highly placed within the Order's hierarchy, and he had
both the power and the influence to win the Pope's
ear, and the intellect and charm to make his ideas
appear attractive to the pontiff.

There was no denying that Pope Urban's emotional
call to arms had solved his most chronic and pressing
problem—and relieved his embarrassment—more efficiently than anyone could have imagined beforehand,
by providing Christian knights everywhere with an
opportunity to fight in a glorious cause on the far side
of the world, and to achieve salvation in a Holy War
against the enemies of their Christian God. The Pope
had turned an idea into reality, and in so doing had
created a ravening monster with a blood lust that
threatened to consume everyone exposed to it.

In spite of knowing that he might never know the
truth, Hugh became increasingly certain that his godfather had, in fact, planted the seed in Pope Urban's
mind, and he found the knowledge that he himself,
Hugh de Payens, had conceived the original idea to be

both appalling and pleasing. Appalling because of the catastrophe that the idea had loosed upon the world and the cataclysmic loss of life on all sides, little of it yet having anything to do with real warfare, and pleasing because he had been instrumental in furthering the objectives of the Order of Rebirth.

Suddenly uncomfortable with what was in his mind, he stood up and looked about him, sensing the dark bulk of the city's walls at his back and aware that his friends were watching him curiously. He kept his face expressionless and bade them good night, then made his way to his bedroll, trying to convince himself as he went that he was not being cynical. He knew he had much to be cynical about, witnessing daily the atrocious behavior of the people around him, the so-called Armies of God and their illustrious leaders, and it was plain to anyone who had eyes that there was more fighting for personal gain going on here among the powerful men in Outremer than there was fighting for the glory of God and His Holy Places, for they had not yet even begun to approach the Holy Places, and Hugh feared that he might not be able to conceal his distaste for his fellow travelers for much longer if their behavior did not improve. It would be many more months yet, however, before Hugh de Payens could will himself to acknowledge that the heathens against whom they were fighting were, in many ways, more Christian and more admirable than were their Cross-wearing adversaries, for whom the shouted phrase "Deus le veult!" had grown to mean *I want that!*

Hugh's disenchantment had begun early in their voyage, when the first horror stories of the earliest expeditions began to trickle back to those who followed. Thousands of ordinary people, serfs and peasants, had been caught up in the enthusiasm and hysteria of the Pope's war, and spurred by visions of salvation through pilgrimage, and an escape from the appalling hardship of their ordinary lives by winning a better life in Heaven in return for their sacrifice, they had immediately left their homes to go campaigning, intent only on traveling to the Holy Land and wresting it, bare handed, from the Turks. But their soaring hopes were soon dashed, for within the distance of a few weeks' travel from the homes that they had never left before, they had begun starving to death, because the vast numbers on the move, throughout all the lands of Christendom, had been unplanned for, and the hordes of eager, hopeful transients had devoured every scrap of food from every source, leaving nothing in reserve. Thousands died before they even reached the boundaries of their own lands, and within a month of leaving their home in Champagne, the Count's retainers were listening with horror to tales of cannibalism in the fairest regions of France.

Until that point, some remnant of Hugh's boyhood faith and training had kept him clinging to the hope that all might yet be well, and that for this new venture, the Church and the men who ran it might, for once, deny their baser motivations and mobilize the forces of Heaven on behalf of the masses of people who came flocking in response to the Pope's summons. But tales had filtered back to the advancing army of a crazed, messianic figure called Peter the Hermit, who had led a tattered horde of starving peasants—their numbers had been estimated at twenty thousand—all the way to the borders of Byzantium, ravaging and pillaging everywhere they went, in their desperate search for food. Godfrey reported a solid rumor that the horde had sacked Belgrade and slaughtered thousands of Hungarians as they passed by. By the time they reached Byzantium, they had apparently been uncontrollable, and the Emperor Alexius had closed his gates and banned them from Constantinople. Shortly afterwards, they were annihilated by the Turks. Their journey to redeem the Holy City had lasted no more than six months, and not a soul among their thousands ever set eyes on the land of Jesus.

When Hugh heard about the fate of Peter's tragic followers long afterwards, from people who had witnessed the events and others who had merely been appalled by hearing about them, his burgeoning cynicism towards the Church and its acolytes became set in his soul. He was not yet prepared, however, for what he was to encounter in Jerusalem.

EIGHT

"That's more like it! By the bowels of Christ, lads, I swear to you we'll be inside by noon. Would anyone care to make a small wager on that?"

"Fools we may be, Goff, but we are not entirely stupid. No wagers this time." Montdidier was the only one who answered him, shouting to make himself heard over the noise of falling masonry as he cuffed his friend's helmed head playfully. The others, Hugh and Arlo, were both too rapt to pay any attention to them, staring up at the pockmarked walls of Jerusalem, less than fifty paces from where they stood, as Montdidier continued. "None of us is mad enough to bet against that. Look at it, in God's name! Nothing could withstand that kind of battering. And there goes the whole façade. Look, it's coming down!"

Sure enough, as he spoke, a long fissure split in the wall directly in front of them, spreading from one hole to another and radiating from there to other breaches, so that the entire surface seemed to crumple all at once and slide forward, stripping the outer shell to expose the rubble with which the interior of the fortifications had been filled. No sooner had the shell stopped sliding, however, than another missile exploded into the rubble-filled center, dislodging a huge amount of debris, and it was plain to see that, within a very short time, the wall at this point would collapse completely beneath the constant hammering of the barrage.

Hugh straightened up from where he had been leaning against the low ruins of an ancient mud wall and sheathed his sword before beckoning to one of his men-at-arms. He pointed to the wall.

"You see that damage there? You know what it means?" The soldier nodded, and Hugh punched him lightly in the upper arm. "Good man. Go you then and find His Grace the Count. He should be in or close by his quarters at this time of day. Bid him good day from me and tell him it is my opinion that the wall will come down this morning ... probably within the hour. Advise him, with my compliments, that should he wish to be among the first to enter the city, he should make his way—discreetly, mind you—back here with you. Do you understand the message?"

"Aye, sir."

"Good. Tell it to me, then." He listened carefully and then nodded. "So be it. Go now, and waste no time. And remember, this is for the Count's ear alone. From me to you to him is the only route for these words to take, so say nothing to anyone else, not even should one of the kings ask you. Off with you now."

He watched the man leave and then he turned back to the others, flinching reflexively as a particularly heavy concussion sent stone splinters thrumming past them.

"Well, my friends, it seems that for once in our lives, we find ourselves in the right spot at the right time. Once the word spreads that the breach is here—and the people creating it will spread the word—others will swarm to it. But I, for one, intend to be at the point of the first group through that gap, so let's form up and make sure no one eases in ahead of us."

They formed a tight knot immediately, and began to move forward slowly, Hugh in the center, Godfrey on his right, and Payn, who was left handed, on his left. One pace behind them, positioned slightly to Payn's left and carrying the standard of Baron Hugo de Payens, Arlo advanced with them, his face expressionless, his eyes shifting constantly, even although he knew that the sole danger they faced at this point was the danger of flying splinters.

It was Friday, the fifteenth day of July in the year 1099, and the enormous siege artillery the Franks had built had been hurling great stones at the city walls for days on end, but here in front of their vantage point, the effects were becoming more noticeable with every missile that struck the crumbling façade. The stretch of wall directly ahead of where they stood had been identified three days before as the weakest stretch on this side of the city, and three of the largest and most powerful siege engines ever built had been brought forward and aligned so that their missiles could all strike the same spot. The smallest of the stones being hurled was as big as a heavy man, while the others were the size of a horse, so that the loaders had a backbreaking task loading them into the trebuchets. From the moment all three had been aimed, the barrage they launched had been incessant, with a single, massive stone striking the weakest point of the wall every minute.

Antioch had withstood a siege by four thousand knights and thirty thousand infantry for eight months. Now, a full year later, Jerusalem was about to fall within six weeks, to a besieging Frankish army numbering less than one third of the one that had captured Antioch. But the Franks who were now about to take Jerusalem were an army of hardened and bitter veterans, each of them a survivor of a nightmarish journey, half a year in duration, from Antioch. Famine had plagued them all along the route, and more than a few of the wild-eyed warriors had turned cannibal, eating the flesh of slain enemies in order to stay alive. Jerusalem, the end of their odyssey and the symbol of all their dreams, had no hope of keeping them out with mere walls. After losing more than half of their force in the 350-mile march south from Antioch, fighting every step of the way towards their objective, the Frankish survivors never doubted the outcome or their own righteousness. The Holy City was theirs. God willed it.

Some time later that morning—it might have been an hour, or perhaps even less, because no one had any sense of the passage of time—Hugh and his three companions were dangerously close to the walls, exposed to lethal splinters from every massive stone projectile that arced down from the huge catapults at their backs, and to the lesser risk of well-aimed arrows from the defenders on the city walls on each side of the target area. The four of them huddled close together, their knees bent and their shields raised high, but they were more concerned about being overtaken than they were about anything else, for in the time that had elapsed since Hugh sent word to the Count, a throng of watchful warriors had gathered in the previously empty space before the walls, eyeing the damaged stonework and waiting for the first full breach to occur. So far at least, the quartet from Payens had managed to keep the point position and they were not prepared to yield it to anyone save Count Raymond, with whom they would share it, should he wish to join them.

"Here he comes now," Payn grunted, having glanced back over his shoulder to make sure no other group was coming too close to them. "Count Raymond and—" He made a quick tally, gazing back to where the Count's party was claiming right-of-way through the throng behind their own group. "Six, no, seven knights. De Passy's there with him, and de Vitrebon. Don't know—"

His last words were lost in the thunderous crash of falling masonry as boiling dust erupted ahead of them like smoke, hiding the walls completely from view, and for long moments there was no sound to be heard other than those of the aftermath of the collapsing rubble. The sound of falling, pattering fragments finally died away, and as the dust began to settle noticeably, Hugh spoke almost under his breath.

"This will be it, lads. That was a breach, or I'm a Burgundian." He hefted the spiked mace that had hung by his right side and settled the shield more comfortably against his left shoulder. "Now, with any luck, the spotters will see the break and they'll stop the bombardment. If they don't, we might find it unpleasant approaching the walls ... Arlo, start counting. We'll move as soon as we know the stones have stopped and it's clear enough to see the way ahead."

In the hushed silence at their backs, Arlo's voice, counting in cadence, sounded ludicrously loud, but it provided a necessary discipline. In the normal scheme of the bombardment, the next projectile should arrive before his count had reached eighty, but he reached eighty and counted on through one hundred before Hugh nodded. "Good, they've stopped. My lord Count, welcome. Do you wish to take command?"

Count Raymond, who had silently joined them, shook his head. "No, Sir Hugh, you appear to have it well in hand. Carry on."

Hugh nodded again and slowly raised his mace over his head, signaling the crowd behind him to make ready. "Right," he said, his voice almost conversational, "the barrage has certainly stopped now, so we can go. Another minute or so, to let the dust clear. Mind where you step, now, but keep your heads up—they'll be waiting for us and you don't want to die looking down at your feet. Steady now ... wait for it ..." An eddy of wind sprang up and whirled the dust aside, revealing a break in the formerly even line of the wall's top.

"There! It's a breach, sure enough, so here we go, up and over. With me, now!"

They broke out of the dust cloud right at the top of the piled rubble in front of the break in the walls to find the city's defenders waiting for them. Hugh, in the lead, found himself alone for the briefest of moments, gazing down at the swarthy faces of the massed defenders below, all of whom appeared to be glaring up at him with hatred in their eyes. He was aware of a feeling of calm detachment, a sensation of silent unreality, and yet conscious at the same time of the insecurity of the rubble beneath his feet as he fought for balance, and then an arrow pierced his shield, sudden and jarring, punching the device solidly back against him and sending him reeling off balance. His heel caught on something and he sat down, hard, his backside jarring painfully on a sharp-edged stone, and then his hearing returned and he clambered back to his feet, aware of the chaos of sight and sound around him and slightly surprised by how many scores of his own men were ahead of him now, having surged by him when he fell.

Ignoring the sharp pain of his bruised buttock, he leapt nimbly down the rubble slope inside the walls and found himself face to face with an armored, grim-faced Muslim swinging a bright-bladed scimitar. Hugh blocked the swing with his shield and swung his mace in a short, chopping arc, plunging the spike on its end through the Muslim's helmet. The man fell away, and Hugh barely felt the tug as he wrenched his mace free again and jumped to his left, swinging an overhead chop at another defender who was on his knees over a Frankish soldier, struggling to stab him with a hooked dagger. The point of the spike crunched into the exposed nape of the man's neck and killed him instantly, but before the fellow could even begin to fall, Hugh sensed another presence lunging towards him from his unprotected right and knew he had no time to free his mace.

He released his grip and spun away to the left, turning hard on his heel and swinging his shield down and inward in a desperate attempt to cover his side as he drew his dagger with his right hand. He heard a quick intake of breath close to his ear, a muttered curse, and then a whiff of some fragrance he had smelled before, and someone's back came hard against his own. He dropped instantly to his left knee and turned again, hard, sweeping his dagger in a tight arc outwards and up until he felt the blade sink into yielding flesh. And then, in a weltering crush of grappling bodies, hearing the clang and grating of blades and the heavier thuds of blows from other weapons, all mixed with the sobbing, grunting, hissing, screaming sounds of men in torment, he sensed a looming shadow—had no time to really see it—and felt a rushing pressure of air as something swept down and smashed into his head, hammering him into blackness.

HE FOUND THAT he could not move his body and it hurt almost beyond tolerance when he tried to open his eyes, and so he lay still for a while, allowing his head to clear and collecting his thoughts. A short time later he tried again to open his eyes, cautiously this time, and was able to do so, but the pain was no less intense than before, and although he could see light this time, he could discern nothing else that made sense to him and he still could not move. And so he slowly closed his eyes and willed himself to lie still and breathe steadily, fighting the urge to panic, until his heartbeat returned to its normal pace. He flexed his fingers slowly, happy beyond belief that he could and that they worked, and then he braced them and pushed hard, straightening his arms. Something yielded at his back and he pushed harder, and whatever was on top of him fell away suddenly. And then he opened his eyes for the third time. It still hurt abominably, but this time he could see, although everything was heavily blurred.

It took him several moments longer to extricate himself and twist his body into a sitting posture, but by then he understood that he had been lying head downward, near the base of the rubble pile behind the city wall, his shoulder caught on a fragment of broken masonry and his face thrust into the debris surrounding it. His eyes were full of dust and grit, and the weight pinning him in place had been contributed by two dead men, one of them Muslim, the other Frankish. The fighting had passed him by—he could hear the sounds of it in the distance—and he became aware of a steady flow of Frankish warriors, knights and men-at-arms, all filing quickly down from the top of the breach in the wall and dispersing into the streets and alleyways of the city ahead of him, moving rapidly as though they feared the fighting might be over before they arrived. None of them paid him the slightest attention.

Hugh rose to his feet but quickly discovered that he was not yet ready to go anywhere, for the world tilted alarmingly sideways and he fell back to his seat again. In falling, however, he felt the heavy weight of his water bottle banging against his side. He pulled a kerchief from inside his mail coat and soaked it from the bottle, then washed the sand and grit from his eyes, hissing against the pain of it yet feeling the relief and improvement immediately. He repeated the treatment with fresh water, and now that he could see better, he looked around the spot where he had fallen, seeing bodies everywhere. He noticed that there appeared to be an equal division of defenders and attackers among the corpses, but he was relieved that he saw no one among the casualties whom he recognized, and he wondered where St. Omer and the others were, and why they had left him behind. The only explanation he could think of—and he suspected it must be accurate, since Arlo had never quit his side before— was that they had lost him in the whirl of the original fighting, which had been utterly chaotic. They must have thought him ahead of them and gone surging forward in search of him.

Knowing he was in no danger here, he removed his flat steel helmet, loosened the thongs at his neck and pushed the chain-mail hood back from his head, grateful that he could feel no obvious rents in the mail with his bare hands. He then soaked his kerchief thoroughly one last time and wiped his face, head, and hands. His skull was pounding from a massive headache, from the blow that had struck him down, he assumed, but there had been no blood on his kerchief and the remainder of his body felt surprisingly well, its various parts responding when called upon to move. He rinsed out his mouth and spat out the dislodged grit, then swallowed a mouthful of water, sealed the bottle, and replaced his hood and helmet, refastening the ties at his chin before he rose once more to his feet, his arms outstretched for balance. Beyond a tiny sway on reaching his full height, this time he was stable.

His sword was where it should be, still in its sheath, but his shield and his dagger were nowhere to be seen, and he stood blinking for a moment, looking around for them before he saw the well-known painted shaft of his spiked mace. Its spike was still buried in the spine of the last man he had struck with it, and he tried not to wonder who the fellow had been as he twisted and pulled at the weapon until it ripped noisily free. He looked at the clotted spike, then struck it into the ground, cleaning the worst of the gore off it, and glanced around in search of his dagger. Realizing that it could be anywhere, hidden under any of the bodies littering the scene, he abandoned trying to find it and drew his long sword from its sheath instead. Then, clutching the mace firmly in his left hand and the long sword in his right, Hugh de Payens stepped forward and finally entered the Holy City of Jerusalem.

He carried both weapons all day long, but he was never even tempted again to use either one of them, except, on three separate occasions, against his own people, when he found them committing atrocities against people who could never, by any stretch of anyone's imagination, have taken any part in the defense of Jerusalem—old and young women, some of the latter pregnant, and helpless, terrified children.

Towards nightfall, after walking around the fallen city for hours on end, he left through the Damascus Gate, passing St. Omer and Montdidier with no sign of recognition and making no response to their shouts. Perplexed, but knowing him well enough to know they would earn no thanks by accosting him, his two friends stood and watched him walk away into the gathering dusk. The faithful Arlo, who had been searching frantically for his friend and master all day long, stayed up the entire night, waiting for him to return. They had assumed he would return to their encampment, but they were wrong.

Weeks passed, and everyone, including his three closest friends, believed that Hugh de Payens was dead. Arlo grew gaunt, for he alone of the remaining three friends had had time to dwell upon Hugh's loss and to wonder what had befallen him. Godfrey and Payn had been kept mercifully busy by the demands of Count Raymond, who was well aware of the dangers inherent in the loss of a bosom friend. Arlo, lowborn as he was, expected and received no such consideration, and thus was left to his own devices. By the end of the third day, after making widespread enquiries, he had become convinced that Hugh had fallen among thieves and been killed, his body hidden in some hole. He had prowled the length and breadth of the city after that, searching every street and every empty house and cave for a sign of his master's corpse before the chaos of the city's sacking had been cleared away, the decomposing bodies gathered up and burned, and the thoroughfares cleaned up and made habitable again.

That initial cleansing, a leviathan undertaking by anyone's estimate, had taken fifteen clear days of back-breaking work by every man-at-arms and every prisoner fit enough to ply a shovel or a broom, but still the stench of blood and death lingered in narrow, shaded places of the city, as though baked into the very stones by the intense heat. And when all his searching had led to nothing, Arlo had spoken individually to everyone in authority among the Pope's armies. No one had seen Sir Hugh de Payens, and no one knew or appeared to care what might have happened to him.

And then one morning, without explanation, Hugh returned, walking into camp soon after dawn, dressed in rags beneath a tattered homespun robe, and leading a donkey piled high with bundled packages. He ignored Arlo's stupefaction, merely nodding quietly to him as if he had seen him only moments earlier, then began unloading the donkey's cargo, which transpired to be his chain-mail hauberk, his quilted tunic, his armor, and his mace and sword. He offered no word of explanation of what he had been doing, and when Arlo eventually asked him directly where he had been, he answered only, "By myself, thinking." Arlo said nothing more, but he recognized that the Hugh de Payens who returned that morning was not the man who had led the charge into the breached city three weeks earlier.

Arlo immediately sent word of Hugh's return to St. Omer and Montdidier, and both men came by Hugh's camp within the hour, only to find that their friend was soundly asleep and that Arlo would not permit them to waken him, pointing out that his master must be exhausted, since he would never otherwise permit himself to be abed at such a time of day. Accepting that as self-evident, the other two demanded that Arlo tell them everything he knew. Arlo, of course, knew nothing more than they did. He told them of Hugh's unheralded return, of his unusual reticence and quietude, but there was nothing more he could add.

That same evening, the two knights returned and found Hugh sitting quietly in front of a fire of horse and camel dung, wrapped in the homespun robe he had acquired and staring into the glowing embers. He greeted them cordially enough, but would respond to none of their questions, and when they became insistent, he would speak to one of them while plainly avoiding answering the other. They suffered it for an hour and then withdrew, shaking their heads.

They returned the next night to discover that nothing had changed, but Godfrey sat narrow-eyed, watching and listening and saying little, his mouth pursed. On the following evening he returned alone and sat in silence for more than an hour, staring into the fire beside his friend. Hugh seemed grateful for his companionship, and they sat in comfortable silence until Godfrey cleared his throat and spoke.

"I was angry at you, you know, the day the walls went down, and I've been angry at you ever since."

The silence that followed was long, but just as St. Omer was beginning to think Hugh would not respond, the other man cocked his head and looked at him sideways. "Why?"

"Why? How can you even ask me that, Hugh? Why? Because I needed you, and you weren't there—Crusty and I both needed you, more than we ever have. You are the only person we can trust without a doubt, and you vanished when we needed you the most. Where did you disappear to, in the name of God?"

Hugh de Payens straightened up in his seat as though he had been hit, and for a moment his face was transformed, his ears drawing backward and the skin over his cheekbones stretching tight in response, the crease lines by his eyes showing pale against the sunburnt bronze of his face.

"In the name of God? You ask where I went in the name of *God*? I went nowhere in the name of God. I ran in shame and terror *from* the name of God, out into the darkness of the desert to where I could no longer hear His name being screamed by madmen. I heard enough of the name of God that day to sicken me for a thousand lifetimes, and I never wish to hear His name again."

St. Omer forced himself to sit quietly, counting from one to twenty, before he asked, his voice quiet,

"What are you talking about, Hugh? I don't understand what you are saying."

The silence stretched again for what seemed like an age before de Payens responded, his voice softer than it had any right to be, considering the weight of what he now said. "God *willed* what happened in Jerusalem that day, Goff. God willed it. I looked in the face of a bishop for whom I had gone searching, to confess my sins for the first time since I joined our Order, and I saw blood matted in his beard and in his hair, and I saw the madness of the blood lust in his eyes and the slashed stain on his robe where he had wiped his blade clean of the blood he had spilled that day. It hung from a belt across his chest, a long, rusted old sword, clotted with gore, and I thought, *This man is a bishop, one of God's anointed shepherds, and he is stained and defiled with human blood ... a priest, forbidden to kill!* And then, and only then, I understood that I alone, of all the people in Jerusalem that day, saw anything morally wrong in what was happening, in what we had done and were doing. How could we be wrong? We were carrying out God's will. *Deus le veult!*

"How many did we kill that day, do you know?"

St. Omer gazed down at his feet. "Aye, Hugh, I know. The number was made known. Everyone was very proud of it. The greatest victory in the history of Christendom ... the redemption of Jerusalem from the hands of the Infidel ..."

"How many, Goff?"

St. Omer sucked in a great, deep breath. "Ninety thousand."

"Ninety ... thousand. Ninety thousand souls ..." Hugh turned and looked at his friend squarely. "Think about that, Goff. Think back. Do you remember how proud we were to belong to our splendid army on the day we set out from Constantinople into Turkey? That was four armies combined into one, and it was less than forty-five thousand strong ... less than half the number killed in Jerusalem that day. Do you remember how *vast* it seemed to us then, that gathering of forty-odd thousand, with its four thousand, five hundred mounted knights and its thirty thousand infantry? Do you remember the sheer *size* of it, the awe-inspiring *mass* of it? And here were ninety thousand, a gathering twice as large as that great army but composed of men and women and children, all of them starving, frail and sick and ailing, walled up in one city, helpless and at our mercy. And we slew them because *God willed it* ..."

His voice failed him and he stood up and crossed his arms, his chin sinking onto his breast, and when he spoke again he held one hand over his eyes, pinching them shut. "I knew the number had to be huge, because there were times when I was wading in blood and guts to my ankles ... places where the drainage was poor and the walls were high ... where there were houses full of wealthy people and family retainers, slaughtered in their homes. And I believe the screams I heard that day—and still can hear today—will never again permit me to hear silence."

St. Omer raised his hands and then let them drop helplessly into his lap. "Hugh—"

"Please tell me you were not about to say that it was not as bad as I remember, Goff, because it was, and worse. I saw men whom I have known my entire life, Christian knights, transformed into beasts, slaughtering women and children wantonly, some of them dragging cloths stuffed with booty they could not have carried. I killed one man myself, a knight from Chartres, whom I found ravishing a girl who could not have been older than seven. He glared at me, demented, and screamed that he was doing God's work, driving the devil out of her. I took his head off with one stroke and left him sprawled over her, because she was already dead. He had killed her before violating her. Because God willed it, Goff ... Because God willed it, through his priests and followers. Don't ever talk to me of God again."

"I will not. You may rely on that."

Something in St. Omer's tone penetrated the other man's awareness and he cocked his head suddenly, curious again. "Why were you angry at me that day? I don't believe you told me."

"Yes, I did. You disappeared. That's what we've been talking about. And now you will doubtless be surprised to hear that I am even angrier than I was then."

He twisted in his seat to stare stonily at Hugh. "How can you say you were the only one who felt the way you did that day? How can you even think such a thing? How can you ... can you have that much ... what's the word old Anselm used to use for pride, the dangerous kind? Hubris, that's it. How can you have that much hubris, Hugh? That is insulting. Insulting to the point of inviting a slap in the face. It's insulting to me, and to Crusty, and to your father the Baron, and the Count himself, and to every other member of our Order who was in the city that day. None of us could avoid being there, if you'll but throw your mind back. We had marched halfway across the world to be there that day, seeing it as a bounden duty, and so we all went in there willingly.

"But not all of us enjoyed what happened there, and what we saw being done sickened more good men than you near to death. You were not the only man to be repelled by what went on that day in that place. I can name you a hundred men I know in person, all of whom are sick at heart over what happened here, but what can they do to change any of it? The treasures that were captured are all gone, into the coffers of the bishops and the nobility. The people who owned those treasures are all dead. The city is uninhabitable, a stinking charnel house, and I would wager no one will live there for the next ten years or more. Titus destroyed Jerusalem twelve hundred years ago, and now the Church of Jesus Christ, a Jew who lived here at that time, has destroyed it again, and somehow you have convinced yourself that you alone can see that? That truly is hubris, my friend, and it is too much so for me. I'll bid you a good night."

St. Omer stood up abruptly and turned to walk away.

"Wait, Goff, wait, wait. Turn around, if you will, and look at me." Godfrey did so, and Hugh immediately looked away, gazing into the fire for a spell, aware of Godfrey's eyes on him, and then looked up at his friend, and shook his head as if clearing it. "Forgive me, in the spirit of our ancient Order. You are correct in every word. I have been steeped in hubris—pickled in it—and unable to see beyond the end of my own stubborn, self-pitying nose. Please, my friend, sit down."

Half an hour later, having talked in depth about their innermost feelings and the experiences of others of like mind, Hugh said, "Thank you for this, Goff. You have made me feel much better, knowing that so many others share my anger and my grief. But there are still those others who do not …"

"And what do you intend to do about them, Hugh?"

"Nothing at all. Providing they leave me to my own affairs, I intend to ignore them."

"Ignore them?" St. Omer seemed on the verge of smiling. "All of them?"

"Every one of them. Why does that make you smile?"

"Simply because of the way you said it. But what if they refuse to leave you to your own affairs, what then?"

Hugh de Payens's face was utterly without humor or compassion when he said, flatly, "Then I will kill a few of them, as they killed in Jerusalem. That will convince them quickly to leave me alone, and I will do it without hesitation if I must. In my eyes, they have lost any vestige of humanity they might have had before coming here, and I wish nothing to do with them. My liege lord, while I am here in Palestine, is Count Raymond, and to him I will dedicate my life and duty as I did before. Beginning once again tomorrow, I will go where he sends me, do what he bids me do, and if it should transpire that I must share duties or fight alongside these others, then I shall do so. But I will have nothing to do with any of them otherwise."

"But—"

"But what, Goff?" Now Hugh smiled, his old nature showing through for the first time. "Think about it, lad—about me, and about what you are saying. I have never willingly had anything to do with any of them ere now anyway. I spend my spare time only with my friends, and all my friends are within the Order." He paused, then said, "What about you and Crusty, what will you do, now that you have seen how wondrously the Holy City was saved for all good Christian souls?"

St. Omer shrugged. "The same as you. We will address ourselves to our sworn duty, in obedience to our lord the Count. Which reminds me, I am summoned to attend him at daybreak, so I had best be on my way. I have a feeling he intends to send me somewhere. Not Crusty, just me. But if he does not, then I'll be back tomorrow night, with Crusty."

"So be it, and may Fortuna ride with you if he sends you out. Be careful and come back safely."

St. Omer nodded and turned to leave, then swung back yet again. "We will be going home soon, you know, now that the campaign is complete. The army is breaking up, did you know that?"

"Breaking up?" Hugh sat blinking for the space of several heartbeats. "What does that mean, *breaking up*?

That would be utter folly, Goff. The army can't break up. The moment that happens, the Turks will sweep back in here like avenging devils, with no one to stop them, and we will have achieved nothing. Where did you hear that nonsense?"

St. Omer stood frowning for a moment. "I don't know where I first heard it, really, but now everyone's talking about it—about going home, I mean. We need to go home, Hugh, particularly those of us who have wives and children. We have been gone for four years already, and even if we were to leave tonight, it would be nigh on six years by the time we win home." He hesitated. "Besides, it's not as if everyone is leaving. There is too much at stake for that. Kingdoms and duchies and counties are being created even as we speak, and they will have to be defended."

De Payens frowned. "Kingdoms? What are you talking about, Goff? Kingdoms, here in God's homeland? Where are these kingdoms?"

St. Omer threw his hands in the air. "They are nowhere, Hugh, not yet. It is all talk at this stage. But there is talk of establishing a Kingdom of Jerusalem, for the protection of the Holy Places. The barons and nobles wanted de Bouillon to be king, and named him such ten days ago, while you were absent, but he refused, saying no mere man should wear a crown of gold where Jesus wore a crown of thorns. He has accepted the lesser title, however, of Advocate of the Holy Sepulcher."

"Hmm. What does that mean?" Hugh knew and admired Geoffroi de Bouillon, the Duke of Lower

Louraine, who had been the undisputed leader of the
Christian armies on the march to Jerusalem, and he
thought it typical of the man that he would have the
moral strength to refuse a kingdom because of his beliefs.
De Bouillon was modest, and even self-effacing, and his
undoubted honesty and integrity were the true reasons
underlying his popularity and the high regard in which
he was held. Now, as he thought about it, it became plain
to Hugh that de Bouillon's refusal would provide an
opportunity for someone else, for the kingship, once
dreamed up, would not go long unclaimed, but as soon
as Hugh mentioned this, Godfrey shook his head.

"Not an issue," he said. "De Bouillon's new title,
Advocate of the Holy Sepulcher, usurps all the powers
of kingship without using the name. It is a pretty piece
of politicking, but it may serve all our needs."

"Aye, for as long as Geoffroi lives. Who else is
involved?"

St. Omer shrugged. "The usual crowd, I should think.
Geoffroi's brother Baldwin won't be far away from the
pickings. A cold fish, that one. Then there's Bohemond
of Taranto. They say he is already laying claim to Antioch,
naming it his own fiefdom and calling himself the Prince
of Antioch. And they say, too, that Baldwin, for his own
protection, while keeping one eye on his brother's claim
to the crown of Jerusalem, is pressing himself forward to
claim Edessa, as its Count. There are wheels turning
within wheels among those three ... And then there are
the two Roberts, of Normandy and Flanders, and their
cohort, Stephen of Blois, who wed the Conqueror's

daughter in a moment of weakness and has rued it ever since. Also, of course, there is our own Count's liege, Count Raymond of Toulouse. They are all looking around like hawks, preening and peering to see what pickings are available to them."

Hugh was staring back into the fire again, nodding his head intently at whatever he could see in the glow of the coals. "I need to speak with Count Raymond," he said, more to himself than to his friend. "I shall be there before you leave him at first light, hoping that he will speak with me. Go now and find your bed, my friend, and sleep well."

NINE

"There is no one close enough to overhear us out here, Brother Hugh, so you may speak plainly. What is it that concerns you?"

It was still early enough in the morning for the shadows to be long, although the sun was climbing rapidly now, its glare strengthening with every passing minute, but Hugh was heartened by Raymond's intuitive understanding of his needs. He had been appalled to find the Count surrounded by a throng of courtiers that morning, many of them supplicants, many of them subordinates, and very few of them brethren of the Order. Godfrey must have been there ahead of his appointed time and received his instructions from the Count before Hugh arrived, because there was no sign of him. The guards had immediately permitted Hugh to enter the enormous tent below the banner of Toulouse, but he had stopped short just within the entry, looking about him, unwilling to penetrate the mass of milling bodies. He spotted the Count, in the middle of the large space and surrounded by half a score of men, but elsewhere in the crowd he saw several people whom he had last seen in Jerusalem, creating havoc, and he had no wish to deal with any of them.

Fortunately, the Count had seen Hugh standing alone and had excused himself from his entourage and embraced him as a brother. He had been glad to hear from St. Omer that Hugh had returned, he said, and Hugh was surprised—but also grateful—that he did not go on to ask where he had been during the three weeks of his absence. Instead, Raymond leaned back and eyed him questioningly, then glanced around at the watching crowd before asking him, quietly, "Did you wish to speak to me of fraternal matters?" When Hugh nodded, he added, "Is it sufficiently important to interrupt this gathering?" Hugh nodded again, and the Count gripped his arm above the elbow, speaking now for the ears of others. "Come then, Sir Hugh, and walk with me in the morning air for a spell. I need to stretch my legs and I am curious to hear of your adventures in the desert."

Now, far removed from the tent and its occupants, Hugh stopped walking and looked directly at his liege. "I hear talk, my lord, of disbanding the army, now that Jerusalem has been retaken."

Count Raymond nodded. "I hear the same, but the reports are less than accurate. There is no possibility of the army being disbanded. That would be sheer madness."

"But some of our people will be returning home, is that not so?"

"Aye, it is, and there is nothing I can do about that. Most of the men here took the Cross voluntarily, to win back the Holy Places, and now that has been done and their aim has been achieved, they believe, with good reason, that their duty has been done, and now they wish to return home. Surely you can understand that?"

"Aye, my lord, I can. But what of us? What of our Order and its intent, here in Jerusalem?"

"The same applies there. Our objective was to establish a presence here from the outset of things. We have done that, earning our right to be here by sharing in the conquest of the Holy City."

"Conquest is not a word I would have chosen there, my lord."

The Count started to frown, but then restrained himself and merely nodded his head, once. "No, and I know why. But you deal in hard, cold pragmatism, Sir Hugh, whereas I must deal in political reality. Thus you may award yourself the privilege of feeling anger and outrage, but I may not. Accept that, if you would please me, and do not question my motives."

"Pardon me, my lord, I would not question anything you do, and I never have. I merely wondered what will become of our mission here when everyone goes home."

"Not everyone will go home. Some of us—some of our brotherhood—will remain behind."

"I would like to be one of those who remain, if it pleases you, my lord."

The handsome Count almost smiled, but dipped his head instead in affirmation. "And you would, under normal circumstances, Sir Hugh. Indeed, you were the first person I thought of when I was considering my plan of action in this matter, prior to the taking of the city. I thought to promote you in the field and leave you in charge of the Order's affairs here, but ..." He shrugged, spreading his hands. "But then you were reported missing, believed dead. That was weeks ago. And then, ten days ago, a courier arrived, bearing word from the Council, and in those dispatches you were named specifically and directed to return home to your father's barony, where the Council has work for you. Believing you dead, I wrote back to that effect ... But fortunately the mail has not been sent, so I will reclaim the letter and destroy it, and you will take the first available vessel headed out of here for Cyprus and home."

"But—"

Raymond's voice held but the slightest trace of censure. "But what, Sir Hugh? But you would rather remain here in Jerusalem with all the people who endeared themselves to you the day you disappeared? Or do you presume to believe that you know better what the Order needs from you than the Governing Council does? Hear me now, for I have thought much on this already today and would have sent for you before the day was out had you not come of your own accord. Here is my opinion: we have achieved entry here in Jerusalem, but for the time being there is nothing we can do, because the city lies empty and stinking to the heavens of blood and offal, and were it not for the fact that the Holy Sepulcher is here, none of us would remain close by. As the smell begins to fade, however, men will begin to plot and political maneuvering will have its day. It has already begun. You know about de Bouillon's refusal of the crown, I presume?"

Seeing Hugh's nod, he continued. "Whatever the outcome of that situation, other events will be occurring here within the next few years. There will be a Kingdom of Jerusalem, just as there is already a Principality of Antioch—Bohemond wasted no time on that development. There will also be a Kingdom, perhaps, of Edessa, and counties in other areas. All of that will transpire over the course of the coming four or five years, and in the meantime we are all of us surrounded by more Muslim enemies than anyone could possibly compute. We have won back God's Homeland from the Infidel, but we will have our hands full, trying to keep it ...

"In the meantime, we would be able to do nothing on behalf of the Order here, even if we knew what the requirements were. You do not know what is required of us, or of you, but I know a little more, at least, than you do. You are required to return home and to study further the Lore of our Order. Then, when you know enough, you will return here, either to perform an assigned task or to await further instructions. St. Omer and Montdidier will accompany you home, and you will carry dispatches from me to your liege of Champagne. Now, return with me, if you will, to where my supplicants await me, and then you may set about gathering your belongings for your voyage."

It took mere moments for them to return, and Hugh was aware of the curious faces peering at them.

He paid none of them any attention, however, and when Count Raymond extended his hand, Hugh bowed over it.

"Go in peace," the Count murmured, "and go with our God, Hugh de Payens. You will see this land again, I promise you."

AWAKENINGS

ONE

"A traveler went down from Jerusalem to Jericho and fell among thieves …"

Hugh de Payens did not know who had spoken, and did not even turn his head to see, for what would be taken elsewhere as a biblical quotation was a banality here on the road to Jericho, which had not changed one iota for the better since the days of the Good Samaritan. The dead men in front of them took up all Hugh's attention. They had been stripped of everything of value and everything that might identify them; their naked corpses, red faced and fish-belly-white everywhere else, confirmed only that they had been from the other end of the earth, from Christendom. They had been slaughtered, then despoiled and left where they had fallen among the desert boulders near the road, and it had happened very recently, for their white-skinned flesh was still largely intact. The vultures had barely begun to feast on them, and black swarms of flies heaved and seethed not only on their wounds but on the pools of blackening, clotted blood that stained the sandy ground. On a boulder above him, one of the carrion eaters stirred and flapped its great, black wings, but made no move to return to its interrupted meal. The newcomers were too close, and it knew from experience that they would attack it.

"Seven of them," Hugh said to the man sitting beside him. "They must have run into a strong party."

"Needn't have been that strong," the other remarked, his eyes moving restlessly from corpse to corpse. "These fellows have all been arrow shot. Take a look at the holes in them. Not a sword slash or a chop cut anywhere. Three or four archers could have done that. I suppose you'll want to give them a Christian burial?"

"I think not, Arlo. We don't even know they were Christian. They might have been Jews, or Levantines. Besides, we have no shovels and it will soon be dark. We can change nothing here. They are dead and thus beyond our help, so let us leave them as they are. No point in even hauling them together into one pile. They'll only stink the more and take longer to rot. As they are, the vultures and the desert beasts will make short work of them." He raised his voice so that everyone could hear him. "Shall we ride on, my friends? There's naught to be done here and we are yet six miles from Jericho, with less than an hour of light remaining. De Beaufort, lead us on, if you will."

As the group began to move again, de Payens scanned them quickly, then kicked his horse towards the head of the column, where Julian de Beaufort rode straight-backed, his shield slung behind him and the butt of his long spear resting in the cup at his right stirrup, his eyes moving constantly from side to side, on the lookout for brigands. There were eighteen men in the group, all well mounted and heavily armed and armored, wearing chain-mail hauberks, helmets, and leggings, their surcoats marked with the various emblems of the nobles to whom they paid allegiance. Sir Hugh knew most of their faces but few of their names, but all of them knew who he was.

Hugh de Payens, at forty-six years of age, was regarded with awe by everyone who met him. A veteran of the sacking of Jerusalem seventeen years earlier, he had become an honored champion of Christendom and a warrior whose prowess was legendary throughout the Holy Lands, not merely in the Kingdom of Jerusalem but in northern Antioch and the other, lesser kingdoms of the region known by then to the Frankish conquerors as Outremer, "the land beyond the sea." He had taken command of this traveling band by natural ranking, not because anyone had appointed him, and there was not a man among them who objected.

Even after seventeen years of occupation, travel within the Kingdom of Jerusalem was more hazardous than it had ever been, because the hills between Jerusalem and Joppa, thirty miles west on the coast, and between Jerusalem and Jericho, which lay about half as far away in the other direction, swarmed with bandits and brigands who preyed on those people—always Franks and usually pilgrims—who used the country's roads to travel between the Holy Places. Thus it was a matter of mere common sense to wait until a journey, no matter how important it might be or what it might entail, could be undertaken in a large group for common safety and self-defense. This was exactly such a group, although by some strange chance, it was composed purely of knights and men-at-arms, with no pilgrims and no merchants. But even among these professionals, there was a grateful acknowledgment that, under Hugh's command, they were in the company of a veteran who knew exactly what he was doing.

Hugh rode in silence for a while, alongside Sir Julian, and he was aware, without any need to look, that Arlo rode close behind him, as he had for the past four decades. But he knew, too, that neither he nor his faithful retainer felt completely at ease here, because this journey to Jericho had been unplanned, and they had long since learned that survival in Outremer relied upon careful planning before committing to any journey. Only a few days earlier, however, a man had come looking for Hugh de Payens, with word from his oldest friend, Godfrey St. Omer. According to the messenger, whom Hugh had distrusted on sight as a shifty-eyed, duplicitous scoundrel who would tell any lie in the hope of profit, St. Omer was now in the care of the recently formed Order of the Knights of the Hospital at their secondary hospice in Jericho, recovering from atrocities inflicted upon him while he had been a slave in the hands of the Muslims.

That had been an astounding piece of information, because Hugh had not seen or heard from Godfrey in years, and his first reaction was that this summons must be a hoax. St. Omer had remained at home on his family estates in Picardy years earlier, in 1107, when

Hugh himself had returned to Outremer. Godfrey had retired there with the full concurrence of Count Hugh of Champagne, to be with his ailing wife, Louise, who had fallen gravely ill of some paralyzing affliction five years earlier, soon after Godfrey had returned from Palestine. But a full decade had elapsed since then, and Hugh was convinced that if Goff had intended to return to Outremer he would have contacted his old friend and brother-in-law through the Order of Rebirth. And so he instinctively distrusted the bearer of the message from Jericho.

On reflection, however, he had quickly understood that his suspicions made no sense, since had Godfrey not been in Jericho, the fellow would have had no basis for his tale, and so he had told Arlo to make ready for a journey and to find a suitable party with whom they could travel as soon as possible.

Count Hugh himself had returned to his County of Champagne the previous year, after a brief stay of little more than a year in Jerusalem, and so Hugh obtained permission to travel to Jericho from Lucien of Troyes, the Count's deputy in the Holy Land. De Troyes, a fellow member of the Order of Rebirth, knew Godfrey of St. Omer well, so his permission had been immediate, even while he himself was preparing to return to France within the coming few days.

"So, Sir Hugh, may I ask what takes you to Jericho so hastily?" De Beaufort had turned in the saddle to address de Payens, but as the older man jerked his head and looked back at him, startled out of his reverie, the other raised a hand quickly. "Forgive me, I was merely being curious. I had no wish to pry. But you did say you had not planned to make this journey."

De Payens waved a hand, dismissing de Beaufort's apology. "I am not offended. I received word that an old friend is in the care of the hospital in Jericho, released but recently from captivity among the Turks. I had not known he was even in the Holy Land, let alone that he had been taken by the Mussulman. For many years I relied upon his wife, my sister, Louise, for all my information, but I have not received a letter from her in more years than I care to count, and now I find I do not even know if she is still alive. Have you—?" De Payens glanced at the younger man and answered his own question. "No, you have not. You are too young. You will find, however, that as you grow older, time has a way of accelerating. I had no idea until two days ago that twenty years have passed since I first came to Outremer, although I have been home since then ... but seven years have fled since I last heard word from my sister."

Riding behind the two knights, Arlo listened to what was being said, smiling to himself and taking note of the way de Beaufort listened wide-eyed to every word Sir Hugh uttered, for he knew de Beaufort would benefit by this encounter and the conversation that was taking place. Sir Hugh de Payens was famed for many things, but being friendly and talkative with strangers was not one of them. He was, in fact, notorious for being brusque and taciturn, a man of high principles, dark moods, and unflinching opinions who preferred his own company and actively encouraged the world to avoid him. That he was actually passing the time of day and sharing personal information with de Beaufort was extremely unusual and would not go unremarked.

DE PAYENS HAD NOT ALWAYS been unfriendly or distrustful. That had been a gradual transition, brought about over a decade of hard living and life lessons harshly learned, but Arlo knew that the final phase of the transformation had been triggered on the day Jerusalem fell, on the fifteenth of July, a Friday, in 1099. It had been Hugh's twenty-ninth birthday. The full extent of his transformation proved to be deeply unsettling, leaving many of the knights unsure of how to deal with this man they had thought they knew.

They need not have bothered to wonder, for de Payens had simply stopped dealing with them, having decided that he desired no truck or commerce with any of the self-styled "Christian" warriors and their blood-lusting hypocrisy. Hugh de Payens lived in a self-imposed exile of silence, surrounded by others but interacting with none of them, except when his duty demanded that he act as part of the army. When one knight, noted for his intolerance and hot temper, believed he had been slighted by Hugh's silence, he grasped de Payens from behind, to wrench him around and face him. Hugh spun and felled him with a single, straight-armed blow to the forehead that left the man senseless. Later that day, as evening approached and the other knight felt sufficiently recovered to convince himself that he had been caught unawares, the fellow renewed the quarrel, attacking Hugh with a bare blade, which was against all the laws of the armies. De Payens disarmed him immediately and almost casually, using a heavy oak cudgel to snap the man's sword blade, and then he thrashed him severely enough to remove all doubts from everyone's mind about the wisdom of trying to thrust themselves uninvited into the awareness of the knight from Payens.

After that, word spread quickly that de Payens was crazed and, except in the execution of his knightly duties, would speak to no one other than his servant. In the eyes of his fellow knights, he had crossed out of heroism and into madness, but no one ever sought, or attempted to supply, an explanation for his bizarre behavior. It was simply accepted that he had been accursed somehow during the sack of Jerusalem. And thus Sir Hugh had become something of a soldiers' legend, his exploits and his eccentricities widely reported and remarked upon, so that even after he returned to Christendom, men continued to talk about him, his strange notions, and the reputation for military prowess, ferocity, and bravery that no one begrudged him.

Summoned home with his friends by their liege lord, Hugh had returned to Champagne in the year after Jerusalem's capture, and there, for the first six years of the new century, he had immersed himself in studying the Lore of the Order of Rebirth, traveling the length and breadth of his home country, from northern Flanders to Languedoc in the far southeast, to study with some of its most learned scholars and teachers. Thinking privately about that time in later years, Hugh regarded the period as the most enjoyable time of his life. Surrounded by his peers, none of whom bore any guilt for what had happened in Jerusalem, he had lived what was, for him, a full and normal life, where his daily weapons training was the only diversion open to him and his entire duty otherwise revolved around study and learning.

Early in 1107, however, he had been summoned before a plenary meeting of the Order's Governing Council and had been charged with returning immediately to Outremer, there to establish contact with as many brethren of the Order as he could find, and to keep them aware of their oaths while they awaited further instructions from home on how they must proceed when the time was judged to be right. It crossed Hugh's mind at the time, right there in front of the entire tribunal, to ask for more specific information regarding that timing and its rightness, but he resisted the impulse, telling himself that he would be informed of everything he needed to know when that need arose. In the meantime, he was informed, he would ride as one of a company of one hundred knights and three hundred men-at-arms raised by the Duchies of Burgundy, Anjou, and Aquitaine in response to requests from the King and the Patriarch Archbishop of Jerusalem. He would be attached to the contingent from Anjou, and would come under the command of whomever was appointed by Count Fulk to represent him in Outremer.

Excited by the prospect of putting his newly

acquired learning to good use, he had gone looking for Montdidier, to try to persuade Payn to sail back with him, but Payn had been in England, visiting his wife's father at Sir Stephen's great castle in Yorkshire, and Godfrey, Hugh already knew, was unable to accompany him either, being at his home in Picardy, looking after his sick wife. Hugh had felt guilty about not having made the time to go and visit his ailing sister, whom he had not seen since the death of their mother five years earlier, and now he found there was not enough time for him to travel to Picardy to see her. He had contented himself with writing to her, a long, rambling letter of the kind he enjoyed writing and he knew Louise loved to read, and then, reluctantly, he had set sail for Outremer without his friends, on his way to Malta, the ship's first port of call, within two weeks of his meeting with the Council. Less than half a year after that, he was back in Jerusalem, noticing the changes that had been effected in his absence.

Primary among those was that the Kingdom of Jerusalem had become a reality. The scruples expressed by Geoffroi de Bouillon, when he refused to wear a golden crown where Jesus had worn thorns, had not extended to his more ambitious brother Baldwin, and when de Bouillon had died after only a year as Advocate of the Holy Sepulcher, Baldwin had been quick to claim the throne. Since then, he had been working hard, and admirably, people said, to consolidate and strengthen his new kingdom, and hand in glove with that to stabilize Christendom's hold in Outremer, including the

Principality of Antioch and the Counties of Edessa and Tripoli, deftly juggling the ambitions of the various lords involved and ensuring that each of them contributed to the support of Jerusalem itself as the administrative center of all Outremer.

The city no longer stank of corruption, its stench burned away by the desert sun years earlier, but apart from its occupying garrison it still lay virtually derelict, with only a few civilian inhabitants, most of those Christians. The King himself had taken over the magnificent al-Aqsa Mosque, the site of the Dome of the Rock, and had converted it into his royal palace. The fact that in doing so he had scandalized and offended all devout Muslims mattered nothing to Baldwin, but it had also done nothing to help his efforts to repopulate the city.

The newcomers from the great duchies were made welcome with great panoply and pomp by King Baldwin, and he made no secret of how great his need for them had been, and would remain. His kingdom was small—as indeed was the total area of all the "redeemed" lands of Outremer, a slender chain of holdings running north to south, with the Mediterranean Sea lying on its western flank—and it was threatened along its entire western perimeter by an enormous host of Muslims, outnumbering the Frankish conquerors by more than twenty to one, according to highly conservative and optimistic estimates. That reality forced Baldwin and his military commanders to maintain a constant readiness, poised to respond at once to any threat to their borders, grateful for a lack of cohesion on the side of the enemy. The Seljuk Turks, the nominal overlords of an empire that had lasted for a hundred years, had never recovered from their ignominious defeats by the Frankish armies in 1098 and 1099. They had forfeited their supremacy among the Muslim peoples of the desert and no one else had yet stepped forward to take it up, so that the Frankish army, small as it was, had never had to be deployed against any major alliance of Muslim groups and had succeeded, to this point in 1116, in fighting off any invasion of its territories. The newcomers from Christendom, four hundred strong and both self-sufficient and adequately equipped, represented a considerable improvement in the strength and readiness of Baldwin's forces, and after an effusive welcome, they were absorbed into the military fabric of life in Outremer.

Hugh's re-entry into the daily life of Jerusalem and its kingdom forced him to make a decision that was to affect his entire life. During the years he had spent at home after his return, he had been content among his own brotherhood, immersing himself wholeheartedly in duty, work, and study and requiring little in the way of what other men considered normal. He had developed little interest in women, not because he disliked them but simply because he seldom found himself in female company and felt no compelling urge to pursue it, but he would have been surprised to realize that many people who knew him thought of his life as verging on monastic. Hugh had known a few women carnally, from time to time, but he had never been tempted to develop any kind of relationship with any of them, and early in his manhood he had come to accept that he could, whenever he so wished, allay any insuperable sexual longings without great difficulty, since women, when he sought them out, appeared to find him attractive. The fundamental truth of his existence, although it was one that he never thought of, was that chastity became an incidental product of a way of life dominated by attendance to duty, responsibility, and solitary study.

Among his own family and his brethren in the Order of Rebirth, Hugh de Payens could be himself, with no inhibitions and no constraints on his behavior. His view of other men, however, knights who were not of the Brotherhood of the Order, had been gravely distorted by what he had witnessed in Jerusalem on his twenty-ninth birthday, so that Hugh now accepted, rightly or wrongly, that hypocrisy, hatred, bigotry, and ruthless intolerance contaminated the entire Christian Church and its military adherents.

In consequence of that, soon after his arrival back in Outremer, Hugh had voluntarily cut himself off again from all intercourse with anyone who did not belong to the Order of Rebirth and had concentrated all his attention on finding other brethren. He soon discovered, however, that the task he had been assigned by the Order was a far from simple one, and the information from which he had to work was tenuous at best. According to the reports compiled by the armies after the capture of Jerusalem and verified by the Order from its own records, there had been a total of thirty-two knights of the Order in Outremer at the beginning of the century, but the challenge of finding them would be enormously difficult, and convening them after that, Hugh knew, would be nigh on impossible. He was skeptical of the reliability of the lists of survivors compiled after the capture of the city, for the casualties among the Christian armies before the victory, on the route from Constantinople via Antioch, had been appalling, and the powers-that-be had been at great pains to present their conquest in the best possible light. That, in turn, had led to many dead men being reported as having voluntarily remained in Outremer.

Despite that and other difficulties, however, Hugh had managed to establish contact with several of his brethren within the first year, but he had been unable to arrange for any of them to attend a gathering of the kind the Order used so effectively at home. That failure, coupled with the distances involved in traveling anywhere in Outremer and amplified by the dangers presented by the swarming hordes of Muslim soldiers infesting the desert hills flanking all the roads, made it inevitable that, over the course of time, Hugh would forfeit his enthusiasm for such an unrewarding task.

Year after year elapsed with no word reaching him from Champagne or from the Order of Rebirth. Of course, silence and secrecy being what they were to him, he said nothing to Arlo about his doubts and disappointments about his superiors in the Order and their failure to do anything more about promoting the brotherhood's supposed mission in the Holy Land, but he found himself growing cynical about the Order as the years passed in silence and nothing happened.

For his part, Arlo, being loyal to his very core, watched and listened carefully to everything he was told, and he missed nothing, frequently divining things that Hugh would have been appalled to think he had let slip. Now, listening to Sir Hugh conversing openly with the younger de Beaufort, Arlo reflected that, at last, Hugh seemed to be emerging from his self-imposed silence, and he was glad of it. They made good time on the road, coming into sight of Jericho just before the quickly fading day leached the last of the whiteness from the distant buildings. It was full night by the time they reached the first of the two hostelries in the small town, and their farewells were short.

TWO

De Payens and Arlo were astir long before dawn the next day, breaking their fast on sliced cold salted meat between slabs of fresh unleavened bread and washing the food down with clear, cold water from the inn's deep, stone-lined well before they set out to find the Jericho Hospital. It was a temporary hospice, established only recently on the very outskirts of the town by the Knights of the Hospital in Jerusalem, in response to a virulent outbreak of pestilence among the Frankish pilgrims, and it was not expected to be long in use.

Early as they were, however, they found the place by the noise already coming from it, and were surprised to see a thriving, almost self-sufficient hamlet that had newly sprung into being around the mud-brick walls of the hospital. It was clearly a market day, and a common meeting place directly in front of the main gates of the hospital was jammed with hastily erected stalls and donkey-drawn carts from which hawkers were selling a bewildering array of foodstuffs and general goods.

Arlo saw one of the two mounted guards in front of the main gates take note of their approach and sit straighter in his saddle, drawing his companion's attention to them with a single word, barked from the side of his mouth, and he turned in his own saddle, calling Hugh's attention to the guards.

"King's men, over there on guard. You can see their shoulder patches even from here. They've taken note of us. I saw the one on the left alert his mate when he saw us come into the square. They're obviously guarding something."

"Aye, they're guarding the hospital and its knights. The Hospital knights fulfill a valuable function—far too valuable for Baldwin and the Church to jeopardize— and so they are deemed worthy of royal protection, and rightfully so. Let's approach them and identify ourselves. It might make things easier if they are kindly disposed to us later."

That thought of royal protection preoccupied de Payens as he made his way over the last few hundred paces to where the guards sat watching his approach. The name itself, Knights of the Hospital, suggested that the new order—it had been officially founded and named only a few years earlier—should be responsible for its own defense, its members capable, as knights, of fighting on their own behalf. Hugh knew, however, that the suggestion was purely that—a suggestion, exaggerated and inaccurate. The Knights of the Hospital existed solely to minister to Christian pilgrims who fell sick on pilgrimage, on their way to or from the birthplace of Jesus Christ. They were monks, following the ancient monastic Rule of Saint Benedict, and their order had operated a hospice in Jerusalem since AD 600, when Pope Gregory the Great had instructed their abbot, Probus, to build and operate

a hospice for Christian pilgrims. The Benedictine Order
had done so ever since, with only one interruption, when
a zealous anti-Christian caliph destroyed the hospice in
1005. Twenty years thereafter, with the caliph safely
dead, it was rebuilt, and the brothers resumed their
Jerusalem operations, running the hospice efficiently and
without fuss ever since. They had been given the grand-
sounding title of Knights of the Hospital in 1113—
purely to enable them to raise funds more easily for the
pursuit of their work—but they were resolute in their
pacific and religious dedication, possessing not a single
offensive weapon among them.

Hugh remembered spending an almost sleepless
night close to a small group of the Hospitallers some six
months earlier, at a caravanserai six nights' journey from
Jerusalem. The entire inn was overrun by travelers, and
he, along with many others, had been forced to bed
down in the open, huddling close to one of a half score
of large watch fires that kept the chill of the desert night
at bay. For some reason that night, perhaps because
they were away from the discipline of their normal
monastic surroundings, the Hospital knights had been
in no hurry to fall asleep after their evening devotions,
and some of them had lain awake far into the night,
talking of the condition of the roads in the kingdom
and the circumstances facing the Christian pilgrims.

Everyone had known since the early days of the
Christian conquest that the situation on the roads of the
Holy Land was a disgrace crying out for attention, but it
was one of those topics that no one ever brought up for

discussion, simply because no one could really think of anything that might reasonably be done to ease the problem, let alone solve it. It was the classic situation of sheep attracting wolves, in this case naïve, starry-eyed, and weaponless Christian pilgrims attracting ever-increasing hordes of nomadic bandits lured by the prospect of easy pickings and no resistance. The situation had long since passed the point of being embarrassing. It had become a scandal that no self-respecting knight or warrior could countenance in good faith. And yet still, year after year, nothing was done about it.

King Baldwin of Jerusalem declared it impossible for him to divert any of his troops away from their primary duties. The war against the Turks might be over, he maintained, but the Kingdom of Jerusalem was still a new and fragile presence in the Holy Land, surrounded by hungry and angry enemies against whom he must be eternally vigilant. The departure of so many of the triumphant Frankish conquerors for home at the end of the first great conflict had left Baldwin in command of only a very small army with which to garrison and police his kingdom, and his resources were chronically stretched to their utmost limits.

That, unfortunately—and this had been the theme of the conversation that had held Hugh so enthralled—had given rise to an astonishingly widespread perception among the populace that the newly titled Knights of the Hospital should take it upon themselves to look after not merely the health and welfare of the pilgrims but their physical safety and well-being, too, by taking arms against the bandit marauders who infested the hills along the major roads. But of course, the knights were Benedictine monks, bound to pacifism by tradition, the dictates of the Church, and their holy vows of poverty, chastity, and obedience. Their knighthood was merely an honorary entitlement; they could not fight as true knights because they were both monastics and ecclesiastics.

The Knights of the Hospital were being dragged into the political considerations of the kingdom nevertheless, and that fact, and the reasons surrounding it, was the major bone of contention in the debate that night. One of the monks was far angrier than his fellows, incensed by the latest information he had received that very day. The King, it appeared, was talking seriously about attracting settlers to his new kingdom, promising them land and water rights if only they would come. New settlers: that was something unheard of until now in Outremer. There were pilgrims aplenty, passing through the land at all times and in all weathers, but they were all transient by definition, on their way to somewhere else. Settlers, on the other hand, would give up everything they owned in other parts of the world in order to travel to Jerusalem and take up residence there, farm the land, and set down roots. They were to be cherished and encouraged by every means available.

The monk's anger had nothing to do with the settlers themselves. He was completely in support of that initiative. What had infuriated him was the news that the King remained unwilling to commit any of his troops to cleaning up the travel routes and making the roads safe for the very settlers he hoped to attract. How, the monk demanded, could any sane person expect farmers, simple, peaceful, hardworking men with wives and children, to assume the risk of bringing those families into a place where their lives would be in constant, daily jeopardy?

There were those among the monk's own group who sought reasons to justify the King's position, and back and forth the argument went, with a few of the knights muttering that they might one day be tempted to take up the sword, if things grew bad enough. But the consensus was that little was likely to be done about the bandits until the eventual, and some thought inevitable, emergence of a new law-enforcement group, probably mercenary in structure, that would be dedicated solely to making the roads of Jerusalem safe for travelers.

Hugh had fallen off to sleep that night with a half smile on his lips, occasioned by the naïve optimism of the Hospital knights in their hope for a corps of high-principled mercenaries. He had been in the Holy Land long enough by then to find the mere notion of an altruistic motivation, on the part of anyone at all in this harsh land, to be laughable, and nothing he had heard that night had made him think otherwise.

He had admired the brethren of the Hospital unequivocally ever since that night, however, and he believed wholeheartedly that they deserved any assistance that could be rendered them in their work, so he was glad to see that the guards awaiting him that morning as he approached the hospital were alert and conscientious. He introduced himself and stated his business, and the senior guard directed him inside with instructions on where to go and whom to ask for.

In a surprisingly short time, Hugh and Arlo were standing over a cot containing a man who seemed at first glance far too small to be the Godfrey St. Omer they both remembered. It was he, nevertheless, and both men immediately found themselves struggling to conceal the shock of seeing him in such condition. He was emaciated, shriveled and wasted from lack of proper food, but there was no mistaking his gladness at the sight of them, for he smiled and stirred weakly, his lips drawing back from his teeth in a skeletal grin.

"Goff, old friend." De Payens leaned over the bed and squeezed St. Omer's hand gently. "By God, it's wonderful to see you." He watched as St. Omer nodded his head, and then he waved to indicate Arlo. "You probably wouldn't recognize this old fraud, after so long a time, but it's Arlo … fatter and balder and older, like all the rest of us." St. Omer smiled again and raised a frail and languid hand to wave, but Hugh interrupted him before he could begin to say anything. "Don't try to speak. We're here now, so your troubles are all over. We came as soon as we received your message, and now we'll make arrangements to take you back to Jerusalem with us. You'll be much better off there, you'll see. It's changed a great deal since last you saw it." He realized that he was babbling, and so he bade his old friend wait a little while longer and set out, followed by Arlo, to find the man in charge of the Jericho hospital.

As it turned out, their timing could not have been better. The monks had been working for the previous seven days to assemble a caravan, including a large party of returning knights, to travel to Jerusalem, carrying the sickest of their charges to where they could obtain better care in the larger Jerusalem facility, and preparations were being completed that day. The caravan would depart at sunrise the following day, but the brethren had only five horse-drawn wagons capable of making the journey and every inch of space within them had long since been allocated to people far sicker than Godfrey. Undismayed, de Payens and Arlo spent the better part of the day searching for another wagon and eventually found a two-wheeled cart drawn by a single horse, the only vehicle left available in Jericho. Its bed was roomy enough to hold two people lying side by side on deep-piled straw, and it could be protected from the sun by a cloth awning, stretched between hoops that slotted into the sides of the vehicle. Its owner refused to sell the cart, but since Hugh did not need it for longer than the single journey, he arranged to hire it, with its owner-driver, for the length of time required to drive it to Jerusalem, and the driver, knowing that Sir Hugh himself would be riding as escort to his friend, agreed to the knight's terms without a deal of argument.

THREE

Hugh and Arlo were back in their own quarters in Jerusalem within five days, having left St. Omer safely installed in the ancient hospice in the monastery of Saint John the Baptist, close by the Church of the Holy Sepulcher, where the Hospitallers would keep him under close watch and nurse him back to full health. Despite his weakened condition, however, and much to Hugh's surprise, St. Omer had been strong enough on the journey to tell them the story of his misadventure with the followers of Mohammed and his stay among them, chained to an oar on a corsair's galley.

They had covered less than half the twenty-mile distance that first day, constrained by the need to travel slowly for the comfort of the sick and injured men in the six wagons, but they were a strong, well-armed party, and no one had any worries about braving the dangers of the night ahead as they set up camp along the road. Hugh and Arlo had lifted St. Omer's stretcher down from the wagon bed and placed him near their cooking fire, and after their meal, fortified with a draft of wine from the full skin Arlo had brought with him, St. Omer had begun to talk.

"I want to ask you something," he said, his voice

whispery and fragile. "When you first went home to Payens, after the first campaign, did you find it utterly different?"

"Different?" Hugh thought about that for a few moments, looking over to where Arlo sat watching them. "Aye, now that I come to think of it, I did. What makes you ask that?"

St. Omer nodded, barely moving his head, and muttered, "Because I did, too, but I thought I might be the only one. None of the others seemed to feel that way."

Hugh sat musing for a moment longer, then frowned. "I don't think it was home that had changed, Goff, not really. It was me ..."

"Me too." St. Omer drew several deep breaths, then began again, speaking clearly but very quietly. "I had nothing in common with any of ... any of my old friends who had not been out there with us. And I couldn't talk to any of them about what it had been like, at Antioch or any of the other places. They all wanted to know ... but I couldn't tell them. I didn't want to talk about it, because ... because I knew they couldn't imagine ... the reality of it. And besides, all they wanted to hear was what they thought they knew already. The priests had told them everything they needed to know about the glorious Holy War, and anything I tried to say, at the start of things, anything that seemed to ... to contradict the priests shocked and frightened them. They did not really want to hear what I ... what I had to say, Hugh."

Hugh had been nodding his head from time to time as he listened, and now he reached out and gripped St. Omer by the wrist. "I learned the same things, just as quickly as you did, but by then you had gone home to Picardy and I was stuck in Payens."

"I had to go, as soon as I got home. I had no choice, as you know. Louise was sick and I had … I had been away from her too long … She died eight years ago, in '08. Did you know that?"

"No, my friend, but I suspected it, for I have not heard from her since then, and she was a great writer of letters. I knew that only death or grave infirmity could stop her from writing to me. Where is she buried? Did you take her home to Champagne?"

St. Omer's headshake was barely discernible. "No. She rests in the garden of our home in Picardy … She loved it there. Did you hear … Have you heard of your father?"

"No. What of him? Is he dead, too?"

"Aye … soon after you set sail to return here. He had … he had no will to live without your mother …"

Hugh's mother had died while he was studying in the Languedoc, and he had been shocked by his father's condition at her funeral, some part of his awareness recognizing that the Baron showed no interest in continuing to live.

"So William is now Baron of Payens?"

"Aye."

"And how came you to Outremer again? Do you feel well enough to talk about that, or should we leave you to rest?"

"I am ... tired. Forgive me, my friend. But we will talk again tomorrow, and every day thereafter."

St. Omer was asleep by the time Hugh rose and moved to make him comfortable. Arlo brought an extra blanket from the wagon and wrapped it round the sleeping man, after which he and Hugh both lay down to sleep.

It was late the following day by the time they delivered St. Omer to the hospital along with the other invalids from Jericho, and so they had had no time to talk that night, and Hugh was on duty all day long the day after that, so that Arlo visited St. Omer alone the second night, sitting with the knight and talking of inconsequential things from time to time when St. Omer felt like speaking. Hugh returned with Arlo the evening after that, and he was more than pleased to find St. Omer already far stronger and with better facial color than when he had last seen him, three days earlier.

"The other night, you were about to tell me how you came to Outremer again," Hugh began, grinning. "But it must be a very dull story, because the mere thought of it sent you to sleep."

St. Omer smiled back at him, a shadow of his former irreverent and irrepressible grin. "I will not do that to you tonight, I promise ... not for some time yet, at least."

"What *did* happen over there, Goff? Why did you come back? I thought you never would."

St. Omer grimaced. "I could not settle down. I was like a fish out of water in Amiens from the moment I returned. And then after Louise died, I lost all will to live without her ... much like your father after your mother's death. I never knew how much I loved my wife until she grew sick and I lost her, and then I was burdened with guilt over all the years I had spent away from her, playing at being a knight when I could have been with her instead. I tell you, Hugh, I wanted to die. I thought I would never recover from the grief and the guilt ... I even thought of killing myself. But I couldn't. I had inherited everything, against all odds, all my elder brothers having gone before me, one way or another. I had become the paterfamilias, responsible for my entire damned clan and all its holdings. I never wished for it and God knows I never sought it, but it happened anyway and I wanted no part of it. And so I sought advice and assistance from ... a trusted friend." The hesitation was barely perceptible, but Hugh had seen the flickering glance towards Arlo and knew that the friend had been the Order of Rebirth.

"I see, and what came of that?"

"Excellent advice, and assistance from my own resources. I wished I had consulted my friend earlier, because the solution, once pointed out to me, was self-evident. As soon as my official year of mourning reached its end, I signed over my entire inheritance, lands and holdings, to my closest relative, a younger cousin from Picardy, from the town of Rouen, retaining only sufficient funds to cover the expense of arming and re-equipping myself and a small group of retainers and mounted men-at-arms to return to Outremer. My farewells were few, so there was nothing to detain us from leaving immediately. We went directly from Amiens to le Havre, then by ship to Marseille, and from there we set sail for Cyprus and eventually Outremer."

He grunted deep in his chest, a derisive sound, as though he were sneering at his own folly. "We never came near to Cyprus. We were severely damaged in a collision with a sister ship during a violent summer storm in the Straits of Gibraltar, and less than a day after that we were attacked and sunk by corsairs. They didn't want to sink us, of course. They wanted our cargo, but the ship went down. I suspect it might have foundered even without their attack, for it was badly holed. Anyway, I was one of only three survivors."

"Only three?" Hugh's voice showed his surprise. "How many died, then?"

Once again, St. Omer's headshake was barely discernible. "It shames me to admit that I have no idea, because I paid no attention to such things, too tied up was I in my own problems to take note of what was happening around me. And then, when I needed to know, it was too late. But there were a lot of them. I had a score of men-at-arms, and half as many again of servants, cooks and the like—I had no intention of starving in Outremer this time. Then there were a score and a half of horses and mules, so it was a large ship, with a large crew ... perhaps a score of seamen, perhaps even more. But they all died. I was taken at the outset, struck down from behind and then dragged aboard their vessel and chained to the mast, where I could see everything. My men-at-arms fought well for a while, until the deck went down beneath them, and they were armored, so they sank like stones.

"They took us ashore somewhere in Africa and I never saw the other two prisoners again. My captors could tell from my dress that I was wealthy, so they held me for ransom. One of them spoke our tongue, and so I told him how to contact my fortunate young cousin in Rouen.

"A year passed by, and then I found out that my cousin had suffered a grievous loss of recollection and had no knowledge of my name or who I was, swearing that he had never known or heard of me."

"Aha—" Hugh caught himself on the verge of commenting that the cousin was obviously not a member of the Order. He had completely forgotten that Arlo was sitting there listening. He managed, however, to recover well, he thought. "Tell me, if you will, why that leaves me disgusted but not surprised? Am I becoming cynical? Hmm ... So what happened then?"

"They sold me, as a galley slave. I spent the next four years shackled to an oar. Four years of never having enough food and always having too much work. Four years of whippings, of pain and despair, and of having no friends. Galley slaves have no friends, you know. That's something you never think about until you find yourself chained to an oar. Their entire life is focused upon staying alive, and their survival depends absolutely upon their own efforts and their own inner strength."

He sighed, his eyes focused on some distant point. "One day I fell sick, and I grew worse from day to day. Finally, when I was too weak to stand up and be shackled to my rowing tier, they decided I was finished. One night they picked me up by the wrists and ankles and threw me over the side."

He ignored the shocked reactions of his two listeners, his attention still focused on whatever it was he could see in his mind. "That should have been the end of me. But it wasn't, as you can see ... The thing I have never been able to understand is that they threw me overboard with my wrists still manacled together, still wearing chains. They should not have done that. I've seen it half a score of times: a man dies at his oar; they strike off his leg irons, to get him away from the oar so his place can be taken by another slave; then they strike off his manacles, because the rusted iron is worth more than the dead man, and only then do they throw the man over the side. It didn't happen that way with me, I don't know why ... it might have been because I wasn't shackled to the tier, so they didn't have to strike off my leg irons. Or maybe they simply didn't care, or didn't notice, but whatever the reason, they threw me over wearing iron chains, and against all logic, that saved my life."

Now his gaze sharpened and he looked at both his listeners, drawing them into his story. "It was dark, remember, so none of them had noticed that there was a dead log floating alongside. I must have landed right on top of it and knocked myself senseless, but somehow—and I only worked this out later, when I had time to think about it—those chains snagged on or around a stubby projection on one side of the log. The weight of my body must have shifted the balance of the thing and made it roll, because when I woke up I was lying across it, one wrist trapped beneath the water on one side and my legs trailing on the other, but my head was above the water ..."

"What happened then?" Arlo was leaning forward, his face avid.

St. Omer grunted again and his body moved, as though he were stretching beneath the covers. "I remember I woke up in agony. My arm was twisted up behind me and stretched as though it must break, and once I had regained consciousness I screamed with the pain of it. And then I began to struggle. That was a mistake, for I upset the balance of the log again, and it rolled over. I almost drowned then, but without knowing what I was about, I managed to throw the chains around the log and make it roll again, and that's when I saw the roots. It was an old tree, not a cut log, and I worked my way along it until I could wrap some chain around the roots and float with my head above water again.

"And then I spent a full day in the water, feeling the salt crusting on my skin and suffering the agonies of Hell while I fought against the temptation to drink the salt water. I swear there is no greater torment on God's earth than thirst, but to suffer thirst while immersed in water is unimaginably painful. I knew I would do it, sooner or later—drink the water, I mean—but I fought it for a long, long time and I think I must have gone out of my mind at one point, for I woke up suddenly with my head underwater, and I panicked. But even as I began to kick and flail I heard a shout and felt hands pulling at me, at my hands and arms and hair, and dragging me out of the water. And that, my friends, is when I began believing in miracles.

"I had been saved by a fishing vessel out of Malta. My tree had drifted towards an islet where they had been fishing. They only saw me when their vessel bumped against my tree. But having saved me, they fed me and tended me until I was strong enough to work, and then they kept me working, ceaselessly but not cruelly, for more than a month. By the time we returned to Valetta, their home port, thanks to good food and simple labor, I had regained much of my health and former strength.

"I stayed in Valetta for another month, working as a cobbler's assistant and fighting a congestion in my lungs, and then I picked up a berth on an Italian trader out of Ostia, sailing to Cyprus. I worked my way from there to Jaffa, but I had little money for food and I was growing weaker again by the day. By the time I reached Jericho, where someone had told me I would find the new hospital, I was barely strong enough to walk. The monks took me in, and when I was able to talk again and tell them who I am, they sent word to you."

De Payens sat silent for some time, his mouth pursed in a thoughtful moue, and then he inhaled sharply and spoke almost to himself. "Aye, they did ... They sent word to me." He sat straighter. "You've been on quite an odyssey, Goff, but it's over now. You're safe among your friends ... or perhaps I should say *between* your friends, since there's only Arlo and myself. But our sole priority now is to have you back on your feet, with meat on your bones and the fire back in your eye. After that, we'll put you back atop a horse and have you swinging a blade with the best of us, as is your right. I spoke with the brother preceptor today and he told me you should be able to leave here within ten days. By that time, Arlo will have found a place for us all to live ... a decent place, with some space and plenty of light and a spot where we can exercise and drill and practice swordplay.

"In the meantime, you have to work on winning free from here, so sleep and eat well and rebuild your strength. One of us, at least, will visit you each day, to keep you from being too depressed, but I have to ride out tomorrow to escort a group of pilgrims to Jericho. I will be gone for four days, and I will see you as soon as I return. Sleep well, my friend."

BY THE TIME de Payens and St. Omer spoke again, five more days had elapsed and Godfrey had improved beyond all Hugh's expectations. He could get up from his bed and move around easily, leaning lightly on a walking stick, and his voice was full and strong. His eyes were bright and sparkling again, and his skin had taken on a healthy, ruddy glow simply from spending an hour or two outdoors each day.

After the dinner hour that night the two men were finally alone, sitting on folding chairs by the side of one of the cooking fires, with no one close enough to hear what they were saying.

St. Omer massaged the palm of his right hand with his left thumb, wiggling his fingers and watching them move. "I'm stiffening up," he said. "I'm growing old."

"All of us are, Goff. No one ever grows younger."

"Arlo tells me you went back to your old solitary ways as soon as you returned here, and now you are famed as the knight who never speaks. Why is that?"

Hugh was momentarily thrown off by the non sequitur, an unexpected challenge, but he merely shrugged. "We've been through all this before, Goff."

"Aye, but that was years ago. You were angry then—with reason, I agree—over the sins committed in Jerusalem."

"There are no buts, Goff. Nothing has changed, despite the passing of the years. The men, the godly knights who are here now, are the same men who were here before. They have different names, and many of them are younger, but, given the opportunity, they would behave in exactly the same way the others did, screaming 'God wills it!' as they slaughter women and children."

"I doubt that, Hugh."

"You *doubt* it?" De Payens's voice was low, pitched little above an angry whisper, but his face was twisted into a grimace. "Look about you, Goff, and listen when these people speak of who they are and what they are resolved to do in God's high, holy name. Because of them, and what they are and what they have done, the name *Christian* stinks in my nostrils. I have been looking since we came back here, Arlo and I, and I have seen but little Christianity among our allies, or even among our own ranks. There is no love or tolerance, forgiveness or enlightenment among the Christian armies that come here. And believe me, my friend, I searched high and low for months, among leaders, lords, barons, counts, knights, and men-at-arms. I found nothing but greed and avarice, cupidity and lust. I saw men everywhere paying tribute with their voices to the All-High and belching forth prayers of humility and gratitude, while all the time grasping and clutching at anything and everything they could find to steal, and fighting among themselves to win power and position here in this new world they were creating.

"We came here in the beginning, all those years ago, to free God's Holy City, and those of us in the Order came to seek God's truth as it is laid out in our Lore. Instead, we founded kingdoms for ourselves. The Kingdom of Jerusalem, the Principality of Antioch, the County of Edessa! We have set up an empire of our own among the holiest places on this earth, and there is precious little of our God or of the Christian Jesus to be found in any part of it."

De Payens lapsed into silence, aware that St. Omer was looking at him from beneath raised eyebrows.

"Tell me, if you will, why that should surprise you," the sick man asked.

Hugh blinked at him. "I don't understand. Why should what surprise me?"

His friend was unfazed by his lack of comprehension. "That our Christian brethren should be the way they are? You know better than to be surprised at that, Hugh. You've spent years studying the mysteries of our Order. Have you stopped believing in the truth you've learned?"

"No, I have not." Hugh's response was instant and indignant. "But the rites I studied were arcane, and those truths were hardly relevant to this world in which we live nowadays. That has been borne out to me since my return by the silence from home, from the Order itself. We expected—I expected—instructions, guidance on what to do, how to proceed. Instead we have heard nothing."

"Strange, but I have been thinking quite the opposite, these past five years and more." St. Omer shook his head gently and smiled at his friend. "While I was shackled to that oar, it seemed to me that the lessons the Order taught us, back in our youth, concerning how we ought to live and what we might expect to learn from our devout Christian brethren were the closest thing I have ever found to the real truth—the truth that prevails in the world in which we have to live. And while much of what we learned back there in our homeland was based upon the Order's accepted Lore, even more of it was based upon supposition ... upon what we might expect, if this and that transpired. Now our entire world is changed, Hugh, and what we were warned to look for has occurred."

St. Omer paused, regarding his friend levelly from sunken eyes. "How long has it been since you last had any real communication with our brethren?"

De Payens shrugged. "Too long, at least five years … But I doubt they have been trying to reach me, for I have not been in hiding." He thought for a moment, and then went on. "But it has been a long time since I spoke with a brother, other than yourself. There was a time, back when I first returned here, when I would sometimes meet others of our Order, and we would invariably talk of gathering together to rehearse our rituals at the very least, even if we were too small in numbers to celebrate them. Rehearsal was even more important than performance, we all knew, for the rites themselves would survive without us, and could pass for years without being celebrated. But the brotherhood, the brethren themselves, relying as we do on memory and repetition to retain the words and format, need to practice the rituals constantly—the content of them, if not the form. Most of us managed, over the years, to remain close to at least one of the other brothers, so that we could act as catechizers to each other. I kept close company at that time with a knight called Philippe of Mansur. Philippe and I fought together and practiced our ritual work together until he was killed in a skirmish on the road to Jaffa, about a year after I returned.

Since then, I have done nothing. My disillusionment began soon after that ...

"But then there is another thing to consider. I can read and write—I am one of the few people around here who can—so that made the task of revising and relearning words far easier for me than it could be for any of the others. And so, for a time in the beginning, as I told you, we tried to foregather from time to time. But you know what it's like as well as I do, to try to arrange something for personal motives while on active duty in the middle of a war. The men I knew in those days were all contemporaries, and we had all known each other before the Pope's war. But then we came to Outremer with our different liege lords, and that alone kept us all far apart from one another. And men were constantly dying, too, so that where there had been a few score of us in the beginning, there were soon less than one score, and reports kept coming in of yet another and another who had fallen in battle or succumbed to one of the plagues and pestilences that thrive here."

St. Omer watched him closely as de Payens sat with lowered head, rubbing the bony bridge of his nose between thumb and forefinger. In a moment, however, Hugh sat erect again and resumed where he had left off speaking.

"Then, for another while, there came a succession of new faces, eager young men, hungry for glory, with shining eyes and peeling, sunburnt faces, who had come out from France and went about shaking hands with everyone they met until they received a correct response. Those ones were always eager to meet elder brethren and spread the word from home. We almost made it once, nine of us, but on the very day we were to meet, a caravan was attacked within three miles of where we had assembled, and we spent the ensuing night scouring the desert and rescuing hostages." Hugh's eyes narrowed to slits as he remembered.

"In those days, the brotherhood would still come looking for me whenever they found themselves near my camp, or, if I heard tidings of one of them being in my vicinity, I would send Arlo to make contact with him, and he would arrange for me to meet with the newcomer in secret. But that could only apply, obviously, to those brethren whom I knew in person. The others, the newcomers, had no way of reaching me, and I had no means of learning who they were. And thus I fell into a growing pattern of silence that extended even to my oath-brothers and the Order itself. I know that is reprehensible. It might even be unforgivable, but I can offer no excuse, other than eccentricity."

St. Omer was peering up at Hugh from beneath his furrowed brows, and now he nodded. "Aye, which some might think of as willfulness." The words were condemnatory, but the tone in which he uttered them was mild.

De Payens nodded. "They might. That is true. But what about you? When did you last have dealings with the Order?"

St. Omer twisted in his seat and glanced over his shoulder, checking to make sure that they were still alone by the smoldering fire before he responded. "Five years ago, and they were directly concerned with you, my friend. I was carrying instructions for you from Amiens when I fell into the hands of the Turks."

"For me, from Amiens? I know no one in Amiens."

"You knew me."

"Aside from you, I mean. Who else would write to me from there?"

"The Order. The letter was from the Seneschal himself, Jean Toussaint, Seigneur of Amiens, second in rank only to the Grand Master."

"Toussaint wrote to me? Why? What could he want of me now?"

"Many things, apparently, judging from the bulk of the dispatches. Unfortunately, however, I lost them when our ship was sunk at sea."

"You lost them ..." De Payens sat blinking at him, then nodded his head. "Well, you must have. You lost everything, except your life, thank God. And had you no indication of what the letters contained?"

"Absolutely none. Why should I? Like you, I am decently literate, but they were none of my concern. I was coming to rejoin you, as a friend, at the suggestion of the Order, which needed my compliance to deliver documents to you. I thought no more of bringing them than I would of scratching myself. I knew that you would read them when we met, and that if you chose to tell me what was involved, it would mean that the senior brethren at home had wished me to know. But to wonder what was in there before they were delivered would have been to invite the temptation to pry, during the long nights of travel, to the imperilment of my sacred oath. Anyway, now that years have elapsed, I presume that the brethren at home have learned that I did not arrive here in Outremer and have either abandoned their intentions for you or switched them to another recipient. You have heard nothing at all from them in the interim?"

"Not a word, written or spoken. And that is really strange, because you must have left Amiens more than a year before Count Hugh left Champagne to come back here. He arrived two, nigh on three years ago, in 1114, and remained for almost a year. I was on duty in Edessa much of that time, but I did see him, albeit briefly, on several occasions, yet he made no mention of anything being sent to me. Nor did he know anything of your misadventure, now that I come to think of it. Your name was never mentioned, and we would have spoken of your disappearance, as a fellow member of the Order, had the Count known anything about it ..." Hugh sat frowning for a moment. "That is passing strange, for the Count is high in the Governing Council, so I would think he must know of anything involving me."

St. Omer waved a hand. "Not so, Hugh. The Council may have seen no need to inform anyone else of what they had required of you the previous year. After a year had passed it might have seemed less urgent, or they might not have expected to hear from you for some time to come ... At any rate, we cannot begin to guess at the instructions they had issued you. It might be a good idea, however, for you to send word back now, somehow, that you are back in communication."

"I will, rest assured on that. Lucien of Troyes is leaving to return to Champagne tomorrow, and once there he will report directly to Count Hugh, as his deputy. Now I shall find him again and tell him all that you have told me, and he will take the word back for us."

"Is he one of us?"

"Of course he is, otherwise I would not dream of trusting him with word of mouth. He is senior to me in membership by two years, but he is from the Argonne, so you might never have met him."

"Excellent ... So be it that he is of the Order." St. Omer nodded, then pushed himself to his feet, where he stood swaying for a moment, waving away Hugh's offer of help. "I am well, stay where you are. But I'm getting tired and it is growing cold. Go you now, and find this Lucien of Troyes, and be sure to tell him everything, so that he can report you had no knowledge of any task being assigned you. I can find my own cot. Sleep well, and we will talk again tomorrow."

Hugh bade his friend good night and went looking for Lucien of Troyes, who was in the final stages of preparing for departure. The magnificent Roman rooms that the Count and his deputy had occupied for the past three years lay empty now, their furnishings cleaned out and packed for travel by de Troyes's men, and Hugh's steps echoed emptily as he strode across the tessellated floors. He found Sir Lucien in a tiny sleeping chamber by the front entrance to his quarters, and the knight listened intently as Hugh told him all that he had just discovered, making no interruption and nodding deeply at the conclusion of the tale, after which he promised to waste no time in reporting Sir Hugh's story to Count Hugh, and to ask him to pass it along to the senior members of the Governing Council.

The following morning, Hugh was on hand to watch Sir Lucien depart for home, accompanied by a small but heavily armed retinue that struck out towards the coast, where a ship waited to transport them to Cyprus and from there, by various stages, home to Christendom. He knew he would hear more from the Order, now that he had broken his silence, but he had no way of knowing when that might be. For the time being he was content to wait, and to assist his friend Godfrey to regain his health and strength. He watched until the knight of Troyes and his party had disappeared from view, then turned and beckoned to Arlo, bidding him bring their swords and other weapons for sharpening.

FOUR

"There's a damsel in the marketplace asking about you."

De Payens lowered the blade he had been polishing until it rested on his knee, and raised his head slowly to look at Arlo from beneath the border of the cloth that shielded his head from the blazing sun. "Do we know him?"

"No. How could we? He's a damsel, I told you."

"Did you tell him where to find me?"

"What am I, a fool? If he's to find you, he'll do it on his own. I know how to earn your thanks, and it's damn hard work. And it's never through telling people how to find you. All I ever get from that is the rough edge of your tongue ..."

Even as Arlo spoke, however, de Payens could see the stranger approaching behind him, from the gates of the caravanserai, closely followed by a servant leading a mule with a wooden chest strapped to its back, and he lost awareness of Arlo's mutterings as he took stock of the newcomer, the damsel, as Arlo had called him.

It took no great amount of brain power to understand where the name damsel came from, or what it stood for. The newcomer was tall and pinkly pale in the way of all newcomers to Outremer, people who had not yet had time to adjust to the searing glare of the desert sun and the parching blast of the hot winds that blew the sand like living rasps against exposed skin. They were instantly recognizable, their clothing too new and too unsuitable for the climate here, their colors all too bright and vibrant, their chain mail and armor still rusted and damp between the links with the moistures of Christendom and the sea passage they had just endured. It would take months in the dry desert air before their mail took on the burnished, sand-scoured look that would brand its wearer as a veteran.

Damsels were everything that the name suggested: virgins among carnivores; innocents among satyrs; pallid equestrian neophytes still untried against the fiercest horse-borne warriors in the world. The jest in Outremer was that the damsel's pallor came of the anticipated fear of seeing his first Turkish janissary in full charge.

This one was a perfect example of the breed, with that unmistakable freshness of the new arrival. His clothing still bore the brightness of non-desert climes, and his bright, eager eyes betrayed that he had yet to see a hostile Mussulman, let alone fight one. He came striding right up to Hugh's fire and addressed him directly. "I seek Sir Hugh de Payens and was told I would find him here. Do you know where he might be?"

"You've found him." Hugh, who was sitting on a

rock close by his cooking fire, set down his long-bladed sword, its point towards the fire, and drew himself up, aware of the surprise on the new man's face and of the reason underlying it, for Hugh was dressed as no Christian knight. He was unarmored and wore the long, loose-fitting garments of the local desert nomads, and now he stood up, throwing the ends of his burnoose back to hang behind his shoulders.

"I am Hugh de Payens. Who are you?"

The man took three steps forward and dropped to one knee beside the fire, reaching for Hugh's hand and seizing it before the surprised knight could snatch it away. "Your pardon, Sir Hugh, for my tardiness in reaching you, but I have been searching for you ever since landing at Joppa more than a month ago." He looked up at Hugh, who was still too astonished to take back his hand. "My name is Gaspard de Fermond. You are a hard man to find, my lord."

"I'm not your lord, man. I am a simple knight in fee to Count Hugh of Champagne and you should have had no difficulty in finding me. I live openly here, among the other knights."

The newcomer flushed, but nodded his head, acknowledging that, and still refusing to relinquish the hand that de Payens was trying to withdraw. "I know that now, my lord, but when I came here at first, enquiring after you, someone sent me to Jericho, swearing you were there."

"I told you, I am not your lord." De Payens tilted his head to one side, looking at the man through narrowed eyes. "Now, why have you been searching for me? Who sent you to find me?"

"Pardon me, my lord, but you *are* my lord, in truth. Your late father knighted me with his own hand and gave me property within his barony, so you are my liege lord. As for who sent me, that I think you must know, if you but reflect on who knows you are here." As he said these words, the damsel's hand moved in Hugh's, pressing on the knuckle and then moving in an unmistakable manner. Given how the man had kept hold of his hand, however, Hugh was prepared for something of the kind, and allowed no reaction to show on his face. He merely returned the proper response of recognition and finally took his hand away, beckoning with it to where another stone sat close to his.

"Sit down, Fermond," he said, "and accept a word of advice. Never ignore the opportunity to collect a suitable fireside stone for your encampment. There are surprisingly few of them lying around in this land, and Frankish knights do not take kindly to sitting on the ground. Stones of the proper size are prized for sitting on. If you spend any time at all here, you will come to know how true that is. Now sit, and tell me what you have for me." Hugh pointed with his thumb. "This is Arlo, also from Payens. He has been with me since we were boys together and is both my friend and my good right hand."

When the two men had exchanged greetings, Hugh continued. "When did you last eat and drink? We have a skin of wine, sour but safe to drink, some bread from yesterday, and some goat cheese. Arlo, will you bring them?" He watched Arlo depart and then turned back to de Fermond. "Arlo is trustworthy, but he is not of the Order. What do you have for me?"

"First, the proof that I am who I say I am. I attended your Raising."

Hugh was astounded, but he had been schooling himself for years to allow his face to betray nothing of what he was thinking, and so he sat motionless although his thoughts were racing. He had absolutely no recollection of this man. Neither his face nor his name were familiar, and there was nothing at all about the fellow that rang the slightest chime of memory. Besides, he would have sworn that de Fermond must be at least three years his junior, and yet if the man had attended the Raising in Payens, then he must be at least a year older than Hugh.

Within minutes, however, de Fermond had proved that he spoke the truth, for not only did he recall the occasion clearly, he knew who else had been there and what they had spoken about afterwards at the celebration, and he even recalled an amusing story Hugh's grandfather had told about the night his son, Hugh's father the Baron, had been raised to the same honor. Hugh listened with enjoyment, and when his guest was finished, he nodded.

"You obviously are who you say you are, so if you will, tell me what you have to tell me."

De Fermond cleared his throat and looked about him. "Is there a spot nearby, perhaps, in which to walk and think, perhaps to talk, without being overheard?"

Hugh looked at him in surprise. "In a caravanserai?

Of course there is, providing you wish to have your throat cut. There is no such 'safe' place in any hostelry that I know of in all Outremer, save for this one." He grinned widely. "You are fortunate, because this hostelry is unique. Its owner is an honest man with eight big, strapping sons, which is why I stay here every time I travel from Jerusalem. There is a stream nearby, flowing from the oasis into the desert for a way before it sinks beneath the sand. We can walk there. But here comes Arlo. We will eat first, and then we will walk and talk."

Once they had eaten, they made their way out of the caravanserai to find the stream, and now they were walking along a path, lined with tall grasses, that followed its banks. When de Fermond was confident of their privacy, he spoke directly, asking Hugh, "Have you heard about the death of Sir Godfrey St. Omer?"

"Godfrey St. Omer is dead?"

"Aye, my lord. He was taken and killed by pirates, five years ago, on his way here from France."

"He will be most displeased to hear that, because he was in fine health ten days ago, when last I spoke with him."

De Payens smiled at the other man's open-mouthed stupefaction. "Godfrey was captured, my friend, taken at sea and sold into slavery, but he was not killed. I sent word of his survival home to France six months ago, but you must have passed it on your way. He spent four years as a galley slave and then was miraculously able to escape with his life almost a year ago, thanks be to God. He made his way to Jericho and sent word to me, and I brought him back to Jerusalem, where he is now returned to full health. He told me that he was carrying missives for me from the Council when he was taken. They were lost with the ship on which he sailed."

De Fermond closed his gaping mouth and nodded soberly. "Thanks be to God indeed, that he survived. We had heard nothing from him since he left, and we had scarce expected to, but the Council was beginning to grow anxious over having heard nothing from you since then, after several years. And then came word that Sir Godfrey's ship had been taken by corsairs, with the loss of all hands. Soon after that I was dispatched, one of four in all, to find you ... Have you heard from any of the others?"

"No, you are the first to reach me, and I confess I am now very curious as to what this is all about."

"It is very simple, my lord. I have been sent by the Seneschal and the Governing Council of the Order to remind you of your responsibilities to your brethren at home in France."

"My responsibilities. I see ... Now tell me, if you will, who is Seneschal of the Order nowadays, and what are these *responsibilities* of which you speak so blithely?"

De Fermond blinked slowly, unsure whether he was being twitted. "The Count is Seneschal today—Count Hugh. He was appointed on his return to France last year, soon after the death of Jean Toussaint, Seigneur of Amiens. Did you not know that?"

"No more than you knew of the safe return of Godfrey St. Omer. How could I know it, man? Our Order is a closed society, Fermond, and secretive above all else. That means that word of such things travels slowly and seldom makes a noise. Count Hugh will be an excellent Seneschal. He has the temperament, and his governance will benefit everyone, including the Order itself. Speaking of which, tell me more about these responsibilities you spoke of. What are they and how do they affect me?"

The other man gaped again. "Your responsibilities," he repeated, waving one hand indeterminately. "To the Order … its history and all its teachings."

De Payens stopped walking and pretended to adjust the drape of his flowing robe as he made sure that no one was close by. "You are making noises, de Fermond, but not much sense. How can I be responsible for the Order and all its teachings?"

"Not responsible *for,* my lord … I meant responsible *to* … as we all are." He cleared his throat and his tone became markedly more solemn as he delivered a memo-rized message. "For hundreds of years—and these are the Count's own words to me, to be passed on to you—everything our Order has done has been aimed towards the fulfillment of the situation—the circumstances—that now exist in Outremer, in the Kingdom, and in the City, of Jerusalem. The Seneschal saw the evidence of this unfolding while he himself was here before, a Councillor but not yet Seneschal, but he had been sent at that time to observe and take notes, and had no authority to do anything on his own initiative. His orders were to return home to report all that he had seen and learned to his fellows on the Council. But he left you behind deliberately, *in situ,* even although he had not been permitted to tell you anything of what he had been about in his brief visit—for he was here but for a few months, is that not so?"

"Aye, less than a year."

"Well, he has sent you a gift. You may have noticed that I came accompanied by a man leading a mule."

"Aye, I saw that."

"The chest is for you, from the Seneschal in person. It is locked and sealed, and you are to check most solemnly upon opening it to see that it has not been tampered with or opened."

"What's in it, regalia?"

De Fermond blinked in surprise. "Aye. How could you know that?"

De Payens smiled. "Nothing magical involved. The last time that the Count and I were together, we talked about that. The Count himself had owned all the devices of the Order, but they had been lost in a surprise raid on the caravan that was bringing them to Jerusalem from Joppa, years ago. And of course, we had no way of replacing them, without sending someone to France to bring back a new set."

De Fermond inclined his head gravely. "Well, Sir Hugh, now that the insignia and regalia of the Order are restored to you and the other brethren here in Outremer, it is my solemn duty to instruct you thus: the

Seneschal charges you, Sir Hugh de Payens, to think back upon the mysteries of which you learned in preparation for your entry into the brotherhood, and to look about you now, in the conduct of your duties in the Holy Land, for ways and means of bringing those mysteries to a culmination."

Hugh stopped walking. He crossed his left arm over his chest and rested his right elbow against the back of his hand, flicking his front teeth with his thumbnail. "Bringing those mysteries to a culmination," he said after a while, speaking as though to himself. "As I said before, noises, but no sense. Do you know what that means, Fermond, what you have just said? Because I certainly don't."

Fermond responded with a question of his own. "Have you heard of Count Fulk of Anjou?"

"Is there a Frank anywhere who has not? Anjou is filled with Count Fulks. I have met both Fulk III and Fulk IV, father and son. Which one are you talking about?"

"Neither, my lord. Both of those are dead. The Count in power now is Count Fulk V. He is a senior officer of our Order."

"Of course he is, as were his ancestors."

"Aye, well, I have been instructed to tell you that Count Fulk will be coming out to Outremer, within the coming year, if all goes well, to take charge of the Order's activities here and to control and coordinate your efforts in your primary task."

"By whom were you instructed?"

"By the Council."

"I see ... And the Count is to control and coordinate my efforts in *what* primary task?"

Fermond hawked and cleared his throat, then began walking again, keeping his voice low as a veiled woman approached them, carrying a long-necked water jug on her head with ease and grace.

"Not your *personal* efforts, my lord—the efforts of the brethren in the Holy Land. You are instructed to gather and organize all of the brethren you can find in Outremer, to re-establish the customs and rituals of the Order, and to devise some means of undertaking an excavation of the ruins of King Solomon's Temple, to rediscover the treasures and the artifacts that our Lore tells us lie buried there."

Hugh walked in silence for several more steps, his head bowed, but then he began to laugh, snorting at first in disbelief, and then throwing his head back to guffaw, his booming voice frightening the birds from the nearest date palms. Fermond looked askance at him, but kept walking and said nothing until Hugh's mirth had died away. When he drew breath to speak, however, Sir Hugh cut him off with a swiftly upraised palm.

"Hold! Say nothing for the moment, if you will. Give me time to think about what I must now say to you. You have had months to consider what you would say to me, and you have said it. I have had mere minutes to absorb it, and now I must think." He walked slowly and resolutely, his head still lowered, watching the puffs of powdery dust stirred up from the pathway by his sandaled feet. Finally he snorted again and reached out to lay a heavy hand on his companion's shoulder, bringing him to a halt and turning him around so that they could look each other in the eye.

"Upon your honor now, Fermond, did these instructions of yours originate with Count Hugh, or did they come to you from the Governing Council?"

De Fermond looked mystified, but then he shrugged, as if to ask if it made any difference. De Payens waited.

"From the Council. They had already been under preparation before the death of Monseigneur Toussaint. Count Hugh merely passed them along as one of his first duties as Seneschal. But it was he who sent the insignia."

"Aye, that is what I thought. Now look here. I want to be practical, Fermond, to deal only with the realities of what you are suggesting, but I cannot. I have never heard anything as asinine as what you have just proposed. That I am to—what was it?—to devise some means of undertaking an excavation of the ruins of King Solomon's Temple? Is that not what you said?"

Gaspard de Fermond cleared his throat again and nodded sheepishly. He had no idea what he had said that was asinine, but it was evident that de Payens thought him a fool. De Payens, however, was now nodding his head emphatically.

"Aye, well," he said. "There would be no grave difficulty there, on the face of it, other than gathering the brethren in one place for any length of time. We all have different lords, you see, Fermond—you know that—different masters, and they are scattered throughout the

kingdom and the counties, spread out over all the Holy
Lands, in fact. All of those various lords make differing
demands of their men, in duty and attendance, and since
few of them are of our Order in the first place, that alone
makes what you are proposing very difficult, since you
are suggesting that we gather the brethren together in a
working group and keep them in Jerusalem—perhaps
for months on end—without offering an explanation to
anyone. An explanation that might be widely demanded,
of who we are and why we are assembled here in such
numbers, and in such a way, and for such a long time, for
Jerusalem is not like any city in Christendom.

"The people who issued these instructions you bring
us have no idea of what Jerusalem truly *is*. This is a city
being reborn as we speak. We sacked it in our first
campaign, and you may think you know what that
means, but let me assure you that you do not. We
destroyed the city, and we destroyed its people, wading
knee deep in blood on the day the city fell to us. We
killed everyone who lived there ... everyone we could
find, that is, for a few, a very small few escaped. Then,
for the next ten years, the city lay abandoned, a stinking
charnel house. Only a scattering of people lived there,
until a few years ago, when King Baldwin realized that
this was the center of his kingdom and it was not even
strong enough to close its gates to brigands.

"Since then things have changed. The city is being
repopulated, and that was not a simple thing to achieve.
It is isolated, close to no other fortified bastion, and it
has no port to serve it, other than Joppa, thirty miles

distant. Baldwin began by bringing in Syrian Christians from the lands across the Jordan, offering them land and houses for their families, and somehow he found men to rebuild and extend the city's northern walls. But he had to feed them, too, and Jerusalem has never been rich in farmland. So he abolished all taxes on food being brought into the city, and at the same time imposed heavy taxes on all food going out. He made it possible, in other words, for a stable citizenry to live here again.

"That does nothing, however, to change the fundamental fact that Jerusalem is landlocked and poor. It has no reason for existence other than as a religious center, to receive the pilgrims who flock to it to visit the Holy Places. And therefore it offers no means of concealing the kind of activities demanded by these instructions you have brought.

"But leave that, for now, and think about this. Were we able to gather all our brethren together by some miracle, we could simply start to dig. No difficulty there. The ruins of the temple are clearly evident, unconcealed and plain to see, and abandoned these thousand years and more. It is never used for anything, other than being the base on which the famed al-Aqsa Mosque was built by the Muslims. Have you seen the mosque yet?"

De Fermond shook his head. "No, my lord. As I said, I am but newly arrived. I visited the city but briefly, then went down to Jericho, looking for you."

"Ah, well, in that case you might have seen it, but

you would not have known it for what it was. In fact, however, it is no longer a mosque. It is now the official residence of the newly crowned King of Jerusalem, Baldwin le Bourcq, the second King Baldwin to hold that rank. And thus, the King's palace sits atop the ruins of the temple far beneath.

"But then, you see, to make matters more difficult, that temple is really *Herod's* temple, even while everyone assumes it to be Solomon's. Not so. It isn't Solomon's at all. The ruined temple visible here was built by Herod a thousand years ago, and it was completed just in time to be destroyed when the Romans finally grew sick and tired of Hebrew rebellions and unrest and decided to kill all the Jews and destroy the troublesome Province of Judea once and for all. I have been told the temple that is there now was never used for proper worship, that it was destroyed before it could be completed. I have also heard that it was built atop the site of Solomon's Temple, but we have no means of proving or disproving it today."

He eyed de Fermond again, one eyebrow slightly raised and a mocking little smile on his lips. "Even so, had we the proof that Solomon's Temple is really there, there would be no great difficulty entailed in excavating it. We would simply apply for permission to King Baldwin—he is the King of Jerusalem and, as such, he owns the city and the temple. I have no doubt that permission would be swiftly granted. Most particularly so when we inform him of the treasure for which we are searching."

"But—"

"Ah yes, the 'but.' But we can tell no one about the treasure, can we? It must be secret, sacrosanct, as are our operations. So we must excavate the temple in secrecy, somehow accommodating the fact that it sits atop a hill within the city, and we must do that while maintaining the secrecy of the very existence of our own brotherhood and Order, all of this in full view of a surrounding city full of people, and without raising any suspicions or curiosity, even among our own knightly but uninitiated comrades, as to what we are about."

He allowed what he had said to reverberate with his listener, then continued. "Tell me, my friend, without compromising your loyalty to the Seneschal, or to the Councillors who compiled these orders and imposed upon him to send them—for I cannot believe Count Hugh would be the originator of such stupidity—have you any ideas about how we might approach this task you have defined for us? If you have, upon my oath, I will bare my head and bow to you, and I will resist the temptation to tell you to go home to the idiots who sent you here and bid them to come and see for themselves what they are so stupidly and arrogantly demanding."

De Fermond stood without speaking, his cheeks flaring with color, and de Payens grasped his upper arm. "Understand me, my friend, I know you are not to blame in this. You are merely the messenger. But tomorrow night we will be back in Jerusalem, and the day after that, I will take you and show you the Temple Mount. You will see instantly, the moment you set eyes on it, that the men who sent you here with these demands have never seen or imagined the reality of what they would have us face."

The flush on Fermond's face had given way to a pallid waxiness. "Are you saying, Sir Hugh, that you will not obey the commands of the Council?"

"Not at all. I am saying that it does not seem possible that anyone, including the Seneschal and the Councillors themselves, could achieve the task set for me and my brethren here in Jerusalem. But your instructions were that I am to attempt to devise a means whereby I can achieve the objective you have described, is that not so? I can promise you I will obey that order faithfully. I will examine everything that I can imagine, in seeking a way to obey the Seneschal. I have no idea how long it will take, but if Count Fulk of Anjou comes here within the year, I will have something to show him—even though it be only the outlines of the plans I have considered and rejected. How long will you remain with us?"

Fermond shook his head. "I cannot remain at all, other than to deliver certain messages that are my charge. Immediately after that, I am bound for Cyprus, to meet with several of our brotherhood there."

"Then I will wish you well on your journey, for these are ill times for travelers, and I suspect you will not be journeying among a great company."

"No, but if God is with us, I will survive to deliver my tidings."

FIVE

"Clearly, God was not with us in this matter, at least."

The news of Gaspard de Fermond's death had been delivered mere moments earlier, and these were the first words spoken since the announcement. Arlo had brought the word from the marketplace, where he had received it from a knight he knew, who had been told of it by another knight, who had known de Fermond and had recognized his mutilated body where it had been found by a roadside, less than two leagues from the city gates.

Arlo was still standing where he had delivered the news, and Godfrey St. Omer was sitting slack-jawed at the table, clutching a loaf of bread in both hands, stilled in the act of tearing it apart. Hugh pushed himself up with both hands on the tabletop and walked away towards the open window, sucking in a great breath.

St. Omer's voice was uncertain when he spoke. "What do you mean, Hugh, God was not with us in this?"

"Those were almost the last words de Fermond spoke to me, three days ago. He said he must travel next to Cyprus and I told him to be careful—"

"Cyprus?"

Hugh spun around, impatient with St. Omer's slowness. "Aye, Cyprus. He had tidings to deliver there, from Count Hugh to ... certain people of the Count's acquaintance, I know not whom." Hugh barely caught himself before he blurted out the truth, forgetting that Arlo was present, and although he did not as much as glance in the man's direction, the slightest twitch of one of Arlo's eyebrows revealed that he had caught the minor hesitation and had interpreted it correctly. "He said that the messages were important and that if God was on our side, he would be kept safe until such time as he fulfilled his mission. I hope he died quickly." He made the sign of the cross and looked around for verification of that from Arlo, and was surprised to see that he had left.

"Another death on the Holy Roads." St. Omer's voice was low and rife with disgust. "It really is becoming unbearable."

Hugh turned back to him. "No, Goff, not unbearable. People will bear it because they must. The only alternative is to remain at home for ever and go nowhere. No one can stomach the thought of that. No amount of terror will keep people from traveling—at least, not for long."

St. Omer had finally broken the bread and now dipped a portion into a small bowl of olive oil and chewed it for a while, his eyes fixed on some midair point ahead of him. Then he drew a deep breath and continued. "I saw you with him three days ago, up on the Temple Mount. What were you doing up there?"

"He wanted to see the temple."

"And was he thrilled with it? There's nothing there except those old stables, and no one has used those in a hundred years."

"He wanted us to dig there."

St. Omer's eyes widened. "He what? He wanted us to *dig*? Knights?"

"No, not knights ... brothers of the Order."

"Hmm ..." A short silence as he considered that, then, "Dig where? In the mountain?"

"Aye, but downward, into the ruins of the temple—beneath them, in fact. He brought word from the Council that I am to call the brotherhood together—all who are here in Outremer—and devise some means of excavating the temple and finding the treasure our Lore tells us is buried there."

St. Omer sat silent for a few moments longer, then shook his head, as if trying to clear it. "Aye, our Lore tells us there is treasure hidden there, Hugh, but it is *lore,* nothing more. There is no demonstrable truth to it. It is legend, tradition. We do not even know for a certainty that the ruins of Solomon's Temple underlie Herod's."

"Agreed, and without debate, but it might be true nonetheless, Goff. I have been thinking about it ever since de Fermond mentioned it, and I don't think it can be done ... But I now have to think seriously about doing it, so I would appreciate your doing the same."

"Oh, no." St. Omer raised a hand in protest. "Do

not place that on me, Hugh de Payens, because you have just defined the impossible. It might be your task to achieve it, and if so, you have my warmest sympathies, but it is not my responsibility in any way, and I have no wish to share in it."

"Then damn you for a parasitic ingrate, after all the pain and effort I've expended on your behalf, nursing you back to health with my own gentle hands." The tone was nowhere near as caustic as the words themselves, and neither man said anything else for a few moments until Hugh resumed. "Seriously, Goff, there must be a way we can do something ... make an effort, at least."

St. Omer sighed. "Aye, there might well be, as you say, but I couldn't even begin to guess about where we should even start. How many of the brethren are there in Outremer nowadays?"

"I have no idea. Damnation, de Fermond might have known that. I should have asked him."

"Too late now. What about sending Arlo out to look for tidings of the Friendly Families? Would that be possible?"

"Aye, if he's willing to go. It's not the kind of thing I would normally ask of him, because it might involve a lot of travel, and we all know too well how dangerous it is out there. But Arlo has been my eyes and ears ever since I withdrew from the world, so he might know those things already. Let's ask him."

Arlo came back at Hugh's summons and listened to the question, then nodded and counted off names on his fingers as he recited them. "Archibald St. Agnan. Gondemare of Arles. Payn Montdidier. Roland de Rossal. Geoffrey Bissot. And you two, of course."

"Payn? Montdidier's here in Outremer?"

Arlo shrugged when he saw the look on Hugh's face. "He comes and goes, or so I'm told."

"Who told you, and why didn't you tell me?"

"Archibald St. Agnan told me, and you were in one of your solitary spells at the time ... It was years ago. I forgot about it after that, thinking that if Payn wanted to see us, he would come by. He never did."

Hugh blinked at that, but said nothing more about it because he had become acutely aware that he had asked about members of the Friendly Families, and every name Arlo had mentioned belonged to one of the brethren of the Order. He cleared his throat. "Those are the only names you know, of all the Families in Outremer?"

"No." Arlo's face betrayed absolutely nothing of what he was thinking. "With the exception of Payn, those are the names of the only members of the Families who came asking after you, time and again, while you were ... being private. I judged them to be the names you would be most interested to hear of."

"Aye, indeed." Hugh flashed a sideways glance at St. Omer, whose face was utterly blank. "I know most but not all of them. Archibald and Payn most obviously, of course. Geoffrey Bissot, too. And Gondemare— although I have never met the man, I like what I have heard. And this Rossal fellow, who is he?"

"Another newcomer … if seven years here still counts as newly come. He came looking for you as soon as he arrived, and however much I would not permit him to come near you, he kept coming back, hoping to meet with you. Since you showed no interest in meeting him, I left you to it."

"Hmm. Well, I want to meet him now. And the others, too." Hugh turned to St. Omer. "What think you, Goff?" The other knight shrugged elaborately but nodded in agreement, and Hugh turned back to Arlo. "Can you arrange a meeting?"

"Depends on when you want to meet."

"As soon as may be, but that will depend on the time it takes you to find them and summon them here. How long will you need, think you?"

Arlo scratched at his chin. "Depends on where they are. Give me half a month to find out how long it will take to contact them, and I'll be able to say then. Can you do that?"

De Payens smiled. "Aye, my friend, easily. With all the 'depending' going on in what you say, we have no other choice. Take all the time you require, so be it you waste none. But tell me, Arlo, truly, why you selected those particular names, out of all the others you have met."

Arlo straightened up to his full height and looked from his employer to Godfrey St. Omer and back again, then shook his head as though he could not believe he was being asked to explain anything so obvious.

"Sir Hugh," he said, leaning heavily on the pronunciation of the honorific, "I have been with you, day and night, ever since we were tads together, and you know that I am neither blind nor deaf. I hope you know, too, that I keep my mouth shut about your concerns and those of your friends, because if you don't know that, I'll be forced to think you've considered me completely witless all these years."

De Payens nodded, somewhat taken aback. "Ah … well, now that you mention it, I have always relied on your discretion absolutely, without even thinking about it, or about the thought that you are, as you say, neither deaf nor blind." He allowed himself a tiny smile. "I suppose that means all that's left to do is to decide whether or not to kill you for what you've learned?"

"Kill me for what I've learned? What about guilt over what you've let slip? Your point's moot, Sir Hugh. Fall on your own sword, if you will, but I've no need to be so foolish. I have already passed along all the information I had about you and been richly rewarded for my treachery. When d'you want me to start asking after these fellows?"

"Now, today, at once."

Arlo nodded. "Right, tomorrow it is. I'll take Jamal with me and travel as one of his people, and I'll come back when I've discovered where all your friends are. In the meantime I'll arrange to have Jubal look after the two of you while I'm away. Otherwise you'll probably starve." He turned and walked away, leaving the two friends alone.

"That was a very sudden decision, to summon everyone here, was it not?"

De Payens acknowledged the question with a shrug. "I suppose it was, but it's long overdue. You and I have talked about the need for a Gathering. Now it seems to be the right time, if we can assemble everyone. Even if we can do nothing about the excavation the Council wants us to undertake, it will be good for the brethren to come together and revisit the ritual after such a long time."

"Aye, if anyone can remember any of it."

"I can, Godfrey, and so can you, because we can read and relearn it all between now and then, if need be. It will not be too difficult, for us or for anyone else. The material was well entrenched in the beginning, so it will come back to mind quickly. I am sure of that."

"You're probably right ... There may be others out there, too, you know. Younger members of the brotherhood who have simply not come forward."

"True, but for this first assembly I will be happy to confine our activities to people I know and whom I know I can trust, which is probably more important." He quirked one eyebrow. "I know, because I can see it in your eyes, that you are about to ask me if I would distrust any of the brotherhood. And the answer is yes, I would. They are all men, Godfrey, subject to men's weaknesses, and I have seen enough of men and their weaknesses, here in the desert, to convince me that I have no desire to trust any man before I have had time to study him closely. You may find that appalling, but that is how I am nowadays."

St. Omer stood up and stretched hugely, rising on his toes and grunting with the pleasure of it. "I don't find it appalling at all," he said when he had finished. "I feel exactly the same way you do, albeit for different reasons. Four years chained to an oar, and you learn how few people there are in the world who are worthy of being allowed to live, let alone of being trusted. So there will be just the few of us."

"Aye, for the first time at least, and we will leave the timing to Arlo. He will not disappoint us."

"Where will you put them? All this rehearsal and repetition will be vocal, so we will have to be careful about where we do all this. It will probably be far from easy, in fact, now that I come to think of it. There may be all kinds of conniving and political secrecy being practiced here, but that is all among the priests and nobles, and most of it occurs within the confines of the palaces. It will be another matter altogether for a gathering of knights such as us to keep our meetings and our intentions from being seen, let alone our secret rituals."

"Ibrahim Farraq. You don't know him yet, but I do. I saved his favorite son's life a long time ago and we became friends. He understands what it means to be silent and discreet and he runs the finest hostelry in Outremer, with the assistance of eight sons. I will arrange for us all to stay there when we convene, and Ibrahim will see to it that we are unobserved and undisturbed for the duration of our stay. Trust me, my friend, there is no need for concern on that matter."

ARLO DID NOT DISAPPOINT THEM. He discovered the whereabouts of all five of the other knights within the two weeks he had asked for, and after consulting with de Payens about the most suitable date, he set out again on the second day of October, once again dressed in the long, flowing robes of the local inhabitants, to find each of them in person and summon them to attend a Gathering in Jerusalem on the last day of the month, the Feast of All Saints. Hugh had had no concept of how long their convocation might take, and so he had instructed Arlo to request that each of them come prepared to spend at least seven days, and perhaps as many as ten, in the city.

The appointed day arrived, and both Godfrey and Hugh were excited at the prospect of meeting their old friends again. Arlo had returned a full week earlier, with word that all five men, including Payn Montdidier, would make the journey, and de Payens had informed his superior, the man in charge of the Champagne contingent now that Count Hugh and his deputy had both returned to France, that he would be taking a two-week furlough in order to spend time with several old friends from his home region, whom he had not seen for many years. That done, he had visited the large hostelry run by Ibrahim Farraq and his eight sons and had made arrangements for his guests to be quartered and fed there, and he was now reasonably satisfied that everything was prepared for his friends' arrival.

His friends, however, were taking far too long to arrive for Hugh's liking. He had recognized, now that his self-imposed solitude was coming to an end, how important they were to him. They, like his servant Arlo, were among the very few men who had remained untainted in his mind after the atrocity of the sack of Jerusalem. With the exception of the men called Gondemare and Rossal, he had known all of them too well and for far too long ever to think, let alone believe, that they would have anything to do with the horrors that had so alienated him. And from all that he had heard of Gondemare, he was prepared to believe the same of him.

And they arrived at last, the first pair of them, riding side by side, emerging from a dense cloud of dust stirred up by the arrival of an enormous caravan, including at least a hundred camels, all of them fully laden with the spoils of other lands. But caked and layered dust and the sweat lines born of a hundred miles of desert roads did little to disguise the well-remembered bulk of Archibald St. Agnan, a formidable warrior and companion, and Payn Montdidier, whom Hugh had not seen in more than a decade. Fortunately, Hugh, Godfrey, Arlo, and the man Jubal, who had attached himself to Godfrey St. Omer as servant and bodyguard, had been waiting for them close to Ibrahim Farraq's caravanserai, and they had warned the proprietor, well in advance, of the prodigious thirst likely to be evinced by their arriving guests.

St. Agnan and Montdidier, each of them accompanied by a trusted man, had arrived through the northern gate in the city walls. Where the others would appear was anyone's guess, for Arlo had found both of them to the south of Jerusalem, Gondemare in the region close to Bethlehem, and Roland de Rossal in the vicinity of Jericho. It was Arlo who suggested that they go and await the other two at the southeastern gate, on the supposition that the road leading there was broader and better traveled, and therefore safer, than any other. By that time, having consumed more than a few jugs of the local bitter beer, they saddled up and made their way southward, around the outside of the city walls to a slight elevation from which they could watch the approaching travelers as they came within sight of the safety of Jerusalem's walls.

Daylight faded into dusk, however, with no sign of any travelers approaching the southeastern gate, and long before that, the two new arrivals had begun to complain, albeit humorously, about the inconvenience to which they were being subjected. They had traveled long and uncomfortably to reach the city, they pointed out, and then, instead of being allowed to eat and rest, they had been asked to drink potent beer and then sit for hours in the hot sun, awaiting the arrival of people who seemed determined not to arrive.

It was a difficult argument to refute, but just as de Payens was preparing to address it, he saw Arlo, from the corner of his eye, tense suddenly and sit upright in the saddle, automatically raising his spear point to the vertical.

"What?" he snapped, apprehensive for no good reason.

Arlo made no answer, his body bent forward over his horse's ears, his eyes fixed intently on the darkening horizon.

"Damnation, are you deaf? What is it, Arlo? What do you see?"

"Grief. Look yonder, by the rocks to the right of us, in the shadow of the mountain."

De Payens squinted into the purple shadows of the thickening dusk, and caught a flicker of movement. There were people out there, and as his eyes adjusted to the different light, he saw what had alarmed Arlo: a cluster of people not quite running for their lives but moving as quickly as they could. Their dusty clothing rendered them almost invisible against the sand from so far away, and his first impression was that they were being chased by a group of horsemen. Almost immediately, however, he realized that they were, in fact, being protected by the horsemen, who were pushing them from behind, prodding them as fast as they could go, and forming a protective screen between them and whoever was pursuing them.

"Pilgrims," Hugh grunted, "and seven horsemen. Could these be our friends, seven of them instead of three?"

St. Omer answered from behind his left flank. "It could be. They might have picked up some fellow travelers. I recognize Rossal, even from here, so two of those with him must be Gondemare and Bissot. The others could be anyone. But why are they—?" He broke off as another hard-riding group of horsemen swept into view around the edge of a spur of rock less than half a league from where he and his companions sat watching, making the answer to his unformed question obvious. De Payens was already calculating distances, speed, and time.

"Bandits. They'll be on top of those pilgrims before we can reach half way to them, but if we move now, we might distract them. Are we as one?"

He heard the familiar sound of weapons being drawn and metal helms being tapped and slapped into place on their wearers' heads, but by then he was already leaning into his saddle, raking his horse's flanks with his roweled spurs and pointing his long spear towards the distant enemy. There were fifteen or sixteen of them— he could not see well enough for an accurate count— but that was far and away more than sufficient to overwhelm a group of seven opponents. Like bandits everywhere, however, they were undisciplined and disinclined to be heroic in the face of odds that were not overwhelmingly in their favor, and de Payens was hoping that the mere sight of him and his seven companions riding to assist the other group would demoralize them.

His initial estimate of speed and distance had been accurate, for the bandits had come within striking distance of their prey long before de Payens and his hard-charging newcomers were close enough to offer any threat. But the speed of their determined approach was enough to give the attackers pause, and the seven defending horsemen took full advantage of their indecision, grouping themselves in a disciplined line abreast and charging straight towards the center of the enemy, splitting them into two groups and leaving two of them sprawled motionless on the ground.

The bandits checked and swung away, attempting to regroup before turning back to attack the defenseless pilgrims, but their victims were no longer helpless. The rescuing group had already closed more than half the distance again, and events were moving quickly. The bandits could now hear the heavy drumming of the shod hooves of the Frankish war horses, and in mere moments, they knew, their numerical advantage would shrink from eight to nil. They broke again and spurred away, clearly expecting that the Franks would give up the pursuit and allow them to escape.

De Payens, however, had no intention of letting these marauders ride away unscathed. His blood was up, and he tightened his reins and urged his horse to greater speed, knowing instinctively that his seven companions were forming a compact group at his back, but he had not anticipated that the other seven riders would also come riding to join their charge, so that the fifteen of them, knights and companions, fell naturally into a powerful arrowhead formation that gave the now routed enemy no time to do anything other than flee.

For more than a league they gave chase, until de Payens realized that night was almost upon them and the bandits, with their lighter mounts, were leading him and his men deeper and deeper into the desert, where, as nomads, they would quickly regain the advantage they had lost. Reluctantly, he drew rein and turned his group back towards the city, which had long since fallen from view in the gathering darkness. The mood among the men was jubilant and lighthearted, the good feelings from their reunion and from the lengthy chase slow to dissipate, and they rode back towards Jerusalem in high good humor.

Gondemare, Rossal, and Bissot were all there, but the other four men were strangers. Two of them were knights, and each of those had an attendant man-at-arms with him. Although they were nominally in the service of Baldwin II, King of Jerusalem, they were visitors to Jerusalem on an official journey that had brought them from their base in the ancient garrison town of Caesarea. The seven had joined forces three days previously, traveling together for mutual support and protection, in the sure knowledge that only a strong and confident group would dare attack seven armored and well-mounted Franks. They had caught up with the group of pilgrims only that morning, and had ridden with them thereafter, and they had become aware of being stalked by the brigands only a short time before Hugh and his group discovered them.

There was no sign of the pilgrims by the time the riders returned to where they had left them, but that surprised no one. They had been within sight and walking distance of the city walls when the rescuers swept by them, and they had plainly decided to seek the safety of the city at once, before night fell, rather than to wait in the darkness for their saviors in order to express their gratitude, because for all they knew, de Payens and his men had gone charging off to their deaths, and the enemy might return to finish what they had begun.

One of the two knights from Caesarea, the younger of the pair, was incredulous over how close the brigands had come to the city walls, but he had been in Outremer for a mere two years and had spent none of that time near Jerusalem. This young firebrand, whose name was Anthony something—de Payens never did learn his full name—was alight with the fiery zeal of youth and innocence, and he was appalled that discipline should be so lax here in the very center and hub of the kingdom that a daring enemy would think nothing of venturing right up to the walls. De Payens and the others listened to his outrage and glanced at one another, twisting their lips and scowling from time to time, although none of them wanted to be the one to disillusion the young knight by telling him the true state of things in and around the city.

The evening—what little remained of it after the seven brethren had all settled in to Ibrahim Farraq's hostelry—was spent in conviviality, several of the knights not having seen one another in years, although all of them were veterans of the capture of Jerusalem and the founding of the kingdom. Eventually, they made arrangements to assemble the following day, first to rehearse each other in the long-unpracticed rituals of their Order and then, in the late afternoon, to celebrate the rites themselves for the first time that any of them knew of in the Holy Land. De Payens then ordered them all to bed, knowing that they would benefit more from a solid night's sleep than they would from exchanging gossip far into the predawn hours. They went without a word of protest, and he did, too, but he was amazed at first, then angry, to discover that he could not sleep, and he lay awake long into the night, his mind seething with ideas.

SIX

The seven Brothers of the Order of Rebirth spent much of the following day, from early morning to mid-afternoon, revising and rehearsing the rituals governing the celebration that would take place later, but they began by sealing off one of the windowless main rooms in the central part of the caravanserai, and placing guards outside it, front and rear, while the others did what they could to transform the chamber into an approximation of the standard ritual lodge of the Order of Rebirth. They opened up the chest of regalia sent by Count Hugh and removed its contents, which, they discovered, included several large rectangular sheets of heavy cloth in both black and white, and by arranging those in appropriate places, they succeeded in transforming the large room to resemble, as closely as possible, the austere temples of their own Gatherings at home. They lacked the tessellated floor of alternating tiles, but everything else in the darkened chamber was as it should be, either stark black or blazing white. When the arrangements were complete, they locked the doors, then dispersed to their own quarters to prepare for the afternoon's ritual.

The long-awaited ceremony went smoothly, with de Payens officiating and each of the other knights playing a key role, and by the time it was over, they were all aware of a feeling of substantial achievement.

Unwilling to lose the feelings of enjoyment they had shared, the knights dined together again in the hostelry that night, in the now-stripped room that they had used earlier as their temple, and afterwards, sitting around the table, they talked idly about a number of things, including the way pilgrims to the Holy Places continued to suffer from unchecked banditry on the roads. That led them into speculation about the true reasons underlying King Baldwin's apparently indefensible and self-serving behavior on that matter, and eventually they graduated to the ever-present subject of the venality of the Church, or at least of its clerical representatives. When they had all had an opportunity to vent their spleen and their indignation began to flag naturally, de Payens decided that the time was right to introduce the most important topic he wanted to discuss with them: the strange instructions brought to him from the Council of Rebirth in Amiens by Gaspard de Fermond. Claiming their attention then, he repeated the instructions from the Council verbatim, offering no commentary of his own, but merely asking his fellow knights for their opinions.

He had no qualms about having any of them speak forthrightly and openly that night. The room in which they were gathered had only two entrances, one of which led in from the kitchens, and both were well guarded against intruders or eavesdroppers, notwithstanding the fact that de Payens knew Ibrahim would permit no one to come near his guests. Arlo stood guard outside the main door, and Jubal stood outside the entrance from the kitchens.

The initial response of the five newcomers on hearing the orders from France was angry disbelief, for they immediately saw the impossibility of what they had been ordered to do, as had de Payens and St. Omer before them. De Payens sat quietly and listened to all they had to say, studiously avoiding showing judgment or opinion. At the end of it all, however, only one real opinion had been voiced, albeit in five different versions: the command from home was a tomfoolery that could not be carried out without betraying the all-important secret of the Order's existence. The matter of the hidden treasure was barely worthy of mention next to the reality that every man there accepted unquestioningly: to proceed as they had been instructed would invite, and even guarantee, official scrutiny from Church and state, and would set their ancient Order's anonymity at hazard.

When the flow of righteous anger began to abate and de Payens held up his hand, everyone fell silent and six pairs of eyes turned to him. He looked from one to the other in turn and then nodded his head as if acknowledging to himself that he had done the right thing, and began to speak slowly, almost haltingly, his gaze moving from face to face and eye to eye.

"I have a plan, my friends, to which I would have you listen. It is an idea that came to me only last night, and I confess to all of you, freely, that when it first occurred to me, I thought it was sheer madness. But I lay awake for hours, considering all the pros and contras that my sanity could throw up. I slept for no more than a short time, I know, because I feel now as if I have not closed my eyes at all since last night. But I woke up at dawn believing that this outrageous and insane-sounding strategy I had dreamed up might actually work. And the more I thought about it today— it was in my mind throughout our temple ceremonies— the more convinced I became that it is not only possible but feasible, and it offers us the possibility of becoming invisible in full view of all the world."

He sat back in his chair, waiting for a reaction with his arms crossed on his chest. It was plain from their faces that every one of them was waiting to hear this plan he was talking about, and he found himself enjoying the ability to keep them waiting and wondering. Suppressing the smile he felt welling up inside, he sniffed instead and took a pull from the goblet that one of them had placed in front of him while he was speaking. The strong red wine made his lips pucker. He wiped his mouth with the back of his hand.

"There are two people at the top of the pecking order here in Jerusalem, and in many ways they are rivals, so I imagine they resent and probably dislike each other. They are the King, Baldwin II, and Warmund of Picquigny, the Patriarch Archbishop of Jerusalem. Two powerful men, each secure in his own primacy, within his own environment—the state and the Church. They live in tolerable harmony, because they have no choice, and they are mutually dependent, working together on most things.

"There is one matter, however, on which they are greatly at odds, and that is this banditry that so outraged our young companion from Caesarea yesterday." Hugh had already told the story of the young knight's unwillingness to believe that what he had seen on his brief journey was an accurate reflection of the way things were in Jerusalem, and they had already discussed the notorious reluctance of the Kings, both Baldwin I and his successor and namesake, to commit any of their meager resources of men and weaponry to fight against what they and their ministers, at least, saw as a minor nuisance. "This Baldwin is only newly crowned," he continued, "but he has adopted the stance taken by his predecessor on this issue, so the Patriarch Archbishop obtained no relief on the death of the old King. Those two had been arguing with each other about this for years, and now that the new King is in power, Church and monarchy are no closer to arriving at an arrangement than they ever were."

None of his listeners moved, their entire awareness tightly focused on what he was telling them, even although he had said nothing that was unknown to them. They knew, however, perhaps from his intensity alone, that they were about to hear something new, perhaps something of momentous import.

"Every year, now that the Holy Land is *perceived* to be safe and free from the Seljuk Turks," de Payens continued, "more and more pilgrims come flocking to visit the Holy Places, and they all fall within the jurisdiction and responsibility of the Patriarch Archbishop. And because of that, the Archbishop is forever beseeching the King to do something to protect these pilgrims, who are surely the most stupid, sheepish breed of willing victims ever to have lived.

"They come, for the most part, bearing no weapons other than the wooden staff that seems to be their badge of identity and office. Few of them even carry knives, and fewer than one in a thousand ever carries a sword or an axe, or even a bow. They come convinced that, simply by making their pilgrimage, they will evade all their earthly guilt and win absolution and eternal salvation. They come trusting blindly that God and His holy angels will protect them, and they take no precautions whatsoever for their own safety, make no effort to protect themselves. They come like sheep to the slaughter, and these swarming bandits delight in greeting them. Most of them come this way from Joppa, and they walk the thirty miles from there to Jerusalem along a route that takes them close to the town of Ascalon, which is, as you all know, a nest of vipers—a city that exists purely for its denizens to prey on defenseless Christian pilgrims. Every year there are more pilgrims, and because pilgrims are such easy victims, every year there are more brigands—bigger bands of them appearing all the time, some of them forming veritable armies, and all of them becoming increasingly daring in their depredations, because they know no one is going to come hunting them, looking for vengeance and retribution."

He looked again from man to man. "I listened to the very same argument being made by the Hospital knights one night near Jericho. The situation here has become so scandalous that people are now beginning to expect, in all sincerity, that the Knights of the Hospital will ride out to do something about it. And that, my friends, is both ludicrous and frightening, because the Knights of the Hospital, as all of you know, are knights in name alone. They are monks. They have always been monks, monastics of the Order of Saint Benedict, bound by their sacred vows to a life of piety and sacrifice. Those men cannot fight. They don't know how, in the first place, and they are expressly forbidden by their Order to do so."

"Why won't the King do anything?"

The questioner was Gondemare, and de Payens looked at him, frowning in mild perplexity, then shrugged almost imperceptibly. "We have just been through that, and you know the answer as well as I do. He says he can't, says he has neither the men nor the resources. And I believe him. His armies are stretched thin, patrolling the borders and garrisoning the major fortresses and castles, and their prime responsibility is to keep the kingdom safe from the threat of invasion. The truth of it is plain to see, for anyone who cares to look without bias. Baldwin has to defend the borders and the welfare of the Kingdom of Jerusalem as a whole. He cannot afford to weaken his defenses simply to defend the roads against wandering bands of ragamuffin brigands. And yet, to have his city prosper, he can neither logically nor practically permit the current situation to continue. To maintain his city, Baldwin must find some way to protect his roads, and their travelers, from this brigandage."

"Then nothing is likely to be done." This was Archibald St. Agnan, his voice sounding plaintive, and de Payens turned to look directly at him.

"That is correct, nothing ... for the time being, at least. There is simply nothing in place—no suitable armed force—that would serve the required purpose without disrupting other things, perhaps fatally, so until such an entity comes along, nothing will be done."

"And the pilgrims will keep on dying."

"Aye. I fear so."

Payn Montdidier spoke up. "What's this plan you spoke of, Hugh? You said you had a plan to enable us to excavate the temple, did you not?"

"I did."

"And does it have any bearing on this matter of the pilgrims?"

"It might. It could."

"How so? Come on, man, tell us how we can do the impossible, on two counts."

Hugh scratched the back of his neck. "I'm not sure we can, but didn't you enjoy chasing those brigands yesterday? I know I did, and I would do it again right now, if I could. But do you realize ... have you even thought about what we did?" He saw the blankness on their faces. "We *outfaced* them. We frightened them off, and had there been twice as many of them as there were, it would have made no difference. What we did was so unexpected that they had no means of counteracting it, and so they turned tail and ran. That may have been the first time in years that anyone—*anyone* in Jerusalem—has shown any fight or willingness to strike back at these animals. But we did it. We drove them off, and that sowed the first seeds of what is now in my mind. The rest of it grew from there."

"Come on then, Hugh, tell us what it is! Or will you keep us here all night, wondering?"

De Payens made a moue and dipped his head to one side. "That *is* it. I thought we could provide the group for the pilgrim task, or at least the beginnings of a group."

St. Agnan came back at him immediately. "You're dreaming, Hugh. Even were that a thing we wanted to do, Cherbourg would never give me leave to quit his service for such a purpose—to go charging off into the desert to protect unwashed, unimportant pilgrim nobodies while he himself has real work for me to do. I'll wager none of your lords would, either. Why should they? We are honor bound to do our duty to our liege lords obediently and patiently, and our allegiance is lifelong."

"I have thought about that," de Payens responded quietly. "And I think about it still. How long have you been in service to the lord of Cherbourg?"

"Since before the Pope launched the first war, so that's twenty years."

"And don't you think you have served him sufficiently?"

"Who, the Pope, or Charles of Cherbourg? And
sufficiently for what? You are sounding strange, Hugh."

"No, with respect, I disagree, Archibald. On the
contrary, I am tired, I am weary, and I have been given a
set of instructions that seem unachievable, so I am
looking for alternatives. I have been thinking of retiring."

St. Agnan glowered at him. "What does that mean,
retiring? You mean withdrawing your services from
Count Hugh? You can't do that. None of us can. We
are bound for life by our knightly vows."

"Which may be superseded by higher, more solemn
vows." That earned a stunned, uncomprehending
silence that lasted until Montdidier spoke up.

"More *solemn* vows? You mean ... as in clerical,
priestly vows?"

"Aye, although I was thinking more of monastic
vows than priestly ones. I thought I might become a
monk." He looked around at their gaping faces and
broke into a broad grin. "I told you it seemed insane
to me at first, did I not? Well, now it might seem
insane to you for a while, but bear with me and listen.
I don't yet understand all the ins and outs of what I
might be proposing here, but there is something
inside me telling me I'm thinking along the right lines.
Listen, now."

He stood up from the table and began to pace,
letting the thoughts spill from his lips as they occurred
to him, and using his hands in broad gestures to

emphasize his points, ticking them off on his fingertips as he made them.

"Two men, remember—a King and a Patriarch Archbishop. Both have the same concerns—an urgent, pressing need to restore order, to safeguard the roads, and to protect the pilgrims traveling in ever-increasing numbers to this holiest of lands—and neither one can solve them. The King will not—cannot—strategically give up a single knight to serve in this regard, and the Archbishop, as a cleric, *has* no fighting men of his own that he can use to relieve his own embarrassment.

"Now, in addition to this nuisance, there is another element, added but recently to the cauldron but already raising difficulties of its own. The King and the Archbishop both want to encourage settlement here in the kingdom, for reasons obvious to anyone who sees the need for economic growth."

He stopped, and waited until they were all looking at him again before he continued, in a changed voice. "Look, I know none of this interests any of you. It is the kind of petty, bothersome detail we prefer to leave to those who find pleasure in such things, providing they leave us free, in turn, to live our lives and follow the dictates of our knightly code and our conscience. But hear me out in this, for it concerns all of us, and in several different ways, so we have to pay attention to it *now*. We *must*, this once, if never again.

"The Kingdom of Jerusalem, both Church and state, needs to encourage settlers if it is to grow and thrive. It needs farmers and merchants—citizens—not merely soldiers but people who produce the food and materiel that people like us need in order to survive.

"But those settlers, peaceable farmers in the main, will not come here until they know they can come in safety. They will not bring their families, their wives and children, into a dangerous, untamed land. Anyone who would seriously expect them to do that is living in a fool's paradise. And yet, even knowing that, the King will do nothing, claiming his hands are tied." He paused, his gaze moving from man to man.

"Now, bearing all that in mind, suppose for a moment that I were to go to Archbishop Warmund de Picquigny, saying that I myself, along with several of my oldest companions, all veterans, all greatly honored Warriors of the Cross, have grown tired of fighting and campaigning, sickened by the continuing savagery and slaughter we have seen and known, and that we have decided accordingly that we would like to withdraw ourselves from active military service, do penance for our sins, and embrace the monastic life.

"Among the seven of us, only two have left wives and children in Christendom, and neither one of those expects, or is expected, to return. Furthermore, all of us, without exception, have come to love this country more than the one that gave us birth, because this Outremer has nurtured and inspired us for two decades now, and so we can think of nothing better or more desirable than to withdraw from worldly things by swearing binding monastic vows and living out the remainder of our lives here in this Holy Land that has become our spiritual home, in prayer, peace, and solitude. How would he respond, think you?"

"He'd have you locked up for a madman," St. Agnan growled. "You're a knight, a soldier. You're not fit to be a monk. That's as clear as a white patch on a black cat."

A few of the men smiled at that, although uncertainly, and de Payens looked from face to face among them, awaiting their responses. Montdidier coughed and shuffled his feet, then coughed again.

"Ridiculous as your story sounds, Hugh, he might be tempted to permit it ... save that it would be of no use to him."

Hugh glanced at St. Omer, raising one eyebrow quizzically, then looked back at Montdidier. "Explain that, Payn."

"Well, the only reason I can think of for him to listen to your tale at all is that we, you and your friends, *are* all veteran knights. He could use our skills and experience. But then, if we became monks, as you suggest, our fighting skills would be lost and useless to him. Monks are forbidden to fight, even verbally, among themselves, although they do that all the time. But to fight with weapons, as we do? That's anathema."

"That's right, Crusty. Anathema. That is exactly correct. Were he to accept us as monks, all our prowess, our training, our disciplines, and our skills would be useless to him. We would be no more useful to him than are the Hospital knights."

"But the Hospital knights are very useful, Hugh."

St. Omer's objection was immediate. "In their own way, doing what they do best, they are invaluable."

De Payens smiled. "Aye, that's right, too, Goff. They are, are they not? You know that better than any of us. And the Archbishop knows it, too. He also knows that the foolish people of Jerusalem are expecting the monks of the Hospital to fight like knights."

Godfrey sat blinking for a few moments, then asked, "What are you saying, Hugh?" His voice was quiet enough to make everyone else sit forward, watching his mouth. "You sound as though you might be talking sense, but everything you say comes out as a riddle."

De Payens shrugged. "Not if you marshal your thoughts from a different direction. Warmund de Picquigny, the Patriarch Archbishop of Jerusalem, has all the power here in Outremer that the Pope possesses back in Christendom. He can make kings, counts, dukes, and knights, and he can make and unmake bishops. It follows, therefore, that he can make monks."

"Well of course he can. No one is disputing that."

"Imagine warrior monks, Godfrey. Fighting monks. *Veteran* fighting monks who would answer to Warmund de Picquigny alone, as their ecclesiastical superior. Think you that thought might intrigue him?"

This time the silence was profound, reflecting the unthinkable tenor of what de Payens had suggested, and he allowed it to hover palpably above all of them before he continued. "Think about it seriously, lads, and forget about all the rules that would tell you a thousand times why this could never be. The times today are different, demanding different measures, different directions, and different solutions to different problems. So imagine, if you will, fighting monks, religious warriors bound by vows, answerable only to the Patriarch. Not to the King, and not to feudal lords. Were we such monks, we could then dedicate ourselves to patrolling the roads and protecting the pilgrims, ridding both Warmund and King Baldwin of their greatest headache. And being bound by the vow of poverty, we would not require to be paid—merely supported through the charity and alms of the Church."

"Fighting monks?" Archibald St. Agnan's scornful tone expressed all their skepticism. "Fighting *monks*? That is ridiculous, Hugh. Who ever heard of such a thing? It's as logical as copulating virgins."

This time no single man smiled in response to St. Agnan's rough humor, and de Payens nodded. "That is true, Archibald, but you are a knight, so you should know better than any cleric that logic has little place in the middle of a fight—and make no mistake, a fight is what we are discussing here. We are about to become engaged, like it or not, in a fight for our ancient Order's very survival, and to win it, we will have to fight the battles of the Christian Church, protecting its pilgrims, certainly—and I see nothing wrong with that—but upholding and appearing to endorse its hegemony, and defending the existence of this Christian Kingdom of Jerusalem, even though that entails a breakdown of sense and logic."

He fell silent for a count of five heartbeats, then said, "Listen now, all of you, and hear what I am saying. No one has ever heard of fighting monks *because there has never been such a thing.* But that idea will stop being ridiculous as soon as the first order of fighting monks is created to confront circumstances extraordinary enough to warrant such a thing. Warmund de Picquigny has the power and the authority to do that, and I believe the circumstances in force here are extraordinary enough to warrant that."

"But why would we even think about doing such a thing, Sir Hugh?" This was Gondemare again, and de Payens smiled at him.

"It would provide us with the means of obeying our orders from the Seneschal."

"What?" St. Agnan's tone was skeptical. "You mean about excavating the temple? We all agreed that's impossible. How can it be less so now?"

De Payens was ready for him, his answer spilling out almost before the question was complete.

"Because we are considering becoming penniless warrior monks, my friend. Once we become that we will have horses, but we will lack the wherewithal to provide feed and shelter for them—and for ourselves, be it said. And so, as partial payment for our services, we will ask leave of the King and the Archbishop to install ourselves and our mounts in the old stables above the temple ruins.

"Warmund de Picquigny will not object to that, I promise you, having gained our military skills for his own ends. Nor will the King object to having a reliable force of knights quartered in his own grounds. And once we are installed in the stables, we can begin to dig, in safety and in privacy. That should solve our most immediate problems for a while, at least."

"Hugh, you have the mind of a Pope," St. Omer growled. "That is brilliant, my friend."

"Aye, you might well be right," St. Agnan said, "but do we have to become monks? I know but little of how monks are made, but I mislike the idea of taking monkish vows. How much of that would we have to endure, were we to go ahead with this?"

"Three, Archibald, no more. Poverty, chastity, and obedience."

"Swear me to chastity? Never!"

De Payens winked at St. Omer. "Come, now, St. Agnan, and be truthful," he challenged the big knight. "When did you last have an unchaste thought of anything other than a pretty goat? How old are you now? Forty? Older? And you have been here in the desert for half your life. You smell like a rancid goat, as do we all, and no self-respecting woman would come near you, even were self-respecting women of our own kind to be found here. Truly, I ask you, what matters chastity to you?"

St. Agnan grunted and grinned, not even slightly offended. "Aye, fair enough, I might grant you that one. But what about the others? Obedience? And *poverty*, in God's name?"

"You already live by those two, my friend. And in God's name, too. That's what the ritual we observed here today is all about. You undertook both of the vows you are questioning now, with only very minor differences, when you were Raised to the Order. You swore to obey the superiors set over you by God, and you swore to hold all things in common with your brethren in the Order, is that not correct?" He waited for St. Agnan's nod, then smiled. "Aye, I'm glad you remember. You swore vows of obedience then, Archibald, and, for all intents and purposes, of poverty."

No one appeared to have anything to add after that, and de Payens looked around at them, catching each man's eye in turn until he was sure they were all waiting for what he would say next, and then a very small smile played along his lips. "Look, my friends," he began, "I can see that you all have doubts about this, and I admit to you freely that until mere hours ago, I shared most of them. But lying awake last night, I thought about many things, and only now do I see that all of those things centered upon this dilemma we face, so let me share them with you.

"You all know of my self-imposed exile, these past years, shutting myself off from everyone." He hesitated, thinking for a moment, then continued slowly, as though examining each word before he spoke it. "That mood, that frame of mind, was born of disappointment ... and of something close to despair—despair for my fellow man, and for myself and my beliefs and my defaced ideals, because everywhere I looked, I seemed to see men wading through blood, befouled by the kind of filth I was taught to detest as a boy. Our Christian brethren, as all of you know, make much of their faith and the power of it. They call it a supernatural gift of God, and priests speak of losing faith as one of the greatest disasters that can befall a man, causing the loss of his very soul. And they say the greatest sin against faith is despair, because it denies the existence of hope.

"Well, my friends, I was in despair for all those years, a despair caused by what I had been watching in my fellow man all my life, and by the ease with which the behavior that inspired my despair can be forgiven, and *is* forgiven, by the Church, leaving men mysteriously cleansed, absolved of guilt, and free and able to go out and commit the same atrocities again and again and again. There is no sin, we are all taught, that cannot be forgiven merely by confessing it to a priest."

He straightened his back and closed his hands over his face, squeezing his eyes shut as he said, "But most priests are just as venal and corrupt as the very men they forgive, citing God's clemency."

He lowered his hands, blinking to clear his eyes. "Most of them are, I said. Not all of them. There may well be some out there who are completely sincere in their beliefs, but I have never met one in person. That is the truth, and it appalls me. I was brought up, as were all of you, among knights and warriors, and I learned the laws of chivalry when I could barely walk. I also learned the laws of God and of the Church at the same time, but I had not grown beyond mid-boyhood before I also learned that few people beyond my family's circle paid any attention at all to God's laws. Most of them—

lords, knights, and soldiers—heeded only those laws that had the power to punish and hurt them in this world. The other world they left wholly to the priests. And the priests, the clerics, gave all of their time towards the care of themselves. They spoke of the goodwill of others, but only insofar as it enriched them in real terms: money, power, and status.

"And then, after several years of increasing discouragement through all of that, I was initiated into this Order of Rebirth and discovered that the love of God, and my faith in God, can thrive outside the framework of the Church. That transformed my whole life, for it taught me to see and appreciate, for the very first time in my life, that every single thing that people do in life is influenced and dictated by the Church, and that the Church today is run by venal, grasping, corrupt, and self-aggrandizing men. Oh, we are expected to believe the Church fathers are all God-chosen and God-blessed, and we are encouraged and expected to entrust our priests with the care of our immortal souls, but who tells us such things? They do, of course. The priests tell us what to do and what to think, in everything to do with God—and in everything else, if the truth be told. They proclaim God's infinite mercy and they claim that they embody God's voice in this world ... and they make it perfectly clear that if we disobey them, or if we choose not to believe them, they have the power to punish us, to condemn and even damn us to eternal perdition."

He looked again from man to man, all of them rapt by what he was saying. "They damn people, brothers, to eternal perdition. Think about that again, for a moment, for it is something we tend to shy away from. Priests consign ordinary people maliciously to the everlasting fires of Hell and they do it simply because they *can*, because they possess and enjoy the power and the willfulness to rule men's lives and dispossess their souls. And while they are doing it, they preach about God's eternal and bottomless mercy. And who is to gainsay them, believing that they have the ear of God?"

His voice took on an edge that had not been there before. "Our Order taught us that we may change all that. Do you not recall the excitement of discovering that? Of knowing that we might someday change the entire world into a better place? The Church, as we know it today, was built by men, not by God, and not by his supposedly man-born son, Jesus. Jesus was man-born, certainly, but what is believed to be his Church was usurped, then shaped and fashioned long after his death, by Paul the gentile and by his Roman associates and advisers. But our Order, the Order of Rebirth in Sion, held out to us the hope of changing all of that someday, not by killing all the ungodly and unworthy priests but by bringing the truth, the *real* truth of what happened a millennium ago, here in Jerusalem, to light.

"I had forgotten that, my friends. I had lost sight of it among all the carnage and the filth of what has happened here since first we came. I had lost sight of it because no word was reaching us, I believed, from the Order itself. But I was wrong, and now that word has come, strange as it may seem in our ears, and I have come to see and to know now what I believe. I have no faith in men for their own sake, but I believe that God has brought us here, every man of us, for a purpose. And I believe that purpose is what brought this plan into my mind last night, while I lay abed.

"We are being asked—or ordered, if you wish—to find, to rediscover, the truth of our Order's Lore. And when we have found it, we will make a start on righting all the wrongs that the real loss of faith—the manipulation and distortion of the real teachings of Jesus and his Jewish brethren—has visited upon this world. And we will change it. And when it is changed, although our names will be long forgotten, people will remember and talk about what we achieved." He stopped, and the silence held until he asked them, "So, what say you? What do you want to do?"

"We shave our heads and dig," came St. Agnan's voice from among the circle of nodding heads.

THAT NIGHT, when he finally made his way to bed, Hugh failed to fall asleep and soon rolled on to his back, aware that he was facing another restless night. Normally he would fall asleep as soon as he lay down and would wake up refreshed, no matter how long or short his rest might have been. He could even nap, if the need arose, standing on his feet or propped in his saddle. Invariably, a failure to drop off instantly meant that something was troubling him, but this time he was unaware of anything that might be niggling at him and so, after a period of tossing and turning, he threw back his coverings and swung his legs out of bed, deciding to take a walk in the cool night air. He shrugged into the long, flowing Arab robe that, like most of his companions, he wore for comfort and convenience when he was not armored, then slipped one arm through the loop of his sword belt and settled it across his shoulder before making his way to the main doors leading to the courtyard. There he yawned and scratched his head, shivering slightly in the chill of the desert night.

"Why aren't you asleep?"

Hugh spun around and saw Payn Montdidier sitting on a bench against the wall behind him on his right, lit by the full moon and the flickering flames of a burning cresset.

"Crusty! You startled me ... But I'll return your question: why aren't *you* asleep?"

"I should be. But I'm going in now, because I'm chilled to the bone. I've been sitting here thinking."

"About what?"

"Margaret ... and my son, Charles, and Helen, my daughter. Helen will be eight years old tomorrow and I had forgotten, until tonight, when you mentioned that only two of us have families, back in Christendom ..."

Hugh was appalled by his own thoughtlessness. Until Montdidier spoke, he had not considered what effect his earlier statement might have had on the two men in question, Montdidier and Gondemare. Now the pain in his friend's voice was too obvious to miss.

"Payn," he said, "forgive me. I had no—"

"I know that, Hugh. You simply spoke the truth,

and you said nothing that came to me as a surprise. The die was cast on that affair long years ago, to everyone's consent, Margaret's as well as mine. But you caught me unprepared when you brought the matter up so suddenly ..." His voice faded, and he stared into nothingness before he resumed. "Remembering my daughter's birthday ... it made me think about the pattern of our lives—of *all* our lives—and how it has changed so completely from what we anticipated when we were young and bright-eyed and full of great ideas." He smiled, looking down at his feet, then shook his head and looked up at Hugh, his smile still in place.

"D'you remember how horrified we were when we found out that they knew about us? We thought they had discovered all about the Order. That was the most disastrous thing we could imagine at the time. May God help us!"

Hugh smiled, too. "Well, it was quite dramatic, I recall."

"Now it seems laughable."

Hugh cocked his head, intrigued by something in his friend's tone. "Laughable? How so? I never thought to laugh. The women have made a tremendous sacrifice, without so much as the comfort of knowing what that sacrifice is for. And they stood back and allowed us to do what we needed to do. They could have wept and screamed. They chose not to, and they prepared themselves for lives without their men. God bless them, I say."

"Aye, as you say, God bless them ..." Montdidier stood up and moved towards the door, then hesitated and reached out to grasp Hugh's shoulder. "It has just occurred to me that I do not even know if Margaret is still alive. She could be dead by now."

Hugh looked his friend in the eye and nodded. "Aye, she could be, but if so, it could only have been in the past year. I think we would have heard word of her passing by now, were it otherwise. She is probably as alive and hale as you are, living happily in Payens."

Montdidier stood for a few more moments without moving, then nodded his head. "Aye, you're probably right. I hope you are. Now I'm going to bed, and you should, too, at least to rest, if not to sleep."

Hugh pulled his robe about him before turning to walk back inside the hostel with his friend.

SEVEN

By mid-morning on the following day, with the cooperation of his six companions, de Payens had a plan of action that would take his proposal to the next stage. They had been together since before dawn, discussing the question of how best to make the first approach to Warmund de Picquigny, and Hugh was now confident that his ideas were well enough fleshed out, and based on sufficiently solid grounds, to permit him to proceed immediately. And so, an hour before noon, he was striding along the main route to the Archbishop's residence, dressed in his finest clothes and armor and accompanied by St. Omer, St. Agnan, and Montdidier, all three of them dressed similarly, in the parade-best clothing they had brought to wear to their inaugural temple Gathering. It never occurred to him to wonder if the Patriarch Archbishop might, for whatever reason, be unable or unwilling to receive him and his friends. He had known and liked Warmund de Picquigny for years and he knew that the liking was mutual, so he was looking forward to the coming meeting and reviewing once again what he would say to the Patriarch, when he felt St. Agnan's arm being thrust across his chest, pulling him to a halt.

Startled back to awareness of where he was, he looked up to see twin lines of men come jogging from his right, then stop and link arms along each side of the narrow thoroughfare, preventing anyone from crossing. They were King's Men of the palace guard, and he turned to see whom they were escorting, but all he could see was a closed coach. As it trundled past, he took note of the heavily curtained windows and of the escort accompanying the cumbersome vehicle, a half score of well-armed, uniformed men in front of the carriage and another half score behind it, all of them wearing the same heraldic insignia: a stylized fountain in bright blue on a field of white. De Payens stifled a surge of impatience at being held there, because he knew they would not be kept waiting long. The King's Guard who lined the street, facing stoically towards the people watching, were long accustomed to their procedure. They waited until the carriage had passed behind their backs, no doubt counting in silent cadence all the while, and then the last section of them disengaged smoothly and ran forward to take up position ahead of the procession, leaving the street behind them free for those who had been waiting to cross.

St. Agnan made no effort to cross the street, but stood and watched until the carriage had disappeared around the next bend. "Who was that?" he asked when it had gone.

"Royal family," Hugh told him. "Probably one of the King's daughters, judging by the closed curtains, and even more probably the second eldest of them, Alice, since the escort were wearing Bishop Odo's colors."

"Who's Bishop Odo?"

"Erstwhile Bishop of Fontainebleau, now secretary to the Patriarch Archbishop, and the Archbishop's liaison with the King."

St. Agnan turned slowly to look directly at Hugh, the beginnings of a frown between his brows. "So why would you associate him with one of the King's daughters and not the others? Is there something going on between them?"

"Come." De Payens stepped out and started to cross the narrow street. "It is generally accepted that Bishop Odo is ... fond of the princess. But she is not yet fifteen, I think, while he is close to our age, so I doubt very seriously that anything is 'going on between them,' as you put it."

The big knight's frown did not abate. "Very well, she's but a child and he's fond of her ... Fond enough to offer her an escort at all times?"

"Not at all times, no, but he has known the princess since she was a child, although from what I've heard, she is a child no longer. But Odo has been one of her father's most loyal counselors for years, when Baldwin was Count of Edessa, long before he became King of Jerusalem. Here, we go this way." The entrance to a narrow alley was barely discernible among the shadows, and his companions, who had been listening attentively, followed closely as he took them along the short length of the alley and then across another narrow passageway that led them out onto a broad street, across from the main entrance to an imposing, well-guarded building.

"The Patriarch's palace," he said. "Stay close."

He made his way deftly through the traffic on the noisy thoroughfare, weaving through a sea of livestock that contained camels, horses, cattle, swine, and goats and a colorful, polyglot mass of people, and presented himself to the guard at the main entrance. Having been duly recognized and acknowledged as presenting no threat to the Archbishop, he and his three companions were shown into a high-ceilinged, richly furnished chamber where they were asked to wait until the Patriarch could see them.

They barely had time to examine the room's treasures, let alone grow bored, before the Patriarch Archbishop swept into the room unattended, smiling widely and welcoming de Payens effusively before turning to put his friends at ease with equal warmth and courtesy. Warmund de Picquigny carried himself with the air of a born politician and was an attractive man by anyone's standards, tall and silver haired with an imperiously hooked nose and fine, white, even teeth. He seemed to smile constantly, even when he was displeased. He was a gracious host and quickly made his visitors feel welcome, but they spent little time in small talk, because all four of his visitors were soldiers, unaccustomed to the niceties of social intercourse and protocol. As soon as they were all seated, de Payens began to deliver the plea he had prepared, and from the moment the Archbishop discerned what was being asked of him, he sat rapt, making no move to interrupt the speaker or spoil the flow of what was being said.

When de Payens eventually fell silent, Warmund de Picquigny sat frowning into the middle distance, and then he reached for a small silver bell, rang it, and replaced it on the small table by his elbow.

"Your request is unique, my friend," he said as the silver chimes died away. "In truth, I have never heard its like. It will require much thought." The door at the end of the long room opened and a tall, dark-featured man wearing the purple of a bishop approached the Patriarch, who held up a restraining hand towards de Payens. "Forgive me," he said quietly and turned to the newcomer. "Has word arrived from Acre?"

"It has, my lord."

"Excellent." The Patriarch turned back to his visitors. "You must excuse me, my friends, but we have been awaiting word most urgently from our associates in Acre, and I must plead the pressure of necessity in leaving you alone while I attend to it. I have merely to read the missive and make a decision based upon its contents. Once I have done that, Bishop Odo here will attend, on my behalf, to whatever must be done thereafter. It will not take long, so please do not feel any need to leave. I will have my people bring you food and drink, and I should be back here even before they have had time to do so. Please, I pray you, be at ease here and await me."

"He's not going to grant it," St. Agnan said as soon as the door had closed behind the Patriarch.

They all looked at him, but St. Omer was the first to

respond. "What makes you think that, Archibald?"

"He made it obvious, didn't he? To walk away and leave us sitting here before he's heard us out? That's a bad sign."

"He heard us out, Archibald, be in no doubt of that," de Payens said. "And his leaving the room is the best sign we could have. He wants time alone now, to think about the pros and contras of what we are proposing. And the longer he remains away, the more thought he will be giving to our suggestions. Had he decided to reject our plea, he would have done so immediately and we would be on our way back to the caravanserai now. This man did not become Patriarch of Jerusalem by being stupid or indecisive."

"What about this Acre urgency, won't that claim all his attention?"

St. Agnan's concern brought a smile to one corner of de Payens's mouth. "There is no word from Acre. That bell is merely a tool the Patriarch uses to give himself time. Whoever comes in answer to the summons agrees to whatever the Archbishop asks or suggests, and an excuse is provided for the Archbishop to leave for as long as he may wish, without offending anyone unduly. In this instance, his departure works in our favor. The Archbishop is considering our case. We have done all we can do, and I don't think we could have presented ourselves better than we did, so now we must wait for him to deliberate and reach the conclusion that will be most advantageous to him in both his personal and official capacities.

"But I feel confident. He could have asked us to return tomorrow, or next week. That he has asked us to remain tells me that he is intrigued by our proposal. But what we are suggesting here would be deemed heresy by any other priest to whom we mentioned it, and we must not lose sight of that. De Picquigny is made of different stuff, however, and he has needs that exist nowhere else. All that remains now—and it is already out of our hands—is for him to decide whether the benefits of what we are proposing would be large enough to outweigh the risks involved for him should he decide to proceed."

The Patriarch's house servants, all of them monks, bustled around them silently and efficiently for an hour, laying out a light but delicious meal of cold fowl, new-baked bread, fresh dates, and goat cheese, served with a variety of sherbets and chilled fruit drinks, and the four knights had barely finished clearing off everything on the table when Warmund de Picquigny returned. He graciously waved away any suggestion that he himself partake of the food—there was still a substantial platter of dates on the table—and poured himself a cup of some sparkling liquid before sitting down in the spot where he had sat originally, by the table with the silver bell. He made no mention of anything to do with Acre and instead launched straight into what the knights had come to talk about, speaking primarily to de Payens but looking constantly from one man to another, so that they all felt included in what he had to say.

"Now, I need to understand, quite clearly and

beyond doubt, exactly what it is that you are suggesting, because from what I have already heard, your proposal could make my life extremely difficult on several grounds. You are asking me to intercede on your behalf with your liege lords, because among you, you owe fealty to several noblemen, in order to persuade them to accept the loss of your services for a higher purpose and to permit all of you to commit yourselves to a life of penance, prayer, and seclusion. Is that correct?"

Hugh de Payens nodded. "Aye, my lord Patriarch, that is the gist of it. We wish to be permitted to dedicate ourselves to God now, after a lifetime of dedicated service to our masters and our knightly vows."

There was a lengthy silence before de Picquigny solemnly shook his head. "I do not think I can achieve that for you, my friends," he said quietly. "Not even with the best will in the world. Those knightly vows of which you speak are binding. They cannot be terminated at the will of any man, this side of death."

De Payens raised a hand as if in surprise. "Not even for the purposes of serving God better?"

"As monks, you mean?" The Patriarch shook his head dubiously. "Who is to define the meaning of *better*? And does the improvement entail prayer alone? If so, I fear your cause is weakened, perhaps fatally. There is no shortage of monks in this land today, and all of them pray, some of them, I fear, better and more effectively than others. But all of them have another purpose, a function—a task or a duty, if you will—in addition to daily prayer and piety. The Knights of the

Hospital are probably the most obvious example. They are nominally knights nowadays, but they are monks and always will be. Their function, unchanged since the day of their formation five hundred years ago, has always been to serve the sick and ailing pilgrims visiting the Holy Places. That is what they do, and as Patriarch of Jerusalem, I rely heavily on their abundant and unstinting services, self-sacrifice, and goodwill. But they are monks, adhering to the Rule of Saint Benedict, and all that they do is predicated upon, and subservient to, that sacred Rule. It gives them their authority and it adds structure to their lives ... rigid structure ... to *every minute* of their lives." He looked from one to the other of them, the hint of a smile hovering on his lips. "Would you be willing to subject yourselves to the Rule of Saint Benedict, or have you other thoughts on that matter?"

St. Agnan cleared his throat nervously. "Could we not have a rule of our own?"

The Archbishop barked a laugh. "Aye, you could, and easily, once you had spent twenty to thirty years establishing yourselves and your dedication to discipline and prayer and a way of life that sets you far apart from any other order of monastics. But I suspect you might have something more immediate than that in mind. No?" He turned his eyes once more to Hugh de Payens. "Tell me, my friend, for I am curious: what ... what *prompted* this? What was the thought, or argument, or incident that led to your decision to take this step and to come here seeking my support?"

Placed squarely on the spot, Hugh felt his face flushing even as chagrin churned in the depths of his belly. He had always prided himself on his truthfulness, and had never knowingly told an outright lie to anyone, so even in this extremity, with so much of import depending on his next response, he could not, nor would he, lie directly to the Patriarch Archbishop. He shrugged his shoulders and had begun to spread his hands helplessly, on the point of admitting his entire design, when the truth came to him suddenly enough to make the pit of his stomach feel hollow. He did not question the intuition as anything other than direct revelation, and shaken as he was, he merely changed his gesture into one that suggested mild embarrassment, then clapped his palms together quietly, his mind racing as he sought the words that would serve him best without committing him to a deliberate lie.

"I received …" He paused, frowned, and then began again, more emphatically, raising his eyes in pious suggestion towards the ceiling as he did so. "I *received* … unforeseen and unbelievable instructions, my lord Archbishop. Instructions that came to me in the beginning as unconditional demands, yet proved later to be formless, unreasonable, and without substance. They contained no guidance, nothing that I could see as concrete or absolute. I simply became aware that I was under a moral constraint to follow these demands, and that, my life being what it is today, I was, and I seemed destined to remain, incapable of obeying them or carrying them out. I awoke one morning with that impossibility lodged in my mind, and I have not been free of the urge to change it since that day."

The Archbishop's eyebrows had risen high. "That is ... impressive, Master de Payens. And might I be entitled to ask the substance of these ... instructions?"

"Aye, my lord, most certainly. And if you understand them more readily than I have, I will be grateful for any enlightenment you may shed on them. I was commanded to think back upon my life, to re-examine everything of import that had taken place since my boyhood, and then to bend my mind to finding ways and means of using all my skills and my abilities to bring about great changes in Jerusalem and to discover and reveal the truth underlying the heart of the Kingdom and the Holy City of Jerusalem."

Warmund de Picquigny sat silent, only the blankness of his expression indicating his inability to react immediately to this astonishing statement, and then he pulled himself together.

"*Your* skills and abilities, you said. Yours alone." He waved a hand to indicate St. Omer and the others. "And what about your friends?"

De Payens shrugged, feeling very pleased with himself. The bait was cast, and he could sense the interest of the fish teasing at it. "I told them about my dilemma, shared my thoughts with them, and they became convinced that I had received a calling, a direct command, obscure as it might be, and they wished to aid me in my prosecution of it. That is why we are here."

"I see. And are there others who share your vision?"

"Seven of us, my lord."

"Hmm ..."

"But we could be more. I told only my closest friends. Of the six I told, all decided to join me, but already they have other names, of friends of theirs, whom they would like to enroll."

"The noblemen would see this as a mutiny. You know that, do you not? They would see it as weakening their resources."

"How could it do that, my lord Archbishop? Even were our numbers doubled, we would not amount to twenty knights, all growing old after a lifetime of hard and loyal service. That could hardly be called a dilution of the strength of Jerusalem's armies."

"Nonetheless, Sir Hugh, twenty veteran knights—"

"Twenty *aging* knights, my lord Patriarch, and less than half of that, in truth, all of us past our prime."

The Patriarch pursed his lips, and de Payens continued. "Even so, my lord, I have to hark back to what you said before, about each order of monks having its own tasks, its own duty in addition to its daily routine of prayer and piety. We have no such incentive, no such direction. But we could have, were one selected for us that we found appropriate to what we are." His voice, which had begun that statement full of enthusiasm, quickly dropped and became dispirited. "Ah, but then all we know how to do is fight, and monks do not fight ..." He smiled and shook his head. "Ah, my lord Archbishop, were there such a thing as an order of warrior *monks* ... what a contribution we could make to that! Now *there* would be a way for us to serve our God in piety and to great purpose. Pity such a thing may not be. Still, we can learn to deal with other tasks. We can adapt. We would not lack in willingness to tackle anything assigned to us."

He stopped talking then, hearing the silence of his friends and imagining the creaking of wheels within the Archbishop's mind. And then Warmund de Picquigny stood up and raised his right hand to bless them, so that they all knelt in front of him with their heads lowered.

"Come again tomorrow, Hugh de Payens, at the same hour. I will think upon what you have said and will have an answer for you when you arrive. It may be one that you will wish to discuss afterwards with your friends here, but you may come alone to receive it. Afterwards, if there is more to be discussed, we will have time to do that. But for now, no word to anyone, from any of you, on what we have discussed today. Is that understood? Now go in peace."

GODFREY ST. OMER looked up from the board game he had been playing with Payn Montdidier, attracted by the movement as the door swung open noiselessly. "Ah," he cried, "finally. We thought you were never coming back."

Hugh de Payens stood just inside the door, holding it open as he waited for his eyes to adjust to the shadows of the interior after the brightness of the early afternoon outside. St. Omer, Bissot, and Montdidier sat gazing at him from the brightly lit table by the window, and behind them, on a couch against the wall where he had been lying in semi-darkness, Gondemare was raising himself on one elbow. De Payens noticed the absence of St. Agnan and de Rossal, but before he had time to ask where they were they crowded through the door at his back, requiring him to move into the middle of the room, where they all began to throw questions at him.

"Enough, in God's name! Listen to yourselves, like a pack of old women. You can't all talk at once if you seriously want answers. Give me time to take off my cloak and lay down my weapons and catch my breath and I'll tell you everything. But I am not going to stand here like a street huckster and be shouted at. St. Agnan, find Ibrahim and ask him to bring us some food and drink, if you will, and the rest of you, sit down around the table like civil creatures."

De Payens took a few moments to rid himself of his long, sheathed sword and the belt that held the dagger and the scrip at his waist. Then, when he had stripped off his long outer garment and the flowing headdress that he chose to wear instead of an iron Frankish helmet, he moved to seat himself at the head of the table, where he waited for St. Agnan to return from his errand. No one spoke to him in the interim, but every eye in the room was on him, trying to detect some hint of what he had to tell, and as soon as all six of them were assembled, he spoke, wasting no time on preliminaries.

"He said yes. We will have our permission."

He waited for the first outburst of approval to die down, then quelled the last of it by simply raising one hand. "It will not happen today or tomorrow. It might take a year to achieve, perhaps even longer. But it will happen. The Patriarch wants it to happen."

"How? What did he say?" This was St. Agnan, eager as always.

"He outlined what he wants, and made it very plain, although he approached it with some subtlety. In fact, had we not taken the pains we did to suggest exactly what we wanted from him, I might have thought he had come up with the idea himself. Certes, he himself believes he did, and that is the finest result we could have won.

"He was waiting for me when I arrived, and his secretary, Bishop Odo, led me right into his presence, in the small room where he works daily, not the audience chamber where we were received yesterday. He then dismissed Odo and followed him to the outer door to check that he was gone from the anteroom before we began to talk."

"Odo would not have liked that," St. Agnan growled. "I had the feeling yesterday that he is the kind of fellow who likes to know everything that's going on everywhere."

"Aye, he was not happy, but Warmund de Picquigny is not a man to be crossed lightly.

"Anyway, as soon as we were alone, the Patriarch reminded me of what I had said about being willing to assume a task like other monkish orders, should someone wish to assign us one that seemed appropriate, and he revisited my comments about the misfortune of not having such a thing as an order of warrior monks, although he did not dwell on any of that. Instead, he talked then about the problem of brigandage on the roads, and the escalating threats to the safety and welfare of pilgrims to the Holy Places. Of course, he knew that we are all familiar with the situation and understand it to be a chronic thorn in the side of the administration of the kingdom, but he went to great lengths to explain, and to justify, why the King is unable to do anything about the problem, contentious as it is. And he went to even greater lengths to make sure that I was fully informed about his own responsibilities as Patriarch and Archbishop, which make him nominally responsible for the safety of the entire Church in Jerusalem, including the priests and clerics who administer the daily affairs of the Church, and the pilgrims who entrust themselves to the authority and supervision of the Church within the Holy Land—"

His eyes widened, and he sat up straighter and looked at each of his friends around the table. "Do you know," he continued in a voice tinged with wonder, "it has but now occurred to me that he spoke invariably of the Holy Land. Not once did he call this place the Kingdom of Jerusalem, and the name Outremer never arose in our conversation, and only now does that lead me to see that our Patriarch perceives his position, and his responsibilities, as having nothing even remotely to do with King Baldwin, or with the King's ambitions for Jerusalem, or his visions of the kingdom as a civil state.

Our Warmund de Picquigny has eyes only for the *religious* reality of Jerusalem—the Holy City in the Holy Land. As far as he is concerned, nothing else has any significance, and the King and his nobles are mere nuisances, interfering with the conduct of the Patriarch's ecclesiastical affairs."

He became aware of the blank looks on his listeners' faces and cleared his throat. "Aye, well … He asked me then to give him my own personal opinion about what might be done—what *needed* to be done—about the situation on the roads, and I did not have much to say. But I told him of our little escapade of two or three nights ago, when we chased the brigands out into the desert, and that led me to speculate on how little actual armed force might be required to halt the depredations of these people. I opined, and he agreed with me, that the difficulties are expanding, and the bandits are proliferating in numbers, simply because they are encountering no opposition at all. That would change rapidly, I told him, if only someone could field even a tiny force of determined, disciplined invigilators to patrol the roads. The mere threat of their presence, I said, once that presence was established and expected, would probably reduce the number of such incidents dramatically.

"And then, having said that, I said no more."

A soft knock sounded at the door, and de Payens waved a warning hand, silencing everyone as the innkeeper himself opened the doors wide and stepped inside, ahead of a pair of grinning servants carrying a stretcher of food slung from their shoulders and another, this one a giant, who carried an enormous copper tray laden with potables. The talk dwindled into triviality as the servants fussed about, setting out the food, and after they were alone again, none of the knights paid any attention to anything other than the food in front of them: fresh-baked bread, still warm, with fresh-made, creamy goat cheese; a dish of olives glistening with oil and herbs; three kinds of fresh fruit; hard cheeses of several kinds and shapes; two cold fowl and a number of dried sausages. No one spoke again for some time, until the food had been depleted and they sat back, belching softly in satisfaction.

Eventually, it was Rossal who brought everyone back to the subject at hand. "Hugh," he said, "there is something I do not understand. You said you believe the Patriarch favors your request, and that it suits all his personal purposes, but that it might take a year or more for him to be able to put it into effect. I thought the Patriarch of Jerusalem has all the spiritual power in Outremer that the Pope in Rome enjoys throughout Christendom. Is that not true? And if it is, why would it take so long for him to make it possible for you to do what you wish to do?"

De Payens wiped his chin and rinsed his mouth with a draft of chilled grape juice before he answered, and even the least attentive of the others could see that he was thinking carefully about how he would respond. Eventually, however, he sat back and stroked his beard. "Nothing is ever as straightforward as it seems, Roland. What to us may seem a simple matter of logic, cause and effect, is seldom seen as such by those whose concern it is to keep the world's affairs proceeding smoothly.

"Warmund of Picquigny, even although he is Patriarch Archbishop of Jerusalem and therefore spiritual leader of his flock in Outremer, is none the less constrained to live in harmony with his temporal coequals. He could go straight ahead and do as he wishes, secure in his awareness of superiority as God's representative here in the Holy Land, but by doing so he would probably alienate—needlessly—every king, every count, and every other nobly born man of power and means within his own dominion. That would be stupid, in my opinion, and if you but think on it for a moment, I have no doubt that you will agree with me. There is an ancient saying, from the New Testament, that the spirit is willing but the flesh is weak. That is a very simple truth, except that, in its self-avowed weakness, the flesh can sometimes be brutally strong, and that is what the Patriarch has to consider.

"He could turn around tomorrow and issue a decree, backed by the absolute power of the Church, that one knight in every three, for example, must be seconded to the Church's affairs for the duration, answerable only to himself as the Church's senior representative here in the Holy Land. He could do that, beyond any trace of doubt, for he has the authority, in theory at least. And the chances are that many of the lords would submit to it, in the belief that God speaks directly through His representatives here on earth. But there would be many others who would balk at it, interpreting his idea as an unwarranted intrusion by the Church—or by cynical churchmen—upon their legal and justifiable affairs. That entire realm of perceptions, beliefs, and interpretations is a quagmire into which no sane and forward-thinking man would ever wish to blunder, for once that refusal has been evoked, and the bit of disobedience is firmly clamped between the teeth of the rebels, who is to say what mutinies might follow or how long it might take to resolve the differences stirred up?"

No one spoke in response to that, until St. Agnan asked, "So what will happen next?"

De Payens spread his hands. "I have no idea. First, the Archbishop will have to convince the King that what he is proposing—this idea of using us as a counteractive invigilator force—has self-evident merit. On that point, I anticipate he will have little difficulty. The King is in dire need of an alternative solution, to divert some of the heat from his own skillet. This that we are offering might well be exactly what he is looking for.

"But it is not the King who concerns us most. He has a keen mind and can be trusted to look to his own advantage. Unfortunately, much the same can be said of the very people to whom we owe our feudal allegiance. They, too, are never without an eye to their own advantage, and in this instance there is nothing, in any part of this proposal, that redounds to their benefit. They lose on all fronts, because they are the people who have to absorb the loss—the permanent loss, without compensation—of our services. Those are the people whom Warmund de Picquigny will have to convince of the soundness of his thinking in this matter, and I have no slightest idea of how he might approach that task. I do know, however, that I wish him well of it."

He thought for a while, then nodded his head emphatically. "That is all I have to say. I believe that what we have petitioned will come into effect. I have no knowledge of what will be entailed, in the final reckoning, other than that we will become Christian monks, supported out of churchly funds, and that we will bind ourselves by the same solemn vows that bind us, for the most part, already, and that we will hold ourselves accountable primarily, albeit purely on the surface, to Warmund de Picquigny, the Patriarch Archbishop."

St. Omer raised a hand. "Did you remember to ask about the stables?"

"Of course I did, and the Archbishop agreed without the slightest hesitation. The stables will be ours, from the moment King Baldwin concurs and our plans achieve reality. He did not even pause to consider my request before granting it. And why should he? Those stables have lain abandoned and unused for hundreds of years. And now he sees them being put to good use, in a manner that will cost him and the King nothing. So mote it be."

His companions joined him instantly in the ancient benison of their Order. "So mote it be."

MONKS OF THE MOUNT

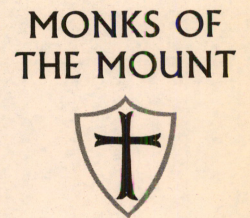

ONE

Trapped and helpless in her swaying carriage and surrounded by battling, screaming men, Morfia of Melitene had no wish to believe that her life was about to end, but she was too pragmatic to doubt the reality of what was happening to her. It had already happened to her escort, Sir Alexander Guillardame, and now he sprawled inelegantly in front of her, face down on the seat opposite hers, the blood and brains from his shattered head all over the skirts of her gown, the stench of his loosened bowels filling the tiny space of the box in which she was confined. He had been the second of the two young knights in the carriage with her when the attack began, both of them lolling at their ease, their helmets on the floor by their feet and their chain-mail cowls thrust back from their heads as they made pleasant conversation, earnestly trying to amuse and divert her on the long journey. But then had come a commotion of some kind and the vehicle had lurched, swayed, and tilted dangerously to one side, its panicked horses pulling it off the road and then coming to a halt as the screams and shouts of angry, frightened men sprang up from every direction.

Before any of the three people in the carriage could even begin to comprehend the sudden change, they had

heard the thunder of hooves as a large group of horsemen—Morfia had been too confused and frightened at
the time even to wonder who they were—arrived
among them, and before she had time even to ask what
was happening, her two knightly escorts were scrambling towards the carriage door, blocking each other's
movements in their haste and fumbling for their
weapons as they went, their helmets forgotten on the
floor.

Antoine de Bourgogne threw open the door and
leapt out first, unaware that he had grasped his lady's
arm for leverage as he thrust himself forward.
Momentarily aware of the fleeting pain of his wrench-
ing grip, Morfia watched him land on his feet and fall
straight to his knees, his hands clawing at the impossibly long spear shaft that had transfixed him as he
jumped. As he toppled forward, her view of him was cut
off by the bulk of young Alex Guillardame as he, too,
fought for balance in the cramped doorway of the
swaying carriage. She then heard a short, violent ripping
noise that ended in a solid, shocking impact that
reminded her, incongruously, of the sound of an axe
hitting a tree stump, and then had come a choking
grunt from the young knight as he spun quickly back
from the door to face her, his entire face ruined, his
skull blown apart by the force of the iron crossbow bolt
that had struck the peak of his unguarded forehead.

As her eyes widened in horror, the dead knight kept
turning, spun perhaps by the impetus of the missile that
had killed him, pulling the door shut again with his

sagging weight so that the heavy curtains blocked out all sight, but not sound, of what was happening outside. Petrified, Morfia watched as the dead man's knees finally gave way and he toppled slowly towards her, the liquescent mass of what had been the contents of his skull spilling from his head to fall with a wet, slapping sound. Only then did she react in horror, screaming and kicking out with both feet in the violence of panic and outrage. Her feet, close together, struck Guillardame's shoulder with great force, and the impact thrust him upright again and turned him around, so that he fell away from her this time, face down onto the bench where he had been sitting moments earlier. She heard the liquid gurgle as his anal sphincter gave way, and then had come a period of time about which she remembered nothing.

When her senses returned to her, the fighting outside was still going on, and she felt herself overwhelmed by panic once again. This time, however, her presence of mind had returned to her sufficiently to allow her to fight off the waves of helplessness and look about her for some means of defending herself.

The hilt of Guillardame's dagger was right in front of her, thrusting up from the belt about his waist, and she grasped it and pulled it free just as her carriage was rocked violently by a heavy impact that sent her reeling against the side of the vehicle. As she sprawled there, arms spread in the angle of the corner but still clutching the dagger in one hand, an arm came through the window across from her and wrenched the curtain from its mounting, revealing the leering, black-toothed face of the man who had leapt up onto the carriage and was now assessing her, savoring his prize.

Morfia pushed herself upright and gripped the dagger more tightly, preparing to launch herself at the fellow the moment he made any attempt to pull open the carriage door or come closer to her, and her breath caught in her throat as she saw his clawed fingers reach for her, even although she knew he could not possibly touch her from where he was. And then, more quickly than it took her to realize what had happened, he was gone, bludgeoned away and ripped backward into death by a trio of small, heavy, spiked metal balls attached to chains that smashed into his head and shoulder with lethal force. She saw the balls strike. One of them crushed the side of his face, another his cloth-bound head, and the third hit high on his shoulder, but they hit as one, producing only a single violent crunching sound. She felt another surge of nausea, but fought it down, grimly determined to do whatever might be necessary to save her own life from then on, and then she saw a gauntleted, mail-clad arm beneath a bright blue surcoat, reaching in to grasp the pillar of her door, and the carriage lurched yet again as another man transferred his weight to her wagon and thrust his head into her window.

He was a young-looking man, wearing a flat metal helm over a hood of mail that framed a deeply tanned face with a short-cropped dark beard and blazing blue eyes that went wide with shock when he saw her gazing at him. He hung where he was, face to face with her for long moments, then turned away and looked back over his shoulder at what was going on behind him.

"Your horses are dead, my lady," he said, not quite shouting at her, "so I can't take you away to some place safer, and it's too dangerous here to risk your life on my horse's back, so I will stay here and watch over you for a while. Jubal!" This last was a bellow, accompanied by a sweeping wave of the arm to attract another's attention, as her savior released his hold on the door and dropped to the ground, his back to her. "Jubal!" It obviously worked, for as she moved forward to look down at him, the knight cupped his hands about his mouth and shouted, "Here, to me, with three others!"

He turned back to where the Queen had approached the window and was gazing out at the carnage surrounding them. The fighting had moved away, but there were still knots of men fighting, it seemed, wherever she looked.

"My man Jubal will be here directly, my lady, and he will see that you are kept safe until we have finished here." The man came hurrying up as the knight spoke, followed by three others, all of them identically dressed in plain brown fustian over serviceable mail. The blue-coated knight turned to him. "See to the lady, Jubal. Keep her secure. I'll be back." He glanced back at the Queen and raised a knuckle to his helmed forehead, then swung away and caught his horse's reins. A moment later he had mounted and was spurring towards the now distant fighting.

Morfia felt empty inside, as though her vitals had

been scooped out without warning; her mouth was bone dry, her tongue stuck to its roof. She tried to swallow but could not, and as the first stirrings of reaction welled up in her, the man called Jubal muttered something to his three companions and stepped forward to pull open the door of her carriage. His eyes went wide as he saw the bloody corpse, and his nostrils wrinkled as the smell reached him.

"Ugh!" he grunted, waving a hand in front of his face, "We'll have you out o' there, milady, right this minute. Take my hand and I'll help you down."

Born and raised in Armenia, Morfia had never been to France, but she had been married to a Frank for many years now, and something in the way this man spoke sounded strange to her ears, although his speech was fluent and authoritative. She guessed that he was not originally from France. She grasped his proffered hand, feeling the thick ridges of sword-worn calluses on his palm and fingers and reflecting, almost unconsciously, that she had never in her life taken the hand of an underling so gladly or willingly. She stepped through the door and balanced on the step there for a moment, trying not to look at the body of young Antoine de Bourgogne on the ground, kneeling obscenely forward and prevented from falling by the broken shaft of the spear that had killed him. Feeling the nausea flicker at the back of her throat again, she closed her eyes tightly, took a deep breath, and then opened them again and stepped down. The big man beside her kept a firm hold of her hand until he was sure she would not fall, and then he released her. His three companions stood with their backs to her, facing outward at different angles, their swords in their hands, shields braced on their free arm.

"Ector, where are the horses?" Jubal's voice was quiet, but filled with tension, his eyes moving constantly as he squinted into the distance, anticipating a direct attack. The man he had spoken to raised his shield arm and pointed off to their left, where a knot of four horses stood together, ground-tethered by their trailing reins.

"Aye, right. Well, we'll just walk over there and get them. Keep your eyes skinned. This would not be a good place or a good day to die, so let us take pains not to do that. Milady, are you able to walk with us, across to those horses yonder?"

Morfia nodded, still not quite able to speak, but she was feeling stronger by the moment. The four men surrounded her, and they began to walk in a tight knot towards the horses, and Morfia was both pleased and surprised to discover that she was still clutching Guillardame's dagger. She was less pleased to discover that the skirts of her gown were plastered against her legs, cold and wet, rubbing heavily and unpleasantly against her thighs as she walked, and remembering what it was that had landed in her lap, she forced herself not to look down. No matter how steadfastly she tried to ignore the sensation after that, however, her imagination was engaged by it, and she could actually feel the glutinous mass of bloody matter slipping slowly down towards her knees, until her imagination flashed a picture into her mind and she could bear it no longer. With a moan of disgust, she dropped to her knees, her stomach heaving, and pulled the clinging fabric away from her skin with both hands, dislodging the mass of unpleasantness there and then scrubbing at the stained cloth with handfuls of sandy soil while her four escorts stood gazing steadily down at her.

When she had finally stopped retching, the man called Jubal stretched out his hand wordlessly and helped her to her feet. She drew in a deep, shuddering breath, and began walking slowly but steadily towards the horses. And as she walked, secure among the four thickset men surrounding her, she set her teeth grimly, reminded herself who she was, and began to reconstruct her normal persona.

She was Morfia of Melitene, now Morfia of Jerusalem, wife of the most powerful man in Outremer: Baldwin the Second, newly crowned King of Jerusalem, who until only a year earlier had been Count Baldwin le Bourcq, lord of the County of Edessa, far to the north of Jerusalem and close to the Armenian city of her birth. The first King Baldwin of Jerusalem had been the brother of Geoffroi de Bouillon, the Champion who had led the victorious Frankish legions in the First Expedition to the Holy Land, and he had ruled for eighteen years, after which, when he had died without an heir the previous year, the kingship had gone to Morfia's husband, his namesake and closest relative.

Morfia had married her Baldwin in 1102, soon after he had become Count of Edessa, and had since borne him four surviving children, all of them daughters. The eldest, Melisende, had been born in 1105 and was now fourteen, and the youngest, Joveta, had not yet reached her seventh birthday. Morfia had been a good and loyal wife and mother, and she had greatly enjoyed being the wife of the widely admired Count of Edessa, but no one had been more surprised than she when they offered the kingship to Baldwin on the death of his cousin. And now she was Queen of Jerusalem, consort to an inexperienced but determined King whose realm was being threatened by an alliance of the same Seljuk Turks the Franks had defeated in 1099. Her rank and title were very new to her, and she was acutely conscious of the responsibility that went with them. And now that she had begun to believe she would not be required to die that day, she felt a determination swelling in her to force her husband to do something about the disgraceful situation on the roads of his kingdom.

They had reached the horses, and as Ector and another man gathered up the animals' reins, Morfia looked about her at the carnage that surrounded them. She had set out on this journey with a large escort, more than twice as large as she would normally have taken, purely because Baldwin had insisted on it. Her destination had been al Assad, an oasis less than ten miles from the city, where King Baldwin I had maintained a pleasure house for his own use and for the enjoyment of friends and visiting dignitaries, and where her own best and oldest friend, Alixi of Melitene, was currently awaiting her. She and Alixi had known each other all their lives, their fathers both Armenian noblemen, as well as trading partners and comrades since their own boyhood, and Morfia had named her second daughter, Alice, in honor of Alixi. She herself had been confined to bed for several days after Alixi's recent arrival, suffering from an ague of some kind, and, unwilling to be seen at less than her best, she had decreed that her friend and several other guests should go ahead of her to the oasis and enjoy themselves while they awaited her there.

The oasis at al Assad had always been a safe place in the past, justifiably famed for its beauty and tranquility, but a credible report had come to the King, on the morning of the day before Morfia was to leave to join her friends, that bandit activity appeared to be strongly on the increase in the region surrounding the oasis, although there had been no activity indicating brigands at or near the oasis itself.

Morfia, cured of her ailment and quietly determined to enjoy the next few days away from the demands of her children, had laughed at Baldwin's concern when, after reading the report on the brigands, he immediately began to fret over her travel arrangements and her safety. Her patience wearing thin after a few hours of listening to his fretting, however, she had begun to grow angry at what she saw as his silliness, until, in a burst of fury that astonished and silenced her, the King had decreed that either she would take a greatly increased escort with her or he would place her under open arrest within the palace.

She had bowed to his anger, swallowed her own, and

taken the larger escort. And now they lay scattered everywhere around her on the rock-strewn sand, inert piles of
bloody rags that were twisted, unnaturally sprawled men,
the majority of them dressed in the heraldic colors of the
Kingdom of Jerusalem. There were others among them,
it was true, brigands identifiable by their clothing and
weaponry, but even a woman who knew nothing of
fighting could see plainly that the attackers had suffered
far less in the assault than had her defenders. Now, as
she scanned the battlefield, she saw that the fighting
appeared to be over. The last of the enemy had vanished
or been killed, and most of the men she could now see
converging slowly on the spot where she stood with Jubal
and the others were unknown to her. She saw a few of
her own men among them, but the others, with the
exception of two knights in blue surcoats, all wore the
same plain brown fustian tunics as Jubal and his three
companions, and she turned towards Jubal, frowning.

"Who are you men? I have never seen any of you
before. Where have you come from?"

Jubal turned to gaze at her, his face expressionless.
"We are from here, Lady, from Jerusalem. We were on
our way home, at the end of an uneventful sweep, and
we saw you by the merest chance from over yonder." He
pointed to a low ridge in the middle distance, perhaps
three miles from where they stood. "We saw sunlight
reflected off your weaponry and stopped to look, and
then, because we were looking down from above, we
saw the others approaching you from behind your backs,
over there." He pointed in a different direction. "We

knew you could not have seen them, and we knew, from their numbers, that you would need help, and so we came. But they reached you long before we could." He shrugged wide shoulders. "Nevertheless, we arrived in time to save you, milady, so that is a blessing. Here comes Sir Godfrey. He commands us."

"But who *are* you?" Her voice was brittle with tension, and he looked at her in surprise, as if she ought to know who they were.

"I am Jubal, milady, of the Patriarch's Patrol."

The Patriarch's Patrol! She had heard the name, of course. Everyone had, by this time, although she had heard of them first from Baldwin. The name had originally been pejorative—a slur bestowed disdainfully in jest at the very outset of things, when the word first emerged that the Patriarch Archbishop had acquired the services of a small band of veteran knights, to whom he had granted the privilege of taking monkish vows in return for dedicating their lives, service, and fighting skills to the Church in Jerusalem in the protection and defense of pilgrims and travelers.

It had been cause for great hilarity at first, this matter of knightly monks or monkish knights. The Knights of the Hospital were healers, not fighters, their "knighthood" granted simply to give them status for the purpose of raising funds for their work. But these newcomers were being spoken of as *fighting* monks— military clerics! The initial mirth had swelled when it was learned that there were only seven of these foolish people in the beginning. Seven elderly knights—for in this instance, the term "veteran" had been taken instantly by everyone to mean venerable—undertaking to patrol and pacify all the roads in the Kingdom of Jerusalem. The mere idea was ludicrous.

Everyone agreed, however, that there was a grave need for something to be done, for the most recent and outrageous incident had seen a daylight attack on a large party of pilgrims and other travelers almost within sight of the city walls of Jerusalem. A huge band of marauders had killed in excess of three hundred pilgrims and taken more than sixty prisoners to be held for ransom. The King had steadfastly refused to become involved in seeking retribution, claiming, as he always had, that pilgrims and travelers were no concern of his and that common sense dictated that he needed to keep all his forces where they would do most good in the event of an invasion by the Seljuk armies that were massing on his borders. The Patriarch had been, everyone agreed, at his wits' end, and most people conceded that he had then acted out of desperation in this matter of the veteran knights, clutching at whatever straws he could see bobbing on the surface of the waters. *But still,* people said disparagingly, *seven elderly men ...*

And then reports had begun to drift in from the desert roads, amazing, awe-stricken tales of small bands of efficient, fearsomely skillful mail-clad warriors wreaking havoc on any brigands foolish or unfortunate enough to come within their ken, then ruthlessly hunting down and exterminating those who thought they had been fortunate enough to escape retribution.

The activities of the brigand bands had quickly become less scandalously visible, and daylight attacks had ceased almost completely within weeks of the first appearance of the new force, so that nowadays, several months later, most of the roads in the kingdom, although certainly not all of them, were clear of threats to travelers, and the only raids reported anywhere in the kingdom were those carried out by large, organized bands like the one that had struck Morfia's party this day.

People had long since stopped laughing at the Patriarch's Patrol. The name had gone from being an insult to being an honor.

Now Morfia stood watching the leader of this particular patrol approaching her. His brow furrowed in thought, he was clearly unaware of her presence, and Morfia of Melitene was not accustomed to being unnoticed. She stepped forward and placed herself right in front of him, staring directly into his startlingly vivid blue eyes, and she saw them flare in surprise as he reared back.

Elderly? she thought. *This fellow is not elderly. He is mature, but there is nothing old about him. And see how he looks me up and down. Covered in blood as I am, I must look monstrous.* She spoke up, forcing him to look up from her stained clothing and meet her eyes.

"I wish to thank you, sir, for my life. I am deeply in your debt, and my husband's gratitude will, I promise you, be no less than mine."

A tiny tic appeared between his brows and deepened

into a frown. "I would gladly forgo his gratitude and yours, my lady, were your husband to undertake never to do anything so foolish as to allow you to travel these roads again without a much larger escort."

Her head snapped up in indignation, although she knew he was right. "You are insolent, sir."

His frown deepened, and he made no pretense of seeking to placate her. "Is that so, my lady? From gratitude to hostility is not a long journey in your world, it seems. Had we not come upon you when we did, you would have been taken by this time, probably alive, and would now be begging and praying for death. If you think me insolent in saying that, take you a look about you at your dead."

One of her knights stepped forward, chopping his arm in the air to cut the other short. "Enough, sir," he snapped. "How dare you speak thus to your Queen!"

Godfrey barely glanced at the man who had challenged him, but his eyes widened again and he repeated her title, pronouncing it slowly and turning it into a question. "My Queen?" His eyes swept her again from head to foot, taking in the condition of her clothing and, no doubt, the disarray of her hair, and probably, now that she came to think of it, her dirt-encrusted face, doubtless smeared with blood from her sticky fingers.

"Aye," the King's knight snapped, "the Lady Morfia of Melitene, wife to King Baldwin and Queen of Jerusalem. Kneel and salute her."

The man Godfrey turned his head slightly and looked at the fellow in obvious disdain, then ignored him completely, turning back to the Queen without another glance at the flushing knight.

"Your pardon, my lady. Had I known who you are, I would have been less vocal with my criticism. But what I said is true, none the less."

Morfia inclined her head. "I know it is, Sir Knight. I took offense where none was offered. Might I ask you for your name?" Morfia smiled her widest, most effective smile at him, and the knight nodded.

"Aye, my lady. I am Godfrey St. Omer ... or I *was* Godfrey St. Omer. Now I am plain Brother Godfrey."

The Queen smiled again. "I understand your difficulty. For many years I was Countess of Edessa, but now I am Queen of Jerusalem. These titles require ... an adjustment before they become familiar. Well then, Brother Sir Godfrey St. Omer, if you will call upon me at the palace, I shall be pleased to express my gratitude, and that of my husband and my children, more formally, and more graciously. When may we expect you?"

The knight drew himself erect and held his clenched right fist to his left breast, nodding his head in salutation as he did so. "Forgive me, my lady, but I fear I may not do that. I am a monk now, and albeit but a novice, I am bound by anticipated vows that preclude me from commingling with women, even when those women are gracious and queenly—" He hesitated, then continued, with the merest hint of a smile. "Or perhaps that should be *particularly* when those women are gracious and queenly. Nevertheless, I appreciate the thought of it." He glanced about him, unsmiling now, then nodded again. "Now, if you will permit me, I shall organize some horses and a conveyance for you—since the carriage in which you came is unfit for use—and we will escort you back to the city ... Presuming, of course, that you wish to return there, rather than continue your journey."

Morfia nodded. "You are correct, sir. Foolish to continue when so many of my escort have been killed. I shall return to my husband. You may continue with your arrangements."

A moment later he was gone about his business, and Morfia was left alone to wait while her rescuers organized the means of leading her safely home to her family. She was far from unhappy or impatient over being left to her own devices, however, for she had learned, chillingly and with appalling clarity, that when churchmen said *in the midst of life, we are in death,* they were being literally truthful. Her own survival of the slaughter that had just occurred was a small miracle that she clutched warmly yet still hazily within her own awareness, taking note of the marvels all around her, now that her life was safe. She was also aware of a need to think about doing something concrete to reward these people who had come to her aid so selflessly, these warrior monks who sought nothing in the way of reward. Although she had uncaringly accepted the common belief that the veteran patrolmen were incompetent and inconsequential, now she owed them her life, and she would never again permit anyone of her acquaintance to demean them or treat them with disdain. Only a fool, she now knew beyond dispute, would accept the opinions of others about anything without making some attempt to determine the truth of them for herself, and Morfia of Melitene was no fool.

TWO

The twin entrances to the stables that had been bequeathed by the King to house the Patriarch Archbishop's new peacemakers were barely discernible as entrances to anything, unless you knew what you were looking for, St. Omer thought as they came into view, but even so, they looked strangely deserted, the only visible signs of life being the slow milling of the small herd of horses in the railed paddock close to the ancient southern wall. As he drew closer, however, his eyes adjusting to the glare reflected from the blank stone walls, he made out the shape of a single man, sitting on a leather-backed chair by the larger of the two vaguely rectangular openings. With his chair tilted back against the wall, the fellow looked as though he might be sound asleep, but he was wearing one of the same unremarkable brown fustian tunics that St. Omer's companions wore, and they all knew he was on guard duty, set there to ensure that no one who did not belong there would set foot in or even near the stables.

Even close up, the stable entrances looked nothing like doorways. They were merely holes knocked out of the walls that had been built across the wide front of an ancient cavern at the southwest corner of the

Temple Mount to create a storage space of some kind. They were neither regular nor similar to each other, and looking idly at them, an observer would see only two gaping black spaces, ragged edged and unworthy of notice, because above them, dwarfing them into insignificance, soared the great landscaped mound topped by the former al-Aqsa Mosque, the site of the Dome of the Rock, one of the three greatest shrines of Islam, along with Mecca and Medina. Since the capture of Jerusalem in 1099, the magnificent al-Aqsa had been desecrated and profaned, converted into a royal palace to house the Christian kings of Jerusalem, and it was now the home of King Baldwin and his wife, Morfia.

The guard opened his eyes and stood up, yawning and stretching, as St. Omer and his party approached, and then he ambled across and opened the barred gate to the paddock, holding it wide until all the new arrivals had ridden in and dismounted. St. Omer and Gondemare unsaddled their own mounts, but before they could begin to brush them down, they were approached by the guard, who informed them that there was a Gathering in progress among the knights and that they were expected to join their brethren as soon as they returned. As the two knights glanced at each other, the man Jubal took St. Omer's reins from his hands.

"I'll see to the horses," he said. "You two had better join the others. Don't forget to tell them you met the Queen."

St. Omer straightened up, scanning the other man's face for humor, but Jubal's expression was unreadable.

"Thank you, Jubal, I will not forget," St. Omer said, and nodded to Gondemare to accompany him into the stables.

Both entrances gave onto the same broad common space, but a little way inside, the remnants of a second wall, a weather barrier built of mud bricks and showing evidence that it had once contained two sets of wide wooden doors, stretched laterally, and from its midpoint another, at right angles to the first, divided the enormous area into two sections. The ceiling was high, perhaps the height of two tall men, and carved out of the rock itself, but it sank lower, in a gradual arch, as it extended to right and left. The whole interior smelled of hay and horses, and the space on the right of the dividing wall contained individual stalls that were now being rebuilt after being unused for many decades, while the section on the left had already been partitioned into simple living accommodations, with truckle cots, a few rudimentary tables and chairs, and several other crude pieces of furniture.

At the very rear of this living section, farthest from the entrance, a high, solid old wooden partition with a single narrow door divided the room again, laterally this time, and provided space for the monks to meet and pray in private. Another solitary guard stood in front of that door, this one a knight with no visible escutcheon, dressed in a simple white surcoat over a full suit of mail. He drew himself upright as soon as St. Omer and

Gondemare stepped through the main entrance and stood watching them until they stopped directly in front of him, at which time he asked them, in a formal, stilted voice, the reason for their being there. Each man in turn then stepped forward and whispered something into the guard's ear, after which he nodded and relaxed visibly.

"I'm always afraid someone's going to forget the watchword," he murmured, keeping his voice low. "It's been too long without regular Gatherings. Good to see you fellows safely back. Did you have any fun?"

St. Omer took off the belt supporting his sheathed sword and laid it on the ground at the other man's feet. "Aye, we did, at the last minute. Broke an attack earlier today, less than five miles from here. Big group, too." Beside him, Gondemare was straightening up from laying his weapons down beside St. Omer's. He nodded towards the closed door. "What's happening in there?"

The guard, Geoffrey Bissot, shrugged. "Your guess is as good as mine, but whatever it is, it was important enough to call for a full council meeting. I'll find out what's happening eventually, but a new man arrived today, so I know it has something to do with that. André de Montbard. D'you know him?"

Gondemare shook his head, but St. Omer said, "Aye, I know him ... at least, I used to. Haven't heard of him in years, not since I was a tad. Where did he come from, do you know?"

"Straight out from France, by the look of him. A damsel. Arrived today, in the middle of the afternoon, and Sir Hugh sent out word immediately for everyone to gather. They only started a short time ago, not even half an hour, so they'll still be in the ritual. Hold on, I'll announce you."

He unsheathed his dagger and turned to pound its hilt on the door, and when it opened in response to his summons, he saluted the inner guard, then stepped inside and announced the newcomers by name, Sir Gondemare of Arles and Sir Godfrey St. Omer. No mention of their monkish titles. Both men then entered the candlelit space, and Bissot closed the door behind them and returned to his guard duty.

In spite of the glow from many lamps and candles, it took St. Omer a few moments before he could see clearly enough to identify the various people gathered in the shadowed depths in front of him, but eventually he saw Hugh de Payens standing in the eastern corner of the long, narrow, rectangular room, dressed in the black-and-white regalia of their Order of Rebirth in Sion, and he bowed deeply towards him and offering the traditional greeting of the latecomer to the Gathering. Beside him, Gondemare did the same, repeating the greeting word for word. De Payens inclined his head formally in acceptance of their salutations, and as he did so, the man on his right, whom St. Omer now recognized as a much-aged version of the André de Montbard he remembered from his boyhood, inclined his head, too, in welcome. De Payens then held up his hand in a signal to the two newcomers to remain where they were, and launched into the closing prayers of the Gathering ceremony. Everyone waited in silence, heads bowed, until the closing exhortation, "So mote it be," which they repeated, and then they relaxed and began to make themselves comfortable, sitting on whatever they could find, some on crudely made three- and four-legged stools, others on logs and soot-stained fireside boulders. De Payens himself seated André de Montbard on the single wooden chair they owned, then turned to address his fellows.

"Our visitor brings word from home, brethren, and so I think he should speak first, since none of us knows what that word may be." He turned to Montbard. "Sir André, will you address us?"

De Montbard twisted in his chair and looked around the room until he had met the eye of each of the six men surrounding him, and when he had done so, he rubbed the ridge of his long nose between finger and thumb.

"Well," he began. "I have no great amount of things that are new to tell you, but yet I have much to say, and much to learn from you, so let me begin by offering the blessings and good wishes of Count Hugh of Champagne, Seneschal of our Order, and also those of the Governing Council. My primary mission is to inform you that Count Fulk of Anjou, who was supposed to visit you within the year, will not be able to come. The Count has pressing concerns that will keep him close to home this year, but he hopes to have all of them resolved in ample time to enable him to come next year."

He looked about him again, then waved a hand to indicate the room in which they sat. "I must say now that this astounds me. All of it astounds me—what you have achieved, what you have done, the brief time, slightly more than a year, within which you have been able to do it. And still I do not know what you have really done ... What *have* you done, in truth?"

De Payens barked a deep laugh. "We've become monks, complete with shaven heads."

"Aye, I see that. But yet you are not, are you? You have not really taken up the cloth."

"No, not really. We remain novices. We have not yet finalized our vows. But we are in training, committed and dedicated to undertake those vows, in all solemnity, when the time is right."

"But why, in God's name? Why did you think it necessary to do that?"

"Because God's name was the only thing we could imagine that would afford us even a minor chance of carrying out the impossibly wrong-headed instructions we last received from France. As monks, quartered here *in situ,* we have at least an opportunity to try."

"Well, certainly the orders you received were foolish and impractical," de Montbard replied. "That is a large part of my reason for being here, sent out to modify those instructions after examining the facts of your situation. You should understand that Count Hugh knew nothing of what had been demanded of you. The instructions you received through Gaspard de Fermond were issued and dispatched without the Count ever having set eyes on them. None of the Councillors responsible for issuing the commands had ever visited

Jerusalem, as you must have guessed. Now please, if you will, tell me the entire tale of how you came to be here, ordained as monks and living in these ... stables."

Half an hour later, he knew everything there was to know about the brotherhood's activities in Jerusalem within the previous year, and when de Payens finally fell silent, de Montbard sat without speaking for a while, shaking his head in admiration and wonder, before he began to ask questions.

"So, you said the Patriarch anticipated thorny problems in convincing the King to grant this petition of yours, but he obviously overcame them. What did he do?"

Godfrey St. Omer grunted, then spoke up in the clear, dry tones that bespoke his keen intellect and education. "He did the simplest thing possible. He told the King precisely what we were hoping to do. But he did it in such a way that Baldwin immediately saw the advantages to himself in what was being proposed. As King and Commander in Chief of the Army of Jerusalem, threatened with invasion from all sides, he had always refused to deplete his defensive forces in any way—but we were not, strictly speaking, in his army, you see. We had liege lords of our own to whom we owed our primary fealty, while they in turn owed theirs to him. Therefore, being the King, he could assert his authority over them by removing us from their governance legitimately, in the name of Mother Church, while making sure at the same time that his own reputation would profit from his taking an action—a salutary, revolutionary action—that everyone would clearly see as a solid step towards the destruction of the brigands who were glutting on the pilgrims and travelers." St. Omer waved a beckoning finger to de Payens, who took over smoothly.

"Baldwin is no fool, and we appreciated that going in, and presented our case with that clearly in mind. He appreciated at first glance that we would *cost* him nothing, and that he had nothing to lose by allowing us to do what we wished to do. At worst, he decided, we would be ineffectual, but we would still provide a visible military presence on the roads that he could point to as proof that he had made an effort. At best, on the other hand, and still at no cost to him, we might achieve at least a lessening of the pressures on the road system and the pilgrims. And so he gave us his royal leave to bind ourselves to the Church, as warrior monks—monastics—our primary fealty transferred to Archbishop Warmund and our mere existence enhancing his own reputation as a sagacious king and leader."

"Warrior monks ... I am amazed that the Pope would permit such a thing."

"Out here, brother, Warmund, Patriarch of Jerusalem, *is* Pope, in all but name, and his needs overrode all other considerations."

"And there are how many, seven of you?"

"Aye, seven."

"And will be eight." De Montbard looked around, acknowledging each of them. "I would be honored to join you, if you will have me. Count Hugh has given me his leave to do so, and to remain here in Outremer as one of you if I so wish. Providing, as I have said, that you will have me ..."

Hugh de Payens smiled. "Why would we not? You are already one of us, bound by the same vows—save that you will need now to swear a vow of chastity, in addition. Will that deter you?"

De Montbard grinned back at him. "At my age? Not in the slightest. My wife died six years ago, and even before that, the fires had cooled. No, a vow of chastity will neither vex nor perplex me. But ... But you have others here, among your number, who are neither knights nor brethren of our Order. I saw six of them, at least, when I arrived this morning, all of them dressed alike, in plain brown tunics and chain mail. Who are those men, and what function do they serve?"

De Payens turned to St. Omer. "Godfrey, would you like to answer that? It was your idea to conscript them in the first place."

"Aye." St. Omer rose to his feet and nodded towards Montbard. "Good day to you, Master de Montbard. You will not remember me, but I recall you clearly from my boyhood, when you used to come visiting my father, Henri St. Omer of Picardy."

De Montbard nodded graciously. "I remember your father very well, Master St. Omer, although I fear I have no memory of you."

"Nor should you. I was but a boy when last I set eyes on you, and you were already a knight of renown." He stopped speaking for a moment, then waved a hand and began again. "Those men you ask about are the main reason for our being able to do what we do. We call them sergeants, and although they be neither knights nor brethren of the Order, we trust them completely because there is not a single unknown quantity among them. They came out here with us, for the most part, when first we set out to fight the Turks, and they have been with us ever since, as servants, comrades, bodyguards, and companions in arms. Their loyalty and good faith towards us and ours is beyond question.

"When we committed to the monkish life, we were obliged to relinquish our former identities and all the heraldic trappings that went with them, and as part of that, we were also required to release all our dependents and followers, for we had renounced the world. Unfortunately, however—and this was something we had failed to consider beforehand—these faithful men had nowhere to go when we did that, and no means of going there, for they were indeed, dependents, relying on us to provide them with everything they required, in return for their strength, support, and loyalty. To our chagrin, we discovered that we had not set them free at all. What we had done was to imprison them without resources, in an alien world from which they could not reasonably hope to escape. And so they refused to be dismissed. They argued, convincingly, that they had been protecting us and underpinning us for many years, and that our taking vows as monks had little bearing on the truth that we would continue to need that support and underpinning, since we did not intend to give up fighting. We were continuing to be knights, as well as becoming monks, and that meant that they ought to be able to continue to serve us in our knightly capacity, if not the monkish one. It was a very persuasive argument, most particularly so when we considered that, if the seven of us were to patrol the roads alone—and it seemed at that time that we might have no other choice—none of us would be able to do any work on our excavations. Hugh?"

De Payens continued. "We spoke to the Patriarch about involving these men as sergeant volunteers and installing them as lay brethren, bound by our prayer schedule and the Rule we would follow, but free of binding vows." He shrugged his wide shoulders self-deprecatingly. "Each of us had at least two such people, a few of us had more, and many of those had people of their own—friends and family, brothers in arms, and veterans who had lost their own knights to sickness or battle. So now we are seven knights—eight, once you join us—and twenty-three sergeants."

"They all look uniform. Where did you find the funds to dress them all the same way?"

"The uniforms were a gift from the Patriarch Archbishop, probably as a gesture to make his contribution to the kingdom's welfare more readily identifiable. We accepted his largesse gratefully, without questioning his motives."

"And what about your vows of poverty?"

"An astute question. We have arrived at a compromise on that, after discussion with the Patriarch. He requires us to maintain ourselves as a fighting force, but, like the King, he has no wish to be responsible for equipping us. He says his diocese cannot afford such ongoing expenditures. Godfrey here took careful note of that and reminded us later of exactly what the Patriarch had said, with the result that we fastened upon his own expression—'*ongoing* expenditures'—and pointed out to him that we ourselves are not without means. In the normal course of things, we would contribute all our possessions to Mother Church upon taking our vows, in return for her complete support. We suggested to the Archbishop, therefore, that we might modify the standard vow of poverty to accommodate our—and his—special requirements here in Jerusalem. Each of us, as monks, would undertake personal poverty henceforth, on oath, but instead of donating all our wealth and possessions to the Church, we would undertake instead to hold all things in common with our brethren, for the good of our fraternity and its endeavors."

De Montbard's eyes were wide with disbelief. "But that is *our* vow—the same vow we all swore on joining the Order of Rebirth: to hold all things in common, for the common good."

"Of course it is." De Payens's grin lit up his entire face. "But we said nothing about that to the Patriarch, and he was happy to accept our suggestion, since it relieved him of any future need to worry about supplying us with armor, equipment, weaponry, saddlery, or horses. And so we are reasonably well equipped, and capable of providing for our own day-to-day needs, so be it they are modest."

De Montbard was shaking his head. "You are amazing, all of you ... And all of you ride out on these patrols?"

"Aye, for the time being." De Payens stood up and stretched his arms widely, grunting with the pleasure of it. "The time will come, we hope, when only the youngest of us, and no more than two or three at any time, will ride out, accompanied by sergeants. That will work well for us."

"Aye," St. Agnan agreed, "it will, because nobody knows or cares which knights ride out, or how often, or where they go, so be it the roads are kept safe. So a few of us will spend most of our time patrolling, while the others spend most of theirs excavating."

"But can you trust these sergeants that far?" De Montbard addressed himself to de Payens. "You have told me you do, and I can see you believe what you are saying, but still, I have to express my strong doubt, since these men are outsiders and know nothing of our Order or its secrets. How will you keep the excavations secret from them? I cannot see that being possible over any extended length of time."

De Payens shrugged, his face untroubled. "We do not yet know, but we *will* keep them secret. We have no intention of allowing anyone not of the brother-hood to suspect, or even imagine, that there are things happening here of which they have no knowledge. That would be sheerest stupidity. So it may mean that the brother sergeants will eventually have quarters separate from ours. That would raise no concerns, since it has ever been thus, we being knights and they being commoners. Now that we are to be monks bound by solemn vows, while they remain lay brethren, the same division will apply. Separate lives and separate quarters. And separate activities—carried out, in our case, in secret."

"What will you call yourselves—ourselves?"

"What d'you mean?"

"You need a name, Hugh, you and your brethren. If you are to become monks, you are going to need a name suitable to who you are and what you do. The Patriarch's Patrol is hardly a proper name for a fraternity of monks."

"What is wrong with it?" Gondemare said. "It describes us well, I think."

"It lacks dignity. You—we—need something more fitting. Something that reflects our purpose."

"What about Knights of the Temple Mount?" Montdidier was normally silent in conference and now he bridled when everyone turned to look at him. "Well that's what everyone seems to be calling us nowadays," he said defensively.

"Is that true?" De Montbard looked around at the others, and when he saw the nods of assent he grimaced and turned back to Payn, shaking his head. "It is a ... straightforward name, I suppose, and one can see how it might become popular, but ..." He grimaced again. "It seems to me that the best thing we can hope for is that

that particular name will simply fade away. It places too much emphasis on both who we are and where we are. *Knights* of the *Temple Mount* ... It could attract undesirable attention to our endeavors. I think we had best forget that one. Does anyone else have a suggestion?"

"The Poor Fellow Soldiers of Jesus Christ." It was Hugh de Payens who spoke this time, and his words attracted every eye in the chamber. The silence afterwards was profound as each man thought about what he had just heard.

"Where did that come from?" de Montbard asked.

"I don't know. The words simply came into my mind."

"It is perfect. What say you others?"

Only Montdidier disagreed. "I think it is hypocritical," he said.

Hugh stared at him. "Hypocritical? How can you say that, Payn?"

"Easily, Hugh, because it is. It's hypocritical of us to use the name of Jesus, and particularly the full name, Jesus Christ, believing what we all believe ... And the hypocrisy of the Church is what appalls us most."

De Payens sighed, sharp and loud. "Crusty, we have been through this a hundred times. We all agree on the importance of the task facing us. We also agree and believe that the Christian Church is an invalid creation. We all agree, further, that only by pretending to conform to the Church's dictates and expectations can we have any expectation of completing our task. And we have proceeded to this point upon those agreements.

This new name conforms to everything we have agreed to do: it will enable us to go about our work without being harried by anyone, and it will lend us, tacitly, an air of probity and trustworthiness. I say we should keep the name. All those who agree, raise your hands."

The vote was six to one, and Montdidier threw up his hands in resignation, muttering that he would withdraw his objection. The name sat well with all the others, every man present repeating it to himself at least once, and when they were finished, they all looked at de Payens.

"So mote it be," he said. "From this day forth, we will call ourselves the Poor Fellow Soldiers of Jesus Christ, and let us pray that through it we may live up to the responsibility placed upon us."

"Amen, so mote it be," came the chorus.

"In the meantime, however, we have other, pressing responsibilities," de Montbard said. "That is why we are here. When do you think you will begin to dig?"

The question evoked a wry grin from de Payens, who rose to his feet and walked towards the middle of the long, narrow chamber. "Come and see this," he said, beckoning with a crooked finger, and de Montbard rose and followed him obediently to where a hole had been dug in the floor. It was a wide but shallow hole, barely three fingers deep, and its bottom had been brushed clean of dirt and dust, showing the exposed bedrock.

"That is what we are sitting on," de Payens said, crouching to sweep his hand across the bare stone. "It is exactly like the stone vaults over our heads. This is not called the Temple Mount without reason. It *is* a mountain. But if there is a ruined temple down there beneath our feet, as our Order's Lore would have us believe, then it must have been dug at great cost, and there is no mention of such a thing anywhere in the scriptures." He shrugged his shoulders and spread his hands. "Until we can discover more about our search—where to set about it, for example—I fear there is little we can do. None of us would have great objections to tunneling through solid rock, if that is what is truly required, but until we know the direction in which to dig our tunnel, it would be sheerest folly to begin."

André de Montbard was frowning down into the shallow depression in front of him, his arms crossed on his chest as he nibbled his lower lip between his teeth, but then he turned on his heel and looked all about him, gazing at the walls as though he could see through them. Finally he turned to de Payens, nodding as though he had arrived at a decision.

"I may have the solution to that. I bring you documents from the Seneschal, and one is a map, copied with great care from the Order's archives. It purports to be a map of the layout of Solomon's Temple, and of the labyrinth of tunnels surrounding it." He held up a hand quickly, to forestall any interruption. "It *purports*, I say. It is a faithful copy of an ancient document, but its age is all that can be warranted. It has belonged to the Order for a millennium, according to our records, but it was ancient long before that and its accuracy has never been tested, as far as we know. I do, however, have it here with me. It is in the long, wooden travel case among my belongings in the other room, and if you have anything similar—a plan or map of the city as it is today—we should be able to compare the two."

"Indeed we should." De Payens was already clicking his fingers for attention. "Montdidier, and Gondemare, bring Sir André's wooden case in here, if you would."

A short time later, all of them were crowded around the table, looking at the chart that had been spread out and anchored with small rocks at all four corners, and for a long time no one spoke, as they all tried to make some sense of what they were looking at, attempting vainly, for the most part, to superimpose the lines of the drawing in front of them upon the landscape surrounding them.

In the end it was Archibald St. Agnan who reached out an index finger to touch the map. "There," he growled. "Isn't that where we are now? Look, you can see the line of the wall, there, and it runs along the dip here, where the wavy lines are. That's where we are now, in the stables."

"There are no stables marked here, St. Agnan."

St. Agnan did not even look up to see who had spoken. "No, of course not. The King's palace isn't shown, either, even as the al-Aqsa Mosque that it once was. This entire place was the temple when this map was drawn. These stables were walled into the cavern later, here in the precincts, after the *new* temple was destroyed and probably after the mosque was built, and that was more than six hundred years after the destruction of that same new temple. When was the original temple destroyed, and how long ago might this map have been drawn, Hugh?"

De Payens shrugged and looked at André de Montbard, who made a wry face and said, "The original? I can only guess ... two thousand years? It must have been at least that long ago. Titus destroyed Herod's temple forty years after the death of Christ, and that was a thousand and two hundred years ago. This map is of *Solomon's* Temple, which was built many hundreds of years before that."

"Well, in the name of all we aspire to, I hope you are wrong, St. Agnan." De Payens's voice was heavy, prompting more than one pair of eyes to glance his way.

"How so? I have to be right, according to what is here in front of us. And if I am ..." St. Agnan hesitated, frowning, then stabbed a finger at the same point. "If I am, we are standing right *there,* at this moment."

"I accept that," de Payens said. "But if you are correct, and we are standing there, we are ... permit me ..." He bent forward and placed his thumb on the point St. Agnan had selected, then stretched his hand to lay the point of his middle finger in the center of what was indicated on the drawing as being the main body of the temple. He held it there, his entire hand stretched widely, and stared at the distance involved, pursing his lips in thought before he continued. "I would say we are at least three score of long paces— strides might even be a better word in fact—three score of strides removed from the outer wall of the temple proper, where we wish to be. And that makes no consideration for our being above ground, while our target is deep below ground."

"Well, what of that?" St. Agnan sounded genuinely perplexed. "We knew from the outset we would have to excavate. That was explicit in our instructions."

No one else said anything, but it was evident from the faces of several of the others, from the way their eyes shifted uncomfortably from St. Agnan to de Payens, that some of them agreed with St. Agnan. Only St. Omer, Montdidier, and de Montbard kept their faces blank, and it was St. Omer who spoke next.

"What Hugh is saying, Archibald, is that the King's palace is directly at our backs, so that the only direction in which we can dig our tunnel is straight down, and then sideways, until we can turn again and strike towards the temple foundations. And the space between us and our target is filled by the Temple Mount. Filled completely by it. If we are to dig a passage underground from here to where we wish to be, it will have to be through solid bedrock, all the way. That will take years, and we have no tools, nor are we engineers."

St. Agnan's ears flushed red as the truth of St. Omer's words sank home to him, but André de Montbard stood staring down at the drawing, tapping one finger thoughtfully against the spot the big knight had indicated.

"St. Agnan might be wrong," he mused. "We may be misreading what is here, but even so, there's no doubting that we are standing on a rock. We need to find out more about this place. We need to know where to dig, and how to proceed. So where will we find more information on that kind of thing?"

There was silence for a time until St. Omer spoke up again, making a wry face. "You are not going to like this, André, but the answer to that question lies within our own archives, at home, where someone clearly should have done more searching than they did before sending you out here. Our Order has more accurate information about Jerusalem and its temple in its archives than any other source anywhere. What happened here in these very precincts is our history, after all, and our ancestors took their records with them when they left, holding them safe against theft, pollution, and destruction. No one—no person, no organization, no entity anywhere—possesses better or more accurate information on this topic than our Order does." He looked about him at his friends and companions. "I should not need to remind anyone here of that, since that is why we are here, after all, and faced with this task."

"But we are *here* and the information we require is back *there*," de Payens murmured. "We can retrieve it, but that will take time, perhaps too much time. So what are we to do in the meantime? De Montbard, have you any thoughts on that?"

"Aye, I have," the other answered. "Two things. The first is to examine all the other documents I brought with me. I have not even looked at them, for Count Hugh told me to deliver them to you privily, and in person, but I know there is no shortage of material. The only thing I actually saw was this chart, because the Count himself was proud of its workmanship and showed it to me before I left—you saw that it is enclosed with several other drawings in its own container. For all I know, the remainder of those documents might contain all the information that we need, because the Count was fully aware of what had been asked of you and what you would be obliged to do about it." He half turned and indicated the case that he had opened to find the drawing they had been studying. Its lid gaped open, revealing a thick leather wallet underlying the long cylinder that had contained the drawing of the temple and several other, smaller charts. "I suspect now that every sheet of parchment, every document and every drawing in that wallet will have a direct bearing on what we are discussing."

De Payens, who had been gazing at the package like everyone else, nodded. "You may be right. We'll go through them all carefully, as soon as we have finished here. But you said there were two things we could do. What's the other one?"

"Verify or disprove St. Agnan's suspicions about the layout of the map, because if he is correct, the treasure we are looking for could lie beneath the foundations of the palace itself ... under the mosque." He ignored de Payens's sharp intake of breath and carried on, muttering in a low voice as though speaking to himself. "If that be the case, our task could be less time consuming. Not less arduous—we would still be tunneling through stone—but we might have less far to travel. Still

requiring years of work, perhaps, but fewer of them ..."
He looked up, his voice reverting to its normal tone.
"We need to find another, more recent map of the city
and locate the temple site on that. Then we can
compare the two and find out exactly what we have in
this drawing. Where would we find such a thing?"

"I doubt that there is one." Every eye in the place
turned to look at Payn Montdidier, who had not spoken
since withdrawing his objection to their new name. He
smiled, nervously, and held up his hands. "If there is," he
continued, "then there are but two places it could be,
and neither of those is desirable from our viewpoint:
either the King might have one in his palace, or the
Patriarch Archbishop might have one in his residence.
No one else would ever have a need for such a thing, and
were we even to ask about it, we would probably fall
under suspicion of plotting something before the request
was fully uttered. But if you want me to, I'll ask some
questions next time I go to the Archbishop's residence.
I have befriended one of the senior clerics there, and if I
give it enough thought beforehand, I might be able to
find a way of asking him a question like that casually, as
though in passing, without arousing his suspicions."

"Good, Crusty. Do that," de Payens said, then
turned to Godfrey St. Omer. "How went your patrol,
Godfrey? Anything of interest to report?"

St. Omer stood up to deliver his report formally, but
he spoke his opening words for effect. "Aye, Master de
Payens. We saved the life of the King's wife today,
Queen Morfia, and she thanked us most warmly."

Having ensured that every man there hung on his every word, he went on to describe the patrol in meticulous detail, omitting nothing.

It had become customary for each patrol leader to report in person to the brethren upon his return to the stables on the Mount, and to answer any questions that anyone might want to ask, because in the earliest days following their formation, when their patrol activities were new and unanticipated by the brigand bands, every sortie had been different and worth studying, and everyone had been highly aware that a lesson learned from one patrol might be of vital importance to a later one. As time passed, however, and brigands grew less and less aggressive in the face of what had rapidly become certain pursuit and punishment, only those patrols that yielded something extraordinary ever occasioned close questioning. The name of Queen Morfia caused a stir on first mention, but once it became clear that nothing serious had happened to her in the course of the attack, the knights quickly lost interest in her. Everyone was acutely aware that the most important business of the day concerned the documents that André de Montbard had brought to them from overseas.

The meeting was adjourned as soon as St. Omer completed his report, the documents were laid out for study, and before the shadows of that afternoon had lengthened into evening, de Payens, St. Omer, and de Montbard, the only three of the brethren who could read with any kind of ease or fluency, had discovered that they had no need of finding a contemporary map of Jerusalem. Almost all of the information they needed was provided, in some form, in the documents from the Seneschal. Hugh of Champagne, in a letter to de Payens written in his own hand, explained how he understood exactly the difficulties that Hugh and his companions would face in carrying out the task assigned to them, and how he had gone to great lengths to supply them with painstakingly accurate copies of every document he could find that had a bearing on the temple in Jerusalem and the site of the treasure for which they were to search. These copies, he reminded de Payens, were themselves made from copies of copies, for the originals were of such great antiquity that they were preserved and protected with great care, hermetically sealed against air and dampness lest they rot or fade or be otherwise corrupted. The copies, however, were as perfect as the expertise of his best clerics could make them, and each had been closely scrutinized to ensure that it matched its original in every detail. He had enclosed two copies of each item, one in the original script in which the information had been set down, and another in the common Latin into which the documents had all been translated after their arrival in ancient Gaul, a full millennium earlier.

By the end of the following few days, the three knights had catalogued and cross-referenced every single item of information in the Count's dispatches, and they had established, beyond dispute, that their target lay, at least partially, beneath the foundations of the al-Aqsa Mosque. A minimum distance of sixty paces separated them, they estimated, from their objective in the bowels of the ancient temple, and much of that distance involved bedrock. The lower levels of the Temple Mount itself, they had learned from their reading, were riddled with networks and mazes of tunnels dug over the millennia, but all access to those tunnels appeared to have been confined to the inner precincts of the temple. Only people inside the temple had been able to enter the tunnels, and the temple had been destroyed, its subterranean interior demolished and filled in a thousand years earlier by the Jewish priests themselves, in order to defeat and frustrate Titus's rapacious legions. The new diggers knew that while it was at least conceivable that they might intersect an ancient tunnel in the course of their excavations, and be faced thereafter with merely clearing out the debris that had accumulated since the tunnels were last used, the odds against such an occurrence were incalculable.

Hugh de Payens put the entire situation into words for the other knights at their next official Gathering, while the sergeant brothers were in the city, celebrating a local feast day.

"The situation with the temple—our distance from it—is as we suspected. We are a long way removed from where we wish to be. But there are other, additional considerations that, together with everything else, will make all our lives more interesting in future. We have been poring over the information sent us by the Seneschal, and we can tell you several things with absolute certainty, based upon what we have discovered in the documents he has supplied.

"Prime among those is that the treasure we are looking for is there. We have no doubt of that, and we are confident that we know exactly where it is.

"Unfortunately, the task of finding it, or more accurately, the task of *reaching* it in the first place, threatens to be a labor worthy of Hercules. The rock beneath the temple foundations is honeycombed with passages and tunnels, but there are no known entrances to any of them and we have no way of reaching them by what anyone would think of as normal means. You all know we cannot simply go outside and start digging beside the palace walls, and so we have to dig straight down, through the solid stone of the mountain, from here in our own quarters, these stables." He paused to allow his listeners to absorb that, then added, "We estimate that we will have to dig as far as thirty paces—one hundred feet—straight down, then angle straight inward from there, beneath the foundations of the palace behind us, which we believe are also the foundations of the earliest temple, Solomon's Temple ... perhaps an additional fifty to sixty feet. It will take years, but with luck and strong security, we can do it."

"What d'you mean, security?" Sir Geoffrey Bissot's voice was a low rumble of sound, and de Payens looked at him and smiled.

"Protection, brother. We will have safeguards to ensure that no one from outside will ever come close enough to suspect that we are digging tunnels."

"How will you do that, especially in the beginning? Digging through hard rock with chisels and steel mauls makes a deal of noise. And who do you mean when you say no one *from outside*? Mean you from outside our commune here, or from outside our Order? Because if that last is what you mean, then I agree with Brother de Montbard—our own sergeants will probably be the undoing of all our plans. These are not stupid men, Hugh, and if you think you can gull them into being unaware for years of what we are about, you are deceiving yourself gravely."

"Suicidally so, in fact," de Payens concurred, nodding his head. "But that is not what I am saying at all. We could not disguise the fact that we are digging in the rock, not from our own men. But we could suggest a feasible purpose for our digging, without telling them everything about what we are doing. Say, for example, that we are digging out a subterranean monastery—cells from the living rock—as a penitential exercise to God's glory. We will have excellent reasons for our excavations, I promise you, reasons sound enough to be accepted instantly by our sergeant brethren. But when I spoke of people from outside, I meant exactly that—people from outside our little commune here in these stables. We are an order of monks, or we will be in the fullness of time, and that means we will have removed ourselves from the world. And so the world will have no cause, and no encouragement, to impose itself upon us or our affairs. No one will bother us, and no one will intrude upon our privacy and solitude. As for the noise of steel on steel at the outset, that will be transitory. It will continue for as long as the work continues, but it will fade beyond hearing as the shaft sinks deeper below the level of the floors."

"How wide will this tunnel be and who will do the digging?"

"All of us will dig, and the vertical tunnel will be as narrow as we can make it. Wide enough for one man to swing a hammer and another to kneel and support the chisel bit, and for one or both to ply a shovel in reasonable comfort, but not for much more. We will need driving bars—chisels, Jubal the sergeant calls them—and tongs to hold them with, and heavy hammers, as well as pickaxes and shovels and several other kinds of tools. Once we dig down far enough, we will need hoists and pulleys to raise the debris from the pit floor. But all of that will present itself later, when there is need to know such things."

De Payens stopped then, aware of the silence of his listeners, and looked from man to man, meeting the eye of each in turn before he continued. "We will probably work, initially at least, in shifts of two, for whatever length of time may prove to be acceptable. That is something else that we will learn only from experience. And eventually, as we develop a routine and the shaft sinks deeper, we will need others working at the top, to raise and clear the debris. But, God willing, the work will continue day and night without pause, and throughout the passage of time, we will maintain our schedule of patrols, policing the roads. Patrols will continue without respite, and will be conducted by ten-man squads of sergeants, each accompanied by at least one knight, but sometimes, for effect, by two or more. Thus, the surface work will continue while the subterranean work is being carried out."

Bissot nodded sagely, fingering his beard. "It sounds ... complex."

"It is, and it will be, but not impossibly so, Brother." De Payens straightened up, his gaze taking in the entire assembly. "This is all very new, of course, and everything appears to have come together very quickly, but we have achieved much in these past few days. Our planning is going well, and within the month the real work will begin. In the meantime, our patrols are effective, and it will not hurt our cause to have been instrumental in saving the life of Queen Morfia. Let us pray that our good fortune will continue, Brethren. So mote it be."

THREE

The continuance of their good fortune began the following day with a summons for de Payens and St. Omer to attend the King that afternoon, and when they presented themselves at the palace at the appointed hour, they were admitted to the royal presence without delay, an event so startling in its novelty that both men felt a certain degree of trepidation as they were led into the audience chamber.

Baldwin le Bourcq, King of Jerusalem, welcomed them with extreme cordiality, clasping their hands warmly and dismissing his guards with a request that one of them should send in his wife and children. From the speed with which Morfia and her daughters appeared after that, accompanied by the children's nurse, it was evident that they had been standing nearby, awaiting the summons. The King introduced the two knights to his four daughters, explaining that these were the knights who had saved their mother's life from the Muslim bandits the previous day, and each of the little girls curtsied prettily, dipping her head in turn, as she had been taught, to each of the two knights, whispering her thanks as she did so. Only the eldest, Melisende, at fourteen years of age, gave the impression of sincerity, as befitted a young princess. Her next sister, Alice, at two years younger, appeared sullen and truculent, frowning beneath lowered brows. The two youngest children, Hodierna and Joveta, were typical little girls, with lisps and dimples and appropriate giggles. As soon as the little ceremony was over, their father clapped his hands and shooed them all off with their nurse, smiling fondly at their retreating backs until the doors closed firmly behind them.

Before he could fully turn back towards his guests, de Payens spoke up.

"Your Grace, I must point out that I was not one of the two who rescued my lady the Queen—"

"I know that, Master de Payens, as does my wife"— the Queen smiled and inclined her head to de Payens— "but I saw no point in confusing the children. Two knights saved their mother's life, and they met and thanked two knights. That is all they will remember. Now please, be seated, and Morfia and I will join you."

The knights exchanged speculative glances as they moved to the table the King had indicated, and the royal couple sat and waved to them to sit at the same time. A tray with glass cups and a tall, silver ewer was already in place there, the long neck of the jug beaded with moisture, and Queen Morfia herself poured drinks for them. When they had tasted the deliciously sweet, lemony concoction and praised the excellence of its flavor, the King sat back and cleared his throat before launching himself into what he wanted to say, and de Payens, at least, was well aware of how closely the

Queen was watching her husband, her eyes flickering between his lips and his eyes.

"There are no words, I suppose, to express adequately how much I am in your debt," he said eventually, and a smile flickered unexpectedly at one corner of his mouth. "My wife has impressed that upon me most profoundly. Even without her instructions, however, I should still be sitting here facing you and saying the same thing. Until yesterday, after your people brought her home, I had never really thought about the consequences of losing her—not merely to brigands, but in any way at all. Her misadventure yesterday, and your timely arrival, brought the narrowness of her escape home to me and made me see, very clearly, just what the loss of this woman would mean to me. I am not exaggerating when I say that I have no words with which I could even begin to describe such a thing. And so ..."

It was clear from the tone of his voice that he had paused merely to consider what he would say next, and neither of the men facing him moved a muscle.

"When you and your friends first came to my notice, Sir Hugh, I thought you might prove to be an annoyance and a source of irritation—" He held up a peremptory hand as though he believed that either man might attempt to contradict him. "I have since changed my mind on all of that, because the value of your contribution to our state became obvious very quickly, even to your most virulent detractors. I was never one of those, but in the beginning I was never slow to join others in sharing a jest at your expense. As King of Jerusalem, however, and this is something I know you are well aware of, I have been plagued since the day I accepted the crown and assumed the throne, by the very problem you elected to attack—the brigandage that now seems to threaten the very existence of this state.

"We are surrounded—our kingdom is surrounded—by Mussulman armies, all of them battle ready and poised to attack us. In the beginning, they were all Seljuk Turks and we were not too greatly concerned, for we had already defeated them and cast them out of Jerusalem, in '99. But that was almost two decades ago. Now we are in a new millennium, and we find ourselves being faced by a new breed of enemies, a race of warlike people who call themselves Saracens. We know little of them at this time, but I have no doubt that we are destined to learn more, and that learning will be greatly to our cost. For the moment, I know only that my spies insist the Saracens are out there, in the deserts of Syria, biding their time just beyond our borders. The only thing that keeps them at bay and deters them from advancing against us immediately is the current readiness and vigilance of our own army, and that readiness would be fatally impaired, I believe, the moment I diverted personnel into what I know would be a futile attempt to entrap and fight such an elusive and highly mobile enemy as these brigand bands. Indeed, for all I know, the worst of them may not be brigands at all, but infiltrators sent by these Saracens to pester us and tempt me to do just that—to divide my forces in an attempt to fight them.

"Then you and your people came along and

presented yourselves to de Picquigny, who, although he is a churchman, is none the less an able strategist and a pragmatist with no fear of fighting the good fight. He brought your request to me, as you know, and he pointed out that I could do myself much good, at little or no cost, by freeing you from your knightly duties to your lieges and reassigning you to his authority, providing you would be willing to maintain your fighting skills and patrol the roads.

"That very suggestion shocked me at first. Fighting knights, certainly. That is fitting and as God intended. But fighting *monks*? God's word on that is plain and unequivocal, written in the stone tablets Moses brought down from the mountain: *Thou shalt not kill.*

"But our Patriarch, a devout and holy man, was sufficiently pious and enlightened to discern that God provides His own solutions to threats against His teachings and His Church. I thought about that for a long time and eventually decided Warmund was right, and so I did as he advised.

"But I was strongly motivated by the thought that I could have your services at no cost to myself. I freely admit to you that, had that not been the case, I would never have agreed to release you from your former duties. Now I can see—and again, I emphasize, without need of my wife's prompting—that I was wrong in being so …" He shook his head. "I do not even know the word I need. Cynical? Greedy? Perhaps both."

The King sat back and reached out his hand sideways towards his wife, who took it in her own. "I know you ask for nothing for yourselves, and I know that you intend to undertake vows of poverty. And my Queen has made it very clear to me that she believes you to be utterly sincere in what you are about. But yet I feel that there must be something I can contribute—some way in which I can be of *practical* assistance to you in the work you have undertaken, whether it be in the form of weaponry, armor, or horses. I can certainly extend my protection and patronage to you, and I hereby do so and will have my wishes recorded in writing." He smiled again. "That will at least guarantee that no one will sneer openly at you from this day forth, and that, in turn, will save you from having to sin in fighting against supposedly Christian oafs and louts, simply to defend your honor." He looked from one man to the other then, all trace of humor vanishing from his expression. "Now, is there anything I can do for you, in return for what you did for me in person yesterday?"

De Payens glanced sideways at St. Omer, who looked back at him, shaking his head.

"What? What is it?" the King said at once. "You have something you do not agree upon. Tell me what it is."

De Payens looked at him and shrugged. "Your Grace, it is an internal matter, one that we have been debating now for months."

"An internal matter? Concerning what?"

The other man looked askance again at his companion. "It concerns the stables in which we are quartered, my lord King."

"Ah! Well, that is understandable, they must be intolerable. I will find other quarters for you immediately."

"No!" De Payens blinked at his own vehemence and immediately bowed his head. "Forgive me, my lord, but we are not at all unhappy with our quarters, other than that some of our brethren think they may be too luxurious."

The King became aware of the increasing pressure of his wife's fingers on his own and glanced over at her. She was staring fixedly at him, one eyebrow raised in an expression he knew well from his dealings with her and his children. *Ask him what he means,* it said, louder than words. He coughed throatily and turned back to de Payens.

"Too ... luxurious," he said. "I am not quite sure I understand what you mean by that, Sir Hugh."

"We are very new monks, my lord," de Payens said, "mere novices in fact, and under the sole instruction of Archbishop de Picquigny, and our lives have been ... less than exemplary, in many cases, and decidedly lacking in many of the Christian virtues. And so several of our brethren—there are but seven of us, as you know, although we have an eighth currently wishing to join us—several of our brethren believe that we should be more zealous in our striving for enlightenment and salvation. They believe that our current quarters in the stables are too warm, too comfortable, and too conducive to sloth and idleness and inattentiveness to duty. And so they would seek to alter things."

"To make them less luxurious?" The King was

frowning. "Tell me, man, how in the name of God Himself do they intend to do that?"

Hugh de Payens shrugged his shoulders expressively, giving the impression that he himself could not understand, either. "What they would like us all to consider, my lord, is the undertaking of a truly penitential task. They are proposing that, in whatever amount of time the brethren have, free of duties and obligations, they should all work on excavating a real monastery beneath the stables, in the living rock of the Temple Mount."

"Excavating a real monastery?"

The Queen bent forward, interrupting for the first time. "I think, Husband, if I may speak, that Sir Hugh is talking about digging monastic cells into the rock. Am I correct, Sir Hugh?"

De Payens flushed. "You are, my lady, but if I might make a request, please call me Brother Hugh, rather than Sir Hugh. But you are right, save that we are talking of digging into the floor, rather than the walls."

"You mean tunneling *downward?*" The King was incredulous. "Why in God's holy name would you do that?"

"For the honor of God's holy name, my lord. Monks do that kind of thing. By tunneling downward, we will be increasing the work required, and thereby increasing the penitential value of what we are doing, while at the same time taking ourselves down beneath the level of the warmth and comfort generated by the bodies and the physical presence of the horses and kine in the stables. It would take us a long time, probably years, but eventually we would excavate a central shaft leading to a chapel, and branching out from there, each monk would then dig out and complete his own cell."

"And you believe, truly, that this ... thing ... this endeavor ... would be a worthwhile task?"

De Payens smiled at both royal personages. "Well, it would provide a focal point for our dedication when we are not patrolling or joined in formal prayer. It would keep us from slothfulness and from growing bored."

"What would you use to dig your hole?"

"I know not, my lord. I am a soldier, not an engineer, but one of our people knows. He talks of chisel bars and hammers and tongs, and eventually the addition of pulleys and ropes and carts to take away the debris. I am sure he has all the necessary details in his mind."

"And do you yourself subscribe to this idea as being worthwhile? I had the impression for a while there that you do not."

"Oh no, my lord, not so. I think it is an excellent notion, in principle. But it would be costly to initiate, and for that reason I have not been fully supportive of it. But I certainly have no doubts about the value of the idea."

"And what if you find treasure?"

De Payens managed to keep his face impassive. "Treasure, my lord? Forgive me, but I fail to understand. We would be digging into solid rock."

"Aye, but mayhap not all the time. You might find *something* in all your digging—a hidden hoard of gold or precious stones. Such things happen. What would you do with whatever you found?"

The knight shook his head. "I ... I do not know, my lord. I had not considered anything of that nature."

Baldwin laughed. "Well, I have. Bear in mind two things: you are sworn to poverty, and Jerusalem is mine. Thus, any treasure, be it coin, bullion, or gemstones, belongs to me. I will pay you a portion of it in fair return for your labor. Will you agree to that?"

"Aye, my lord King, and happily, but—"

"Excellent, so be it! Talk then to your man with the knowledge and find out what tools you will require for your excavation. I myself will purchase and supply them, on behalf of the Queen. Is there anything else you can think of?"

"No, my lord. Nothing at all, other than the need to express our thanks."

The King surged to his feet, still holding the Queen's hand and drawing her up with him. "It was our thanks that needed to be expressed, Brother Hugh, and our friendship extended. Should you have need of anything further, let me know immediately." He stopped, peering at de Payens. "What is it? You look as though something else has occurred to you."

"No, my lord, nothing new. I simply thought of the need for privacy. If people hear the sounds of our digging, they might wish to know what is going on. But I suppose they will hear nothing, since we will be digging only within our own stables. There is, however, one additional consideration. We have, as I am sure you know, associates whom we call sergeants. They were formerly our servants and personal retainers, before we became monks, and now they assist us as before, but in a different capacity. They are warriors all, and without them we would not be able to do the half of what we do." The King had been nodding as he listened to this, and de Payens concluded, "But they are lay brethren, not monks."

"I don't follow you. Why should that matter?"

"It does not, my lord, save in one respect. When we finalize our vows, they will have to remove themselves to separate quarters, so I would like to have your consent to build barracks for them, out of the stables."

Baldwin made a harrumphing sound and flicked an imaginary crumb from the front of his tunic. "You have my consent. Build what you need. As for others wondering what you do, let them wonder all they want. I will know what is taking place there and that is all that matters. But you are right in thinking that there is no benefit in causing talk, so let this be a secret between us four. Not a word about digging anywhere, and not a single mention of treasure." He raised a finger to his lips in an exaggerated symbol of silence. "Silence and secrecy, my friends, silence and secrecy. Fare ye well."

The two knights stood and bowed, remaining bent at the waist until they were alone, and then they turned and made their way from the royal residence.

"WHERE DID ALL THAT come from?"

De Payens turned towards his friend, already smiling at the hostility in St. Omer's tone. "I've been wondering how long it would take before you started to jump on me. I counted twenty-two paces from the palace."

"I was being discreet. Didn't want to start shouting at you within hearing of the King's guards. They tend to be humorless about disturbances close to the King's person. Now, will you tell me what that ... that *performance* was all about?"

"What are performances always about, Goff? Diversion, amusement, enjoyment, and focus—always *focus*. But we're still too close to the guards to talk about this. We will discuss it later, with the others."

St. Omer stopped in his tracks, but kept his voice low. "No, Hugh, we will discuss it now, because I want to understand what you did this morning, before we even come close to discussing it with the others. I am finding it hard to believe I heard what I heard."

"Very well, but let's walk over that way, across the courtyard where we won't be overheard ... Now, what do you think you heard me say?"

"I don't *think* anything. I heard you betray our plans to the King."

"Are you sure about that, Godfrey? What did I betray?"

"That we intend to tunnel beneath the rock, into the foundations."

"Oh, I see. I mentioned foundations, did I?"

"Well ... no, you did not ... But I knew what you meant."

"But did the King know, Goff? Did *he* know what I meant?"

St. Omer hesitated. "No … He thought you were talking about creating a monastery out of the rock."

"Now that is strange, because that is exactly what I thought I was talking about, too. And did the King grow angry over my presumptuousness?"

"No, but— Damnation!" St. Omer swung around and raised a pointing finger towards his friend, but then he stood silent, his frowning face working independently of his mind as he thought over what he was about to say, and then his brow cleared, his eyes widened, and he began to laugh. "Damn you, Hugh de Payens, you are the most devious, unscrupulous, and brilliantly deceitful manipulator of people I have ever known. You didn't say or do any of the things I thought you had. And you hoodwinked the King himself as completely as you tricked me."

"Oh no. There was no trickery of mine involved in what you thought, my friend. You tricked yourself by worrying too much about how Baldwin might see into my mind and read my true intentions. I could see that in your face, so I stopped looking at you after a time, lest someone else should see your concern as clearly as I could. And as for hoodwinking the King, I did no such thing. Nor did I lie to him. The brethren had that very discussion I described, about pretending to dig out a monastery. You were there, so you must remember it. We talked about everything I described to Baldwin."

"Aye, I know. I knew that when you were talking about it, too, but I could not understand what you were doing, and I suppose I panicked. But you were astounding, now that I see the truth of what was happening.

You disarmed the King, completely destroyed any possibility that his suspicions might be aroused now by some idle report of unusual noises or activities, and then you convinced him, without even seeming to try, that he should provide and pay for all the tools we will need in our excavations. I simply cannot believe you did all that in less than a single hour."

"Don't forget the treasure."

"Aye, the treasure ... When first he began to speak of it, I was convinced he knew what we were about and was speaking of the treasure *we* are seeking. I thought I might vomit from the fear that sprang up in me. But then I realized he was only talking about ordinary treasure, gold and jewels, and not our treasure at all."

"And he has little hope of our finding anything at all, for even he knows that there are no treasures buried in the heart of solid rock."

St. Omer was frowning again. "What will we do if there should be gold and gemstones among the treasures we are looking for?"

"There will be. The archives speak of it quite clearly, mentioning precious artifacts, temple accoutrement, and jewels of great value. We are seeking a temple treasure, Godfrey. Irrespective of what it may contain for our Order's purposes of knowledge and Lore, it will also contain specie. When did you ever know or hear of a priest or a temple without wealth of some description? But that is a bridge we can cross when we reach it. In the meantime, the King does not really expect us to find anything. He is perfectly content to leave us digging in the stony heart of the mount, so be it we continue to patrol the roads and byways. And so we shall, Godfrey. So we shall. *Now* may we go and share these tidings with the others?"

St. Omer grinned and waved an open hand in an invitation to precede him, and the two men began to make their way towards the southwest corner of the Temple Mount, de Payens whistling quietly and tune-lessly through his teeth.

THE TEMPTRESS

ONE

"The man appears to be indefatigable." The speaker was the Patriarch Archbishop of Jerusalem, and Hugh de Payens half smiled in response, his eyes on the spectacle being enacted in front of them.

"He appears to be," he agreed. "But you, of all men, should know that one should never trust appearances. He will grow as tired as any other man, but the difference you are seeing is that he is far younger than the others, with all the added strength and stamina of youth. Ha! Look at that. He moves like a cat. I wish I had four more like him."

They were watching a contest, a training fight involving five swordsmen, grouped four against one, and the single man, the youngest of them, was making all four of his opponents look foolish and ineffectual. He held a large, two-handed sword with a long, tapering blade that made his adversaries' weapons look puny, and he was wielding it with brilliant mastery, transforming it into a whirling, impenetrable curtain of shimmering movement. Two of his opponents had converged on him simultaneously, one of them catching his blade with his own, while the other seized the advantage and leapt forward to close with him, but even as he did so, the younger man spun nimbly and sprang away, his outstretched foot finding the top of a low wall that had been at his back. For a moment he hung there, his knees bent as he sought balance, and then he leapt away again, doubling the distance between himself and the others before any of them could react to his first move, and when his feet touched the ground again he laughed and grounded the point of his sword, signaling a rest, which his winded opponents were happy to share.

"Well done, Stephen," de Payens shouted as the group relaxed and tried to catch their breath, and the Patriarch turned to him, smiling.

"I can see why you are so impressed, but why should you not have four more like him? And why only four? Why not a score like him?"

De Payens laughed aloud. "Why not? I should have a score like him, as you say, but I never will, because the lad is a phenomenon. He is … he surpasses credulity. I still have difficulty believing he is here and one of us. I mean it, my lord Archbishop, every word of it. Very few young men of his age, perhaps no more than one in five or even ten thousand, possess those fighting skills this one uses so effortlessly. But not one in a thousand of those few, young as they are, and puissant, filled with the rising sap and immortality of youth, could ever be tempted to give up the pleasures facing them in order to take up the cloth and live their lives as monks."

"Aye, I grant you that. The world and the flesh have great attraction for young men. But where, then, did this one spring from? You brought me out here to see him, but you have not even told me his name, or anything about him."

"I inherited him, I suppose." A half smile played about de Payens's lips as he watched the young knight's performance, and he spoke to the Patriarch without looking at him. "His grandfather was my godfather, old Sir Stephen St. Clair. *The* Sir Stephen St. Clair, who invaded England with the Normans in 1066 and later became the trusted friend and close companion of William the Bastard, Duke of Normandy and King of England. You must have heard of him, surely?"

He looked over at the Patriarch, who was shaking his head politely.

"You've never heard of him at all? Sir Stephen St. Clair? That is astonishing. He was reputed to be the man who killed King Harold during the invasion of 1066. St. Clair always denied it, but King William himself claimed to have seen it happen, and swore he won his crown because of it."

"So how does that lead to his grandson's being here in Outremer, and looking to become a monk?"

"Young Stephen's father and I were friends when we were young, not close, but close enough to think highly of each other, despite his being five years my senior. Anyway, Robert married young, to a first cousin of mine, and she bore him the one son, young Stephen, then died soon after, of a virulent pox that killed her and all seven of her women. They were living in the northeast of England then, in one of King William's territorial castles, built to subjugate the local Saxons and keep them obedient to the King's new laws. It was hostile territory and they had no allies within riding distance, so that, in the absence of women, the boy was nurtured and reared by the monks and churchmen his father had brought with him to preach the gospel to the local Saxons. Everyone liked the lad, but his upbringing among monks, as you would expect, made an indelible impression on him. He also turned out to be a spectacular fighter—two sides of a single coin—encouraged and trained by his father's master-at-arms and his cronies, once they began to discern just how gifted the boy was.

"His father Robert's life was a full one, his duties leaving him no time to search for, let alone find, another wife, or even to pay much attention to his son's upbringing. By the time the lad had grown to manhood, he was invincible in the arena and in the lists, but every moment that he spent away from his military training was passed in prayer. His father thought that was unnatural—most fathers would, I suppose. But then there came a twist that worked to my advantage. You may remember that Count Fulk of Anjou came out here to visit us two years ago?" The Patriarch nodded. "Well, when he returned to Anjou, he found Count Hugh of Champagne there, in residence and awaiting Fulk's return. The St. Clairs were there, too, father and son, visiting the family holdings in the region, and at dinner one night, the two Counts talked about our newly formed brotherhood, apparently with great enthusiasm. Sufficiently so, it transpired, to excite

young Stephen's father. Robert recognized me by
name, although we two had not met in more than a
score of years, and it seemed to him that what we are
doing here in the Holy Land would be attractive to his
son, and young Stephen agreed. A short time later,
young Stephen met with Count Hugh, who recruited
him immediately, and the lad was on a ship, outward
bound for Cyprus on his way here, not too very long
after that. He is very young, but it seems he is perfectly
suited to—"

The Patriarch waited for the space of two heartbeats
and then asked, "Perfectly suited to what?" But de
Payens was watching something else, and flicked a hand
at him sideways, warning him to be quiet.

The Patriarch drew himself erect, blinking in mild
indignation. "What? What is wrong? Why did you stop
me?" Even as he asked the question, however, he saw
the answer for himself. A magnificently dressed officer,
flanked by three lesser luminaries, had approached
unseen from behind them and had now passed them,
treading carefully on the rock-strewn, uneven ground,
to where the five former fighters stood talking. The
light blue surcoats adorned with gold acorns identified
the newcomers clearly as royal guardsmen, and the five
knights, who were also uniformly garbed, although in
plain brown surcoats with no heraldic devices of any
kind, became aware of them just as the guardsmen were
about to reach them. All five swordsmen turned to face
the guards, their faces wary and their posture radiating
challenge, and the guards halted smartly about two

paces short of them. Payens and the Patriarch were too far away to distinguish what was being said, but the sound of the captain's voice, speaking to the youngest knight, came to them clearly.

De Payens turned completely around to look behind him and saw an enclosed carriage, drawn by a pair of horses and surrounded by a strong escort of guards. The windows of the carriage were curtained and closed.

"Royal coach," he said quietly, drawing de Picquigny's attention. "Enclosed. Could it be the Queen?"

The Patriarch was looking back now, too, and he shook his head. "No, not the Queen, not today. Her Grace is indisposed. Has been for several days. There is a sickness going around, and she came down with it some days ago. Nothing too serious, but sufficient to keep her in her rooms. And it's not the King, either, for if it were, he would be over here, talking to us. No, it must be one of the daughters. That carriage is large enough to hold all four, but I doubt that any of them would ever consent to spend time in the others' company." He glanced over to his left, where the young knight and his companions were now walking quietly with the captain, flanked subtly by the other three guards. Four of them had sheathed their swords, but the youngest, St. Clair, still carried his in his hand, its long, gleaming blade slanting backward to rest casually against his shoulder as he walked towards the enclosed carriage.

"Alice," Warmund de Picquigny said, a strange note of resignation in his voice. "It must be Alice. She is the only one bold enough to flout propriety so blatantly. Your knight may be in danger, de Payens."

"From the princess?" De Payens laughed. "She is but a chip of a thing, not one tenth his size."

"I did not mean physical danger. I meant in danger of sin. He is in mortal jeopardy and we had best walk over there and do what we can to save his soul. I have no doubt the princess will be ... delighted to see me here."

De Payens could hear the sarcasm dripping from the Patriarch's words, but he had no notion of what underlay that, and he quickly decided it might be best to hold his tongue until he was called upon to speak. He matched his pace to the Patriarch's as de Picquigny set out for the carriage.

FROM THE DIMNESS of the interior, Alice saw the two men walking towards her, but they were far away and she paid them no heed after the first glance, dismissing them as elderly and therefore unworthy of interest for the time being. All her attention was tightly focused upon the young man approaching her, an earnest-looking young fellow with eyes that even from a distance were brilliantly blue, and a slight frown creasing the wide expanse of his forehead.

He stopped as he drew near her coach, and thrust his long broadsword into the ground at his feet, unaware that she was watching him through a tiny gap between the leather curtains. Then, using both hands, he loos-ened the drawstring beneath his chin and pried the close-fitting hood of his mailed tunic away from his skin, before thrusting it back off his head to hang at his back, freeing surprisingly long, golden hair and shaking it out like a dog before scrubbing at it with his fingertips, loosening the sweaty tresses to hang around his ears. That done, he combed the long, damp curls roughly with spread fingers, pushing them back behind his ears, and retrieved his sword, clamping it firmly beneath one arm before striding directly to her carriage.

Alice withdrew hurriedly from the curtains, pressing herself back into the rear corner of the vehicle as she heard one of the soldiers outside preparing to open the door, and then in the flood of bright light, the stranger appeared, his shoulders blocking the doorway, and bent forward to stare into the interior.

"My lady, you wished to speak with me?" His eyes moved over her without seeing her, and she did not respond, knowing that he was temporarily sun blinded and that she was free to look at him as closely as she wished for the few moments before his eyes adjusted to the change in light.

Now, seizing the opportunity while she could, she applied herself to examining his perfection: impossibly blue eyes beneath brows of pale gold and fringed with thick lashes; a mouth formed for kissing, its full, wide lips impeccably arched, its teeth perfectly shaped and brilliantly white; and long, golden, silky hair, falling now in curls about his strong, wide neck as he leaned forward, still unable to see her clearly in the gloom of the carriage. Most knights wore long, full beards, but kept their heads close-shorn for reasons of comfort and hygiene, because they wore their tight-fitting chain-mail hoods most of the time. This man did exactly the opposite, shaving his chin and wearing his hair long. Through vanity? She wondered briefly about that, then thrust the thought aside. If he was vain, that would work to her advantage, because he would be easy to flatter, but for now it meant nothing.

That she had noticed him at all in passing was the sheerest accident, for she had been on her way home from the house of a friend, in a foul frame of mind because her friend had inconvenienced her by falling ill, like most of the other people she knew, and had thereby condemned Alice to a long and boring after-noon of unplanned solitude. As a result, Alice had been riding through the streets in self-imposed isolation, sulking by herself in the darkness of her carriage, the leather curtains tightly laced against the blindingly intrusive sunlight. She had heard the clanging of weapons and a series of high-pitched, laughing shouts as she passed a group of idling soldiery. She had no idea why she should have noticed that particular noise, for she had already passed a number of similar groups along the route. Jerusalem was a frontier state, constantly beset by enemies from outside its borders, and her father maintained a large army in a constant state of readiness for war, which meant that among the most familiar sounds in the city were the clash of weapons and the jeering shouts and laughter of men for whom life was an unending sequence of training sessions, practice fights, and unruly brawls.

Something in the noise generated by this particular group of ruffians, however, had attracted her annoyance, and she had snapped back the curtains and bent forward, fully prepared to vent her anger on them in some way, but even as she opened her mouth to call to her guards, she had seen the man now standing in front of her, and had lost awareness of everything else. Even from a distance, featureless and concealed from head to foot in a heavy hauberk of chain mail, he had struck her as being very different from the common herd. It may have been the way he moved, for that in itself was highly distinctive, but from the moment Alice had first glimpsed him, seemingly flying through the air like a leaping, steel-clad leopard, she had eyes for nothing else.

That first impression, of effortless, soaring grace, had been branded into her memory, and she knew she would not soon forget it. All knights were immensely strong. That was such a commonplace that people had lost awareness of it, for when men fought and trained to fight as long and as intensely as knights did, swinging and wielding long, heavy, clumsy weapons for hours and hours on end, each and every day that came along, they developed gigantic muscles. What they seldom developed, however, was lightness of motion, gracefulness, and agility. Bound by the sheer mass of muscle on their bodies, knights on foot tended to move slowly and inexorably, hunched forward in a crouched, bow-legged stance that lent itself to the style of fighting they knew best, armed confrontation, nose to nose and blade to blade until the best man walked away victorious.

This one was a different breed. Alice had seen him first as a blurred shape, moving very quickly, but almost immediately her eyes and mind had adjusted to what she was seeing and she took note of the four crouching figures who were turning in unison, too late, to pursue the opponent who had launched himself at them and over them, using a low wall as a springboard to propel himself upward and over their heads in a whirling somersault. He landed behind them on flexed legs, then spun nimbly and smacked the nearest of the four across the backside with the flat of his blade before turning yet again and leaping upward, seizing a strut hanging from a nearby roof and hoisting himself up, one handed, onto a window ledge, where he turned, laughing, and waved to his companions, then vanished into the interior of the building.

Alice had called to her driver to halt the carriage, and as the young fighter emerged from the building she ordered the captain of her guards, who was not unfamiliar with the princess's whims, to summon him. And now, gazing at the face of the man she had summoned, Alice was very glad of the impulse that had driven her to look outside.

The fellow blinked hard and scrubbed at his eyes, then blinked again, several times, keeping his eyes as wide as he could hold them.

"May I know your name?" Alice asked him, speaking softly, as though afraid of frightening him away.

"My name? It is Stephen, my lady ... Stephen St. Clair, of York and Anjou."

"Well met, then, Sir Stephen. And do you know who I am?"

The young knight shook his head.

"I am Alice le Bourcq."

He nodded, but it was plain that the name meant nothing to him, and she frowned. "Are you new here? Why have I never seen you before?"

"I know not, my lady. I am not new here, but neither have I been here for a long time. I came nigh on three months ago, to join the brothers of the Patriarch's Patrol."

Alice's eyes widened. "The brothers! Are you a monk?"

"I hope to be one soon, my lady. I am a novice at present, a student of the Rule."

"Rule? What rule is that?"

"The Rule of Benedict, my lady. The way of life followed by monastic brethren, designed by Saint Benedict himself."

"Ah! Of course." Watching him closely, Alice could see quite clearly that, beautiful though he might be, he was something of a simpleton, lacking imagination and even the rudiments of a sense of humor. A puff of dust wafted into the carriage from behind him, its motes shimmering in the slanting rays of light that surrounded his bulk, and she coughed delicately into the scrap of linen she clutched in one hand.

"Please come inside and close the door, if you will. I have some questions for you, and would prefer to ask them without inhaling dust each time I open my mouth."

"Questions, my lady? What kind of questions could you have for me? You do not know me at all."

He really was delightful, standing there wide eyed with innocent surprise, and Alice's mouth quirked in the beginnings of an ironic little smile. "That can be quickly remedied, believe me," she murmured, making him bend farther forward to hear what she was saying. "But I know of your brothers. They once saved my mother's life, and although that was several years ago, she still feels grateful to them and has much to do with them. But I would like to know, among other things, where you learned to fly through the air the way you do, wearing a full coat of chain mail and mailed leggings. So come, if you will, and tell me. Come, sit across from me and close the door against the dust and the bright light."

St. Clair's frown deepened, but then he nodded. He removed the broadsword from beneath his arm and reached into the carriage to prop it securely against the seat on his right before he grasped the pillars of the doorway in both hands to hoist himself inside. Before he could do so, however, a deep voice called out his name from behind him, and Alice saw his eyes widen in surprise as he stepped back, turning to face whoever had spoken. Furious that anyone should dare to interfere or interrupt her, Alice pushed herself forward quickly and thrust her head angrily through the doorway, only to find herself face to face with Archbishop Warmund de Picquigny.

"Princess Alice," he cried, in a voice greatly different from the one that had spoken St. Clair's name. "What a delightful and unexpected pleasure to encounter you here, so far from your home. May I be permitted to ask what brings you out here, and might I be of any assistance?"

He had stepped forward to the edge of her door, and now he kicked down the small mounting steps with one foot while he reached out a hand to support her as the princess, with no choice but to comply, stepped carefully down from the carriage, keeping her eyes downcast as she placed her small feet with great care. She had seen the young knight's jaw drop open when he heard de Picquigny address her by her title, and she was incensed, knowing that he would now be overwhelmed by her rank and station and would consequently be, in all probability, more difficult to seduce. She wanted to spit at the foolish old busybody, but forced herself to smile sweetly.

"Thank you, my lord Patriarch, but I have no need of assistance. I merely stopped to ask Sir Stephen how he was enjoying his stay among the brethren of your Patrol."

"Ah, my Patrol ... Forgive me, Princess, but it occurs to me only now that you may not remember my companion here, although I know you have met him. May I present Brother Hugh de Payens, the founding member of the brotherhood to which Brother Stephen belongs? You first met Brother Hugh on the day after your mother's rescue from the Saracen brigands, several years ago." As Alice raised her head to look at de Payens, the Archbishop reached inside her carriage and retrieved St. Clair's long sword.

Alice had turned the full warmth of her smile on de Payens, who raised a mailed fist to his breast in salute, his mouth twisting slightly into the beginnings of a smile in return. "I remember the occasion very well, Brother Hugh, young as I was," she said, demurely. "I had just mentioned the incident to Sir Stephen. Is that not so, Sir Stephen?"

"It is plain Brother Stephen, my lady." St. Clair's golden skin now bore a deep red flush, probably caused, Alice reflected, by his awareness of how blatantly she was lying and involving him.

"Brother Stephen." She nodded. "Of course, you have renounced the world. I had forgotten."

"Not quite true, Princess," the Patriarch murmured, holding out St. Clair's sword to the young man, who took it, blushing fiercely. "Brother Stephen is but a novice today, but in a short time he will take his full vows, undertaking to renounce the world, and more. He will, in fact, renounce the devil, the world, and the flesh in favor of dedicating his life to God. A wonderful destiny for any man."

Alice managed to retain her smile, although she would wonder for months afterwards how she had been able to conceal the rage seething in her at the old hypocrite's barely veiled insolence. But his disapproval mattered not a whit to her because, powerful as he was, with his Patriarchal Archbishopric and his direct access to her father's ear, he had nothing concrete of which he could accuse her. Forewarned of his suspicions about her sexual conduct years earlier, she had taken great pains to make sure that he would have nothing, ever, to report to her father. She had been very careful and even, latterly, very abstemious. She knew, too, that he had suspicions about her behavior in several other areas wherein their paths occasionally crossed. She resented his suspicions, irrespective of the validity underlying them, but she accepted, too, that there was nothing she could do about them. Not yet, while she was still a powerless princess. Once she was Queen—and she had every intention of achieving that status—matters would be vastly different. Then she would be able to put the old catamite in his place, and with him everyone else who shared his opinions of her.

But for now, faced with a situation in which she could not win, Alice accepted the inevitable and bowed to it. She inclined her head graciously to the senior monk, de Payens, and then to the young one, St. Clair, demurely wishing them both well, and then she turned a smile of purest love and admiration on the Patriarch himself, thanking him for his concern and assuring him that she would pass along his kind regards to her ailing mother. That done, she turned back to her carriage and mounted the steps nimbly, her outstretched hand supported again by the Patriarch Archbishop.

As soon as she was safely inside, de Picquigny stepped back and raised a hand to the watching driver, waving him forward. The horses leaned into the traces, the carriage lurched and then rolled forward, and Stephen St. Clair stood at attention, watching the retreating vehicle as though he could see directly through its walls to the young woman inside. He had never seen anyone so beautiful in his entire life, and he had a picture of her in his mind, bending towards him, one hand bunching a long gold chain that hung about her neck, allowing the heavy gold to slip slowly, link by link, down into the other hand she held cupped beneath it. He knew it was dangerous to allow himself to think of her beauty, and that he should pray for strength to resist temptation, but as he heard the disapproving tone of his superior's voice recalling him to his duties, he knew too, beyond doubt, that her smiling face would be the last thing he would see in his mind before he fell asleep that night.

TWO

Alice, safe in the darkness of her carriage, called to her driver to take her home to the palace immediately, and she spent the entire journey weeping in frustrated fury, seething and burning with the humiliation of being thwarted and defeated and even chastised, albeit subtly, by the Archbishop. She wanted to scream and to throw things, but she contented herself with biting down savagely on a twisted skein of cloth wrung from the wrapping she had worn around her hair, knowing that to give in to her rage would be to entertain the servants and escort around her, who would take great glee in talking about her behavior later. Accordingly, she sat in silence, as taut as a drum skin, viciously twisting the cloth in her hand and imagining all the punishments she would love to inflict on the old Archbishop.

There were few things in her life, and even fewer people, that Alice le Bourcq could not completely dominate and govern, but one of those people was Warmund de Picquigny, and it galled her that it should be so. She had sought to put him in his place once before, two years earlier, when his meddling had become intolerable, but the attempt had been a disaster, provoking a rare outbreak of fury from her father, who had excoriated her publicly, in front of an entire gathering of people. From that time forward, Alice had been extremely circumspect in her dealings with the Patriarch, electing to avoid him completely whenever possible and to ignore his existence as much as she could whenever circumstances placed them together.

Her father was another of the few whom she could not dominate, despite the fact that most of the time it might appear to others that Baldwin was too indulgent of her. Alice simply knew, and had known since infancy, that she dared not push her father too far and would never deliberately defy him. Baldwin was an autocrat, answerable to no one, and his rages, few and far between though they were, were unpredictable, violent, and highly dangerous. There was not the slightest doubt in Alice le Bourcq's mind that her father was capable of murder when he was enraged, and so she trod very cautiously around him.

She knew when her carriage began to climb the slope to the main gates of the royal residence, because she heard and felt the difference when the iron-tired wheels clattered onto the cobblestones, and she quickly scrubbed the last of the tears from her face and swathed her head in the folds of the long silken shawl she had worn around her shoulders. When the captain of her escort opened the door, she sat silent and unmoving until he had kicked down the mounting step, and then she climbed down quickly, refusing the assistance of his arm and keeping her head tightly swathed in her shawl, holding a length of it across her face in the Muslim fashion. She went directly indoors, towards her own rooms, without saying a word to anyone, sweeping silently along the high-ceilinged passageways and up the main staircase to the upper floor and pausing only when she saw the open doors to her mother's rooms ahead of her.

She hesitated there, debating whether to walk boldly by, hoping that there would be no one in the first room, or to turn tail and go back down to the floor beneath, then around to the rear passageway that would allow her to enter her own rooms from the other side. She chose the former option and stepped forward boldly, holding her head high, but her mother's voice greeted her as soon as she reached the open doorway, almost as though she had been waiting for her.

"Alice? Alice, in Heaven's name, child, what is the matter with you? You look as though you have been to war and assaulted by bandits. Come in here at once."

Alice stopped dead, muttering words beneath her breath that would have astonished and angered her mother, then turned and looked into the room beyond the open doors, where Queen Morfia stood gazing at her imperiously, surrounded by her women.

"Mother," she said levelly, nodding her head in a tiny greeting, "I thought you were unwell, confined to bed."

"I was." Her mother's tone was icy with disapproval. "But I am restored, and now feel much better than you appear to be. Where have you been, child, and what have you been doing that makes you so disheveled?"

"I've been weeping, Mother. Tears of rage and humiliation." Alice's voice matched her mother's in coolness, completely devoid of inflection.

"Tears? Occasioned by what, may I ask?"

"Occasioned by life, Mother, and no, you may not ask anything more."

Morfia's face smoothed out in anger and she held her head higher. "You are insolent, and although that is unsurprising in itself, nevertheless it ill becomes you. I suggest you go and bathe the puffiness from your eyes before your father sees you. You may return to us when you have overcome your silliness and can at least pretend to be sociable."

Alice turned on her heel and stalked away to her own rooms, aware that none of her mother's women had so much as glanced at her in the course of that exchange. Not that she had expected any of them to do so. They would not dare, because they had to live in the same house as Alice and they knew better than to antagonize her. They were her mother's creatures, but they had learned that, ubiquitous and all-knowing as Morfia seemed at times to be, they could not always rely upon the Queen's presence for protection from Alice's vengeance if they presumed to be amused by Morfia's treatment of her, even as a child.

Morfia of Melitene was her daughter's nemesis, the bane of her life, although Alice held her mother, albeit grudgingly, in great respect. In truth, Alice considered her mother to be ten times the man her father was, for although it had always been incontestably clear that

Baldwin ruled his County of Edessa with an iron hand when it was needed, Alice had known since infancy that her formidable mother ruled the Count with equal severity. For that achievement alone, Alice had respected Morfia ever since she was old enough to know what respect entailed. But respect was not the same as liking, and although Alice had long since stopped caring, there was no liking between mother and daughter.

She had gone through a period, around the age of ten and eleven, when she had examined everything she did, trying to identify what it might be about her—her appearance, her behavior, or her temperament—that unfailingly brought out her mother's dislike and disapproval, but she had never been able to identify anything, and so she had finally decided that it must have something to do with her physical appearance, her resemblance to her father.

Alice had been born with her father's coloring and features, with golden hair, fair skin, and hazel-colored eyes, and she was the only one of the four siblings who resembled him in any way. The other three all favored Morfia, who, even today, as the mother of four grown daughters, was exotically beautiful, her flawless face and delicately sculpted bones proclaiming her aristocratic Armenian ancestry. From the outset, Alice discovered years later, Morfia had been besotted with her firstborn daughter, Melisende, fascinated with the child's perfection and by the indisputable fact that the infant was her mother in miniature. By the time Alice had been born, eighteen months later, she was already too late even to think about competing with her sibling for their mother's affections. Melisende became a diminutive replica of her mother, dressed in the same colors, a tiny creature of astounding beauty who drew sighs and cries of admiration from everyone who ever saw her. Alice's appearance, on the other hand, was commonplace. She was not unattractive, but beside her older sister she was plain and pedestrian. She was, however, quick witted, highly intelligent, and clever, in the way of her father. And as time passed and she developed the ability to discern such things, she found herself becoming more and more aware that her beautiful sister Melisende had been born with great beauty but little in the way of wit or intellect and was, in fact, a lusterless and boring person.

Soon after, Alice turned her developing powers of critical observation upon others around her, and most particularly upon her mother the Countess. She found the exercise to be enthralling, for she became aware, gradually over more than a year's observation, that her mother was a fascinating person in her own right and eminently worthy of study, particularly when removed from her husband the Count and pursuing her own designs. And Morfia, Alice quickly discovered, had many designs and a wide variety of means that she used in executing them.

Watching her mother put those designs into motion, however, was a far more complicated and clandestine process than the mere word *watching* implied, because

Morfia of Melitene had decided, many years earlier, that what she did within her own personal time was very much her own affair. In public with her husband, playing the dutiful spouse to Baldwin, Count of Edessa, she was the embodiment of *dignitas* and decorum; in more intimate surroundings, with her family and friends, she played the role of caring friend and concerned mother perfectly, winning herself a reputation as a living saint whose entire existence was dedicated to the welfare of her husband and her daughters. In private, however, Morfia was Morfia, and rigidly private to the point of being reclusive in her solitude, and people who knew her otherwise would not easily have recognized her. Alice was quickly forced to realize that if she really wished to watch her mother during her hours of isolation, she would have to do so from hiding, as a spy.

Alice found nothing strange in her mother's behavior; on the contrary, she accepted it as being unremarkable because that was the way that she herself, given the choice, would have preferred to live. Within a very short time, she learned the secrets of every nook and alcove, high and low, in the rooms her mother used, and she could make herself invisible, sitting or crouching or lying silent and unseen in any room in the Count's palace. And over time, as she watched and listened, she came to appreciate that her mother had much to teach her. Morfia, however, had made little effort, ever, to teach her anything. And so Alice became almost slavish in studying her mother's ways, learning and absorbing Morfia's techniques for achieving her designs.

For years, throughout Alice's entire childhood, she had been jealous of her elder sister, Melisende, who seemed to receive all the attention her mother had to lavish on anyone but herself, but as the two youngest children matured, their mother had taken note of their resemblance to herself and had begun to spend more time with them, too, fussing over them constantly and grooming them from earliest childhood to be the wives of wealthy and powerful men. Melisende, Morfia had clearly decided, was already taken care of and would present no difficulties when it came time to find a husband for her. But throughout that time, save for the most superficial scrutiny and unfailing, sharply pointed criticism, Morfia had neglected her second daughter, never seeing or sensing the child's need for affection and approbation, and never suspecting that, through her own neglect, she had bred an implacable enemy within her own family. She noticed only that Alice was constantly sullen and unsmiling, ill tempered and waspish, unpleasant and unappealing to her guests, drably and unprepossessingly dressed, and forever requiring correction and reprimand.

For her part, Alice had decided, by the time of her thirteenth birthday, that her primary role in life must be to confound and frustrate her mother in everything to which she could turn her hand. Since the union of Baldwin and Morfia had produced no sons, she knew that her sister Melisende, her father's legitimate firstborn, was the legal heiress, destined to marry the most suitable future Count of Edessa who could be found. But Alice's contempt for her beautiful, empty-headed sister was so great that she anticipated little difficulty in removing Melisende from contention when the time was right, and replacing her as the future Countess. That decision made, she regarded it within her own mind as an inevitability, and she won countless hours of pleasure in contemplating her mother's fury and frustration when it came to pass. And she knew it would come to pass, because her mother had taught Alice, unwittingly, a secret that her sister Melisende would never have the need for, or the brains to use: Morfia had taught Alice how to manipulate men.

Alice had watched, for years, how men behaved in her mother's presence, and how, sometimes surprisingly, her mother herself behaved in the presence of men she wished to influence or bend to her will. She had seen many of these men—for Edessa, and even Outremer in its entirety, was a small community—interacting with her mother in public, where Morfia was the wife of the Count and they, no matter how great their power in other areas, were her husband's feudal subjects. When they came to her mother in privacy, however, Alice paid attention to how they danced to an entirely different pattern, equally formal but more intimate, with nuances of meaning and intent that were the more resonant for being left unstated and unavowed.

In all her hours of watching such encounters, Alice never saw her mother indulge in even the slightest impropriety, but she watched avidly as the men preened like exotic birds around the Countess, strutting and sometimes fawning over her, each of them plainly convinced that he was within grasp of having this haughty and beautiful royal consort succumb to him. And on several occasions, always with an excitement that forced Alice to hold her breath in anticipation of what might happen next, she watched her mother respond alarmingly to such overtures, blatantly flirting, fluttering her eyelids outrageously and sometimes moving in ways that brought her full, ripely female body—Morfia could have been no more than thirty-five or -six at that time—into unmistakable and highly charged erotic prominence. And yet never once did Morfia permit a situation to go beyond her control, or allow a single man to touch her in any way. One man, and only one, had gone so far as to expose himself after such a dalliance, defiantly thrusting his hips and his engorged phallus forward in silent invitation and challenge. Alice, watching from a hiding place on an upper balcony, almost hiccoughed with excitement.

"It is plain, my lord," her mother said, smiling and looking directly up into the man's eyes and betraying no awareness of any threat to her dignity, "that I have something you desire. And to match it, as you know, you have something I desire in turn. Either wish would be simple to gratify, with no one but we two being any the wiser, but the challenge lies in deciding which of us should first commit, does it not? Now, you may quibble and complain and swear that I am in error, but deep in your heart you know, and I do, too, that I would be a fool to be the first to commit in this instance."

The man swayed towards her, but at the first hint of movement Morfia had raised her hand, palm outward in warning, and he had remained as he was, gazing at her as his manhood began to wilt and droop, and then he nodded, brusquely, and readjusted his clothing before telling her that she was correct and should watch his behavior in the coming days. He did not quite say that he would return to claim his prize, but Alice was filled with admiration for her mother's coolness, and took careful note of that word, *commit*, and what it signified.

She learned other lessons, spying thus from conceal-ment, but they all culminated in a powerful awareness that men, faced with erotic possibilities of pleasure and conquest, could be molded like clay in the hands of a cool-headed, determined, and resourceful woman. Alice learned that lesson well in theory, but at the age of thirteen she had yet to put her theory to any kind of test. She had no interest in boys, and none, yet, in sexu-ality for its own sake. She had seen sex in almost all its manifestations, from rutting animals to coupling people, and by the age of eleven she had been well aware of what a man or a boy could do to himself with his hand. She even knew that older women found sex and copulation pleasurable, for she had heard them talking about such things, but from all that she had seen, she had her own doubts about what pleasure might be gained from such a violent and earthy proce-dure. What interested her was the power she could gain from it, and the acquisition and the use of that power through the suggestion of erotic satisfaction. And she knew that when she became Countess of Edessa, she would need all the help she could garner from all the powerful men she had ever known, in order to outwit and outmaneuver her dull and empty-headed older sister. She was prepared to do anything she might have to do in order to enlist that help.

She had long since learned the importance of discretion and subterfuge, for her father would have spilled blood on many occasions, probably including his wife's, had he ever suspected what was happening beneath his roof. She had also become profoundly aware of the awe-inspiring power that could be generated by sexual suggestion and allusion. And perhaps more important than either of those, she had learned the benefits of feelings of guilt, not with any application to herself but when they were brought into play deliberately against a sexual opponent. What she needed then was an opportunity to test herself, and she did so by relying strongly on the restraining powers of guilt as she seduced one of her mother's coterie of friends, an aging bishop called Grosbec, who would soon be returning to the Kingdom of France, to the home in Paris that he had left decades earlier.

Alice had studied this man around her mother for some time, observing how he watched her avidly all the time, but particularly when he thought Morfia was unaware of his gaze. Of course, Alice had quickly become convinced that Morfia was never unaware of

Grosbec's gaze, but merely pretended to be, using that pretense somehow as a means of manipulating the man, who yet wielded a great degree of power and influence among his clerical peers, even as he was preparing to quit the Holy Land forever. Morfia had need of Grosbec's influence at that time, to ensure that she could retain control of one particular matter being weighed by a panel of clerics appointed by the young and zealous Bishop of Edessa, Odo of Fontainebleau. Grosbec, the oldest and most highly respected cleric in the county, had the ear, and the respect, of all the panel members, and so Morfia had gone to greater lengths than usual in seeking to please the elderly bishop and to persuade him to use his influence on her behalf. Inexperienced as she was when she first noticed her mother's peculiar deportment around Grosbec, Alice had been slow to understand what was happening when the two conspirators met, for conspirators they were, and they always met in the chapel closest to the Countess's rooms. They spoke little about anything in particular. And they certainly did not pray together. It seemed strange to Alice that they should spend ages simply sitting together, wasting time to no purpose.

She knew exactly what her mother wanted the bishop to do; she had heard them talking plainly about it on several occasions. But as the days went by, Grosbec would report that the judging panel had not yet come close to ruling on the matter, and then he and Morfia would simply sit together at the front of the chapel, seldom speaking to each other, and Alice could not understand how Morfia, who was not usually religious, could spend so much time doing nothing but staring up at the altar while Grosbec sat staring at her. Puzzled, Alice would sit in her hiding place above and behind the pair of them every day, peering through the dimness of the chapel, her eyes moving constantly from Morfia to Grosbec and back. They always met at the same time, the third hour of the afternoon, and they would remain together for anything from a quarter to half an hour, at the end of which time the bishop would stand up, and Morfia would bow her head for a blessing and then return to her own rooms, leaving Grosbec behind.

It was on a Friday afternoon that the bishop gasped aloud, his entire body quivering suddenly and spastically as he grasped the back of a pew for support, then stood where he was, head down, making no further movement. Morfia had been kneeling on a prie-dieu before the altar, and he had been standing close to her, gazing down at her for some time, swaying slowly, as though swiveling his hips. Morfia had not been praying. She had been sitting erect and staring straight ahead at the altar, her shoulders back so that her breasts, and the dark valley between them, were thrust into prominence. When Grosbec suddenly shuddered and appeared to be choking he almost startled Alice into betraying herself, but she caught herself in time, noticing that Morfia, who was much closer to him than Alice was, appeared to have taken no notice of his outburst. She merely rose to her feet and turned to where he stood facing her. She looked at him for long moments in silence, with a strange expression on her face, a look that Alice had never seen before, and then she bowed her head demurely to await the bishop's blessing. When it was done, she simply left, and Grosbec stood gazing after her, his face drained and haggard.

After thinking about all that had occurred in those few moments, Alice not only understood what had happened but she also grasped, intuitively, the dynamics of the interplay between the two that had been so baffling to her before. Grosbec was a *watcher,* and she knew what that entailed. Even at her young age, she saw nothing shocking in the revelation that Bishop Grosbec was sexually active. Licentious clerics were everywhere, and no one thought anything about it. The only unusual element in what she had learned was that the bishop was a watcher. Alice knew another watcher, a boy living in her father's enclave, a strange character two, perhaps three years older than she was, who liked to watch while other people did those things, and Alice had once watched him as he pleasured himself openly while they did. She had asked about him later, and discovered that he had absolutely no desire to share the act with a girl. His friends laughed at him because of it and called him names, but he made no attempt to change. He enjoyed watching people copulating, and made no secret of it or of how it excited him, and Alice had been surprised to hear how many people encouraged him and even seemed to enjoy having him watch them as they did it. Grosbec, Alice now knew, was a watcher, but more important than simply knowing that, she now realized that Morfia knew it, too, and was using the knowledge for her own purposes.

Three days after that, the clerics brought down their judgment, ruling in Morfia's favor, and she and Grosbec met once more in the chapel that same afternoon. This time, Alice was physically thrilled by the awareness that she knew what to look for. She saw the increasing tension in Grosbec's posture as he gazed at Morfia's seated form, but then Morfia rose and moved forward to the altar, where she lit a number of votive candles. Alice knew, beyond a doubt, that this was a deliberate display of gratitude and a reward to the old bishop, because as the Countess bent forward to select the candles and then stretched upwards to place them high on the rack, at the very top of the candelabrum's arms, her body and its movements were highly provocative, and the effect on Grosbec was immediate. And afterwards, when he had straightened up and squared his shoulders, she knew to the nearest heartbeat the exact moment when Morfia would turn around. This time, however, the Countess smiled openly at the elderly bishop.

"Thank you, my friend, for all your efforts on my behalf in resolving this matter. They will not go unrewarded. Unfortunately, the successful outcome of all our planning has already begun to effect additional demands on my time and attention, and I regret that our delightful times together, times that I have come to enjoy very much over the past month, may be few and far between in the future. I will make sure, however, that you and I see each other again before you depart for France at the end of this month. In the meantime, you have my gratitude."

During the month that followed, Princess Alice le Bourcq learned many valuable lessons that would influence the direction of her life for many years. She learned, not surprisingly, that all the tales she had heard about sexual pursuits being pleasurable were true, and once she had sampled the first fruits of success, with her short-lived and remarkably easy conquest of Bishop Grosbec soon before his departure for France, she rapidly developed the kind of confidence to proceed with all the courage of her convictions. It was her mother's condoning of the lecherous Bishop Grosbec's behavior in her private chapel, however, that gave Alice the insight she needed to defy Morfia from then on, for the knowledge that her supposedly saintly mother was not above being hypocritical was a solid endorsement to Alice's determination to play her mother's game, and to play it blatantly and without any trace of hypocrisy, knowing that her mother would be appalled if she ever heard a word about her daughter's outrageous behavior.

And thus a pattern of living was set within Count Baldwin's family: Alice simply stopped making any pretense of being civil or obedient to her mother, and in response, Morfia intensified her disapproval of Alice, criticizing the girl bitterly and loudly at every opportunity. The Count himself, forced to live with the constant discord between the two women, eventually came to disregard their fighting completely, and made a point of avoiding being in the company of both of them at the same time. Morfia continued to enjoy her "times of solitude" each day, and while she was doing so, her daughter copied her in the privacy of her own rooms. Morfia lived, as she always had, with her own designs and stratagems, manipulating people deviously and ruthlessly to gain her own ends while, unknown to her, her daughter did the same, focusing all her ambitions and her intellectual energies upon the someday theft of her sister's birthright, while she directed her sexual energies towards the acquisition of unassailable power over men, and to her own pleasurable and vengeful defiance of her mother the Countess.

And then had come the death of King Baldwin I of Jerusalem, and the surprising offer of his crown to her own father, who had become King Baldwin II, thereby promoting his wife to the status of Queen, and inspiring his younger daughter's ambitions to seek higher heights than ever before, for now Alice was determined to be Queen of Jerusalem one day.

Until she set eyes on the novice knight monk Brother Stephen, however, Alice had never really sought out any man for the sheer pleasure of anticipating the enjoyment of him, but this man was a monk, and therefore an idealist, and was also attractively strong and virile in his every look and movement. That was enough to spark a new kind of lust in the King's daughter, and she set out to have him.

THREE

In the course of the six weeks that followed their initial meeting, Stephen St. Clair met the princess three more times, apparently by sheerest accident on each occasion. Unworldly as he was, it did not occur to him that Alice might be having him watched, tracing his movements so that she might intercept him whenever she so wished, and he would have been genuinely shocked had anyone suggested to him that she might have any prurient interest in him as a man. But even he, unsophisticated and self-effacing as he was, admitted wonder at the frequency with which he saw the princess during that time, particularly because she was seldom far from his mind and was unwittingly causing him a degree of embarrassment. He had taken to dreaming of her and spilling his seed involuntarily in the night, and whereas there was nothing new in that, he had seldom if ever in the past recalled any specific dream triggering such episodes. They had always been unsettling and vaguely troubling, noticeable only from the evidence they left in passing. Now, however, he had sprung awake shuddering with release several times, with the vision of the princess's face filling his mind, along with the devastatingly tactile but impossible memory of friction, and her flesh burning against his.

The experience, and his inability to prevent it or even to put it from his mind during the day, had begun to cause him grave concern, so that he had determined to seek out a priest and confess to what he believed must be grievous sins. He had not yet done that, because of his training in the Order, but his awareness of the need to do it—to purge himself of the guilt he was feeling— contributed greatly to his reactions to Alice when he found himself face to face with her. The first time, on the morning after his first clearly recalled dream of her, he had not been able to look her in the eye, and his embarrassment would not allow him to speak to her at all. Alice's amusement at his pitiable shyness was almost completely genuine, but she had cut the interview short, releasing him to his misery.

The second meeting had been much the same, except that this time St. Clair had managed to stammer out a few words in answer to several of Alice's questions. Once again, however, Alice had decided that it was not yet time for her to press ahead with her designs for the young knight, and so she had concentrated simply but intently upon making him feel at ease in her company, and lulling him into a belief, eventually, that her feigned interest in his brethren and their activities was genuine.

She was more than three years his junior, eighteen years old to his one-and-twenty, but in life experience Alice le Bourcq was decades older than he was. St. Clair was a virgin; his entire life, lived away from women and dominated by the pious and dedicated men among whom he had been reared in damp, dreary England, had left him ill prepared to deal with feminine beauty. Alice, on the other hand, exulted in the power she could exercise over men, seducing whomever she wished to suborn, but never permitting herself to be seduced, finding great pleasure even in that aspect of her control. She was the architect and arranger of her sexual affairs and she had never encountered failure or resistance.

Now, however, with this attractive but infuriatingly awkward monk, she found herself at a loss, unsure of what to do next, or even of what to say to him, for she had seen with her own eyes that, whenever she ventured into conversational territory with which he was unfamiliar, he tended to panic, and his ability to speak dried up completely. She had no way of knowing that he was terrified to speak for fear of saying something that might betray his lustful thoughts, but she knew that he was eager to spend time with her, because the joy that sprang into his face each time he saw her was impossible to misunderstand. And so she persevered in her assault on him, seething inwardly with impatience, while he squirmed with guilt-ridden pleasure.

It was their third meeting that cast the die and pushed Alice beyond amused tolerance and into anger. She had set spies to watch for St. Clair's return from a long patrol, and she knew from previous observation what his activities would be upon his return to the monks' dwelling place in the temple stables. He would report to his superiors, after which he would sleep for an entire day, recouping the strength he had depleted through long days of riding beneath the desert sun, and then on the next day, he would walk to the marketplace outside the city walls, by the southwestern gate, where he would spend the morning wandering among the stalls, eating and drinking hugely of the variety of food and beverages available. Later, having sated himself on rich food and the sweet, syrupy drinks and sparkling sherbets of the local vendors, he would make his way back to the Temple Mount, where he would vanish for days on end, doing whatever he and his fellow monks did in the darkness of their quarters, until the time came around again for him to ride out on a new patrol. He was as predictable as sunrise and nightfall, his routine never varying, his route to and from the marketplace the same every time.

SULEIMAN AL KHARIF knew that something was distracting the *ferenghi* princess, for she was one of his most valued but most critical customers, thoroughly schooled in the finer points of rug making despite her youth, and difficult to please at the best of times. Today she was, he knew, preoccupied by something other than the quality of his merchandise, but he was too old and well schooled in the ways of the marketplace to betray that awareness, and too accustomed to the blessings of Allah's compassion to take her lack of concentration as other than what it was, a beneficence. The princess had already paid exorbitantly for two rugs that she would not even have considered on any other day, and it was clear to the old merchant, from the way her eyes strayed constantly to the people passing in the street outside his stall, that she had no interest in his goods on this day, but was merely using his premises, waiting for someone to come along. And so, aware that he had already profited well from her preoccupation, he left her and climbed up to the platform that held his proprietorial chair and permitted him to overlook his entire stall. There he stood patiently waiting to see what would develop, allowing her to pretend to be examining his wares while he, standing above her, was able to peer over the hanging racks of his rugs and scan the crowded street outside.

He had no idea whom she might be expecting, but there was not the slightest doubt in Suleiman's mind that she was waiting for a man. Gazing out at the crowd, therefore, he wondered idly if he might perhaps be able to identify the man she was waiting for before she herself saw the fellow coming, for his vantage point was far superior to hers. And then he saw a towering figure at the far end of the street, head and shoulders taller than everyone around him, and he knew he had no need to wonder further. The approaching man was a gigantic young yellow-haired *ferenghi* with shoulders the width of the street and blue eyes so bright that Suleiman, even with his ancient eyes, could see them from fifty paces, and as he passed among the crowd, every head turned to watch him go by.

Suleiman watched the princess, aware that she had not yet had the time or opportunity to notice the man approaching. She was an alluring young woman, this Princess of the Franks, and paradoxically she was well regarded among the local people, Suleiman's people, many of whom could barely stomach the sight of the *ferenghis,* with their sunburnt faces and arrogant bearing, their heavy chain hauberks and their long swords. Alice, however, had been born among the faithful, and despite her Christianity, she spoke flawless Arabic and conducted herself in public as a Muslim woman should, concealing her face modestly and wearing heavy, shapeless outer garments that caused no offense to anyone. He had heard rumors that among her own she was regarded as something of a disgrace, but he had seen no signs to warrant such a calumny, and neither had anyone he knew. Today she was veiled and wearing Muslim clothing, mostly in a heavy fabric of blue embroidered with green and gold thread, that concealed her from head to foot, save for her eyes, which flashed wide when she finally saw the blond giant coming towards the stall.

One glance told Suleiman that the golden-haired Frank had no idea that the princess was even there. The fellow, who was dressed in sensible desert clothing rather than suffocating *ferenghi* armor, and carried only a long, straight sword, hanging from a shoulder belt, was drifting along at his own pace, gnawing at a piece of meat and peering about him, his eyes flitting constantly from face to face and stall to stall, missing nothing except the face of the young woman who was now leaning forward eagerly, peering at him through a gap between two of Suleiman's hanging rugs. Suleiman watched her snap her fingers imperiously, then send her servant running to accost the giant and bring him to her. The tall Frank frowned, then grasped the scabbard of the long sword that hung from his shoulder and followed his summoner, clearly unaware of whom he was going to meet. When he straightened up from stooping to enter Suleiman's premises and saw the princess waiting for him, however, his surprise and confusion was comical to behold, and Suleiman, who had been on the point of stepping down from his platform, stayed where he was, watching and listening instead.

"Brother Stephen," the princess greeted him, unveiling her face and smiling at him. "This is a pleasant and welcome surprise. You are the last person I would expect to find wandering through the market. I would have said, had anyone asked me, that you would be out in the desert with your fellow knights, patrolling the roads and terrifying bandits."

The big man was plainly flustered, red faced and ill at ease, and the rug merchant moved marginally closer, straining to hear what he might say.

"My lady Princess," the fellow muttered, close to stammering with nervousness, "forgive me, I did not ... I had no idea ..."

"Of what, that I was here?" The princess laughed. "How could you? I did not know myself, until an hour ago, that I would come this way. This is what is known as an accident ... a meeting brought about through sheer good fortune." She hesitated. "I was just about to have some cake and sherbet. Will you share it with me? It would give me great pleasure."

With an imperious clap of her hands she summoned her servant again and ordered refreshments to be brought for them, then evidently remembered where she was and looked about her for Suleiman, who presented himself immediately, bowing low and smiling in welcome at the giant Frank. When the princess began to ask his permission to eat on his premises, he waved her question away before she could complete it, offering refreshments of his own. Alice would hear none of that, however. Suffice, she said, that he would permit her this privilege; she had brought food and drink with her, intending to eat outdoors later. She was most grateful. Suleiman bowed again and left her with her "unexpected" guest.

For the short time between Suleiman's departure and the return of Alice's servants bearing refreshments, St. Clair stood awkwardly, looking at the carpets that lay piled all around him and hung from suspended poles to give the illusion of walls. His eyes shifted everywhere and anywhere, looking at anything except Alice.

"The rugs are beautiful, are they not?" she asked.

He frowned, almost as though he did not know how to respond, and it took Alice some time to realize that, in truth, he did not know how to respond.

"Can it be—? Have you never seen rugs before, Brother Stephen?"

He shook his head, a deep crease between his brows. "No, Lady. I have never seen the like of these before. But they are beautiful. What are they? What is their purpose?"

"Purpose?" She laughed, delighted by his apparent lack of sophistication. "They have no purpose, Brother Stephen, they simply *are*. They are floor coverings, to be walked upon. Surely you have rugs in Christendom? *Everyone* has rugs."

He swung suddenly to face her, and spoke through clenched teeth, his taut jaw muscles making him look angry, although she knew he was not. "Where I came from, our floors are dirt, Lady, and we spread dried rushes over them to soak up spillage and mud. It rains in England, Princess, and the days are cold and damp and miserable most of the time. Little summer and less sunshine. Items such as these"—he waved a hand at the rugs surrounding them—"if we had anything resembling them, we would hang on walls, to keep out drafts. We do it with tapestries, but our tapestries are stiff and loveless things. We have nothing as rich and beautiful as these, with all these colors and soft, rich textures. It would be sinful to throw such beauty on a packed dirt floor, to be trodden into mud by mailed feet and be shit upon by dogs."

He paused, then cleared his throat before continuing. "Of course, I have seen that such things are very different in this country. Everything is warmer. Cleaner. Spacious and airy. That's the heat. When it's not wet and cold all the time, you can do things differently. But in our quarters, in the stables, our floors are stone and we still have rushes on them, although we call it straw—" He broke off, aware that he was looking directly at her and she was returning his gaze with a wide smile on her lips. She waited, and then, when she saw he would say no more, she laughed aloud.

"You can speak! That is the most I have heard you say since I first met you, Brother Stephen. Were you aware of that?"

He looked troubled. "I am now. And I *am* Brother Stephen. I should not be here."

"Oh, please, please stay and share some food with me. See, here it comes now."

The young knight stood uncertainly, but in response to Alice's waving hand, he finally sank slowly into one of the three chairs Suleiman provided for his clients, and thereafter, for the space of almost an hour, the princess applied herself conscientiously to putting him at his ease and undermining his defenses against her femininity. She fed him honey cakes that her servants had brought especially for her, made with crushed almonds and heavily impregnated with the opiate known as hashish, of which she had an ample and regular supply, delivered by sources about which her father would have been gravely concerned had he known of them.

What Alice had no way of knowing about that day, however, was the extreme fragility of St. Clair's self-confidence, brought about by the simple fact that he had become obsessed with everything about her and knew very well that his attraction to her was unconscionable. He had always been shy and awkward around her, hesi-tant and tongue-tied and unsure of himself since their first meeting, and Alice had quickly come to accept that as normal in him, adding to his charm—the bashful boy in the giant body of a hero. But because she had never seen any other aspect of his character, she was unable to imagine how he might behave when she was not there to influence him and his conduct, and she was, of course, incapable of seeing beyond the exterior he presented to her. There was nothing in his demeanor to indicate to her that he spent much of his life nowadays dreaming of her, awake and asleep, and there was even less evidence that he was racked by guilt because of that, and so Alice moved ahead confidently, unaware of how close her prey was to despair. In her efforts to put him at his ease, she deliberately avoided any attempts to be seductive or alluring, opting instead to treat him as she believed a sister might, and trying to be completely natural in all she did around him. It was a difficult thing for her to do, verging in fact on the impossible.

St. Clair, looking at her as she moved with such apparent lack of artifice, saw far more than she was showing him: in his imagination he saw the way her clothing clung to her beneath the heavy fabric of her shapeless outer garment, shaping the hills and hollows of her form; he saw the way she subsided into her chair, lounging back into it, and in his mind her breasts were thrust into prominence and her rounded thighs, so clearly parted beneath the flimsy stuff of her clothing, became the most all-consuming sight in the universe, and he writhed mentally, believing that his lust for her was an abomination and a crime against a spotless, innocent young woman.

Had Alice even suspected any of what was in his mind, she would have been exultant, and would have shown her feelings far more aggressively, but instead she continued as she had begun, behaving as though there was no such thing as sexuality in her nature, avoiding any of the overtly seductive gestures and smiles that were so much a part of her normal behavior. Believing herself modestly shielded by the weight and thickness of her brocade robe, she fed the fires of the young knight's overheated imagination with a series of uninhibited body movements, of which she was genuinely unaware, that aroused him beyond his power to prevent a sudden crisis. He leapt to his feet, his face pale as death, and fled her presence.

Afterwards, when she had time to think about it calmly, Alice had still been unable to understand what had triggered his astonishing behavior. Her fury had scarcely abated in the time that had since passed. No man, no one, had ever insulted her so grievously, and Alice was determined to have vengeance.

That he was a monk and bound by a vow of chastity meant nothing to her, because she had had many lovers with the same commitment, all of them more highly placed than he, and their vows had never kept them from her bed. Alice believed herself too desirable to be resisted over anything as insubstantial as a simple vow. And thus she went searching for other, more pragmatic reasons for the monk's behavior, beginning with the assumption that he already had a lover who must, by definition, be highly placed and well known, since there were so few Christian women in Jerusalem. Not even Alice would have believed that a devout Christian monk, and most particularly a rigidly humorless one, would have a sexual relationship with a Muslim woman. She had had him spied on and followed before, keeping track of his movements between patrols, but that had been only during daylight hours, since at that time she had had no suspicions that he might be conducting an amatory liaison with anyone. Now she set her spies to watching him night and day.

A full month later, having received the third of the regular ten-day reports of her chief spy in this matter, she was forced to accept, with great reluctance, that Brother Stephen was not involved with any woman, Christian or Muslim. Her people had made sure that he went nowhere without their being in close attendance. They had noted every person he spoke to and every purchase that he made in the markets. Two of them had even followed him into the desert when he went out on patrol, and they had seen nothing that aroused their suspicions in any way.

That acknowledgment left Alice then with the notion that he might be homosexual; it might have been sexual revulsion that drove him to run away from her. She had trouble visualizing that, let alone understanding it, but the possibility at least soothed her bruised sensibilities.

Once again, however, after a month of watching and listening, her spies could provide her with nothing to substantiate her suspicions. His brother monks were St. Clair's only close companions, and he was by far the youngest of them all. They all disappeared inside the stables every night, to sleep, and they were up and about, praying at the oddest hours of the day and night, their entire routine dictated by the Rule of Saint Benedict that they followed. But there was nothing anyone could see, even with the best will in the world, that suggested that any of the monks indulged in sexual activities of any kind.

Alice remained angry and unforgiving, even after two clear months, but she was still infuriatingly incapable of putting the young monk knight out of her mind or her lustful fantasies, imagining on several occasions, when entertaining an ineffectual or unsatisfying lover, that it was Stephen St. Clair straining above her, ravishing her brutally.

FOUR

"Come!"

Bishop Odo de Fontainebleau, formerly the Bishop of Edessa and now Secretary Amanuensis to Baldwin II, King of Jerusalem, did not even look up in response to the knocking on his door, but he recognized the footsteps that entered the room following his summons, and sat back in his chair, setting aside his quill pen and rubbing his eyes with the heels of his hands, then yawning hugely and clasping his hands behind his head. In front of him stood a slight, nondescript little man with too-small eyes and a long, pointed nose, one hand clutching the strap of a leather bag that hung from his shoulder. The fellow's face was expressionless, his manner unassuming, and his dress drab to the point of being unworthy of notice. Had there been one other person in the room to compete with him for attention, the little man would have faded into quasi invisibility.

Odo eyed the fellow for long moments before dropping his hands from behind his head and crossing his arms over his chest. "Speak to me, then. What have you discovered?"

The responding headshake was barely noticeable. "Of what you sent me for, nothing. There's nothing there to find. The princess's spies are everywhere, never less than six of them at any time, and they change over every four hours, but they're all wasting their time and probably being well paid to do it. You set me to watching them, to discover what they were finding out. The answer, my lord Bishop, is that they are finding nothing, but far more astonishing than even that, although it is unsurprising, if you take my meaning, they have no idea what they are looking for. They are set to watch the monk knight—the young one, the fighter—and so they do that, but they don't know why. I spoke with six of them in three days. They all said the same thing: they had seen nothing, found nothing."

"So this has all been a waste of my time and money, in addition to Alice's losses? Is that what you are telling me?"

"No, not at all, my lord. I said I found nothing of what you sent me to find."

"You found something else instead."

"Perhaps. I think I did, but you might disagree. Anyway, I discovered something interesting."

"Something interesting, but not what you were sent to discover. I see. And am I going to have to pay you extra to tell me about it? Spit it out, man."

His visitor was not at all put out by the bishop's nastiness. He reached into his bag and produced a grubby-looking kerchief, which he used to wipe his nose, and then he replaced it carefully in the bag, sniffing daintily.

"There's something going on in the stables."

The bishop's eyes widened in disbelief. "Of course there is something going on in the stables! There's an entire fraternity of monks living in them, with horses."

"Nah, more than that. There's something strange going on."

"Strange ... I see. Are these monks running a bordello in there?"

"They might be. They might even be fornicating with the horses. You couldn't tell by me. I couldn't get close enough to see what was going on, although I got closer than anyone else could. They're a peculiar lot, those fellows. Only the actual monks live in the stables. The ones they call sergeants live in barracks built right in front of the entrance to the stables. And the two don't mix much. The sergeants and the monks, I mean. Mind you, they're all monks, it seems to me, and from what I know, all monks are equal. These ones aren't."

"You know next to nothing, and most of what you think you know is wrong. They are knights and sergeants, for one thing—noblemen and commoners—and then as monks, they are brothers and lay brothers. Two excellent reasons for segregation. Now tell me, if it pleases you, exactly what you suspect is going on in there."

"I told you I don't know, but it's something strange. It looked to me as though there's a door in there that no one who is not one of the nine knights ever gets to enter. And I heard noises coming from there, too, as though they were chiseling into stone."

"Chiseling into stone. Are you aware that those

stables are built right on top of—and in places carved right out of—the Temple Mount? So let us imagine, for a moment, that these knights are desirous of improving their living space. Their only means of doing that might be to enlarge the premises by digging into the rock. Would you agree with that?"

"Aye, perhaps, but—"

"I know, I know. *But* you suspect that something strange is going on in there. Tell me, then, what it is. This door, for example, the one that no one but the knights is ever allowed to enter, where is it?"

"It's inside ... in the darkest part of their living quarters, away at the back."

"Where the *knights* live, you mean?"

"Aye. The place is split into two areas, one for the horses and the other for the monks."

"And the sergeants, you say they live outside?"

"Aye. Some of them work inside the stables, but they don't live in there. They've built a barracks building close against the wall."

"So the only people who live inside the stables are the knights. Why, then, is it strange that only the knights use one particular door, or any other door, if they are the only people in there? Has it occurred to you it might be their latrine?"

"It's not, my lord Bishop. The latrines are over on the other side. The place is a stable, and the sergeants are coming and going, in and out, all the time. But there is always a knight close by that door. He's not obviously on guard duty there, but the truth remains that every time one of the sergeants goes within a certain distance of that door, someone comes out of nowhere and turns him away. Always with great charm and goodwill, but *always,* without fail. Who would set guards on a latrine? I've been watching for weeks now, and I've seen it happen nigh on a score of times. And in the same time, I have never seen one sergeant go in through that door."

"And so you grew suspicious, based upon that, or is there more, something you have not told me?"

The little man shook his head. "No, there's no more."

"I see. Well, you may not care to hear this, but I have no interest in your suspicions, Gregorio, and I do not pay you to be suspicious. I myself can generate all the suspicions I require, about anything and everyone, including you. What I require of you, my small functionary, in due return for the stipend I pay you, is tangible fact, backed with proof. Do you understand me?"

The little man nodded, and the bishop grunted in response, then bent forward and picked up his pen again. "Go, then, and don't come back until you can do so without wasting my time."

Odo was immersed in his work again before Gregorio even turned away, but as soon as the door closed behind the spy, the bishop threw his pen down on the tabletop and rose to his feet. He stalked to the arched window, from which he could look down into one of the lesser courtyards of the King's palace, where a marble fountain splashed pleasantly, surrounded by dense growths of palmettos. He was angry, and he was jealous, and while anger was not a new experience for him, jealousy certainly was, and Odo was having trouble coping with it.

He had no illusions about what he was feeling. He liked to think that it was all the fault of Princess Alice, and had he had anyone to whom he could demonstrate that, he could have laid out details, chapter and verse, of every incident and every occasion that she had used to ensnare him. But of course, it was not something that he could discuss with anyone, and besides, he knew the real truth. It was not Alice's fault at all. She had not forced him to lie with her, not on the first occasion, and not at any other time. He was the one who had allowed himself to become besotted with her, despite his knowing that whenever and wherever she so chose, the princess would spread her legs for anyone who caught her eye. She appeared to be insatiable, she was beautiful, and she was breathtakingly young—eighteen to Odo's forty-two. And therein lay the roots of his jealousy. He was no longer young enough to keep Alice satisfied. He never had been, from the outset, almost four years earlier.

He had known from the start of his involvement with her, too, exactly why she had blessed him with her favors. He had been her confessor for years, and as she grew older he had found himself growing thrilled, and erotically charged, by her increasingly lurid confessions as she began to experiment with herself physically and with her sexuality in general. She related in great detail, and over the course of several months, the attraction she was feeling to one of the younger men in her father's court, and the fantasies she indulged in regarding the fellow. And from there, warming to her task as she progressed, she regaled her confessor with the most intimate and lurid details of her seduction of the hapless man. Of course, once he himself had succumbed to her charms, Odo had discovered that Alice had taken great and perverse delight in the entire exercise, knowing exactly what effect she was having upon the man behind the confessional's screen, and lingering over every salacious element of her adventures. By the time she was ready to seduce him, then, she had already laid all the foundations for his downfall.

And of course, there was a *quid pro quo*. Alice did nothing, gave nothing, without a *quid pro quo*. In return for the privilege of enjoying her magnificent young body, Odo provided the princess with information, confidential and extremely sensitive information on everything that took place within the King's Council Chamber. That Alice had been merely fourteen years old when the arrangement was set into place was insignificant. In her soul and in her mind, Alice le Bourcq, reared as the spoiled favorite of a father pre-eminent among men of power and influence, had never really been a child. Old beyond her years, she was already a woman of great subtlety, possessing the kind of mind that exulted in intrigue, and her own ambitions had been molded and set while her friends and siblings were still playing as children.

Odo had known that, and had known that she would attempt to suborn him for her own designs, and to a great extent he had resented that she should, but when it had come time to weigh his scruples against his lusts, to measure the value of his principles against the yielding pressure of her soft, bare thigh in the palm of his hand, his decision made nonsense of all the high-minded ideals of which he had been so proud.

His current distemper arose from the discovery, made almost two months earlier by one of his many spies, that Alice had become fascinated by the young knight monk, St. Clair. The spy in question was a menial female servant who was close enough to Alice most of the time to have become invisible, her constant presence taken for granted, and so her evidence was trustworthy. She it was who had overheard the instructions Alice gave to her majordomo, a eunuch by the name of Ishtar, to set up a watch on Brother Stephen, as he called himself, and keep her informed about who his lovers were and what he did with them.

Of course they had found no lovers, and no evidence of St. Clair's doing anything amiss, but that had only inspired Alice to dig deeper, and despite his knowing that St. Clair was innocent of any wrongdoing, as he saw her obsession with this knight monk growing, Odo himself had set his spies to watching hers, hoping to find something that he could use to discredit the monk and make him *persona non grata* to everyone, including Alice. Now, staring down into the courtyard and thinking about what Gregorio had said—his conviction that something "strange" was going on in the stables—Odo recognized the first faint glimmerings of an idea that he could use against Alice, to stir her up, at least, and make her aware again of him and of his desire for her. As the outlines of a plan began to form in his mind, he made his way back to his worktable, whistling tunelessly under his breath, a sure sign to all who knew him that the bishop was deep in thought.

FIVE

"Really, Odo, you are being thoroughly tiresome today. I sent for you in the hope that you would entertain me and divert me this afternoon, but you have done nothing but mope like an old dotard."

"Nonsense, my dear princess, let us tell the truth and put the devil to shame. You sent for me in the hope that you could pump me for information, on whatever topic holds most interest for you at this time. When was it ever otherwise? But I have not been able to tell you anything this time, much as I love you and wish to please you, because I do *not* know what you *want*. If you insist on playing games and not asking me directly about whatever it is you wish to know, then you can hardly hold me responsible for being incapable at times of deciphering your true intent."

Alice le Bourcq remained silent for a count of ten, staring at him through narrowed eyes. "I am very glad you were smiling when you said that, my lord Bishop," she said then, precisely when he knew she would. "Otherwise I might have thought you were being insolent. As it is, you have succeeded in amusing me for the first time since you arrived, so come over here and sit close to me. I wish to whisper secrets in your ear."

Marveling for perhaps the thousandth time how anyone so young could sound so worldly, Bishop Odo rose slowly to his feet and crossed silently and obediently to where she reclined on a couch, watching him, her feet tucked modestly up beneath her long skirts. For all her surprising sophistication, he thought, her lack of years and experience could not be completely concealed all the time. Although she may have been schooled to astonishing depths in the ways of men and women, in some respects her youthfulness was yet as transparent as fine glass, and this wheedling, teasing eagerness to have her own way was one of those.

He had played his own part to perfection this afternoon, he thought as he approached her, achieving an air so faultlessly poised between distraction and preoccupation that it had piqued the princess's interest while annoying her intensely at the same time. And once her interest had been attracted, it had been merely a matter of time until, notwithstanding her annoyance, she had been compelled to act upon her curiosity. Now she was visibly intrigued, knowing that he was thinking about something for which he was prepared to risk her anger, and Odo knew she would stop at nothing now until she was satisfied that she had drained him of every drop of information he possessed, despite the possibility that it might hold no interest at all for her.

He stood directly in front of her, towering over her so that she had to tilt back her head to look up at him, exposing the snowy perfection of her long neck and a swooping expanse of smooth skin that ended in the first swelling of her breasts, and he felt his loins stir in response to her nearness. She raised a hand languidly, wiggling her fingers until he took them in his own, at which point she closed her hand and pulled him down towards her.

"Come, sit with me."

She tightened her grip and pulled him closer, arching her back and pushing her buttocks against the rear of her couch to make enough room for him to sit close against her, in the curled crescent of her body. As he lowered himself to sit, he felt her body pressing against his lower back, and she laid her right hand flat against his belly, just above his pubic bone, pressing him closer until he relaxed and leaned back against her, his right arm resting on the curve of her hip where it swept down to her waist, his left elbow on her thigh, the back of his fingers aware of the warmth of the soft skin behind her knee, beneath the diaphanous robe.

"There! Are you comfortable?"

He dipped his head, allowing his hand to settle on the curve of her waist, flexing his fingers gently in a caress. She made a contented little sound, and he pressed harder, kneading the pliant flesh more firmly as the fingers of his other hand spread and grasped the back of her leg above the knee.

"Aah, you beast," she murmured, smiling at him as she slowly raised her leg high, bracing her heel against the couch's back and permitting his questing fingers to slide down along the length of her thigh to the join of her body while her own hand moved with the ease of long practice to penetrate his episcopal robes.

Odo permitted himself only a short time to luxuriate in the sensation that followed, before he thrust his right hand forward to grasp her wrist tightly, for he knew how quickly those milking fingers could bring the seed spuming, and once it was spilt, he would probably lack the time required to regenerate his stock.

"Hold, my dear. Be patient for a while."

Alice cocked one eyebrow as if she were wondering what could possibly be wrong with him, but her grip had slackened to a less intense, but still pleasurable, level, and Odo allowed his own hand to relax in the same way as he continued, his voice calm and deliberate.

"We have much to talk about here if I am to tell you what is on my mind today, because I am still thinking through the possibilities of what has come to me, and I am sure you would prefer, as would I, to keep me alert in the telling, rather than risk having me lose focus by being too soon tired—if you take my meaning. Would you agree with that?"

Alice continued to gaze at him for several moments, her eyes speculative, and then she nodded, her fingers like butterfly wings fluttering against him, fingertips suddenly transformed to lightest gossamer. "I agree," she said. "Far better to keep a storyteller awake and alert to his surroundings while he performs than to risk having him fall asleep in a distant corner through lack of interest in his ... tale." She raised an eyebrow then, and her hand pulled his robes apart, folding them back and away from him. "So, what is this story to be about? You have my entire attention."

"As you have mine, my lady."

A long silence ensued, broken only by an occasional gasp and some lingering, deep-drawn breaths until the princess pushed herself up to her feet from behind him, then straddled him on her knees. Moments later, she held him firmly lodged and she leaned back on her haunches, pinning him with her full weight. "There, now," she whispered. "If you stay there, without moving for a while, you should be able to concentrate upon what you have to tell me. Keep me interested, my lord Bishop, keep me listening, for only thus will you be able to avoid a sudden ending to this bliss. Tell me what has been distracting you so noticeably today."

Odo closed his eyes, gathering his thoughts, and then he began to talk, pausing only very occasionally to shift slightly, and each time he did, Alice moved with him, her hands gripping his shoulders lightly, her eyes intent upon his, watching his every flicker of expression while accommodating him, acknowledging his lust without inflaming him beyond where he already was.

"It's those damnable monks," he began. "The upstarts created by Warmund."

"Why would you call them damnable?" Alice took great care to keep her face expressionless and made her voice sound bored. "My understanding is that they have proved themselves useful on many occasions, and they are very modest in their desires. What have they got to do with you?"

"Nothing, on the surface, but underneath, they are becoming a nuisance, taking up too much of my time— time I can ill afford to waste on them."

"How so?" Alice shifted her position minutely, sideways and back, merely enough to focus his attention where she wanted it.

He grunted and closed his eyes for a moment, then returned to his topic. "Well, they are not so modest now, not so self-effacing. It has been years since they were last called the Patriarch's Patrol. They call themselves nowadays the Poor Fellow Soldiers of Jesus Christ." He made no attempt to hide his disdain for the knight monks or for their new name, but he was acutely aware of the need to name no names and to avoid, in particular, any mention of the youngest one, St. Clair, for were Alice to discover that he suspected her interest in the fellow, her reactions would be unpredictable, and Odo had no wish to incur her anger.

Alice laughed aloud. "The *what*? What a ridiculous and ludicrous name! The Poor Fellow Soldiers of Jesus Christ ... The poor fellows are obviously delusional. But why should that concern you?"

"It does not ... not at all. I have no interest in what they call themselves. They can call themselves Daughters of the Blessed Virgin, for all I care, so be they keep their stupidities and their apostasies from stinking up the public awareness. No, it's what they are doing that concerns me."

Alice sat motionless now, staring into his eyes. "And what are they doing that concerns you so?"

"I—" Odo sucked in a sudden deep, agonized breath and froze, rigid in bare-toothed concentration, his fingers digging into Alice's thighs until the surging threat of explosion had passed, and then he slumped back, exhaling raggedly. "Sweet Jesus, that was close ..."

"Aye, it was, but it passed by. Tell me, what are these monks doing that concerns you so?"

"Digging." Odo's voice was still unsteady.

Alice released his shoulders and sat back, resting her haunches on his thighs, one outstretched hand touching his chest as she looked into his eyes to see if he meant what he had said. "Digging? In the ground?" Her voice was heavy with disbelief. "Those men are knights, Odo. Monks today, perhaps, but knights by training and breeding. They are no more likely to dig in the ground than you are."

"But that is what they are doing. Digging ... tunneling. I believe the Poor Fellow Soldiers of Jesus Christ are digging a tunnel in their stables."

The princess was staring at him in stupefaction, but then she began to laugh. "In their *stables*? Why would they do that?"

"Because they are obviously searching for something. That is why anyone digs a tunnel. Either to find something at the end of it or to escape to some other place. In this case, had they wished merely to escape to some other place, all they need do was walk away. Ergo, they are searching for something."

"But what on earth could they be searching for? And how did you discover they were doing this?"

So intense had been this last exchange that both of them had temporarily forgotten the other activity that had been engrossing them mere moments earlier. Now Odo shook his head abruptly. "Two questions there. Which do you want answered first?"

"The first one. What are they searching for?"

"I don't know, and that's why I'm so annoyed over this. First, there is no place for them to dig, except downward into the living rock."

"So? What are you saying?"

"I am saying, my lady, that they might well be tunneling straight down into solid stone, but that makes no sense if they are looking for a treasure or what have you, simply because there cannot be a treasure, or anything for that matter, hidden in solid stone."

"No, unless the rock beneath them is less solid than we think, and knowing that, they are digging in search of that less sólid matter …"

"But how would they—?"

"Hush. Let me think. How did you find out they were doing this, this tunneling?"

"One of my people told me."

"What people are those? Are you telling me you have spies among the knight monks?" The bishop shrugged, and Alice disregarded that piece of information for the moment. "Very well, then, what did this spy discover?"

Odo pushed his body against her, but his tumescence had vanished and he felt only warmth and moist soft-ness. He sighed and resigned himself to the inevitable. "That there was something suspicious taking place within the stables, something confined only to the knight monks themselves. The sergeants—the lay brothers—from what he had seen and learned knew nothing of what was happening, or if they did know something, they were being highly protective of their knowledge. My man came to believe eventually that they truly knew nothing, and that in itself is remarkable, within such a small and tight-knit community as theirs."

"And what *did* he know, this man of yours? What did he see?"

"He *saw* nothing ... nothing absolute. But he observed what was going on for months and took careful note of everything that happened."

"And what about the digging, did he see that? Did he see anything that involved digging or tunneling?"

"Well, no, not exactly. But he heard it."

"Heard what?"

"Hammering. Digging into rock. He heard the noises coming from the stables, muffled hammerings, at night, when everything else was quiet."

"Your man might be a lying fool, Odo, and I would be a fool to believe you without more evidence than you evidently have."

"Aye, you are right, Princess. I have no proof, but I have suspicions, and I have ample grounds for believing those suspicions to be valid. And so I would be a fool myself were I not to take my suspicions to your father the King. The stables are his property, and no matter what those monks are doing there, if they are digging, tunneling, or disturbing the status quo in any way, without permission, they must hold themselves liable to the King, as would I were I to fail to report to him what I believe. I believe those knight monks are hiding something, and so an investigation will be launched into their activities. And when that is complete, whatever it is that they are hiding will have come to light."

Alice had grown pensive as she listened, and now she sat nodding her head slowly. Odo cleared his throat, but before he could speak again she made a shushing sound, soothing him to silence, and placed one hand flat against his sternum as her other sought down at the join of them, her probing fingers bringing him back to life as if by magic until he filled her again. Then, for a while, he lay with his head thrown back while she reared above him, taking him slowly to the point at which he began to tremble and thrust blindly, then stopping him before he could achieve completion. Odo was close to ecstasy, shuddering with deferred pleasure, whereas Alice, watching him, was deep in thought, and as she saw him begin to regain awareness of who and where he was, she began to move again, knowing that he would be determined to finish this time. She allowed him to work towards that, seeing the half smile on his face develop into a rictus. And then, judging the moment to within half a heartbeat, she straightened her legs and stood up, dislodging him and holding him away with a straight arm until he finally subsided, gasping, and asked her what in God's name she was doing.

She smiled sweetly at him. "I am withholding pleasure, my lord, prolonging the excitement. You do enjoy me, do you not? You love the pleasure and the sinful-

ness of what I do to you and what I permit you to do
to me. Your lust for me makes you wild and keeps you
young, and the danger of it keeps you coming back to
me for more. You wallow in the enjoyment of fornicating with the King's daughter, of debauching her and
being debauched by her in all her wicked youthfulness,
despite the fact—or perhaps *because* of the fact—that
being caught doing so would be the death of you. Is
that not so? I know it is, dear Odo, because you have
often told me so. And thus I want you to consider
very carefully what I have to say next, and to believe
that I am being completely truthful. Then, once I am
convinced that you really understand and believe what
I will tell you, we can continue, and I will explain to
you what is in *my* mind for a change. Are we agreed?"

Odo nodded, but his eyes fastened on the matted
tangle of hair so lewdly exposed by the way she held
her skirts clutched up around her waist.

"Are we agreed, Odo? Look in my eyes and
answer me."

Reluctantly he raised his eyes to hers. "Agreed."

"Good. Now listen carefully." She bent her knees
and lowered her center towards him again, stopping
just beyond his reach but holding herself brazenly open
to his inspection. "Look at me, Odo. See what I have
here and think of this. You will never see, or feel, kiss or
caress or enjoy this body in any way, ever again, if you
breathe one single word of what we have talked about
here to anyone, be it my father the King or his Most
Holy Patriarch Archbishop." Odo had reared back as far

as he could, his eyebrows rising in disbelief, and she pounced, lowering herself onto him until she felt him penetrate her. "Feel me, Odo, feel that, then ask yourself if you believe I mean what I say." She withdrew her heat again as quickly as she had delivered it, and stood, dropping her skirts to conceal her legs.

"*Do* you believe?"

Odo of Fontainebleau nodded, slowly, and his eyes were filled with conviction. "I believe you. Absolutely and completely. I have no idea why you should make such a demand on me, or what would make you utter such a threat, but it is a potent one, and I have no wish to see it come to pass. I will say nothing, tell no one. But I may go to my grave wondering why."

Alice's wide grin was a sudden explosion of joy, one of those breathtakingly beautiful and all too rare demonstrations that she was, in fact, little more than a child, with a child's enthusiasm and delight still flickering within her. Odo's heart turned over, as it always did when he saw the fleeting magic of it.

"No, you will not," she exclaimed, spinning on one foot, the other in the air. "No need for that, my lord. I'm going to tell you now exactly why it must be so." She paused, hesitating on tiptoe, her eyes still flaring in little-girlish enjoyment. "At least I shall, in a moment, when we have finished our delights." She gathered up her skirts again, holding them bunched around her waist, and moved slowly back towards him, licking her lips, slack mouthed and lascivious, and watching his response as she drew near him.

This time there was no restraint and no withholding, and their melding was brief and incandescent, finished almost before it began. For a while they lay intertwined, too spent to move, and when Odo spoke again the shadows in the room had shifted visibly.

"Why would you punish me so severely for speaking of this to your father?"

They were respectable again, seated at a table by the window, drinking chilled wine and eating sweetmeats, their clothing showing no signs of their earlier activities.

"First, you must tell me something. Do you really believe the knight monks are digging in the Temple Mount?"

"Yes, I do."

"Very well. What lies beneath it, do you know?"

"Nothing, I suspect, unless a mountain has roots."

"Whence came its name, do you know?"

Odo shrugged. "It was named because the Hebrew temple built by Herod stood on top of it."

"On top of it, beside it, and around it. The temple was large, Odo, larger than you would expect in looking at what remains of it. And its precincts were extensive. I know, because Warmund told me himself. He is greatly interested in the history of Jerusalem, and of the temple in particular. Do you know when it was destroyed?"

"I know it was a long time ago."

"It was. The city, its temple, and most of its citizens were destroyed by the Roman general Titus more than a millennium ago, and those who survived scattered to the four winds. Think of that, Odo, a thousand years and more. The city was rebuilt, but not by Jews, for there were virtually none of those left alive in all Judea, and without Jewish worshippers, the temple could never be rebuilt. Its ruins have lain abandoned ever since, unused for one good and solid reason: the Romans destroyed the place, and Roman destruction was nothing if not thorough."

"Is that significant?"

"Of course it is significant, as significant as the fact that you believe these knight monks are digging in the Temple Mount. Why would anyone want to waste time digging through a mountain to find the rubble of a building that was destroyed a thousand years ago? What could they possibly be looking for?"

"Buried treasure?"

"After a thousand years? What kind of treasure could be there and how would they have found out about it?"

Odo's eyes brightened. "They have a map. They must have."

"A map of what, and from where, and drawn by whom?" Her voice was heavy with skepticism, but she was still deep in thought, merely musing aloud. "Warmund told me that the temple of Herod was newly built at the time of Jesus, completed only a short time before its destruction. And we know that the Romans would have hunted down and confiscated anything of value that remained in or around the temple, because that is what they always did. But Warmund also told me that, according to what he has been told, Herod's temple was supposedly built on the site of a smaller, far more ancient temple, the original temple of Solomon."

"You mean King Solomon, the Lawgiver?"

"Do you know of any other Solomon who built a temple?"

Odo sat silent, ignoring her sarcasm until she spoke again.

"But what I cannot understand is this: if those people are in fact digging, as you suggest, then why would they dig *there*, in the old stables, and directly into rock?"

"Because they can." To Odo it was self-evident, and he crossed his arms on his chest, plucking at his lower lip as he continued. "Consider it. They can dig there in secrecy, whereas were they to dig anywhere else, people would take note and start asking questions. The stables are theirs, given them by the King's own dispensation. So even though the work is far more difficult and arduous, there is little mystery behind the reason for their digging there: secrecy, security, and convenience, despite the inconvenience."

"No. I do not doubt your reasoning, as far as it goes, but there must be more to the truth than that. The treasure must lie close by. They would hardly start digging in the stables, despite all you have said, if their goal lay a mile away."

"That is logical."

"Therefore they must have found something that tells them there is a genuine and worthwhile reason for searching there ... a buried treasure of some kind. They *must* have found something. And bear in mind, they are monks, *new* monks, Odo, filled with enthusiasm and sworn to poverty, so we might reasonably expect them to be immune to the temptations of greed. Whatever it may be that they have chanced upon, therefore, it clearly has sufficient value to induce them to abandon their newly undertaken vows." She held up a hand to silence the bishop, although he had made no effort to speak. "And so you now, noble and dutiful creature that you are, would take this information to my father, as is your duty. And my father will then investigate your report and discover the truth of it, and whatever is uncovered will be taken immediately into the royal treasury for the good of the realm. And who knows, depending upon the value of what is found, you might even receive a small reward for your loyalty."

"You sound as though you do not believe that would be a good thing."

"Oh no, not at all. It would be an excellent thing, for my father. A source of wealth, perhaps of uncountable wealth, the existence of which he had never suspected. And he would not have to share it with a soul, because he is the King and the treasure was found in his realm. It would become his ... entirely his."

"It would." Odo pursed his lips and nodded slowly before permitting himself a half smile. "And you would rather it became entirely yours?"

Alice fluttered her eyes at him, a dimple forming in her cheek. "Of course I would. Would you not wish the same, were you me? And of course, I would be far more generous towards you than my father ever would. I would have to be, would I not, since you would know my secret?"

"We are speaking of treason here, my lady, of crimes meriting execution."

"Nonsense, my dear lord Bishop. We are speaking of dreams, fantasies, and rich imaginings, no more than that. Mere formless notions, lacking the slightest reality."

"At this time ..."

"That is correct."

"So how might you proceed, my lady, should these notions come to have foundation?"

"I have no idea, but when the time comes, I will know. There are only nine of these knight monks, these Poor Fellow Soldiers of the Christ, and they keep their activities secret even from their own lesser brethren, so it should not be difficult to find some means to interrupt them when the time is right." She grinned. "I am sure we will be able to find some way of compensating the poor fellows, even for treasonous activities. So, my dear, are you prepared to work with me in this?"

The bishop's hesitation was deliberate. "It is dangerous. Should the King find out about it ..." Then he began to nod his head, very slowly at first, then more emphatically. "But yes. Yes, I am with you."

"Excellent, Odo." Alice's voice had dwindled into a contented, soft-throated purr. "Now come over here to me and let us see if we can find some way, between the two of us, to seal our pact."

SIX

When Odo finally departed that afternoon, Alice lay down again on her divan, fanning herself languidly and thinking long and carefully. Odo had been in her quarters for close to three hours, a scandalous length of time for any man to be closeted alone with a woman, young or otherwise, but that concerned Alice not at all. Her personal staff were all fully aware that their discretion in such matters was the key to their continuing enjoyment of a life of great privilege. None of them, she knew, would dare to breathe a word of what she did with her private, personal life, on peril of their own lives.

Despite what she had said to Odo, Alice really had no idea of how to uncover the secret of the knight monks. She knew Hugh de Payens only slightly, but even that was enough to make it clear to her that she would be wasting her time to try bending him to her will and wishes. For one thing, the man was too unyielding, and too set in his warrior ways even to consider a dalliance with a woman young enough to be his granddaughter. His closest associate, Godfrey St. Omer, was cut from the same cloth, likable enough but impermeable when it came to resisting blandishment.

Alice had met men of their ilk before, and she found them, without exception, to be humorless and intractable, the only male animals in the world whom she could not sway to her will.

That left her with only one remaining source of information, Stephen St. Clair, and she felt sufficiently uncomfortable about her chances of success with him that she found herself unable to consider him objectively. He was the only *young* man in all her experience who had successfully resisted a full frontal assault from her, and she had no confidence at all that she could change anything on another meeting, because it seemed to her that she had used all her cunning, and all of it uselessly, in their last, ill-fated encounter. For months afterwards, she had been furious that he should run away from her, as a frightened peasant might flee the plague, and yet she had made no effort to punish him. She told herself that her reasons for that were humane, because he was a monk and therefore unworldly and socially inept, but she knew that she had left him unmolested purely for her own protection. No one knew anything about her and him, and she was afraid that should she pursue the matter, someone might learn the truth of what had happened, and she would become a laughingstock.

Out of sheer necessity, she had eventually convinced herself that the young monk knight's behavior that day had been a personal thing, born of his own inner conflicts and containing nothing insulting to her. His terrified pallor and his abject flight from her presence might have been born purely out of his religious conviction, although—and this was something she had come to consider only long after the event—it might equally have been born of simple nausea, engendered by the hashish that had been liberally mixed into the honeyed cakes they had eaten that afternoon. After years of using the drug, she herself was immune to the nausea it sometimes caused, but to a neophyte like St. Clair, it could have devastating results.

Be that as it may, however, Alice found little to look forward to in the prospect of facing the monk knight again, and yet she knew she would have to were she to have any hope of discovering anything about what they were up to, there in their holy stables. She knew she could not simply go riding in there, not even as Alice, Princess Royal of Jerusalem. The temple stables were now genuinely regarded as holy ground, given to the knight monks by her own father, and since dedicated to their use by the Patriarch Archbishop himself. As a woman, Alice had no right to enter there. She had known that for months, but she knew, too, that no *man* who was not of their brotherhood was allowed to enter there either. Only the knights of the Order of the Poor Fellow Soldiers of Jesus Christ were admitted, and they were very few.

An idea, unsought and unbidden, flickered at the edge of her consciousness. She picked up a tiny set of three brass bells and rang it, and within moments Ishtar, the head of her household staff, came in response.

"Princess?"

Alice looked at him, frowning in thought. "Did you tell me yesterday that Hassan the horse trader is back?"

"I did, Princess. He rode into the market with a new herd—a very small herd, I noticed—while I was there, just after dawn."

"Did you notice anything spectacular in his small herd?"

"Aye, my lady, I did. Two things, in fact. He has a pair of white ponies that look to be litter twins. From the little I saw, they appeared to be flawless."

Alice nodded, her upper lip caught between her teeth. Ishtar had been born and raised among horses, and she valued his opinions, since horses were the single thing in her life that she found she could trust and love without reservation. "Summon him, as soon as you can. Have him come directly to me. I will await him here."

Ishtar bowed deeply and hurried away to do her bidding, and Alice moved to stand by a window, hugging herself, elbows in hands, as she stared out into the late-afternoon light, seeing nothing except the images in her mind.

SEVEN

Hassan the horse trader was far more than he appeared to be, and Alice had known him now for five years, ever since her thirteenth birthday, in Edessa, when he had delivered her birthday gift from her father, a pure black Arab filly that Alice had immediately named Midnight. From that time on, for nigh on three years, Alice had visited the merchant's premises and spent time with him and his horses every time he returned to Edessa, and when she moved with her family to live in Jerusalem as Princess Royal, her patronage of his establishment there continued seamlessly. Since first she met Hassan, she had bought seven magnificent horses from him, but she had also come to rely upon him for much more than horses.

A new aspect of their relationship had come into existence after two years of developing familiarity between the pair of them, and it had nothing to do with sex or sexuality. Hassan was not an old man, but he was an austere one, with strongly held convictions of what was and was not permissible within society—society including, in his eyes, both the Muslim and the Christian communities. He was confident of his status with his God, and the name of Allah was never far from his lips, and Alice had learned that his convictions burned with the intensity of a zealot's.

In the autumn of Alice's sixteenth year, still several months short of her sixteenth birthday, one of her closest friends had been violated and cruelly beaten within the city's confines. The girl, whose name was Farrah, was Muslim, of an age with Alice, and the only daughter of an itinerant Arabian merchant. Alice had befriended her years earlier, as a child in Edessa, when Farrah's father settled there, and he had since set up a thriving enterprise in the city, a trading hub serviced by suppliers from around the world who brought him everything from spices to fabrics and from perfumes to exotic jewelry. Farrah had been waylaid in daylight, on her way homeward from a friend's house, and had been left lying in an alley near her father's place of business. She was found that same evening, but no one had seen or heard anything of what had happened to her, and no one seemed to have any idea of who might have done such a dreadful thing. The only possible means of identifying the miscreant had been provided by an earring, found in Farrah's clenched fist. It was of gold, and it bore traces of blood, indicating that she had ripped it from her assailant's earlobe.

Alice had let her fury be known, offering a substantial reward for any information leading to the capture of the rapist, but nothing had come of it until she visited Hassan's encampment almost a month later, when he next returned to Edessa. There, while sitting in his tent, discussing the points of a particularly fine horse, he had offered her a small box, removing the lid to show her a carefully folded scrap of velvet cloth. Alice had reached for it, to unfold the cloth, but Hassan stopped her, waving a finger in warning, then tipped the box upside down so that its contents fell to the tabletop. It took Alice several moments to recognize what lay there as two severed human ears, one of them with a lobe that was still torn and scabbed over, while the other bore a solid-gold earring.

Her initial shock had been followed by a surge of nausea that she fought down stubbornly, already aware of the exultation that was swiftly replacing everything else within her. There, on the tabletop in front of her, lay her vengeance and her vindication for seeking it when everyone she knew, it seemed, had been urging her to forget the episode. Gritting her teeth, she had forced herself to lean forward and pick up the ear that held the ring. It felt like nothing she had ever handled before, hard and cold and lacking in any kind of texture that would suggest it had ever been human or warm and alive. When she opened her fingers and let it fall to the tabletop again, the ring made a heavy, clacking sound. She sat back and looked at Hassan.

"Where is he? Where are you holding the rest of him?" She forced herself to look and sound moved, asking the question flatly, without emphasis, in the flawless Arabic she preferred to her father's native language.

A tiny tic that might have been the beginnings of a stillborn smile flickered at one side of Hassan's mouth,

but he shook his head and no trace of humor material-
ized. "I am not. The man is dead, killed while being
taken. That was some time ago." He wiggled a thumb
to indicate the ears. "These were brought to me yesterday, packed in salt."

Careful to keep her face expressionless, Alice nodded
her head once. "I will have the reward sent to you this
afternoon."

"There is no need. I seek no reward. I have no need
of money."

"Perhaps not, but the man who brought this about
probably does."

Hassan's headshake was small but decisive. "He has
been paid already. I rewarded him when he delivered
the evidence."

"I see. You mean he did this for you, not for me or
my reward." It was a statement, not a question, and
when the Muslim inclined his head in agreement, Alice
sat up straighter. "Then why did you order this? What
do you want from me?"

Now Hassan smiled. "I want nothing from you,
Princess Alice ... nothing." When he saw that she was
about to speak again, he resumed smoothly. "You are an
entirely remarkable young woman for your years,
Princess Alice, and I anticipate that you are destined to
generate great change in these lands, for both Muslim
and Christian. In the course of time, I feel convinced,
you will replace your able father as ruler here, for there
is nothing anywhere to forbid the ruler of any of your
Frankish lands from being a woman. And I believe you

will be a finer, stronger ruler even than he."

"I will be. You may rely on that." Her voice had been deadly serious, and her listener gave no sign of doubting her as she continued. "But how, or why, should that have any significance to you, a Muslim and a trader in horse flesh?"

"Because I am far more than either one of those." Alice's brows had drawn together in a frown, but Hassan was grinning broadly. "To do what I must truly do in Allah's holy name, I am required to be a student of humanity. Thus, when I see you frown and your eyes flash the way they did a moment ago, I have great hope for the future, because you are not afraid to do what you perceive needs to be done." His finger flicked idly towards the ears on the tabletop. "You have no fear of speaking the truth, no fear of demanding and taking what you want and what you believe to be right. That makes you unique among the others who surround you, most of whom would rather suffer shame and swallow insults than speak up and utter truths that might later come back to cause them discomfort. Within a society where compromise and corruption are commonplace, you represent, even at your very young age, a cleansing breeze. A fresh wind, in fact."

Hassan's face was sober now, no vestige of levity or humor to be seen in it. "You will find, as you pass through life, that there will be people who will offend you, grieve you, inconvenience you, and infuriate you. Some of them will thwart you, undermine you and your reputation, work to confound your best efforts and designs, and generally make nuisances of themselves. Many of those you will be able to deal with on your own terms. I have no doubt that you have already mastered the means of keeping most of such people firmly in their places. But there will always be a few, Princess, who will prove to be intolerable, their enmity a constant source of aggravation and frustration." He indicated the severed ears again. "The owner of those adornments will never be seen again. He has vanished from the earth and from the awareness of men."

Hassan paused again, and then said, deliberately, so that there could be no ambiguity or misunderstanding, "Anyone can vanish, Princess. Anyone. There is no person alive in the world today who cannot be made to disappear, suddenly, completely, and mysteriously. But it is also true that there is no person alive in the world today who cannot be made to die violently and shockingly, and highly visibly, in any public place at any hour of the day."

Alice's mouth had gone dry and she had to moisten her lips before she could respond, for she understood exactly what he was saying. "You mean, killed for the effect the killing will create."

"Precisely."

"Like the Assassins. They kill for effect, and to spread terror."

Hassan shrugged his shoulders eloquently. "It surprises me that you should know the name, but yes, if you so wish, like the Assassins. The Hashshashin. But it is most unwise to speak openly of the Hashshashin or their activities. And it is also unnecessary. Mothers use their name to frighten their children and make them behave, but most people do not really believe that the Hashshashin truly exist.

"Between us two, however, conversing alone and privately, suffice it to say that such matters as we have discussed are simple to arrange, and highly effective in their execution. You need simply call on me, at any time, and the matter is concluded."

Now, looking back on that conversation, Alice reflected that she had come to know the man himself well enough that she would not hesitate to call upon him should the need ever arise. He was unlike any other man of her acquaintance. From the outset of their relationship, he had clearly decided to trust Alice implicitly, for reasons of his own that he never explained to her— she was, after all, a woman *and* a Christian Frank, both of which should have precluded any interaction between the two of them—and she had always been deeply aware of the honor he had accorded her in the doing of it. And she respected and admired him greatly, ignoring the fact that her father would have had him executed out of hand had he known Hassan's true identity. His name, for one thing, was not really Hassan. That was merely a title, indicating his rank and status to those who knew anything of the organization to which he belonged. He was, as she had suspected, an Assassin, the senior member of that secretive and greatly feared organization in the Frankish lands of Outremer. An Ismaili Shi'ite Muslim, he had been born in the Yemen, like the founder of his organization centuries earlier, and had been raised to be one of the fedayeen, zealots prepared to sacrifice their lives for the cause in which they believed and for which they fought.

He told her that he had taken the name Hassan in honor of Al-Hassan, Hasan-I Sabbah, the Sheikh of Alamut, who was spoken of nowadays in hushed, awe-stricken tones as the Old Man of the Mountain, founder of the Assassins. The cult had existed since the eighth century, but in recent years, after the fall of the Alamut fortress, the charismatic Al-Hassan had reorganized his followers as single-mindedly religious enforcers, dedicated to the destruction of the ruling Sunni Abbasid caliphs. Since that time, the Shiite Assassins had pursued a campaign of ruthless terror centered around fearlessly executed public murders of prominent Sunni figures. Their weapon of choice was a dagger, they were meticulous in killing only the targeted individual, and they often performed their murders in mosques.

The fact that they used only daggers ensured that their killings were always sudden, unexpected, and violent, and their attacks had the appearance of being inescapable. The killer would frequently wear a disguise, enabling him to penetrate close to the target, and the subsequent murder would spread terror and confusion among the enemy. Because they were so close to their victim, the killers were frequently unable to escape the scene of their crime, but faced with certain death, the Assassins never committed suicide.

They much preferred the notoriety attached to being killed by their captors.

Hassan explained to Alice that their name, the Hashshashin, which the Franks had corrupted to Assassins, supposedly meant "the eaters of hashish," and it was commonly believed to have been given to them by their implacable enemies, the Sunni Muslims. The eaters of hashish, the orthodox Sunni claimed, defiled their bodies by polluting themselves with drugs in order to induce the trance-like state that permitted them to kill with such cold-blooded savagery and lack of conscience, even in holy places.

Hassan rejected the Sunni contention as ludicrous, saying that it was demonstrably political and self-serving. He admitted readily that his people used hashish, but he maintained that they used it for religious reasons, as part of their initiation ritual when they joined the ranks of the secretive organization, and thereafter as an aid to meditation. He reminded Alice of her own experiences under the influence of the drug, which his people supplied regularly for her own use. It was a relaxant, not a stimulant, and its users were generally rendered comatose to some extent, and certainly incapable of violence. The Assassins did not use it, in any sense, to bolster their courage or their dedication in any of their endeavors, and no one who knew anything about the noble and austere Al-Hassan, he told Alice, could ever believe that the devout sheikh would indulge in the taking of debilitating drugs. Hassan's own belief was that the name Hashshashin had originally meant "the followers of Al-Hassan" in the dialect of the Ismailis of the Yemen.

Alice had no illusions about Hassan's openness with her; she knew that he had something in mind in courting her goodwill the way he had, something that would work to his advantage and fit his agenda at some time in the future. That was to be expected in the world in which she lived, and it bothered her not at all. Everyone in power, anywhere, worked constantly towards safeguarding and increasing that power. Besides, knowing what she knew about who and what Hassan was, she was also forewarned, and therefore forearmed against anything he might attempt in future, and she knew he was fully aware of that.

Now she heard the swish and click of beaded curtains at her back and turned to face her visitor.

"You sent for me, Princess. How may I serve you?"

"As well as you always do. Be seated, Hassan, and hear what I have to say. I have a problem that I do not think I can resolve without your help—" She saw the flare of interest in his eyes and quickly held up a hand, smiling. "No, I do not desire to have someone vanish, but there is an individual—a man—with whom I need specific help."

Hassan's grin was instantaneous. "*You* need help with a man?"

Alice ignored his raillery and proceeded to tell him about the knight monk St. Clair and how he had proved to be immune to the power of her regular hashish. She was careful to give Hassan no indication that what she sought from the monk was information, merely asking him if he knew of any drug, or combination of drugs, that would render a man incapable of remembering what happened to him while he was drugged. She was more than content to leave Hassan to draw whatever lascivious conclusions he wished from what she was asking, and after a while he stood up and bowed deeply to her, waving his hand in salaam, from his forehead, to his lips, to his heart. He left then as silently as he had appeared, but Alice was content knowing that by the same hour of the following day she would have in her possession the means to overcome all conceivable resistance on the part of Brother Stephen St. Clair.

EIGHT

St. Clair was dreaming, a very pleasant, lethargic yet somehow frightening dream that had him struggling for wakefulness. It was not the woman in his dream who was causing him the concern, for he could see practically nothing of her, muffled in heavy garments as she was, and his only physical contact with her was the painful grip she had on his wrist, pulling him along behind her faster than he wanted to move, so that he staggered occasionally, unable to keep pace. He knew, vaguely, that she had a comely face, dark skinned with enormous brown eyes, but had anyone asked him how he knew that, he could not have told them.

This dream woman had come to him in a darkened room, shaking him into semi-wakefulness and talking unintelligibly in tones of great urgency, tugging and pulling at him all the while until he arose from the bed. He suspected that she might have helped him to dress, although he had no clear memory of such a thing, but then she had led him through a nightmarish maze of ill-lit, twisting passageways, each indistinguishable from its neighbors, tugging at him to move faster every time he tried to slow his steps, and stopping occasionally and inexplicably to push him against a wall, leaning her weight against him and holding a hand over his mouth, as though to prevent him from crying out. Each time she did that, he seemed to recall, he had felt as though someone was burning his wrists. They had come to a doorway and passed through it, and the light had blinded him, so that he had closed his eyes tightly against the glare of it. But still she had pulled him along, hurrying and bullying him.

Now, however, she had stopped, and he had stopped with her, standing without moving for the first time in what seemed like hours or even days. His wrists still felt as though they were on fire, and there was an ache in his chest that grew unbearable whenever he tried to breathe too hard or too deeply, but he knew he was no longer dreaming. The pains he felt were real pains. There were noises now, too, coming from somewhere, but they sounded muffled, distant and distorted. He concentrated on listening, and pushed himself harder towards wakefulness. The woman no longer held his wrist, the light was no longer so abrasive against his eyelids, and he could feel the surface of a wall against his back, although he had no memory of leaning against any wall.

Dreams could be extremely confusing, he knew and accepted that, but he was becoming frustrated now. He opened his eyes slowly, cringing only a little, and straightened up from the wall, turning his head to look at the woman beside him, but she had vanished, if she had ever been there at all, and he was alone, in an alley of some description, between high, blank walls and near a junction with a thoroughfare that was the source of all the noises he could hear. That much he saw and was aware of before the ground came rushing up towards him.

"BROTHER STEPHEN!"

The voice came again, calling his name from a great distance, but it was hard edged and insistent and he could not continue to ignore it, although he shook his head in protest and tried to turn away, seeking refuge in sleep again.

"Brother Stephen! Master St. Clair, wake up!"

He opened his eyes, squinting against the light, and saw someone looming above him, and his conditioning took control of him, so that he rolled away, throwing himself violently backward and reaching down for his dagger. But there was no dagger in his belt. He was wearing no belt. And his lightning-like roll was a sluggish, wallowing upheaval worthy of a besotted drunkard. He frowned again, still squinting against the outrageous light, and peered up at the shape above him.

"Brother Stephen? It is you, is it not? You are Brother Stephen, of the Poor Fellow Soldiers of Christ?"

"Who're you?"

The question emerged as a mumble, but it earned an immediate response. "It *is* you! Praise be to God, we all thought you dead."

St. Clair made a mighty effort to pull himself together, shaking his head to clear it, and when he tried to sit up the other man supported him against his knee, one arm around his shoulders. Stephen did not even have the strength to push the fellow away, and so he remained there for a moment, leaning against the man and breathing deeply, fighting down fear and panic. A few moments later, he pushed himself until he was sitting more upright and looked down at himself, peering at his open hands, seeing raw-skinned bracelets of red and angry-looking flesh around his wrists, and then his eyes focused down between them at the material of a rough brown knee-length tunic that was completely unfamiliar.

He attempted to speak, but his mouth appeared to be gummed shut. He hawked and spat weakly, then tried again, this time finding a croak that appeared to be all the voice he had. "Where am I ... and who are you? Tell me that first."

"Giacomo Versace, Brother Stephen. I'm one of your sergeants ... well, not *yours,* but I'm new. You don't know me, but I have seen you several times since I joined."

St. Clair was still working his mouth, gathering saliva that would allow him to speak. "Thank God for that, then," he croaked, "because I thought I ought to know you and was unable to. Where am I, and how came I here?"

"We are in an alley near the souk, but I have no idea how you came here or whence you came. I was passing by, on my way to the street of goldsmiths, and saw you lying here. I thought you dead, or drunk, and would have passed on by without stopping had I not seen the whiteness of your skin. Thanks be to

God that I did stop, for I have found a miracle: Lazarus arisen from the grave."

Stephen thought about that for a moment, trying to understand what the other man had said, and then he cocked his head. "Lazarus? You mean me?"

"Aye, most certainly. We said the Holy Requiem for your soul a month and more ago, believing you waylaid and murdered somewhere, for you had vanished without trace ten days before and we had swept the entire land in search of you. Where were you? Where have you been?"

"What mean you, where have I been? I have been here, in Jerusalem, since I returned from patrol ..." He hesitated. "When was that, yesterday? It must have been. We lost two men—the Englishman, Osbert of York, and Grimwald of Brussels, in a skirmish with a Saracen band."

"That was more than a month agone, Brother Stephen. Since then you have been missing, and we all believed you dead."

Stephen sat silent for a long time before he stretched out his hand. "Help me up, if you will. I think you had best return me to my brethren without further ado. I feel most devilishly sick and my mind is not functioning properly. Take me back to the Temple Mount."

WHEN HE AWOKE the next time, St. Clair knew he was back in the stables on the Temple Mount. He remembered that his return had caused a great commotion, and that the analogy used by his sergeant rescuer, about

Lazarus arisen, proved to be an apt one. All his friends and brothers crowded around him, staring open mouthed for the most part, touching him and fingering his clothing as though to assure themselves that he was, in fact, there among them and alive, and then the questions had begun, questions that St. Clair found himself incapable of answering because he could recall nothing of what had happened to him since what his friends referred to as his disappearance. They told him that he had returned from a long and arduous patrol, in which he and his men had ridden as far as the robbers' town of Ascalon, twenty-two miles to the northwest, in pursuit of a band of Saracen marauders who had raided and robbed a caravan that had traveled unmolested all the way from Edessa, only to be waylaid within a few hours' ride of Jerusalem.

Stephen and his men had arrived at the scene of the attack less than an hour after the raiders had departed, and he had decided to give chase immediately. Two days later, having spent hours on end quartering stony ground for the quarry's trail, which had been expertly concealed, he and his troop had been ambushed crossing a dry streambed, and although they had won the encounter and recaptured the goods stolen from the caravan, two of their number had been killed in the fighting.

Safely home again, and in no mood to celebrate, Stephen had made his report to the brotherhood and had then gone into the city, as was his habit, simply to be alone and to escape from the talking of his friends in order to mourn the loss of his two men in his own way.

He had not returned that night, and a massive search of the city turned up no evidence that he had ever been to any of his favorite places. The search had lasted for three days and had involved the Royal Guard and a large number of knights who volunteered their time out of appreciation for the efforts of the Poor Fellows in general and for St. Clair in particular, for his youthfulness and prowess had made him very popular despite his monkishness. Eventually, however, there came a point at which it had to be admitted that there was no place left that had not been searched, and that not a single gram of evidence had been generated to show where Brother Stephen might have gone or what might have happened to him.

It had been Hugh de Payens himself, after consulting with his brethren and the Patriarch Archbishop, who had, in the absence of St. Clair's body but with complete conviction that everything had been done that could be done to find the knight, formally declared him dead after an absence of fifteen days, pronouncing him abducted and killed by persons unknown, probably in retaliation for his activities against the brigands. Masses had been said for the repose of the dead knight's soul, and all of them had been well attended, several of them by the King himself, accompanied by his Queen and their daughters.

But now Stephen St. Clair was returned, miraculously restored, it seemed, if not to life at least to duty, for he appeared to be in reasonably good health. The Patriarch himself came to the stables on the afternoon of his rescue, to visit the prodigal and to welcome him back into the fold of his brothers' concern, and announced that he would personally offer several masses in thanks for the young knight's safe return. St. Clair had remained awake and alert throughout the activities that day, and he had even eaten a hearty dinner that night with his fellow monks, but then he had retired to his cot and fallen deeply asleep, and the prayer cycle of the night and the following day had not disturbed him at all. When he awoke later that second evening, he had been raving mad, and his fellow monks had been forced to restrain him, binding him to his cot with wide leather cargo straps from the stables and watching over him in shifts as, for five days and more, he behaved like an injured beast, gibbering and moaning and incapable of retaining food.

Now, unaware of how much time had passed, he awoke at mid-morning, feeling rested, fit, and hungry enough to eat his own horse, only to find that they would not yet let him out of bed, and so he was forced to remain there while they brought him bowl after bowl of hot, nourishing stew with crusty, fresh-baked bread. He was aware that everyone was watching him closely, but no one made any attempt to question him further than they had on the day of his rescue.

Towards mid-afternoon, he was visited by de Payens and St. Omer, and he knew from the outset that they had come in their official capacities, because they asked Gondemare and Roland, who were visiting him when they arrived, to leave. Stephen greeted the newcomers with a nod, then eased himself up until he was sitting erect, his back against the wall of his small cubicle.

"It is good to see you are become yourself again, Brother Stephen," de Payens began, "because for several days we have been considering an exorcism to cast the evil spirits out of you. The Patriarch visited you himself at that time, however, and he decided that what you required was merely sufficient time in which to recover yourself. It pleases me to see he was correct." He paused. "We have been making enquiries based upon what you told us when you first returned, and we now agree that you were abducted. That appears obvious now, and there is no mystery there. But even so, we have been unable to discover where you were held, or anything at all about the why of it, and that presents us with more mysteries than we can count."

St. Clair frowned. "I don't understand."

"No more do we, Brother, but the mysteries are there." De Payens began to tick off items on his fingers. "You were abducted. But why? Certainly not for ransom, because no demands were made and no one was informed you had been taken. And your disappearance most certainly had nothing to do with your high station, since you are no longer Sir Stephen St. Clair but a penniless monk, newly sworn to poverty. So why else would anyone wish to abduct you? Clearly not for revenge or punishment for some wrong, fancied or real, else you would be dead in truth.

"And you were tortured. You have burns and broken ribs and your entire body is a mass of bruising. Your wrists and ankles bear the scars of chains and manacles, too, yet there is mystery even there, for you had been missing for a month and more and yet, according to the physicians who examined you on your return, there was no injury or blemish on your body that appeared to be more than ten days old." He shook his head. "Even more than that, however, you were clean."

St. Clair's eyes went wide in astonishment. "What d'you mean, *clean*?"

"I mean clean, as in recently washed, laved, bathed ... *Saracen* clean."

"Recently? That is impossible. I last bathed at Easter, with everyone else, as part of the Easter Rites. You are mistaken."

De Payens shrugged. "I am not mistaken. It was the physician who examined you when you first returned— he was set to the task in person by the Archbishop— who remarked upon it. He said that you bore the scars of torture, but that your body had plainly been bathed and ... what was it he said, Godfrey? Pampered, yes, that was it. Your body had been bathed and pampered mere weeks agone. When we asked him to explain, he told us your toenails and your fingernails had been pared and tended to—'polished' was the word he used—and that all dirt between your toes and in your body crevices had been washed away."

"But that is impossible, Brother Hugh! I would remember such an outrage being committed upon me."

De Payens shrugged again, but not unsympathetically. "How can anyone explain such things, Brother

Stephen?" He held up a warning hand. "I pray you, do not be angry. Denial is acceptable, but bear in mind that you also have no memory of *anything* that happened during all those days when you were gone. Nothing at all. No memories. No awareness. And yet you were clearly alive *somewhere*, and presumably awake throughout that time.

"Thus I must ask you again, and beg you to be patient in obeying: can you think of anything that might help us find an answer to these questions? It might be something of which you have lost awareness, or something in your memory that you ignore for some reason, or even some thought, some image or idea that you have dismissed as insignificant."

St. Clair sat silent for a count of five and then began to speak, nodding his head as if in agreement with what he was seeing in his mind. "Abduction. Yes, you're right. I remember now what happened ... or some of it. I was in the marketplace, walking among the stalls, going nowhere special ... A thief stole a merchant's purse, right in front of me, and he saw me seeing what he did. He stood there looking at me, the purse in one hand, a little knife in the other, and then he turned and ran. He had a limp, and I ran after him, into an alley. It was dark in there, but I could see him ahead of me, still running, and then I saw other shapes moving on each side of me, coming at me, and something hit me hard ... The next thing I remember is waking up in the alley, perhaps the same alley, the day the sergeant brought me home."

"And you can remember nothing else? Think hard. Anything you can recall might be important."

St. Clair shook his head. "No, nothing else. Except the woman, and she was only a dream."

"How do you know she was nothing more than a dream?"

"Because she wasn't there when I opened my eyes and turned to thank her. I was alone in the alley."

"But she had led you there." St. Clair merely shrugged, neither confirming nor denying, and de Payens harried him. "What? You doubt that? If she did not, then how did you get there? Or do you think it *was* the same alley and you lay there for an entire month before being discovered?"

"Wait." St. Clair held up his hand, frowning in thought. "There's more ... I remember her coming to me more than once. Yes. I was on a cot of some kind, the first time, in a dark room, and I could not move. I was in great pain, I recall ... or I think I do. She carried a lamp and she leaned over me, peering into my eyes, and then she wiped my face with a cold cloth and went away, but I saw her nodding as she went, as though to someone on the other side of the room, someone beyond my sight. I remember I tried to turn and look, but the turning caused a pain in my back, so intense that I lost awareness of everything."

"And she came to you again, like this?"

"Aye, once more, when she roused me up and took me away. There was no one else there on that occasion, and all the doors were unlocked. She led me directly out of the place, wherever it was, and through a wending maze of tunnels to the alley where the sergeant found me, and as soon as we arrived there, while I was sun-blinded, she must have slipped away again, back to where she had come from."

"Sergeant Giacomo will remember where you were found, so we should find your escape route if we explore every entrance to the alley. The sergeant will take us back." De Payens and St. Omer, who had not spoken a single word, rose to their feet, and de Payens bent forward to clap St. Clair on the upper arm. "Stay well and rest easy. We will find the place, and that will lead us to your abductors."

Sergeant Giacomo remembered the exact location where he had found the young knight, but a painstaking search of all the surrounding buildings produced nothing positive that anyone could use to find either Brother Stephen's abductors or the place where he had been confined. After a time, as month followed month, other matters emerged to claim the monks' attention, so that the mystery of St. Clair's disappearance eventually dwindled to become a part of the lore of the new brotherhood, forgotten by everyone save on odd occasions when it would resurface and be discussed briefly, before sinking back into oblivion.

CONFESSIONS

ONE

Hugh de Payens stopped moving for a moment and used the back of a gauntlet-clad hand to wipe away the annoying bead of sweat that hung from the peak of his eyebrow. His eyes were already smarting from the steady trickle of sweat that ran down his temples from the mailed cowl covering his head, and inside his heavy, metal-backed gloves, his hands were hot and slick. The skin of his chest and back seemed afire, hotter than he could ever remember, and he could feel one stream of perspiration running down the center of his chest and another trickling in the groove of his spine and pooling at the top of his buttocks. He cursed silently and blinked his eyes rapidly, knowing he was beaten, but refusing to admit that he was too old to be fighting this hard in the full sunlight of mid-afternoon.

Across from him, having grounded the tip of his long sword, Stephen St. Clair had also stopped moving, patiently waiting for his superior to collect himself and start advancing again. The two men had been exercising together for almost an hour, in full armor, with swords and heavy shields, but de Payens noted, to his chagrin, that St. Clair seemed scarcely aware of the heat or of the length of time they had been pounding at each other.

Ah, God, to be young again, he thought, and impulsively threw away his shield, grasping the hilt of his sword with both hands and springing directly towards his younger opponent, hoping to take him by surprise and win a momentary advantage.

St. Clair saw him coming and raised his shield high above his head to block the great two-handed chop that de Payens aimed at him, but even as he did so, he dropped to one knee and lunged forward, sweeping his blade around in a silver arc to bring the flat of it crashing against the older man's knee with sufficient force to bring de Payens down, then pushing himself back and up, in a mighty heave, to regain his feet. He was on his toes again as quickly as his opponent fell, and stepped forward to press the point of his sword against the other man's mail-covered neck.

"Yield," he said.

De Payens lay glaring up at him for long moments, and then nodded. "Aye, and gladly. Help me up."

Moments later, they had both thrown down their weapons and heavy gauntlets and removed their mailed cowls and were scrubbing their fingers in their sweat-matted hair, the shaven squares of their tonsured scalps gleaming white in the sunlight. When they had set their pates a-tingling, they subsided, side by side, against a horse-sized boulder and sat staring up the hill to the entrance to their stables. Where once the paired entrances had been gaping holes in the lower wall topping the hill, demanding the eyes' attention, their obviousness had now been lessened by a nearby cluster of blockhouses and barracks, built over a period of several years to accommodate the lay brothers known as the Sergeants of the Order. There were sergeants everywhere de Payens looked now, all of them involved in matters of their own, and none paid any attention to the two knights sitting in the full glare of the sun. There was no shade where they sat, staring up the hill, but it was still too soon, the distance too great, for de Payens to contemplate climbing all the way up there to the coolness of the darkened stables. He would do it, eventually, but not until his breathing had slowed down and the fiery, prickling heat had lessened on his skin.

Neither man made any attempt to speak, and within moments de Payens became aware that his companion was nodding off, his chin sinking low on his chest, as though he were too tired to hold up his head. Frowning, de Payens was on the point of reaching out to prod St. Clair when the younger man started and snapped his head up, looking about him wide eyed.

"I need to speak with you, Master Hugh," he said, "if you will grant me the time. It is a matter of grave urgency, and I have been intending to approach you now for a long time, but I have always found some reason conveniently to hand for not doing so."

De Payens narrowed his lips, wondering what could be coming, but he was not really surprised. He had been aware for some time that all was not well with the youngest of his brethren, and St. Clair's use of the term "Master" spoke volumes, for although Hugh was the bona fide Master of their fraternity, appointed to that status by the Seneschal of the Order of Rebirth in Sion, the title was seldom spoken aloud within their brotherhood.

The young knight sniffed and wiped away another bead of sweat with a curled finger.

"Then we should go up to the stables," de Payens suggested. "It's cooler up there and we will be able to talk in comfort and in privacy. Besides, we're being disgracefully slothful sitting here in the sun. God may smite us both with sunstroke. Come on, then, up with you, and let's away."

Once on their feet again they gathered up their weapons and gear, then made their way up the hill into the shadows of the cavern that housed the stables, pausing just inside the entrance until their eyes adjusted to the darkness. The cavern had undergone great changes since the knight monks had first moved in, almost eight years earlier. Where there had once been two roughly equal divisions under the arching stone roof, there now appeared to be only one, on the right of the entrance, and it was divided into neat rows of well-made stalls for horses, with a sturdy platform hayloft above the stalls that was reached by stairs made from thick, solid planking—no small achievement in an environment where wood of any kind was hard to come by, and where finished lumber was a precious and sought-after commodity.

It was the area on the left of the entrance, however, that had seen the greatest changes. What had been a vast, empty space in the beginning was now a maze of roofless rooms, all of them open to the soaring stone vault above them and all solidly built, with thick, strong walls made from stone fragments mixed with mortar. Most of these rooms were used for storage, although some provided sleeping quarters for the nine brothers— Spartan and bare and without creature comforts, in the tradition of monkish cells. There was also a spacious chapel there, and a refectory, although the kitchens, for obvious reasons, were housed outside the cavern, in a stone building constructed specifically to hold them. At the rear of the place, close by the chapel, was another, more spacious room, equipped with tables and chairs and shelving, that served as a scriptorium and records-keeping center for the Master and his clerics. The rear wall was blank, save for a single door that was covered in heavy curtains of thick, felted wool that served to muffle any errant sound that might emerge from behind it. This was the sole entrance to the excavations that had been going on here now, without pause, for eight years, and those excavations were the source of the plentiful supply of stone chips and fragments that had been used to build the walls inside the cavern and to construct the sergeants' barracks buildings on the sloping ground outside.

The two men went directly to the records room where most of the clerical affairs of the small commu-nity—and of the Order of Rebirth—were carried out. There was no one there at this time of the day, and de Payens waved the younger man towards a chair, while he himself opened a cupboard and brought out a large jug of water and two cups, and poured for each of them. They sat and drank attentively for a while, concentrating on the enjoyment of their refreshment as de Payens downed two full cups and St. Clair emptied his third. Then, relaxing visibly, de Payens stretched and leaned back in his chair, rubbing his flattened palms against his armored belly.

"Very well then, Brother, speak. You have my full attention."

St. Clair sat thinking for a time, then raised his head. "I am beset by demons."

"You are beset ..." De Payens's voice died away almost completely. He had expected nothing close to what he had heard. "Demons?"

"Devils ... a devil."

"A devil. I see ... What kind of devil, do you know?"

"Aye. A succubus."

"Ah! A succubus ... That is ... That is a very common devil. A female devil."

"Aye, I know. Too well do I know that. I am possessed."

"Well, Stephen, I do not think I would go so far as to say that." De Payens knew this conversation was beyond his experience, but he knew, too, that he could not avoid it, and so he tried to lessen the importance of the issue by being placatory. "We are all of us, as men, and celibates, troubled by the succubus from time to time."

"I know that, Master de Payens. It has always been thus, and I have been as aware of it as everyone else is, from the age at which I first became a man. But that seemed normal, somehow, something that happened once a month, or sometimes twice, and was forgotten almost as it happened. This curse that plagues me now is different."

"Different ... How so?"

"In every way. Before this began, I would have dreams on certain nights, dreams vaguely remembered and formless, unknowable save that they left evidence of having happened. Spilt seed." He shrugged, managing to convey both awkwardness and embarrassment in one movement. "But all of that has changed ... Now this is a nightly occurrence. Every night. And I have dreams that I remember, sometimes very clearly, with places I can almost recognize although I know I have never been in any of them ... and sensations so intense that I can *feel* the reality of them. Every night, Master Hugh. Prayer has no effect on it, nor does tiredness, and yet I struggle every night against falling asleep. But then I do sleep, and I dream. And I am close to despair."

There was a long silence during which de Payens sat gazing at the younger knight, seeing his obvious and genuine misery, and in the course of it another of their number, Archibald St. Agnan, came to the door and hovered on the threshold, looking from one to the other of them and clearly realizing that there was something going on between them that was not for his ears. He raised an eyebrow at de Payens, who shook his head gently and sent him on his way with a wave of the hand. De Payens turned back to St. Clair.

"You said 'before this began.' Do you remember when it began? Is there a specific date or event in your mind associated with its onset?"

St. Clair sighed. "No, nothing that clear. But it began after my ... illness."

"You mean your abduction."

"Aye, abduction, illness. Whatever we call it. But it was after that that this began to happen to me."

"But that was nigh on eight months ago. When did these dreams begin?"

"I don't know, Master Hugh, but I think now it was perhaps three or even four months after my return. I was aware of ... certain things, certain inconsistencies in my body's functions. As time passed by, I grew more and more aware of them, because the incidence increased, from once or twice a month to three or four times, and then to once a week, and twice a week. Now, as I have said, it is nightly and I have no control over myself. I am possessed."

De Payens rose to his feet and began to pace the room, his hands clasped behind his back, his chin sunk on his chest, and St. Clair sat staring straight ahead as the older man moved from side to side. Finally de Payens stopped and stood facing him. "I cannot help you with this, Brother Stephen. It is beyond my capabilities and my experience. But I do not believe you are possessed, and so I want you to go and talk with the Patriarch, Archbishop Warmund. Tell him all you have told me. He will know far better than I how to help you. I am a mere knight, like you, a warrior, not a priest, and therefore I have no knowledge of possessions and such things."

St. Clair's face fell. "Aye, Master Hugh, but the Archbishop is a Christian. Have I need of Christian prayers now, think you, after so long without?"

"You have need of prayers, Brother, and of the understanding and assistance of a good and noble man who can intercede for you with his God, who is the same as your own. Our ancient Order has never quarreled with that kinship. Our concerns stem only from the misdirection that Christians have received from other men, over more than a millennium, concerning the allegations that the man called Jesus was the son of God Himself. That alone is the basis of our difference. Unfortunately, however, we suspect with good reason that it would quickly prove to be a lethal difference were it to come to light, and so our brotherhood has learned to live with the inevitable hypocrisies involved in being non-Christian yet living and behaving as Christians in a Christian world. It seems invidious and yet it is no more than simple self-preservation."

He paused, mulling over his next thoughts, and finally added, "There is far more to it than that, of course, although few of us in the brotherhood ever appear to think about it. I am referring to our own strictest rule: one family member, at most, from each generation." He looked St. Clair directly in the eye. "I have lost many hours of sleep over that, from year to year, since joining the Order, and I still have not yet come to terms with it. Every man of our brotherhood has kinsmen, brothers, cousins, and friends among the

Families—and I am not even referring to wives and female relatives—who do not belong to the Order and therefore live as Christians, never suspecting what we know to be true. And we live among them and they have no knowledge of who we truly are.

"Does that difference make us better men than they are? Does it disqualify them from being admirable, or make them lesser in any way? No, it does not. We know, through the Order, that they have been duped. But that is not a weakness, for the entire world, Christendom itself, grew out of that duplicity. And so, for the sake of our own sanity, we must accept that despite all the atrocities and abuses, the corruption and the disgraceful behavior that we see perpetrated around us in the name of Jesus Christ, this world is none the less peopled, by and large, with men of genuine goodwill, admirable men, governed by conscience and their own sense of propriety and the fitness of things."

He squinted at St. Clair from beneath furrowed brows, then nodded decisively. "Such a man is Warmund de Picquigny. I have no slightest doubt of that. The error of his beliefs is unimportant in this matter, compared to the strength of his convictions and his personal integrity, and I am *equally* sure of that. And as your Master, I tell you that you may believe the same with absolute certainty. Do you have any doubts of that?"

"No, Master Hugh."

"Excellent. Then I will go now, today, to talk to him and ensure that he will see you as soon as may be. In the interim, I will ask you to spend the remainder of this day in prayer, and wait for me to summon you. Now go, and be at peace. Archbishop Warmund will give you peace of mind, and if he feels you are indeed possessed, he will exorcise whatever demon dwells within you. Go now."

TWO

The Patriarch Archbishop of Jerusalem stood musing by an open window, his right elbow supported on his left fist as he leaned against a wall, stroking his nose with the tip of one finger and gazing out absently into the courtyard by his chambers. Behind him, in the Archbishop's private chapel, Hugh de Payens's youngest knight knelt alone in front of the altar, awaiting the Archbishop's return. The Patriarch, however, had no intention of returning before he had taken the time to decipher everything the young man had told him, and already he was faced with a mystery that he suspected might be insoluble. He knew beyond a doubt that young St. Clair was not possessed by devils. Bewitched, perhaps—and that thought, as it came to him out of nowhere, elicited a grim little twitch of one side of the Archbishop's mouth.

Although he was saddened by all St. Clair had told him, he was unsurprised, because it merely confirmed what he had suspected since the day of the young monk's unexpected return. He had asked one particular question of his supplicant, a question about color, prompted by something St. Clair had said, and the response had confirmed his suspicions and made clear to him some, but not all, of the many frustrating elements of this situation. Warmund de Picquigny now knew who had abducted St. Clair, but he was utterly mystified as to what might have prompted the abduction.

From the hazy details of the young man's ill-remembered dreams, and a specific color he had uncertainly recalled in response to the Patriarch's probing question, the Archbishop had clearly identified the royal palace, the former al-Aqsa Mosque, as the place in which St. Clair had been held captive, and with that he had known that there was only one possible abductor: the King's wayward and hard-headed daughter, Princess Alice. That was the source of Warmund's present perplexity, for although he held absolutely no illusions about what kind of person the King's daughter was, the Archbishop could see no sense of any kind in what he had just learned, unless the entire abduction and confinement had been dictated by sheer, unrequited lust. He could clearly remember the occasion on which he had rescued the unworldly young monk from Alice's clutches, and he had seen how angry she was with him at the time for his interference. Even so, he could barely give credence to the idea that Alice would go to such lengths simply to have her way with a complete innocent.

Alice le Bourcq, he knew beyond dispute, was a voluptuary and a hedonist, never having known the restraints of life in Christendom. Born and raised in the East as a child spoiled by doting servants and an indulgent father, she had been accustomed early to the luxuries and the exotic pleasures she enjoyed so shamelessly. It made no sense, therefore, in any slightest, conceivable degree, that accustomed since infancy to all the pleasures and perfumed delights of the bathing habits of the Arabs and Turks among whom she lived, she would stoop to abduct a foul-smelling, dirt-encrusted, ascetic, and penniless monk knight, heroic and laudable though that monk may be in his military aspects. And it made even less sense that she would do so in secrecy, and then go to such extreme lengths as must have been necessary in order to ensure his safe return to his brethren, after having tortured him for the final weeks of his captivity. That, in de Picquigny's estimation, was the final, imponderable facet of this puzzle. The Patriarch heaved a deep, heartfelt sigh and straightened up from his slouch.

Brother Stephen, de Picquigny could tell, was completely under Alice's sexual thrall. The color—violet—that the knight had mentioned in connection with his dreams of fornication existed only in one place in all the Kingdom of Jerusalem, to the Patriarch's certain knowledge: within the bedroom of the Princess Alice. De Picquigny had no slightest doubt of that because it was he who had been instrumental in importing the pigment from Italy, on behalf of the King, for the princess's fourteenth birthday. It had been extraordinarily difficult to find and outrageously expensive to purchase, and they had imported only sufficient for the princess's needs.

De Picquigny also knew, from his spies, that the princess frequently used opiates and narcotics to enhance her physical pleasures, and he knew, too, from personal experience, how stunningly effective opiates could be. He had been thrown from a horse, years earlier, and suffered a massive and complex fracture of his left thigh bone, in which the splintered end of the bone had been driven through the flesh of his leg and had then refused to heal, leaving him in constant pain and in danger of death, should the wound turn gangrenous. The physicians had been powerless to do anything for him, and in desperation his staff had engaged the services of the famed Muslim physician Ibn Az-Zahir, of Aleppo. The Syrian physician had immediately ordered the application of opiates, and the dementing pain had abated within moments, to Warmund's shocked but formidably grateful disbelief.

Warmund's priestly colleagues, forgetting their former helplessness, had at once started muttering jealously about sorcery and witchcraft, but he quickly silenced them. He had known about opiates for years, he told them, from information gleaned from his wide-ranging reading. He knew that the Roman legionary surgeons and physicians had used opiates for hundreds of years, and he had read many examples of how their painkilling powers had verged upon the magical. What he had not been able to imagine, until he experienced them for himself, was just how magically analgesic the opiates would prove to be. Under their influence he had lost all awareness, and all memory, of the pain from which they protected him.

But he had become addicted to them, too, and being weaned away from them once his wounds had healed was one of the most harrowing experiences he had ever known. Seeing the intense and debilitating sickness that the young knight monk had suffered in the days following his return, Warmund had recognized the symptoms of withdrawal that he himself had endured years earlier. He had said nothing to anyone, merely intimating that he would pray for the young knight and that the man would regain his senses within a short time.

Now there was no doubt in the Archbishop's mind that Stephen St. Clair had been abducted by the princess, for reasons known only to herself, and that he had been heavily drugged for the duration of his captivity.

The question bedeviling the Patriarch Archbishop at the moment was, what to do next? He could see no benefit at all in telling the young knight, or his fellow monks, what he now knew, because he knew St. Clair, hothead that he sometimes was, would be likely to go storming off in search of the princess, demanding an explanation, and that would lead to nothing but grief. Besides, if he were to inform the young man, or anyone else for that matter, that he had been abducted by the princess, he would virtually guarantee the loss of all hope of discovering what underlay the abduction.

Pushing himself away from the window, the Archbishop moved to sit at the long work table against the eastern wall, where he sat drumming his fingers on the tabletop for a long time before he rose again and went to the chapel where St. Clair awaited him.

"These dreams, my son," he said as he entered. "I have been thinking about them and about what you have gone through. You say you recall some of them clearly after awakening. Do you recall them with pleasure?"

The younger man had sprung to his feet as the Archbishop entered, and now his eyes went wide with consternation. "No, my lord Patriarch, I—"

"Do you anticipate them with pleasure before going to bed, or falling asleep?"

"No, my lo—"

"And do you compose your mind to accept the dreams before you fall asleep?"

"No—"

"I thought not, and I am glad of it. But I had to ask."

St. Clair's mouth hung slightly open and his brow was furrowed in incomprehension. Warmund beckoned with one hand.

"Come with me, if you will."

He led the other man out of the chapel and into the room with the table, where he pulled out a chair for St. Clair, bidding him sit, and perched himself on one corner of the table.

"You may have forgotten this," he said, "but the primary constituent of a mortal sin—the single element without which there can *be* no sin—is *intent*. Intent to sin. And intent to sin entails two things: the clear recognition that a given course of action will result in the commission of a mortal sin, and a decision, after that, to go ahead and sin deliberately, despite that certain knowledge. Do you understand?"

St. Clair shook his head, and Warmund sighed and spoke more slowly, enunciating each point clearly and emphasizing each one with a raised finger.

"I am telling you, as Patriarch Archbishop of Jerusalem, that I detect no sin in you, Brother Stephen. You have done nothing to incur guilt. These events are beyond your control. They are inflicted upon you without your volition, and therefore you are innocent of intent, and innocent of sin.

"I believe that much of the pain you are feeling is caused by your belief that you are sinning in these matters, so hear me clearly now in this, my son: you are not. Believe that, and it is my sincere belief that these dreams will pass from your awareness. Not at first, you must understand, and not quickly, but slowly and surely they will fade. Pray to God for sustenance and guidance, and place yourself in His hands. He will not abandon you. Now go in peace and remember me to Brother Hugh."

THREE

"**B**rother Hugh, Brother Stephen is back." Payn de Montdidier hesitated, seeing the incomprehension in his superior's eyes, then added, "Brother Stephen. You asked me to let you know when he returned, from his meeting with the Patriarch."

"The Patriarch?" Hugh de Payens continued to look befuddled, but then, as he pronounced the words, his face cleared. "Ah, Brother Stephen, yes, of course. Have him come to me at once, if you will, Brother Payn." As the other swung away in obedience, de Payens returned to the document over which he had been poring, his pointing fingertip once again tracing the lines on the ancient chart.

That morning, shortly after Stephen St. Clair's departure for the Patriarch's palace, the word they had all been anticipating for years had finally arrived. But it had not come from Anjou. It had come from the ground beneath their feet, where against all odds, the two brothers working the early-morning shift in the tunnels had broken through into an older tunnel that ran above and slightly to the left of the one in which they had been working. The breakthrough had been accidental, signaled only by a sudden rift in the roof of the tunnel.

The roof of that tunnel had, for years, been solid stone, yet now there was a hole, through which a stream of debris and dust was falling. As soon as the initial fall had abated, the monks had gone forward, with great care, to investigate, and it became immediately obvious that they had encountered something beyond their experience.

Hugh had no doubt that they had found one of the very tunnels shown on the map he was now scrutinizing, one of a series of charts carefully copied from the ancient original in the Order's archives. The tunnels it depicted were of unimaginable antiquity, dug deep beneath the Temple Mount itself, in the days following the flight of the Hebrews from Egypt.

By sheer coincidence, Hugh himself had been the first person Gondemare and Geoffrey Bissot had seen when they came bursting from the tunnel entrance full of the news of their discovery and as stunned as he was by the unimaginable magnitude of what their find signified. He had none the less retained sufficient presence of mind to rein in their enthusiasm quickly, before their exuberance could endanger any of the secrecy the brothers had worked so hard to maintain. The two monks had been abashed and slightly chastened by his warnings to be cautious, but their eagerness had been irrepressible, and so he had sent them back to work temporarily, until he could have the opportunity to assemble the brethren for the announcement of their tidings.

He had not yet had time to do that. He had not yet had time even to settle the turmoil in his own breast, for this discovery was the first sign they had encountered, in eight years of solid, grindingly brutal labor, that there might, in truth, be substance to the legendary lore they were pursuing, and a solid core of facts underlying all their hopes and endeavors. His first act, after sending the monks back to work in the tunnel, had been to retrieve the old map from the case in which it was stored and to check it against the direction in which they had been digging for the previous five months. They had sunk their primary shaft vertically for eighty-six feet, by Montbard's calculations, and then, relying on the most careful mathematical analysis of which they were capable—and two of the brethren were highly capable in that field—they had established a sound method of directional digging, striking northeastward at a depth they had gauged likely to lead them to intercept another tunnel. None of them, Hugh was secretly convinced, had expected anything to come of it, for everyone knew that the odds against such an intersection were great enough to defy calculation. It was nothing short of madness to think that they could dig vertically, then horizontally, and actually find another excavation dug thousands of years before.

Yet that was exactly what they had done.

A noise from behind him made him turn quickly enough to surprise St. Clair, who had just entered. The younger monk drew himself up and bowed his head slightly. "You sent for me, Brother Hugh."

"I did, Stephen, I did. How went your interview with the Patriarch?"

St. Clair nodded, his face somber. "Well enough, I think. He does not believe me possessed."

"I knew that. I told you so myself, did I not? What did he say to you?"

"Not much. He listened closely while I told him everything you had bidden me tell him, and then he made me tell the whole tale again, interrupting me this time with many questions, some of them very strange and seemingly lacking in logic."

"Such as what?"

St. Clair huffed a deep, sharp sigh. "The colors in my dreams held great interest for him, although I had scarce been aware of any colors."

"Colors?"

"Aye, he was insistent that I think of those, and as I did, they came back to me ... strange colors I could scarce describe ... yellows and purples and reds. Then, when I had finally remembered them, he lost interest in them, it seemed to me. Finally he told me to put my faith in God, who would not abandon me, and he said he believes that much of my torment comes from my own belief that I have sinned sorely. He attempted to convince me that I could not have sinned, since I had no intent to sin. But I've seen too many knights standing over butchered bodies that they had not meant to kill in the beginning to believe in that. A killing is a killing. A sin is a sin."

"I see. Did he say no more?"

"Only that I should pray, and that the torment, whatever is causing it, will recede eventually."

"So he believes you should return to your patrol duties?"

The look that St. Clair shot back at him was filled with cynicism. "Did you expect otherwise, Master Hugh? I draw four patrols to every other brother's one. Of course he would want me to return to my patrol duties, but he did not say so."

De Payens grunted, deep in his chest, and bit back the impulse to chastise the younger monk for his angry tone, reminding himself that St. Clair had been under great strain recently. Instead, he walked away, scratching with one finger at a sudden itch in his ear. "I don't think I want you to return to patrol duties. Not yet, not for a while." He turned back and waved an open hand towards the table and the chairs beside it. "Sit you down."

As St. Clair moved slowly to obey, de Payens continued. "I believe it might not be in your best interests at this time to be too much out there in the world you have so recently sworn to forsake, and so I intend to keep you walled in here for a time, away from the world of ordinary men. I have work for those young muscles of yours—work that your elder brethren will be glad to see you undertake." A wide, kindly smile took any sting from his words, and he sat down on the other side of the table.

"We have had great news this day, Stephen, news that justifies everything we have been doing since we came here. Gondemare and Bissot broke into a tunnel this morning. I have not seen it yet, and none of the others know it has even happened—I'll be telling them all as soon as you and I are finished here. It is, of course, an ancient excavation, and it appears to have been filled in deliberately. Gondemare and Bissot both agree on that. The passageway is filled with rubble. That means it is likely to be one of the tunnels sealed and filled in by Titus's legionaries after the capture of Jerusalem. That was a thousand years and more ago, Stephen, eleven hundred and fifty years, in fact. Think of that. It defies comprehension." He sat quietly for a time, trying in his own mind to grasp that time span.

"The work will be easier from now on, but it will still be arduous. We will no longer be piercing solid rock with every hammer blow, but we will now be faced with removing far more detritus, far more quickly than we have been required to in the past. You wish to ask me something?"

"What about—? How will we know where we are down there? I remember hearing you say once, long ago, that there are scores, perhaps hundreds, of passages down there."

"Mathematics." De Payens smiled. "Our first task will be to find an intersection with another tunnel. Our tunnel has done its work, and from now on it will function only as an adit to the workings. Once we find that new intersection, we will be able to work out where we are on this map. It may take us a long time, perhaps even more years, but at least we know now that we are within reach of our goal, and that the goal is real. So, will you be content to work beneath the ground for a while, away from the sunlight?"

St. Clair nodded, his face devoid of expression. "I will, Master Hugh."

FOUR

O ver the course of the ensuing weeks and months, they found that there were areas within the newly discovered network of tunnels where the air was better, purer, than it was in others, and this appeared to depend upon the undulations of the tunnels themselves, for they were by no means regular. Sometimes one branch would stretch levelly for scores of paces and then, for no discernible reason, the grade would tilt up or down for a distance, sometimes returning to the original level, sometimes not. Montdidier had been the first to remark that the air always seemed thicker and more foul at the bottom of these variances than it ever did at the top. In saying that, he had stirred up controversy, for there was little else down there to capture the attention of his brethren, but after months of arguing back and forth and pro and contra his observation, a consensus had formed, accepting his opinion.

Stephen had been in one of the sweet-air regions the previous week, and he knew that he might not have seen what he found there in another spot, for one of the main advantages of the sweet-air zones was that the light of their lanterns and candles always seemed brighter in such places, as though the very flames themselves rejoiced in the clean air. He had been working smoothly that day, shoveling rubble into the small, wheeled carts they had built to haul away the detritus. As he filled up each cart, he would pull on the rope attached to it, and whoever was working behind him at that point would pull the filled cart away, then push an empty one back up to him. Perhaps twenty or thirty paces distant now, to the rear of where they were digging, there was a lateral split in the tunnel, a shift formed by some upheaval in the earth that had taken place since the tunnel was dug, and one side of the split fell away into a deep crevasse. It was less dangerous than it appeared to be at first glance, for the rift was barely more than a stride across, but it seemed endlessly deep, for a stone dropped into it produced no sound of impact beneath, and the tunnelers had been tipping all their refuse into it now for months.

The space where he had been working that day was narrower than usual, and St. Clair had been stooped over, alone at the end of the tunnel, when he thought he saw a metallic glint among the stone fragments ahead of him. Curious, he had picked up the nearby lamp and stepped forward, and the glint grew stronger, reflecting the light. He had found a jewel, a translucent blue stone, teardrop-shaped and almost as large as the pad of his thumb, its narrow end clasped in a silver loop that was clearly designed to hold a chain. He had held the bauble up to his light to examine it, and found himself smiling at the beauty of it, its color and its texture, smooth and cool to the touch, and then he had dropped it into his scrip and taken up his shovel again, his lamp safely returned to where it had been. It was far from being the first treasure they had unearthed since finding the tunnels. They had found more than a score already, including several magnificent pieces of jewelry and a number of copper, silver, and even gold coins bearing the likenesses of several Caesars, predominantly Augustus and Tiberius, although a few were of Nero.

Now, a week later and twenty paces farther down the tunnel, the wall ahead of him subsided slightly as he pulled out yet another shovelful of small stones and dust, and he found himself looking at a gap between the top of the dirt wall and the tunnel roof. Within moments he had clambered up and crawled carefully, sheltering his candle flame, into one of the infrequent stretches of tunnel that had not been filled with dirt. He had barely entered the place, however, when his candle began to gutter and its flame shrank to a fraction of its normal size, indicating that the air in there was foul, and so he struggled out again.

He had barely escaped, and with only his head and shoulders projecting from the narrow crawl space, he choked on the acrid smoke from the candle's smoldering wick and was shaken by how close he had come to losing consciousness. He sprawled face down on the slope of the rubble and sucked air into his lungs in great, whooping gulps until he felt strong enough to struggle forward and slide free. Then, after rolling onto his back at the base of the pile, he sat up and pushed himself on his heels to where he could prop himself against the wall and look up at the narrow gap near the roof.

Before anyone else tried to enter that section of tunnel, he knew, all the rubble blocking it would have to be cleared away, allowing fresh air to penetrate the space and make it habitable, but he felt no driving urge to leap up and tackle the task immediately. He had come close to panicking while he was scrambling out of there, fighting off waves of nausea and dizziness as he struggled to draw a breath, and he was content, for the time being, to relish the pleasure of simply breathing clean air. Farther back along the tunnel behind him, he could hear voices and rumbling wheels as his shift mates, Montdidier and Rossal, worked at emptying the last trolley he had sent back to them, so he knew that, despite the disorientation caused by his misadventure, he had not been long away from his work. His stomach tightened and heaved without warning, and he rolled onto all fours and vomited up the foulness of whatever it was that had almost overcome him. Then, feeling better, he rolled onto his back, looking up at the arched roof as he concentrated upon breathing deeply and regularly, enjoying the cool, clear air, seemingly far more fresh than usual, that was flowing from somewhere nearby.

A short time later his hand moved to his breast, where the blue stone bauble now hung from a string about his neck, and he began to rub the smooth surface gently between his thumb and his forefinger, his attention drifting away from his surroundings. He had not turned the jewel over to Brother Godfrey as he should have at the end of his shift the day he found it, and even as he had walked by him, he had wondered at his own behavior. He had no intention of stealing the thing; that thought had not occurred to him at all. The jewel held no value for him, or for any of his brothers, unless they might wish to sell it, which would have been sheer madness. St. Clair felt no lust to own it, and no desire even to look at it, for in the permanent semi-darkness of his sleeping quarters its beauty would have been invisible. The simple truth was that he had found something formlessly comforting in the smoothness of its texture between his fingers, and he had decided that he did not wish to part with it straightaway. The thing itself was a mere trinket, with no intrinsic worth, but it gave him solace, so he was content that he had committed no sin in temporarily keeping it for himself. He did not permit himself to wonder why he should need solace, but he did tell himself frequently that he was doing no wrong.

There had been moments throughout that time, however, when his conscience had bothered him, because do what he would, his mind kept throwing up whispered reminders of oaths and vows undertaken, and it did little good to attempt, at such moments, to rationalize the underlying logic of his stance. That had been bothering him increasingly, and now he thought of it again, hearing Rossal's harsh, characteristic bark of laughter in the distance as Montdidier made a jest of some kind.

He and his eight brethren of the Poor Fellow Soldiers of Jesus Christ, supported and sustained by their sergeant brothers, had built themselves a rock-solid reputation over the years they had spent as warrior monks here in Jerusalem. They were generally perceived as being friends and valuable allies of the Church authorities, dependable, lacking in worldly ambitions, and therefore trustworthy in a world where few men inspired or deserved trust. The Patriarch Archbishop relied upon them heavily for the protection of the growing streams of pilgrims forever coming to the city, and King Baldwin made no secret of the fact that the activities of the brotherhood, to whom he referred as "his" monks, greatly simplified his task of defending his borders and maintaining what he called "the peace of Christ" within his domain.

St. Clair found that ironic, and he frequently wondered how his brethren felt about it, although he had never spoken of it with any of them. An unwritten law had come into existence since their formation here in Jerusalem forbidding them to discuss any of the things that marked them as being different from others, save in the conclave of their ritual Gatherings as the Order of Rebirth. Even there, however, the irony of their situation was never mentioned, since the Gatherings occurred so seldom nowadays and the need for absolute security was serious enough to ban any discussion of sensitive Order-related topics. There were too many ears around, and too little real privacy within the stables, to permit regular Gatherings. One day, perhaps, they might be able to acquire secure, defensible quarters in which they could safely conduct their rites and ceremonies, but in the meantime they lived together each and every day, their behavior and their way of life constant reminders of their duties and responsibilities. That awareness, allied with the risks of being overheard by profane ears, ensured that they did not speak among themselves of the things that only they knew.

Stephen St. Clair, however, could not stop marveling at the contradictory nature of their very existence, and he spent much of his time thinking about the cold reality, and the staggering cynicism, involved in being a warrior monk.

"What's wrong with you?"

The voice startled him, and he opened his eyes to find Montdidier staring down at him. Stephen grunted and hoisted himself onto one elbow, then pointed to the tiny space at the top of the slide.

"I went—" He was surprised to find that his tongue and lips were coated with thick, powdery dust. He spat, drily and with great difficulty, and tried uselessly to moisten his lips with his tongue before speaking again. This time his voice emerged as a dust-blurred croak. "I went through there. The air's foul."

Montdidier looked up at the narrow strip of blackness. "Idiotic thing to do, my friend. You would have had my hide had you caught me doing such a thing. Here, drink." He handed St. Clair his flask of water. "What's back there?"

St. Clair rinsed his mouth and spat, then swallowed a mouthful of water before passing the flask back. "A stretch of empty tunnel. I broke through into it, then crawled in to see how long it was, but I had to turn back before I could see anything. We'll have to clear the entrance and let the air change before we go inside."

"That was a fool's trick, Brother. You know better than to do a thing like that without calling for support before you go in. Are you all right?"

"I will be in a few moments. But I thank you."

"Hmm. I thought it was taking a long time for you to send down the next truck, so I came up to see what you were doing. You're absolutely thick with dust—did you know that? Caked with it. Even your face."

St. Clair scrubbed at one cheek with the back of his hand, feeling the coating on his skin. "It's from the rubble, where I crawled through … it's like flour in there."

Montdidier shrugged, unimpressed. "Well, I'm glad you're not as bad as you look. I thought you were dead when I saw you lying there. Looked like you'd been turned to stone. But then I saw you breathing. That foul air can kill you faster than you can snatch a breath—you know that. You could have been dead even before I thought of coming to look."

"Help me up, I'm fine." Montdidier hauled him to his feet and St. Clair brushed off the worst of the dust that coated him, then retrieved his shovel and was back to work before the other man had begun to walk away, and as he shoveled, he forgot about the space behind the rubble and began to think again about what had been preoccupying him earlier, the great secret of his Order and its place within the Kingdom of Jerusalem.

Cynicism was what he had been thinking about

when Montdidier interrupted his thoughts, and now he returned to thinking of it, acknowledging that hypocrisy had walked hand in hand with it in the inauguration of the fighting monks of the Temple Mount, and that, irrespective of the noble motivations underlying their establishment, he and his fellow monks were living a lie simply by being here, pretending to be Christian while they searched surreptitiously for evidence that could destroy the Christian faith. What else, he asked himself wryly, could that attitude encompass besides hypocrisy?

St. Clair knew, although he seldom stopped to think about it, that he was one of the rarest of rarities in his own age—a literate, educated knight who had been gently reared within a good and devoutly Christian environment. He had spent much of his youth in the company of the small, devout fraternity of monks who lived and labored industriously on a small corner of his father's lands and who adopted the boy as their special favorite, much as they might have taken in a stray dog.

As they began to see young Stephen's potential, the monks grew serious in tending to his education, so that the youngster spent fully half of his time with them, absorbing what they taught him, and the remainder of each day with his father's veteran master-at-arms, Pachim of Arles, who had elected to see to the boy's military education in person. Learning from both sources, Stephen had been taught, as a matter of course, to be ethical, judicious, and temperate in everything he undertook, and now that he was a full-blown knight with duties of his own, he frequently found himself recalling those days and wondering when the magic that had illuminated them died. He knew that disillusionment had killed it, if magic it had been, and that it had occurred long before he joined the Order of Rebirth and, hand-picked, had set sail for Outremer, at the direct order of Count Hugh of Champagne.

As a young knight, from the moment he came of age to bear arms, Stephen had lived and served as an ordinary knight-at-arms in the service of Count Hugh, although he had never set eyes upon the Count. But the experience, to which he had looked forward with keen pleasure, had been disastrous, and Stephen had been appalled by the casual and mindless depravity, the venality and the corruption of his fellow knights. None of them, he quickly came to see, betrayed the slightest interest in anything other than the pursuit of pleasure and satiation. Their entire lives were dedicated to armed violence, and to the violation of women, with rape and ravishment accepted as part of the reward for serving in the armies. He was sufficiently disgusted to give serious consideration to joining the fraternity of his friends the monks, but bound by his feudal duty to his liege lord and driven by the need to be scrupulous and exact in fulfilling his commitments, he had first sought out Count Hugh in person and explained why he wished to do such an unheard-of thing in forsaking the world of arms for that of prayer.

Count Hugh, astonished as he had seldom been, had taken close notice of this remarkable young man, knowing already that St. Clair was a firstborn son of one of the

Friendly Families. Discovering soon afterwards—for he launched immediate enquiries—that St. Clair had been approved several years earlier for admission into the Order of Rebirth, but had left home to travel and fight abroad before he could be initiated, the Count had promptly set about arranging matters so that the Order could benefit from the young knight's sterling abilities, a melding of the radically opposed professions of arms and the priesthood, by using him for its own purposes in Outremer. At that time, Hugh himself had but recently returned to his county in Champagne from Jerusalem, and he was one of the handful of men in the entire world who knew that the Order's purposes there had multiplied in recent years, since the revolution initiated by Warmund de Picquigny when he formed the Patriarch's Patrol.

Since the early beginnings of knighthood, there had been little love lost between churchmen and the warrior class, and the differences between the two estates had widened since then. The knights of Christendom, only nominally Christian at the best of times, knew no containment and nothing of moderation, and they had no fear of reprisals for anything they did, since reprisals, when all was said and done, entailed fighting, and fighting was the be-all and the end-all of their existence. There were countless thousands of them, each a law unto himself, and until Pope Urban had conscripted all of them to free the Holy Land from the grip of the infidel Muslim, they had threatened all of Christendom with utter anarchy.

Nowadays, the Holy Land was filled with knights,

few of whom bore any resemblance to Christians in the traditional sense, removed as they were from any vestigial remnants of the civilizing influences of wives, families, and social responsibilities. They were warriors all, and savage in the way of warriors. Many of them were guilty of heinous crimes, both at home and in Outremer, and most of them were still so ungovernable that until the formation by Warmund de Picquigny of the new order of warrior monks in Jerusalem, no sane person would have believed that such a thing would ever be possible. Until the Patriarch Archbishop took that unprecedented step, no cleric had ever been permitted to bear weapons, let alone take human life. The fifth commandment, "Thou shalt not kill," was unequivocal, and its application universal.

Warmund de Picquigny, however, had viewed things from a different and greatly troubled perspective: that of a senior prelate faced with the apparently hopeless task of protecting an entire patriarchy against destruction by a hostile, anti-Christian presence that surrounded it. Spurred by urgent and unrelenting need, he had applied some moral definitions of his own that were both radical and innovative, bluntly stating that men sworn to the service of God must, by definition, have a Christian duty to defend their God and His works against faithless unbelievers who sought to destroy His servants in His earthly kingdom. The Patriarch had, in effect, propounded a justification for creating a new breed of churchmen, making it not merely forgivable but laudable for priests and monks to fight and kill other men in the name of God and His Holy Church, and it was clear that, as Patriarch Archbishop of Jerusalem, he saw neither cynicism nor hypocrisy in such a blatant warping of rules, criteria, and interdictions that had existed for centuries in order to suit the political exigencies of the moment.

Count Hugh, as Seneschal of the Order of Rebirth, had, on one level, been involved with the new order of knight monks from soon after its inception. At another, secret level, however, he had been one of those responsible for making the entire thing possible, in order to further the designs of the Order of Rebirth, and he had clearly seen the advantages to having a young knight of St. Clair's caliber within his camp. Sir Stephen St. Clair had quickly been taken into the Count's household and enrolled as a potential entrant to the Order, under the Count's personal sponsorship, and he had responded so favorably and enthusiastically to his tutors that he was Raised to full membership in a remarkably short time. A bare three years later, carrying the Count's own instructions as Seneschal, he had been dispatched to Jerusalem, to join the brethren of the fledgling order of knight monks.

Now an admired and honored veteran of the Poor Fellow Soldiers of Jesus Christ, who were looked up to by the entire populace as champions of the holy faith, St. Clair frequently found himself shaking his head in rueful disbelief and reflecting on the irony of their situation.

That he and his eight brethren were not Christian was

the single biggest secret of their fraternity, and they guarded it, literally, with their lives, for they would all be condemned to die instantly were the truth to become known or even suspected. Each man among them came from a Christian family, and their parents and siblings were all Christians, as were their servants and associates, the sergeant brothers who supported them and bore the brunt of their patrolling duties. The nine knights themselves, however, had relinquished Christianity when they were Raised to the Order of Rebirth.

Even the contemplation of that, after so many years, still had the power to astonish St. Clair, for that single act of relinquishment had been, for him and for each of his brethren, the most momentous and far-reaching commitment of their lives, and it was one that none of them could have accepted had it been presented to them in any other way. They had not been asked to abjure their former religion, nor to condemn it. Instead, surrounded by the warmth and trust of their nearest and dearest friends and relatives, some of them sponsors, all of them brethren, and knowing that each one of them had taken the selfsame route in earlier years, the neophytes had simply learned that there were other, older traditions of enlightenment than the Christianity that was pre-eminent in their world at that time, and that they and their ancestors had sprung from one such tradition. That their particular tradition was firmly rooted in Judaic principles was an anomaly that surprised most of the newly Raised members, but they soon came to accept that, after a millennium of careful nurturing and close attention to the content and form of its official Lore and rituals, the Order's fundamental Jewishness was no more surprising, and no less Jewish, than the origins of Christianity itself.

Stephen St. Clair had been unwilling to concede that understanding without a struggle, and he could still remember, almost verbatim, the discussion that had triggered his conversion, although it had, in truth, been more of a forceful argument than a measured debate and it had left him—or so he had thought at the time—unconvinced. Now, as his body settled into the easy, driving rhythm of shoveling rubble into the carts for disposal in the crevasse, he thought about it again, and it was still the foremost thing in his mind when, many hours later and bone-weary, he lowered himself to the boards of his cot, only to toss and turn for much of the night, remembering that far-off afternoon clearly and unable to find sleep in spite of his tiredness.

FIVE

W hat Stephen remembered most about his uncle, Sir William St. Clair—and it amused him, as always, that this should be the first thing to spring into his mind even after so many years—was that he seemed too *young* to be an uncle. Uncles, Stephen had always supposed, were on a par with fathers, members of an older generation and therefore beyond the understanding of young men of his age. This particular uncle, however, had been his father's youngest half-brother, born to Stephen's aging grandfather and a new, young wife who had replaced Stephen's long-dead grandmother. And the truth was that Sir William St. Clair deserved to be remembered and respected for much more than his astonishing youth, for he was the natural successor to his own father, the austere and distinguished Sir Stephen St. Clair who had landed at Hastings with William the Bastard in 1066.

More than any of his several brothers, William possessed and used all his father's attributes—his massive stature and strength, his charm and wit, his intelligence, and his unparalleled skill with every imaginable weapon. He had ridden to the wars against the Seljuk Turks in Outremer at an early age and had earned himself a fearsome reputation for valor and prowess, before being struck down by a Seljuk arrow in a minor battle near Damascus, after which he had lain out in the desert for a day and a half before being found by Cedric, his loyal attendant, who had brought him home to Christendom after a long convalescence.

Their journey from Outremer had been long and slow, and they had landed eventually in southern France, where William had made his way to Champagne, to visit his seldom-seen cousin Count Hugh, arriving by coincidence just in time to attend the Raising of his never-before-met nephew Stephen, who was no more than three years his junior. William had every intention of returning home to England eventually, he said, but for the time being, he was content to remain in France, eating and drinking in the sunshine and building the strength back into his huge body.

Stephen liked him from the moment they met, and he knew the liking was mutual, although at first he had found his uncle's natural exuberance and his outspokenness to be disconcerting. In his soldiering days, he had quickly learned that the best way to deal with the constant shouting of his fellow knights was simply to keep to himself as much as he could, and once his companions had uncovered his disapproval of them, he had had no difficulty in keeping to himself constantly. He had no desire to avoid his uncle William, however, and so he soon grew inured to the loudness and ebullience, finding it oddly pleasing after a while.

On the day of the argument that had made such an

impression on Stephen, Sir William had taken a blow from a practice sword on his injured shoulder, and he was still pale and pinched about the mouth when Stephen walked in to where he was sitting with the Count, sharing a jug of wine in front of a roaring fire. It was already late on a wintry afternoon, and an unusually cold day for that part of France. Two hours yet remained before dinner in the great hall, and normally Sir William would still have been out in the practice yards and the Count would have been busy with his clerics, tending to accounts. Sir William's shoulder injury had changed all that, however, and both men were enjoying the respite from routine. The Count waved Stephen to a chair near the fireplace, inviting him to help himself to some wine, and when the younger man refused and remained standing, the Count tilted his head sideways and asked, "What's wrong? You look unhappy. Did you wish to speak with me?"

Stephen shrugged. "Yes, my lord, but it can wait. I did not know you were with Uncle William. I'll come back later."

"No, we will talk about it now, because I suspect it has something to do with your studies on the Order, and if that is the case, then William's opinions will be every bit as valid as mine. Is that what this is about?" He saw Stephen's nod and responded with one of his own. "So be it, then, what are you worried about?"

"It's ... it is difficult to ..."

"No, it's not. It never is, once it boils down to being

truthful. You're simply afraid of it. Come on, spit it out."

"I'm having difficulty believing what I've been told about Saint Paul."

Neither of his listeners showed even the slightest sign of surprise, and the Count barked a laugh. "And so you should, after a lifetime of being taught to revere him. What you are hearing now, from us, sounds like blasphemy. Having difficulty with that merely proves that you are alive and thinking properly."

"Aye, well …"

"Well nothing, lad. Accept it. What you are learning now, within our Order, is the truth, written down in the beginning and unchanged in more than a thousand years. Everything you've learned about such things *until* now, on the other hand, is the *manufactured* truth, as perceived by the men who built the world's Christian community."

"But Saint Paul is the greatest saint in the Church's calendar."

"Aye, he is. But that makes no recognition of any possibility that the Church might be in error. And devout and dutiful Christians dare not wonder whether Paul might be the greatest saint of the Church only because he appointed himself to that position." He paused, watching Stephen, then asked, "Do you know who the Maccabees were?"

"Er … They were Jews … No, I don't know."

"And what about the Seleucids. Does that mean anything to you?"

"No."

"Well, it will, once you have learned a bit more. The Maccabees were the hereditary high priests of the Jewish temple before the advent of the Seleucids and the Romans." The Count turned to his cousin William. "Why don't you tell him about the Seleucids. But keep it simple."

Sir William spoke to Stephen, inclining his head in the direction of the Count. "He never stops testing, this one. Very well, but before I begin, know this, Nephew. This difficulty you are having is not new. We have all known it, suffered the same fears, felt the same uncertainties, experienced the same reactions. Every one of us within the Order of Rebirth has had to grapple with this doubt, the very question you are debating now, so you are not alone. Bear that in mind through everything we tell you here. Do you understand me?"

Stephen nodded.

"Excellent. Now listen closely. We have evidence—and you will soon see it for yourself—supporting *all* of what you are about to hear, and it was all written down more than a millennium ago. The Seleucids were a very powerful dynasty, a line of kings directly descended from one of Alexander of Macedon's generals, and they ruled Syria for hundreds of years."

"Alexander of Macedon. You mean Alexander the Great?"

"Aye. What do you know of him?"

"He was Greek. Conquered the world three hundred

or so years before the Christ was born."

"Aye, he was Greek. So were his generals, who divided up his empire when he died. Macedonians, all of them—Hellenic. One of them was Ptolemy, who took over Egypt and founded the dynasty that bred Cleopatra, and another was Seleucus, who founded the dynasty that ruled Asia Minor and Sicily for hundreds of years, intermarrying and diluting their Hellenic blood with the Arabs to produce a bastard race. Nothing wrong with that, as the Romans proved.

"But then these Seleucids whelped a fellow called Herod—called himself 'the Great'—who made himself king of the Jews after marrying Miriamne, the last princess of the Maccabees. He then wiped out the remainder of the Maccabean royal family and proceeded to spawn an entire brood of his own, the most famous of whom, from our viewpoint, was Herod Antipas, the tetrarch of Galilee. The Herod clan itself, and everyone associated with it, became known as Herodians, and the Jews—especially the fanatically nationalist Jews, the Zealots—detested them all, for being gentiles, of mixed, unclean, and non-Jewish blood. Herod's biggest sin in the eyes of the Jews, however, was that he replaced all the Maccabean priests of the temple with priests of his own—the Pharisees. The Jews—the real, devout Jews—saw that as the worst kind of sacrilege: unclean gentiles and false priests defiling the temple."

He paused as though seeking something inside him, then went on. "You will find it easier to understand much of this, Nephew, if you understand this one thing:

false priests defiling the temple may not seem like much of a sacrilege to us today, but that is because we are accustomed to seeing Christian churches defiled by ungodly priests, and to thinking of churches—all of them, from basilicas to cathedrals to small chapels—as the house of God. By that we mean they are places of prayer and worship, places in which we can gather to pay homage to God.

"But the Jews believed no such thing. They had only one temple. It stood in Jerusalem, and it literally was *the* house of God. Jahweh, their God with the unutterable name, lived right inside it, in the Holy of Holies, which was why there was so much ritual involved in approaching the place. People who entered there were entering, in fact, into the presence of God Himself. He was there, in the Holy of Holies. He did not live in Heaven, or in Paradise. He lived among His chosen people, in the temple they had built to house Him. And so when Herod appointed his *own* priests, *Seleucid* priests, to tend the temple, and then invited the Romans to oversee their safety, he outraged everyone who took the slightest pride in being Jewish.

"So there you have the political lines that were drawn in Judea at the time of the Christ's birth. In power, you had the gentile Herodians, under Herod Antipas, backed by the armies of Rome, and against them, beneath them but all around them, the Jews—the Hebrews and Israelites—seething in half a hundred sects and factions, most of them awaiting the Messiah, the Jewish King who would free them, and all of them screaming for inde-

pendence, self-rule, and freedom from the Roman overlords. Their viewpoints and some of their activities may
have varied wildly, but for all intents and purposes they
were united as a single movement to throw off the
foreign chains that bound them." He squinted at young
Stephen. "Did you follow everything I said there?"

"Aye, I did, I think."

"Good. Now comes the next level of understanding." William glanced at the Count, raising his
eyebrows. "Do you want to continue from here?"

Count Hugh smiled and shook his head. "No, you
are doing remarkably well."

"Right." William pursed his lips for a moment,
considering his next words, then launched himself. "It's
difficult to make this brief, but I said all the Jewish sects
were united in a *movement*, and so they were, although
there's no single name for it. But we know it was revolutionary, because it ended up in a revolt against Rome
and the destruction of the Jewish nation.

"Be that as it may, this ... movement was character-
ized by its opponents, the Pharisees and their
Herodian allies, as a Messianic and therefore a
warmongering movement, aimed at overthrowing the
Jewish authorities and establishing a revolutionary
nationalist government. The Herodians, in consequence of that, represented themselves to the Romans
as the forces of peace and order, dedicated to maintaining the status quo and the stability of the Jewish
state. And since the status quo was pro-Roman, the
die was cast accordingly.

"But it was more convoluted that that—far more complex." Sir William was frowning, concentrating hard upon what he was attempting to say. "There was more involved in the movement than simple patriotism in the Roman sense. To the Romans, patriotism was, plainly and simply, a love of their homeland, Rome itself. But to the Jews, far more was involved. Their patriotism involved the love of God, and of God's chosen people as an entity, and of their homeland—God's homeland. And that's what gave rise to all the trouble that followed." His voice faded away, and Stephen, impatient, prompted him.

"What happened?"

"Nothing that's easily explained, as I said before, but I'll try. There was a common element among most of the Jewish sects around that time, and it was all about poor-versus-rich politics, those who had nothing against those who had everything. The governing class in Judea was Herodian. They owned everything, simply because they had usurped it with the backing of the Romans, who were happy to have a vassal king in power who was sympathetic to Rome and willing to keep the contentious Jews and the remaining adherents of the Maccabees in their place."

"Wait. What exactly do you mean when you say Herodian?"

Sir William cocked an eyebrow at that, then grunted and said, "Think about it, lad. Herod's family held all the power, and they used it to create new priests, tax collectors, and a hundred other forms of support for themselves, and all of those people owed their livelihood to the Herods. Their loyalties, therefore, were Herodian, as vassals to liege lords."

Stephen nodded, understanding the feudal equivalent, and Sir William continued. "The Jews, on the other hand, whose country Judea was, had nothing. Less than nothing, in fact, for most of them were heavily indebted to the Herodian moneylenders. The system under which they lived *forced* them to borrow heavily in order to survive, for that was how their entire society had been structured, ever since the Herod clan had come to power. Increasing taxes, including tithes to the temple, kept the people mired in poverty, and they were forced to borrow to be able to pay their tithes, plus their next round of taxes. It was a vicious, killing circle.

"And so this tradition—this *cult*—of poverty grounded in unyielding righteousness had come into being, and the Zealots were among its prime supporters. Another sect, Ebionites or Essenes, called themselves the Poor Ones, or sometimes the Poor, Righteous Ones. Or even more simply the Poor."

William cocked his head towards the Count, who was listening closely, his face expressionless. "Am I missing anything?"

The Count shook his head, as though surprised at being addressed. "Nothing important. I am fascinated by how much you can remember without prompting."

William turned his eyes back to his nephew. "*The Poor*. Do you recall Jesus' words about the camel climbing through the eye of the needle?"

"Aye, of course. It's an impossibility, equal to the chances of a rich man gaining entry to the kingdom of Heaven."

"Exactly. Rich men, to the Jews of Jesus' time, were either Herodians or Romans, which meant that they were definitely not Jewish, and the Jews of Judea were the most self-righteous race in the world—God's chosen people.

"It means nothing to us today, but it must have been intolerable to them to have their country, and the temple that embodied their religion, ruled and owned by a mongrel race, half Arab, half Greek, and both halves unacceptable in the eyes of Jehovah. And then, simply because they were so stiff necked and unbending, it must have been even worse to be forced to live with the Pharisees, Herod's false priests. Think then, how their frustration must have been inflamed by having to endure the scorn of the temple moneylenders and the indignity of having to deal with them in the first place, and to know there was nothing they could do about it because the power was all in the hands of the rich, with the hated Romans—who had attempted to set up an idol of their blasphemous emperor inside the Holy of Holies in the temple itself—providing the force that kept the usurpers safe from harm."

Sir William was silent for a moment, giving Stephen time to think about what he had said, before he continued. "The Jews lived in a world of black and white, Stephen, with nothing between the two extremes, no middle ground. Anyone who was not Jewish was gentile, and could not inherit the Kingdom of God.

"But even for a Jew, the way to God's good graces was a rocky and uncomfortable one, and among the Messianic sects was a group from among the Ebionites, or the Essenes, although some called them Nazarites or Nazarenes, who had set themselves up as a small community in Jerusalem, a community more strictly law-bound and conservative in some ways than were the Zealots—a community of righteousness, founded upon the expectation of the coming of the Messiah and the triumph of the Jews and their God over the whole world. One of that group's leaders was a man called Yeshua Ben David—we call him Jesus—and according to the records in our Order's possession, he never laid claim at any time to being the Messiah and never had any thought of being the Christ, the redeemer of the world. He was just a man, extraordinary in some ways. But he was involved in revolutionary politics, so that he fell afoul of the Pharisees, the upstart High Priests, and they denounced him to the Romans, who crucified him."

William St. Clair rose to his feet and crossed to the ewer of wine on a table by the wall, where he filled his own cup before offering some to the others. The Count accepted, but Stephen waved away the offer. William drank deeply, refilled his cup, and finally set the wine jug down, leaning his buttocks against the edge of the table.

"Thirsty work, talking. Doesn't matter whether you talk well or badly, clearly or confusingly. Have you understood what I've been telling you?"

"So far, yes. But I can't see what any of it has to do with Saint Paul."

Sir William looked quickly at Count Hugh, and then back at Stephen. "Paul was a Seleucid."

Stephen sat blinking. "You mean, half Greek and half Arab? No, he was a gentile, a Roman citizen, from Tarsus."

"The Seleucids were gentiles, and many of them were Roman citizens, too. And perhaps he *was* from Tarsus. That's certainly what he wanted everyone to believe later in his life. But the truth is, no one today really knows who Paul was or where he came from. No one knows anything about his early life, until the moment when God supposedly knocked him off his horse, after which he admitted openly that he had been a persecutor of Christians. But there were no Christians at that time, Stephen. There were only Jews. Christianity had not yet been defined or named.

"Our records, however, which name him clearly as the man you call Saint Paul, indicate that he was a Herodian—and a family member, at that, blood cousin to Herod—by the name of Saulus, and that he was the man sent as ambassador from the Herodian 'peacekeepers' to invite the Roman army that was camped outside Jerusalem to enter the city. The same Saulus sent a report of the event, at the time, to Nero's headquarters in Corinth, in Greece, a favorite haunt of Paul's in later years. Anyway, we were talking about the Crucifixion." He turned to Count Hugh. "You tell him about the Crucifixion, Hugh. You were the one who told me about it, and I've never forgotten what you said."

The Count at first demurred, saying he preferred to listen and enjoy rather than to think laboriously, but William would have none of it, and eventually Hugh shrugged his shoulders in resignation and sighed deeply.

"Much is made of the Cross today, Stephen, and of the fact that the Jews crucified the Christ. You know that, of course."

"Of course, my lord. Everyone knows that."

"Ah, *everyone* does. *Every* man knows that." Sir William's tone was somber and he shook his head gravely. "You must always be careful of those words, young Stephen, because they tend to mean the opposite of what they appear to say. Things that *everyone* knows are seldom what they appear to be, and they are seldom true.

"So, let us begin with the absolute truth, that which we can *prove* to be true: the Jews did not crucify the Christ. We can go even further than that: the Jews did not *hate* the Christ, because the Jews had never *heard* of the Christ. No one had heard of the Christ because the name did not exist until Saul, or Paul if you wish, first used it, years after Jesus was dead, speaking of him as Jesus, the Christ. 'Christos' was an obscure Greek word, meaning a redeemer of things, before Saul personalized it to Jesus, to indicate his supposed divinity. So the argument condemning the Jews as the slayers of Christ is a total fabrication. It is a vicious lie, created for political purposes.

"Nor can it be argued that the Jews hated Jesus the *man,* even setting aside the 'Christ' part, because hatred requires great effort and dedication, and they had no reason to hate Jesus collectively. He was one of them, a member of their movement and a citizen of Judea. There was hatred enough to go around in those days, God knows, but it was all used up between the Seleucid family of Herod and his supporters and the people of Judea, the Jews. It flowed in equal measure from both sides, one to the other. But the Jews, most certainly, would not have hated Jesus, simply because he was one of them, the people who were God's chosen. He was a Jew.

"And they certainly did not crucify him, either, because that was simply beyond their power. Crucifixion was a *Roman* punishment. Nor did the Jews—as a mob—ever scream for Jesus' blood and call down God's wrath upon themselves and upon their children for his death. That is the worst kind of madness to claim, *and* to believe. Think about it calmly for a moment. Can you imagine *any* crowd of people, or even any mob, calling down the wrath of God upon their own heads and their children's heads, and doing it not only voluntarily but in *unison,* unrehearsed? It defies belief, and yet people believe it. You do, don't you?"

"Believe it?" Stephen floundered, open mouthed, before his uncle took pity on him.

"Of course you do, because you have no choice. Because throughout your life, ever since you were old enough to understand, the most important people in your life have been telling you that's the truth, that you *have* to believe it, because if you don't, you'll be excommunicated, you will be damned to burn in everlasting fires. The Church tells you that. The priests tell you that. A monk will tell you that if you stop one on the road and ask him. And there is nothing, anywhere, to suggest otherwise, or to teach you otherwise, or to explain anything in alternative terms. Nothing. So what else can you do but believe what you are told?" He stopped suddenly, dramatically, holding up one hand towards the younger man.

"But let us think about crucifixion, you and I, for just a while longer before we move on to other things— about *the* Crucifixion, about the way the Romans and the Jews sought to humiliate the Son of God by hanging him on a cross for all the world to mock, as though crucifixion were a special invention designed to shame and humiliate Jesus. You know all about that, don't you?"

"I ..." Stephen hesitated, then raised a shoulder defensively. "*All* about that? I would have said yes moments ago, but now ..."

"Quite right you are, too. Right to doubt. Right to question, because there was nothing special involved in any part of the Crucifixion, except perhaps for the man to whom it happened. It was a commonplace event. Crucifixion was the most common form of death for criminals in Roman times, whether the criminals were thieves, miscreants, murderers, rebels, political dissidents, or deserters from the Roman armies. If you were deemed worthy of death by the Romans, you died. If you were wealthy or well connected, you might die quickly, beheaded or garroted, but if your death was required by the state, as a public spectacle, a lesson and a deterrent to others, you were crucified and died slowly, in great pain. Jesus was condemned as a political criminal—a rebel. And that was how he died. And apart from the people who knew him and were close to him, no one really cared."

There was silence among the three men for some time after that, for neither of the two older men wished to add anything at that point, and Stephen plainly did not even know how to begin formulating a response. After a while, he rose to his feet and crossed to the table, where he helped himself to a cup of wine and stood sipping at it, staring at the wall in front of him while the other two waited, watching him. Finally, he gulped one great mouthful and swung around to face both of them, his voice truculent and challenging.

"You still have said nothing about how all this has anything to do with Saint Paul."

Sir William raised his injured arm high and cupped his shoulder with his other hand as he flexed the joint, grimacing in discomfort. "You phrased your comment wrongly, Stephen. It was *Paul* who had to do with all this," he said through gritted teeth. He lowered his arm and released pent-up air explosively between his lips. "Paul changed everything, Stephen, from what it was then into what it is today—from Jewish to gentile. It was all Paul's doing. He stripped what was there in Jerusalem—the movement that Jesus and his followers called the Way—of all its Jewishness, and thereby of all its true meaning, and turned it into something inoffensive and innocuous, an idea bland enough to be accepted by the Romans. He stripped away all the rigid, unyielding, and unpopular Jewish morality and rewrapped the story in the style of his ancient Greek ancestors, with their love of fantastic, dramatic, fictitious, and completely implausible tales. And in so doing, he changed Jesus from a simple Jewish man of high ideals and stern patriotism into the Son of God, born of a virgin."

The Count rose to his feet and stretched mightily. "You have heard enough here this afternoon to set your head a-spinning," he said to Stephen. "So much information, and all so sudden and so unexpected. I know that, and so does William here. But remember what we said earlier, about time. You have your entire lifetime in which to explore and re-examine what we have told you, and you have full access to all the records in our archives, together with equal access to our most learned brethren, who will be happy and honored to share their knowledge and their studies with you.

"All that we require of you is that you keep an open mind and be aware that there are always other points of view on any topic that the human mind can countenance. In this particular instance of the man known as Saint Paul, you will learn that there are voices from the past, from his own time, that state quite clearly that he was not who he appeared to be, and that he was not altogether wholesome in many aspects of his character, including his truthfulness. There are others, equally strong and cogent, who maintain that his vaunted

Romanness led to his being a toady and a confidant and spy of the emperor Nero. Still others indicate—and I make no accusations here, I am merely saying they *indicate*—that he may have been directly involved in the murder of James, the brother of Jesus. After the death of Jesus, James took his place as leader of the movement that we in the Order call the Jerusalem Assembly. James had no time for Paul and made no secret of his disapproval of the man, while Paul clearly saw James—and said so in his own writings—as a threat, a deterrent and a hindrance to the spreading of God's word to the gentiles. He denounced and denigrated James accordingly as being worthy of arrest and punishment. There is no doubt that he was right about the hindrance, for James was a Jew, one of the people chosen by God to be His own, and there was no place in James's world for gentiles.

"There is far more to all of this, of course, than most men know, but we in the Order, who can trace our direct descent from the Essenes, the Poor Men of the Jerusalem Assembly itself, and who acknowledge the Way that they perceived and by which they lived, have a duty to maintain a clear line of sight from here to where this all began. Bear that in mind at all times from this moment on, and be true to the vows you made in being Raised." He stopped and eyed Stephen sympathetically. "You look baffled. And so you should. But now you need to go away and think about everything we have said here today. And if you have more questions, come back and ask them, of either one of us. Go now in peace."

SIX

The seeds that had been sown in Stephen's mind that day rooted strongly, and in the two years that followed, before he was shipped off to join the new fraternity in Jerusalem, Stephen St. Clair developed an insatiable appetite for any information that bore upon the Jerusalem Assembly, the Way of the Essenes, and the earliest days of what would, thanks to the man Paul, become Christianity as the world knew it twelve hundred years later. He soon lost count of the hours spent in a score of locations throughout the country, listening to his elder brethren, the archivists of the Order of Rebirth, recounting and translating the Lore that they safeguarded. The archives were a source of constant amazement to him, for although they were extensive in their scope, they were surprisingly small in physical mass, being mainly, although not exclusively, in the form of scrolls, which were far lighter and less bulky than the heavily bound books known as codices. They were decentralized, too, scattered among the main houses of the Friendly Families and guarded painstakingly by the senior brethren who had undertaken to study and conserve them.

He became thoroughly versed in the politics of Judea in Herodian times and in the aims and beliefs of the various sects and subsects at all levels of the Messianic movement, and he quickly learned to trust his own judgment in evaluating information, and to rely upon his intuitions when they were backed by intensive reading and research.

He had quickly discovered, for example, that one of the archives, near the ancient town of Carcassonne in the Languedoc, contained copies of the original writings of the Jewish historian Josephus, and from his studies of those, with the assistance of his mentors who had studied them for years, he came to appreciate that, uniquely self-serving as his writings were, Josephus had provided minute and exquisitely detailed recordings of the political and military situation within Judea and Palestine in his own time. It was by comparing Josephus's viewpoints and depictions in his two best-known works, *The Jewish War* and *Antiquities,* to those in Christian teachings and writings that Stephen had come to understand, and to believe beyond doubt or question, how Paul the Evangelist had sanitized the Jerusalem Assembly's teachings and used them to create Christianity in his own image and for his own ends, soon after the destruction of Jerusalem, stripping the old religion of its original anti-Roman Jewish nationalism and its anti-gentile prohibitions to make it politically acceptable to the Imperial authorities and to the polyglot citizenry of the Roman Empire.

He had also been fascinated by the emergence of Imperial Christianity hundreds of years later, from the moment in the fourth century when the emperor

Constantine had romanized the Church, extracting and destroying the revolutionary teeth that had attracted his attention to it in the first place. In an act of what St. Clair's predecessors in the Order had conceded to be unprecedented political genius, Constantine had made the Church an integrated part of the establishment of the Empire by transforming its Pope and cardinals into imperial princes, and the crowning achievement of his stratagem had lain in endowing them with an earthly palace that would forever afterwards symbolize their worldly importance and would mark, for those few who cared, or dared, to look, the true death of the movement established by Jesus, James, and the other original adherents of the Jerusalem Assembly.

St. Clair would never forget the exhilaration he felt on first reading and hearing such things, for this was heady and frightening information, reeking, at first, of apostasy and heresy. But it had been made clear to him by then, by his sponsors, that the Order of Rebirth had documented everything of which it spoke, and the evidence it possessed, smuggled out of Judea by the fugitive priests and their families, was impressive in its scope, its great age, and its obvious authenticity. There was sufficient material there, as Stephen had since seen for himself, for several lifetimes of study, and many of his predecessors, archivists and antiquarians down through an entire millennium, had dedicated their lives to investigating, translating, and interpreting what was there.

He now believed implicitly that the ancient Order of Rebirth in Sion was the sole legitimate descendant of the Jerusalem Assembly remaining on earth, and that should its existence be discovered, it would be eradicated instantly by Saint Paul's creation, the Christian Church, which in the course of twelve hundred years had systematically rooted out and destroyed all opposition, even the most supposedly benign, in a ruthless and sustained effort to protect its own power and values and to keep the entire world subjugated to its will—a will that had been indisputably created and formulated by men. That latter was an important point, for these so-called representatives of God, whether they called themselves bishops, archbishops, cardinals, popes, or patriarchs, were all men, mortal men who, by their lives and actions, demonstrated daily that they knew little and cared less about their supposedly immortal progenitor, the man who had lived so long ago in Judea and died on a cross for fomenting rebellion against Rome.

Paul, St. Clair now believed, had been much more a self-serving cynic than he had been a saint. He had had the acumen, and an opportunistic instinct, that had enabled him to recognize a magnificent concept when it confronted him. And so he had usurped it, cleansed it of everything that non-Jews might find offensive, and then built it inexorably into a self-perpetuating organism, such a potent force for revolution and reformation, but ultimately for gathering revenues, that centuries later the emperor Constantine—Paul's equal, at least, in self-serving opportunism—had been inspired to adapt it to his own benefit.

By the time of that transformation by Constantine,

however, three hundred years after the destruction of Jerusalem, the families that nurtured the Order of Rebirth had lived in the south of ancient Gaul for more than fifteen generations, on the land where they had settled after their arrival there, and no one, including themselves, would ever have suspected that their ancestral origins lay far from where they now lived in prosperity. The Friendly Families, as they called themselves, had blended seamlessly into their adopted society and had become friendly clans, for while the thirty original families were still there, their numbers had expanded enormously, and while all were aware that the bonds that held them in such close amity were ancient and even sacred in some arcane and unknowable way, few of them ever wondered over the why of such a thing. Their relationship to all the other Friendly Families was a given, a fact of life that had existed before the parents of their grandparents were born and would continue to exist long after they themselves and their own grandchildren were gone. They took their interrelationship, and their undoubted Christianity, for granted.

Only in the deepest recesses of their families' most close-held secrets, guarded jealously and conscientiously by perhaps one single member of each family in each generation, was the truth about their origins enshrined and passed down through the generations in compliance with a sacred duty. And it was a truth that none of their relatives would have believed.

Their ancestors, the founders of the Friendly Families, had all been priests of the Jerusalem Assembly, adherents of the original Ecclesia of Jesus and James the Just. The death of Jesus, at the hands of the Romans, had been taken in stride by the people of Jerusalem and of Judea, but when his brother James was brutally murdered in turn, beaten to death with a fuller's club by unknown assassins, the resultant outcry had precipitated the final Jewish uprising against the Herodians and Rome, and had brought Vespasian and his son Titus, with their remorseless armies, to wipe out the Jewish troublemakers once and for all time.

Towards the end of the siege of Jerusalem, when the destruction of their city and its temple was seen to be inevitable, the priests of the Assembly had hidden their most sacred artifacts, records, and relics deep beneath the ground, securely beyond the reach of the rapacious Romans. Only then, when they were sure they had done all that they could do to safeguard what they could not carry with them, did they join the thousands of people fleeing Judea. They made their way through the Mediterranean lands, traveling for many years as a large and seemingly loose but none the less tight-knit and self-sufficient group, until they reached the south of Iberia, and from there they struck northward into southern Gaul, settling eventually throughout the area known as the Languedoc. And there they remained, consolidating their possessions, their knowledge, and their most sacred traditions, finally entrusting the guardianship of their most precious secrets to a secret guild that they formed from the most trustworthy men among their families.

St. Clair found it bitterly ironic that he, who had been raised, to a great extent, by monks and warriors, and had dreamed himself of being a Christian monk in his ancestral province of Anjou, should now be numbered among the nine most anomalous beings in the annals of the Christian Church: the warrior monks of the Order of the Poor Fellow Soldiers of Jesus Christ. He found it even more ludicrous, however, that he should have been the one to become so obsessed by the history of Christianity that he was now close to having the ability, if not to destroy it, to cast genuine doubts at least upon the authenticity of its central tenets.

COMMITMENT

ONE

Brother Stephen came awake blustering in panic, his head ringing with what might have been the echo of a strangled cry, and found that he was sitting bolt upright, shoulders hunched defensively, hands outstretched as though to fend off a blow. It took a few seconds longer for him to realize that he could not see a thing, that his mouth was dry from fright, that his heart was thudding hard, almost painfully, and that he was holding his breath. He swallowed hard and lowered his arms cautiously, then scrubbed at his eyes with the heels of both hands and peered around at the darkness surrounding him. It was black as pitch, but his rump recognized the hard slats of his own cot, and as his heartbeat slowed towards normal, he began to hear the familiar nighttime sounds made by his companions sleeping nearby, grunts and murmurs and the occasional snore. He was not, as he had feared at first, back in that hellish dream room in which he had been chained hand and foot to a bed of narrow plank boards.

Shuddering with relief, he strained to hear anything unusual. Something had awakened him, he knew, and it must have been something threatening, to have startled him out of a deep sleep the way it had. But he could hear nothing out of the ordinary, and after a while he eased himself off the cot, straightening to his full height without a sound and reaching out surely in the blackness to where his sheathed sword hung from the armor tree against the wall, by the prie-dieu in the corner. He eased the blade silently from its sheath, laid the empty scabbard on the cot, then moved quietly to the doorless entrance to his cell, where he stood still again, listening intently, his bare blade held at the ready.

Within moments, he had identified the breathing of each of his sleeping companions and had almost assured himself that there was no one else breathing there in the darkness of the communal space in front of him, dimly lit as it was by a solitary, long-burning candle. What, then, had wakened him? Judging from the overall stillness surrounding him, St. Clair estimated that it was deep in the middle of the night, and he knew that, had he and his brethren really belonged to a Christian order of monks, they would all be up and in chapel at this time, reciting the psalms and prayers of the Night Order of Saint Benedict. As it was, having worked long and brutal hours all day long in the tunnels, as they did every day, his brothers were sleeping deeply, fortifying their bodies against the day ahead.

Bissot, whose cell lay opposite where Stephen stood, was always the noisiest sleeper among them, and now he erupted in an explosive, spluttering snore and turned heavily on his cot, breaking wind loudly. One of his neighbors—it sounded like Rossal—cursed him drowsily from a neighboring cell, less than half awake but aware of the sudden disturbance, and St. Clair permitted himself a quiet smile.

All was well, he finally decided, and he had merely been startled awake by a bad dream. But even in accepting that, he wondered what kind of dream could have awakened him so violently. In the past, his worst experiences had been caused by those nocturnal episodes of overwhelming sexuality that he had come to abhor deeply, but those had all been more disgusting and morally repugnant than truly frightening. He had awakened terrified this time, his heart pounding in fear and distress.

He returned to his cell and found a candle that he took and lit from the single flame burning in the common area outside. He sheathed his sword and returned it to its peg on the armor tree in his cell, then lay down on his cot again, hands behind his head, fingers interlaced as he gazed up at the ceiling and wondered what he had been dreaming about.

The flickering image of a face flashed against the back of his eyelids, frightening him so badly that he hunched forward again in a reflexive, cowering gesture, whipping his elbows down towards his navel, as though to protect his ribs. What was he thinking of? he asked himself frantically, screaming the question out into the silence of his mind. But even as he asked, the face that had frightened him came back to him, unmistakable and intransigent in its arrogant beauty, yet with a vulnerable softness to the pouting curve of the lips edging the imperious mouth. Whimpering aloud in disbelief, he squirmed sideways to sit on the edge of his cot and lowered his feet to the floor, squeezing his eyes tightly shut and clasping his hands despairingly over his head to block his ears.

He would not, *could* not, allow himself to believe that this was anything other than a visitation from the Devil himself. And yet, even as he told himself that, he saw images that were intensely, achingly familiar: the blue jewel now hanging from the string about his neck had in his dream been suspended from a golden chain, a chain that he had held in his hand as he dangled the suspended bauble to nestle between the breasts of the woman who lay beside him in the sumptuous bed on wrinkled, silken sheets, the woman whose warm, naked thigh was draped over his hip, holding him captive. The woman whose smiling face brought him surging to his feet again, to stand swaying in panic.

There was no possibility of error, and he made no attempt to delude himself or excuse himself. The woman in his dream was Alice, the Princess Royal of Jerusalem, King Baldwin's second daughter, and he knew, suddenly and crushingly, that he had lain and rutted with her. The heavy, yielding weight of her breasts in his hands was as real as the solid, unmistakably remembered weight of her thigh. He could even recall the musky perfume she wore, and the sensation of probing the tip of his tongue into the deep well of her navel, the tautly sculpted smoothness of her warm belly against his face.

In less time than it takes to tell, he was fully dressed

and armored, pulling his linen surcoat over his head and
fastening his heavy sword belt over it before cramming
his flat-topped steel helmet beneath his arm and snatch-
ing up his three-balled flail in a gloved right hand. He
strode almost noiselessly through the common area
beyond his cell, his booted feet making only the slightest of swishing sounds in the thick straw on the floor,
and the single guard on duty in the stables merely
huffed once in his sleep and then settled his shoulder
more comfortably against the wall. No one expected
anyone to attempt to steal anything from the monks of
the temple stables.

St. Clair bridled and saddled his horse expertly,
barely making a sound, and led it slowly to the exit,
making no attempt to mount until he was safely outside
beneath the stars. Once there, he stopped to place his
helm firmly on his head, then hung his flail from its
saddle hook and transferred his short, heavy battle-axe
from the belt at his waist to a corresponding hook on
the other side of his saddle. That done, he dropped the
reins and went quickly back into the stables, where he
took a spear and a shield from the racks inside the door,
then returned directly to mount his horse. He spurred
the animal hard, down towards the scattering of buildings that separated him from the South Gate, where he
roused the guards, told them who he was and that he
was on a mission for the Patriarch, and passed quickly
through the portal before the heavy gates were fully
open.

He gave no thought to what his brethren might

think of his disappearance, because in his own mind he knew he was unlikely to see any of them again. They had mourned him as dead once already, and in his despair he now doubted that they would care to do so again, and he reflected grimly how much better it would have been for everyone had he been dead in truth at that time. He had no idea where he was going. He knew only that it would be far from where anyone would know him by his name or his face, and if that meant he had to ride away and die in Syria, fighting alone against a Saracen horde, then he would be content to do so, in the hope that his death might atone for the heinous nature of his sins. He had lain with the King's daughter, fornicating with her like a rutting beast, and the memories of it were now swarming in him, shaming him to the depths of his soul.

Only once, and then very briefly, did he stop in his headlong flight from Jerusalem, and that was when the thought occurred to him that one part, at least, of what he had experienced in his dream was an impossibility. He reined in his mount and sat still, staring towards the lightening eastern horizon. The blue bauble that he wore around his neck had been buried deep underground throughout the time of his abduction. He had not found it until months after his return, which meant that his "memory" of what he did with it was false and that he had, in fact, been dreaming. He felt his heart leap in his chest as he realized and accepted that; felt his chest expanding with hope that was like a great intake of fresh breath as the possibilities of error rang through his mind like the jangling clamor of the spring-mounted bell above the door of the cook's room in his mother's kitchen.

No sooner had he thanked God for the impossibility of the blue bauble's presence, however, than he began to think about the chain from which it had hung suspended: a thick, heavy, snake-like chain of solid, hand-wrought links of buttery yellow gold, supple and slippery smooth, strong and beautifully made, and far and away the single most valuable item he had ever held in his hands. And he *had* held it in his hands, many times. He had cupped one hand often to enjoy the feeling of the solid links pile up in his palm as he lowered the chain into it from above, his upheld hand clearly limned against the pale purple perfection of the walls of the princess's bedchamber. And he had placed the chain around Alice's neck, too, on several occasions, and then carefully inserted his own head into its loop, so that the two of them, he and she, had been bound close together by it, unclothed breasts touching, naked and raging with riotous lust.

He had broken his vow of chastity. Now his entire body felt leaden as he kicked his horse gently forward again, prodding it to a walk. Warmund of Picquigny had told him he was free of sin so long as he had remained free of *intent* to sin. St. Clair had believed him and had, in fact, begun to mend. The nightly visits from the succubus had waned noticeably in recent weeks, and Stephen had been feeling better about himself, about his life and his duties. Now, however, he was again at an impasse. Had there been volition involved in his fornications with the princess?

His own painfully restored memory of what had occurred made it seem scarcely possible that he had not willingly engaged in the activities he was now recalling more and more clearly with every passing moment. Pleasure, certainly, he knew had been there; pleasure had been there in indescribable amounts, as had voluptuous abandon and wanton excesses. He was crushingly aware of all of those things. But there was still one small, stubborn voice in his mind that insisted upon asking him over and over again if his *volition* had been involved. Had he participated in the debauchery willingly and knowingly? Parts of him had, certainly, he knew beyond dispute, for he recalled the deliberate and sensual way he had insinuated his head into the chain binding the two of them together, but still the voice persisted: had his bodily responses been dictated, or regulated, by his conscious will? This was a question more suited for clerics than for soldiers, Stephen knew, yet even as he mentally threw up his hands at his inability to answer the question with any confidence, he knew too that both the question and its answer, infuriatingly vague as they were, were of crucial importance.

And then, after a long period of agonized self-doubt, his mind began to present him with things he could consider sanely, snippets of memory, and long, real gaps in his memory, the awareness of periods of time, both long and short, when he had absolutely no memories of anything. And then, eventually, it brought memories of very strange *behaviors:* of staring at Alice, seeing her as though poorly reflected in an untrue mirror, watching her closely, convinced that her body, so strangely shimmering and flowing, was about to dissolve into nothingness, and feeling his head spin while the chamber revolved around him and he laughed like a man demented ... There had been times, he came to accept then, when he had not been in control of himself at all, and that mystified him, for throughout his life, he had always kept himself under strict and tight control.

Thus there was something unwholesome, or at least mystifying, about the period of his abduction. There was no connection, for example, and no transition between his memories of the sexual lust he enjoyed in the purple bedchamber and the torture he had undergone in the place where they had chained him to a bed. And he had no knowledge of how he had arrived in either place, or of how he had escaped, other than the vaguest memory of the unknown, half-seen woman who had pulled him along behind her with a strong grip on his injured wrist, apparently leading him to freedom and then leaving him there alone.

And then, just as he was beginning to believe that there might be a glimmer of light in the darkness that surrounded him on all sides, he became aware of the blue jewel that hung from the string around his neck. He had reached up almost unconsciously to take it between his finger and thumb, in a movement that had become habitual over the past few weeks, and with that simple action unleashed an entirely new set of revelations and self-recrimination. He had retained—and he immediately corrected himself ruthlessly, emphasizing the truth—he had *kept*, secreted and in fact *stolen* the bauble, uncaring of its true value, whether it be jewel or worthless glass, on a purely personal whim, and in his determination to keep hold of it simply because he wanted to keep it, he had broken another of his vows, the one that was not quite a vow of poverty but rather a promise to hold all things in common with his brethren and to keep nothing for himself.

He felt the weight of that realization settling about his shoulders like a millstone, and if he had been capable of tears by then, he would have wept. But there were no tears within him, and he felt his self-loathing multiply. The blue jewel was worthless, a mere piece of stone, prettily shaped and pleasant to touch, deceptively soft-seeming in its hardness and smoothly warm in a way that reminded him of the inner intimacies of Alice le Bourcq's flawless thighs. And with that association newly sprung to mind and instantly acknowledged, he ripped the thing from his neck, breaking the string, and threw it away, seeing its flight clearly against the dawn sky and noting where it fell against a good-sized boulder. He sat there staring at the place where it had fallen, unable to see the blue stone itself, but thinking of other things, of how that tiny piece of blue stone had been involved in his triple dereliction, the breaking of the only three sacred vows he had ever made, to God or man. Chastity, poverty, and obedience. He was thrice damned and undeserving of life, and the thought came back to him that all that was left for him to do now was to ride out and sacrifice his life in battle against the Infidel.

And so Sir Stephen St. Clair, Brother of the Order of the Poor Fellow Soldiers of Jesus Christ, climbed down from his saddle and retrieved the bauble he had just thrown away, then, with the string that was still attached to it, he tied it carefully and tightly about the cross-guard of his sword. That done, he sheathed the sword, gathered up his reins, secured the butt of his spear in the holder by his stirrup and, with his shield slung over his left arm, spurred his horse again and rode defiantly eastward into the new day, resolved to die quickly and bravely in the name, and for the glory, of his God.

TWO

The word of St. Clair's disappearance reached the princess before the supper hour of the second day after he left the city, for his brother monks, remembering his earlier abduction, were determined that he should be found this time, no matter where he had gone or who might have abducted him again, and for several days all eight of the remaining brothers were out and about in the streets of Jerusalem, along with all the sergeants of the Order, questioning everyone on the whereabouts of the heroic Brother Stephen.

On the morning of the third day, an envoy appeared at the entrance to the stables, asking to see Brother Hugh, and some time after that, looking distinctly mystified, Brother Hugh handed over his duties to Brother Godfrey and departed with the envoy, having said only that he was summoned to the royal palace on some matter to do with Brother Stephen's disappearance.

On his arrival there, he was escorted directly to a private audience with the princess, in her own rooms, where she was accompanied only by two of her ladies. Hugh de Payens, amply accustomed to commanding and controlling men, was completely out of his depth with women, and within a very short time he had been stripped of everything he knew or suspected about the disappearance of his youngest knight monk. He told the princess that Brother Stephen had vanished once before, abducted, evidently without any reason that made sense, by persons unknown, and that he had been increasingly troubled, recently, by memories of tortures he had undergone in the course of that abduction.

Alice had been all concern, asking for more and more details on what had happened to the young monk, and fishing for details of the memories that had been troubling him, for she had not expected to hear anything resembling that. She was feeling the first stirrings of anxiety over St. Clair's apparent recall of the tortures she had had her people inflict upon him months before, for she had been assured that the drugs he had consumed would make it impossible for him to remember anything. The tortures had been mild—barely tortures at all. She had ordered him confined in such a way that his wrists and ankles would show clear signs of manacling, and she had ordered him flogged once, simply to break the skin upon his back and create scabbing, if not lasting scars, for she had known how strange it would have been to release him unharmed. She had also had him scrubbed down during that "torture" period with animal dung and filth, to disguise the fact that he had been regularly bathed and kept clean throughout his captivity. That he remembered anything at all about that time worried her deeply.

She had been curious, but no more than that, when she heard, the previous evening, about the knight's second disappearance, but she had quickly ruled out the possibility of someone else's having abducted him, either for information or for sexual pleasure. The only person she could think of who might do such a thing was Bishop Odo, and she knew Odo had neither the will nor the courage to defy her. Her father would have taken direct action had he wished to have anything to do with the monk, as would the Patriarch Archbishop. Neither of those two had any need to deal in subterfuge. She had considered going to de Picquigny at first, to find out what he knew or suspected, but she had quickly given up on that as a bad idea, knowing that the Patriarch Archbishop had no time for her and would do nothing for her that he thought might assist her in anything. And so she had gone to the source, approaching de Payens himself, offering to help find his missing monk.

After questioning de Payens extensively, however, and discovering that he really had no faintest idea of how to go about finding the missing man, she sat silent for a long time, debating with herself, before telling the senior monk that she might be able to help him. She had a friend among the Muslims, she told him, who had extensive and far-reaching connections throughout Outremer. She would talk to this friend and ask him what he might be able to do, and she would send word to de Payens as soon as she had anything to report.

De Payens bowed deeply and thanked her once again for her generous offer. And as soon as the door of her chambers had closed behind him, Alice summoned her factotum, Ishtar, and sent him to find Hassan the horse trader and bring him to her.

Ishtar was slow to return, and when he did arrive back, late in the afternoon, it was to bring word to his mistress that Hassan the Syrian was not in the city, and that no one knew where he was. He had been on his own premises the night before, apparently conducting his affairs as usual, after a successful day that had seen the sale of four fine animals, and he had spoken with his head groom just at dusk, supervising the feeding and grooming of his stock in his normal fashion, but he had been gone before dawn and had left no word with anyone of where he had gone or when he might return. The head groom, whose name was Nabib, questioned by Ishtar, had suggested three possible places where his master might have gone, all of them in or close to the city, but a search had turned up no trace of Hassan, and Ishtar had finally returned to leave instructions with Nabib to have his master come to speak with the princess on a matter of great urgency as soon as he returned.

Alice was not at all pleased with Ishtar's tidings, unaccustomed to having people place themselves beyond her instant call, but there was nothing she could do other than fume impotently and cause all her attendants to find good reasons to stay far away from her until her mood should improve. Fortunately for all of them, however, Hassan himself came in answer to her summons a mere hour after Ishtar's return, and Alice's fury diminished instantly, for she knew well that she could not turn the cutting edge of her tongue on the Assassin. They spent an hour cloistered together, during which Alice outlined in detail the requirements she had in mind for Hassan, and he left on the verge of nightfall. St. Clair had been missing for three full days by that time.

Mere moments after Hassan's departure, with the bar not yet lowered into place on the courtyard gates to the princess's quarters, another man, this one elderly, glided through the darkening shadows in the courtyard and made his presence known to Alice's guards. The Captain of the Guard came to attention and led the newcomer indoors, straight to the main reception room where his mistress preferred to meet her official visitors, for this particular visitor was highly official. It was the knight Sir Bertrand de Perigord, a renowned warrior who had waded through infidel blood at the sack of Jerusalem in 1099 and was now a senior adviser to its King. Perigord, a grim, humorless martinet who was there solely because the King had dispatched him in person, refused to sit and remained standing, drumming his fingers impatiently against the heavy, beaten silver cross on his breast until the princess arrived. She paused imperiously on the threshold of the room, scowling at Perigord, who glowered back at her with a dislike to match her own, and informed her brusquely that her father the King required her presence at once. His message delivered and his duty done, the veteran warrior turned his back on her and left without another word.

Alice spat at his retreating back as the door closed behind him, but then she wasted no time. She clapped

her hands for Ishtar and sent him to summon her hand-
maids to aid her in changing her clothing and preparing
herself for the meeting with her father. As she surrendered herself to their ministrations, she tried to recall
who was here in court at this time, and which of them
might have occasioned this summons to her father. She
had no concerns, for once, about being the subject of
the King's displeasure, because her conscience was
absolutely and unusually clear, but she was intrigued
about what her father could want. He seldom
summoned her privately and he never did so at night, so
close to the main mealtime of the day, because that was
invariably when he was most deeply involved with the
constant progression of guests who came and went
without respite, from the other counties and territories
of Outremer, and with almost equal frequency from
Rome and the many royal courts of Christendom. As
monarch of the Kingdom of Jerusalem, her father was
ten times busier than he had ever been when he was
merely Baldwin le Bourcq, Count of Edessa.

Half an hour later, when the royal guards admitted
her to the audience chamber, she was greatly surprised
to find her father waiting for her, not merely alone but
in high good humor. He stood up as soon as he saw the
doors opening, but by then she had already seen him
perched inelegantly on the arm of the great, gilded
chair and reading a parchment, holding it up with both
hands to the flaring torch that burned in a high bronze
stand behind his head. He released the scroll as she
entered, allowing it to roll itself up again as he stepped

quickly down from the dais to greet her, his face wreathed in a broad smile.

Returning his smile, albeit tentatively, Alice curtsied rapidly, then kissed him on both cheeks, calling him Papa as she always did, and using all her skills to keep her looks modest and decorous. No one looking at her, including her father, would have thought that she saw anything out of the ordinary in meeting her august parent without a surrounding throng of courtiers, supplicants, and sycophants constantly coming between the two of them and making real conversation impossible. This easy, informal encounter was the way she remembered meeting her father daily, once upon a time long years before.

Now he squeezed both her hands gently within his own, raised them to his lips and kissed them before releasing her and turning away to a table against one wall, where a profusion of documents and packages showed that Baldwin was a working king. He hesitated for a moment, scanning the piles in front of him, then picked up a small, leather-wrapped object, hefting it speculatively in one hand as he looked back at her over his shoulder.

"Are you aware of the envoys who arrived from France today, my dear?"

Alice shook her head, genuinely surprised, for there was little that escaped her attention in the comings and goings of her father's court. "No, I had no idea there were any. When did they arrive, Papa?"

"This afternoon, early. They came from Jaffa, and had to wait for a caravan to assemble, to be sure of safe

passage. For more than a week they waited. Eight days
to assemble their party, then three more for the journey
here. Far, far too long."

"Is the Jaffa road still that dangerous? I thought the
knight monks were taking care of that now."

"They are, my dear, they are, but they are not super-
human. They have a firm pattern of regular patrols on
the roads from here to Jericho and Jaffa, but of the two,
the Jaffa road is altogether longer and more difficult to
police, and it carries fewer pilgrims."

"Since when are pilgrims more important than regal
and vice-regal envoys from Christendom?"

Her father smiled fondly at her. "That depends upon
whose eyes are doing the looking. The Patriarch, along
with Brother Hugh and his excellent brethren, is most
intimately and consistently concerned with the welfare
of the pilgrims. There is little we can do to change that
now. Anyway, my dear, the envoys arrived, and they
brought this for you."

The package, slightly larger than her open hand, was
flat, rectangular, and quite heavy, and at first she could
not make her fingers work at undoing the intricate knot
that held the decorative leather wrapping in place. She
could have cut the thong easily, she knew, but for some
reason she instead worked doggedly and delicately to
unravel the knot until it came apart in her fingers. She
unwrapped the package quickly then and stood staring
wide eyed at the miniature portrait she held, painted on
a small panel of densely grained wood and edged with
an elaborately carved and gilded border of what she

recognized as classical acanthus leaves. The subject of the portrait was a young man, with curling golden hair and bright blue, smiling eyes. Even allowing for the natural exaggeration of a painter unwilling to offend his subject, it was plain to Alice that if the artist's abilities were one tenth as skilled as they appeared to be, the man in the painting must be remarkably comely and well made.

At first glance, she had thought that she was looking at a portrait of the Angevin Count Fulk of Anjou, who had become betrothed to her elder sister, Melisende, two years earlier, while on a brief visit to the Holy Land. Some anomalous and illogical impulse suggested, although for no more than the briefest of moments, that her father had erred and had sent for her instead of Melisende. She knew within the same heartbeat, however, that the error was wholly hers and that the man in the picture resembled Fulk of Anjou in no way. Where this man was golden blond, Fulk was swarthy and dark and a full decade or more older. Alice knew Fulk well, but as a rival for her father's crown and kingdom, not as an admired brother-to-be. She felt a surge of detestation for the Count and his empty-headed wife-to-be, and then a corresponding surge of curiosity about the stranger in her hand. She finally looked up at her father.

"Who is he, Papa?"

The King's smile grew broader. "His name is Bohemond, Prince of Antioch. His father, Bohemond I, was my friend. His son, now Bohemond II, is to be your husband."

"My husband." The words came out sounding flat, but then her head snapped back and her eyes flared. "My *husband*? I will have no husband, Papa. Have you gone mad, expecting me to wed this wretch? I have never even *heard* of him."

"You had no need to, until this moment. Nor have you any need to risk my anger by being provocative." The words were spoken mildly, but Alice required no reminder of the razor's edge of her father's impatience, and she bit the inside of her lip in fury, forcing her face to show nothing more of her thoughts as he gazed levelly into her eyes, searching for further defiance. Finally he nodded, and continued in the same gentle tone. "Be at peace, Daughter. He will suit you well."

Reacting sweetly to such an obvious inanity strained every fiber of Alice's patience, but she succeeded somehow, and when she spoke again there was nothing but meekness in her response. "But how can you be sure of such a thing, dear Papa? How can you know, beyond doubt, that this man will not break my heart with sadness? I have never been to Antioch, so how may I hope that he will suit me well, a complete stranger? Has he ever seen me? Does he know who I am?"

"He has seen as much of you as you have of him." The King gestured towards the miniature she held. "I sent him one of those, two years ago. You must surely recall sitting for the painter. The boy is nineteen now, almost the same age as you, and he lives not in Antioch but in Italy, where he has spent his life to this point. He is Prince of Taranto, as was his father before him, and he is a cousin to the King of Italy. He is also the grandson of the King of France, and now that he is come of age he is on his way here to assume his place as Prince of Antioch, next to our own holdings, the richest seat in all of Outremer. He may be here within the month, and then again, he may be here within the year. It all depends, as such things ever do, upon winds and weather and the vagaries of Fortune. When he does arrive, however, you will be wed and become his queen as soon as may be. You and he have been betrothed since you were children, the agreement witnessed by the Pope himself."

"But Papa!" Words failed her for a moment and she had to steady herself before saying what was in her mind, keeping her voice reasonable despite the angry tenor of her words. "The man might be a simpering clown!"

Baldwin raised a peremptory hand even as his lips twisted in a half smile. "No, Daughter. Grant me at least the wit and fatherly good sense to think of such concerns. The prince is well thought of and well spoken of. I have had him under close observation for several years now, for I have been acting for him, during his minority, as regent of Antioch, governing from here and through an intermediary. I have never met him, obviously, but he is very tall, I am told, head and shoulders taller than most of his companions, and he is apparently comely enough to have women fighting over him—although that should concern you not at all. He has long, fair, curling hair, as you can see, almost golden blond, with fine white, even teeth and large blue eyes. He is said to be responsible in all things, including his spending habits, and is reputedly kind to his servants and gentle with his animals. In addition to that, I am told, the men he commands admire and respect him and would do anything he asked of them. He is a warrior of promise and some renown already, despite his youth, and he dreams of doing great things here in Outremer for the glory of God and His Holy Church."

Alice sat silent after that, not thinking about Bohemond at all but still nonplussed by her father's comment about her having no need for concern over the prince's attractiveness to other women. She never quite knew how to respond to such comments from him, and he had been making them with something approaching frequency in recent months. His facial expressions were always inscrutable at such times and his tone of voice invariably left room for doubt about his true meaning, as it did about the depth of his under-standing, or even his misunderstanding, of her sexual affairs and proclivities, so that now she found herself wondering, as she had so many times before, what her father really thought of her, beneath the mask of his fatherly concern. Was he saying that, faced with a husband's infidelity, she would find it easy to console herself with others? Or did he mean that her own beauty was sufficient in itself to safeguard her against the predatory efforts of other women? She could not tell which of the two meanings might be closer to the mark, and she wondered, for the briefest of moments, if her mother might have said something. She dismissed the thought, however, for she and her mother had

finally arrived at a truce of kinds, after years of squab-
bling. It was not complete, and at times it was decidedly
uneasy, but it had been in effect now for more than a
year, and Alice doubted that Morfia would want to
endanger it by saying anything inflammatory to her
husband.

Morfia had found out about her daughter's dalliances
around the time of Alice's seventeenth birthday—Alice
had no idea how, or from whom—and had attacked
forthwith, threatening to tell the King unless Alice
promised her, on the spot, that she would mend her ways
and behave as a Princess of Jerusalem might be expected
to behave, with modesty, graciousness, and decorum.

"Pray tell, how might a Countess be expected to
behave, or a Queen of Jerusalem?" Alice had flung the
question back at her and then swept onward, naming
the names of men she knew, beginning with old Bishop
Grosbec. Her mother had been stunned at first, then
furious, stating what Alice knew from her own observations to be true: that she had never touched or been
touched by any man, other than her husband. Alice had
been ready for that, however, and she had raised the
specter of appearances. What would the Count have
said or done, she asked, had he known or suspected that
his wife, while ostensibly doing nothing, had obtained
favors and compliance through willingly lending herself
to an elderly bishop's lustful fantasies, so that he spilt
himself frequently, even daily, watching her?

The discussion had been lengthy and fiery, filled with
mutual condemnation, yet strangely quiet because of

the need to be discreet, to avoid being overheard, and by the end of it this tense and sharp-edged truce had evolved, with each of the two women developing a new respect and wariness of the other. They had not discussed terms of behavior, or how they might deal with each other afterwards, but they had not had another confrontation of any kind from that day forth, and when they met nowadays, which they did more often and more openly than ever before, they were civil to, and tolerant of, each other.

Alice became aware that she and her father were sharing a long silence, and that the King might be awaiting a response from her, to something he had said or asked. She inhaled sharply, smiled brightly at him and shook her head, as if dismissing an amusing thought. He pursed his lips, his face grave.

"Very well, Daughter. I will leave you with this thought, but be warned that it is not open to change, or even to discussion with an eye to that end, so inure yourself to accepting the duties of a King's daughter. You will wed the Prince of Antioch, and as soon as it may be arranged. That is your destiny, so embrace it willingly and be aware that you could fare far worse. The young man has everything to recommend him: born of the noblest bloodlines in Christendom, he is rich, highly regarded by all who know him, in excellent health, and filled with eagerness to be your husband. He has no desire to hold the Crown of Jerusalem, knowing your sister Melisende is my firstborn and betrothed to Fulk of Anjou, who will one day rule here when I am gone. He is content to have his own Principality of Antioch, the richest seat in Outremer save only Jerusalem itself. Antioch is large and wealthy as it stands today, but Bohemond has plans to extend its borders to the south and east, far into Seljuk Syria, to Aleppo and perhaps even as far south as Damascus. You and he will build a kingdom of your own, to rival this of mine and perhaps even to outshine it someday."

Alice stared down at the portrait in her hand and thought about what her father had said, her mind automatically selecting those attributes she most wished to consider: handsome, well disposed, golden haired, dashing, adventurous, and brave above all else. And even as she thought those things, she was aware of her own lip curling in a sneer. She had come to know many men in a very brief time and she had never yet met any single one of them who possessed more than one or two of those attributes.

"Well? Have you heard what I have told you?"

Alice widened her eyes innocently. "Of course I have, Papa. I am slightly overwhelmed, perhaps, but I have no wish to displease you. I have it in mind now, and I will give it all my attention from this time on, and in the meantime I will await further word from you on how the matter is progressing." She hesitated, knowing she was being daring. "Does Mama know of this?"

"Of course she does. She was present when the matter was arranged, while you were but a child in arms, but she and I had not spoken of the matter in years, until two years ago. It was arranged, but you two were a world

apart, and so I decided that the less said of it the better it
might be for all concerned. Thus, if anything untoward
occurred to the young man while he was growing up,
you would not feel deprived or disconsolate."

"So you forbade Mama to tell me of it?"

"No, not at all. We decided together, your mother
and I, that the betrothal was the best arrangement we
could make for you at the time, but that nothing would
be gained by having you aware of it while you were yet
too young to understand what it might mean to you. I
have never regretted that decision, nor has your mother,
and the wisdom of it was brought home to us several
years ago, when another young man was killed in a
hunting accident, his neck broken when thrown from a
horse. He had been similarly betrothed to your sister
Melisende. His name would mean nothing to her today,
but had she known herself to be betrothed to him, she
would have grieved. So, best not to have known, do you
not agree?"

On the point of saying something more, Alice caught
herself and bowed her head submissively, the picture of
an obedient daughter, then curtsied deeply and asked,
"May I, then, speak to Mama about this matter now?"

"You may, but the dinner hour is upon us and we
have many guests this night—eight envoys from France
and six from the court of Italy, so perhaps it might be
better were you to wait until tomorrow. Go now and
prepare to act the Princess of Jerusalem and Antioch."

Alice bowed again and left her father alone, her head
spinning, and a tight, tense appreciation in the center of

her chest told her she might be on the threshold of something profoundly exciting, completely unlike anything she had ever experienced. She was to be Princess of Antioch, wed to a golden prince of great beauty and prowess, and that might work to her advantage. Fulk of Anjou was her father's official successor. There was no getting around that, unless Fulk died ... and if that happened, he would be replaced. Alice had no doubt that her father already had a list of potential replacements drawn up. But Fulk, if anything, was suitable; he was stern, somewhat forbidding in his personality, and utterly humorless, the sort of man who alienates others, an opponent, she thought, who could feasibly be dealt with, and most particularly so by a golden-haired champion with the ability to win the hearts of men, a prince with dreams and ambitions of expanding his principality beyond recognition.

It crossed Alice's mind then that her current crop of lovers were likely to be most unhappy about this new development, particularly since she would be moving to her new husband's home in Antioch, hundreds of miles to the north. Bishop Odo would probably be the most vocal of those, and probably the most carping, because although she kept him on a short leash, in the matter of permitting him access to her favors, he was yet accustomed to having his own way and could be snappish and almost womanly in his nastiness when he was crossed. Fortunately for Alice, however, Odo was also the most vulnerable of her lovers and the one who would be easiest to control, for several reasons, all of which she intended to look after assiduously in the time ahead.

As Alice prepared for bed that night she was still deep in thought about her father's tidings and the changes they would necessitate in her life, and long before she ever fell asleep, she had completely forgotten Hassan the horse trader and the errand on which she had dispatched him.

THREE

S t. Clair heard the crackling of fierce-burning flames and felt their searing heat on his face, and then the bright agony of having a burning ember land on the web of his hand brought him fully awake, shouting wordlessly in pain, cursing and writhing with tightly bound limbs as he tried to escape the torture. Above him, leering down with mindless malice, the halfwit he called the Torturer was still holding the smoking twist of burning reeds that he had used to burn St. Clair's hand. The knight quickly looked around for any of the others, hoping for rescue, but the two of them were alone and St. Clair's heart sank, knowing that his tormentor must have dragged him bodily to the edge of the fire, although neither reason nor logic could inform him why the sullen brute had stopped short of throwing him onto the fire itself. He might easily have done so, for there was no capacity to reason in whatever passed for the creature's mind.

The others in the small band who were the knight's captors, knowing their dim-witted companion's love of inflicting pain on others, had thus far discouraged him from going too far, clearly hoping to win a ransom for their prisoner, and aware that he would be useless to them if they allowed the simpleton to kill him. None of them spoke any form of intelligible language that St. Clair understood. Their conversation was gibberish to him, lightning-fast and sibilant, rather than throaty and guttural like most of the Arab tongues with which he was familiar. And so he had been unable to disabuse them of the notion that he was a Frankish knight and therefore must be wealthy and worthy of ransom, valuable to someone.

He had lost awareness of how long they had been holding him, but he knew he must have been close to death when they found him, raving with thirst and unable to defend himself. The fact that he was here at all attested to the utter helplessness that must have bound him at the time of his capture, but he had no knowledge of how much time had elapsed since then. He knew only that he had returned to consciousness one day, weak but clear headed, to discover that he was a captive, wearing only the soiled remnants of the tunic he had been wearing the night he left the stables in Jerusalem. He had no way of knowing whether days, weeks, or months had passed in the interim, although his reason, and his observations of his captors, told him that it was probably a matter of days. They would have made no effort to prolong his life, other than giving him water, and had he not improved noticeably in a short time, they would have killed him or left him to die.

He had no recollection of what had happened to his horse, or to his mail armor and weapons, but he had seen no signs of them since regaining his awareness, and so he assumed that he had rid himself of them before being found by these people. He remembered that he had ridden for days in the desert, looking for death, but had seen no single person with whom he might fight, and eventually he had arrived at a water hole that no longer contained water. Only slightly dismayed, he remembered, he had set out for the next water hole along the desert route. He had traveled it many times before and knew all the watering places, but on this occasion, long before he drew near the deep, ancient sump that sustained all the life for an enormous distance around it, he had seen vultures circling above the site and had arrived to find the place defiled, its water fouled and rendered undrinkable by bloated, stinking corpses so long dead that they were indistinguishable by sex and barely recognizable as human.

Appalled, he had fallen to his knees and cursed the abject folly and criminal irresponsibility of his fellow Franks, for he knew beyond question that no Muslim would have committed such a crime. It required all the posturing self-righteousness and unbridled stupidity of an arrogant, hatred-flushed Christian to murder defenseless nomads such as these—for the emaciated and pathetic condition of their slaughtered livestock left St. Clair in no doubt as to the status of the people who had died—and then to throw their bodies into the only sweet water source for hundreds of miles around, condemning to death not only the people of the surrounding land but all the desert creatures who depended on the water hole for life. Unable to pray to a

God who would condone such iniquity, he had saddled
up and ridden onward, dangerously low on water now
and fully aware that he would be hard-driven to reach
the next hole he knew of before thirst drove him mad.

He had obviously failed to make the trek. He
remembered riding through a series of wind storms that
first confused and then confounded him, and the next
time he became aware of himself or his surroundings,
he was a prisoner.

Soon after regaining consciousness that first time, he
had his first encounter with the mindless Torturer, who
simply loved to cause pain, not merely to St. Clair but
to any living creature that fell into his power and could
not retaliate. He would push a sharpened sliver of bone
into St. Clair's flesh—he carried the thing tucked into
his belt and St. Clair knew he was far from being the
first person on whom it had been used—for the sheer
pleasure of watching the way St. Clair reacted, and all
the while he would grin that empty, evil grin, the
stumps of his rotted teeth glistening wetly in the cavern
of his drooling mouth.

Now the Torturer squatted, still grinning, and
thrust his twist of reeds at St. Clair's face, but the
flames had already died out and what was left of the
reeds was no more than warm. The charred ends
broke off against St. Clair's skin, and he felt dribbles
of powdery soot roll down towards his chin. As the
Torturer sat back and began to fumble for the bone
sliver at his belt, there came the sound of raised voices
as the others in the band returned, and the halfwit

lurched to his feet and shambled off to greet them.

Moments later, one of the others appeared, bent forward under the weight of a large goat that was slung across his shoulders. He dumped the eviscerated carcass on the ground by the fire, then looked at St. Clair, his eyes moving to the fire and seeing that the prisoner lay far too close to it. He muttered a curse and shuffled forward, calling for help as he began to pull the knight away from the heat. A second man joined him, and between them, none too gently, they picked the Frank up and carried him back to where he had previously been sitting. St. Clair clacked his mouth open and shut noisily, making the sound they recognized as a request for water, and one of them returned with a small clay cup, which he held to the bound knight's mouth.

St. Clair drank thirstily, rinsing his mouth thoroughly with the last drops before swallowing them, and as he did so he heard a curious but familiar sound that ended with a solid, jarring thump. It was the hissing strike of a hard-shot arrow. The missile struck the man kneeling over him, taking him somewhere high in the back and hurling him violently sideways, leaving St. Clair stiffening in shock. The sound was repeated four times after that, clearly audible each time above the rising clamor of frightened voices, and each time, the babble of voices lessened, punctuated by the noise of a body falling. And then the arrows stopped.

St. Clair knew there had been eight men in the band that had captured him. Five of them, he now suspected, were dead. It occurred to him, inanely, that they might simply have been severely wounded, but he doubted that even as the thought came to him. But where, then, were the other three?

He heard a sharp, sibilant whisper, answered promptly by two others. All three men were there, close by, crouching unseen for the time being, presumably safe from the arrows of the lurking enemy beyond the firelight. He turned his head as far as he could to his left, hoping to see where his remaining captors were, but all he could see was a single corpse, his erstwhile nemesis the Torturer, belly down in a lifeless sprawl, his eyes staring emptily at St. Clair, his ever-open mouth finally closed by the ground beneath his chin. A single arrow protruded from his back, its feathers daintily fletched and cunningly fashioned. St. Clair had seen many such missiles, all of them made in Syria by the Seljuk Turks. He was, he decided ruefully, about to exchange one batch of captors for another. The burn in the web of his hand began to throb again.

He sensed movement behind his right shoulder and turned back quickly to look beyond the fire, where he saw an apparition walk into the light. The newcomer was tall and slim, hawk faced and bearded, wearing a tall, conical helmet of shining steel from which hung a net, almost an open veil, of delicate, finely made chain mail. The fellow shimmered as he moved, covered from neck to ankles in a long coat of the same supple mail. His right hand held a long, glittering scimitar and his left a curved dagger, while a small round Saracen shield was mounted on his left forearm, covering it from biceps to wrist when the elbow was bent. There came a cry and a scuffle from the three remaining men behind St. Clair's shoulder, and then he heard running feet approaching him and a smashing blow hammered him into oblivion.

"SANGLAHR."

St. Clair had been awake for some time, but he had not yet opened his eyes, for he had known from the moment of his awakening that he was still a captive, feeling the bonds that yet confined his arms and legs. His head ached from the blow he had taken, but not as badly as he might have expected, and that surprised him. He was in no rush, however, to open his eyes to the light, and for two good reasons, both of them involving risk: the light might inflame whatever it was that caused his head pains, and someone might see that he was awake. And so he lay still and listened, trying to form a picture of what was happening around him.

He knew he had been brought back to awareness by the delicious smell of roasting meat, and one of the last things he remembered, just before the arrival of the enemy from beyond the firelight, was the sight and sound of the goat's gutted carcass being dropped by the fire. Since then, evidently, sufficient time had passed for someone to win the ensuing fight—it had been three against one, he remembered, and hand to hand, since the attacker had obviously set aside his bow and come forward with bared blades. Unless, of course, there had been more than one of them out there in the darkness. He abandoned that train of thought and returned to

where he had been going originally: someone had won
the fight, and had then had time to spit and cook the
goat over the fire of dried camel dung, which meant
that St. Clair must have been unconscious for considerably more than an hour.

"Sanglahr."

The voice spoke again, more clearly and emphatically
this time, and St. Clair knew the outsider had won the
fight, for none of his former captives, with their sibilant
jabbering, had possessed that sonorous depth of voice.

"Sanglahr!" This time the voice was very close, and
a hand grasped him by the shoulder and shook him
hard. He opened his eyes and found dark, flashing eyes
with startling whites peering down into his own. He
thought it must be the outsider in the high, conical
helmet, but the play of light and shadows was too
intense for him to be sure, and by the time he had gathered himself, the other man had moved away to sit
across the fire from him, his back resting against a camel
saddle. He sat with one knee raised, supporting his
elbow, and he held a short, curved, sharp-looking
dagger, dangling it by the hilt, between thumb and
forefinger. In his other hand, lying on the ground by his
left side, he held a set of light, rust-brown manacles.

"I do not own your *ferenghi* tongue, Sanglahr. Do
you have me?"

The language was recognizably French, and
ferenghi—an Arabic corruption of *Frankish*—was the
term used by the local people to describe anything
having to do with the Christian warriors who occupied

their lands. St. Clair sat blinking for long moments, trying to decipher what he had heard. And then it came to him and he shrugged his shoulders, answering in Arabic. "Very little. I am newly come here, a few years only. I do not speak with your people very much ... to learn the language."

The hawk-faced man nodded, and his fine chain mail rattled gently as his helmet moved. "You speak my tongue better than I speak yours, so we will use mine. How long have your legs been bound like that?"

St. Clair looked down at his legs and then shook his head. "I don't know. Several days."

"I will have to cut the ties. You will not enjoy the aftermath. But if Allah wills it, you may recover the full use of your legs. Your arms will be the same, but less severe, I think. Brace yourself." He stood up and stepped back to where St. Clair lay looking up at him, and then he bent and quickly slashed the leather straps binding the knight's legs together before returning to his seat by the fire, where he sat waiting, narrow eyed.

St. Clair took a deep breath and braced himself as instructed, waiting for the pain to come, but for a long time nothing happened and he saw, without under-standing, a deepening frown beginning to form on the stranger's face. But then the first stab of feeling pierced him as the returning blood forced its way back into veins that had been tied off for days on end. The pain was overwhelming, dementing, and finally unen-durable, so that he lost consciousness again, albeit only briefly this time. When he reopened his eyes, the helmed man had not moved and the pain in St. Clair's legs was slightly, and slowly, abating. He gritted his teeth and fought against the urge to moan aloud.

"Try moving them. Bend your knees."

It seemed at first that his legs might never function again, for no matter how hard he tried to make them respond, nothing happened, and a great, surging fear began to rise in him. He had wanted to die when he left Jerusalem and rode out into the desert, but it was a quick death he had sought, an honorable death in battle against infidels like the man across from him now. This—this lingering death in life, unable to move and in constant pain—was not at all what he had had in mind.

"Stop, then. Stop. Think about your feet, your toes. Try to flex your toes, even a little."

St. Clair squeezed his eyes shut against the pain and the fear and concentrated all his mental powers on his right foot, willing the toes to stir, but he felt nothing and his stomach churned in despair.

"There, you see? Now do it again."

"Do what?"

The stranger looked at him in surprise. "Move them. Move your toes again."

"My toes moved? Are you sure?"

"Of course I am sure. Did you not see them?"

"My eyes were shut."

"Then keep them open and watch this time. Now do it again."

The toes moved, and moments later, the toes of his left foot did, too.

"Good. If the toes work now, the legs will work later. Time is all they will require. Now, your arms. This will hurt, too, but perhaps not so badly. Here, drink first. Did these animals feed you?"

St. Clair drank from the cup the man held, then nodded. "Yes, they did. Not much, and not often, but they fed me as often as they fed themselves. Who were they?"

"Animals. Eaters of offal, unclean and unworthy of notice. Better off dead. Now, be still." He cut again, his blade slicing easily through the leather bindings, and this time the pain came more quickly but with less intensity. It wore off more quickly too, and by the time St. Clair was able to stretch and flex his fingers, gritting his teeth against the pain of it, the man across the fire had removed the goat flesh from the spit and spread it, succulent and steaming, on an oval dish of metal that he had dug from one of his bags, along with a long, narrow oval of unleavened bread and a small container of olive oil. He set all these aside for a moment, then knelt quickly in front of St. Clair and snapped the manacles about the knight's wrists and ankles. St. Clair tried to resist, but he was far too weak to do more than sputter in protest, and the Muslim ignored him until he was back in his own place, where he leaned forward and pushed the metal plate towards his prisoner.

"Here, eat. The meat is flavored with garlic—a Frankish taste I picked up while living among you *ferenghi*, years ago. The bread and salt are our own people's, and the pressed oil of olives is Allah's gift to a grateful world. Eat. You will need your strength."

St. Clair ate, and discovered that he was ravenous, and when he was full, his captor gave him more water to drink, and then told him to sleep, as they would probably be traveling in the morning. St. Clair listened to his footsteps moving completely around the perimeter of the little camp. It was only as he was drifting off to sleep, strangely grateful for the loose metal bands about his wrists and ankles after the cruel leather bindings, that he realized that the stranger knew who he was; had known him all along. The first word he had spoken, and repeated, "Sanglahr," had been as close as his tongue could come to pronouncing St. Clair. All thoughts of sleep suddenly banished, St. Clair sat up and shouted, looking about him and trying to see where the stranger had gone, but there was nothing to see. The fire had died down, its fuel exhausted, and there was no response to his shouts.

"SANGLAHR."

The infidel was bending over him again, but this time when St. Clair opened his eyes he felt better, physically, than he had since the morning he left Jerusalem. His hands and feet felt better, almost completely free, the restriction of the loose shackles as nothing to the discomfort he had recently been undergoing. It was still almost dark, the sky above the other man's head paling but not yet discernibly blue.

"How do you know my name? Sanglahr—that is my name, is it not?"

The man facing him blinked, puzzled. "Is it not? You are Sanglahr."

"I am. But how did you know that?"

"I have been looking for you. Was asked to find you."

"By whom? Who sent you?"

The infidel shrugged noncommittally. "A friend."

"Whose friend, yours or mine?"

A hint of a smile flickered at the edge of the other's lips. "Ask that question of yourself, Sanglahr. Would any friend of yours send you out into the desert alone to look for a lost infidel?"

"How did you find me? How did you even know where to look?"

The stranger smiled. "It was not so difficult, Sanglahr. This is my country."

"It may be, but that is not a good enough answer. How did you know where to begin your search? No one, not even I myself, knew where I was going when I left Jerusalem. And I rode for many days without meeting a soul."

"Aye, but because you did not meet a soul does not mean that not a soul saw you. I sent out the word among my people that I was seeking you, a single, crazed *ferenghi*, and that you were not to be approached. It was Allah's will that you were seen soon after that, and the word came swiftly back to me. By the time I drew close to you, you had been captured by the unclean ones. I found you, and they refused to give you to me. Now enough talking, for you know the rest and we have much to do. I have some clothing for you, to cover the whiteness of your *ferenghi* skin from Allah's sun, but the garments are my own and I have no wish to see you wear them over the disease-ridden filth that encrusts you, so before we do anything, or go anywhere, you will bathe and cleanse yourself."

St. Clair blinked in shock. "In the water hole?"

"No, Allah forbid! There are creatures nobler than you who must drink there. You will bathe by the side of the hole, on the bank, and I will keep watch to protect you from any jackal that comes to drink while you are there. Thus, the water that cleanses you will be cleansed again as it drains through the sand before re-entering the hole. I have a bucket. Come now."

He reached out a hand and pulled St. Clair to his feet, and half an hour later, with the sun now high enough in the sky to dry him, the Frankish knight was clean again, scrubbed until his skin was pink, and he felt utterly reinvigorated. He suspected that it might be sinful to enjoy the sensation as much as he did, but he had come to enjoy a guilty pleasure in bathing occasionally.

Above him on the sloping bank, the tall infidel stood watching in silence as St. Clair eventually realized that it was impossible to dress himself while his hands and feet were shackled, and when the knight turned mutely to him with his arms extended and his wrists held apart, he made a show of pondering the request before moving slowly down towards St. Clair, pulling a key from the sash at his waist.

"Where would you run to?" he mused as he unlocked the irons. "But you will put them on again as soon as you are clothed, no?"

St. Clair made no attempt to answer but busied himself instead with donning the long, flowing robes the other had lent him. He had no difficulty with any of them, having discovered, as most of his fellows had soon after arriving in the Holy Land, that the local native dress was far more comfortable than the heavy, scratchy garments worn by the Franks. Only when he had finished winding the burnoose about his head did he pause and look up appraisingly towards the tall figure who stood watching him, seeing the way the fellow's own natural height and slimness were emphasized and enhanced by the smooth, vertical lines of his armor and mail coat, topped off by the tall, slender, conical helmet. The breastplate and the mailed coat were all of burnished metal, glinting silver in the morning sun, but the rest of the man's clothing, the tunic beneath the mail and the trousers tucked into the high boots, was all black, as were the boots themselves, fashioned of supple leather and thickly soled against the desert terrain. A long, black cape hung from the man's shoulders to the ground. He looked not merely fierce but wealthy.

"Are you a Janissary?" St. Clair asked him. "You look as though you might be. I have never seen a Janissary, so I have no way of knowing. Are you?"

The man almost smiled, one cheek twitching wryly. "What do you know of Janissaries, Sanglahr?" When he saw that St. Clair was not going to respond, he continued. "No, Sanglahr, answer the question. I ask without anger. What do you know of Janissaries? Tell me, if you will."

"They are the finest warriors in Syria, from what I have heard. Specially selected and hand picked as the personal fighting troops of the caliph."

The tall man inclined his head. "They are, as you have been told, everything as you say, save that they are not the finest warriors in Syria. They cannot be, in the eyes of Allah. They are Sunni."

"And you are not? Is that what you are telling me?"

"I am Shi'a. Do you know the difference, Sanglahr?"

St. Clair permitted his expression to show nothing of what was in his mind, and then he nodded slowly. "I know a little. I know, mainly, that there are very few Shi'a in this part of the world. Almost every Muslim I know is Sunni. I know, too, that you of the Shi'a Ali— or many of you—are not great lovers of the caliphs. Which would explain your poor opinion of the Janissaries."

"You surprise me, Sanglahr. I thought you would know nothing. And do you know, then, why we of the Shi'a despise the caliphate?"

"Aye, I do. Because you believe they usurped your faith and used their earthly rank and power to take over the work of the Prophet Mohammed, work you believe had been entrusted by the Prophet himself to his cousin and son-in-law, Ali ibn Abu Talib. But what I am wondering is why you can dare to ride around so openly, professing yourself a Shi'a, in such a Sunni stronghold."

The infidel's eyebrows had risen high as St. Clair spoke, and now he shook his head, as though in admiration, but his words were dismissive. "We are in Syria, Sanglahr. You wandered a long way from Jerusalem before your strength gave out. This is Shi'a country more than it is Sunni, and you have reminded me that we have a long way to go. Now I must place you in restraint again, so will you permit me to do so, or should I simply hit you on the head and chain you while you are asleep?"

St. Clair looked at him through narrowed eyes and cocked his head. "Have you a name, then, or must I call you Infidel? My name is St. Clair, as you know."

"Call me Hassan."

"Well, Hassan, hear this. I am afoot, and I have no weapons and no armor, and I would guess that my stamina, what remains of it, is close to its lowest ebb, so I doubt that I could escape from you even if I wanted to."

"I have a horse for you."

"Excellent. I am grateful for that, but I will not be able to mount it if my legs are shackled."

"You will mount first, and I will shackle you beneath the belly of the beast."

"Uncomfortable, and not convenient for me, for you, or for the beast. Would you consent to leave me unshackled if I gave you my solemn word not to try to flee?"

"Your solemn word? The word of a *ferenghi* Christian?"

St. Clair pursed his lips and sniffed. "You have a point there, and I will not try to argue against it. But no, not the word of a Frankish Christian. The word of a warrior who values his honor." He did not allow himself to remember how he had come to be here in the first place, but to his surprise the black-clad Shi'a nodded without hesitation.

"Yes, I will accept that. Is it given?"

"Aye, freely."

"Good, then we may put these back whence they came." Hassan stuffed the shackles into a bag beside him and then hesitated before turning back and tossing something to St. Clair. "Is this yours, by chance?"

St. Clair caught the flying object and stood gaping at the small blue jewel. "Where did you find this?"

"On one of the animals I killed last night. It was tied around his wrist, but I knew it could not be his."

Only then did St. Clair realize, to his own disbelief, that he had not once thought about the fate of his former captors since awakening. Now he looked around, wide eyed, but he could see no sign of them anywhere.

"Where are they? What happened to them?"

Hassan's lips twisted into a sardonic little smile. "I did, Sanglahr. I happened to them. But I think you meant, where are they now. I used the horses to drag the bodies away from the well this morning. They are lying in a wadi, far enough removed for their stink to remain well clear of the water once they begin to rot."

"Who were they, do you know?"

"I have no idea. They were merely nomads, far traveled, from nowhere near here. I tried to speak to them yesterday but could not understand a single word of what they said. Strange language, strange men. But they were Sunni, so the world is better off without them. Now we should go. Are you ready?"

"Aye, but I would like to find my sword. This bauble was tied around the hilt of it."

Hassan shook his head. "I saw no sign of a *ferenghi* sword. The weapons that those fools possessed were poor things, worthless. They would not have left a fine sword behind had they found one. You must have removed the bauble before you abandoned the weapon. Now pick up, and let's away."

St. Clair could only shake his head in bafflement as he hoisted up the heavy bag containing the chains he was to have worn and followed Hassan to where two magnificent white horses and a pack camel stood tethered beneath a stand of palm trees. Hassan secured the bag and two full skins of water to the camel's back, and then led the way southward into the desert.

COMPLICITIES

ONE

The Bishop of Fontainebleau was working himself into a very unepiscopal fury, pacing the length and breadth of Princess Alice's bedchamber and growling unintelligibly, not daring to throw back his head and howl out his outrage the way he wanted to. So swift was his pacing that the silken stuff of his clerical gown floated about him like a cape, the front of it plastered against his naked body as he swept one way and then the other. His testicles ached from the way Alice had handled them, and where before he had been pleasantly drained and sated, he now felt abused and maltreated, insulted openly and left alone to chew upon his own response to the ultimatum the bitch had delivered to him before she left him there. He had not noticed, in the throes of their copulations, that someone had entered the room and made off with all his outer garments, and now that he was aware of it, he had no doubt who the interloper had been—the raddled old slut called Esther, who had been with Alice since her infancy.

Odo had not the slightest flutter of concern that the old bawd might have seen him rutting with her mistress. She had seen that many times before, he knew. What infuriated him was that she had stolen his clothing, depriving him of even the pretense of being able to leave this room, and keeping him dangling at the mercy and pleasure of her damnable harpy of an employer, who had taken so much gloating pleasure in humiliating him.

Odo, she had said to him, in so many words, *this is your last time here. You will not see me again after today—not like this, at least—unless, of course, I change my mind and summon you one last time for nostalgia's sake. But I will see you are looked after well. I am to wed, soon now, and my betrothed is on his way to Outremer to claim me as his bride. Obviously, therefore, I must mend my ways from this time on, and cast off my bad habits. And you, my sweet, are one of those bad habits.*

Betrothed! And to whom? Some popinjay from France or Italy, coming to claim her as his bride! The whore of Babylon herself, and she claimed rights to bridehood? Odo had been so angry that his throat closed up, threatening to choke him, but none of his frantic, screaming questions or accusations had actually emerged from his mouth. Who would wed her? he asked in his mind. What man in his right mind would even ...? But at that point he had answered his own question. Any man who thought he might have the opportunity to wed Alice le Bourcq would climb over a mountain of corpses to claim the privilege.

She had sat watching him as he strove to digest what she had said, hungrily following the play of his emotions on his face and in his eyes as he absorbed her tidings, and then she had laughed and stood up and tapped him with the whisk she used against the ubiquitous sand flies. *Think about it,* she had said. *Think about it quietly for a spell, and I will do the same, for I know what you need and I know where to find it. Now stay, if you will, and wait for me.* And she had gone, leaving two guards at her door and Odo alone, with nothing but a silken undershirt to cover his nakedness. It was too much to bear.

He heard the door opening quietly at his back and spun on his heel, prepared to rend her with his tongue, but she forestalled him with an upraised hand and waved to the woman Esther who was with her. Wordless, the old woman stepped forward and, with a sweeping movement of her right arm, smoothed the material of Odo's outer garment as she draped it across a chair.

"There," Alice said. "No trace of your little accident to be seen."

Odo opened his mouth to snarl, but then closed it without uttering a sound. He had had a mishap, that was true, but in the light of what had happened since then, he was sure it had been no accident. In the excitement of their first meeting after a separation of several weeks, he had been somewhat over-eager, and in her willingness to accommodate him, Alice had contrived to have him spill his seed on the pale green silk front of his outer clothing. He had paid little attention to it at the time, apart from a passing awareness that he would have to wash out the stains before they set, because Alice had been more than simply amorous that day, she had been all over him. Now he knew why: she had wanted to distract him while the old sow stole his clothing in order to make sure he could not safely leave before Alice wished him to. But why? Why had she not simply permitted him to leave, nursing his anger?

As though she had been reading his mind, Alice held up her hand again to still him, and waved Esther away with the other, watching until the old woman had closed the door solidly behind her. Only then did she turn back to face the glowering bishop, who stood teetering, red faced, his hands clenching and unclenching at his sides.

"Danger," she said. "You thrill to risk and danger, Odo."

"I—" He swallowed his outrage and forced himself to speak slowly and clearly. "What are you talking about, my lady?"

If Alice noticed the stiffness of his lips or the tight constriction of his speech she gave no sign of it. "Dress yourself first, then come and sit." She indicated the couch beside her. "Sit, and calm yourself. You are going to enjoy this, I promise you."

She watched wordlessly as Odo dressed himself, then smiled to herself as he slumped onto the couch head down, like a sullen boy. "You will forgive me, I hope, if I fail to see how," he growled.

"You will, believe me. Now listen to what I have to say. Shortly before you arrived today, I received an urgent summons, a *very* urgent summons that I could not ignore. You arrived immediately afterwards, and thus I did not wish to leave." She flashed him a seductive smile, so unexpected that it disarmed him for a moment, distracting him from the anger he had been nurturing, but she was already talking again, the smile still in place. "And so I stayed with you for as long as I could. But I knew by then that, if I left after giving you the tidings of my wedding, you would be angry and would rush away and simmer yourself to a boil in that stuffy old house of yours where I could not reach you. And therefore I arranged to have Esther steal your clothes. Can you forgive me?"

In mere moments, she had pulled every tooth in Odo's maw of anger, and he now sat blinking at her. "I still do not understand. Why then did you not simply tell me what you were about? I would have waited."

"Perhaps you would have, perhaps not, but I did not want you being angry at me from afar. Better, I thought, to have you angry here, where I could explain matters to you once I returned. I had no time to think of anything better or more elaborate to do or to tell you, and besides, I did not know what I would hear when I reached the envoy with whom I had to meet."

"And what did you hear? Who was this envoy?"

"Do you remember our last discussion of the matter of the knightly monks?"

Odo nodded, frowning slightly. "Very clearly, and I confess I have been wondering why you have said no more about it. It has been several months, but we agreed that I would say nothing to anyone, and you would attempt to find some way to discover what they are about in that cavern of theirs. Have you discovered something?"

Alice shook her head. "Nothing that is certain. Nothing that I can use as a weapon. But there is one of them, the youngest of them, whose activities have begun to interest me. They call him Brother Stephen."

The name was like a slap in the face, but Odo, by that time, had mastered his emotions well enough to allow no trace of his jealousy to show. "Stephen, the one who disappeared, you mean? I remember the furor surrounding his disappearance. They turned the city inside out looking for him. But then I heard tell he reappeared from somewhere, professing to have lost his memory." He laughed, a single deep grunt of scorn. "Would he had come to me for his confession! I would have jogged his memory."

"His brethren believed him," Alice said soberly. "And I believed that. The two senior men there, the knights de Payens and St. Omer, are no one's fools. But then the wandering brother disappeared again, less than a month ago, and has not been seen since."

"Where did he go, do you know?" He saw the flash in her eyes and recognized the banality of his question. "Forgive me, that was stupid. Of course you do not know."

"No, I do not, neither where he went nor where he has been since. But I now know that he is on his way back here, accompanied by a trusted ... associate of mine."

Odo gave no sign of having noticed the tiny hesitation, a heavy frown already forming between his brows. "How would you learn such a thing, my lady, and why would you even care about the fate of a filthy, scrofulous monk?"

The princess arched her eyebrows as though she could not believe his lack of wit. "Because of who and what he is, of course. Do you not see, Odo? He is the one among them all who travels most and farthest, the only one who ever leaves those stables for any length of time. And when he disappeared a second time I asked myself, where does he go during these disappearances? Who does he visit? With whom does he speak, and what, above all, might he take with him or bring back with him when these events occur?"

She watched Odo's face as he examined what she had said, and at length he sat back and nodded. "And so you set your spies to look for him?"

"I set one spy to look for him—one spy whose influence extends to every grain of sand in the desert. You do not know the man, nor will you, but he has found the knight monk and he is bringing him back here."

"To meet with you?"

"No, to rejoin his brethren. After that, I want you to speak with him. I will tell you what to ask him, and you will conduct the interrogation. Then you will bring his information back to me."

"But you have barely finished telling me I will not see you again."

"No, not so." Alice tilted her head slightly to one side. "I told you that our delightful fornications are over—that I can no longer afford to indulge myself with our shared pleasures. It would be far too dangerous now, not to mention foolish. I cannot be betrothed to a powerful prince and risk being caught rutting with a bishop of God's Church."

Odo marked the reference to the "powerful prince" and wondered fleetingly who it could be, but for the moment his petulance would tolerate no further distraction. "It never bothered you in the past," he snapped, furious with himself for stating the obvious, even before the words had left his mouth.

"I was not betrothed to anyone in the past. Now I am to wed Prince Bohemond of Antioch."

That silenced Odo. Bohemond of Antioch was a powerful and ominous name, even although he knew they were speaking of the son and not the father. Bohemond I's reputation for prickly honor, ill temper, and drastic, bloody solutions to all kinds of problems had been legendary even in his own lifetime, and Odo had no desire at all to risk the displeasure of his son. He cleared his throat uncertainly and asked Alice how long she had known of this, and she shook her head dismissively.

"I knew nothing of it until recently, but our fathers were friends and I have discovered that we have been betrothed since we were infants."

Odo had already made his decision to remain prudently clear of the princess from that time on, but for the sake of appearances, he allowed himself one last, disillusioned grumble. "Ah," he grunted. "I see how it is. So I am now expected to disappear discreetly. This is my thanks for faithful service?"

"No, your thanks for faithful service will be recognized in the fact that I have found a replacement for myself, on your behalf."

"I—" Odo's mouth hung open, and Alice laughed. "Come now, I can see you thinking all kinds of things that you ought not to be thinking, but listen to me for a moment. Listen, and then see if I am not right. Will you listen?"

He nodded, still speechless, and the princess knelt in front of him, one hand on his knee as she stared into his eyes. "I said once before that you thrill to risk and danger, and that is why you have enjoyed our liaison so much. I was fourteen when you and I first had each other, and had we ever been discovered, my father would have had your head off your shoulders that same day, bishop or no. And therein lay your pleasure and the thrill of the risk, am I not right? Be truthful."

"And if you are? I fail to see what my admission will achieve."

"It will gain you a new mistress, younger than I, and as discreet, surrounded by even more perils and hazards than I pose to you."

The bishop's eyes narrowed in suspicion. "Do I know her? Does she know me?"

"Yes ... and no."

"What does that mean? You tease me with riddles?"

"No, by my soul. Do you recall the night we made a three?"

Odo sat up straighter, for he remembered the

occasion very well indeed, the only time he had ever passed an entire night with Alice and the only time she had ever brought a third party to join them, a very young woman, a girl in truth, who had come to them in darkness and had intertwined with them all night, saying no single word but sharing all their debaucheries before vanishing with the approaching dawn. She had been very young, he remembered, her breasts tiny and still unformed, her small body pliant and avid, but as hard and resilient as a street urchin's. He nodded, swallowing hard.

"She is the one. You have enjoyed her, but not seen her. She has enjoyed you, and would see more of you."

"She is very young." His voice was a raspy whisper, so dry was his mouth.

"Barely fourteen. Younger than I was at first, but no less willing and already better trained."

"By whom?"

"Why, by me, of course." Her laugh was a tinkling cascade of sounds. "She and I have become great friends."

"Then what ...?" He swallowed again. "Wherein lies the risk you spoke of?"

Alice's smile faded. "Her name is Arouna. She is Muslim, of good family. Her father, Fakhr Ad-Kamil, is a sheikh, placid and law abiding at this time but noted for his ferocity in times not so long past. Should he ever discover you in this, or have even the most fleeting suspicion that you may have looked sideways at his daughter, he will cause you to die a lingering, agonizing death." She shrugged. "Against that, you have to weigh Arouna—young, bright, beautiful, passionate, depraved ... She has no wish to be who she is, would far rather live among the Franks and enjoy their ways, but she knows that she will soon be called upon, like me, to wed her father's choice. She will then enter the seraglio of some hawk-beaked old warrior and her life of pleasure will be over. In the meantime, she has her father under her thumb and subject to her every wish, and he permits her, as my special friend, to spend most of her time with me, living here in the palace, a situation she intends to keep unchanged for as long as ever she may."

"So how long would I have her?"

"A year, perhaps two, then things will change. But what more could you desire? A secret mistress, young and dangerous, with a lust for love—indeed a love for lust—that will fulfill your every wish and fantasy. Would you like to meet her?"

"Aye. When?"

"Soon. I will make the arrangements. But are you completely sure you wish to do this?"

"Of course I am."

"Even despite the risk that her father, who is a barbarous old villain, will slit your scrotum and cook your testicles before your eyes, then eat them while his men flay you alive? Will you risk all that, simply for the pleasure of having young, tight flesh to pleasure you?"

"Aye, all of it. You know I will."

"Good." Alice stood up and clapped her hands to summon Ishtar, then lay one hand lightly on Odo's arm. "I will call for you as soon as I know anything. In the meantime, be you prepared to question the knight monk Brother Stephen when he returns. Ah, Ishtar. His lordship the Bishop is leaving now."

TWO

B y the time Stephen St. Clair arrived in sight of the walls of Jerusalem again, he had changed greatly, in some ways, from the man he had been when Hassan rescued him from the nomads, because he and the Shi'a had ridden and lived together for several hundreds of miles by then, and the major part of their time together had been spent in talking, once they had begun to grow accustomed to each other. He had learned, much to his surprise, since it went directly against much of what he had been taught, that the Muslims, in their adherence to the religion of Islam, considered both Christians and Jews to be close to equal to themselves, and as fellow worshippers of the One God, referred to them as People of the Book. It was unimportant that each of the three peoples had a different name for the Book; what mattered was that each *had* a Book, witnessing their involvement with the One God. That idea, that Jews, Christians, and Muslims were interrelated through their God, novel as it was, was none the less logical to a member of the Order of Rebirth in Sion, no matter how close to anathema it might appear to a devout Christian.

He had discovered, too, not only that a Saracen warrior could be an ideal companion in the desert but that he might also possess many of the attributes that St. Clair had found so signally lacking in his own knightly Christian counterparts, such things as dignity, nobility, honor, and an inbred, natural sense of decorum. In fact he had become convinced, purely from watching the behavior and listening to the opinions of the man called Hassan, that those very attributes must be considered commonplace among the warriors of Allah and His Prophet.

They had even talked about religion during their long journey, although St. Clair had presented himself as nothing more than an ordinary Christian knight, and Hassan had taken pains to clarify for St. Clair the differences between the Shi'a Muslims and their more numerous Sunni counterparts, and to explore the schism between the two Islamic factions. St. Clair had found the explanations interesting, but he had none the less found himself being largely unimpressed by any of it, and because he had wondered why that should be, and had then thought about it afterwards, he knew that his lack of interest had sprung from the perception that Islam's leading figure was a mere man, the Prophet Mohammed, whereas Christianity had the Christ himself, the living Son of God, at its peak. That realization had dumbfounded him, because it was illogical and, he now honestly believed, blatantly superstitious. The logical part of his mind knew and accepted from his own studies that Jesus, the man of Galilee, had been no more than what that term implied: a human but extraordinary man set apart by Destiny and, at most, a prophet, just as was Mohammed, the man of Mecca, six hundred years later.

The main thing he had discovered, however, was that this enigmatic, black-clad warrior with the exotic chain-mail armor, who ought, by every criterion known to St. Clair, to have been an enemy, had, in the space of a few days' companionship, become closer to being a real friend than anyone else St. Clair had met since first leaving home as a knight years before. He was unprepared, therefore, when they came in sight of the distant towers of Jerusalem, for Hassan to stop, release him from his obligation not to attempt to escape, and send him on his way alone, while he himself vanished back into the desert behind them. When St. Clair had tried to argue against him, Hassan merely smiled and indicated himself with a downward sweep of his hand. *Look at me,* the gesture said plainly. *I am a desert warrior, a Saracen. I would not survive the day were I to ride into the city.*

St. Clair could not gainsay the truth of that, knowing that he himself was incapable of providing Hassan with any kind of protection or any guarantee of safety or immunity from attack by the first person to set eyes on him. Had he himself encountered Hassan mere days earlier, and seen the man dressed as he was, an obvious representative of every threat that existed to the Frankish kingdom, he would have drawn his own blade and attacked him instantly. And so the two men exchanged farewells and parted, Hassan to return to the desert and St. Clair to seek out his brethren on the

Temple Mount, in all humility and penitence.

He was aware, because he had discussed the matter at great length with the infidel Hassan one night, beside a fire of dried camel dung, that he had come perilously close to losing his soul to the demon of Despair, whose depredations were every bit as lethal to devout Muslims as they were to Frankish Christians. Now, knowing how close he had come to losing everything he valued, St. Clair was prepared to return and confess and acknowledge all his weaknesses. His sole remaining regret, he realized as he rode towards the city's walls, was the loss of his new friend, and he would have been astonished to know that he had passed many times, and would continue to pass in future, within mere paces of Hassan's permanent encampment in the city, because even had he come face to face with Hassan the humble horse trader, it would never have crossed his mind that he might be looking at Hassan the aristocratic Shi'a warrior.

His reappearance at the stables created nowhere near as much of a furor as his first one had. His brethren were glad to see him, and they made no secret of it, but he was extremely conscious from the moment of his return that a gulf had opened up between him and them. It was obvious that they were all curious about what had happened to him and where he had been, but it was equally clear that none of them knew what to say to him or how to treat him. Not a single person commented upon his lack of weapons, and he found that ludicrous, because if there was one major truth governing all their lives in Outremer, it was that no one could expect to live for any length of time unarmed in the desert. He was amused, at first, but quickly grew awkward himself, and within little more than an hour he was speaking to no one, and nursing his injured feelings in resentful silence.

Later that evening, he was summoned to meet with the two senior brethren, Godfrey St. Omer and Hugh de Payens, and when he entered the main recording room at the rear of the stables, he found them waiting for him, their faces studiously devoid of expression. The interview that followed was an awkward and one-sided one, until the moment when St. Clair realized that his own formless shame was driving him to behave with a stubborn pride and arrogance that was utterly beyond justification.

The two men who were questioning him had nothing but his own best interests at heart. There was no question in his mind concerning that. They were not disapproving churchmen, looking to condemn him for moral dereliction, nor were they fathers confessor demanding penitence. They were knights and soldiers, plainspoken and straightforward in their dealings with all men, and they were his sworn brothers in the Order of Rebirth, genuinely concerned for his physical and mental welfare and entirely confident that, as a man of honor, bound by their common code, any moral dilemma in which he found himself involved would be solved to the best of his own abilities and without detriment to them or their Order.

St. Omer had started to ask him another question, assuming that the previous one would go unanswered as had all the others, when St. Clair held up a hand to stop him, and then launched into a detailed explanation of everything that had happened to him in the recent past, beginning with his discovery of the blue stone and omitting only the identity of the woman whom he had recognized in his dreams, and who had precipitated the entire chain of events. Apart from that, he held nothing back and made no attempt to conceal the fact that he believed himself guilty of having broken all three of his vows, and that he had ridden out in search of death, hoping to expiate his sins in suffering some form of martyrdom. He described how he had been taken captive and then rescued and delivered by Hassan the Shi'a.

From the moment St. Clair began to speak, St. Omer, who had known nothing of the dreaming or of St. Clair's struggles with the succubus, sat listening open mouthed and wide eyed with astonishment. Not so de Payens. Sir Hugh sat without speaking, too, as rapt as was his colleague, but for different reasons. He had been unsurprised by the young knight's revelations about his broken vows, for he had suspected something of the kind, something connected to the woman in the younger man's dreams and to St. Clair's long and unusual confinement in the tunnels of the Temple Mount, for he knew that, among all of them, Stephen St. Clair had been the one most accustomed to the freedom of patrolling and spending the major part of his time beneath the open skies.

He found the matter of the Shi'a warrior far more intriguing, because from the moment St. Clair mentioned that an unnamed "friend" had apparently sent the Shi'a searching for him, de Payens had been seeing Princess Alice's face in the forefront of his mind, remembering what she had said to him when they met, about setting a Muslim friend to find St. Clair. He had heard rumors that Alice had friends and allies among the desert nomads, but he could not quite bring himself to believe that the princess's contacts could be sufficiently extensive to enable her, young as she was, to reach out into the wilds of the desert sands and command the attention and obedience of a man like this warrior Hassan, who was formidable by any standards. But St. Clair's evidence indicated clearly that *someone* had done precisely that, and Hugh could think of no one else whom it might be. He said nothing to St. Clair of what he suspected, however, and contented himself with asking the knight if he had any idea of who this mysterious "friend" might be, accepting without comment the headshake he received in response.

When the younger knight's story was complete, the two older brothers sat mulling over all that he had told them, and finally it was de Payens who spoke up.

"Well, Brother Stephen, you have obviously been close to despair, and equally obviously, you have survived it and passed by it. That is good. On the matter of your conscience and your self-doubt over the sins you think you have committed, I can say nothing, save to express my own belief that you appear, to me, to have broken none of your vows irrevocably. As I see it, having listened to you describe what occurred, I can discern fleeting weaknesses, perhaps a lapse in judgment, but nothing of willful rebellion or disobedience. Of course that is not my province, and so I am unqualified to judge. My suggestion, however, would be that you return and visit Patriarch Warmund. He is the man who can advise you best on what you ought to be doing about all that is troubling you. I have to be close by his place tomorrow, so I will visit him and ask if you might talk with him again, and when."

"The Patriarch is not here, Hugh." St. Omer's voice was low. "He left for Antioch yesterday, and will be gone for a month, do you not recall? We saw him off together."

Hugh de Payens raised his eyes to the heavens and clasped his hands prayerfully in front of him. "One more instance, Lord God, of the tyranny of advancing age. Too many things on my mind these days." He turned back to St. Clair. "So, that will have to wait, Brother Stephen. As soon as the Patriarch Archbishop returns, I will make the arrangement for you to meet with him, and in the meantime the weeks will pass quickly. I promise, you will not be bored." He glanced at St. Omer. "For the time being, if the matter of the jewel continues to trouble you, and it evidently does, then that is easily resolved. Give it into the custody of Brother Godfrey here, and we will say no more about it. That done, relieve your mind of any guilt concerning it and rest yourself here, among your brothers. You have been long away. Tell them where you have been, and of the adventures you have had, for although they may not ask, they would love to know. Now go in peace and fret no more until the month has passed and you have spoken to Warmund de Picquigny."

THREE

Hugh de Payens was proved correct, for the month flew by and was gone before St. Clair ever had time to think about time's passing, so busy had he been since his return. He spent much of the time underground, laboring hard with his fellows, and much of the remaining time he spent in prayer, and in studying the mystifying charts of the underground labyrinth that had come from France. Those were kept in a chest in the records room in the monks' quarters, and St. Clair found them fascinating, for the workings they depicted were immense and complex, and yet nothing the knights had found came anywhere close to being identifiable in the drawings.

He was working there one day, deep in concentration on one map, when André de Montbard interrupted him to deliver a summons for him to attend upon Warmund de Picquigny at his earliest convenience. Because St. Clair had been expecting the invitation, he made his way immediately to the Archbishop's palace. He reported to the guard at the main entrance and then was led by one of the Patriarch's cowled clerical functionaries through a maze of rooms and corridors, none of which he remembered from his previous visits. He

thought nothing of that, simply assuming that the
Patriarch would have his own reasons for being wherever he happened to be that day.

The cleric led him past the end of one wide gallery
that St. Clair remembered as leading to the Patriarch's
personal quarters, because he recognized a magnificent
tapestry that hung there. They passed by, however, and
his guide conducted him beyond, to a high-ceilinged
room with stone walls, a flagged, rush-strewn floor, and
small, high-set windows that managed to imbue the
place with a dank, chilled air that reminded St. Clair far
more of northern Anjou than any other place he had
seen in Outremer. His escort waved him, none too
amicably, towards a high-backed chair and then withdrew, leaving him alone to sit and wait.

He had been waiting for what he estimated to be
the better part of a half hour, and had long since lost
the battle to restrain his growing impatience, when the
heavy door at his back swung open and he rose to his
feet, turning to acknowledge the Patriarch. It was not
Warmund de Picquigny who strode towards him,
however. Instead, it was the man he recognized from a
previous visit as being the Archbishop's amanuensis, a
bishop whose name would not come to mind. St. Clair
merely inclined his head, prepared to hear that the
Patriarch had been detained and was unable to keep
their appointment, and so he was taken aback when the
newcomer fixed him with a withering, unfriendly glare
and waved him back into his seat without a word of
cordiality or greeting. St. Clair subsided into his chair

again, clasping the end of one of its arms gently in his right hand and adjusting the dagger at his belt with the other.

The bishop took a chair behind the table by the empty fireplace, where he began to pore over a document he had brought in with him, leaving St. Clair, once again, to wait in silence. The bishop sat reading for some time, frowning portentously, St. Clair thought, and then, just as the knight was preparing to stand up and walk out in protest at such unconscionable treatment, the cleric sighed loudly, threw down the parchment—it immediately sprang back into its cylindrical shape—and peered at St. Clair, pinching the bridge of his nose between thumb and fingertip.

"Stephen St. Clair," he said. "Do you know who I am?"

Stephen bit back the retort that sprang to his tongue but refused to be browbeaten by a cleric, no matter how highly ranked, and so he merely shrugged. "A bishop?"

"I am Odo de St. Florent, Bishop of Fontainebleau, secretary amanuensis to his Grace Warmund, Patriarch Archbishop of Jerusalem." He fell silent and waited, presumably to observe the effect of his pronouncement, so St. Clair kept his face expressionless for a count of five heartbeats and then nodded, once.

"I see."

"The Patriarch has empowered me to interrogate you on his behalf, since his business will not permit him the time or opportunity to follow this affair in person."

"What affair?"

Odo glared at him. "You will address me as 'my lord Bishop,' and you will not speak at all until required to."

"What affair, Bishop Odo? I do not know what you are talking about."

"This—" Odo waved a hand towards the parchment scroll on the tabletop. "The affair under investigation."

St. Clair was ill at ease with this development, but not as badly disconcerted as Odo had presumed he would be. He knew he had done nothing wrong— nothing, at least, to warrant interrogation by Odo of Fontainebleau or any other churchman, including the Patriarch himself. Confession and absolution was one thing, between a man, his God, and the priest or bishop who served as interlocutor, but he had done nothing to merit this kind of treatment. And yet ... Unsure of himself, he sat back into his chair.

"What are you investigating? Tell me what it is you want to know."

"It is a matter concerning your abduction of several months ago, and this more recent disappearance of the past few weeks. It has come to the Patriarch's attention that there are inconsistencies and irregularities in what you have said about them to your superiors and what he has been told about them from other sources. I now wish to hear the pertinent details again, so that between the two of us, his Grace and I may reach a conclusion regarding your truthfulness, or the lack of it, in this nonsensical affair."

"Explain what you mean by nonsensical."

There was an edge to St. Clair's voice, and Odo's

head jerked back as though he had been slapped. "How dare you question me! You are insolent! Remember who I am, and do not force me to have you reminded." He held up the heavy, jeweled pectoral cross of his bishop's rank. "This is a symbol of who I am and what I represent, and you would be well advised not to lose sight of it. You are a menial brother in a small and irregular fraternity of friars. You will therefore address me with the respect to which I am entitled."

St. Clair shifted in his seat and leaned forward, deliberately hooking his thumb around the cross-hilt of his dagger and pushing it into prominence at his waist. "Aye, my lord Bishop," he said quietly, "at times we all need symbols to remind ourselves and others of what we are and what we represent." He saw Odo's eyes grow wide, and was satisfied that he had made his point. "You have come close to accusing me of lying to the Patriarch and to my brethren, Bishop Odo, and therefore I claim privilege on two counts, as knight and monk: I wish to discuss this matter with my superiors in the Order, and I wish to speak again with the Patriarch in person."

There was a long silence, and then Odo managed to say, "Again? You wish to speak with the Patriarch *again*?"

"Of course I do, as would you yourself in similar plight. When last I spoke with Master Warmund, at the instigation of my superior, Brother Hugh de Payens, his lordship graciously heard my confession on these very matters that you say are now troubling him, and found me blameless. He sent me away that day shriven of all guilt. Thus, if he wishes to question me further on this matter, I will confess myself puzzled, but I will submit to his authority, so be it I may do so in person." St. Clair waited, and then asked, "Did you not know that? The Patriarch said nothing of it to you?"

Odo somehow managed to keep his face expressionless, but his eyes betrayed his panic and confusion, and it was suddenly clear to St. Clair that the bishop had been lying. Whatever the purpose underlying this interview might be, it had nothing to do with Warmund de Picquigny. Odo had been unmasked, and now, while he scrabbled frantically for words with which to reassert himself, it was St. Clair's turn to sit and frown, and he did so with great aplomb, leaning back into the uncomfortable chair and folding his arms on his chest, waiting for Odo of Fontainebleau to speak.

Odo, however, was in no hurry, simply because he did not know what to say. He knew he had erred badly and destroyed his own credibility, but now he had no faintest idea of how to proceed, for no matter what he attempted now, the man facing him would refuse to comply, and Odo, still vividly conscious of the dagger at the fellow's belt, was afraid of pushing him too far. Alice, he knew, would be livid at such a pathetic failure, after coaching him on exactly which questions to ask.

He was saved from further agonizing by St. Clair, who addressed him in a voice that evinced nothing but courtesy.

"I propose, Master Bishop, that we begin again. Clearly you brought me here under false pretenses, hoping to gain some advantage by intimidating me while interrogating me. No need to protest, my lord— I know I am correct. I have no idea what it was you wanted, but I have nothing to hide, and I confess I am curious to know what you are looking for, so if you would care to start afresh, we can proceed."

Odo sat staring at the young knight through narrowed eyes, fury simmering inside him hotly enough to scald his throat, although he allowed nothing to show on his face. He knew he was being offered a way out, but he was still unable to grasp it, to see the route he had to take. And finally it came to him that Alice herself would be the one best suited to resolve this entire charade.

"There is ... a lady," he began. "A lady whom I know. A patroness of great wealth and influence who is ... desirous of meeting with you, to discuss matters of mutual interest."

"That is not possible. I am a monk. There can be no mutuality of interest between me and any woman." St. Clair had known instantly who the woman was, because he clearly remembered de Payens remarking, the very first time St. Clair had ever seen Bishop Odo, that the cleric spent much time in the company of the King's second-eldest daughter. It had seemed to St. Clair at the time that there might even have been a suggestion of *too much* time attached to the comment, but he saw no point now in naming the princess. Even as he spoke, however, Odo was already shaking his head.

"Believe me, Brother Stephen, you need have no

fears on the grounds of propriety. The lady to whom I refer is—"

"I know exactly to which lady your refer, my lord Bishop, but not even the Princess Royal can claim exemption from the laws of God. I am surprised to hear you suggest otherwise."

For the second time in the brief course of this interview, Odo was stunned into slack-jawed speechlessness, and St. Clair realized he might have said too much. Clearly the bishop knew nothing about his abduction by the princess, and he, as the simple monk he professed to be, could have had no plausible reason for his assertiveness. He pressed on, giving Odo no time to recover either his wits or his wind, recalling the few occasions when he had met the princess harmlessly in public, and explaining, with a sheepish smile that felt as false to him as a wooden mask, why the princess's name had come to him so unerringly. Odo had spoken, he said, of a woman of wealth and influence, and the princess and her mother were the only Christian women of wealth and influence whom St. Clair had seen since his arrival in Jerusalem. In fact, he added shyly, should the truth be known, the princess was the only woman of rank that he had ever met since leaving his home in France as a boy, to travel and soldier with his liege lord. Thus hers was the only name in his mind when Odo spoke of a lady of influence and he had assumed ... He allowed his voice to fade out, then mumbled that he could not imagine what the lady could conceivably wish to discuss with a simple, unwashed knight monk.

The bishop frowned, then nodded, too intent upon salvaging his own situation to be suspicious of the other man's motives, and when he spoke, clearing his throat self-consciously to give his voice its most commanding timbre, his words were somber and measured, his delivery pompous and unconvincing.

"I can understand your mystification, Brother Stephen, but perhaps it might relieve your mind to know that there is nothing personal involved in the lady's desire to speak with you. To the contrary, in fact, the princess has the utmost faith in your goodwill and in your honor and integrity."

St. Clair marveled at the way in which this bishop could so easily spout one thing at one moment and then turn completely about and say the very opposite mere minutes later. It was clear to him that the man assumed, simply because he was speaking to a knight and not to an educated cleric, that he had no need to deal with intelligence and even less need to consider his listener's ability to differentiate between falsehood and flattery.

"The princess is deeply perturbed because of certain matters ... certain *information* that has been brought to her attention recently. I have no knowledge of what, precisely, is entailed, nothing, in fact, on which to base my judgment other than my own observations of the princess herself. I gather, however, from what I have seen and heard, that there are strange but ... *unspecified* goings-on, occurring within the confines of the stables in the Temple Mount. I suspect it may have something to do with the foundations, although I know not what that might entail.

"Whatever it is, whatever is involved, the Princess Alice now finds herself in a dilemma of great urgency. Her natural wish, and indeed her filial duty, is to present these reports to her father the King, but such is her regard for your superior, Brother Hugh, and for yourself, that she is hesitant to proceed without making some enquiries of her own, aware that such a report, unsubstantiated and anonymous as it is, could provoke a host of troubles for you and your brethren, and most probably without need. Therefore she charged me with the task of questioning you, rather than summoning you directly into her presence. I, unfortunately, knowing nothing of the background to this affair, chose to conduct my task, as I now see, improperly and inappropriately. It would have been better, I now understand, to have been open with you from the outset."

"Aye." St. Clair's tone was as dry as the bishop's was orotund, but he said no more, and Odo hesitated.

"Aye, indeed ..." He then rushed on, before St. Clair could say anything more. "Would you be willing to come with me right now and put the lady's mind at rest on these matters?"

St. Clair covered his mouth with his hand, thinking furiously. Odo's mention of the foundations had distressed him. Anything else the knight could have taken in stride, for it was common knowledge that everyone was interested in the strange knight monks of the Temple Mount and their apparently bizarre life in

the stables there, but the specific mention of the foundations of the stables was of great concern. A face-to-face
encounter with Alice might have been something he
would welcome, given sufficient time to prepare himself
for it, because he had been thinking deeply about her
during his last few days in the desert with Hassan, and
about what she represented to his life in the future. The
dreams that had haunted him were now a thing of the
past; he had not had a single recurrence of the incidents
since the night he recognized the truth and fled from
Jerusalem. And so he felt, with some small degree of
confidence, that he might be able to confront his fears
by confronting Alice herself. It was, however, and he had
admitted this to himself wryly and frequently during the
preceding few days, a very small degree of confidence.
Nevertheless, he had been willing to face the possibility
of one more, final encounter with the princess.

This specific mention of foundations and the temple,
unexpected as it was, had pushed all such considerations
aside and filled his mind to capacity with thoughts of
danger, interference, and betrayal. Odo's mention of
the brotherhood's most closely held secret had set every
warning bell in St. Clair's mental watchtower jangling
discordantly, because he understood immediately that if
Alice, and by extension this creature, Odo, knew of the
activities beneath the stables, that meant, beyond
doubt, that someone, one of his own brethren, had
betrayed the Order of Rebirth, and the entire world
might find out about their activities at any moment.
Even in his momentary panic, St. Clair did not believe

for an instant that anyone had deliberately betrayed them. One of the brothers must simply have been careless in some way. That was the only reasonable explanation he could imagine, because it was plain that despite all of their secrecy and their meticulous and painstaking precautions since beginning their excavations years earlier, their activities had been noted, and with sufficient precision to specify the underground location of their work: the *foundations.*

The how and why of it, to his surprise, were insignificant beside the disastrous consequence that the clandestine efforts of the Jerusalem brethren on behalf of the Order of Rebirth in Sion were about to come to an abrupt end, with foreseeable catastrophic effect upon the Order itself.

Unless—and there he had to stop and brace himself physically, tightening his belly muscles—*unless* he were somehow able to convince Princess Alice, and through her Bishop Odo, that her suspicions were groundless. The prospect made him want to groan aloud, for he knew precisely how inept and pathetic his previous behavior had been around the princess. To hope for anything different now would be folly. It was far too late to defer to de Payens and St. Omer; matters were much too far progressed for anyone to hope that those two could go in and face the princess unprepared, without knowing in advance what information she had received and how she had chosen to interpret it. He, at least, had an existing relationship with Alice, shameful and degrading as it might have been, and so he found himself considering, much to his own ludicrous disbelief, that there might be some hope, some magical possibility, that he might be able, despite the inherent impossibility of any such thing, to put that former association to use, and to disarm or defer Alice's suspicions for as long as would be required for de Payens and St. Omer to evolve a counterstrategy based upon what he could report back to them. And so he simply had to try—he had to face Alice, and then face her down, no matter what became of him and his newfound resolution of chastity. He shook his head in disbelief as the thought came to him that this final encounter with the woman who had abducted, detained, and debauched him would probably be the most important interview in the history of the Order of Rebirth in Sion.

"Very well," he said. "Take me to the princess."

FOUR

St. Clair stood alone in an anteroom, staring vacantly at an enormous tapestry covering one entire wall that depicted a deer hunt in some wooded valley in Christendom. His stomach rumbled uncomfortably and sent hot bile spurting up to burn the back of his throat. He had no idea how long he had been waiting since Bishop Odo had ushered him into this room and closed the door behind him while he went in search of Princess Alice. Since then, he knew only that he had examined every detail of the tapestry—the only object in the room other than a few ungainly pieces of furniture— deciding almost immediately that the composition of the piece was ill conceived and poorly executed, and although he looked at it still, it no longer occupied any portion of his awareness.

He was also acutely conscious, for the first time that he could ever recall, of not being *clean,* and that was a consideration that troubled him greatly, because cleanliness was not something that a man of his kind concerned himself about. In truth, cleanliness, in the sense of washing oneself in order to render oneself odorless and inoffensive to others, was regarded by some as a weakness almost akin to effeminacy and by others as being sinfully effete and hedonistic. St. Clair had not washed since the day by the water hole in the Syrian desert where Hassan the Shi'a had found him, and on that occasion he had done so only because Hassan refused to lend him any of his clothing until he washed the encrusted filth from his body, which had been fouled with refuse and excrement during his captivity. Even so, he thought now, that had been mere weeks before, and as a monk he was required to wash no more than two or three times in any year.

His discomfort, he knew, was caused by his knowledge of the Princess Alice and her habits. Alice loved to bathe, he remembered, and had always done so, from the days of her earliest childhood. She had been raised by servants in her parents' household in Edessa, and as servants will with small children, they had spoiled her outrageously, lavishing love on the child and making sure she had the best of everything that life could provide. They were of mixed races, these servants, from a host of differing tribes and nationalities, but all of them were Muslim, and they had imbued in the child a love of cleanliness, encouraging her to use the magnificent baths in her father's city that had been built by the Romans many centuries earlier and used by the Arabs ever since. In consequence of that, Alice had grown to womanhood as a sweet-smelling rose among foul-smelling men, and St. Clair knew, because he clearly remembered now how and when she had confided in him, that she refused to have unwashed people about her. Even her guardsmen were clean and fresh smelling, although they did stop short of being perfumed.

His thoughts were interrupted when the doors at his back swung open and Bishop Odo re-entered, accompanied by the princess herself, who stopped dramatically on the threshold and gazed imperiously and questioningly at St. Clair, her chin held high, one eyebrow slightly raised, her expression unreadable. She was wearing a shimmering robe of the most beautiful fabric St. Clair had ever seen, so flimsy and diaphanous that it appeared to be made of mist. It was of palest purple—he had seen the precise color before, somewhere, in a flower, he thought, but could not remember where or when—and beneath it she wore another garment altogether, this one of denser material in a glorious pink. She paused there only for a brief moment, but to St. Clair it seemed to be an age, for not a single word of greeting suggested itself to him and he felt his face and neck begin to redden.

"Upon my life, it *is* the celebrated Brother Sir Stephen, in the flesh! I confess I am flattered and delighted both, even if incredulous. When my lord Bishop here told me you had come a-visiting, I thought he must surely be mistaken, for it is said that only the shy desert fox is more elusive and more hard to spot than this noble knight monk ... albeit I am told that the fox is not *quite* as adept at vanishing from view, run as he might."

There was no trace of humor on her face or in her eyes, but St. Clair knew she was twitting him, referring to the time they had met in the marketplace, and he felt his face flush crimson. "Well, Brother Stephen, have you no greeting for me? No surly grunt to warn me of my place?"

St. Clair cleared his throat, and as he did so he had a vision from years before, when he had witnessed the first meeting of one of his cousins and the woman who would become his wife. "I rejoice to meet you again, my lady," he said smoothly, recalling his cousin's words. "Your presence brightens even the sunlit morning." *There*, he thought, even as the princess's eyes widened in surprise, *that was easy*. "Bishop Odo told me that you wish to speak with me, and so I came at once."

She blinked at him, once only. "Yes, I can see you did, and I am grateful. Come, if you will, accompany me." She turned and led the way back towards the chamber she used as a reception room, walking quickly, straight backed and square shouldered, while Odo and St. Clair followed her. A single armed guard at the entrance opened the door and stood at attention beside it until they should pass through, but on the point of entering, Alice stopped and looked at Odo.

"My thanks to you, my lord of Fontainebleau, you have been of great service, as you always are, but I am sure you have other matters to attend to and so I will not keep you. You may return to your affairs. Brother Stephen and I have much to discuss."

The bishop nodded, stone faced, but the knotted muscles in his jaw betrayed tightly clenched teeth, and St. Clair sensed that Odo was seething with anger, having no doubt expected to sit in on the conversation between him and the princess, and he half smiled, enjoying the realization that Bishop Odo of Fontainebleau was not one of the princess's favorite people.

As Odo stalked away, his heels thumping angrily, Alice crooked a finger at St. Clair, and she swept through the door and into the beautifully appointed rooms beyond. He swallowed nervously and entered close behind her, his nostrils filled with her perfume, then moved to the chair she indicated, where he remained standing, waiting for her to seat herself. She smiled at him and sat down, and he lowered himself carefully onto the chair, noting thankfully that a substantial space now separated them and that he could no longer smell the scent she was wearing. And that reminded him, inevitably, of his own odorous condition, for he realized that Alice had seated herself far enough away to avoid the unwashed smell of him.

They sat without speaking for a count of perhaps ten heartbeats, each of them looking at the other, and then the princess cleared her throat gently.

"I was being truthful when I said how surprised I am to see you here, Brother Stephen. I would not have believed you would come here."

What does that mean? he thought. *Does she mean voluntarily, and if she does, does that mean she expects me to remember having been here before?*

Alice continued in the same tone. "It has been my impression that you and your brethren prefer to keep yourselves and your concerns close held among yourselves."

He knew he had to say something, so he attempted

to look as though he had no notion of what she meant as he replied, "Well, my lady, we are monks, bound by our sacred vows to abjure the world and the things of the world."

"You mean the *people* of the world, do you not, sir knight? Your vows I will accept—for the moment at least—because they are common knowledge, but the Poor Fellow Soldiers of Jesus Christ are a different breed of monks, are they not? Monks who fight and kill are scarcely like other monks. That, to me, is a profound distinction."

She would accept his vows, for the moment? He had no idea what she meant, but he nodded, surprised that the tension fluttering in his breast had largely died away. "That is true, my lady. We are different, and dedicated to a new purpose—a purpose that has never existed prior to this time and place."

"And a laudable purpose, no?"

He shrugged, sensing a trap somewhere. "In the eyes of the Patriarch Archbishop and your father the King, that would appear to be the case."

"Aye, laudable indeed. To fight and kill men in the name of God, and beneath His own banner, in clear, but somehow suddenly justifiable, defiance of the clarity of His commandment 'Thou shalt not kill.'"

St. Clair gave a brief jerk of the head. "Your point is clear, my lady, and barbed. But the men against whom we fight—the Muslim infidels—despise our God and would drive His presence from this land."

"Not so, Brother Stephen. That is not true. In fact it

is specious. No devout Muslim despises our God, for
He is the same God to whom they pray. They call Him
Allah, whereas we call him God—*le bon Dieu*—the
Good God. But He is the same deity. He is the *sole*
deity." Alice's face had grown pinched with disapproval,
and St. Clair found himself watching her closely, seeing
how her eyes narrowed with a passionate belief in what
she was saying, and he felt a stirring of admiration for
her intensity, in the light of the journey he had just
undertaken with Hassan the Shi'a and the conversations
they had shared in the course of it. But she had not yet
finished. "The hatred and the killing, all of it, Brother
Stephen, from the first moment our most Christian
armies descended upon this land under the leadership of
Geoffroi de Bouillon and with the blessing of the Pope
in Rome, has been carried out in the name of God, but
for the convenience and enrichment of the men who
believe themselves entitled to interpret God's holy will.
And my father ranks highly among them."

The unexpectedness of this denunciation, and the
ferocity with which it was delivered, rendered St. Clair
speechless, for he had been witness, no matter how
unwillingly or unwittingly, to a statement that would be
deemed worthy of death had anyone in power overheard
it. Moreover, it was a statement with which he agreed in
every sense, and in his enthusiasm he came close to
saying so. He opened his mouth to speak, but discovered in doing so that there was nothing he could dare to
say, and so he closed it again, quickly, his mind reeling
with the revelation that had just occurred to him.

He had spent months now believing that this woman was a spoiled, malevolent, self-centered child with no thought in her mind except debauchery and sensual pleasures, but in the space of moments she had shown him another, entirely unsuspected facet of her nature: a fiery passion allied with a withering contempt for the powerful men of her acquaintance. He was convinced, quite suddenly and unexpectedly, that he was out of his depths in this confrontation, if, in fact, it was a confrontation. He shook his head, as if trying to clear the clutter of his thoughts, then made a valiant attempt to redirect the conversation, which had become far too dangerous for comfort.

"I cannot find it in my heart to disagree with you, my lady, but the sin is not all one-sided. The men against whom my brethren and I fight are not devout Muslims. They are godless and they are murderous, bandits and marauders and more than deserving of the justice meted out to them when we find them. Were they Christian Franks, guilty of the same transgressions, we would treat them no differently.

"But I suspect that has nothing to do with why you sent for me, although I may be wrong. Was it this you wished to speak with me about? If so—"

Alice smiled again. "No, Brother Stephen, it was not, so you may set your mind at rest, even on this matter of my treasonous speech. I am a dutiful daughter and I love my father dearly, as a just and indulgent parent. It is only with his *kingship* that I struggle—his manhood, masculinity, male pride, call it what you will. I think of it as that element in his nature that prevents him from seeing the world through a woman's eyes. And since you are a monk, self-sacrificingly severed from such worldly things, and devoted single-mindedly to the pleasure and the glory of doing God's real will, I may not include you in my general condemnation of men."

St. Clair blinked. "You condemn *all* men, my lady?"

"Most men, Brother Stephen, and most particularly the majority of those men with whom I have to spend much of my life. The more powerful a man becomes, I find, the less pleasurable is his company, and those men involved in acquiring power, like our admirable Bishop of Fontainebleau, are totally intolerable. I abhor men who are grasping for power, because all of them crush lesser men beneath their lusts." She saw the expression on his face and continued. "Yet I know too, believe me, that lesser men, ordinary men, can be just as swinish and as evil as their so-called betters, so do not misconstrue what I am saying. All that I mean is that our system of feudal tenure exists solely for the benefit of those men who hold power. That means, Brother Stephen, that it exists to the detriment of everyone, for even those on the pinnacles of power are all too often destroyed by being atop the pinnacle. I would change that, if I could, but I cannot. I am a mere woman, and women are more powerless than serfs in this world of men. What is it? You look as though you have something you would like to add."

"No, my lady. Nothing at all."

"Very well, then, let us begin to *begin*, you and I."

She raised her hands and clapped sharply, and an old man entered through the doors at the far end of the room and came to her. "Ishtar," she said, her eyes still on St. Clair, "this is Brother Stephen, of the brotherhood from the stables on the Temple Mount, but he is here this day as Sir Stephen St. Clair, in order to assist me. Conduct him to the baths, if you will. Sir Stephen?"

Her right eyebrow had risen high on her forehead, whether in challenge or in curiosity St. Clair had no idea, but he permitted nothing to show on his face as he debated with himself. He had gone through all this in his mind before even entering these rooms, knowing that she would, in all probability, insist upon his bathing, and he was well aware of the dangers to his chastity—a chastity already compromised to the point of risibility—that were involved therein. She would not approach him while he was unwashed, rank and offensive to her nostrils, but once he had emerged from the hot water baths, all steamed and scrubbed and perfumed, he would face another reception altogether. She would not scruple to approach him then, and he had but little confidence in his own ability, or even in his willingness, to withstand the blandishments she might bestow upon him. And this time, if he succumbed to her, there would be no matter of *intent* to debate.

Having bathed within the previous month, and therefore being less rank than usual, he thought he might stand upon his vows and refuse her invitation, and he had earlier surmised that he would probably be

able to win the confrontation that would undoubtedly
follow, depending upon how badly she needed and
wanted his cooperation and whatever information she
thought she could obtain from him. Against that, he
now had to weigh the astonishing attitude Alice le
Bourcq had so newly revealed to him. If he refused now
to bathe at her request, he would incur her hostility and
forfeit the amiable, forthright, and unprecedented
reception she had accorded him so far.

And there came the crux of the matter, because he
could imagine nothing more important—to himself and
to his brothers in the Order of Rebirth—than to
discover as much as he could about what she knew and
what she hoped to discover. It made sense, then, that he
should accede to her wishes in this matter of bathing
and use the goodwill generated by that to extract whatever information he could amiably, rather than hope to
glean it in an adversarial encounter.

He stood up without speaking, and her head tilted
backward, holding his gaze, that single eyebrow still
raised—in what, he wondered, reflecting that if it were
anticipation, he was incapable of guessing what
prompted it.

"I remember, my lady." He had not meant to say
that. The words had sprung to his tongue and spilled
out before he even knew he had formed them, and now
he saw her eyes widen in surprise, mingled with something else—confusion, he thought, or perhaps consternation. When she spoke, however, there was no sign of
any such thing in her voice.

"*What* do you remember, Brother Stephen?"

He smiled slightly, amazed at the ease with which his response came to him, and dipped his head. "What I had heard. Not that you dislike men, but that you dislike the stink of *unwashed* men."

She continued to stare at him for a moment, her eyes narrow, then nodded. "You heard correctly, Brother. Go you now with Ishtar. And Ishtar, send Esther to me, if you will." She looked back at St. Clair. "I shall be here when you are ready."

St. Clair followed the old eunuch through the maze of passageways and courtyards within the walls of what had been the great al-Aqsa Mosque, looking about him as he went for anything that he might recognize. He saw nothing that was even vaguely familiar, however, which confirmed his own belief that he must have been barely conscious—or perhaps more accurately, barely aware of his surroundings—when he was confined here previously. The bathing rooms were completely unfamiliar, too, and that surprised him greatly, for among the most persistent memories he had were those of long, pleasant hours spent in the warmth and luxury of the baths.

"I do not remember this place." He spoke the thought aloud, merely to express his confusion, if only to himself.

"And why should you? You have never been here."

St. Clair, barely aware of the eunuch's presence, had not expected a response, and so it took him a moment to realize that Ishtar was unsurprised to hear him hint, even as vaguely as he had, that he was aware of having been here before. He looked keenly at the old man. "Are there, then, other baths here?"

"Hah!" It was more of a bark than a laugh, but St. Clair could see that the old fellow was amused. "I imagine so. There are six more, all separate."

"Then which one did I use?"

Ishtar gazed back at him, blank eyed. "Today, *ferenghi*, you use this one. Achmed, whom I will send to you, will be your masseur. I will wait for you outside and take you back when you are ready." He bowed and moved away without another word.

Less than an hour later, bathed and pummeled, oiled and scented, and dressed in fresh clothing, St. Clair re-entered the princess's audience room and found her deeply involved with several of her women in some project that involved countless lengths of bright fabrics and materials, strewn over every available surface in a riotous explosion of vibrant colors. She saw him enter behind Ishtar and dismissed the women immediately, sending them scurrying away, burdened with armloads of fabrics, and she stood up to welcome him back. He nodded politely but made no attempt at conversation, knowing that she knew she had won in the matter of the bathing, and that the conducting of this interview was hers to dictate. She waved him to a couch and sat beside him, facing him far more closely than she had before, so that the smell of her perfume filled his nostrils, tightened his chest, and set his blood stirring again.

"There, now I can approach you, at least." She

paused, awaiting a reaction that he successfully suppressed, and then she smiled. "Bravo! I expected you to move away when I said that, but you barely flinched. And yet I suspect you may be even more skittish and nervous around women nowadays than you were before, Brother Stephen, now that you are a monk in fact. Am I correct?"

He pursed his lips, wondering what was coming next, but nodded. "Aye, my lady, you are correct. I am."

"And yet you were a knight for many years before you ever thought to turn monk. Surely you knew no lack of women in those years?"

That was a statement, he decided, not a question, and so he merely shrugged his shoulders.

"Well?"

It had been a question after all, and the princess wished him to answer it. He thought for a while, then said, "My mother died when I was but a babe and I had no sisters or female relatives, my lady. I was brought up in an unusual household, in England, a country where the people still hate us as the Norman invaders who conquered them no more than fifty years ago. It was a household lacking in women, yet one in which antique values and standards were espoused and nurtured, even revered. My upbringing was built around those values and was supervised throughout my boyhood by a group of wise, devout, and learned men." He paused for a while before continuing. "They taught me many things for which I have been grateful for many years, but none among them, alas, was an adept in the knowledge of women, so my learning there was severely limited."

Again he stopped, a tiny frown on his face, deep in thought now and unaware that the princess was watching him closely.

"Fortunately for me, I had the natural aptitudes of a soldier, in addition to being scholarly, and so I was knighted early. And then, being very, very young, I rushed out into the world, eager to fight for all the things that I had been taught to believe in and to revere. And that, I fear, was the end of my youth. I quickly discovered that I had little in common with my fellow knights, and even less with the women who surrounded them.

"That first year of knighthood outside of my home was a time of revelations, none of them pleasant. I quickly learned the difference between the world of ideas and ideals in which I had been raised, and the real world of bestial brutality within which most men live.

"I discovered that my fellow knights were not as I had envisioned them. They were barely civilized and lacked even the rudiments of what I had been taught was Christian conduct. I saw the undeniable reality of godlessness everywhere: hypocrisy, cynicism, venality, simony, and unbridled carnality even among priests and clerics. I could not approve, but neither could I disapprove too loudly, for I would not have lasted a month once the word of my disapproval was out. And so I held my peace and sought to live my own life for myself. I lived in solitary misery, by choice. I made no friends, and I knew no women. My sole companions were my own servitors. I fought much and volunteered for every task at every opportunity until I was sorely wounded and sent home to die. But even there, I went my own way. And soon after that, I came here, and I met you for the first time."

He saw the princess staring at him in amazement and he was unsurprised, because he was equally amazed at himself. He had had no thought, before he began speaking, to say any of what had come spouting from his mouth, but then had found himself matching her candor with his own.

Alice looked down at her hands. "Aye, Sir Stephen, I remember that first meeting. And now we may be meeting for the last time."

"How so, my lady?" He felt a surge of alarm, his mind connecting what she had just said with the reason underlying his presence here—the information she had uncovered.

"I will soon be leaving Jerusalem," she said. "I am to be wed to Prince Bohemond of Antioch, who is on his way here now from Italy to claim his throne and to succeed his father."

His first thought was that this might be a reprieve from the threat of being seduced, but he realized the true significance of what she had said immediately after that. He cleared his throat. "Then I am glad for you, my lady. How soon is the prince expected?"

She shook her head. "No one can tell me. It depends upon too many things other than winds and weather, which are of course the most important of all. He could be here in a week, or a month, or half a year. Only one thing do I know with certainty: when he arrives, we shall be wed. That is why there was so much cloth fabric in evidence here when you came in. My women are working at all hours to prepare my new clothing. What are you people doing in the stables?"

He opened his mouth and closed it again, taken aback by the swift change of subject.

"I have received reports that you and your fellow monks are involved in something within your stables, something nefarious, it seems, and although the reports vary, I am satisfied that I know what is going on."

Her words hung in the air, and St. Clair could hear his heart thudding in his chest. She was watching him closely, scanning his face for some hint of what he was thinking, and he schooled himself to show nothing as he tilted his head slightly to one side. "I beg your pardon, my lady, but I do not ... What do you believe is *going on,* as you say?"

"Digging. You and your brethren are digging in the earth, in the foundations there, in search of some treasure buried there long ages ago."

"Wha—? What would make you even suspect such a thing, my lady?" He felt himself almost breathless.

"Information! I told you, I have heard reports that something is going on."

"Aye, and I have no wish to contradict you, but you also said that those reports conflicted with each other, did you not, and that you had therefore drawn your own conclusions on what they said?"

"I did. What are you saying?"

He spread his hands far apart. "Simply that I would like to hear these conclusions at which you have arrived. May I ask that of you?"

"I spoke of treasure, Brother Stephen. I now believe that you and your brotherhood have somehow acquired secret information—ancient knowledge of some kind—and are using it to lead you towards some great discovery."

St. Clair froze. His mouth went dry, his tongue cleaving to his palate as the words thundered in his head. All his convictions about the integrity of his brethren turned to ashy powder in his mouth, so that he barely heard Alice as she continued.

"I can only interpret that to mean that you are all apostate, ignoring and defying the sacred vows you undertook so recently, in the hope of unearthing riches that rightfully belong to others." She stopped, eyeing him and pursing her lips. "This is the Kingdom of Jerusalem, Brother Stephen. Everything herein, above and below the ground, belongs to my father the King. Whatever treasure you seek belongs to him, no matter where or when you find it, and no matter whether or no he knew of it before you found it. But I suspect that means nothing to you, does it? When you and your associates uncover these riches, this treasure that you seek, you intend to abscond with it, abandoning all your duties and responsibilities."

St. Clair could barely think, his mind was reeling so. They had a traitor among their tiny number. Who could it be? In a daze, he began to summon up the faces of his brother knights, gazing at each of them in his mind, trying to see some weakness, some hint of treachery.

"Answer me! Is that not what you intend?"

He blinked and focused his eyes on the princess's angry face. "Forgive me, my lady, but what is it that you think we intend to do?"

"You are going to steal the treasure and make off with it. But I will not allow it."

"Make off with it? Make *off* with it? With *what*, my lady? We are monks, not brigands."

"Hah! Then I give you back your own words of moments ago, sir, when you were condemning the atrocities committed by priests and clerics. Am I to imagine, in the light of what I now know, that monks are different?"

"But we are, my lady! Do you not recall? A new order, different from any other." Despite the angry edge to his voice, St. Clair was growing confused, because the sole denunciation he was hearing here centered upon the theft of treasure, of portable wealth. There was nothing of secret societies or underhanded plotting or treachery; nothing that bore directly upon the Order of Rebirth, or of which he truly needed to be afraid. Nothing, in fact, that threw any light at all upon the extent of the woman's knowledge of what was truly going on in the stables. He rose to his feet, but kept his tone moderate.

"Tell me, if you will, my lady, what you propose to do with this information and what you need from me in regard to it."

"I intend to denounce your activities to my father. And also to the Patriarch Archbishop, since it was to him that your brethren swore their original false loyalty."

"Denounce us? Do you really believe that we are hatching treachery?"

"How else am I to believe?" She sat straight backed, glaring at him accusingly. "Your conduct has left me no other choice, and my own conscience permits me no other course of action. Ever since I became convinced of what you were doing, I have been unable to sleep, fearful of being the direct cause of the deaths of nine monks who have shown themselves to be heroic in some ways."

She was lying, he knew, protesting her helplessness too much. There was no doubt of it in his mind. The woman who had so shamelessly abducted him was not the kind of woman who would suddenly be overcome by a crisis of conscience such as she was claiming now. He changed tack.

"Only nine of us, my lady? What of the sergeant brothers?"

"No, not them." Her denial was emphatic. "The sergeants are innocent of all complicity in this. I know that beyond question, for I have become sure—as sure as I now am of the perfidy of the nine knights—that the lesser brothers know nothing at all of what has been going on beneath their feet. The guilt in this lies squarely with you knights, all of you nobly born and therefore able, by birth and knightly training, to distinguish right and wrong even before you took your sacred vows." She stopped for a moment, frowning at him. "How could you do such a thing, after the events and the realizations of your earlier life, those things you spoke so bitterly about such a short time ago?"

He resisted the urge to challenge her with his own knowledge of her former conduct, but he turned away from her instead and looked about the silent, sunlit room, nodding as though considering what she had said, and then he sighed and sat down again, looking directly at her.

"Tell me then, my lady, if I may ask so boldly. How did all this—what did you call it? this nefarious activity come to your notice?"

He knew from the way she blinked at him that she had not expected the question, but she rallied quickly. "At first?"

"Yes, from the earliest moment."

"I know not. Not precisely. I have been told it all grew out of perfectly innocent observations from some of the local merchants who supplied the temple garrison ... and supplied fodder and equipment to your stables. They were the first to notice that there was one area into which they were never permitted to wander."

"We are a closed community, my lady. No one who is not of our order is permitted to pass beyond our outer precincts."

"I know nothing of that, never having been there, but that is what I was told, on sound authority. It was observed that there is a locked and guarded doorway that no one other than the knight monks themselves is ever permitted to pass through."

"That is true. Such a door exists. It is the entrance to our living quarters and our chapel. None may enter there save our brethren."

"Ah. Well, it was noticed, and the matter was brought to my attention soon afterwards. I was reluctant to believe anything of what I heard at first, and so, mindful of my duty to my father, I sent people of my own to observe what they could and report back to me."

"I see. And what did they report to you?"

"That they had seen ... things that were inexplicable. And thus I decided to approach my father the King and advise him that something ... something untoward was happening."

"So this discovery was recent?"

"Recent enough. That is why you are here."

"And why *am* I here, my lady? Why would you summon me? If, as you suspect, there is something clandestine going on in the stables, then I must be one of the perpetrators. Why would you bring me here instead of denouncing me immediately to the King and to the Patriarch?" St. Clair was watching her closely, attempting to read her eyes, and he was amused, despite all his apprehension, to realize that he was, beyond belief, enjoying himself. Somehow, in realizing that he was clearly not to be seduced on this occasion, he had been able to rally resources he had not known he possessed, and had begun to feel that the situation might not be as bleak as he had feared.

Seeing a flicker of uncertainty in her expression, he pressed on.

"Tell me what it is you want to know. What kind of treasure are you so convinced we seek? I promise you, I have heard nothing of hidden hoards of gold, but I will answer your questions openly and truthfully, as well as I may."

She hesitated, and he held his breath, knowing that this would be the moment of no return. Her first question would be as instructive as it was probing. Finally, he saw a stiffening of her lips and braced himself.

"You are digging—there, in the stables. The noises have been heard, and you are using the chips of stone you unearth to build walls inside the cavern. What treasure are you searching for?"

His heart leapt exultantly and he wanted to spring to his feet and shout with relief. *What treasure are you searching for?* The question liberated him as suddenly as if she had cut a taut rope. *What treasure are you searching for?* No mention of the Order of Rebirth, no nuanced phrase leading deeper into where he could not go. The simplicity of the question spoke of greed—greed and curiosity—nothing more, nothing less. It also meant, and far more significantly, that no brother had betrayed his trust, and that the princess had nothing more than suspicions on which to base her claims. He felt a surge of liberation so enormous that he had to brace himself to permit no slightest hint of it to show on his face or in his eyes. Instead, he pretended to frown, as though befuddled, and then he allowed his face to clear, and surrendered to the urge to laugh aloud, venting his pleasure and incredulity.

"Treasure, my lady," he said through his laughter, making no attempt to disguise his feelings now. "We seek the treasure that all men of God are sworn to seek— the treasure of His enlightenment, through service and through prayer."

"Do you dare to mock me, sir, here in my own house? Explain yourself and this unseemly mirth."

St. Clair threw up his hands. "Lady, forgive my laughter, I beg of you. It is born of relief, not mockery, for now I see what you have been fretting over. My brothers and I have been laboring underground, as you suspect, and have been doing so for years, but what we do has nothing of the illicit or seditious in its nature. We have had the blessing of your father the King on our labors since the outset. But—but you spoke of the *foundations* of the stables. The stables have no foundations, my lady. They sit upon the solid rock of the Temple Mount, and that is what we have been digging. And you will quickly see, if you but stop to think of it, that there can be no treasure hidden within solid rock. May I explain?"

"I think it would be wise." The chill in her voice reminded him of icy alpine winters in his native land. He cleared his throat and made a show of collecting his thoughts.

"We are a new order, as you know, my lady, and bound by vows to poverty in our way of life, and new as we are, and zealous, we have imposed new disciplines and penances upon ourselves in all we do."

"Continue."

"The stables—our quarters—are adequate to our needs, for the time being, but some of our brethren initially thought they were too comfortable, with their natural profusion of straw and the warmth generated by our horses. Comfort and luxury are both conducive to sloth and indolence, and injurious to discipline and asceticism. Would you not agree?"

The princess glanced around her luxurious chamber, and if not quite mollified, her voice was less frigid when she spoke next. "I might, were I that way inclined. Go on."

"Well, several of our brotherhood decided among themselves, long before I came here, that it would be right and fitting were they to dedicate themselves to creating a truly monastic dwelling in the living rock beneath their feet, each man carving out his own cell in time, and offering the hard work and discipline of doing so to God, in recognition of His greatness and bounty. And that is the digging that has been brought to your attention. Brother Hugh sought and received permission from your father before the work began, and King Baldwin was gracious enough to accord his blessing on the work."

The princess was now wide eyed. "But— Then why all the secrecy?"

"There is no secrecy, my lady. At least, there was never meant to be. But my brothers live in close-mouthed discipline, praying often but seldom speaking among themselves, let alone communing socially with people outside their own small circle. And so I suppose the silence simply grew, over the years, and became ingrained. But there is neither mystery nor nefarious behavior involved. I confess, you had me profoundly disturbed there for a time, wondering if I myself had been blind to something. I shall give thanks tonight, before I sleep, that I was mistaken—and, if I may dare to say so, that you were, too."

The princess slumped suddenly and settled back against the rear of her couch, staring at him through slitted eyes, and her new posture reminded him again, for the first time since this strange conversation began, of the ripeness of her body beneath her garments. He gritted his teeth slightly and stared off into the distance beyond her shoulder, grimly refusing to allow his eyes to rest on her form.

For her part, Alice was mulling over all that St. Clair had said, and in spite of herself and all her wishes to the contrary, she found herself believing him. His mention of her father's blessing on their digging—a detail that would be too easy to verify—had convinced her more than any other thing the knight had said. That, plus the self-evident truth of his statement about the stables being built upon solid rock. She had known that from the outset, having seen the outcrops of it among the rubble of the temple ruins, but she had chosen to disregard it in her eagerness to set her hands upon a treasure of her own. Now, looking at the knight monk, she decided that if she were asked to wager on which was more feasible—the monks digging out living quarters for themselves from the solid rock or, alternatively, the monks hewing through solid rock in search of some unknown treasure, she would know enough to place her money on the former. That fool Odo really was a fool, she mused, and she would find some way to make him painfully aware that she knew he was.

In the meantime, however, she saw the way the strange monk knight opposite her was trying not to look at her, and she sighed and rose to her feet, admitting to herself that she had caused him enough grief for one day. And besides, she thought, she herself had to be about her affairs, selecting the fabrics for her wedding gown.

She smiled pleasantly at St. Clair, thanked him courteously for his explanations, and clapped her hands to summon Ishtar, who escorted Brother Stephen to the palace gates and saw him safely on his way back to the stables below, one arm clutching a bundle that contained the clothes he had worn when he arrived at the palace.

FIVE

A profoundly scandalized silence descended upon the entire community of the Poor Fellow Soldiers of Jesus Christ from the moment Brother Stephen was first spotted approaching the stable precincts, dressed as he was in silks and muslin, with his face scrubbed pinkly clean and sweet odors wafting in his wake as he passed. Such was the euphoria that still gripped him, however, that he found himself grinning widely to everyone he met, calling each of them loudly by name and greeting them effusively as he swept past, into the interior of the stables, and leaving all of them, without exception, staring after him open mouthed and speechless.

He found Brother Hugh, as he expected, in colloquy with Brother Godfrey in the records room and stepped directly inside, closing the doors at his back and smiling at the expressions on their faces as they took in his appearance from head to foot. It was de Payens who first recovered his voice and his aplomb. He sat back in his chair, his eyebrows settling back into their normal position, and crossed his hands upon his flat belly. "We shall assume, in the hope of salvation, that you will be able, thanks to God's ample blessings, to explain why you come to us dressed like an effeminate from some sultan's seraglio, my son."

"I will, indeed, Brother Hugh, and I thank you for the opportunity to do so, and for the forbearance that you show in not upbraiding me first and questioning me after. I have much to tell you, and when you have heard it, you will understand my appearance here today."

Quickly then, wasting no words but omitting no single detail, he explained to them everything that had occurred that day, from the moment of being summoned to meet with the Patriarch, who was, he had since learned, in a spiritual retreat from which he would not emerge for several days. Brother Hugh nodded gravely at that, confirming that it was so, but that was the only gesture of any kind that either of the two senior brethren made until St. Clair had told them everything.

When he was finished, both elders sat silent, their heads bowed as if in prayer while they digested what he had told them.

"Did you lie to the princess?" This was Brother Godfrey.

"No, Brother, I did not. I said only that I had heard nothing of hidden hoards of gold. I made no mention of other kinds of wealth, for by then it was plain to me that the princess had no interest in anything but specie—portable treasure."

"And she believed you."

St. Clair turned to Brother Hugh. "Aye, she did. She believed the explanation that I offered, that there could be no treasure in solid rock."

"Unless it had been there since the Creation."

"Yes, Brother, that was what I implied."

"What have you in the bundle beneath your arm?"

"Oh! This is the clothing I was wearing when I left here this morning."

"Excellent tidings, for which we are grateful. Be so good then as to put it on again, as quickly as you may, and bring those"—Brother Hugh waved a hand in the younger monk's direction—"*garments* back here to me. I will see that they are returned to the palace with your gratitude."

St. Clair bowed his head and turned to go, but de Payens stopped him before he could begin to move away. "You have done well, Brother Stephen, and the brethren will know of it. I shall inform them tonight, after evening prayers, how bravely you have ... suffered on their behalf. Now go you and change, then return here, for I doubt you will have heard the latest tidings, and you should. Quickly now. But, if it please you, make some attempt to lave away the perfumed stuff in which I fear you have been bathing."

St. Clair returned in less than half an hour, dressed in his oldest tunic and hose, both impregnated with years of sweat, his own and his horse's, and wearing his mail hauberk, which smelled redolently of old sweat, oily leather, and rust, and de Payens sniffed appreciatively and grinned. "There, that is a much more becoming odor for a Poor Fellow Soldier of Christ. Sit down now, and listen. We found a new tunnel this morning, almost as soon as work began. St. Agnan came across a wall of masonry closing off the tunnel he was in. He sent back word to ask what he should do, and Brother Godfrey instructed him to go ahead and breach the wall."

"And? What did he find?"

"Another passageway, crossing the one he was in and walling it off from the other three arms of a crossroads. But it was clear of debris and had a current of clear air blowing through it, and when Brother Archibald and his companions, Brothers Bissot and Montbard, followed each of the three arms, they found another tunnel, then another and another. In fact, they found a labyrinth. When is your next patrol?"

"My first patrol, you mean, Master Hugh. The first in months." St. Clair thought for a moment. "Tomorrow? What day is this? Yes, it must be tomorrow. Gondemare and Montdidier are out now, between here and Jericho. They should be back tonight, and I am due to leave for Jaffa with Rossal and a full patrol as soon as they are back."

"Would you postpone it?"

"If you see a need, yes, of course. But why? We never have postponed a patrol before, and the frequency of our sweeps is part of what keeps them successful."

"Because we will need every man to explore these new tunnels. I have a feeling we can match them to our map this time. And if any of them are blocked, by cave-ins or anything else, and have to be cleared, your muscles are younger and stronger than any others among us."

St. Clair nodded. "You spoke of a labyrinth, Master

Hugh. How many of these new tunnels are there?"

De Payens thrust out his lower lip and shook his head. "I cannot say at this time. But I would hazard, from what I have been told, that there are more than a score of junctions down there, each of those leading into others. Labyrinth is the proper word, I believe. Why did you ask me that?"

"In hopes it would confirm what I suspected, and it does. Let me ride out tomorrow as planned, Master Hugh. The Jaffa patrol is a ten-day sweep, and I think it might be unwise to neglect it now. I have a feeling that band of brigands de Montbard could not find is still out there, somewhere along the Jaffa road. It is only a feeling, but it's a strong one, and I've learned to trust such things within myself. They were a large party, according to what de Montbard was told, and we have heard nothing about them since he came home, but that is not to say they are not out there, and it's been a month since he was last there. I would prefer to go and make the sweep, simply for my own peace of mind, and while I am away, the rest of the brethren can explore the tunnels and make note of any that are blocked. When I return, I will gladly tackle any digging that needs to be done."

De Payens pursed his lips, then nodded. "So be it. Make your patrol, and if you find these creatures, sweep them from the earth. By the time you return, we'll be ready for you."

SIX

S t. Clair had learned the art of dozing in the saddle long before he ever went to Outremer, and on long desert patrols the ability served him well, permitting him to shorten the lengthy days considerably while yet covering long distances. But because he was asleep when the alarum was sounded on the afternoon of their third day out from Jerusalem, he did not know who had been the first to see the threatening figure by the cliff above the road.

He snapped awake when someone called his name, and by then he had already registered the first warning shouts that rang out, and his sergeants were beginning to deploy their men in their fighting formations while the two light commissary wagons were wheeling into their positions in what would be the center of their defensive perimeter. Of his co-commander he saw nothing in those first few moments, learning only later that Rossal had ridden off with a small party a short time earlier to examine a large swathe of tracks found by their scouts. Frowning at his own ignorance of what was happening, he kicked his horse forward, reining it in where Bernard de la Pierre, their senior sergeant, sat with two of his subordinates, scrutinizing the cliffs to the north of the road.

"What is it, Sergeant Bernard?"

The sergeant pointed almost casually towards the cliffs. "Over there, sir, among the rocks at the bottom, on the right. Only one man, so far, but he's making no effort to conceal himself, so it's almost certainly a trap. He must think we are really stupid if he expects us to go charging after him without an exploration first."

St. Clair could not see the man at first, but eventually the fellow moved, and as he focused on the movement, St. Clair suddenly sat up straighter in his saddle and shaded his eyes against the sun's glare, peering forward to where the distant stranger stood on the blurred edge between two blocks of brightness and shade. The fellow, whoever he was, was afoot, but too far away for anyone in their group to see him clearly. St. Clair felt a tiny tugging at his gut.

"He may think we are stupid, Sergeant, but then again, he may not. Follow me, two ranks, line abreast." He kicked his horse to a walk and moved off the road, directly towards the distant man, and as he did so, sunlight flashed off metal as the fellow moved again. *Now he will run away,* St. Clair thought, *and expect us to follow him to where his friends can kill us all.* But when he looked again, the distant man was in the same place, still partially obscured in shadow but growing easier to see as St. Clair and his double line of mounted sergeants approached. And then, when he judged the time to be right, he stepped out into the full glare of the sun.

Shocked by his first clear sight of the fellow, St. Clair threw up his hand immediately, stopping the troopers advancing behind him. There could be no mistaking the identity of the stranger facing them. It was Hassan the Shi'a warrior, dressed exactly as he had been the last time St. Clair had seen him, from the tip of his high, slender helmet to the bottom of his high black boots.

"Sergeant Bernard, hold your line here, if you will. I will go forward alone. I know this man. He is a friend. He saved my life when I was lost and dying of thirst in the desert, then led me home. He obviously wants to speak with me. Wait here."

"But Sir Stephen, if harm should come to you—"

"I told you, Sergeant, he is a friend. No harm will come to me."

He left his patrol behind and rode forward steadily until he was within a few paces of Hassan.

"Well met, Hassan, if unexpectedly. What brings you here?" He swung his leg over the saddle's high cantle and slid to the ground, then embraced the other man, inhaling the familiar, strangely masculine scent of cinnamon that always clung to him. Hassan returned the embrace with a smile.

"Sala'am Aleikhem, Sanglahr, and accept the gratitude of this humble wayfarer that you have chosen to smell more like a man than a camel since last we met. Allah be praised. As for what brings me here, the answer is that you bring me here. What else would? This region is not exactly the Garden of the Houris. I have information for you, and a favor to request. I also have a camp nearby with sweet water, among these rocks. Will you come there?"

St. Clair shook his head. "No, my friend, I cannot do that and leave my men sitting out in the midday sun, but you will be welcome to ride with us to where we are going."

Hassan's teeth flashed in a sardonic smile. "To Jaffa, amid an armed throng of *ferenghi,* and dressed like this? I think not, my friend. But I am grateful for the offer of companionship, none the less. So come, sit with me here in the shade, upon Allah's firm ground, and let us talk, you and I."

To sit thus and talk was more easily said than done in St. Clair's case, for he was wearing his mailed hauberk, a hooded, ankle-length overcoat of heavy leather entirely covered by chain-mail links. It was bulky, uncomfortable, and unyielding, and he had to unlace the front of it and spread its armored skirts about him as a woman does before he could lower himself to sit with his legs comfortably crossed in the manner of the desert nomads. When he was eventually seated, he laid his sword belt down by his side, removed his metal helmet, and undid the thong beneath his chin before pushing the mailed hood back off his head and scrubbing at his scalp with clawed fingers.

The Arab grinned, watching him. "I find it remarkable that, no matter what a man's faith or belief may be, and no matter how far away he may have been born from any other people, the first instinct of any warrior, on baring his head, is to scrub at his scalp like a dog scratching at fleas." Both men laughed, and then Hassan reached into an ornate silver-buckled, black leather bag at his waist and withdrew a carefully wrapped and bound package, less than a foot long by one third of that in width. He held it out to St. Clair. "I have a cousin in Jerusalem, with whom I share my name. He is Hassan the horse trader, and he has a permanent stall in the central market there."

St. Clair took the package and hefted it in one hand. It was very light, wrapped in soft, supple leather of a bright yellow hue, and he noticed the beaded emblem of a tiny crescent moon, barely the size of his smallest fingernail, sewn into one edge of it with silver thread. Judging from its size and weight, he guessed it contained a document of some kind. "Hassan the horse trader," he said, smiling. "I know that name. I know exactly where his stall is, too. It stands close to the premises of Suleiman, the trader in rugs."

Hassan cocked his head, clearly surprised. "That is correct, Sanglahr, it does. But how would you know Suleiman? You are a monk, are you not? What need does a monk have of costly rugs?"

St. Clair was on the point of saying that he had visited the stall to meet a lady, but realizing how that might sound, he hesitated. "No need at all," he said. "But a monk does not forsake either his eyesight or his ability to speak when he forsakes the world. I am not blind to beauty, be it in rugs or horses. I had occasion to pause at Suleiman's one day, and spoke with him while I admired his merchandise, just as I had stopped to admire your cousin's horses in passing, moments before that." He indicated the package he was still holding. "I presume you would like me to deliver this to your cousin?"

"I would, Sanglahr, and you will earn my gratitude by doing so. My cousin will not be there when you arrive, as I discovered only days ago, in talking to a sheikh whose fire I shared and who knows him well. Hassan will be gone for most of a month, according to the sheikh, and I have other matters to look after. That is why, when I knew it was you approaching, I decided to ask you to deliver the package for me on your return to Jerusalem. If you would leave it with Nabib, who runs the place when my cousin goes away in search of new stock, he will see that it reaches the person for whom it is intended, and I will be most grateful."

"Of course I will." St. Clair was already stuffing the package into the breast of his hauberk. "You said you had information for me, although I am mystified how you could know I ... But then, had anyone told me, a minute before you first appeared out of the night when we first met, that you would come and rescue me, I would not have believed them. So, what startling information do you have for me on this occasion?"

"Sufficiently startling to save your life, Sanglahr, and the lives of all your men."

St. Clair's face sobered instantly. "That is more than startling, my friend. It is alarming. Tell me about it, for it is a subject on which I have no wish to jest."

"There is a group of brigands close by here—a large group."

"I know that. We are hunting them."

The shake of Hassan's head made his veil of fine mail hiss and rattle. "No, Sanglahr, they are hunting you. They found you yesterday and have been leading you ever since. Your companion—the other knight—"

"Rossal?"

"I do not know his name—the one who rides with you, in joint command. He was lured away an hour ago to look at the tracks of many mounted men, leading from here out into the high desert, tracks that your scouts were led to today, deliberately—tracks that were carefully prepared and then disguised last night to make them appear older than they are. He will return soon, with word that he has found these tracks and that they lead to an encampment by an oasis, less than ten miles from here, and that you and your men can be close to there by nightfall, in time to rest and attack with the morning light at your back."

"I see. You are telling me to pay no heed to his advice."

"No, I am telling you that no matter what you do, or where you decide to go, you are already in a trap. Your enemy is at your back even as we speak. Those who prepared the tracks leading into the trap near the oasis are but a few, leading riderless horses. They know you are *ferenghi,* that you have no skill in tracking in the sand. They know you will follow the tracks, and they will follow you. Then, when you lie down to rest before your dawn attack, they will fall upon you from behind and wipe you out."

St. Clair drew back his head and looked steadily at the other man, no trace of humor or raillery to be seen now in his expression. "How come you to know all this?"

Hassan shrugged his shoulders and dipped his head, an elegant gesture. "I have informants among them. I have spoken with two of them, one last night and another this morning. That is how I knew you were coming this way, although I did not know until I saw your face myself that you were leading the patrol."

"When did you see my face?" St. Clair made no attempt to hide the nascent hostility in his voice, and Hassan shrugged again.

"Earlier today. You passed within a score of paces from where I lay watching. I would have called a greeting, save that I might not have lived to hear you return it. Your men are vigilant."

"Not vigilant enough, it seems, if you could come that close and these others could manipulate us so easily. Tell me about these informants of yours."

Hassan extended a cupped fist, then opened it to demonstrate that it was empty. "Do not blame yourself for failing to stop the wind, Sanglahr. Its power lies in the will of Allah. There was but one way you could come here, and I had been in hiding by the pathway long before you and your people came along. Your men could not possibly have found me unless I betrayed myself. The same applies to what your enemy has done to you. Do you imagine your pattern of patrols has not been noted? Your every move is charted nowadays and you have been under constant watch from the moment

you first emerged from your city gates. Even the variances that you use are carefully scrutinized. The people
against whom you are now pitted have been waiting for
you to come back for more than a month, and they have
been patient, their plans laid long since. Everything that
happens takes place in accordance with the will of Allah.
If you are to die tomorrow, it is already written. If you
are to prevail, that, too, is written. But until the
outcome of whatever happens, only Allah Himself will
know how it is written."

"Hmm. And these informants of yours?"

"What of them? They told me everything they know."

"And why would they do that?"

"Because I asked them, and they are in my debt and
have no wish to anger me. Besides, why should they not
tell me? I am no *ferenghi*. I represent no threat to them.
It would never occur to any of them that I might have
a friend among your ranks."

St. Clair sat silent for a moment longer, then asked,
"Well, then, tell me this. Had you not seen me here,
would you have warned whoever came along instead
of me?"

"I have been asking myself that same question,
Sanglahr, and the answer is, I do not know. I may have,
and I may not. But you did come, and thus I was spared
the pain of having to decide."

"Why would you even be concerned? As a Muslim
warrior, you should regard us as your enemies."

"But I am Ismaili Shi'a, of the Nizari, in the land you
call Persia, and these people of whom we speak are of

the Abassid. That will mean nothing to you, Sanglahr, but it has great significance among my people, the fedayeen. The Abassid are Sunni, followers of the caliphs, and they believe we are not true Muslims. They have a word for us, 'Batini,' which is a slur, suggesting that we are not true followers of the Prophet. They would deny us life itself, not merely the freedom to worship as we please, and thus they are no friends of mine. I would probably have warned your friends, therefore, even had you not been with them. But it was written that you would be with them."

"Well then," St. Clair said, shaking his head in wonderment, "we should be glad that you are ... What was the word you used? Batini?"

Hassan frowned. "You should never use that word, Sanglahr, even in friendly jest. Heard by the wrong ears, it could be the death of you. Trust me in this."

"I will. The word will never cross my lips again, for I can see how it offends you. Now, what should I do in this matter of the trap that is set for us? Can you advise me?"

"Of course. They are all around you now, so there is nothing you can do to avoid them, and thus you must turn the trap on them. Proceed as they expect you to, and make camp where you would have made it had you been unwarned—there is only one suitable place, set among the dunes but within striking distance of the oasis. Then have your men prepare under cover of darkness for the attack that will come in the dead of night. The Abassid will come on foot, in silence, with knives

and swords, to take you while you sleep. They have three
to every one of you, but they will not expect to find you
waiting for them. It will be a hard and bitter fight, but
the advantage will be yours. And it appears that Allah
Himself is watching over you, for the moon will be full
tonight and you will have light by which to fight."

"And where will you be then? Will you watch from
a distance?"

The Shi'a smiled. "Aye, I will, from within bowshot.
I too will have light by which to add my contribution,
for the sand is pale there, almost white, and moving
men will stand out clearly in the moonlight. Besides, I
cannot be too far away, for if you are killed I will have
to reclaim my cousin's package and deliver it myself.
And now you should go, before one of the Abassid sees
us together. But before you do, there is one other thing
I wished to ask you. My friend Ad-Kamil, whose fire I
shared two nights ago, asked me about one of your
churchmen, a bishop by the name of Odo. Do you
know anything of this man?"

St. Clair snorted, half laugh, half grunt. "Odo de St.
Florent, Bishop of Fontainebleau. I know him well
enough to have spent some time with him several days
ago. What would you care to know of him?"

"What manner of man is he, Sanglahr?"

St. Clair shook his head slowly and deliberately.
"That I cannot tell you, my friend, other than that he
is a very pompous and humorless bishop, much given
to the enjoyment of listening to his own voice. He is
secretary and amanuensis to Warmund de Picquigny,

who, as you no doubt know, is the senior churchman in Jerusalem, the Patriarch Archbishop."

"Aman—amanuen— What is this word?"

"An amanuensis is what you would call a scribe, a cleric so skilled in writing that he can capture and write down words as they are spoken. He is a keeper, and a creator, of written records. Odo keeps written records of all the affairs upon which the Patriarch is engaged."

"Ah, I see. So this man is an intimate of your Patriarch?"

"A close associate, but not an intimate. I do not believe Odo has intimates. The man appears to have no friends among his peers. He is not amiable."

"You do not like him, Sanglahr?"

St. Clair smiled. "No, Hassan, I do not like him, but I do not know him well at all, so he will not die of my dislike."

"But he might of the dislike of others. Is that what you are saying?"

"No, not at all. That was no more than a silly comment, a Frankish way of speaking."

Hassan stood up and stepped deeper into the shade beneath the rock face. "So be it, Sanglahr. Go you now and prepare your men, and may Allah watch over you this night and keep you and my cousin's package safe. Go with God."

"And you too, my friend. But tell me, if I were to set out men with crossbows among the dunes, would they be able to see well enough to shoot?"

"As well as I will, but they will be visible, too, in the light of the full moon. How will you deal with that?"

"They may not be too visible at the outset. Their cloaks are brown. I'll have them lie down in the sand and cover themselves until the time comes to attack. As soon as the fighting starts, it will be every man for himself."

"Allah willing, that should succeed, giving you surprise. But they had best be all in place before the rise of the moon, Sanglahr, and that will be soon after nightfall."

SEVEN

S t. Clair had assured Hassan that his men would be safely in position before moonrise, but it was a promise made without any more forethought than a feeling in his gut. In spite of that, however, he made sure to keep his word. Rossal had returned from his reconnaissance soon after St. Clair took his leave of Hassan, and he had brought exactly the tidings that the Shi'a had said he would. He had then led the patrol slightly north and east towards the oasis where the trap was to be set for them.

It was only long after they had set out on the route they were supposed to follow that St. Clair, by now having developed a plan that he believed would have a chance of success, pulled Rossal aside to ride with him in private and told him of Hassan's warning. Rossal listened without interrupting, then called their troop leaders to gather around. When they were all there, riding in a tight cluster, St. Clair quickly explained the situation and what he proposed to do about it. St. Clair had expected some skepticism, if not outright resistance, and had been marshaling an argument strong enough to convince them, he hoped, to trust him, but they had accepted what he told them without demur, and he realized, humbly, that they trusted him completely, in spite of all his recent scandals, accepting his own trust of Hassan and according him a degree of confidence that went beyond mere loyalty to a patrol commander, although bolstered, perhaps, by a desire not to put their own lives at risk unnecessarily.

Of the forty sergeants in their company, eighteen carried crossbows, and in one of the wagons they had an ample supply of the steel bolts they used as ammunition. Rossal assumed command of the eighteen as a separate contingent, and throughout the afternoon, each time they paused to rest themselves and their mounts, he had two, and sometimes three, of his eighteen chosen sergeants pass by the wagon and help themselves uncer-emoniously to an extra bundle of ammunition, while the rest of the patrol moved around busily enough to disguise what was going on from the people they now knew were watching them from the surrounding dunes.

The transition from daylight to darkness is very brief in the desert, so St. Clair, riding knee to knee with Rossal, found himself governing the approach to the oasis with care, relying heavily on the reports and observations of his scouts, for he had no wish to arrive at the designated camping spot too soon, and he wanted to do nothing that might arouse suspicion in the minds of those undoubtedly watching. And yet he knew they could not afford to be one moment later arriving there than they must be, since the interval between the set of the sun and the rise of the moon that night would be a short one. He had planned well, however, and everything went smoothly, aided by an unusual accumulation of heavy cloud banks that added to the gathering darkness.

The men made camp among the dunes, within striking distance of the oasis to the north, and although they all knew that the attack would come from behind them, they gave no indication to any watching eyes that they were even mildly suspicious or apprehensive. As darkness finally fell, while the horses were being roped in their lines on the outer edge of the encampment, Rossal and his half of the group calmly positioned their bedrolls to make it appear they were asleep, and then they moved swiftly and stealthily away from the campsite and buried themselves under their spread brown cloaks in the sand on the sides of the dunes overlooking the tiny cooking fires. They were within easy bowshot of the camp, and thereafter they lay in utter stillness and silence, waiting for the enemy to come to them.

For a long time that night, the skies remained obscured with clouds, and the moonlight broke through only intermittently and unpredictably, keeping the watching enemy pinned down and hampered, unwilling to risk being exposed by a sudden gap in the clouds before they were ready to attack. And so they stayed concealed for so long that St. Clair began to fret that the attack was taking too long to develop, for absolutely nothing marred the stillness of the desert. He sat for so long, his eyes and ears straining against the utter stillness, that he had to stand up, eventually, and move around quietly, even while he knew the movement might bring arrows from the blackness beyond the fires. Even as he did so, however, the clouds parted and the moonlight broke through, shining even more brilliantly than it might have otherwise, thanks to the darkness of the night to that point.

He was aware, of course, that no one else in the entire camp had been able to sleep either, and that they had all been lying as tense and as wide awake as he was, and so he forced himself to walk around the fires for a while after the moonlight sprang up, affecting unconcern and talking quietly with the guards, while encouraging everyone else, in a lower voice, to remain as they were and pretend to be asleep. Then, when he judged the time to be about right, he sat down by the fire and allowed himself, to all outward appearances, to slump towards sleep, although his every nerve was strained to catch the first sounds of anyone approaching.

He found it amazingly difficult to sit still, and quite impossible to empty his mind of worries, and as time passed and nothing happened, he began to experience difficulty in breathing normally. No matter how much air he inhaled, he felt that he could not fill up his lungs, and so he began to breathe more and more rapidly until finally, afraid that he was about to swoon, he had to stand up, cautiously and with tooth-grinding difficulty, and move about. That helped, and as his breathing slowly returned to normal he realized that the attack he had just undergone, whatever it had been, had been caused by fear. He stood erect, holding his head high, and turned slowly in a complete circle, gazing out into the darkness of the desert night, and he saw and heard nothing. Then, in an effort to distract himself, he sat down again and made himself think back to Jerusalem, and to the night in the tunnels when he had almost suffocated on the foul air, and he began to feel calmer. He remembered sprawling at the foot of the dirt pile after thrusting himself back out from the tiny entrance and into the clean air. His entire body had been thickly coated with clinging dust and his mouth had felt full of it, devoid of moisture, and he remembered the pleasure with which he had spat his mouth clear and then rolled onto his back against the wall, feeling the cool breeze blowing from the side against his face ...

He heard a gasp and a curse, followed immediately by a loud challenge that was drowned in a warlike, ululating wail, and then the night was full of sounds, the clashing of steel blades and the hissing of crossbow bolts that terminated in solid, meaty thumps, and a rising chorus of battle cries that quickly gave way to screams of panic and alarm as the attackers realized that the enemy was at their backs and that they had been tricked. They had penetrated the camp as they had planned to do, and in so doing they had passed through and among Rossal's buried crossbowmen without discovering a single one of them. Rossal's people had watched them pass by and had then waited, high on the sides of the dunes, choosing their time deliberately and then opening fire in volleys, with murderous effect.

"Hold still!" he shouted to the men around him.

"Count the volleys! Then on three, rise up with me!"

The second volley struck home, causing carnage among the attacking Muslims while the sergeants around the fires remained on the ground, leaving the killing to the crossbowmen for the third and final volley, and then, as the enemy began to rally slightly in the pause that followed the second flight of bolts, he shouted again, warning his men to stay where they were and wait for the third volley. It came, and those of the enemy who were left on their feet in the aftermath were turning about, first one way and then another, not knowing what to do or where to run.

"Now, lads! Take them!" As he scrambled to his feet, the loose sand making him feel unusually slow and cumbersome, a man came charging at him, waving a long-bladed scimitar, but before he could come within striking distance, he jerked forward headlong, grunting as if in surprise, and fell to his knees. His open mouth filled up with blood, black in the moonlight, that spewed down the front of his clothing, and he came to rest face down between St. Clair's feet. Stephen leapt forward over the man's body, his sword swinging as he sought an opponent close enough to fight. It was all over quickly, however, and he failed to cross swords with a single attacker.

His remaining sergeants were swarming everywhere, relieved now of the strain of having to lie helpless in the face of an advancing enemy while their companions above on the dunes did all the killing, and the attackers who had planned on slaughtering them as they slept had lost all appetite for the contest now that they had chain-mailed and angry opponents in front of them and at their backs with long-bladed swords and maces and axes. Those among them who were fleet enough of foot vanished into the desert in any direction they could reach, and within minutes of the first blow being struck, the fighting was over.

Rossal was already restoring calm, enquiring after casualties, and he glanced at Stephen and winked. "One man dead, two wounded, neither one seriously. And as far as I can tell, perhaps a score and a half on the other side of the tally. Are we taking prisoners?"

St. Clair had been looking about him, half expecting to see Hassan somewhere close by, but there was no sign of the Shi'a warrior, and now he shook his head in response to Rossal's question. "No time for that, not if we're to hit the oasis as we planned. Put the dead man and the two wounded on one of the wagons. I'll rally the others and get us underway." He raised his voice. "Sergeant Bernard, to me, if you will. All men to be mounted and ready to move out within the quarter hour. See to it."

They hit the encampment shortly more than an hour later, and found the place empty of life, although there was much evidence around to show that the camp had been hurriedly abandoned mere minutes before they arrived. They set up a perimeter then and settled down to make use of the water hole, and within the day, they established that they had slain approximately one in four or five of the men they had been seeking. They found no wounded Muslims, although there were bloodstains aplenty, and their scouts estimated that the remnants of the enemy band had scattered to the four winds. St. Clair did not disagree, but he wondered what had happened to Hassan.

That night, before he fell asleep, he lay in his bedroll by the fire, talking to Rossal, and the last question he asked him before falling silent left Rossal frowning and wondering what his friend was thinking of.

"Imagine yourself lying on the floor in one of the tunnels under the Mount," St. Clair had said. "The wall is against you, on your left, and you are flat on your back, and there's a breeze blowing over you ... You've been digging and sweating and the breeze is cool and fresh. Delightful. But it's blowing sideways, cooling your neck and the side of your face ... The left side of your face. What can you learn from that?"

EIGHT

"Well, what *did* you learn from that?" It was eight days later, and Hugh de Payens's face was unreadable, but there was no doubting his curiosity, and across from him, Godfrey St. Omer was leaning forward, his eyes intent on St. Clair, who shrugged, the beginnings of a smile tugging at his lips.

"Nothing that I can prove, Brethren. Not yet, at least. I came here directly from stabling my horse, leaving Rossal to dismiss the men and complete the patrol, my first duty being to report to you on our progress and condition. Now that I have done so, I am free, I presume, to tend to my own affairs for a while. As soon as I leave here and remove this armor, therefore, I intend to go underground and investigate my suspicions. After that, I will be able to answer your question."

The two senior brothers exchanged glances, and de Payens inclined his head. "So be it, then. Our business here is concluded, but I think I am safe in saying that Brother Godfrey here is as curious as I am about your tidings. Would it displease you if I asked you to take us with you when you go down into the tunnels?"

It was only a very short time later when the three men passed the vertical rift in the tunnel floor where the tunnelers had been disposing of their detritus for many months, and less than a hundred paces beyond that, St. Clair hesitated and stopped, holding his flaming torch high as he gazed about him, looking back the way they had come and then turning to stare down the passageway that stretched into darkness ahead of them.

"This should be the place," he said at length. "It should be, but it looks nothing like what I remember. There was a wall of rubble here, filling the passageway completely, last time I was here. I climbed over it and squeezed through the opening at the top, then almost suffocated on the other side and barely made it back out. That's when I collapsed against the wall and felt the fresh air. There has been a lot of work down here since then, to clear the debris away, but in the doing of that, the few reference points I had have been removed, too. The spot where I lay and felt the draft could be anywhere from where I'm standing up to a score of paces in either direction." He looked around again and then waved his hand towards the passageway stretching ahead of them. "The only thing I know with certainty is that I was lying with my feet pointing down that way, towards the blockage, so the draft came from some-where along this wall here, on the left."

"Taper," St. Omer said. "We need a taper, or a candle, and a long handle." He glanced from one to the other of his listeners and shrugged. "Alternatively, you could get down on your hands and knees and crawl the length of the passage, feeling for the draft, but it strikes me that it would be easier to tie a lit taper to the end of a long stick of some kind, or even a sword, and walk along the wall with it. If there's still a current of air blowing through, it will affect the flame."

"No tapers down here," St. Clair responded. "But we have oil lamps and mattocks, so we should be able to achieve the same effect. I'll attach a lamp to the blade of a mattock. We'll have to be careful not to tilt the lamp and spill the oil. There are some old tools over here, against the wall. Now, then ..."

It took no more than a few minutes to attach a lamp to the end of a mattock shaft, and when they had it firmly bound there, they lit the wick with one of their torches. The lamp burned slowly, its bare wick generating much sooty smoke, but that was an advantage, and they found the vent in the wall almost as soon as they began to search for it. The lamp's flame guttered quickly, blown sideways with surprising strength and sending black, greasy smoke swirling fitfully across the passageway. St. Clair looked at his two companions from beneath raised eyebrows, then brought the open flame back to the same spot, holding it this time in a stream of air so strong and steady that it set the lamp's flame fluttering audibly. He knelt quickly then, setting the lamp aside and reaching out with his bare hands to feel the flow of cool air from the base of the wall.

"It's strong, but the hole is very small. Bring one of those torches down here and give me some light." He lowered himself farther, taking his weight on his hands and moving his legs back until he could lie on his belly, then he thrust his fingers into the small hole. The other two men moved back to give him room, although St. Omer held the torch carefully out and down at arm's length to provide the light he had been asked for.

St. Clair inched forward until his face was ludicrously close to the wall, and then he shook his head and rolled away. "The air's blowing upward, but where could it be coming from? This tunnel wall is solid stone, so what we have found must be some kind of a crack in the rock. It makes no sense." He looked around, then pushed himself back up to his feet and crossed to the pile of tools, where he selected a long pry bar of solid steel and returned to attack the tiny air vent, trying to enlarge it. Moments later, the wedge-shaped point of the bar broke through, enlarging the hole considerably, and once the penetration had begun it progressed swiftly until the opening was the size of a man's head. It had begun with the chink at the base of the wall, but as St. Clair kept chipping and picking away at it, the cavity proved to be more in the floor than in the wall, and at one point, prizing at a jagged edge that gave way more suddenly than expected, he staggered and lost his grip on the bar, and it disappeared into the blackness of the hole. All three men stood motionless, listening to the silence until the clanging echo of the bar's landing came up to them. None of them needed to point out to the others that it had fallen a long way.

Shortly after that, they tied one of their torches to a length of rope and lowered it into the darkness below, but it showed them nothing other than an apparently vast blackness, and watching the flame flicker and eventually burn out far below—the rope was more than twenty paces long—St. Clair shivered, feeling apprehension crawling between his shoulder blades.

They would not appreciate the reality of what had happened until long afterwards, when logic and exploration had made it clear beyond any doubt, but there, at the beginning of it all, the three men were completely at a loss for understanding of what they had found. It was St. Omer who would eventually arrive at the analogy that explained it to all of them, comparing the chamber below—for it was a vast, square chamber that they had found—and the tunnel in which they stood to a cube and a tube. The cylindrical tube of the tunnel had touched precisely on one of the upper corners of the chamber, closely enough to break through at that single point and create the hole that became the conduit for the air from the chamber beneath. Had the tunnel been dug as little as a hand's breadth to the right of where it was, the discovery would never have been made and the presence of the chamber underneath might never have been suspected. But the contact was made, the flow of air was noted, and therein some men thought afterwards to see the Hand of God.

None of the three men present that afternoon had a single thought in his mind of God or divine intervention. They were nonplussed and unsure of what to do next, and as they stood there, gazing down into the hole in the floor, their last remaining torch began to flicker towards oblivion, its fuel depleted.

"Whatever we do next, it is going to require thought, and planning," de Payens growled, "and we are going to need the others down here. Come, we'll return later, once we have decided what we should do."

They returned to the surface, replenishing their torches as they went, and the climb up through the excavations was a silent one, each of the three men involved with his own thoughts on what they had found. As soon as they regained the stables, de Payens called all the brothers to attend a Gathering. St. Agnan and Payn de Montdidier had been on the point of riding out at the head of their scheduled patrol, but the sergeant messenger caught them in time and they came to the Gathering room with everyone else, wondering what was afoot.

De Payens cut to the essence of his summons as soon as the outer door was securely locked and guarded, once again by Geoffrey Bissot, whose duties as guard of the Gatherings seemed to occur on every occasion when something new and important had to be discussed. Hugh began by acknowledging St. Agnan and Montdidier, and the fact that their projected patrol would take them out of the city for the following eight days, but he assured them that by the time they returned, God willing, there would be much for them to do. He instructed St. Agnan to have his men stand down for the night but be prepared for an early departure the following morning.

They waited, muttering among themselves, while St. Agnan hurried off to find someone to carry that word to his senior patrol sergeant, and as soon as he returned, de Payens proceeded to describe St. Clair's discovery and the reflection and re-examination that had led to it. Now, de Payens concluded, thanks to that, and to the accident of the pry bar falling into the abyss, they knew there was *something,* some vast, empty space, beneath the floor of the tunnel in which they had been working at the time of St. Clair's near-suffocation, and he required all of them to abandon whatever they were working on in the tunnels immediately and to pool their labor and resources, to exploit the new discovery and find out just where, if anywhere, it led.

It was approaching time for the evening meal by then, and they adjourned their formal Gathering but remained in the room behind closed doors, joined now by Bissot, where they could talk freely about the discovery and plan their work for the coming days.

They had accumulated a considerable amount of equipment over their years of excavation, and there was no shortage of blocks, pulleys, ropes, and hoisting tackle at hand, and by the next morning the tunnel lengths to right and left of the opening from the day before were lined with materials to be used in the new excavation. But the task facing them was a daunting and disturbing one. They had been told that an enormous space lay beneath them, yet none among them was able to imagine what was there. They knew absolutely nothing, and they were afraid to let their imaginations run away with them.

All that they knew, and the realization was a chasten-

ing and worrisome one, was that everything they
dislodged beneath their feet fell away into nothingness,
dropping silently into a black abyss for a long way
before shattering against the rocks, or whatever else, lay
directly underneath. Accordingly, after one single near-
disaster when Montdidier almost fell into the pit, every
man who worked at enlarging the cavity did so wearing
a safety harness, with ropes securely attached to an overhead anchoring tripod. It was only after many hours of
work by alternating two-man shifts that someone
noticed—and no one could remember afterwards who
had remarked upon it first—that the hole at their feet
was distinctly triangular, converging in a deep V-shape,
and that what were apparently walls stretched down and
away on each side from what could only be a ceiling.

It soon became obvious that they were looking down
into a man-made structure. They had tried several times
to illuminate the space beneath, throwing half a score of
lit torches down into the blackness, but only half of
those had survived the fall, and they lay guttering on
the surface below, revealing nothing, until they burned
themselves out. Even those torches lowered on a rope
showed nothing of what was beneath, and the men had
grown bored with looking at them even before they
guttered and died out. But the mere fact that they
could feel the rush of clean air, and that the torches had
burned out naturally, proved that the air down there
was breathable, and once they had accepted that they
were looking down into a chamber of some description,
they agreed that someone ought to go down there and

have a look at whatever there was to see. St. Clair, as the youngest among them, and also the one who had made the discovery, was the first to be lowered, in a large basket suspended from a hoist, clutching a newly lit torch in one hand and fingering the dagger at his waist with the other, while he gazed about him, dropping lower and lower into the blackness with an elbow hooked around one of the basket's supporting ropes.

The first thing he discovered, mere moments after leaving the surface above, was that he was in fact in the corner of a room, for his basket swung into the juncture of the walls, and when he brought up his torch to look at them, he saw that they were a dull black, coated with a pitch-like substance so that they absorbed light and radiated none.

He shouted that information up to his companions, and then concentrated on looking about him, breathing deeply and trying not to give in to the feeling that he was being stifled and that the blackness surrounding him was growing ever heavier and more dense as they lowered him deeper and deeper. His mind focused suddenly on the fact that his sword, which was seldom far from his hand, now lay far above him, on the bed in his sleeping cell where he had thrown it before coming down into the tunnels, and although logic told him he would have no need of it here, he felt defenseless none the less, and aware of the puniness of the dagger at his waist.

He became aware, quite unexpectedly, that the basket had reached the floor of the enormous chamber, but so gently had it touched down that only the cessation of movement told him he was resting on a solid surface. He held the torch as high as he could above his head, peering into the surrounding gloom, but he could see nothing at all.

"I'm down," he called to the watchers above. "Unloading now." He reached down and grasped one of the dry torches piled about his legs, then swung his right leg carefully over the edge of the basket and stepped out. He lit the fresh torch from the one he was holding and stooped close to the ground, waving both lights back and forth to see what he could see.

The floor was level, and paved in square stone slabs, each a good long pace to a side, and there was a thin coating of dust on the stones, far less than one might have expected, he thought, until he remembered the steady current of cool air that had been blowing around him since the start of his descent. He stooped lower, looking for a hole in or between the flagstones, something into which he would be able to tuck one of the torches, but there was nothing to be seen, not the slightest crack or unevenness into which he might insert a dagger point. He straightened up again and turned slowly in a complete revolution, peering into the blackness all around and waving his torches widely in the hope of catching a reflection of some kind from whatever might be there beyond his sight.

Finally, he took a deep breath and stood with his back to the angle of the corner, taking his bearings as well as he was able. When he felt confident that he could maintain a course by following the edges of the flagstones under his feet, he began to walk slowly forward diagonally, stepping from corner to corner, stone by stone, into the chamber, holding one torch low to light his way across the floor and the other high to show him anything that might be seen, while he counted his steps aloud. Then he stopped and glanced up, his eye attracted by movement up there in the corner behind him, and he made out the shape of one of his companions being lowered to join him, another torch flickering in his hand as he sank downward. St. Clair had not been aware of the basket being raised again, his attention had been so tightly focused upon what he was doing. He turned back to his task and kept walking, the cadence of his counting unbroken.

He had reached thirty when he saw the first dim outline of a different shape on the floor ahead of him and he stopped, raising both torches high to give himself as much light as possible. As he did so, he heard a soft step at his back, and André de Montbard spoke into his ear.

"What is it? You see something?"

St. Clair made no attempt to answer, knowing Montbard could see for himself. Instead, he crouched slightly lower and took another step forward, and then another as Montbard drew abreast of him on his left.

"Something there."

Again St. Clair offered no response other than to continue to advance until he could see what was in front of him. It appeared to be a jar, or an urn of some kind, and it was merely the closest of an entire array, all uniform in shape and size. He walked until he stood in a wide gap between two ranks of the things, and he could see files of them stretching away from him, disappearing into the gloom ahead. He counted eight on each side, and could see at least ten more parallel ranks of them, eight to a side, with a wide aisle stretching between them.

"They are jars, plain clay jars." He went closer, until he could see the tops of them. "And they're sealed, with some kind of wax, I think … They are all sealed. Sealed *jars*?" He looked at de Montbard and raised his hands in a gesture of helplessness. "Jars of *what*? What's in them? And why so many of them?" He reached out a hand towards the nearest one, as though to grasp it and tilt it, but before he could touch it de Montbard caught his sleeve, restraining him gently.

"Careful, Stephen. They could be full of oil, or even wine, but if they are what I believe they might be, then we have found what we came looking for, my friend. We have found our treasure."

"Treasure?" St. Clair's voice was strained, his disappointment almost tangible. "This is the treasure we've been seeking for so long? In clay *pots*?"

"Clay pots, true, but ask yourself what they might contain, Stephen. Ask yourself, too, how long it might have been since anyone but we set foot in this chamber. And ask yourself then why these jars should have been laid out so carefully here on this floor and then left there. Now, if I am right, there should be an altar somewhere ahead of us."

On the point of asking how de Montbard could

possibly know that, St. Clair bit back his question and was bleakly unsurprised when they found the promised altar within twenty paces. Despite his lingering disappointment over the clay jars, however, this newest discovery immediately set his pulse hammering again, for it was hardly the kind of altar he had been expecting, and its sheer bulk humbled him. It was immense, unlike any altar he had seen before, larger by far than any altar in any Christian church or basilica that he had visited.

It came into view slowly, seeming to solidify out of the surrounding darkness as they came closer to it, and they heard the footsteps approaching from behind them as Hugh de Payens caught up to them, bringing new light to add to their own. He said nothing to either of them, all his attention reserved for the altar that towered above them, and for a time the three men stood silent, their eyes scanning the planes and highlights of its cliff-like heights. They had approached it from the side, and it was clear from the outset that the top of its sacrificial table could be reached only by means of a broad, high flight of shallow steps that descended from its rear, the bottom-most steps only dimly visible from where they stood. Its frontal surface, stretching left of them, plain and unadorned as it seemed at first sight, revealed itself on closer inspection as being intricately carved and shaped, and covered with thousands upon thousands of tiny carved glyphs.

"And there it is," Montbard whispered. "Exactly as our records described it. The Lore is accurate. The

Order is founded on truth."

"It's ..." St. Clair swallowed, the sounds as he tried to moisten his suddenly dry mouth clearly audible to the others. "This place is not Jewish at all. It cannot be. They abhor graven images."

De Montbard tilted his head back to gaze upward. "It's Egyptian." A long pause ensued, and then he added, "Everything that is now Jewish came out of Egypt in the beginning, brought out by Moses and his Israelites after centuries of slavery. Our own Lore tells us that. The changes came later, as changes always do, but in the beginning, at the very start of it, it was all Egyptian. And we are looking at the proof of that. This place is ancient beyond imagining, my friends. Moses never returned here to their promised land, but his sons and grandchildren may have stood right here, where we are today, looking up there just like us. We have found the proof of our Order's tenets."

"You sound as though you doubted that until now." St. Clair's attempt at raillery fell flat, the challenge in his words lost in the fact that he, too, spoke in a hushed whisper.

"Not for a moment," Montbard replied in the same tone. "What I meant to say was that our Order is founded upon *demonstrable* proof with this discovery."

"So be it. I believe you. But what *have* we found?"

"Knowledge, Brother Stephen. And an altar that is not what it appears to be."

"Someone else is coming," Stephen said. They could see another light in the distance. "Is there anything we are not permitted to know? Any sacred secrets?"

It was de Payens who answered this time. "All of these things are secrets, Stephen, and all of them are sacred. Ah, Goff, I thought that might be you. Look at what we have found. André believes our search is at an end."

"I confess, I am impressed. It is huge. What is it?" Godfrey St. Omer was craning his neck to look up at the altar.

"It's an altar, Godfrey," de Montbard answered. "The Lore said it would be here."

"Did it, by God? Then it must be here for a purpose. Is it hollow? Can we get into it?"

De Montbard shrugged, although St. Omer did not see the gesture. "I don't know. It is too soon to tell. We will explore it later."

"Hmm. What about all those jars back there? What's in them?"

"The treasure we have been looking for."

That got St. Omer's attention. He turned his head sharply to look at de Payens, making no attempt to hide his skepticism. "Those things hold the *treasure*?"

His friend nodded. "De Montbard thinks they do ... But he also thinks his altar is not what it appears to be, and that has me curious. Come."

He led them around to the left, to the front of the altar, until it reared vertically above them, the project-ing shelf of its table forming a straight-edged ceiling above their flickering torches, and St. Clair leaned back on his heels to stare up at it.

"It must be the height of four tall men," he said, then hesitated. "What's that up there, that large pattern on the stone? Is it a cross? Here, step back and hold up your torches."

The light from their combined torches revealed a shallow incision high in the stone, the shape of a cross with a loop at its upper end.

"It is a cross," St. Omer said, his voice filled with surprise. "Is this then a Christian place?"

Again it was André de Montbard who provided the answer. "It is not a cross, my friend, it is an ankh."

"A what?"

"An ankh."

"Then I did hear you correctly. An ankh, is it? What's an ankh, is it something Jewish, some Hebrew symbol of religious significance? I thought the Jews abhorred graven images."

"That is true. Stephen made the same point, just before you arrived. They do." De Montbard's voice was reflective, almost musing, and his neck was still craned backward as he gazed up at the ankh above their heads. "The ankh is a symbol of religious significance, but it is not Jewish, Goff, it is Egyptian, a symbol of life and prosperity, not merely in this world but in the next, the afterworld."

St. Omer was staring at Montbard, his brows creased in a frown. "But we are in King Solomon's Temple here. Are you saying that the ancient Hebrews subscribed to Egyptian beliefs?"

"Well, first of all, we are not in the Temple of

Solomon. We must be close by it, perhaps even beneath it, but we are not *in* it. This place is far too large to be the temple. We know that was very small." He flicked a sideways glance at de Payens, and then his eyes dropped to scan the ground at their feet. "And why should the ancient Hebrews *not* have subscribed to Egyptian beliefs? They lived there for hundreds of years. It is more than possible that they admired elements, at least, of what the Egyptians believed. But that is no concern of ours for the moment. What concerns us is this other ankh."

He held his torch low now, pointing at the floor, and they looked down to see a second ankh, not quite as large as the one above them but far more deeply incised into the stone on which Montbard was standing. Before any of them could say anything, he dropped to one knee and waved to St. Clair to do the same, facing him. "Here," he said, "feel what's in here." He dug the fingers of one hand into his end of the cross-arm of the ankh and tried to pry out the dust and dirt that had filled the gap between the outline of the carved figure and the surrounding flagstone, but although some of the material came away, the remainder was too tightly packed. Montbard stopped and looked at St. Clair, who had achieved the same result on his side.

"Would you be surprised to know that what you are holding is a handle?"

St. Clair shrugged. "I would not have thought it, but if you say it is, then I believe you."

De Montbard nodded, then looked around him at

the torches they were holding. "How are these torches doing? How many fresh ones have we left?"

St. Omer did a quick tally. "Six that I can see. The others are in various stages of strength."

"Damn! Damnation and perdition. I should have anticipated this."

No one knew what he was talking about, and they all looked blankly at one another until St. Clair asked, "Anticipated what?"

"We are losing the light ... the torches. We are about to be plunged back into darkness, and we need far more illumination than we have if we are to complete this task and uncover the remaining treasures."

"But we have more torches up above, plenty of them."

"No, we have some, but nowhere near close to as many as we will need. That's why I think it better to stop now and lay in supplies *before* we find something exciting and are forced to abandon it in darkness." He looked at his three listeners, his eyes shifting from face to face, and he could barely contain his glee.

"This is a great day, my friends. We have found what we sought, what our Lore told us was here, and if we find no more than the jars, we will have found enough to justify the existence of our ancient Order. But I would suggest we need to return to the surface and tell the others what we have found. They deserve to know, as much as we do. After that, we will need to gather as much fuel as we can find, for banishing this darkness, and while we are doing that, we should also be purchasing oil lamps, as many as we can obtain, and large, fat candles that can burn for hours on end. If we are to work down here for the length of time I am beginning to think might be necessary, then we are going to need as much light as we can manufacture by any and all means. So we had better climb back out of here and set to work, for the sooner we gather what we need, the sooner we can come back and finish our task."

NINE

It took a full week of hard work, collecting wagonloads of wood—always in scarce supply in Palestine—before the monks, impatient with what they saw as yet another frustrating impediment to their success, had assembled enough fuel and torches to enable them to go back to work exploring the chamber, but it could have taken much longer had not Montdidier remembered hearing a report, several months earlier, of a wildfire that had destroyed a large olive grove a few days' journey to the southeast. A train of five rented wagons, accompanied by a strong escort of sergeants, was sent out in search of the grove and, by one means or another, they managed to bring back four complete wagonloads of heavy, charred tree trunks, suitable for splitting and making into torches. Every candle maker in Jerusalem had been bought out of stock by then, and an entire barrel of pitch, purchased from one of the Arab traders, had been set in place below ground, and the monks began immediately making torches that would burn long and cleanly.

St. Clair was happy enough to find himself unin-volved in the search for fuel that week; de Payens, mindful that the younger knight had returned from patrol and gone straight to work on the underground explorations, granted him a three-day rest period, completely free of duties. St. Clair spent much of the first day simply lying around in slothful bliss, enjoying the sheer simplicity of doing nothing, but it was not in his nature to remain idle for long, and the following morning, after attending to the few allocated chores he had, he set out with the package that he had promised to deliver to Hassan the horse trader from his cousin and namesake, Hassan the Shi'a warrior. He had felt no urgency about the task until then, and undertook it when he did simply for diversion, because he knew that the trader would not yet have returned to the city.

Even before he left the stable precincts that morning, however, Stephen became aware that something unusual was afoot, because the streets were crowded and he could hear the hubbub even from a distance. None of the sergeants on guard was able to tell him what was happening, but it was clear the mood of the throng below was festive, and so he slung his sword belt comfortably over his shoulders, out of the way and yet easily reachable, and struck out for the marketplace beyond the walls, where Hassan's horse stalls were located. He had an inbred distrust of exposing himself needlessly to the dangers of being a Frankish knight alone in a close-packed crowd of potential enemies, but the mood of the crowd seemed benign, and he felt reasonably sure that his heavy, mailed hauberk would protect him against the kind of sneak attack that would involve nothing heavier, in such circumstances, than a sly knife. He entered the flow of bodies and was quickly hemmed in on every side, the press growing thicker as he began to approach the city walls, and by the time the enormous wooden gates came into view over the heads of the people around him he was barely making any progress at all.

Finally, no more than thirty paces from the gates, he could go no farther. The huge, wooden barriers were closed, which was unheard of at this time of day when there was no attack expected, and now he saw that the crowd ahead of him was being held in check by a line of the King's Guard, who had linked arms and were facing into the crowd, their backs to the empty street. He began to push his way forward to the front, ignoring the complaints of the people he displaced, many of whom turned to see who was pushing and then bit back their angry protests at the sight of the towering, blue-eyed *ferenghi* in the mailed coat. Before he could reach any of the guards to ask what was going on, however, there came a blare of trumpets, and the massive gates began to swing open, the noise of their ponderous groaning quickly drowned out by the excited shouts of the people around him, and the tension on the faces of the guards increased visibly as they hunched even harder against the pushing of the crowd. Knowing then that questions were pointless, St. Clair gave up the struggle to advance and simply stood there, looking over the heads of the people in front of him and waiting to see what would develop.

He could not have been better positioned to witness the arrival in Jerusalem of a truly magnificent cavalcade of newcomers, most of them fitting his concept of what he and his fellow veterans called damsels, in that they were fresh faced and obviously unweathered by the desert climate, their clothing, weapons, and accoutrements new and shining with bright, unfaded colors and heraldic devices he had never seen before. Three score of these bright-eyed warriors rode at the head of the procession, in fifteen ranks of four abreast, preceded by a tight, magnificently burnished and caparisoned formation of twelve of King Baldwin's senior commanders, mounted on the King's finest horses. The newcomers were followed by a group of musicians, drummers and trumpeters, marching to the cadence of a quartet of drums, and after those came the royal party, all aglitter with gilt and jewels and embroidered surcoats. King Baldwin himself sat on a throne mounted on an elaborately decorated bier surmounting three long poles, carried by four men to a pole, twelve in front and twelve behind, and as he passed by, royal servants walking beside his bier threw sweetmeats and honey cakes to the watching throng. And then, riding directly behind the King, on a well-sprung, flat-bottomed wagon drawn by a team of four stocky, well-matched, solid-looking blacks, came the Patriarch Archbishop, seated comfortably on his Bishop's Seat, resplendent in his full episcopal finery and accompanied by his secretary, Bishop Odo of Fontainebleau.

At their rear, separated by another corps of drummers marching to a single drum beat, came yet another band of damsels, their magnificence outshining even

Baldwin's, and the young man who rode at their head, on a breathtakingly splendid horse of pale gold with a silver mane and tail, appeared as the very embodiment of a Christian paladin, tall and broad shouldered, with long, blond hair, darkly bronzed skin, and startling, flashing blue eyes. This was obviously the welcome guest, whoever he might be, St. Clair thought, and he was plainly glad to be here, smiling widely and display-ing perfectly white and even teeth. His armor, in the Byzantine fashion, shimmered as he moved, its cuirass covered in individual leaflike plates of what appeared to be solid gold, and his booted legs, solid and strong looking as young trees, bore greaves of the same fashion, covering him from knee to ankle. From his shoulders, hanging down his back and draped across his horse's withers, a full cape of thick, ivory-colored silk, bearing a brightly embroidered coat of arms, draped flawlessly, prompting St. Clair to wonder, looking at its perfection, if it had somehow been pinned in place.

The magnificent young man rode on proudly, followed by his bodyguard of damsels, who were followed in turn by the rear guard, appropriately another contingent of King Baldwin's own guard, impeccably turned out and marching smartly, despite the age and worn condition of their armor, as though acknowledging that they could not compete with the finery ahead of them but were prepared to fight to keep their guests from being overtaken by the mob before they reached the palace.

As the last of the rear guard passed by, the crowd

began to break up, many of them following the cavalcade but others beginning to go about their normal
business. The guards lining the street formed up in
ranks, preparing to return to their barracks, and St. Clair
recognized the knight who supervised them. He stepped
into the road and called him by his name, and the
knight looked down and recognized him, returning
the greeting.

"What was that all about? Who is the young demi-
god?"

The other man grinned, but barked an order to one
of his subordinates before he turned back. "That was
Prince Bohemond of Antioch, new come from Italy to
claim his father's throne and pausing here to claim the
hand of his betrothed, the Princess Alice. Where have
you been, that you do not know that?"

St. Clair shrugged. "I've been on patrol, smiling at
brigands. Came back but yesterday. The young man
seems impressive. He is to wed the Princess Alice, you
say?"

"Aye, as soon as it may be arranged, for he has a
kingdom—or at least a principality—to set in order. It
has been too long ungoverned." The knight glanced
away, towards his men, then raised a hand in salute to
St. Clair and turned back to his duties.

St. Clair stood where he was for a few moments
longer, watching the other man marshal his troops and
set them marching, but his thoughts were far from what
he was watching. His mind was filled with thoughts of
the princess and her coming nuptials, and he found

himself, without expectation or rational cause, resenting the noble and handsome youth who was to be her husband, aware of a tight ball of envy and frustration forming deep in his chest and sending out discomfiting tendrils to afflict his loins, reminding him of images he had no real wish to recall. He hung there a little longer, hesitant, fighting an unreasonable and ludicrous temptation to follow the parade back to the King's palace, then swung sharply on his heel and stalked away, surprised to find the streets now almost empty.

He was still fighting to empty his mind of thoughts of the princess when he came to the railed enclosure fronting the premises of Hassan the horse trader, and he paused to admire the three animals penned there, one white, one a pale dun color, and the third a beautiful dappled gray. All three were stallions and all bore the clean lines and unmistakable narrow muzzle of the pure Arab bloodlines. He wondered idly what they might be worth, smiling ruefully as he remembered that, even before the days of his joining the Brethren of the Mount, the poorest of the three would have been far beyond the reach of his purse.

"They are magnificent, are they not, Lord St. Clair?"

He swung around to find himself looking at a man he recognized but could not place, and he was sufficiently flustered by being addressed in his own tongue to neglect correcting the fellow's mode of addressing him. Instead, he remembered where he had seen the man before and drew himself up, reaching beneath his surcoat for the package in his belt, then spoke in Arabic.

"You are the man called Nabib, who works for Hassan, are you not?"

The other inclined his head graciously and answered in the same tongue. "I have that honor, praise be to Allah. What may I do for you?"

"Nothing at all. I am merely the bearer of tidings. I was making my way towards your stall in the market when the procession approached." He pulled out the package he was holding and extended it. "I was asked to deliver this to you to give to your master when he returns. It was sent by his cousin Hassan."

The other's eyebrows rose, but he allowed nothing else to show on his face. "His *cousin* Hassan? The warrior Hassan?"

St. Clair nodded. "The warrior. I met him in the desert, close to Jaffa, and he asked me if I would deliver this on my return."

The hint of a smile flickered around one corner of the Arab's mouth, but he merely inclined his head again. "Then it must be of great import, for a Shi'a warrior to entrust a *ferenghi* warrior with its safety. You may be sure of our lasting gratitude, Lord St. Clair."

"Not Lord St. Clair, Nabib. I am but a monk nowadays, known as plain Brother Stephen."

Again Nabib nodded. "The Prophet teaches that we should not belittle others by disbelieving what they say in truth, but in this I have to speak. Brother Stephen you may be today, but no *ferenghi* who can speak of Hassan the Shi'a as a friend could ever be plain. Accept our thanks and go with God, my friend."

On leaving the Arab's enclosure, St. Clair was briefly tempted to stroll through the market and indulge his love of sweetmeats, but the more he sought to forget about her, the more strongly the Princess Alice intruded into his thoughts, and he soon found himself becoming aroused, even in the crowded marketplace, as he pictured her with her new husband in the intimacy of her chambers, so that soon, verging close upon outright panic, he quit the marketplace and strode off homeward, towards the stables and the recent discovery that lay in the tunnels beneath them, renouncing any and all claim on the time off that de Payens had granted him, and uncomfortably aware that in the space of another single day, without the blessing of hard work to distract him, he could be lost again in the morass churned up by his awareness of temptation. He would be better off by far, he knew, floundering through the darkness of the place he had discovered beneath the tunnels of the Temple Mount, and he was relieved beyond words that in merely thinking about the massive chamber and the secrets it contained, he was able to purge his mind of thoughts about Alice le Bourcq.

Some of the brotherhood, he reflected, had begun to refer to the newly discovered chamber as "the Temple" when they withdrew that first day, purely because of its size and scale. But André de Montbard would have none of that and quickly set them to rights. The hall they had discovered lay beneath the level on which the original Temple of Solomon had stood, he told them, and he cited several sources from the Order of Rebirth's own hallowed Lore to reinforce his claims, so that the others had no option but to believe what he said, and the new term for the place they had discovered became "the Hall."

Much as the brothers liked and admired him, André de Montbard had always been something of an incongruity among them, in that he had been sent from France to join them—virtually co-opted to their brotherhood—by Count Hugh of Champagne, the Seneschal of the Order of Rebirth. It was a distinction Montbard shared with St. Clair, but St. Clair's selection had been self-evidently attributable to his youth, strength, piety, and fighting skills, whereas Montbard's abilities lay in other areas, which had only begun to be seen since the discovery of the underground tunnels.

That distinction alone set de Montbard apart, and might have been a serious impediment to his acceptance by the others had he been a different kind of man, for vassal to the Count though he might nominally be, all of them knew that de Montbard was far more wealthy and powerful in his own right than any other among them and could easily have made their lives intolerable simply because of that. That he had chosen not to do so surprised several of the brethren who had initially been prepared to resent him as a spy set to watch them. And thus he was an anomaly—a man of immense personal power in France, choosing to display or pursue no vestige of that power here in Jerusalem, and voluntarily sublimating himself in true fealty to serve as deputy for another. It was the very stuff of feudalism, but few people in the real world of ambitious and venal men ever made even a pretense of placing any other man's demands and priorities—feudal lord or no—ahead of their own best interests.

Following his unexpected arrival, the others had soon come to see that de Montbard was, in fact, exactly what he appeared to be, no more and no less, and they had adjusted to the strangeness of that truth as being simply a part of the man. No one among them had ever had the slightest cause to complain about his bearing or his behavior in any respect, and he had comported himself exactly as one of them from the outset, assuming neither airs nor privileged expectations. Now, however, from the moment of discovering the Hall, de Montbard had begun to dictate requirements and instructions that were obeyed without demur by de Payens and St. Omer, making it clear to all of the brothers, without need of explanation, that he was following long-standing instructions of his own and that this situation was the precise reason for his presence in their midst.

St. Clair found de Montbard waiting for him a few days later when he emerged from his own cell, soon after the return of the wood-gathering expedition, and he paused, almost in mid-step, and cocked his head slightly, his eyebrows rising in curiosity.

"I'm going down," de Montbard said without preamble. "Will you come with me?"

"Aye, give me a moment." He spun on his heel and went back into his cell, emerging a short time later with his belted sword, slinging it over his head so that the belt hung across his chest, the long sword hanging at his back and the sheathed dagger dangling by his belly. De Montbard made no attempt to mask his grin.

"You think we might find opponents down there?"

"You do, too, obviously. I only came for these because you're wearing yours ... You never know, my friend. There might be demons, waiting to suck us into Hell the moment we lift that ankh. Should that be the case, I would rather go clutching my good, sharp sword than anything else I can think of. If it transpires not to be the case, on the other hand, we can use the dagger point to scrape the dirt from the grooves in the stone, and perhaps even use the sword as a lever."

It took the two men the better part of half an hour to reach the subterranean hall and lower themselves to the floor in the basket hoist, with an ample supply of freshly made torches that St. Agnan, who had made them himself, swore would burn for hours. De Montbard carried two armloads of the torches, while St. Clair carried two small iron braziers, modified so that they would stand on the floor and support a brace of burning torches apiece. A short time later, the torches set and placed where they cast most light, the two knights knelt facing each other on each side of the ankh carved into the floor. De Montbard nodded, and they went to work, using dagger points to gouge out the dirt that had settled into the grooves over a millennium. It soon became apparent that de Montbard had been right again: once cleared of dirt, there was sufficient space beneath each cross-arm of the ankh to permit each half to be grasped on its own side like the hilt of a sword.

St. Clair took a firm grip and looked at Montbard. "Ready?"

"I am, but I think you might be better off on this side, too. Then we can lift together, from the same direction."

St. Clair crossed to kneel beside the other man and gripped the "handle" de Montbard had dug out. But before the other man could move, he tilted his head back and looked his companion in the eye, a taut little smile on his lips. "You know," he said, "it occurs to me that what we are about to do here might have a momentous outcome."

De Montbard quirked one eyebrow. "Like what?"

"How could I know that? We haven't done it yet, have we? But we have been scrabbling about in the dark down here like rats for a long time, a very long time, and now we may be about to do something from which there can be no turning back. The world we know might never be the same again once we have pulled on these handles. Should we not, perhaps, say something portentous? Something profound?" He frowned. "I thought I was about to say something tongue in cheek when I began that, but suddenly what I was saying feels true."

De Montbard simply stared at him, unmoved. "Do you have something you wish to say, then?"

"No ..."

"Nor do I, so may we proceed? Together then, on three."

They heaved, steadily, and their combined strength produced not the hint of a movement, as though they were attempting to lift the solid floor, and they released at the same moment, their breath exploding from their lungs.

De Montbard wiped his forehead with the back of his hand. "A thousand years is a long time, I suppose. Moving parts might stiffen up over that long a period."

"Principles of leverage," St. Clair said, staring down at the ankh.

De Montbard stood up and stretched hugely. "Principles of what?"

The younger man sat back on his haunches. "Brother Joachim, an elderly monk I knew in my boyhood, had a great love of the ancients—Archimedes and Euclid and Pythagoras and their mathematics. I remember him saying something about being able to lift up the world if he had a large enough lever. He used to talk about the laws of force and energy, and how there is a correct way to move anything. I think if we squat, knee to knee and face to face, and lift straight up together, using our leg muscles instead of our arms, we might do better."

"Let's try." De Montbard moved immediately into position, and both men reached down between their feet to grasp the handles.

"I just thought of something, something you said last time we were here."

De Montbard raised an eyebrow. "What was that?"

"It was about this being over when we find the treasure. It won't be, will it? Finding the treasure will only be the beginning."

De Montbard tilted his head to one side, a smile beginning to form on his lips. "The beginning of what, Stephen?"

St. Clair shook his head. "The beginning of whatever comes next, I suppose. I don't know, and I would not care to guess at what that might be, but I have no doubt that something is inevitable. I may be no more than a simple soldier monk, but I am not stupid. All those jars over there contain *something*, André, and whatever it is, it must be enormously valuable and of great significance to have been hidden so carefully a thousand years ago. That is an entire millennium, as you said—fifty generations of fathers and sons. And all that time, our Order has been dreaming of finding this place and its contents. But a length of time like that is meaningless to any ordinary man. We cannot grasp the reality involved. We can barely recall our *grandsires*, two generations removed from us, so we cannot begin to comprehend the thought of *ten* generations, let alone fifty.

"And now it appears that after all that time, this hoard, whatever it contains, is to become unhidden. We have unhidden it. Whatever it is, Brother, whatever this treasure may be, or may comprise, I hope you will not insult me by saying it is going to remain a secret, for even I can see that it is far too important.

"And so I am wondering, what then will happen to the Order of Rebirth in Sion? Will it remain secret as it has always been, or will it, too, and all of us, come forth into the light of day, brandishing what we have found?"

De Montbard held up his hands, palms forward. "Too deep for me. I swear to you, Stephen, I have no idea. Those things lie far beyond my capacity to influence, or even to interpret. This much, however, I can promise you: whatever we find here, today, tomorrow, or whenever, will have to be catalogued and recorded, meticulously, before a word of what we have found leaves these tunnels. Depending on what we unearth here, that single task alone could take months and perhaps even years to complete. But it will have to be done. And that we do it is important beyond credence. We must record our findings, in every detail of our discovering them." He grinned again, his teeth gleaming and his features seeming to waver in the flickering torchlight. "But we may find nothing more than those jars. So, what say you, shall we try your leverage idea?" He waited for St. Clair's nod of agreement, then grunted. "So be it. Ready, then? One ... and two ... and *three!*"

They unfolded slowly, straightening and straining in unison, glaring straight forward into each other's eyes, their thigh and calf muscles locked and trembling with the strain they were exerting, and slowly, so gradually that they could only sense it rather than actually feel it, they wrested a degree of yielding from the ankh that lay between them. A moment later, with no lessening of the pressure they were exerting, they felt another shift, this one tiny yet unmistakable.

"One more," St. Clair gasped, his face crimson with sustained effort. "Heave!" This time, however, nothing happened, and it was de Montbard who gave the signal to desist and rest for a while. They had wrested a small amount of motion from the stone, an acknowledgment that movement had been designed into the device, and so they took time to recover from their efforts before trying again. A short time later, with not another word spoken between them, they took their places again and straightened up together, using the full strength of their thigh and leg muscles to push against the force that kept the ankh immobile, and something yielded without warning; the cross-arm they were pulling against rose suddenly, perhaps half a foot, and then stopped. The shift was accompanied by an indistinct yet solid percussive sound, strangely hollow seeming, and that was followed by a brief and muffled barely audible noise, as though of grinding stones, that appeared to come from directly beneath their feet. Even as St. Clair heard it, his mind was registering what had happened to the ankh.

"Straight up," de Montbard said. "It came straight up."

St. Clair had been thinking exactly the same thing, because his expectation had been that the ankh would rise out of its carved niche like a lever, the handles swinging upward and pivoting upon the fixed point that was the lower extremity of its shaft. But that had not happened at all. Instead, the cross-arm of the device had popped free and risen vertically, exposing a rod beneath that vanished into the earth below.

"What was the noise? It sounded like something broke off and fell underground."

"I thought the same, but I think we are unlikely to find out easily. This handle does not appear to have any more travel left in it." De Montbard was pushing at the handle as he spoke, and it seemed to be rock-solid. St. Clair grunted in disgust and pushed himself to his feet, tilting his head back to look up at the other ankh scratched into the face of the altar, but de Montbard was still pulling and pushing at the handle they had raised from the floor.

"I think you may forget about that, my friend," St. Clair said. "It is not about to move again. We may have to come back to it with mauls and pry bars, to dig up the flagstones and let us see what is underneath, although I suspect it is solid earth and nothing more."

"No, it sounded hollow," de Montbard said quietly, gazing down at the shape in the floor. "It makes no sense, but that noise we heard sounded hollow to me."

"How did you know the altar was here? And the ankh?"

De Montbard looked at him. "I was told. Our oldest records deal with it and they described the layout of this chamber perfectly. I never saw those records, but I spent time with a number of the Order's most learned men, absorbing from them everything I could learn about this place before I was sent here. I knew the layout, and I knew the content. Unfortunately, the records that we have give no indication of anything beyond referring to the ankh, and that very obliquely, as the key, so even that reference is not assured. It seems clear, in retrospect, that the survivors of what befell here had no concept of how long they might be gone after they concluded their work. They must have thought they would return within their own lifetimes or those of their children, and that their knowledge would enable them to open the vaults they had so carefully concealed." He smiled, wryly, and clapped his hands together, looking about him. "As you said earlier, no ordinary man can visualize a thousand years ...

"The chamber is truly ancient. I know you know that, speaking of a millennium, but it is even older than you may think. It was built before the Temple of Solomon was even designed. Everything about it, its shape, design, construction, all of it, is Egyptian. It was built in the earliest days of the return of the Hebrews from their bondage in Egypt, and its sole purpose was to house and conceal the temple treasures. It had two entrances, according to our records, and we'll find them as soon as we begin to examine the place more fully, but I suspect we will find that the passages leading to them from outside have been blocked off and sealed, completely hidden from view on the far side. The people who used this place last had no desire to leave any part of it accessible to looters."

"Obviously," St. Clair said quietly, "and they were successful. When will you begin opening the jars?" He took a torch from one of the braziers and walked away towards the nearest row of the clay jars around the altar to the right of where they were, and de Montbard watched him go until he passed beyond the vertical edge of the altar, evidently counting rows, but moments later his voice came back from the darkness.

"André, come and look at this."

Intrigued by St. Clair's tone, de Montbard straightened up, took a torch of his own, and followed the sound of the other man's voice to find him standing rigidly, illuminated by the torch he held and staring fixedly back towards the altar. A glance to see what he was looking at was enough to freeze de Montbard into immobility as well. He saw the dimly lit shape of the flight of steps that rose to the altar table. He knew it was different, but he could not at first see how.

"I don't know what made me look," St. Clair said quietly. "I only saw it from the corner of my eye at first, and we're not close enough to be sure of anything yet, but …"

"The bottom steps are missing."

But as they drew closer and their eyes adjusted, they could see that was inaccurate, because the steps were not missing. They had moved, but they were still there. The bottom portion had merely sunk down into the floor, on some kind of pivot mechanism, revealing an entrance that had not been visible before, and the steps that had formerly stretched up towards the sacrificial table above now led downward into a deep, dark space beneath the great altar. The two knights stood looking down into it for what seemed like a long time until St. Clair said, "That explains the noises we heard. Are we going down there?"

De Montbard cleared his throat before he spoke.

"We are, but I think we should take at least one fresh torch apiece before we do. It doesn't smell bad, but the air might be foul in there."

Holding their torches high and carrying another spare apiece, they made their way slowly down the steps into the space beneath the altar, and stepped forward cautiously, surprised by the size and extent of their discovery, a long, high-ceilinged, rectangular chamber stretching to both sides from the foot of the stairs. St. Clair's immediate impression was that the shape of the place mirrored the dimensions of the altar above and included its hollow height, for the ceiling was at least a score of feet above their heads. He raised his torch even higher and saw that the walls on each side of him, right and left, were lined with stone shelves all the way up to the ceiling, cubic stone boxes, open at their sides, and each a good arm's length, shoulder to fingertip, in height, width, and depth, most of them crammed with exactly the same kind of jars that were ranged on the floor of the Hall above, save that he could see a few chests or cases among them.

De Montbard stood rapt, his head moving from side to side as he scanned the ranked tiers, while St. Clair looked instead at the length of the chamber, trying to estimate the total number of boxes. The gallery was long, and narrow in proportion to its length, and he counted eighteen boxes at floor level on the unbroken wall facing them. He multiplied that by the seven layers from floor to ceiling, doubled the result to accommo-date both sides of the gallery, and then subtracted three tiers for the space occupied by the stairs at their back. He was only slightly surprised at the total of 231 boxes.

There were brackets all along both walls, at head height, to hold torches of the kind they had brought with them, and de Montbard grunted, then reached up and placed his torch in one of them before turning back towards the entranceway.

"Torches," he said, his voice echoing in the confined space. "We'll need more light. Help me load the rest of these sconces, then let's see what's in here."

They quickly brought down more torches from the Hall and, minutes later, the interior of the gallery now brightly lit by half a score of flambeaux, they stood side by side, examining the rows of boxes lining the walls.

"More jars," St. Clair murmured. "These people must have had a manufactory making nothing but clay jars."

"They're not all jars," de Montbard said. "Let's open some of those wooden chests."

The first contained loose pieces of jewelry, some of them barbarically ornate, others delicately made, and all of them reflecting the dancing light from above. They were in no order at all, appearing to have been simply thrown into the chest, and after a glance at them, de Montbard turned to open a second, larger chest that proved to be full of gold coinage, also piled loosely, with no attempt having been made to put the coins in any kind of order. St. Clair glanced over and saw silver pieces gleaming in places among the golden coins, but his attention had been seized by one particular piece of jewelry in the open chest at his feet, and he reached down to pull it free of the other pieces with which it was entangled. It was a glittering necklace, a circle of heavy, woven gold wire from which depended a selection of splendid stones in blue and green, strung on a web of finer gold wire and designed to grace the breast of some wealthy woman. The green stones were rectangular lozenges, long and narrow, but the blue jewels were teardrop shaped, smooth and polished, and the gap where one of them was missing was plainly evident. He knew that the missing piece was the very stone he had found in the tunnels above, and he wondered who had stolen it originally, for there was not the slightest doubt in his mind, seeing the necklace, that someone had stolen it, a thousand years earlier. But then, his curiosity strangely satisfied, he dropped the necklace back into the chest, closed the lid, and turned to see what else de Montbard had found.

The other knight was hauling heavy vessels around, pulling and pushing them this way and that to see what was behind them, and St. Clair, recognizing nothing about them, asked what they were. Montbard's curt response—"ceremonial vessels"—meant nothing to him, but he could see that whatever they were, the vessels were in no way precious. Many of them were made of polished stone, some green and some brown, but the majority appeared to be of bronze, and they all looked clumsy and awkwardly formed, so St. Clair left his companion to whatever he was doing and turned his attention to the other boxes lining the walls.

"More than three quarters of this is jars like those upstairs."

De Montbard straightened up. "I had noticed that. I think what's in here is the most valuable material—the rest of it, upstairs in the main hall, is probably less important."

"Important? To whom? What do the jars contain, Montbard?"

De Montbard shrugged. "Have you seen me look into any of them? We'll find out later what they hold, but my guess is that they contain parchment scrolls, tightly bound and sealed inside the jars with wax to protect them against time and dampness. I believe we will find they are the recorded annals of the priests who left them here."

Disappointed, despite having guessed at something of the sort, St. Clair sighed and looked around him again. "And what about those things there, the ceremonial vessels, what are they for?"

"They would have been used in temple rites. Some of them are probably unimaginably ancient."

"But they're made of stone."

"Aye, most of them. Stone or bronze."

"So they are worth nothing."

"No, not if you wanted to sell them in the souk. Why would you even say that?"

St. Clair grinned wryly. "Because it's beginning to look as though the vaunted treasure that our Lore speaks of is less than might have been expected. So far, one case of jeweled pieces and one more of gold and silver coins. Hardly a massive hoard of wealth."

De Montbard looked him in the eye, smiling.

"That is only because your expectations are born of your experience, my young friend. Treasure, to you, should be treasure in today's meaning. Bear in mind, the churchmen who concealed this trove were not Christian churchmen as we know them. This hoard, as you call it, was buried by the priests of the original Christian Church, the Church that admired poverty and preached the virtues of owning nothing of value."

"Then what about the gold there, and the jewels?"

"Two boxes so far—as you say—out of all of this collection," de Montbard answered. "They were probably collected in the temple, as offerings in lieu of sacrifices. We will never know where they came from or how they were gathered, but proportionally they amount to next to nothing. King Baldwin will be happy to accept all of it, in return for allowing us to keep what is left." He placed one hand flat on the side of the jar nearest to him and patted it gently. "*This* is our Order's treasure, Stephen, here in these jars. And perhaps ..." His voice trailed off and he moved away towards the far end of the gallery, where he stood staring at the blank wall.

"And perhaps what?"

"Does it not strike you as being odd that this wall should be plain and unused, where the other walls are honeycombed with storage cells?"

"Odd? No, I think not. Why should it be odd? This is an end wall."

De Montbard grimaced. "Wrong, Stephen. Disabuse yourself. There is a secret here, somewhere ... Do you see any ankhs carved anywhere?"

"No." Stephen's response was emphatic. "And before you ask, I know there are none because I've been looking for decorations of any kind, merely out of curiosity. There are none. Why would you think there might be?"

De Montbard had knelt down on one knee and was peering at the bottom of the wall. "Because, my youthful friend, there ought to be. There is more in here than meets the eye. I am convinced of that." He stood up again and turned away from the wall, his gaze traveling all over the chamber. "And yet there is nothing," he continued, speaking to himself as much as to St. Clair. "Nothing at all."

"What else did you expect?"

De Montbard rounded on him then, drawing himself up to his full height, his eyes flashing with sudden impatience. "Trickery, Stephen," he snapped. "Subterfuge and deceit. This place was built by the people who built the pyramids in Egypt, the finest stonemasons who ever lived. You saw the workmanship of the opening—the intricacy of that doorway in the steps. Anyone possessing the learning and the craft required to build such a thing would have been more than capable of hiding a simple cavity behind a false wall." He whipped out his sword and slashed backward, underhand, striking its blade loudly and dramatically against the wall behind him. "And I believe this wall is false."

His impatience vanished as quickly as it had appeared, and he turned slowly in a full circle, his eyes sweeping the entire room, floor and walls, including the one at his back. "And if that is true, then there must be a key to opening it, just as the ankh was the key to opening the other. So where could it be?"

"The sconces? They are the only things in the room that are not made of solid stone."

De Montbard's eyebrows shot up. "Of course! Try them. You take that side. I'll handle this one."

The third sconce from the wall turned in St. Clair's hand as he tugged at it, and as he snatched at the torch that tumbled from it, they both heard the same subterranean rumble they had heard earlier, when the first door opened, except that this time it was closer and not at all muffled, as the blank end wall sank slowly into the floor.

Stretching across the cavity revealed a heavy curtain of richly embroidered cloth hung from a thick rod, the colors in the pattern still bright in the torchlight. For a long space neither man moved or appeared to breathe, but finally de Montbard took a tentative step forward, stretching his hand out cautiously to touch the cloth. St. Clair stood spellbound, watching the hanging fabric stir beneath that questing hand until suddenly de Montbard seized the curtain and thrust it violently to one side, letting the light from their torches spill into the darkness beyond.

In spite of himself, St. Clair leapt in fright and uttered a strange, high-pitched sound, then fell to his knees as though he had been smashed with a mace. Beside him, de Montbard reacted similarly, grunting an unintelligible sound, but remaining on his feet despite the shock.

In front of them, awash in the light of the torches they had lit, stretched a chamber as large as the one in which they stood; a long, narrow space of two contrasting colors, black and white. It was a perfect replica of the temples, the ritual gathering places, they had known at home in Christendom, from the alternating marble tiles of black and white upon the floor, to the draped thrones on either side of where they now stood staring into the chamber's depths, to the twin pillars between which they had sworn their oaths. They saw and recognized all of it, and yet each of them knew, within the echoing stillness of his own mind, that this place, this temple, had been shut up in darkness for thousands of years, awaiting their arrival.

De Montbard was the first of them to gather his wits—probably, St. Clair found himself thinking to his own surprise, because he had known enough beforehand to suspect what might be here. He stepped into the chamber slowly, holding a flaming torch high above his head, and St. Clair went with him, matching him step for step and willing his pounding heart to slow down.

"We are in the West," de Montbard said.

"Aye, and facing towards the East," St. Clair responded, barely aware of repeating the ritual words, "where all shall be revealed."

They moved forward together, stepping out resolutely until they were confronted by another curtain, much like the first but narrower. They exchanged glances, and de Montbard reached out yet again and, more cautiously and reverently this time, pulled the curtain aside. Beyond this veil, reflecting the light of their torches in a golden blaze, was something magnificent but unidentifiable: an elongated rectangular shape, solid and substantial and somehow more elaborate—this in defiance of all logic—than any single object St. Clair could ever remember having seen. It took him several more moments to understand that he was looking at an ornate golden chest, and he estimated its size to be about four feet in length by half that in height and width. It was topped with a complex, unrecognizable sculpture, also of gold, and two long, golden poles, held in place by heavy gold rings on each side, were obviously the means of carrying it from place to place. The sheer splendor of it filled St. Clair's entire being with an awe that was almost religious, and for long minutes he simply stood and stared at it, aware that de Montbard was kneeling motionless in front of him, like a man in a trance. He had not seen de Montbard pass him or sink to his knees, but he was not surprised by any of that; since the moment the curtain had been pushed aside, St. Clair had been aware of nothing but the chest. Now he felt a need to move. And he willed himself to go forward, one small step at a time, until he was standing beside the kneeling man. His eyes filled with the golden glory of the thing in front of him, he reached down with one hand to grasp de Montbard's shoulder.

"What is it?" He heard the timidity and awe in his own voice, but his question seemed to break the trance that gripped the other man, for he reached up and grasped St. Clair's arm, using it to pull himself upright.

When he was on his feet, he walked backward, pulling St. Clair with him, to the curtain, and he closed it once again, reverently, concealing the golden chest from view. That done, they continued to back away, looking neither to right nor left, until they reached the foot of the stairway leading to the Hall above. Only there did they turn, to run up the steps to the darkness of the great chamber, and only then, safely out of the other place, did they stop and turn to stare at each other, wide eyed.

"I did not believe," Montbard said then, in a shaky voice. "I did not believe it could be true."

St. Clair was breathing heavily, although he could not have told anyone why. "*What* could be true?" he asked. "What are you talking about? What *is* that thing?"

Now de Montbard gaped at him. "You don't know? You don't know what we have found? *This* is the Order's treasure, Stephen, but a real treasure, spoken of in the Lore but never mentioned as being present here. A treasure greater than any of us could ever have suspected. It is the *Ark*, Stephen. We have found the Ark."

St. Clair stood frowning, uncomprehending, aware only of his companion's profound awe. "What Ark?"

"*The* Ark, Stephen. The Ark of the Covenant, the repository of God's covenant with humanity. It was kept in the Holy of Holies, in the temple. It is the symbol of God Himself ..."

He turned to face St. Clair, his eyes glowing with conviction. "We have to tell the others, Stephen, now, immediately, for this changes everything. This will change the entire world. Nothing will ever be the same again. This is the reason for our Order's formation a thousand years ago."

St. Clair shook his head as though to clear it. "The Ark of the Covenant? I thought our treasure was no more than written records. But now you are telling me that this thing we have found is the Ark of the *Covenant*? From the Holy of Holies? Then I want to look at it again." He ran swiftly down the steps, uncaring whether de Montbard came with him or not, but by the time he paused hesitantly in front of the concealing curtain, he was aware of the other man at his shoulder. He reached out slowly and pushed the curtain aside carefully, hearing the curtain rings slowly sliding along the rod, and then he stood, gazing solemnly at the Ark, marking the way the flickering of their torches was reflected in the lines of the golden surface.

"Solid gold," he said some time later, his voice barely louder than a whisper.

"No, I think not," de Montbard demurred. "The lid is solid gold. But I believe the chest and the carrying poles are carved from *setim*—an imperishable acacia wood—then coated with a covering of pure gold. Were the entire thing made of solid gold, it would be too heavy to carry."

"What about the winged things on the top?"

"Cherubim, cherubs, angels—winged spirits of great power. You see how their wings are spread out and touching each other? They form a protective canopy over the lid of the Ark itself. The ancient Jews believed that God, the God of Moses, lives within that space."

"Not in the Ark itself?" St. Clair's face betrayed his surprise.

"No, in the space beneath the wings of the cherubim."

"But those are graven images. The Jews were forbidden to have those."

Montbard shrugged, his eyes still on the carvings. "Apparently they made an exception, just this once."

"What is in the chest? Do you know?"

De Montbard's response was little more than a whisper. "I did not even know the thing really existed. And no one knows what is inside it, Stephen. But I have heard tell that the Ark contains the tablets of stone Moses brought back from the mountain, bearing the Ten Commandments. It is also said to contain Aaron's famed rod, the one that bore seeds. And some say it also contains manna from Heaven."

"Can we touch it, open it?"

De Montbard's hand came up automatically, as if to forestall a blow. "I think not. Remember, the Jews believed their temple was God's home. He lived in the temple, above this Ark, beneath those very wings. Are you prepared to wager that He is not still there? I would not dare touch that device before doing a great deal of further study. But you may, if you wish, after I am gone from here."

"No, perhaps not ..." St. Clair cocked his head sideways, peering beyond the Ark. "Is that—?" He bent forward, squinting into the darkness behind the golden chest. "There's another curtain there, behind the Ark, a black drape. There may be other treasures back there."

He heard de Montbard sniff. "I doubt that, Stephen. I remember reading that the two carrying poles always touched a veil of some kind behind the Ark—I believe it was the veil that separated the two chambers of the Tabernacle. If so, that drape at the back is probably only symbolic, covering the wall and nothing else." He reached out and prodded St. Clair, to add emphasis to what he was saying. "Besides, what would they want to hide back there? What could be more valuable than the Ark of the Covenant?

St. Clair turned to him in surprise. "Nothing, if you believe in the God of the ancient Jews. But that is not to say there is nothing else of any value here. I'm going to take a look. There's room enough for me to slip by the end of the Ark without touching it."

He waited for an answer from de Montbard, and when none came he turned his head again. "What think you?"

De Montbard shook his head, his lips pursed doubtfully. "I don't know, Stephen. How close must a man approach a lightning bolt before being burned by it? Even were I a doubter, I do not think I would have the bravery, or the foolishness, to shrug by within a hand's breadth of what might be the living God. But apparently you would."

"Hmm." St. Clair did not move, but stood in silence for some time before saying, "Well, since you put it like that, I doubt that I would, in fact. Perhaps I will wait until we hear what Master Hugh has to say. And so we had better go upstairs and tell the others about what we've found. Don't you think so?"

Montbard nodded, smiling. "Aye, I think so. They might, after all, wish to see something of it at least, since they've been digging like moles for eight years and more in the mere hope of finding it. Let us go up, then, and find out."

The hours that followed were a far cry from anything that had been known before, as all nine of the brethren crowded down into the Hall to look at what had been found beneath the altar, and no two men among them had exactly the same reaction to seeing the stark, black and white beauty of the chamber behind the first curtain, and the glory of the fabled Ark of the Covenant within its own curtained niche at the rear of the chamber. Several men wept openly; Geoffrey Bissot dropped to his knees at the foot of the entry stairs, facing the open end wall, and stayed there for three hours without moving, apparently lost in prayer; Godfrey St. Omer chose to kneel within the chamber that housed the Ark, and stayed there for two hours, joined from time to time by others of the brotherhood. All of them moved about in silence, and few of them spoke among themselves. None of them, it seemed, could fully come to terms with the truth that, after all their years of hard labor, scratching and scrabbling at the solid rock of the Temple Mount, they had actually found the treasure they had come to find, and had discovered it to be greater than their wildest imaginings could have made it.

Only Hugh de Payens seemed aloof from the general reaction. He was present the whole time, but he said not a word to anyone, and St. Clair watched him from a distance, with steadily growing concern, as he stood apart from the others, taking note of everything that was done and said but making no attempt to take an active part in any of the activities. Eventually, when the senior knight walked away into the surrounding darkness of the great Hall, St. Clair followed him, maintaining a wide distance but watching anxiously lest his superior fall over or grow ill.

No such thing occurred, however, and de Payens merely seated himself beyond the lights from the altar and continued to watch in silence until, one after another, the knights hoisted themselves up in the basket and retreated to their sleeping quarters far above. Only then, when the last of them had gone, did Hugh de Payens rise to his feet and walk forward into the still-guttering light of the few torches that remained. At the top of the stairs descending into the chamber beneath the altar, he stopped.

"Stephen," he called out. "Come down with me, into the crypt." He went down then, and St. Clair followed behind him, to find him waiting on the open threshold of the black and white chamber. The two of them stood side by side for a time, staring into the shadowy depths, and then de Payens knelt down and placed his hands on two of the marble floor tiles, one of them black, the other white.

"Here it is, Stephen," he said, looking down at his hands. "All of my life, in this one room. Black and white. The colors of our Order, darkness and light, death and life, ignorance and enlightenment, not merely underfoot, on the floor, but all about us, in everything we do." He rose smoothly to his feet and stood with his hands on his hips, then moved forward slowly, pivoting as he went so that his body revolved in a circle.

"You can have no idea how much I have waited for this day, my friend, waiting for it to come, yet not ever knowing even if it would or could. From the moment I found the Order of Rebirth, I dedicated my life to it and to its teachings, hoping against hope that I had not made a foolish choice and a bad decision. For there is nothing, really—no, there *was* nothing, really, to tell us what was true and what was not. Now there is. We have found the proof, and God has blessed us with the knowledge. But before, we had nothing to distinguish us from Christians, gravely misled and believing blindly in hope, and faith, and love. I have believed in what the Order taught, but there have been times when I was close to despair … close to believing we were wrong. Today has changed all that, and that truth has over-whelmed me these past few hours, so that I dared not trust myself to speak, or even to look too closely at my friends. Where is the Ark?"

St. Clair was surprised by the question. "Have you

not seen it? It is back there, behind you, behind the curtain there."

"Come, then, with me."

They reached the closed curtain and de Payens opened it slowly, then stood there mute, staring at the ornate splendor of the golden chest for long moments before he sank slowly to his knees. He reached out a hand, tentatively, and then held it there, less than a hand's breadth from one of the carrying rings on the side of the chest, as though he would lean forward and touch the container, but then he sighed and lowered his hand, and when he turned to look at St. Clair, the younger knight was unsurprised to see tears flowing down his cheeks. He felt a lump in his own throat in response and tried to look away, but found he was incapable of moving. Hugh de Payens blinked, unashamed of his tears, and then swallowed and spoke.

"I am not fit ... no man is fit to lay hands upon the residence of God, the God of Moses and of Abraham, of Jesus and Mohammed. And I have no doubt that this Ark was, and is, that residence. And here it sits, in front of us, solid and real. The world has changed today, Stephen St. Clair, and so has everyone in it. I am grown old suddenly—not that I will die soon, or withdraw from life, but I am come of age, and so, my friend, are you. I must return to Christendom soon, I fear, to deal with all of this, but I will leave you and your brethren here with Brother Godfrey, who will govern in my place, and you will all live different lives from this day forth, thanks to what we have uncovered here today.

Ah! See how the Lord of Hosts bids us to sleep."
Around them, the three remaining torches had begun
to flicker and burn out. "Quickly now, Stephen, take
the last fresh one there and light it while you can. It will
show us the way to our cots, for tomorrow there is
much to do."

TEN

•

On the morning when Princess Alice of Jerusalem was to be wed to Prince Bohemond of Antioch, two men, both up and abroad long before dawn, viewed the occasion differently from the mass of their fellows: Brother Stephen St. Clair of the Poor Fellow Soldiers of Jesus Christ was oblivious to the event and its grandeur, having far more on his mind than any mere wedding or state occasion could usurp, whereas Bishop Odo of Fontainebleau, who would be in attendance at the wedding ceremony, had other plans to occupy himself during the grand reception and banquet celebrations that would follow the marriage ceremony. His intent was to take full advantage of the kind of opportunity that seldom came his way. Neither man gave a thought to the existence of the other, each of them intent on his own affairs.

The wedding itself was sumptuous, the most splendid affair seen in the Holy Land since King Baldwin had assumed the throne. Alice was not his firstborn daughter, and as such she would not inherit his throne; everyone knew that honor would pass to her elder sister, Melisende. And Melisende had been betrothed for years already and would marry, in the fullness of time, but

Alice was the first daughter Baldwin had bestowed in marriage, and young Bohemond, the heir to the Principality of Antioch, was pre-eminently suitable. The Patriarch Archbishop officiated, and the sonorous chant of the massed monks throughout the solemn nuptial Mass moved many of the congregation close to tears. Throughout the entire ceremony, King Baldwin sat proudly beside his beautiful and exotic Armenian wife, Morfia, his head held high. His kingdom was secure, for the time being, and it was commonly understood that this dashing new son-in-law would be a strong and vigilant ally in maintaining the northern outposts of his kingdom against the Turks who posed a constant threat to him in the east.

The Seljuk Turks had been in decline as a fighting force ever since the fall of Jerusalem, almost two full decades earlier, but they were still an ever-present menace. And a recent report had described what might be a new, non-Turkish threat, from Syria. *Saracen* was an unfamiliar word—a generic name for the infidels from that distant part of the world. Now, however, spies were telling the king that a new Muslim horde, calling themselves Saracens, was stirring beyond his borders, in the enormous wastes of Syria, where yet another manifestation of the seething cauldron of political forces that comprised Islam was taking shape.

An outbreak of coughing followed quickly on fresh, thick clouds of incense billowing up from the censers surrounding the bridal couple at the main altar. The

King rose to his feet with the other celebrants and joined the Te Deum chant of rejoicing for the newly wed couple.

A SHORT TIME LATER, having made his formal and prearranged obeisances to monarch and patriarch, Bishop Odo of Fontainebleau stood apart from the throng, watching the royal party depart the church for the grand banquet that would be served in the main hall of the royal palace, and he frowned at the unexpected and unwelcome sight of the spy, Gregorio, approaching him, keeping to the side and out of the way of the departing guests, and looking meaningfully and urgently at the bishop. The fellow came right up to him and stopped, waiting to be acknowledged, and Odo made no attempt to hide his displeasure.

"Are you mad? How dare you approach me openly? I told you never to come near me unless I sent for you."

As usual, the little spy showed no sign of being discomfited by the bishop's displeasure. He merely made a moue and dipped his head to one side, accompanying that with a tiny, disparaging shrug of his shoulders.

"You also told me that I should come to you directly as soon as I had proof that the monks in the temple stables were guilty of anything."

Odo straightened up. "You have proof?"

The spy shrugged again. "As good as. They are talking about a treasure they have found, beneath the temple."

"Beneath the—beneath the *temple*? Are you sure of this?"

"As sure as I can be. One of their sergeants, whom I pay well to listen, overheard two of them talking about it. They have found gold, and jewels, and a trove of documents."

Odo turned away, leaving the little man staring at his back, but he was thinking furiously. He had an assignation this afternoon, long in the planning and carefully arranged, with his young Muslim mistress, Arouna, the daughter of Sheikh Fakhr Ad-Kamil, and he had no wish to forgo it. All her male relatives were here in the palace today, attending the wedding, and this had presented him with a golden opportunity to enjoy an afternoon of lust with the girl without the usual haunting fear of being discovered and killed out of hand, and so he had made arrangements to absent himself from the celebrations, claiming that he had work to do on the Patriarch's behalf and that, besides, he was on the last day of a self-imposed penitential fourteen-day fast.

This new development, inconvenient as it was, was completely unforeseen, but the possibility it presented for enriching himself was unprecedented, and timely beyond belief. A treasure in gold and jewels for the taking … Alice was besotted with her new husband and had been preparing to leave with him for Antioch since before Bohemond's arrival, and Odo knew, beyond doubt, that she had no thought in her head nowadays about the pestilential knight monks and their underground activities. Now if this story of Gregorio's was true to any extent, Odo might have an opportunity to profit beyond his wildest dreams, since no record of any treasure, far less the extent of it, existed. If he could lay his plans quickly enough now, and with sufficient care, he could take action as soon as Alice had safely left Jerusalem, presenting himself in a heroic light to the King, and at the same time sequestering a substantial portion of this treasure for his own, exclusive use.

All that need be done, he was thinking, given that this new information was true, was to summon the knight monks to a meeting with the Patriarch, there to denounce them and have them all taken into custody, while Gregorio conducted a quick search of their excavations before the King had time to organize a search of his own. Gregorio, Odo knew, was devious enough to manage that adroitly, in return for a substantial portion of whatever he was able to extract from the treasure in advance of the King's exploration. How large that portion should be would be negotiable, but Odo was prepared to part with half the total, provided that Gregorio, who was a puny little man, should survive to claim it. He turned back quickly to find the spy looking up at him, waiting patiently. They were alone, everyone having vanished into the palace proper.

"Come with me, then. I have to disrobe. We can talk while I am doing that. Come."

Once they were alone in his chambers, Odo began to strip off his ceremonial vestments. "Who is this sergeant that you have in your pay?"

The little man sniffed. "Giacomo Versace is his

name. He is one of my best. I inserted him into the ranks of the sergeant brothers long ago, when we first started looking for evidence against the monks. He has been one of them for a long time now, and he is trusted. It was he who found the one called Brother Stephen—the St. Clair knight—after his abduction."

"And is he trustworthy?"

"I trust him, but I sense that might be no great recommendation to you. But if you mean can we believe what he says, then yes, we can. I told you, the monks trust him, and he is one of those fortunate people, in my profession, who possess the fine art of becoming invisible when they wish to remain unseen. He is among the knight monks constantly, always working, always unobtrusive, and always listening. The two monks he heard conversing about the treasure are the two called St. Agnan and Gondemare. Versace was in the stables, by sheer good fortune, sitting quietly among the fodder bales when they came in, and they thought they were alone. He heard them talking of chests of gold and silver coins, and cases of jewels, buried for a thousand years in the tunnels beneath the mount, in the very bowels of the temple. They were hoping that they might be able to use them to buy armor and weapons, and horses. Versace listened carefully, then remained where he was, in hiding, until long after they had gone. He had waited for more than a year for that moment and had no wish to jeopardize his safety by being too impatient. Then, once safely out of there, he came directly to me."

"Did you reward him?"

"Aye, with what I had at hand. That was not much, but it would buy him a jug of wine. I had no concerns about that, either, for I know the man well. He is more closemouthed than I am. But I told him, too, that I would reward him more amply later."

"I will want you to point him out to me later ... He has no knowledge, I presume, that you are in my employ?"

"Why should he? He works for me and I see him well rewarded. That is all he cares about."

"Excellent. Now, the two monks involved, what did you say their names are?"

"Archibald St. Agnan and Gondemare. He only has the one name."

"Write those down for me. There is a pen and an inkwell there on the table." The spy wrote down the two names while Odo finished pulling on his outer robe, a plain, brown garment that was entirely nondescript and would permit him to walk the city streets without being recognized and without drawing attention to himself. He took the piece of paper, read the names one more time, then folded it and placed it on the tabletop, covering it with the inkstand.

"Now, I want you to go back and talk to your man Versace again. Question him closely this time, and find out precisely what he overheard, every detail, every word, with particular reference to these tunnels beneath the temple. How do they gain access to the tunnels? That is most important, but be careful not to alert this fellow to how important it is. I would not normally presume to instruct you in your own profession, but pretend to be idly curious for more detail and find out everything there is to know."

"Well, we know how they gain access, do we not? Through the tunnel, or the shaft, that they were excavating years ago."

Odo sniffed. "That may be so. They said they were digging out a monastery in the rock, but I would wager they dug far deeper and farther than anyone could ever suspect. That will remain to be seen. In the meantime, however, I want to be sure we have gained every little piece of knowledge that your man Versace possesses. Come back to me in three days' time, and I will give you final instructions. In the meantime I can promise you this: if all goes well here, you and I will share a large portion of this treasure equally. I will invite the brothers to a gathering, and then I will denounce them while they are with the Patriarch and have them arrested. You, in the meantime, will enter their tunnels and locate the treasure, and once you have done so, you will immediately take our portion, as much as you can comfortably handle, and set it aside where it will not be discovered. I will then accompany the King's Guard on a search of the tunnels, and we will find what remains of the treasure and present it to the King, who will be more than happy with our work. Then, when everything has settled down and the treasure has been removed by the King's men, you and I will divide what remains equally. Are we in agreement?"

The little man eyed him carefully, one eyebrow raised high, almost in mockery. "Aye, my lord Bishop, we are indeed."

"So be it. Make you sure, then, that you drain your man Versace of everything he knows. Now go, and come back in three days."

Odo watched the little man leave and then stood deep in thought for several minutes before taking a light, drab traveling cloak from the cabinet where he kept his episcopal robes. He threw it about his shoulders and made his way out of the building, relieved, in spite of all his planning, to encounter no one between his chambers and the main entrance. Once on the street, he looked in both directions, then quickly made his way across the main thoroughfare and into one of the numerous alleys between the surrounding buildings.

He walked quickly after that, keeping his face covered with the cowl of his cloak to ensure that he would not be recognized if he was seen by anyone he knew, and his confidence grew as he passed out of the precincts of the royal residence into the city proper, where he knew he would blend in with the crowds in the streets as he made his way towards the small house that the Princess Alice le Bourcq had taken for him, through some discreet and faceless intermediary. It stood on the outskirts of the city, close by the eastern wall but far enough from any of the main gates to afford him a measure of anonymity, even although he was obviously a Frank. There were enough *ferenghi* living in Jerusalem by that time for their presence to be accepted without rancor by the populace, and many of them were soldiers who, for one reason or another, mainly involving women and access to women, managed to maintain a private roof over their heads in addition to their formal barracks housing. The danger of his being recognized by any of those, he knew, was minuscule, especially when he was wearing shabby street clothing.

He was impatient to reach his destination and the fleshly delights that awaited him there, because thanks to the chaos that had descended upon Jerusalem with the arrival of the Prince of Antioch nigh on a month earlier, it had now been twelve days since he had last seen Arouna, the beautiful and depraved child mistress who had besotted him. He still could not quite bring himself to believe, after almost four months of delight that outstripped anything he had ever known with the exquisite Princess Alice, that Alice had thought sufficiently highly of him to have endowed him with such a reward in the first place, and had then gone out of her way to provide him with safe accommodations in which to conduct his secretive and highly perilous liaison with the young Arab girl. He knew, and in moments of tranquility could even acknowledge to himself, that he had much to thank the princess for, including this current opportunity to lay hands upon an unsuspected treasure. Had it not been for Alice, he would never have given a thought to the temple monks and their subterranean activities. He knew, too, despite what his vanity might prompt him to believe about his masculine attractiveness, that Alice could easily have simply dismissed him

out of hand when she was done with him, denying him
her favors and defying him to do anything about it.
That she had not done so, and had in fact gone to great
extremes to ensure that his pleasures and his lusts were
amply provided for, in compensation for his loss of her
personal attentions, had become more and more flattering with the passage of time and his growing fascination
with Arouna, the astonishing replacement she had
provided.

Visualizing the lascivious delights he was about to
experience, he felt himself becoming aroused and
lengthened his pace. Gregorio had kept him late, later
than he wanted to be, and Odo resented the spy's
unfortunate timing, even as he thrilled again at the
thought of the possibilities the little man's information
had generated. Ahead of him, he saw the narrow side
street that would take him to his house, but at the same
moment he became aware of the figure walking towards
him in the distance, a tall Frank, wearing a full suit of
gleaming, sand-burnished mail covered by a plain white
surcoat.

The sight was unexpected and unpleasant, for the
white surcoat of the knight monks had become a well-
known sight in Jerusalem in recent years, though they
numbered only nine, and Odo knew from the youthfulness of the approaching man's stride that this could
only be the youngest one, the knight St. Clair, who
called himself Brother Stephen, the one among them
most likely to recognize him. Cursing quietly to
himself, he was heartened a little to see that the knight

was unaccompanied and appeared to be walking like a man in a dream, staring ahead into nothingness and unaware of his surroundings. His heart suddenly hammering in his chest, the bishop extended his stride even more and swung into the alleyway before St. Clair could come close enough to see him.

ELEVEN

St. Clair, for his part, had been walking alone for hours by that time, wandering aimlessly through the city streets as he struggled with a decision he had been pondering all night long. It was a weighty decision, for several reasons, and he had dismissed Arlo before dawn that morning to his own devices, insisting that he had matters on his mind that demanded not merely concentration but isolation within which to concentrate. Arlo had been disgruntled and had made no secret of his displeasure, but St. Clair had never been so determined about such a thing before and so, albeit with a total absence of grace on Arlo's part, the master's wish had overruled the servant's.

The previous afternoon, at a convocation of the brothers, Hugh de Payens had announced that he would be returning to France within the month, and that he would be taking two others of their number to accompany him.

One of those two, for reasons that had previously become obvious, was André de Montbard, but in the spirit of brotherhood, de Payens had announced that the name of the third member of the group would be chosen by lot, ensuring each man an equal opportunity of being selected. Once at home in France, the three knights would report their discoveries to the senior Council of the Order of Rebirth, and would then, with the support and agreement of that body, make a formal approach to a man who, despite his youth, had rapidly become the most influential and powerful figure among the French clergy. This young cleric, who had been born Bernard of Fontaines-les-Dijons, was now known throughout ecclesiastical circles as Bernard of Clairvaux, after the Cistercian monastery he had built and now presided over as abbot. Bernard of Clairvaux was the nephew of André de Montbard, and de Montbard, long before leaving France to come to the Holy Land, had endowed the young man, and by extension the recently formed Cistercian order, with the estates on which the Abbey of Clairvaux now stood. De Montbard was confident that, properly approached, his nephew would be willing to act as intermediary in arranging an audience for them with the Pope, in the course of which the brothers would present evidence of what they had found in the bowels of the temple.

The treasure had by this time been examined and catalogued, and the authenticity of the Ark of the Covenant investigated and ratified beyond any possibility of error, although its contents remained, to this point, undisturbed and unexamined. De Payens, as the senior among them, had not changed his opinion on mere men being worthy or entitled to lay hands, physically, upon such a precious and sanctified relic, and so he had ordered that it be crated and preserved intact until such time as it could be opened and examined by people better qualified than he was to deal with its portent.

Hugh de Payens, after consulting with St. Omer and de Montbard, had decided that the containers found in the crypt beneath the altar were likely to be more important than those stored more openly in the hall above, and accordingly, not knowing the order in which the jars had originally been placed on the shelves, they had selected eight jars, two from each end of the ranked vessels on either wall, one from the top and one from the bottom of each tier of shelves.

It had not surprised St. Clair at all that de Montbard had been the one to take charge at that point, supervising the removal of the eight samples from the crypt to the stables. Under his scrutiny, each jar was roped and cradled, and then carried by two of the brethren to the records room on ground level, where a large array of wooden tables had been laid out, several in each of the four corners, to receive them. A fifth group of tables stood in the center of the room, already covered with documents that the brethren recognized as having been brought by de Montbard himself from France when he first came.

Once safely delivered, a pair of jars, from corresponding positions on each side of the gallery, was placed upon a separate table in one of the corners, then marked and numbered with great precision before de Montbard broke each seal with exquisite caution and gently removed the contents. St. Clair had been present at the time—they all had—anxious to set eyes upon whatever it might be that they had worked so long and so hard to find, and when it became obvious that the jars did indeed contain parchment scrolls, as predicted by Montbard, they all stood silent, watching almost in awe, as de Montbard called for a bowl of water and washed his hands absolutely clean, then dried them thoroughly on a clean towel before sitting down and leaning forward with great deliberation to unroll the first portion of the very first scroll, holding it open with spread fingers. The writing on it was tiny, the letters and symbols exquisitely formed, but to all of them, save perhaps de Montbard himself, it was completely alien and indecipherable.

De Montbard sat transfixed, utterly motionless except for his eyes, which scanned the document eagerly until some of the other men began to shift and fidget. Even de Payens and St. Omer hovered anxiously, their eyes intent upon their companion, their faces making it appear that they were holding their breath, but eventually de Montbard nodded his head, satisfied with something, and sat back, cradling the parchment as it sprang back into its tube shape. He raised his eyes to look at each of the two elders in turn.

"Yes," he said, and nodded again, more emphatically this time. "Yes! This is it. We have it. This is what we came to find."

Hugh de Payens gasped aloud, and St. Omer fetched him a resounding thump on the shoulder, a wide grin breaking out on his seamed, grizzled face while the other six men looked at each other with varying degrees of baffled curiosity and incomprehension. De Montbard was already on his feet and moving to the tables in the center of the room where his own documents were neatly laid out. He shuffled through several before selecting one and bringing it back to the table that held the scroll, and only then did he notice the expressions on the faces of the others. He hesitated, looking from man to man, and then he rested his buttocks against the edge of the table behind him and looked again at each man in turn, his smile widening to a rather rueful grin.

"I can see that none of you really knows what has happened here, so let me try to explain it to you in a way that will make some sense." He paused, aware of the fact that every man there was hanging on his words, then waved to indicate the four pairs of jars in their respective corners. "What you have found, my friends, in these jars and the others down below, *is* the Rebirth in Sion. With this discovery, our ancient Order of Rebirth in Sion *is reborn* in Sion. These scrolls contain the absolute vindication of all that our ancestors have believed, and have striven to find, for centuries, for more than a thousand years. And the honor and glory of having found them is yours."

He was no longer smiling. "We—*you*—found the Ark of the Covenant, the most treasured, fabled relic of Antiquity. We have not touched it since finding it, as you all know, and none of us yet knows what it contains. But the discovery itself is of enormous importance, even if it appears to be nothing more than an elaborate wooden box, perhaps an empty box, covered with a coating of hammered and carved gold. It was made, we are told, to contain the twin tablets of stone that Moses brought down from the mountain—the Ten Commandments—the proof of God's covenant with man, but none of us here would dare or presume to touch it, open it, and look upon what is inside. Therefore we cannot estimate its worth in terms that ordinary men could understand. But is there any of us here who doubts its provenance?"

He waved his hand again towards the jars. "But we also found these. Sealed jars, filled with ancient, brittle scrolls. You have said nothing, but I know that many of you must be disappointed that the treasure you have worked so hard to find seems to have so little substance. Some of you might even think it worthless, a poor reward for so much dedication in time and brutal work. But I promise you, Brothers all, that had every jar we found been full of precious jewels, they would not, could not, have begun to approach the value of what we have found instead. This"—he held up the document in his hand and used it to indicate the others on the table behind him—"and these, are the keys to those." Again he indicated the jars.

"I am not a greatly learned man, but I have spent much time being taught by others who are, and who have studied the Lore and records of our Order throughout their lives, and I have managed to learn enough to enable me, at least, to recognize and to authenticate what we have found here as being the genuine and original records of what our Order calls the Jerusalem Community, the original Assembly, the original *church,* if you will, established by Jesus and his followers here in this city. James, the brother of Jesus, was its first leader, perhaps before his brother's death, but certainly afterwards."

He allowed that to settle in their minds before going on. "I know you all recall the shock and consternation you felt soon after your initiation to the Order, when you first learned of our belief that all is not as it should be within the Christian Church as it exists today. Acceptance of that, the first tenet of the Order, was a harrowing and difficult experience. I know it was for me, as a young man of eighteen, because I had come from a devoutly Christian family, as had every one of you, and it seemed to me that I was being asked to condone and accept a heresy that involved the repudiation of the teachings of the hallowed Saint Paul and the entire New Testament.

"But, like all of you, I became convinced—in a surprisingly short time, I remember—by the scholarship and the logic of my teachers and the Order itself. I quickly came to accept and believe that Simon Peter was not the first leader of the Church; he was not the first Pope, as the Church would have us believe. That honor belonged to James, the brother of Jesus, known to his followers as James the Just. But the Church also teaches that Jesus had no brothers, and indeed how could he have, in their viewpoint, being born of a virgin? Are we to believe that Mary, having experienced divine inter-vention, then became carnal and worldly, a prey to the pleasures of the flesh?

"And so we all had to ask ourselves, at different times, the same profoundly disturbing questions. If

Church doctrine is wrong in so fundamental an error as the identity of its first leader, and if the Church denies the existence of Jesus' brothers and his family structure, then what else, which other aspects of its teachings, might come into question?"

Once again he looked from man to man, including the two senior brothers. "You all know our teachings, based upon the records and the annals in our vaults: Jesus had a family, his mother was Mary, and James the Just was one of his brothers. It was the man Paul, sometimes and confusingly known as Saul, who altered the truth for his own reasons, and most likely to fit his own designs, to make this faith politically and racially acceptable to the Romans, with their fear, distrust, and hatred of anything that was Jewish.

"Jesus was arrested and executed for his radical beliefs, for his political activities. Crucifixion was the fate of political dissidents and rebels.

"The strange thing is, Brothers, and once more you know this from our Order's teachings, that the death of Jesus provoked no significant reaction in Jerusalem or anywhere else. He died, and his brother James continued to direct the affairs of their community. It was in reaction to the murder of *James,* assassinated years later on the steps of the temple of Herod, that civil unrest and open war broke out, and soon after that, sent by his father, Vespasian, the Roman general Titus led an avenging army to obliterate Jerusalem and its insurgents, and to destroy the temple, believing that only thus could they break the spirit of the Jews.

"They were wrong. They destroyed Jerusalem and its temple, but the members of the Assembly saw the end approaching, in time to conceal their precious records—this treasure—and to escape the destruction of the city, carrying with them sufficient written information to ensure that someday, when the troubles had died down and been forgotten, their descendants would be able to return and reclaim their history.

"We, my friends, are those descendants. And that history is what we have rediscovered: the complete record, we believe, of the Jerusalem Community, its achievements, its people and their ancestry, the tenets and articles of their beliefs, and their struggles to redeem their people from the tyranny of the Herod family and the infamous, repressive religion they had foisted upon the entire Hebrew race."

St. Clair sat motionless, holding his breath and feeling the pounding of his heart as de Montbard stopped to think through his next words.

"That is what you have unearthed, Brothers. The true and incontrovertible story of what really happened to Jesus, his family and friends, and the religion, or the beliefs, by which they lived. And now all that remains to be done is to translate these scrolls. It will be a prodigious task and a fearsome responsibility. Your primary work here is now almost done, and from this point forward you will be able to spend more time on your secondary responsibility, the guardianship of the roads of Outremer. My task, in the time that now begins, will be to examine what we have—not to translate it, for I have neither the skills nor the time for that, but to use what little skill I have, aided by the documents entrusted to me by my superiors in the Order, to ensure that everything we have here is intact, and that it is, beyond dispute, what we believe it to be. And so I must begin working immediately, and you may retire to discuss this among yourselves and to ponder the consequences, all of them unforeseeable, that must undoubtedly come to pass in the years ahead.

"I know I have no need to remind you of your oath of secrecy and the need to keep this information absolutely secure and unsuspected by anyone not of our brotherhood, but I also know you will forgive me for bringing it back to your awareness. Be more careful from this day forth than you have ever been in guarding our secrets. And now, with the agreement of Brother Hugh, who is Master here, I thank you all on behalf of every brother in the Order of Rebirth. You have, by your own efforts, brought about that Rebirth."

The meeting broke up at that point and the brethren dispersed, talking quietly among themselves, but St. Clair left the room alone and walked off by himself, his mind filled with the wonders of all that had happened to him and around him in the previous month, and as he walked he felt himself grow buoyant, as though a great weight had been lifted from his shoulders and he was free to blow in the wind, weightless and able to drift where the breeze took him.

THAT EPISODE had occurred almost two months earlier, and St. Clair reflected that de Montbard's work had

continued quietly since then, with none of the brotherhood making any attempt to ask questions about the
progress of his investigations. By and large, work had
continued as before, but with freedom from the years-
long need to dig, the program of patrols had been
expanded and intensified until, the previous evening, de
Payens had announced the impending return to France.
It had been decades since any of the brothers had seen
their homeland, and so the selection of the third envoy
had been viewed with great enthusiasm and suspense.
The draw had been made immediately, and St. Clair, to
the good-natured chagrin of everyone else, had won.

Even as he accepted the position, however, St. Clair
had been aware that Gondemare, who was arguably the
quietest of all the brethren, had been more deeply
disappointed than any of the others, and his conscience
had begun to plague him. Gondemare, like Payn
Montdidier, as St. Clair knew well, had been widowed
early and had come to Outremer soon after the death of
his wife. Unlike Payn, however, Gondemare had left
several young children behind in the care of relatives,
and word had reached him, a few years earlier, that
those children had produced grandchildren. This might
have been Gondemare's only opportunity to meet those
grandchildren, and St. Clair had gone to bed that night
with that knowledge in his mind, and had been unable
to sleep. He had no family of any closeness remaining in
Anjou, and although he would have enjoyed returning
there, it would have been for no real purpose other than
his personal attendance to the duties of his Order—a

task that Gondemare could accomplish just as easily as he. Besides—and this was the awareness that had troubled him more than any other—he, among all of the brotherhood here, was the one who had broken all his vows and proved himself, in his own eyes at least, to be unworthy of the honor involved in representing his brethren on this expedition. And so St. Clair had spent an entirely sleepless night and had arisen well before dawn, to walk the streets and struggle with what he ought to do.

He had finally decided, with great relief, to relinquish his place to Gondemare, and at that point, engrossed in his own thoughts as he was, he might never have become aware of Odo at all, had it not been for the bishop's last spurt of speed in seeking to avoid him. St. Clair sensed, rather than saw, a sudden movement and looked over just in time to see a man's shape vanishing into the alley. He recognized something familiar about it, something in the way the fellow moved, but by the time his attention sharpened sufficiently, the figure had vanished, and St. Clair walked past the alley, glancing casually down its length just in time to see the figure turn left and disappear from view, once again leaving him with an elusive feeling of having recognized the man. He hesitated, aware of an urge to follow, then shrugged and kept walking.

He had gone no more than ten or twelve paces, however, when he realized, against all logic, that the scurrying figure he had seen reminded him unmistakably of the Patriarch's amanuensis, Odo, the Bishop of

Fontainebleau. He knew he must be mistaken, for the man he had twice glimpsed had been shabbily dressed, far too shabbily to be a bishop, but then, as he remembered the shiftiness and untrustworthiness he had sensed in the selfsame bishop, his curiosity became aroused, and he retraced his steps to the mouth of the alley, where he stood for several moments gazing into its shadowed depths and then moved idly forward to the spot where he had last seen the vanishing figure.

There was nothing there. The corner he had seen was merely the entrance to a blind alley with high, blank walls on all three sides, which meant that the hurrying man, whoever he had been, had entered it purely to avoid being seen from where St. Clair had been watching. His curiosity now fully engaged, St. Clair left the alley again and turned left, lengthening his pace in pursuit of the enigmatic shadow, aware that he was in unknown territory and that the few people he saw, all of them men, were staring at him with pronounced hostility. Unperturbed, he shifted his sword belt, bringing his hilt closer to hand, and strode on.

FAR AHEAD OF HIM NOW, and safely concealed by several twists in the narrow, winding street, Odo was congratulating himself on his avoidance of being seen, when he emerged into a small, enclosed square and saw several swarthy, dangerous-looking men straighten up on seeing him, almost as though they had been waiting for him to appear. He knew, of course, that no such thing was possible, and so he swallowed the sudden fear that flared in him and drew himself up to his full height, holding his head high and striding resolutely forward. Even as he did so he heard a sound at his back and turned his head to see two more men converging on him from the rear, both of them holding long, curved daggers. Choking on a strangled cry of fear, he swung around in a complete circle, counting six men, all of whom now held bare blades, and saw that they all came to a halt, surrounding him but several paces distant. He was steeling himself to challenge them, to tell them who he was, when he felt his heart and his soul shrivel within him.

"Bishop." The single word was spoken quietly, but there was no doubting what it was or what it meant, and he turned, suddenly terrified, to face the direction from which it had come. A single man, tall and slim and dressed from head to foot in the long, flowing black robes of a desert nomad, was walking towards him, his face concealed except for his dark, unblinking eyes, which were fixed on Odo's. He approached to within two paces of the bishop, who stood frozen, and then he spoke again, another single, unmistakable word. "Arouna." Then, before Odo could even begin to react to what he had heard, the fellow struck.

For the briefest of moments, Odo thought the man had punched him in the stomach, the blow heavy and solid, driving the wind from him, but then his assailant twisted his wrist, hard, turning the blade in Odo's flesh and dragging its razor-sharp edge up along the inner curve of his ribs and across, eviscerating him so that, as the incredible pain belatedly struck home, Odo felt his bowels sag loose and tumble out into his clothing. His mouth opened and closed, emitting only a high-pitched whine of fear and agony, his voice stilled forever, but before he could lose consciousness, his killer leaned close and breathed into his ear, "This for Princess Alice, a wedding gift, and for Arouna's father, vengeance. You bought this death when you befouled his daughter." He then whipped out his blade and stepped back, watching as Odo fell to his knees and unaware that the bishop's last conscious thought was of Alice, the faithless bitch, and how she would now claim his treasure.

With a wave of his hand, Hassan the Shi'a sent his Assassins melting into the surrounding doors and alleyways before he removed a folded letter from his breast and tucked it carefully into the dead man's clothing where it would not be stained by his blood. Without even wrinkling his nose at the stench of Odo's loosened bowels, he wiped his blade clean on the dead man's cloak and casually walked away, leaving the square deserted.

Mere moments later, St. Clair stepped into the small square.

THE ASSASSINATION of a bishop caused an uproar among the Frankish community, but it was short lived, since the letter found in his clothing detailed the bishop's sins and transgressions, and the murdered body of a young Muslim woman, the daughter of a local sheikh, was discovered a short time later, in the house that was soon proved to be held in Odo's name. Within the day, two more Franks were found dead together, murdered in the same manner, one of them the spy Gregorio, and the other a sergeant brother of the order of the knight monks, Giacomo Versace. This discovery, too, caused little public fuss, since the men's association with Odo was already known, their names written clearly in the letter found on the bishop's body, but the killers of all four went undiscovered.

Only Stephen St. Clair was left with anything to wonder about, and his curiosity was something he could share with no one else, much as he might wish to. It had been he who found the bishop's body, and he who found the neatly penned letter, written in Latin, that, if it did not explain or expunge the crime, at least clarified the corrupt reasons underlying it. Everyone had accepted what was there, seeing it as self-evident after the fact. St. Clair was the only one who gave any significance to the penmanship of the letter—an elegant, delicate, and vaguely, indeterminately feminine script—or to the container in which the condemnatory letter had been wrapped for protection, a soft and supple envelope of bright yellow leather, with a tiny crescent moon stitched carefully into one corner, but he wisely chose to keep his own counsel.

EPILOGUE

"**G**o with God, Brothers, and may He guide your every footstep henceforth."

With those words, Godfrey of St. Omer bade farewell to the three departing delegates who would, within the year, represent the Order of the Poor Fellow Soldiers of Jesus Christ to the Church and the establishment in France and the rest of Christendom. St. Omer was now assuming command of the remaining two thirds of the fraternity of Knights of the Temple Mount, all of whom sat their horses silently at his back, their faces studiedly expressionless as they watched their three friends and comrades salute them one last time and then turn their mounts to ride away downhill, accompanied by their escort of five sergeants, towards the lengthy cavalcade that was already wending its way down to the city gates.

Their personal farewells had all been made long since, and now the homeward-bound contingent would join the procession of the royal newlyweds for the first stage of their journey, northward to Bohemond's principality of Antioch and the port of Alexandria, where the three knight monks would take ship for Cyprus, on the first seagoing leg of their long journey home to France.

Watching the three of them ride away—de Payens, de Montbard, and Gondemare—St. Clair was aware that he was smiling, if only with one side of his mouth, because of a random thought that had come to him moments earlier, reminding him of Princess Alice and her alluring ways. He would feel much more comfortable here in Jerusalem now, he knew, than he would have riding along the route to Antioch with the constant presence of the princess in his awareness. It mattered nothing to him that Alice seemed radiantly happy and obsessed with her magnificently attractive new husband; the simple nearness of her would have disturbed and aroused his own memories intolerably, and he was honest enough with himself now to admit that. He no longer felt sinful or guilty over what had happened between him and her, and his sleep had been untroubled by thoughts of her for months, but he was still young enough, and male enough, to be curious and vulnerable. Better by far, then, that the faithful Gondemare should ride with her, in ignorance and innocence.

As soon as the departing knights had disappeared from view, St. Omer turned to St. Clair. "Have a safe patrol, Brother Stephen," he said, raising one hand in salute. St. Clair nodded in response and pulled his mount around, his eyes seeking and finding his co-commander, Montdidier, and their senior brother sergeant, who was, on this occasion, St. Clair's own man, Arlo. He raised a hand to Arlo and nodded, and the sergeant immediately spurred his horse away downhill, shouting the orders that would bring the already assembled patrol to attention and set them moving.

"One more time, then," Montdidier murmured, reining his mount to where he could ride knee to knee with St. Clair. "Shoulder to shoulder against the Infidel, swords bared, for the glory of God and the safety of the pilgrim. I confess to you, Stephen, I would far rather be riding towards Anjou than to Jericho."

"Ah, but think of how much better off you will be in ten days' time, when you are safely back here in Jerusalem, abed in comfort and scratching idly at your lice, while those poor wanderers are being tossed on stormy seas, wretched and seasick, spewing until their entrails protrude from their heaving gullets. Much better to be here, my friend."

Montdidier grunted. "Perhaps," he said, "but we are not yet through the gates on our outward journey. We may have much to distract us yet, before we win home. *If* we win home ... St. Agnan was saying something last night to de Payens, at supper, about increased bandit activity between here and Jericho. More and more hostiles gathering all the time and creating chaos, he says, although I don't know where he finds his information. I know even less how he processes it, once he has received it. Give Archibald one fact, it seems to me, and he will build a gospel from it."

St. Clair wanted to respond to that with some observations of his own, but he did not have the opportunity, because they had reached the city's eastern gate— chosen on this occasion to avoid the press caused by the royal departure through the southern gate—and his attention was taken up with passing his men through without incident, after which, as soon as they were on the road outside the city, both he and Montdidier had their hands full for a while, organizing their units. It was only long afterwards, when all their scouts were out scanning the terrain ahead of them and the patrol had settled down into the routine it would pursue for the remainder of their ten-day patrol, that he had time and opportunity to return to what Montdidier had said. At first he debated with himself over whether it might be better to say nothing, since he had no wish to upset his friend as he himself had been. In the end, however, he decided to share what he knew.

"I had a fascinating talk with Brother Hugh last night."

"I'm surprised he would have time to talk, with all the preparations for today's departure. What was he talking about, and what was so fascinating about it?"

"About this whole affair … the treasure, the records, his return to France, and the effect that what he has to say will have on the Church. Have you thought much about that?"

Montdidier twisted lazily in his saddle and grinned his slow grin. "Thought about that … you mean about the Church? Me? Please, I pray you, Brother, I have other matters to engage me, and no time to fret over what our worthy religious brethren—outside our own Order, I mean—might be doing with their own holy orders. I would rather keep my blades sharpened for fighting Allah's minions than save my wits for debating with God's benighted brethren of the cloth."

St. Clair nodded, unsurprised. "No more had I, until I asked an idle question of de Payens."

Montdidier cocked his head. "And?"

"And received more than I had bargained for. In the space of moments, our estimable Brother Hugh offered me a glimpse of the depths of my own ignorance. I have been thinking about it ever since."

Montdidier was no longer smiling. Something in St. Clair's demeanor had alerted him that here was something more serious than he would have suspected, and his own bearing changed, his back now straight, his head held high. "That sounds grave, my friend. Tell me about it."

St. Clair glanced over to where his companion sat watching him. "I asked him how long he thought it would take for our discovery to take effect, for the changes we had set in motion to take effect and become apparent. At first he said nothing, simply throwing me what I thought at the time to be a droll look. But then he pulled me away with him to where the two of us could talk alone, he said, without being overheard. We talked for a long time then. Well, he talked, mainly, and I listened. And I was ... shocked, I suppose would be the most accurate word, by what he had to say."

"Stephen, you are making me impatient. What did the man *say*?"

"That nothing is going to change. Nothing is going to happen."

Montdidier tucked in his chin, his eyes narrowing to slits. "But that is patently ridiculous. Things *have* to change now. We have proof that they *need* to be changed, that the reality of the Church's *foundation* is questionable, even that it is based upon lies. How then can de Payens say nothing will change?"

"He said that the established Church will not bend the knee to what we have discovered. They will ignore it if they can, and if they cannot ignore it they will deny it, using the entire weight of their history and worldly authority to reinforce their stance, and anyone who makes it too difficult for that denial to be maintained will be dealt with."

"What do you mean, 'will be dealt with'?"

"What do you suppose I mean, Payn? Do you think I am trying now, having come so far, to be obscure? Think about it for a while. We have a Church that considers itself universal, and for the last what—eight hundred years?—for the last eight hundred years, since the days of Constantine the Great, it has been solidly based in Rome, its well-fed, worldly princes blithely ignoring the beginnings they abandoned so quickly under the flattering, seductive spell of imperial bribery—those beginnings that were founded in poverty and proudly proclaimed that it was easier for a camel to pass through the eye of a needle than it was for a rich man to enter the Kingdom of Heaven.

"This discovery of ours, de Payens pointed out, were it to be made public, would result immediately in the senior hierarchy of the entire Church having to admit the error of their ways, and being forced to relinquish all their wealth, their privilege, and the luxuries they now enjoy. That would be the very least that would happen. The knowledge, revealed, would destroy the Church."

"Well, I hardly think it would go that far ..."

"Oh, really? You don't think people would be angry to discover that they've spent their lives in poverty when they needn't have? That they've starved in their hundreds of thousands, giving most of what they own to the Church, not for the glory of God, or because God asked for it, but for the welfare and benefit of lazy clerics, simply because the priests think that is the way it should be? You think people might not be inclined to rebel and spill blood, seeing the proof that the Church has been exploiting them and their families for hundreds of years?

"Those hierarchical clerics I mentioned, popes and patriarchs and the like, are all men, my friend—not a God or a saint among them. And being men, they will go to any lengths they feel are necessary to protect them and their *livelihood*. To *any* lengths ...

"Should we all vanish from the world tomorrow, we Poor Fellow Soldiers of Jesus Christ, it would not be the first time in history that such a thing has happened. Archbishops and cardinals take great pride in representing God. They have His ear and they are zealous and jealous in preserving their right to pronounce His opinions and His judgments."

"So they might wipe us all out. Is that what you are saying?"

"Aye, of course it is. Like flies."

There was a long pause while they rode in silence, the only sounds being made by their horses' hooves and the occasional creak of saddle leather, and then Montdidier asked, "So what did de Payens end up saying, really?"

"That we have allies and assets. That we are not without power of our own. That our own roots go back further and deeper than those of the Christian Church. That we have access to, and possession of, the documented truth of what we claim, while no one else has. That we have the ability and the intellect to keep our sources—and our treasure—securely hidden. And that we are not stupid enough to put ourselves at risk by wandering into peril, starry eyed and naïve.

"He said we will win, eventually, but not in any way that I, or you, might ever think of. And at the last, he bade me be patient and prepare myself, and all the rest of you, for great and sweeping changes to our world, changes, he said, that would be incomprehensible and unimaginable were he even to attempt to point them out to us now. They have not yet begun to occur, he said, but once they do begin, they will be unstoppable, and we, the Poor Fellow Soldiers of Jesus Christ and the Temple of Solomon, will have the power to change the entire world."

Montdidier sat with his head to one side, eyeing St. Clair askance for several minutes before he grunted and said, "All nine of us? That, if you will forgive me for saying so, sounds like the ravings of a madman. And while we are on the topic of madness, tell me, if you will, Stephen, how we all became soldiers of Christ in the first place, when there is not a Christian among us?"

"Protection." St. Clair did not even hesitate. "Protection, pure and simple. Who would suspect sedition among the Poor Fellow Soldiers of *Christ*? The name allowed us to go about our lives without hindrance while we were seeking the treasure. As for the madness in what de Payens said, I thought the same at first, and then I questioned him more closely. He really does see great changes ahead for us. Recruits, for one thing. He sees us attracting hundreds of them, from all the lands of Christendom."

"From Christendom … You mean Christian recruits? How can that be? I know the Order of Rebirth has been reborn, but it will continue to be a secret society, will it not? How then can we admit Christian knights?"

"Easily, Crusty. That was the first thing I asked de Payens when he mentioned recruitment, and he had already thought the matter through. Our ancient Order will continue to exist within the new order here in Jerusalem, whether we be called the Order of the Temple Knights or something else. The name we call the new order is not important, but its activities will be, and the activities of the Order of Rebirth will continue to be exercised, concealed among its activities. It will take thought, and much organization, but Hugh and St. Omer think it can be achieved. Hugh believes the

Church will be brought to recognize our Order, and that will be the making of us.

"He has great faith in Bernard of Clairvaux, de Montbard's young nephew who is abbot of the Cistercian monastery of Clairvaux. He is confident that, with the backing of Clairvaux, allied with our own Order's Grand Council and all the temporal power that can be brought to bear there by the Angevin Counts, Fulk of Anjou, Hugh of Champagne, and others like them, our Friendly Families will be able to prevail upon the Pope to accept not only the existence and import of our discoveries but also our sincere reassurances that nothing sudden will be forced upon the Church in the near future, until the Church Fathers themselves have had a sufficiency of time to study these matters and decide upon their validity. And in the meantime, he believes, we, and our works here in the Holy Land, will receive the full benison of papal recognition and favor, in return for our cooperation and silence."

"And you believe that." It was not a question.

St. Clair looked at his companion and nodded his head slowly. "I do. It took me some time to accept everything I had been told, but I now believe de Payens is right. In finding what we have found, we may have changed the known world and improved the life of every man, alive and to come, from what it has been to this point. For a thousand years there has been nothing, no dissenting voice, to gainsay the Church, or to threaten it with the loss of its worldly influence. Now we have the power to play that role, and in that way we may have made people's lives better—theirs, and our own. That is worth believing, I think."

Montdidier grinned and removed his flat-capped helmet, thrust the mailed cowl back off his head, then shook his head to loosen his matted hair and scrubbed it with one hand before replacing everything. That done, he drew his long sword and stood up in his stirrups.

"Tonight, friend Stephen, we will drink a cup of wine to that. To the betterment of people's lives throughout the world. But it will still require armies of people with these—" he swung his sword around his head—"to see to their safety. So we will drink a second cup to ourselves, and to our friends and brethren, the monk knights of the temple, Poor Fellows that they are."

FINIS